Agatha Christie is known throughout the world as the Queen of Crime. Her books have sold over a billion copies in English with another billion in foreign languages. She is the most widely published author of all time and in any language, outsold only by the Bible and Shakespeare. She is the author of 80 crime novels and short story collections, 19 plays, and six novels written under the name of Mary Westmacott.

Agatha Christie's first novel, *The Mysterious Affair at Styles*, was written towards the end of the First World War, in which she served as a VAD. In it she created Hercule Poirot, the little Belgian detective who was destined to become the most popular detective in crime fiction since Sherlock Holmes. It was eventually published by The Bodley Head in 1920.

In 1926, after averaging a book a year, Agatha Christie wrote her masterpiece. *The Murder of Roger Ackroyd* was the first of her books to be published by Collins and marked the beginning of an author–publisher relationship which lasted for 50 years and well over 70 books. *The Murder of Roger Ackroyd* was also the first of Agatha Christie's books to be dramatised – under the name *Alibi* – and to have a successful run in London's West End. *The Mousetrap*, her most famous play of all, opened in 1952 and is the longest-running play in history.

Agatha Christie was made a Dame in 1971. She died in 1976, since when a number of books have been published posthumously: the bestselling novel *Sleeping Murder* appeared later that year, followed by her autobiography and the short story collections *Miss Marple's Final Cases*, *Problem at Pollensa Bay* and *While the Light Lasts*. In 1998 *Black Coffee* was the first of her plays to be novelised by another author, Charles Osborne.

THE AGATHA CHRISTIE COLLECTION

The Man in the Brown Suit
The Secret of Chimneys
The Seven Dials Mystery
The Mysterious Mr Quin
The Sittaford Mystery
The Hound of Death
The Listerdale Mystery
Why Didn't They Ask Evans?
Parker Pyne Investigates
Murder is Easy
And Then There Were None
Towards Zero
Death Comes as the End
Sparkling Cyanide
Crooked House
They Came to Baghdad
Destination Unknown
Spider's Web*
The Unexpected Guest*
Ordeal by Innocence
The Pale Horse
Endless Night
Passenger to Frankfurt
Problem at Pollensa Bay
While the Light Lasts

Poirot
The Mysterious Affair at Styles
The Murder on the Links
Poirot Investigates
The Murder of Roger Ackroyd
The Big Four
The Mystery of the Blue Train
Black Coffee*
Peril at End House
Lord Edgware Dies
Murder on the Orient Express
Three Act Tragedy
Death in the Clouds
The ABC Murders
Murder in Mesopotamia
Cards on the Table
Murder in the Mews
Dumb Witness
Death on the Nile
Appointment with Death
Hercule Poirot's Christmas
Sad Cypress
One, Two, Buckle My Shoe
Evil Under the Sun
Five Little Pigs
The Hollow
The Labours of Hercules
Taken at the Flood
Mrs McGinty's Dead
After the Funeral
Hickory Dickory Dock
Dead Man's Folly
Cat Among the Pigeons
The Adventure of the Christmas Pudding
The Clocks
Third Girl
Hallowe'en Party
Elephants Can Remember
Poirot's Early Cases
Curtain: Poirot's Last Case

Marple
The Murder at the Vicarage
The Thirteen Problems
The Body in the Library
The Moving Finger
A Murder is Announced
They Do It With Mirrors
A Pocket Full of Rye
4.50 from Paddington
The Mirror Crack'd from Side to Side
A Caribbean Mystery
At Bertram's Hotel
Nemesis
Sleeping Murder
Miss Marple's Final Cases

Tommy & Tuppence
The Secret Adversary
Partners in Crime
N or M?
By the Pricking of My Thumbs
Postern of Fate

Published as Mary Westmacott
Giant's Bread
Unfinished Portrait
Absent in the Spring
The Rose and the Yew Tree
A Daughter's a Daughter
The Burden

Memoirs
An Autobiography
Come, Tell Me How You Live

Play Collections
The Mousetrap and Selected Plays
Witness for the Prosecution and Selected Plays

* novelised by Charles Osborne

Agatha Christie

POIROT

THE FRENCH COLLECTION

THE MURDER ON THE LINKS

THE MYSTERY OF THE BLUE TRAIN

DEATH IN THE CLOUDS

HarperCollinsPublishers

HarperCollins*Publishers*
77–85 Fulham Palace Road,
Hammersmith, London W6 8JB
www.harpercollins.co.uk

This edition first published 2003
6

ISBN 0 00 717113 7

Typeset in Plantin Light and Gill Sans by
Palimpsest Book Production Limited,
Polmont, Stirlingshire
Printed and bound in Great Britain by
Clays Ltd, St Ives plc

CONTENTS

THE MURDER ON THE LINKS

To My Husband
a fellow enthusiast for detective stories
and to whom I am indebted for much
helpful advice and criticism

CONTENTS

CHAPTER 1

A FELLOW-TRAVELLER

I believe that a well-known anecdote exists to the effect that a young writer, determined to make the commencement of his story forcible and original enough to catch and rivet the attention of the most blasé of editors, penned the following sentence:

'"Hell!" said the Duchess.'

Strangely enough, this tale of mine opens in much the same fashion. Only the lady who gave utterance to the exclamation was not a duchess.

It was a day in early June. I had been transacting some business in Paris and was returning by the morning service to London, where I was still sharing rooms with my old friend, the Belgian ex-detective, Hercule Poirot.

The Calais express was singularly empty – in fact, my own compartment held only one other traveller. I had made a somewhat hurried departure from the hotel and was busy assuring myself that I had duly collected all my traps, when the train started. Up till then I had hardly noticed my companion, but I was now violently recalled to the fact of her existence. Jumping up from her seat, she let down the window and stuck her head out, withdrawing it a moment later with the brief and forcible ejaculation 'Hell!'

Now I am old-fashioned. A woman, I consider, should be womanly. I have no patience with the modern neurotic girl who jazzes from morning to night, smokes like a chimney, and uses language which would make a Billingsgate fishwoman blush!

I looked up, frowning slightly, into a pretty, impudent face, surmounted by a rakish little red hat. A thick cluster of black curls hid each ear. I judged that she was little more than seventeen, but her face was covered with powder, and her lips were quite impossibly scarlet.

Nothing abashed, she returned my glance, and executed an expressive grimace.

'Dear me, we've shocked the kind gentleman!' she observed

to an imaginary audience. 'I apologize for my language! Most unladylike, and all that, but, oh, Lord, there's reason enough for it! Do you know I've lost my only sister?'

'Really?' I said politely. 'How unfortunate.'

'He disapproves!' remarked the lady. 'He disapproves utterly – of me, and my sister – which last is unfair, because he hasn't seen her!'

I opened my mouth, but she forestalled me.

'Say no more! Nobody loves me! I shall go into the garden and eat worms! Boohoo. I am crushed!'

She buried herself behind a large comic French paper. In a minute or two I saw her eyes stealthily peeping at me over the top. In spite of myself I could not help smiling, and in a minute she had tossed the paper aside, and had burst into a merry peal of laughter.

'I knew you weren't such a mutt as you looked,' she cried.

Her laughter was so infectious that I could not help joining in, though I hardly cared for the word 'mutt'.

'There! Now we're friends!' declared the minx. 'Say you're sorry about my sister –'

'I am desolated!'

'That's a good boy!'

'Let me finish. I was going to add that, although I am desolated, I can manage to put up with her absence very well.' I made a little bow.

But this most unaccountable of damsels frowned and shook her head.

'Cut it out. I prefer the "dignified disapproval" stunt. Oh, your face! "Not one of us", it said. And you were right there – though, mind you, it's pretty hard to tell nowadays. It's not everyone who can distinguish between a demi and a duchess. There now, I believe I've shocked you again! You've been dug out of the backwoods, you have. Not that I mind that. We could do with a few more of your sort. I just hate a fellow who gets fresh. It makes me mad.'

She shook her head vigorously.

'What are you like when you're mad?' I inquired with a smile.

'A regular little devil! Don't care what I say, or what I do, either! I nearly did a chap in once. Yes, really. He'd have deserved it too.'

'Well,' I begged, 'don't get mad with me.'

'I shan't. I like you – did the first moment I set eyes on you. But you looked so disapproving that I never thought we should make friends.'

'Well, we have. Tell me something about yourself.'

'I'm an actress. No – not the kind you're thinking of. I've been on the boards since I was a kid of six – tumbling.'

'I beg your pardon,' I said, puzzled.

'Haven't you ever seen child acrobats?'

'Oh, I understand!'

'I'm American born, but I've spent most of my life in England. We've got a new show now –'

'We?'

'My sister and I. Sort of song and dance, and a bit of patter, and a dash of the old business thrown in. It's quite a new idea, and it hits them every time. There's going to be money in it –'

My new acquaintance leaned forward, and discoursed volubly, a great many of her terms being quite unintelligible to me. Yet I found myself evincing an increasing interest in her. She seemed such a curious mixture of child and woman. Though perfectly worldly-wise, and able, as she expressed it, to take care of herself, there was yet something curiously ingenuous in her single-minded attitude towards life, and her wholehearted determination to 'make good'.

We passed through Amiens. The name awakened many memories. My companion seemed to have an intuitive knowledge of what was in my mind.

'Thinking of the War?'

I nodded.

'You were through it, I suppose?'

'Pretty well. I was wounded once, and after the Somme they invalided me out altogether. I'm a sort of private secretary now to an MP.'

'My! That's brainy!'

'No, it isn't. There's really awfully little to do. Usually a couple of hours every day sees me through. It's dull work too. In fact, I don't know what I should do if I hadn't got something to fall back upon.'

'Don't say you collect bugs!'

'No. I share rooms with a very interesting man. He's a Belgian – an ex-detective. He's set up as a private detective in London, and he's doing extraordinarily well. He's really a very marvellous little man. Time and again he has proved to be right where the official police have failed.'

My companion listened with widening eyes.

'Isn't that interesting now? I just adore crime. I go to all the mysteries on the movies. And when there's a murder on I just devour the papers.'

'Do you remember the Styles Case?' I asked.

'Let me see, was that the old lady who was poisoned? Somewhere down in Essex?'

I nodded.

'That was Poirot's first big case. Undoubtedly, but for him the murderer would have escaped scot-free. It was a most wonderful bit of detective work.'

Warming to my subject, I ran over the heads of the affair, working up to the triumphant and unexpected dénouement.

The girl listened spellbound. In fact, we were so absorbed that the train drew into Calais station before we realized it.

I secured a couple of porters, and we alighted on the platform. My companion held out her hand.

'Goodbye, and I'll mind my language better in future.'

'Oh, but surely you'll let me look after you on the boat?'

'Mayn't be on the boat. I've got to see whether that sister of mine got aboard after all anywhere. But thanks, all the same.'

'Oh, but we're going to meet again, surely? Aren't you even going to tell me your name?' I cried, as she turned away.

She looked over her shoulder.

'Cinderella,' she said, and laughed.

But little did I think when and how I should see Cinderella again.

CHAPTER 2

AN APPEAL FOR HELP

It was five minutes past nine when I entered our joint sitting-room for breakfast on the following morning. My friend Poirot, exact to the minute as usual, was just tapping the shell of his second egg.

He beamed upon me as I entered.

'You have slept well, yes? You have recovered from the crossing so terrible? It is a marvel, almost you are exact this morning. *Pardon*, but your tie is not symmetrical. Permit that I rearrange him.'

Elsewhere, I have described Hercule Poirot. An extraordinary little man! Height, five feet four inches, egg-shaped head carried a little to one side, eyes that shone green when he was excited, stiff military moustache, air of dignity immense! He was neat and dandified in appearance. For neatness of any kind he had an absolute passion. To see an ornament set crookedly, or a speck of dust, or a slight disarray in one's attire, was torture to the little man until he could ease his feelings by remedying the matter. 'Order' and 'Method' were his gods. He had a certain disdain for tangible evidence, such as footprints and cigarette ash, and would maintain that, taken by themselves, they would never enable a detective to solve a problem. Then he would tap his egg-shaped head with absurd complacency, and remark with great satisfaction: 'The true work, it is done from *within. The little grey cells* – remember always the little grey cells, *mon ami*.'

I slipped into my seat, and remarked idly, in answer to Poirot's greeting, that an hour's sea passage from Calais to Dover could hardly be dignified by the epithet 'terrible'.

'Anything interesting come by the post?' I asked.

Poirot shook his head with a dissatisfied air.

'I have not yet examined my letters, but nothing of interest arrives nowadays. The great criminals, the criminals of method, they do not exist.'

He shook his head despondently, and I roared with laughter.

'Cheer up, Poirot, the luck will change. Open your letters. For all you know, there may be a great case looming on the horizon.'

Poirot smiled, and taking up the neat little letter opener with which he opened his correspondence he slit the tops of the several envelopes that lay by his plate.

'A bill. Another bill. It is that I grow extravagant in my old age. Aha! a note from Japp.'

'Yes?' I pricked up my ears. The Scotland Yard Inspector had more than once introduced us to an interesting case.

'He merely thanks me (in his fashion) for a little point in the Aberystwyth Case on which I was able to set him right. I am delighted to have been of service to him.'

Poirot continued to read his correspondence placidly.

'A suggestion that I should give a lecture to our local Boy Scouts. The Countess of Forfanock will be obliged if I will call and see her. Another lap-dog without doubt! And now for the last. Ah –'

I looked up, quick to notice the change of tone. Poirot was reading attentively. In a minute he tossed the sheet over to me.

'This is out of the ordinary, *mon ami*. Read for yourself.'

The letter was written on a foreign type of paper, in a bold characteristic hand:

> Villa Geneviève,
> Merlinville-sur-Mer,
> France.
>
> Dear Sir, – I am in need of the services of a detective and, for reasons which I will give you later, do not wish to call in the official police. I have heard of you from several quarters, and all reports go to show that you are not only a man of decided ability, but one who also knows how to be discreet. I do not wish to trust details to the post, but, on account of a secret I possess, I go in daily fear of my life. I am convinced that the danger is imminent, and therefore I beg that you will lose no time in crossing to France, I will send a car to meet you at Calais, if you will wire me when you are arriving. I shall be obliged if you will drop all cases you have on hand, and devote yourself solely to my interests. I am prepared to pay any compensation necessary. I shall probably need your services for a considerable period of time, as it may be necessary for you to go out to Santiago, where I spent several years of my life. I shall be content for you to name your own fee.
>
> Assuring you once more that the matter is *urgent*.
> Yours faithfully,
> P. T. Renauld.

Below the signature was a hastily scrawled line, almost illegible:

'For God's sake, come!'

I handed the letter back with quickened pulses.

'At last!' I said. 'Here is something distinctly out of the ordinary.'

'Yes, indeed,' said Poirot meditatively.

'You will go of course,' I continued.

Poirot nodded. He was thinking deeply. Finally he seemed to make up his mind, and glanced up at the clock. His face was very grave.

'See you, my friend, there is no time to lose. The Continental express leaves Victoria at 11 o'clock. Do not agitate yourself. There is plenty of time. We can allow ten minutes for discussion. You accompany me, *n'est-ce pas?*'

'Well –'

'You told me yourself that your employer needed you not for the next few weeks.'

'Oh, that's all right. But this Mr Renauld hints strongly that his business is private.'

'Ta-ta-ta! I will manage M. Renauld. By the way, I seem to know the name?'

'There's a well-known South American millionaire fellow. His name's Renauld. I don't know whether it could be the same.'

'But without doubt. That explains the mention of Santiago. Santiago is in Chile, and Chile it is in South America! Ah; but we progress finely! You remarked the postscript? How did it strike you?'

I considered.

'Clearly he wrote the letter keeping himself well in hand, but at the end his self-control snapped and, on the impulse of the moment, he scrawled those four desperate words.'

But my friend shook his head energetically.

'You are in error. See you not that while the ink of the signature is nearly black, that of the postscript is quite pale?'

'Well?' I said, puzzled.

'*Mon Dieu, mon ami*, but use your little grey cells. Is it not obvious? Mr Renault wrote his letter. Without blotting it, he re-read it carefully. Then, not on impulse, but deliberately, he added those last words, and blotted the sheet.'

'But why?'

'*Parbleu!* so that it should produce the effect upon me that it has upon you.'

'What?'

'*Mais oui* – to make sure of my coming! He re-read the letter and was dissatisfied. It was not strong enough!'

He paused, and then added softly, his eyes shining with that green light that always betokened inward excitement:

'And so, *mon ami*, since that postscript was added, not on impulse, but soberly, in cold blood, the urgency is very great, and we must reach him as soon as possible.'

'Merlinville,' I murmured thoughtfully. 'I've heard of it, I think.'

Poirot nodded.

'It is a quiet little place – but chic! It lies about midway between Boulogne and Calais. Mr Renauld has a house in England, I suppose?'

'Yes, in Rutland Gate, as far as I remember. Also a big place in the country, somewhere in Hertfordshire. But I really know very little about him, he doesn't do much in a social way. I believe he has large South American interests in the City, and has spent most of his life out in Chile and the Argentine.'

'Well, we shall hear all the details from the man himself. Come, let us pack. A small suit-case each, and then a taxi to Victoria.'

Eleven o'clock saw our departure from Victoria on our way to Dover. Before starting Poirot had dispatched a telegram to Mr Renauld giving the time of our arrival at Calais.

'I'm surprised you haven't invested in a few bottles of some sea sick remedy, Poirot,' I observed maliciously, as I recalled our conversation at breakfast.

My friend, who was anxiously scanning the weather, turned a reproachful face upon me.

'Is it that you have forgotten the method most excellent of Laverguier? His system, I practise it always. One balances oneself, if you remember, turning the head from left to right, breathing in and out, counting six between each breath.'

'H'm,' I demurred. 'You'll be rather tired of balancing yourself and counting six by the time you get to Santiago, or Buenos Aires, or wherever it is you land.'

'*Quelle idée!* You do not figure to yourself that I shall go to Santiago?'

'Mr Renauld suggests it in his letter.'

'He did not know the methods of Hercule Poirot. I do not run to and fro, making journeys, and agitating myself. My work is done from within – *here* –' he tapped his forehead significantly.

As usual, this remark roused my argumentative faculty.

'It's all very well, Poirot, but I think you are falling into the habit of despising certain things too much. A fingerprint has led sometimes to the arrest and conviction of a murderer.'

'And has, without doubt, hanged more than one innocent man,' remarked Poirot dryly.

'But surely the study of fingerprints and footprints, cigarette ash, different kinds of mud, and other clues that comprise the minute observation of details – all these are of vital importance?'

'But certainly. I have never said otherwise. The trained observer, the expert, without doubt he is useful! But the others, the Hercules Poirots, they are above the experts! To them the experts bring the facts, their business is the method of the crime, its logical deduction, the proper sequence and order of the facts; above all, the true psychology of the case. You have hunted the fox, yes?'

'I have hunted a bit, now and again,' I said, rather bewildered by this abrupt change of subject. 'Why?'

'*Eh bien*, this hunting of the fox, you need the dogs, no?'

'Hounds,' I corrected gently. 'Yes, of course.'

'But yet,' Poirot wagged his finger at me. 'You did not descend from your horse and run along the ground smelling with your nose and uttering loud Ow Ows?'

In spite of myself I laughed immoderately. Poirot nodded in a satisfied manner.

'So. You leave the work of the d— hounds to the hounds. Yet you demand that I, Hercule Poirot, should make myself ridiculous by lying down (possibly on damp grass) to study hypothetical footprints, and should scoop up cigarette ash when I do not know one kind from the other. Remember the Plymouth Express mystery. The good Japp departed to make a survey of the railway line. When he returned, I, without having moved from my apartments, was able to tell him exactly what he had found.'

'So you are of the opinion that Japp wasted his time.'

'Not at all, since his evidence confirmed my theory. But *I* should have wasted my time if *I* had gone. It is the same with so called "experts". Remember the handwriting testimony in the Cavendish Case. One counsel's questioning brings out testimony as to the resemblances, the defence brings evidence to show dissimilarity. All the language is very technical. And the result? What we all knew in the first place. The writing was very like that of John Cavendish. And the psychological mind is faced with the question "Why?" Because it was actually his? Or because some one wished us to think it was his? I answered that question, *mon ami*, and answered it correctly.'

And Poirot, having effectually silenced, if not convinced me, leaned back with a satisfied air.

On the boat, I knew better than to disturb my friend's solitude. The weather was gorgeous, and the sea as smooth as the proverbial mill-pond, so I was hardly surprised when a smiling Poirot joined me on disembarking at Calais. A disappointment was in store for us, as no car had been sent to meet us, but Poirot put this down to his telegram having been delayed in transit.

'We will hire a car,' he said cheerfully. And a few minutes later saw us creaking and jolting along, in the most ramshackle of automobiles that ever plied for hire, in the direction of Merlinville.

My spirits were at their highest, but my little friend was observing me gravely.

'You are what the Scotch people call "fey", Hastings. It presages disaster.'

'Nonsense. At any rate, you do not share my feelings.'

'No, but I am afraid.'

'Afraid of what?'

'I do not know. But I have a premonition – a *je ne sais quoi!*'

He spoke so gravely that I was impressed in spite of myself.

'I have a feeling,' he said slowly, 'that this is going to be a big affair – a long, troublesome problem that will not be easy to work out.'

I would have questioned him further, but we were just coming into the little town of Merlinville, and we slowed up to inquire the way to the Villa Geneviève.

'Straight on, monsieur, through the town. The Villa Geneviève is about half a mile the other side. You cannot miss it. A big villa, overlooking the sea.'

We thanked our informant, and drove on, leaving the town behind. A fork in the road brought us to a second halt. A peasant was trudging towards us, and we waited for him to come up to us in order to ask the way again. There was a tiny villa standing right by the road, but it was too small and dilapidated to be the one we wanted. As we waited, the gate of it swung open and a girl came out.

The peasant was passing us now, and the driver leaned forward from his seat and asked for direction.

'The Villa Geneviève? Just a few steps up this road to the right, monsieur. You could see it if it were not for the curve.'

The chauffeur thanked him, and started the car again. My eyes were fascinated by the girl who still stood, with one hand on the gate, watching us. I am an admirer of beauty, and here was one whom nobody could have passed without remark. Very tall, with the proportions of a young goddess, her uncovered golden head gleaming in the sunlight, I swore to myself that she was one of the most beautiful girls I had ever seen. As we swung up the rough road, I turned my head to look after her.

'By Jove, Poirot,' I exclaimed, 'did you see that young goddess?'

Poirot raised his eyebrows.

'*Ça commence!*' he murmured. 'Already you have seen a goddess!'

'But, hang it all, wasn't she?'

'Possibly, I did not remark the fact.'

'Surely you noticed her?'

'*Mon ami*, two people rarely see the same thing. You, for instance, saw a goddess. I –' He hesitated.

'Yes?'

'I saw only a girl with anxious eyes,' said Poirot gravely.

But at that moment we drew up at a big green gate, and, simultaneously, we both uttered an exclamation. Before it stood an imposing *sergent de ville*. He held up his hand to bar our way.

'You cannot pass, messieurs.'

'But we wish to see Mr Renauld,' I cried. 'We have an appointment. This is his villa, isn't it?'

'Yes, monsieur, but –'

Poirot leaned forward.

'But what?'

'Monsieur Renauld was murdered this morning.'

CHAPTER 3

AT THE VILLA GENEVIÈVE

In a moment Poirot had leapt from the car, his eyes blazing with excitement.

'What is that you say? Murdered? When? How?'

The *sergent de ville* drew himself up.

'I cannot answer any questions, monsieur.'

'True. I comprehend.' Poirot reflected for a minute. 'The Commissary of Police, he is without doubt within?'

'Yes, monsieur.'

Poirot took out a card, and scribbled a few words on it.

'*Voilà!* Will you have the goodness to see that this card is sent in to the commissary at once?'

The man took it and, turning his head over his shoulder, whistled. In a few seconds a comrade joined him, and was handed Poirot's message. There was a wait of some minutes, and then a short, stout man with a huge moustache came bustling down to the gate. The *sergent de ville* saluted and stood aside.

'My dear Monsieur Poirot,' cried the newcomer, 'I am delighted to see you. Your arrival is most opportune.'

Poirot's face had lighted up.

'Monsieur Bex! This is indeed a pleasure.' He turned to me. 'This is an English friend of mine, Captain Hastings – Monsieur Lucien Bex.'

The commissary and I bowed to each other ceremoniously, and M. Bex turned once more to Poirot.

'*Mon vieux*, I have not seen you since 1909, that time in Ostend. You have information to give which may assist us?'

'Possibly you know it already. You were aware that I had been sent for?'

'No. By whom?'

'The dead man. It seems that he knew an attempt was going to be made on his life. Unfortunately he sent for me too late.'

'*Sacré tonnerre!*' ejaculated the Frenchman. 'So he foresaw his own murder. That upsets our theories considerably! But come inside.'

He held the gate open, and we commenced walking towards the house. M. Bex continued to talk:

'The examining magistrate, Monsieur Hautet, must hear of this at once. He has just finished examining the scene of the crime and is about to begin his interrogations.'

'When was the crime committed?' asked Poirot.

'The body was discovered this morning about nine o'clock. Madame Renauld's evidence and that of the doctors goes to show that death must have occurred about 2 am. But enter, I pray of you.'

We had arrived at the steps which led up to the front door of the villa. In the hall another *sergent de ville* was sitting. He rose at sight of the commissary.

'Where is Monsieur Hautet now?' inquired the latter.

'In the *salon*, monsieur.'

M. Bex opened a door to the left of the hall, and we passed in. M. Hautet and his clerk were sitting at a big round table. They looked up as we entered. The commissary introduced us, and explained our presence.

M. Hautet, the Juge d'Instruction, was a tall gaunt man, with piercing dark eyes, and a neatly cut grey beard, which he had a habit of caressing as he talked. Standing by the mantelpiece was an elderly man, with slightly stooping shoulders, who was introduced to us as Dr Durand.

'Most extraordinary,' remarked M. Hautet as the commissary finished speaking. 'You have the letter here, monsieur?'

Poirot handed it to him, and the magistrate read it.

'H'm! He speaks of a secret. What a pity he was not more explicit. We are much indebted to you, Monsieur Poirot. I hope you will do us the honour of assisting us in our investigations. Or are you obliged to return to London?'

'Monsieur le juge, I propose to remain. I did not arrive in time to prevent my client's death, but I feel myself bound in honour to discover the assassin.'

The magistrate bowed.

'These sentiments do you honour. Also, without doubt, Madame Renauld will wish to retain your services. We are expecting M. Giraud from the Sûreté in Paris any moment, and I am sure that you and he will be able to give each other mutual assistance in your investigations. In the meantime, I hope that you will do me the honour to be present at my interrogations, and I need hardly say that if there is any assistance you require it is at your disposal.'

'I thank you, monsieur. You will comprehend that at present I am completely in the dark. I know nothing whatever.'

M. Hautet nodded to the commissary, and the latter took up the tale:

'This morning, the old servant Françoise, on descending to start her work, found the front door ajar. Feeling a momentary alarm as to burglars, she looked into the dining-room, but seeing the silver was safe she thought no more about it, concluding that her master had, without doubt, risen early, and gone for a stroll.'

'Pardon, monsieur, for interrupting, but was that a common practice of his?'

'No, it was not, but old Françoise has the common idea as regards the English – that they are mad, and liable to do the most unaccountable things at any moment! Going to call her mistress as usual, a young maid, Léonie, was horrified to discover her gagged and bound, and almost at the same moment news was brought that Monsieur Renauld's body had been discovered, stone dead, stabbed in the back.'

'Where?'

'That is one of the most extraordinary features of the case. Monsieur Poirot, the body was lying face downwards, *in an open grave.*'

'What?'

'Yes. The pit was freshly dug – just a few yards outside the boundary of the villa grounds.'

'And it had been dead – how long?'

Dr Durand answered this.

'I examined the body this morning at ten o'clock. Death must have taken place at least seven, and possibly ten hours previously.'

'H'm! that fixes it at between midnight and 3 am.'

'Exactly, and Mrs Renauld's evidence places it at after 2 am, which narrows the field still farther. Death must have been instantaneous, and naturally could not have been self-inflicted.'

Poirot nodded, and the commissary resumed:

'Madame Renauld was hastily freed from the cords that bound her by the horrified servants. She was in a terrible condition of weakness, almost unconscious from the pain of her bonds. It appears that two masked men entered the bedroom, gagged and bound her, while forcibly abducting her husband. This we know at second hand from the servants. On hearing the tragic news, she fell at once into an alarming state of agitation. On arrival, Dr Durand immediately prescribed a sedative, and we have not yet been able to question her. But without doubt she will awake more calm, and be equal to bearing the strain of the interrogation.'

The commissary paused.

'And the inmates of the house, monsieur?'

'There is old Françoise, the housekeeper, she lived for many years with the former owners of the Villa Geneviève. Then there are two young girls, sisters, Denise and Léonie Oulard. Their home is in Merlinville, and they come of most respectable parents. Then there is the chauffeur whom Monsieur Renauld brought over from England with him, but he is away on a holiday. Finally there are Madame Renauld and her son, Monsieur Jack Renauld. He, too, is away from home at present.'

Poirot bowed his head. M. Hautet spoke:

'Marchaud!'

The *sergent de ville* appeared.

'Bring in the woman Françoise.'

The man saluted, and disappeared. In a moment or two he returned, escorting the frightened Françoise.

'Your name is Françoise Arrichet?'

'Yes, monsieur.'

'You have been a long time in service at the Villa Geneviève?'

'Eleven years with Madame la Vicomtesse. Then when she sold the Villa this spring, I consented to remain on with the English milor'. Never did I imagine –'

The magistrate cut her short.

'Without doubt, without doubt. Now, Françoise, in this matter of the front door, whose business was it to fasten it at night?'

'Mine, monsieur. Always I saw to it myself.'

'And last night?'

'I fastened it as usual.'

'You are sure of that?'

'I swear it by the blessed saints, monsieur.'

'What time would that be?'

'The same time as usual, half past ten, monsieur.'

'What about the rest of the household, had they gone up to bed?'

'Madame had retired some time before. Denise and Léonie went up with me. Monsieur was still in his study.'

'Then, if anyone unfastened the door afterwards, it must have been Monsieur Renauld himself?'

Françoise shrugged her broad shoulders.

'What should he do that for? With robbers and assassins passing every minute! A nice idea! Monsieur was not an imbecile. It is not as though he had had to let the lady out –'

The magistrate interrupted sharply:

'The lady? What lady do you mean?'

'Why, the lady who came to see him.'

'Had a lady been to see him that evening?'

'But yes, monsieur – and many other evenings as well.'

'Who was she? Did you know her?'

A rather cunning look spread over the woman's face.

'How should I know who it was?' she grumbled. 'I did not let her in last night.'

'Aha!' roared the examining magistrate, bringing his hand down with a bang on the table. 'You would trifle with the police, would you? I demand that you tell me at once the name of this woman who came to visit Monsieur Renauld in the evenings.'

'The police – the police,' grumbled Françoise. 'Never did I think that I should be mixed up with the police. But I know well enough who she was. It was Madame Daubreuil.'

The commissary uttered an exclamation, and leaned forward as though in utter astonishment.

'Madame Daubreuil – from the Villa Marguerite just down the road?'

'That is what I said, monsieur. Oh, she is a pretty one.'

The old woman tossed her head scornfully.

'Madame Daubreuil,' murmured the commissary. 'Impossible.'

'*Voilà*,' grumbled Françoise. 'That is all you get for telling the truth.'

'Not at all,' said the examining magistrate soothingly. 'We were surprised, that is all. Madame Daubreuil then, and Monsieur Renauld, they were –?' He paused delicately. 'Eh? It was that without doubt?'

'How should I know? But what will you? Monsieur, he was *milord anglais* – *très riche* – and Madame Daubreuil, she was poor, that one – and *très chic*, for all that she lives so quietly with her daughter. Not a doubt of it, she has had her history! She is no longer young, but *ma foi!* I who speak to you have seen the men's heads turn after her as she goes down the street. Besides lately, she had had more money to spend – all the town knows it. The little economies, they are at an end.' And Françoise shook her head with an air of unalterable certainty.

M. Hautet stroked his beard reflectively.

'And Madame Renauld?' he asked at length. 'How did she take this – friendship?'

Françoise shrugged her shoulders.

'She was always most amiable – most polite. One would say that she suspected nothing. But all the same, is it not so, the heart suffers, monsieur? Day by day, I have watched Madame grow paler and thinner. She was not the same woman who arrived here a month ago. Monsieur, too, has changed. He also has had his worries. One could see that he was on the brink of a crisis of the nerves. And who could wonder, with an affair conducted in such a fashion? No reticence, no discretion. *Style anglais*, without doubt!'

I bounded indignantly in my seat, but the examining magistrate was continuing his questions, undistracted by side issues.

'You say that Monsieur Renauld had not to let Madame Daubreuil out? Had she left, then?'

'Yes, monsieur. I heard them come out of the study and go to the door. Monsieur said goodnight, and shut the door after her.'

'What time was that?'

'About twenty-five minutes after ten, monsieur.'

'Do you know when Monsieur Renauld went to bed?'

'I heard him come up about ten minutes after we did. The stair creaks so that one hears everyone who goes up and down.'

'And that is all? You heard no sound of disturbance during the night?'

'Nothing whatever, monsieur.'

'Which of the servants came down the first in the morning?'

'I did, monsieur. At once I saw the door swinging open.'

'What about the other downstairs windows, were they all fastened?'

'Every one of them. There was nothing suspicious or out of place anywhere.'

'Good. Françoise, you can go.'

The old woman shuffled towards the door. On the threshold she looked back.

'I will tell you one thing, monsieur. That Madame Daubreuil she is a bad one! Oh, yes, one woman knows about another. She is a bad one, remember that.' And, shaking her head sagely, Françoise left the room.

'Léonie Oulard,' called the magistrate.

Léonie appeared dissolved in tears, and inclined to be hysterical. M. Hautet dealt with her adroitly. Her evidence was mainly concerned with the discovery of her mistress gagged and bound, of which she gave rather an exaggerated account. She, like Françoise, had heard nothing during the night.

Her sister, Denise, succeeded her. She agreed that her master had changed greatly of late.

'Every day he became more and more morose. He ate less. He was always depressed.' But Denise had her own theory. 'Without doubt it was the Mafia he had on his track! Two masked men – who else could it be? A terrible society that!'

'It is, of course, possible,' said the magistrate smoothly. 'Now, my girl, was it you who admitted Madame Daubreuil to the house last night?'

'Not *last* night, monsieur, the night before.'

'But Françoise has just told us that Madame Daubreuil was here last night?'

'No, monsieur. A lady *did* come to see Monsieur Renauld last night, but it was not Madame Daubreuil.'

Surprised, the magistrate insisted, but the girl held firm. She knew Madame Daubreuil perfectly by sight. This lady was dark also, but shorter, and much younger. Nothing could shake her statement.

'Had you ever seen this lady before?'

'Never, monsieur.' And then the girl added diffidently: 'But I think she was English.'

'English?'

'Yes, monsieur. She asked for Monsieur Renauld in quite good French, but the accent – however slight one can always tell it. Besides, when they came out of the study they were speaking in English.'

'Did you hear what they said? Could you understand it, I mean?'

'Me, I speak the English very well,' said Denise with pride. 'The lady was speaking too fast for me to catch what she said, but I heard Monsieur's last words as he opened the door for her.' She paused, and then repeated carefully and laboriously: '"Yeas – yeas – but for Gaud's saike go nauw!"'

'Yes, yes, but for God's sake go now!' repeated the magistrate.

He dismissed Denise and, after a moment or two for consideration, recalled Françoise. To her he propounded the question as to whether she had not made a mistake in fixing the night of Madame Daubreuil's visit. Françoise, however, proved unexpectedly obstinate. It was last night that Madame Daubreuil had come. Without doubt it was she. Denise wished to make herself interesting, *voilà tout!* So she had cooked up this fine tale about a strange lady. Airing her knowledge of English, too! Probably Monsieur had never spoken that sentence in English at all, and, even if he had, it proved nothing, for Madame Daubreuil spoke English perfectly, and generally used that language when talking to Monsieur and Madame Renauld. 'You see, Monsieur Jack, the son of Monsieur, was usually here, and he spoke the French very badly.'

The magistrate did not insist. Instead, he inquired about the chauffeur, and learned that only yesterday Monsieur Renauld had declared that he was not likely to use the car, and that Masters might just as well take a holiday.

A perplexed frown was beginning to gather between Poirot's eyes.

'What is it?' I whispered.

He shook his head impatiently, and asked a question:

'Pardon, Monsieur Bex, but without doubt Monsieur Renauld could drive the car himself?'

The commissary looked over at Françoise, and the old woman replied promptly:

'No, Monsieur did not drive himself.'

Poirot's frown deepened.

'I wish you would tell me what is worrying you,' I said impatiently.

'See you not? In his letter Monsieur Renauld speaks of sending the car for me to Calais.'

'Perhaps he meant a hired car,' I suggested.

'Doubtless, that is so. But why hire a car when you have one of your own? Why choose yesterday to send away the chauffeur on a holiday – suddenly, at a moment's notice? Was it that for some reason he wanted him out of the way before we arrived?'

CHAPTER 4

THE LETTER SIGNED 'BELLA'

Françoise had left the room. The magistrate was drumming thoughtfully on the table.

'Monsieur Bex,' he said at length, 'here we have directly conflicting testimony. Which are we to believe, Françoise or Denise?'

'Denise,' said the commissary decidedly. 'It was she who let the visitor in. Françoise is old and obstinate, and has evidently taken a dislike to Madame Daubreuil. Besides, our own knowledge tends to show that Renauld was entangled with another woman.'

'*Tiens!*' cried M. Hautet. 'We have forgotten to inform Monsieur Poirot of that.' He searched among the papers on the table, and finally handed the one he was in search of to my friend. 'This letter, Monsieur Poirot, we found in the pocket of the dead man's overcoat.'

Poirot took it and unfolded it. It was somewhat worn and crumpled, and was written in English in a rather unformed hand:

> My Dearest One, – Why have you not written for so long? You do love me still, don't you? Your letters lately have been so different, cold, and strange, and now this long silence. It makes me afraid. If you were to stop loving me! But that's impossible – what a silly kid I am – always imagining things! But if you *did* stop loving me, I don't know what I should do – kill myself perhaps! I couldn't live without you. Sometimes I fancy another woman is coming between us. Let her look out, that's all – and you too! I'd as soon kill you as let her have you! I mean it.
>
> But there, I'm writing high-flown nonsense. You love me, and I love you – yes, love you, love you, love you!
>
> Your own adoring
>
> Bella.

There was no address or date. Poirot handed it back with a grave face.

'And the assumption is –?'

The examining magistrate shrugged his shoulders.

'Obviously Monsieur Renauld was entangled with this Englishwoman – Bella! He comes over here, meets Madame Daubreuil, and starts an intrigue with her. He cools off to the other, and she instantly suspects something. This letter contains a distinct threat. Monsieur Poirot, at first sight the case seemed simplicity itself. Jealousy! The fact that Monsieur Renauld was stabbed in the back seemed to point distinctly to its being a woman's crime.'

Poirot nodded.

'The stab in the back, yes – but not the grave! That was laborious work, hard work – no woman dug that grave, Monsieur. That was a man's doing.'

The commissary exclaimed excitedly:

'Yes, yes, you are right. We did not think of that.'

'As I said,' continued M. Hautet, 'at first sight the case seemed simple, but the masked men, and the letter you received from Monsieur Renauld, complicate matters. Here we seem to have an entirely different set of circumstances, with no relationship between the two. As regards the letter written to yourself, do you think it is possible that it referred in any way to this "Bella" and her threats?'

Poirot shook his head.

'Hardly. A man like Monsieur Renauld, who had led an adventurous life in out-of-the-way places, would not be likely to ask for protection against a woman.'

The examining magistrate nodded his head emphatically.

'My view exactly. Then we must look for the explanation of the letter –'

'In Santiago,' finished the commissary. 'I shall cable without delay to the police in that city, requesting full details of the murdered man's life out there, his love affairs, his business transactions, his friendships, and any enmities he may have incurred. It will be strange if, after that, we do not hold a clue to his mysterious murder.'

The commissary looked around for approval.

'Excellent!' said Poirot appreciatively.

'You have found no other letters from this Bella among Monsieur Renauld's effects?' asked Poirot.

'No. Of course one of our first proceedings was to search

through his private papers in the study. We found nothing of interest, however. All seemed square and above-board. The only thing at all out of the ordinary was his will. Here it is.'

Poirot ran through the document.

'So. A legacy of a thousand pounds to Mr Stonor – who is he, by the way?'

'Monsieur Renauld's secretary. He remained in England, but was over here once or twice for a weekend.'

'And everything else left unconditionally to his beloved wife, Eloise. Simply drawn up, but perfectly legal. Witnessed by the two servants, Denise and Françoise. Nothing so very unusual about that.' He handed it back.

'Perhaps,' began Bex, 'you did not notice –'

'The date?' twinkled Poirot. 'But, yes, I noticed it. A fortnight ago. Possibly it marks his first intimation of danger. Many rich men die intestate through never considering the likelihood of their demise. But it is dangerous to draw conclusions prematurely. It points, however, to his having a real liking and fondness for his wife, in spite of his amorous intrigues.'

'Yes,' said M. Hautet doubtfully. 'But it is possibly a little unfair on his son, since it leaves him entirely dependent on his mother. If she were to marry again, and her second husband obtained an ascendancy over her, this boy might never touch a penny of his father's money.'

Poirot shrugged his shoulders.

'Man is a vain animal. Monsieur Renauld figured to himself, without doubt, that his widow would never marry again. As to the son, it may have been a wise precaution to leave the money in his mother's hands. The sons of rich men are proverbially wild.'

'It may be as you say. Now, Monsieur Poirot, you would without doubt like to visit the scene of the crime. I am sorry that the body has been removed, but of course photographs have been taken from every conceivable angle, and will be at your disposal as soon as they are available.'

'I thank you, monsieur, for all your courtesy.'

The commissary rose.

'Come with me, messieurs.'

He opened the door, and bowed ceremoniously to Poirot to precede him. Poirot, with equal politeness, drew back and bowed to the commissary.

'Monsieur.'

'Monsieur.'

At last they got out into the hall.

'That room there, it is the study, *hein*?' asked Poirot suddenly, nodding towards the door opposite.

'Yes. You would like to see it?' He threw open the door as he spoke, and we entered.

The room which M. Renauld had chosen for his own particular use was small, but furnished with great taste and comfort. A business-like writing-desk, with many pigeon-holes, stood in the window. Two large leather-covered armchairs faced the fireplace, and between them was a round table covered with the latest books and magazines.

Poirot stood a moment taking in the room, then he stepped forward, passed his hand lightly over the backs of the leather chairs, picked up a magazine from the table, and drew a finger gingerly over the surface of the oak sideboard. His face expressed complete approval.

'No dust?' I asked, with a smile.

He beamed on me, appreciative of my knowledge of his peculiarities.

'Not a particle, *mon ami!* And for once, perhaps, it is a pity.'

His sharp, birdlike eyes darted here and there.

'Ah!' he remarked suddenly, with an intonation of relief. 'The hearth-rug is crooked,' and he bent down to straighten it.

Suddenly he uttered an exclamation and rose. In his hand he held a small fragment of pink paper.

'In France, as in England,' he remarked, 'the domestics omit to sweep under the mats?'

Bex took the fragment from him, and I came close to examine it.

'You recognize it – eh, Hastings?'

I shook my head, puzzled – and yet that particular shade of pink paper was very familiar.

The commissary's mental processes were quicker than mine.

'A fragment of a cheque,' he exclaimed.

The piece of paper was roughly about two inches square. On it was written in ink the word 'Duveen'.

'*Bien!*' said Bex. 'This cheque was payable to, or drawn by, someone named Duveen.'

'The former, I fancy,' said Poirot. 'For, if I am not mistaken, the handwriting is that of Monsieur Renauld.'

That was soon established, by comparing it with a memorandum from the desk.

'Dear me,' murmured the commissary, with a crestfallen air, 'I really cannot imagine how I came to overlook this.'

Poirot laughed.

'The moral of that is, always look under the mats! My friend Hastings here will tell you that anything in the least crooked is a torment to me. As soon as I saw that the hearthrug was out of the straight, I said to myself: "*Tiens!* The legs of the chair caught it in being pushed back. Possibly there may be something beneath it which the good Françoise overlooked."'

'Françoise?'

'Or Denise, or Léonie. Whoever did this room. Since there is no dust, the room *must* have been done this morning. I reconstruct the incident like this. Yesterday, possibly last night, Monsieur Renauld drew a cheque to the order of some one named Duveen. Afterwards it was torn up, and scattered on the floor. This morning –'

But M. Bex was already pulling impatiently at the bell.

Françoise answered it. Yes, there had been a lot of pieces of paper on the floor. What had she done with them? Put them in the kitchen stove of course! What else?

With a gesture of despair, Bex dismissed her. Then, his face lightening, he ran to the desk. In a minute he was hunting through the dead man's cheque book. Then he repeated his former gesture. The last counterfoil was blank.

'Courage!' cried Poirot, clapping him on the back. 'Without doubt, Madame Renauld will be able to tell us all about this mysterious person named Duveen.'

The commissary's face cleared. 'That is true. Let us proceed.'

As we turned to leave the room, Poirot remarked casually: 'It was here that Monsieur Renauld received his guest last night, eh?'

'It was – but how did you know?'

'By *this*. I found it on the back of the leather chair.' And he held up between his finger and thumb a long black hair – a woman's hair!

M. Bex took us out by the back of the house to where there was a small shed leaning against the house. He produced a key from his pocket and unlocked it.

'The body is here. We moved it from the scene of the crime just before you arrived, as the photographers had done with it.'

He opened the door and we passed in. The murdered man lay on the ground, with a sheet over him. M. Bex dexterously whipped off the covering. Renauld was a man of medium height, slender, and lithe in figure. He looked about fifty years of age, and his dark hair was plentifully streaked with grey. He was clean-shaven with a long, thin nose, and eyes set rather close together, and his skin was deeply bronzed, as that of a man who had spent most of his life beneath tropical skies. His lips were drawn back from his teeth and an expression of absolute amazement and terror was stamped on the livid features.

'One can see by his face that he was stabbed in the back,' remarked Poirot.

Very gently, he turned the dead man over. There, between the shoulder-blades, staining the light fawn overcoat, was a round dark patch. In the middle of it there was a slit in the cloth. Poirot examined it narrowly.

'Have you any idea with what weapon the crime was committed?'

'It was left in the wound.' The commissary reached down a large glass jar. In it was a small object that looked to me more like a paper-knife than anything else. It had a black handle and a narrow shining blade. The whole thing was not more than ten inches long. Poirot tested the discoloured point gingerly with his finger-tip.

'*Ma foi!* but it is sharp! A nice easy little tool for murder!'

'Unfortunately, we could find no trace of fingerprints on it,' remarked Bex regretfully. 'The murderer must have worn gloves.'

'Of course he did,' said Poirot contemptuously. 'Even in Santiago they know enough for that. The veriest amateur of an English Mees knows it – thanks to the publicity the Bertillon system has been given in the Press. All the same, it interests me very much that there were no fingerprints. It is so amazingly simple to leave the fingerprints of someone else! And then the police are happy.' He shook his head. 'I very much fear our criminal is not a man of method – either that or he was pressed for time. But we shall see.'

He let the body fall back into its original position.

'He wore only underclothes under his overcoat, I see,' he remarked.

'Yes, the examining magistrate thinks that is rather a curious point.'

At this minute there was a tap on the door which Bex had closed after him. He strode forward and opened it. Françoise was there. She endeavoured to peep in with ghoulish curiosity.

'Well, what is it?' demanded Bex impatiently.

'Madame. She sends a message that she is much recovered and is quite ready to receive the examining magistrate.'

'Good,' said M. Bex briskly. 'Tell Monsieur Hautet and say that we will come at once.'

Poirot lingered a moment, looking back towards the body. I thought for a moment that he was going to apostrophize it, to declare aloud his determination never to rest till he had discovered the murderer. But when he spoke, it was tamely and awkwardly, and his comment was ludicrously inappropriate to the solemnity of the moment.

'He wore his overcoat very long,' he said constrainedly.

CHAPTER 5

MRS RENAULD'S STORY

We found M. Hautet awaiting us in the hall, and we all proceeded upstairs together, Françoise marching ahead to show us the way. Poirot went up in a zigzag fashion which puzzled me, until he whispered with a grimace:

'No wonder the servants heard M. Renauld mounting the stairs, not a board of them but creaks fit to awake the dead!'

At the head of the staircase, a small passage branched off.

'The servants' quarters,' explained Bex.

We continued along a corridor, and Françoise tapped on the last door to the right of it.

A faint voice bade us enter, and we passed into a large, sunny apartment looking out towards the sea, which showed blue and sparkling about a quarter of a mile distant.

On a couch, propped up with cushions, and attended by Dr Durand, lay a tall, striking-looking woman. She was middle-aged, and her once dark hair was now almost entirely silvered, but the intense vitality, and strength of her personality would have made itself felt anywhere. You knew at once that you were in the presence of what the French call *une maîtresse femme.*

She greeted us with a dignified inclination of the head.

'Pray be seated, messieurs.'

We took chairs, and the magistrate's clerk established himself at a round table.

'I hope, madame,' began M. Hautet, 'that it will not distress you unduly to relate to us what occurred last night?'

'Not at all, monsieur. I know the value of time, if these scoundrelly assassins are to be caught and punished.'

'Very well, madame. It will fatigue you less, I think, if I ask you questions and you confine yourself to answering them. At what time did you go to bed last night?'

'At half past nine, monsieur. I was tired.'

'And your husband?'

'About an hour later, I fancy.'

'Did he seem disturbed – upset in any way?'

'No, not more than usual.'

'What happened then?'

'We slept. I was awakened by a hand pressed over my mouth. I tried to scream out, but the hand prevented me. There were two men in the room. They were both masked.'

'Can you describe them at all, madame?'

'One was very tall, and had a long black beard, the other was short and stout. His beard was reddish. They both wore hats pulled down over their eyes.'

'H'm!' said the magistrate thoughtfully. 'Too much beard, I fear.'

'You mean they were false?'

'Yes, madame. But continue your story.'

'It was the short man who was holding me. He forced a gag into my mouth, and then bound me with rope hand and foot. The other man was standing over my husband. He had caught up my little dagger paper-knife from the dressing-table and was holding it with the point just over his heart. When the short man had finished with me, he joined the other, and they forced my husband to get up and accompany them into the dressing-room next door. I was nearly fainting with terror, nevertheless I listened desperately.

'They were speaking in too low a tone for me to hear what they said. But I recognized the language, a bastard Spanish such as is spoken in some parts of South America. They seemed to be demanding something from my husband, and presently they grew angry, and their voices rose a little. I think the tall man was speaking. "You know what we want?" he said. "*The secret!* Where is it?" I do not know what my husband answered, but the other replied fiercely: "You lie! We know you have it. Where are your keys?"

'Then I heard sounds of drawers being pulled out. There is a safe on the wall of my husband's dressing-room in which he always keeps a fairly large amount of ready money. Léonie tells me this has been rifled and the money taken, but evidently what they were looking for was not there, for presently I heard the tall man, with an oath, command my husband to dress himself. Soon after that, I think some noise in the house must have disturbed them, for they hustled my husband out into my room only half dressed.'

'*Pardon*,' interrupted Poirot, 'but is there then no other egress from the dressing-room?'

'No, monsieur, there is only the communicating door into my room. They hurried my husband through, the short man in front, and the tall man behind him with the dagger still in his hand. Paul tried to break away to come to me. I saw his agonized eyes. He turned to his captors. "I must speak to her," he said. Then, coming to the side of the bed, "It is all right, Eloise," he said. "Do not be afraid. I shall return before morning." But, although he tried to make his voice confident, I could see the terror in his eyes. Then they hustled him out of the door, the tall man saying: "One sound – and you are a dead man, remember."

'After that,' continued Mrs Renauld, 'I must have fainted. The next thing I recollect is Léonie rubbing my wrists and giving me brandy.'

'Madame Renauld,' said the magistrate, 'had you any idea what it was for which the assassins were searching?'

'None whatever, monsieur.'

'Had you any knowledge that your husband feared something?'

'Yes. I had seen the change in him.'

'How long ago was that?'

Mrs Renauld reflected.

'Ten days, perhaps.'

'Not longer?'

'Possibly. I only noticed it then.'

'Did you question your husband at all as to the cause?'

'Once. He put me off evasively. Nevertheless, I was convinced that he was suffering some terrible anxiety. However, since he evidently wished to conceal the fact from me, I tried to pretend that I had noticed nothing.'

'Were you aware that he had called in the services of a detective?'

'A detective?' exclaimed Mrs Renauld, very much surprised.

'Yes, this gentleman – Monsieur Hercule Poirot.' Poirot bowed. 'He arrived today in response to a summons from your husband.' And taking the letter written by M. Renauld from his pocket he handed it to the lady.

She read it with apparently genuine astonishment.

'I had no idea of this. Evidently he was fully cognizant of the danger.'

'Now, madame, I will beg of you to be frank with me. Is there any incident in your husband's past life in South America which might throw light on his murder?'

Mrs Renauld reflected deeply, but at last shook her head.

'I can think of none. Certainly my husband had many enemies, people he had got the better of in some way or another, but I can think of no one distinctive case. I do not say there is no such incident – only that I am not aware of it.'

The examining magistrate stroked his beard disconsolately.

'And you can fix the time of this outrage?'

'Yes, I distinctly remember hearing the clock on the mantelpiece strike two.' She nodded towards an eight-day travelling clock in a leather case which stood in the centre of the chimney-piece.

Poirot rose from his seat, scrutinized the clock carefully, and nodded, satisfied.

'And here too,' exclaimed M. Bex, 'is a wristwatch, knocked off the dressing-table by the assassins, without doubt, and smashed to atoms. Little did they know it would testify against them.'

Gently he picked away the fragments of broken glass. Suddenly his face changed to one of utter stupefaction.

'*Mon Dieu!*' he ejaculated.

'What is it?'

'The hands of the watch point to seven o'clock!'

'What?' cried the examining magistrate, astonished.

But Poirot, deft as ever, took the broken trinket from the startled commissary, and held it to his ear. Then he smiled.

'The glass is broken, yes, but the watch itself is still going.'

The explanation of the mystery was greeted with a relieved smile. But the magistrate bethought him of another point.

'But surely it is not seven o'clock now?'

'No,' said Poirot gently, 'it is a few minutes after five. Possibly the watch gains, is that so, madame?'

Mrs Renauld was frowning perplexedly.

'It does gain,' she admitted. 'But I've never known it gain quite so much as that.'

With a gesture of impatience the magistrate left the matter of the watch and proceeded with his interrogatory.

'Madame, the front door was found ajar. It seems almost certain that the murderers entered that way, yet it has not been forced at all. Can you suggest any explanation?'

'Possibly my husband went out for a stroll the last thing, and forgot to latch it when he came in.'

'Is that a likely thing to happen?'

'Very. My husband was the most absent-minded of men.'

There was a slight frown on her brow as she spoke, as though this trait in the dead man's character had at times vexed her.

'There is one inference I think we might draw,' remarked the commissary suddenly. 'Since the men insisted on Monsieur Renauld dressing himself, it looks as though the place they were taking him to, the place where "the secret" was concealed, lay some distance away.'

The magistrate nodded.

'Yes, far, and yet not too far, since he spoke of being back by morning.'

'What time does the last train leave the station of Merlinville?' asked Poirot.

'11.50 one way, and 12.17 the other, but it is more probable that they had a motor waiting.'

'Of course,' agreed Poirot, looking somewhat crestfallen.

'Indeed, that might be one way of tracing them,' continued the magistrate, brightening. 'A motor containing two foreigners is quite likely to have been noticed. That is an excellent point, Monsieur Bex.'

He smiled to himself, and then, becoming grave once more, he said to Mrs Renauld:

'There is another question. Do you know anyone of the name of "Duveen"?'

'Duveen?' Mrs Renauld repeated thoughtfully. 'No, for the moment, I cannot say I do.'

'You have never heard your husband mention anyone of that name.'

'Never.'

'Do you know anyone whose Christian name is Bella?'

He watched Mrs Renauld narrowly as he spoke, seeking to surprise any signs of anger or consciousness, but she merely shook her head in quite a natural manner. He continued his questions.

'Are you aware that your husband had a visitor last night?'

Now he saw the red mount slightly in her cheeks, but she replied composedly:

'No, who was that?'

'A lady.'

'Indeed?'

But for the moment the magistrate was content to say no more. It seemed unlikely that Madame Daubreuil had any connexion with the crime, and he was anxious not to upset Mrs Renauld more than necessary.

He made a sign to the commissary, and the latter replied with a nod. Then rising, he went across the room, and returned with the glass jar we had seen in the outhouse in his hand. From this he took the dagger.

'Madame,' he said gently, 'do you recognize this?'

She gave a little cry.

'Yes, that is my little dagger.' Then she saw the stained point, and she drew back, her eyes widening with horror. 'Is that – blood?'

'Yes, madame. Your husband was killed with this weapon.' He removed it hastily from sight. 'You are quite sure about its being the one that was on your dressing-table last night?'

'Oh, yes. It was a present from my son. He was in the Air Force during the War. He gave his age as older than it was.' There was a touch of the proud mother in her voice. 'This was made from a streamline aeroplane wire, and was given to me by my son as a souvenir of the War.'

'I see, madame. That brings us to another matter. Your son, where is he now? It is necessary that he should be telegraphed to without delay.'

'Jack? He is on his way to Buenos Aires.'

'What?'

'Yes. My husband telegraphed to him yesterday. He had sent him on business to Paris, but yesterday he discovered that it would be necessary for him to proceed without delay to South America. There was a boat leaving Cherbourg for Buenos Aires last night, and he wired him to catch it.'

'Have you any knowledge of what the business in Buenos Aires was?'

'No, monsieur, I know nothing of its nature, but Buenos Aires is not my son's final destination. He was going overland from there to Santiago.'

And, in unison, the magistrate and the commissary exclaimed:

'Santiago! Again Santiago!'

It was at this moment, when we were all stunned by the mention of that word, that Poirot approached Mrs Renauld. He had been standing by the window like a man lost in a dream, and I doubt if he had fully taken in what had passed. He paused by the lady's side with a bow.

'*Pardon*, madame, but may I examine your wrists?'

Though slightly surprised at the request, Mrs Renauld held them out to him. Round each of them was a cruel red mark where the cords had bitten into the flesh. As he examined them, I fancied that a momentary flicker of excitement I had seen in his eyes disappeared.

'They must cause you great pain,' he said, and once more he looked puzzled.

But the magistrate was speaking excitedly.

'Young Monsieur Renauld must be communicated with at once by wireless. It is vital that we should know anything he can tell us about this trip to Santiago.' He hesitated. 'I hoped he might have been near at hand, so that we could have saved you pain, madame.' He paused.

'You mean,' she said in a low voice, 'the identification of my husband's body?'

The magistrate bowed his head.

'I am a strong woman, monsieur. I can bear all that is required of me. I am ready – now.'

'Oh, tomorrow will be quite soon enough, I assure you –'

'I prefer to get it over,' she said in a low tone, a spasm of pain crossing her face. 'If you will be so good as to give me your arm, doctor?'

The doctor hastened forward, a cloak was thrown over Mrs Renauld's shoulders, and a slow procession went down the stairs. M. Bex hurried on ahead to open the door of the shed. In a minute or two Mrs Renauld appeared in the doorway. She was very pale, but resolute. She raised her hand to her face.

'A moment, messieurs, while I steel myself.'

She took her hand away and looked down at the dead man. Then the marvellous self-control which had upheld her so far deserted her.

'Paul!' she cried. 'Husband! Oh, God!' And pitching forward she fell unconscious to the ground.

Instantly Poirot was beside her, he raised the lid of her eye, felt her pulse. When he had satisfied himself that she had really fainted, he drew aside. He caught me by the arm.

'I am an imbecile, my friend! If ever there was love and grief in a woman's voice, I heard it then. My little idea was all wrong. *Eh bien!* I must start again!'

CHAPTER 6

THE SCENE OF THE CRIME

Between them, the doctor and M. Hautet carried the unconscious woman into the house. The commissary looked after them, shaking his head.

'*Pauvre femme*,' he murmured to himself. 'The shock was too much for her. Well, well, we can do nothing. Now, Monsieur Poirot, shall we visit the place where the crime was committed?'

'If you please, Monsieur Bex.'

We passed through the house, and out by the front door. Poirot had looked up at the staircase in passing, and shook his head in a dissatisfied manner.

'It is to me incredible that the servants heard nothing. The creaking of that staircase, with *three* people descending it, would awaken the dead!'

'It was the middle of the night, remember. They were sound asleep by then.'

But Poirot continued to shake his head as though not fully accepting the explanation. On the sweep of the drive he paused, looking up at the house.

'What moved them in the first place to try if the front door were open? It was a most unlikely thing that it should be. It was far more probable that they should at once try to force a window.'

'But all the windows on the ground floor are barred with iron shutters,' objected the commissary.

Poirot pointed to a window on the first floor.

'That is the window of the bedroom we have just come from, is it not? And see – there is a tree by which it would be the easiest thing in the world to mount.'

'Possibly,' admitted the other. 'But they could not have done so without leaving footprints in the flower-bed.'

I saw the justice of his words. There were two large oval flower-beds planted with scarlet geraniums, one each side of the steps leading up to the front door. The tree in question had its roots actually at the back of the bed itself, and it would have been impossible to reach it without stepping on the bed.

'You see,' continued the commissary, 'owing to the dry weather no prints would show on the drive or paths; but, on the soft mould of the flower-bed, it would have been a very different affair.'

Poirot went close to the bed and studied it attentively. As Bex had said, the mould was perfectly smooth. There was not an indentation on it anywhere.

Poirot nodded, as though convinced, and we turned away, but he suddenly darted off and began examining the other flower-bed.

'Monsieur Bex!' he called. 'See here. Here are plenty of traces for you.'

The commissary joined him – and smiled.

'My dear Monsieur Poirot, those are without doubt the footprints of the gardener's large hobnailed boots. In any case, it would have no importance, since this side we have no tree, and consequently no means of gaining access to the upper storey.'

'True,' said Poirot, evidently crestfallen. 'So you think these footprints are of no importance?'

'Not the least in the world.'

Then, to my utter astonishment, Poirot pronounced these words:

'I do not agree with you. I have a little idea that these footprints are the most important things we have seen yet.'

M. Bex said nothing, merely shrugged his shoulders. He was far too courteous to utter his real opinion.

'Shall we proceed?' he asked, instead.

'Certainly. I can investigate this matter of the footprints later,' said Poirot cheerfully.

Instead of following the drive down to the gate, M. Bex turned up a path that branched off at right angles. It led, up a slight incline, round to the right of the house, and was bordered on either side by a kind of shrubbery. Suddenly it emerged into a little clearing from which one obtained a view of the sea. A seat had been placed here, and not far from it was a rather ramshackle shed. A few steps farther on, a neat line of small bushes marked the boundary of the Villa grounds. M. Bex pushed his way through these, and we found ourselves on a wide stretch of open downs. I looked round, and saw something that filled me with astonishment.

'Why, this is a Golf Course,' I cried.

Bex nodded.

'The links are not completed yet,' he explained. 'It is hoped to be able to open them some time next month. It was some of the men working on them who discovered the body early this morning.'

I gave a gasp. A little to my left, where for the moment I had overlooked it, was a long narrow pit and by it, face downwards, was the body of a man! For a moment my heart gave a terrible leap, and I had a wild fancy that the tragedy had been duplicated. But the commissary dispelled my illusion by moving forward with a sharp exclamation of annoyance:

'What have my police been about? They had strict orders to allow no one near the place without proper credentials!'

The man on the ground turned his head over his shoulder.

'But I have proper credentials,' he remarked, and rose slowly to his feet.

'My dear Monsieur Giraud,' cried the commissary. 'I had no idea that you had arrived, even. The examining magistrate has been awaiting you with the utmost impatience.'

As he spoke, I was scanning the newcomer with the keenest curiosity. The famous detective from the Paris Sûreté was familiar to me by name, and I was extremely interested to see him in the flesh. He was very tall, perhaps about thirty years of age, with auburn hair and moustache, and a military carriage. There was a trace of arrogance in his manner which showed that he was fully alive to his own importance. Bex introduced us, presenting Poirot as a colleague. A flicker of interest came into the detective's eye.

'I know you by name, Monsieur Poirot,' he said. 'You cut quite a figure in the old days, didn't you? But methods are very different now.'

'Crimes, though, are very much the same,' remarked Poirot gently.

I saw at once that Giraud was prepared to be hostile. He resented the other being associated with him, and I felt that if he came across any clue of importance he would be more than likely to keep it to himself.

'The examining magistrate –' began Bex again.

But Giraud interrupted rudely:

'A fig for the examining magistrate! The light is the important thing. For all practical purposes it will be gone in another half hour or so. I know all about the case, and the people at the house will do very well until tomorrow; but, if we're going to find a clue to the murderers, here is the spot we shall find it. Is it your police who have been trampling all over the place? I thought they knew better nowadays.'

'Assuredly they do. The marks you complain of were made by the workmen who discovered the body.'

The other grunted disgustedly.

'I can see the tracks where the three of them came through the hedge – but they were cunning. You can just recognize the centre footmarks as those of Monsieur Renauld, but those on either side have been carefully obliterated. Not that there would really be much to see anyway on this hard ground, but they weren't taking any chances.'

'The external sign,' said Poirot. 'That is what you seek, eh?'

The other detective stared.

'Of course.'

A very faint smile came to Poirot's lips. He seemed about to speak, but checked himself. He bent down to where a spade was lying.

'That's what the grave was dug with, right enough,' said Giraud. 'But you'll get nothing from it. It was Renauld's own spade, and the man who used it wore gloves. Here they are.' He gesticulated with his foot to where two soil-stained gloves were lying. 'And they're Renauld's too – or at least his gardener's. I tell you, the men who carried out this crime were taking no chances. The man was stabbed with his own dagger, and would have been buried with his own spade. They counted on leaving no traces! But I'll beat them. There's always *something!* And I mean to find it.'

But Poirot was now apparently interested in something else, a short, discoloured piece of lead-piping which lay beside the spade. He touched it delicately with his finger.

'And does this, too, belong to the murdered man?' he asked, and I thought I detected a subtle flavour of irony in the question.

Giraud shrugged his shoulders to indicate that he neither knew nor cared.

'May have been lying around here for weeks. Anyway, it doesn't interest me.'

'I, on the contrary, find it very interesting,' said Poirot sweetly.

I guessed that he was merely bent on annoying the Paris detective and, if so, he succeeded. The other turned away rudely, remarking that he had no time to waste, and bending down he resumed his minute search of the ground.

Meanwhile, Poirot, as though struck by a sudden idea, stepped back over the boundary, and tried the door of the little shed.

'That's locked,' said Giraud over his shoulder. 'But it's only a place where the gardener keeps his rubbish. The spade didn't come from there, but from the tool-shed up by the house.'

'Marvellous,' murmured M. Bex ecstatically to me. 'He has been here but half an hour, and he already knows everything! What a man! Undoubtedly Giraud is the greatest detective alive today.'

Although I disliked the detective heartily, I nevertheless was secretly impressed. Efficiency seemed to radiate from the man. I could not help feeling that, so far, Poirot had not greatly distinguished himself, and it vexed me. He seemed to be directing his attention to all sorts of silly puerile points that had nothing to do with the case. Indeed, at this juncture, he suddenly asked:

'Monsieur Bex, tell me, I pray you, the meaning of this white-washed line that extends all round the grave. Is it a device of the police?'

'No, Monsieur Poirot, it is an affair of the golf course. It shows that there is here to be a "bunkair", as you call it.'

'A bunkair?' Poirot turned to me. 'That is the irregular hole filled with sand and a bank at one side, is it not?'

I concurred.

'Monsieur Renauld, without doubt he played the golf?'

'Yes, he was a keen golfer. It's mainly owing to him, and to his large subscriptions, that this work is being carried forward. He even had a say in the designing of it.'

Poirot nodded thoughtfully. Then he remarked:

'It was not a very good choice they made – of a spot to bury the body? When the men began to dig up the ground, all would have been discovered.'

'Exactly,' cried Giraud triumphantly. 'And that *proves* that they were strangers to the place. It's an excellent piece of indirect evidence.'

'Yes,' said Poirot doubtfully. 'No one who knew would bury a body there – unless they *wanted* it to be discovered. And that is clearly absurd, is it not?'

Giraud did not even trouble to reply.

'Yes,' said Poirot, in a somewhat dissatisfied voice. 'Yes – undoubtedly – absurd!'

CHAPTER 7

THE MYSTERIOUS MADAME DAUBREUIL

As we retraced our steps to the house, M. Bex excused himself for leaving us, explaining that he must immediately acquaint the examining magistrate with the fact of Giraud's arrival. Giraud himself had been obviously delighted when Poirot declared that he had seen all he wanted. The last thing we observed, as we left the spot, was Giraud, crawling about on all fours, with a thoroughness in his search that I could not but admire. Poirot guessed my thoughts, for as soon as we were alone he remarked ironically:

'At last you have seen the detective you admire – the human foxhound! Is it not so, my friend?'

'At any rate, he's *doing* something,' I said, with asperity. 'If there's anything to find he'll find it. Now you –'

'*Eh bien!* I also have found something! A piece of lead-piping.'

'Nonsense, Poirot. You know very well that's got nothing to do with it. I meant *little* things – traces that may lead us infallibly to the murderers.'

'*Mon ami*, a clue of two feet long is every bit as valuable as one measuring two millimetres! But it is the romantic idea that all important clues must be infinitesimal. As to the piece of lead-piping having nothing to do with the crime, you say that because Giraud told you so. No' – as I was about to interpose a question – 'we will say no more. Leave Giraud to his search, and me to my ideas. The case seems straightforward enough – and yet – and yet, *mon ami*, I am not satisfied! And do you know why? Because of the wristwatch that is two hours fast. And then there are several curious little points that do not seem to fit in. For instance, if the object of the murderers was revenge, why did they not stab Renauld in his sleep and have done with it?'

'They wanted the "secret",' I reminded him.

Poirot brushed a speck of dust from his sleeve with a dissatisfied air.

'Well, where is this "secret"? Presumably some distance away, since they wish him to dress himself. Yet he is found murdered close at hand, almost within ear-shot of the house. Then again, it is pure chance that a weapon such as the dagger should be lying about casually, ready to hand.'

He paused, frowning, and then went on:

'Why did the servants hear nothing? Were they drugged? Was there an accomplice, and did that accomplice see to it that the front door should remain open? I wonder if –'

He stopped abruptly. We had reached the drive in front of the house. Suddenly he turned to me.

'My friend, I am about to surprise you – to please you! I have taken your reproaches to heart! We will examine some footprints!'

'Where?'

'In that right-hand bed yonder. Monsieur Bex says that they are the footmarks of the gardener. Let us see if this is so. See, he approaches with his wheelbarrow.'

Indeed an elderly man was just crossing the drive with a barrowful of seedlings. Poirot called to him, and he set down the barrow and came hobbling towards us.

'You are going to ask him for one of his boots to compare with the footmarks?' I asked breathlessly. My faith in Poirot revived a little. Since he said the footprints in this right-hand bed were important, presumably they *were*.

'Exactly,' said Poirot.

'But won't he think it very odd?'

'He will not think about it at all.'

We could say no more, for the old man had joined us.

'You want me for something, monsieur?'

'Yes. You have been gardener here a long time, haven't you?'

'Twenty-four years, monsieur.'

'And your name is –?'

'Auguste, monsieur.'

'I was admiring these magnificent geraniums. They are truly superb. They have been planted long?'

'Some time, monsieur. But of course, to keep the beds looking smart, one must keep bedding out a few new plants, and remove those that are over, besides keeping the old blooms well picked off.'

'You put in some new plants yesterday, didn't you? Those in the middle there, and in the other bed also.'

'Monsieur has a sharp eye. It takes always a day or so for them to "pick up". Yes, I put ten new plants in each bed last night. As monsieur doubtless knows, one should not put in plants when the sun is hot.' Auguste was charmed with Poirot's interest, and was quite inclined to be garrulous.

'That is a splendid specimen there,' said Poirot, pointing. 'Might I perhaps have a cutting of it?'

'But certainly, monsieur.' The old fellow stepped into the bed, and carefully took a slip from the plant Poirot had admired.

Poirot was profuse in his thanks, and Auguste departed to his barrow.

'You see?' said Poirot with a smile, as he bent over the bed to examine the indentation of the gardener's hobnailed boot. 'It is quite simple.'

'I did not realize –'

'That the foot would be inside the boot? You do not use

your excellent mental capacities sufficiently. Well, what of the footmark?'

I examined the bed carefully.

'All the footmarks in the bed were made by the same boot,' I said at length after a careful study.

'You think so? *Eh bien!* I agree with you,' said Poirot.

He seemed quite uninterested, and as though he were thinking of something else.

'At any rate,' I remarked, 'you will have one bee less in your bonnet now.'

'*Mon Dieu!* But what an idiom! What does it mean?'

'What I meant was that now you will give up your interest in these footmarks.'

But to my surprise Poirot shook his head.

'No, no, *mon ami*. At last I am on the right track. I am still in the dark, but, as I hinted just now to Monsieur Bex, these footmarks are the most important and interesting things in the case! That poor Giraud – I should not be surprised if he took no notice of them whatever.'

At that moment the front door opened, and M. Hautet and the commissary came down the steps.

'Ah, Monsieur Poirot, we were coming to look for you,' said the magistrate. 'It is getting late, but I wish to pay a visit to Madame Daubreuil. Without doubt she will be very much upset by Monsieur Renauld's death, and we may be fortunate enough to get a clue from her. The secret that he did not confide to his wife, it is possible that he may have told it to the woman whose love held him enslaved. We know where our Samsons are weak, don't we?'

We said no more, but fell into line. Poirot walked with the examining magistrate, and the commissary and I followed a few paces behind.

'There is no doubt that Françoise's story is substantially correct,' he remarked to me in a confidential tone. 'I have been telephoning headquarters. It seems that three times in the last six weeks – that is to say since the arrival of Monsieur Renauld at Merlinville – Madame Daubreuil has paid a large sum in notes into her banking account. Altogether the sum totals two hundred thousand francs!'

'Dear me,' I said, considering, 'that must be something like four thousand pounds!'

'Precisely. Yes, there can be no doubt that he was absolutely infatuated. But it remains to be seen whether he confided his secret to her. The examining magistrate is hopeful, but I hardly share his views.'

During this conversation we were walking down the lane towards the fork in the road where our car had halted earlier in the afternoon, and in another moment I realized that the Villa Marguerite, the home of the mysterious Madame Daubreuil, was the small house from which the beautiful girl had emerged.

'She has lived here for many years,' said the commissary nodding his head towards the house. 'Very quietly, very unobtrusively. She seems to have no friends or relations other than the acquaintances she has made in Merlinville. She never refers to the past, nor to her husband. One does not even know if he is alive or dead. There is a mystery about her, you comprehend.'

I nodded, my interest growing.

'And – the daughter?' I ventured.

'A truly beautiful young girl – modest, devout, all that she should be. One pities her, for, though she may know nothing of the past, a man who wants to ask her hand in marriage must necessarily inform himself, and then –' The commissary shrugged his shoulders cynically.

'But it would not be her fault!' I cried, with rising indignation.

'No. But what will you? A man is particular about his wife's antecedents.'

I was prevented from further argument by our arrival at the door. M. Hautet rang the bell. A few minutes elapsed, and then we heard a footfall within, and the door was opened. On the threshold stood my young goddess of that afternoon. When she saw us, the colour left her cheeks, leaving her deathly white, and her eyes widened with apprehension. There was no doubt about it, she was afraid!

'Mademoiselle Daubreuil,' said M. Hautet, sweeping off his hat, 'we regret infinitely to disturb you, but the exigencies of the Law, you comprehend? My compliments to madame your mother, and will she have the goodness to grant me a few moments' interview?'

For a moment the girl stood motionless. Her left hand was pressed to her side, as though to still the sudden unconquerable agitation of her heart. But she mastered herself, and said in a low voice:

'I will go and see. Please come inside.'

She entered a room on the left of the hall, and we heard the low murmur of her voice. And then another voice, much the same in timbre, but with a slightly harder inflection behind its mellow roundness, said:

'But certainly. Ask them to enter.'

In another minute we were face to face with the mysterious Madame Daubreuil.

She was not nearly so tall as her daughter, and the rounded curves of her figure had all the grace of full maturity. Her hair, again unlike her daughter's, was dark, and parted in the middle in the Madonna style. Her eyes, half hidden by the drooping lids, were blue. Though very well preserved, she was certainly no longer young, but her charm was of the quality which is independent of age.

'You wished to see me, monsieur?' she asked.

'Yes, madame.' M. Hautet cleared his throat. 'I am investigating the death of Monsieur Renauld. You have heard of it, no doubt?'

She bowed her head without speaking. Her expression did not change.

'We came to ask you whether you can – er – throw any light upon the circumstances surrounding it?'

'I?' The surprise of her tone was excellent.

'Yes, madame. We have reason to believe that you were in the habit of visiting the dead man at his villa in the evenings. Is that so?'

The colour rose in the lady's pale cheeks, but she replied quietly:

'I deny your right to ask me such a question!'

'Madame, we are investigating a murder.'

'Well, what of it? I had nothing to do with the murder.'

'Madame, we do not say that for a moment. But you knew the dead man well. Did he ever confide in you as to any danger that threatened him?'

'Never.'

'Did he ever mention his life in Santiago, and any enemies he may have made there?'

'No.'

'Then you can give us no help at all?'

'I fear not. I really do not see why you should come to me.

Cannot his wife tell you what you want to know?' Her voice held a slender inflection of irony.

'Mrs Renauld has told us all she can.'

'Ah!' said Madame Daubreuil. 'I wonder –'

'You wonder what, madame?'

'Nothing.'

The examining magistrate looked at her. He was aware that he was fighting a duel, and that he had no mean antagonist.

'You persist in your statement that Monsieur Renauld confided nothing to you?'

'Why should you think it likely that he should confide in me?'

'Because, madame,' said M. Hautet, with calculated brutality, 'a man tells to his mistress what he does not always tell to his wife.'

'Ah!' She sprang forward. Her eyes flashed fire. 'Monsieur, you insult me! And before my daughter! I can tell you nothing. Have the goodness to leave my house!'

The honours undoubtedly rested with the lady. We left the Villa Marguerite like a shamefaced pack of schoolboys. The magistrate muttered angry ejaculations to himself. Poirot seemed lost in thought. Suddenly he came out of his reverie with a start, and inquired of M. Hautet if there was a good hotel near at hand.

'There is a small place, the Hôtel des Bains, on this side of the town. A few hundred yards down the road. It will be handy for your investigations. We shall see you in the morning, then, I presume?'

'Yes, I thank you, Monsieur Hautet.'

With mutual civilities we parted company, Poirot and I going towards Merlinville, and the others returning to the Villa Geneviève.

'The French police system is very marvellous,' said Poirot, looking after them. 'The information they possess about everyone's life, down to the most commonplace detail, is extraordinary. Though he has only been here a little over six weeks, they are perfectly well acquainted with Monsieur Renauld's tastes and pursuits, and at a moment's notice they can produce information as to Madame Daubreuil's banking account, and the sums that have lately been paid in! Undoubtedly the dossier is a great institution. But what is that?' He turned sharply.

A figure was running hatless down the road after us. It was Marthe Daubreuil.

'I beg your pardon,' she cried breathlessly, as she reached us.

'I – I should not do this, I know. You must not tell my mother. But is it true, what the people say, that Monsieur Renauld called in a detective before he died, and – and that you are he?'

'Yes, mademoiselle,' said Poirot gently. 'It is quite true. But how did you learn it?'

'Françoise told our Amélie,' explained Marthe with a blush.

Poirot made a grimace.

'The secrecy, it is impossible in an affair of this kind! Not that it matters. Well, mademoiselle, what is it you want to know?'

The girl hesitated. She seemed longing, yet fearing, to speak. At last, almost in a whisper, she asked:

'Is – anyone suspected?'

Poirot eyed her keenly.

Then he replied evasively:

'Suspicion is in the air at present, mademoiselle.'

'Yes, I know – but – anyone in particular?'

'Why do you want to know?'

The girl seemed frightened by the question. All at once Poirot's words about her earlier in the day occurred to me. The 'girl with the anxious eyes'.

'Monsieur Renauld was always very kind to me,' she replied at last. 'It is natural that I should be interested.'

'I see,' said Poirot. 'Well, mademoiselle, suspicion at present is hovering round two persons.'

'Two?'

I could have sworn there was a note of surprise and relief in her voice.

'Their names are unknown, but they are presumed to be Chileans from Santiago. And now, mademoiselle, you see what comes of being young and beautiful! I have betrayed professional secrets for you!'

The girl laughed merrily, and then, rather shyly, she thanked him.

'I must run back now. *Maman* will miss me.'

And she turned and ran back up the road, looking like a modern Atalanta. I stared after her.

'*Mon ami*,' said Poirot, in his gentle ironical voice, 'is it that we are to remain planted here all night – just because you have seen a beautiful young woman, and your head is in a whirl.'

I laughed and apologized.

'But she *is* beautiful, Poirot. Anyone might be excused for being bowled over by her.'

But to my surprise Poirot shook his head very earnestly.

'Ah, *mon ami*, do not set your heart on Marthe Daubreuil. She is not for you, that one! Take it from Papa Poirot!'

'Why,' I cried, 'the commissary assured me that she was as good as she is beautiful! A perfect angel!'

'Some of the greatest criminals I have known had the faces of angels,' remarked Poirot cheerfully. 'A malformation of the grey cells may coincide quite easily with the face of a Madonna.'

'Poirot,' I cried, horrified, 'you cannot mean that you suspect an innocent child like this!'

'Ta-ta-ta! Do not excite yourself! I have not said that I suspected her. But you must admit that her anxiety to know about the case is somewhat unusual.'

'For once I see farther than you do,' I said. 'Her anxiety is not for herself – but for her mother.'

'My friend,' said Poirot, 'as usual, you see nothing at all. Madame Daubreuil is very well able to look after herself without her daughter worrying about her. I admit I was teasing you just now, but all the same I repeat what I said before. Do not set your heart on that girl. She is not for you! I, Hercule Poirot, know it. *Sacré!* if only I could remember where I had seen that face?'

'What face?' I asked, surprised. 'The daughter's?'

'No. The mother's.'

Noting my surprise, he nodded emphatically.

'But yes – it is as I tell you. It was a long time ago, when I was still with the police in Belgium. I have never actually seen the woman before, but I have seen her picture – and in connexion with some case. I rather fancy –'

'Yes?'

'I may be mistaken, but I rather fancy that it was a murder case!'

CHAPTER 8

AN UNEXPECTED MEETING

We were up at the villa betimes next morning. The man on guard at the gate did not bar our way this time. Instead, he respectfully saluted us, and we passed on to the house. The maid Léonie was just coming down the stairs, and seemed not averse to the prospect of a little conversation.

Poirot inquired after the health of Mrs Renauld.

Léonie shook her head.

'She is terribly upset, the poor lady! She will eat nothing – but nothing! And she is as pale as a ghost. It is heartrending to see her. Ah, it is not I who would grieve like that for a man who had deceived me with another woman!'

Poirot nodded sympathetically.

'What you say is very just, but what will you? The heart of a woman who loves will forgive many blows. Still undoubtedly there must have been many scenes of recrimination between them in the last few months?'

Again Léonie shook her head.

'Never, monsieur. Never have I heard madame utter a word of protest – of reproach, even! She had the temper and disposition of an angel – quite different to monsieur.'

'Monsieur Renauld had not the temper of an angel?'

'Far from it. When he enraged himself, the whole house knew of it. The day that he quarrelled with Monsieur Jack – *ma foi!* they might have been heard in the market-place, they shouted so loud!'

'Indeed,' said Poirot. 'And when did this quarrel take place?'

'Oh, it was just before Monsieur Jack went to Paris. Almost he missed his train. He came out of the library, and caught up his bag which he had left in the hall. The automobile, it was being repaired, and he had to run for the station. I was dusting the *salon*, and I saw him pass, and his face was white – white – with two burning spots of red. Ah, but he was angry!'

Léonie was enjoying her narrative thoroughly.

'And the dispute, what was it about?'

'Ah, that I do not know,' confessed Léonie. 'It is true that they shouted, but their voices were so loud and high, and they spoke so fast, that only one well acquainted with English could have comprehended. But monsieur, he was like a thundercloud all day! Impossible to please him!'

The sound of a door shutting upstairs cut short Léonie's loquacity.

'And Françoise who awaits me!' she exclaimed, awakening to a tardy remembrance of her duties. 'That old one, she always scolds.'

'One moment, mademoiselle. The examining magistrate, where is he?'

'They have gone out to look at the automobile in the garage. Monsieur the commissary had some idea that it might have been used on the night of the murder.'

'*Quelle idée*,' murmured Poirot, as the girl disappeared.

'You will go out and join them?'

'No, I shall await their return in the *salon*. It is cool there on this hot morning.'

This placid way of taking things did not quite commend itself to me.

'If you don't mind –' I said, and hesitated.

'Not in the least. You wish to investigate on your own account, eh?'

'Well, I'd rather like to have a look at Giraud, if he's anywhere about, and see what he's up to.'

'The human foxhound,' murmured Poirot, as he leaned back in a comfortable chair, and closed his eyes. 'By all means, my friend. Au revoir.'

I strolled out of the front door. It was certainly hot. I turned up the path we had taken the day before. I had a mind to study the scene of the crime myself. I did not go directly to the spot, however, but turned aside into the bushes, so as to come out on the links some hundred yards or so farther to the right. The shrubbery here was much denser, and I had quite a struggle to force my way through. When I emerged at last on the course, it was quite unexpectedly and with such vigour that I cannoned heavily into a young lady who had been standing with her back to the plantation.

She not unnaturally gave a suppressed shriek, but I, too, uttered an exclamation of surprise. For it was my friend of the train, Cinderella!

The surprise was mutual.

'You!' we both exclaimed simultaneously.

The young lady recovered herself first.

'My only aunt!' she exclaimed. 'What are you doing here?'

'For the matter of that, what are you?' I retorted.

'When last I saw you, the day before yesterday, you were trotting home to England like a good little boy.'

'When last I saw *you*,' I said, 'you were trotting home with your sister, like a good little girl. By the way, how is your sister?'

A flash of white teeth rewarded me.

'How kind of you to ask! My sister is well, I thank you.'

'She is here with you?'

'She remained in town,' said the minx with dignity.

'I don't believe you've got a sister,' I laughed. 'If you have, her name is Harris!'

'Do you remember mine?' she asked with a smile.

'Cinderella. But you're going to tell me the real one now aren't you?'

She shook her head with a wicked look.

'Not even why you're here?'

'Oh, *that!* I suppose you've heard of members of my profession "resting".'

'At expensive French watering-places?'

'Dirt cheap if you know where to go.'

I eyed her keenly.

'Still, you'd no intention of coming here when I met you two days ago?'

'We all have our disappointments,' said Miss Cinderella sententiously. 'There now, I've told you quite as much as is good for you. Little boys should not be inquisitive. You've not yet told me what *you're* doing here?'

'You remember my telling you that my great friend was a detective?'

'Yes?'

'And perhaps you've heard about this crime – at the Villa Geneviève –?'

She stared at me. Her breast heaved, and her eyes grew wide and round.

'You don't mean – that you're in on *that*?'

I nodded. There was no doubt that I had scored heavily. Her emotion, as she regarded me, was only too evident. For some few seconds she remained silent, staring at me. Then she nodded her head emphatically.

'Well, if that doesn't beat the band! Tote me round. I want to see all the horrors.'

'What do you mean?'

'What I say. Bless the boy, didn't I tell you I doted on crimes? I've been nosing round for hours. It's a real piece of luck happening on you this way. Come on, show me all the sights.'

'But look here – wait a minute – I can't. Nobody's allowed in. They're awfully strict.'

'Aren't you and your friends the big bugs?'

I was loath to relinquish my position of importance.

'Why are you so keen?' I asked weakly. 'And what is it you want to see?'

'Oh, everything! The place where it happened, and the weapon, and the body, and any fingerprints or interesting things like that. I've never had a chance before of being right in on a murder like this. It'll last me all my life.'

I turned away, sickened. What were women coming to nowadays? The girl's ghoulish excitement nauseated me.

'Come off your high horse,' said the lady suddenly. 'And don't give yourself airs. When you got called to this job, did you put your nose in the air and say it was a nasty business, and you wouldn't be mixed up in it?'

'No, but –'

'If you'd been here on a holiday, wouldn't you be nosing round just the same as I am? Of course you would.'

'I'm a man. You're a woman.'

'Your idea of a woman is someone who gets on a chair and shrieks if she sees a mouse. That's all prehistoric. But you *will* show me round, won't you? You see, it might make a big difference to me.'

'In what way?'

'They're keeping all the reporters out. I might make a big scoop with one of the papers. You don't know how much they pay for a bit of inside stuff.'

I hesitated. She slipped a small soft hand into mine.

'*Please* – there's a dear.'

I capitulated. Secretly, I knew that I should rather enjoy the part of showman.

We repaired first to the spot where the body had been discovered. A man was on guard there, who saluted respectfully, knowing me by sight, and raised no questions as to my companion. Presumably he regarded her as vouched for by me. I explained to Cinderella just how the discovery had been made, and she listened attentively, sometimes putting an intelligent question. Then we turned our steps in the direction of the villa. I proceeded rather cautiously, for, truth to tell, I was not at all anxious to meet anyone. I took the girl through the shrubbery round to the back of the house where the small shed was. I recollected that yesterday evening, after relocking the door, M. Bex had left the key with the *sergent de ville*, Marchaud, 'In case Monsieur Giraud should require it while we are upstairs.' I thought it quite likely that the Sûreté detective, after using it, had returned it to Marchaud again. Leaving the girl out of sight in the shrubbery, I entered the house. Marchaud was on duty outside the door of the *salon*. From within came the murmur of voices.

'Monsieur desires Monsieur Hautet? He is within. He is again interrogating Françoise.'

'No,' I said hastily, 'I don't want him. But I should very much like the key of the shed outside if it is not against regulations.'

'But certainly, monsieur.' He produced it. 'Here it is. Monsieur Hautet gave orders that all facilities were to be placed at your disposal. You will return it to me when you have finished out there, that is all.'

'Of course.'

I felt a thrill of satisfaction as I realized that in Marchaud's eyes, at least, I ranked equally in importance with Poirot. The girl was waiting for me. She gave an exclamation of delight as she saw the key in my hand.

'You've got it then?'

'Of course,' I said coolly. 'All the same, you know, what I'm doing is highly irregular.'

'You've been a perfect duck, and I shan't forget it. Come along. They can't see us from the house, can they?'

'Wait a minute.' I arrested her eager advance. 'I won't stop you if you really wish to go in. But do you? You've seen the grave, and the grounds, and you've heard all the details of the affair. Isn't that enough for you? This is going to be gruesome, you know, and – unpleasant.'

She looked at me for a moment with an expression that I could not quite fathom. Then she laughed.

'Me for the horrors,' she said. 'Come along.'

In silence we arrived at the door of the shed. I opened it and we passed in. I walked over to the body, and gently pulled down the sheet as Bex had done the preceding afternoon. A little gasping sound escaped from the girl's lips, and I turned and looked at her. There was horror on her face now, and those debonair high spirits of hers were quenched utterly. She had not chosen to listen to my advice, and she was punished now for her disregard of it. I felt singularly merciless towards her. She should go through with it now. I turned the corpse over gently.

'You see,' I said. 'He was stabbed in the back.'

Her voice was almost soundless.

'With what?'

I nodded towards the glass jar.

'That dagger.'

Suddenly the girl reeled, and then sank down in a heap. I sprang to her assistance.

'You are faint. Come out of here. It has been too much for you.'

'Water,' she murmured. 'Quick. Water.'

I left her, and rushed into the house. Fortunately none of the servants were about, and I was able to secure a glass of water unobserved and add a few drops of brandy from a pocket flask. In a few minutes I was back again. The girl was lying as I had left her, but a few sips of the brandy and water revived her in a marvellous manner.

'Take me out of here – oh, quickly, quickly!' she cried, shuddering.

Supporting her with my arm, I led her out into the air, and she pulled the door to behind her. Then she drew a deep breath.

'That's better. Oh, it was horrible! Why did you ever let me go in?'

I felt this to be so feminine that I could not forbear a smile. Secretly, I was not dissatisfied with her collapse. It proved that she was not quite so callous as I had thought her. After all she was little more than a child, and her curiosity had probably been of the unthinking order.

'I did my best to stop you, you know,' I said gently.

'I suppose you did. Well, goodbye.'

'Look here, you can't start off like that – all alone. You're not fit for it. I insist on accompanying you back to Merlinville.'

'Nonsense. I'm quite all right now.'

'Supposing you felt faint again? No, I shall come with you.'

But this she combated with a good deal of energy. In the end, however, I prevailed so far as to be allowed to accompany her to the outskirts of the town. We retraced our steps over our former route, passing the grave again, and making a detour on to the road. Where the first straggling line of shops began, she stopped and held out her hand.

'Goodbye, and thank you ever so much for coming with me.'

'Are you sure you're all right now?'

'Quite, thanks. I hope you don't get into any trouble over showing me things.'

I disclaimed the idea lightly.

'Well, goodbye.'

'Au revoir,' I corrected. 'If you're staying here, we shall meet again.'

She flashed a smile at me.

'That's so. Au revoir, then.'

'Wait a second, you haven't told me your address.'

'Oh, I'm staying at the Hôtel du Phare. It's a little place, but quite good. Come and look me up tomorrow.'

'I will,' I said, with perhaps rather unnecessary *empressement*.

I watched her out of sight, then turned and retraced my steps to the villa. I remembered that I had not relocked the door of the shed. Fortunately no one had noticed the oversight, and turning the key I removed it and returned it to the *sergent de ville*. And, as I did so, it came upon me suddenly that though Cinderella had given me her address I still did not know her name.

CHAPTER 9

M. GIRAUD FINDS SOME CLUES

In the *salon* I found the examining magistrate busily interrogating the old gardener, Auguste. Poirot and the commissary, who were both present, greeted me respectively with a smile and a polite bow. I slipped quietly into a seat. M. Hautet was painstaking and meticulous in the extreme, but did not succeed in eliciting anything of importance.

The gardening gloves Auguste admitted to be his. He wore them when handling a certain species of primula plant which was poisonous to some people. He could not say when he had worn them last. Certainly he had not missed them. Where were they kept? Sometimes in one place, sometimes in another. The spade was usually to be found in the small tool-shed. Was it locked? Of course it was locked. Where was the key kept? *Parbleu*, it was in the door of course. There was nothing of value to steal. Who would have expected a party of bandits, or assassins? Such things did not happen in Madame la Vicomtesse's time.

M. Hautet signifying that he had finished with him, the old man withdrew, grumbling to the last. Remembering Poirot's unaccountable insistence on the footprints in the flower-beds, I scrutinized him narrowly as he gave his evidence. Either he had nothing to do with the crime or he was a consummate actor. Suddenly, just as he was going out of the door, an idea struck me.

'*Pardon*, Monsieur Hautet,' I cried, 'but will you permit me to ask him one question?'

'But certainly, monsieur.'

Thus encouraged, I turned to Auguste.

'Where do you keep your boots?'

'On my feet,' growled the old man. 'Where else?'

'But when you go to bed at night?'

'Under my bed.'

'But who cleans them?'

'Nobody. Why should they be cleaned? Is it that I promenade myself on the front like a young man? On Sunday I wear the Sunday boots, but otherwise –' He shrugged his shoulders.

I shook my head, discouraged.

'Well, well,' said the magistrate, 'we do not advance very much. Undoubtedly we are held up until we get the return cable from Santiago. Has anyone seen Giraud? In verity that one lacks politeness! I have a very good mind to send for him and –'

'You will not have to send far.'

The quiet voice startled us. Giraud was standing outside looking in through the open window.

He leapt lightly into the room and advanced to the table.

'Here I am, at your service. Accept my excuses for not presenting myself sooner.'

'Not at all – not at all!' said the magistrate, rather confused.

'Of course I am only a detective,' continued the other. 'I know nothing of interrogatories. Were I conducting one, I should be inclined to do so without an open window. Anyone standing outside can so easily hear all that passes. But no matter.'

M. Hautet flushed angrily. There was evidently going to be no love lost between the examining magistrate and the detective in charge of the case. They had fallen foul of each other at the start. Perhaps in any event it would have been much the same. To Giraud, all examining magistrates were fools, and to M. Hautet, who took himself seriously, the casual manner of the Paris detective could not fail to give offence.

'*Eh bien*, Monsieur Giraud,' said the magistrate rather sharply. 'Without doubt you have been employing your time to a marvel! You have the names of the assassins for us, have you not? And also the precise spot where they find themselves now?'

Unmoved by this irony, M. Giraud replied:

'I know at least where they have come from.'

Giraud took two small objects from his pocket and laid them down on the table. We crowded round. The objects were very simple ones: the stub of a cigarette and an unlighted match. The detective wheeled round on Poirot.

'What do you see there?' he asked.

There was something almost brutal in his tone. It made my cheeks flush. But Poirot remained unmoved. He shrugged his shoulders.

'A cigarette end and a match.'

'And what does that tell you?'

Poirot spread out his hands.

'It tells me – nothing.'

'Ah!' said Giraud, in a satisfied voice. 'You haven't made a study of these things. That's not an ordinary match – not in this country at least. It's common enough in South America. Luckily it's unlighted. I mightn't have recognized it otherwise. Evidently one of the men threw away his cigarette and lit another, spilling one match out of the box as he did so.'

'And the other match?' asked Poirot.

'Which match?'

'The one he *did* light his cigarette with. You have found that also?'

'No.'

'Perhaps you didn't search very thoroughly.'

'Not search thoroughly –' For a moment it seemed as though the detective was going to break out angrily, but with an effort he controlled himself. 'I see you love a joke, Monsieur Poirot. But in any case, match or no match, the cigarette end would be sufficient. It is a South American cigarette with liquorice pectoral paper.'

Poirot bowed. The commissary spoke:

'The cigarette end and match might have belonged to Monsieur Renauld. Remember, it is only two years since he returned from South America.'

'No,' replied the other confidently. 'I have already searched among the effects of Monsieur Renauld. The cigarettes he smoked and the matches he used are quite different.'

'You do not think it odd,' asked Poirot, 'that these strangers should come unprovided with a weapon, with gloves, with a spade, and that they should so conveniently find all these things?'

Giraud smiled in a rather superior manner.

'Undoubtedly it is strange. Indeed, without the theory that I hold, it would be inexplicable.'

'Aha!' said M. Hautet. 'An accomplice within the house!'

'Or outside it,' said Giraud, with a peculiar smile.

'But someone must have admitted them. We cannot allow that, by an unparalleled piece of good fortune, they found the door ajar for them to walk in?'

'The door was opened for them; but it could just as easily be opened from outside – by someone who possessed a key.'

'But who *did* possess a key?'

Giraud shrugged his shoulders.

'As for that, no one who possesses one is going to admit the fact if he can help it. But several people *might* have had one. Monsieur Jack Renauld, the son, for instance. It is true that he is on his way to South America, but he might have lost the key or had it stolen from him. Then there is the gardener – he has been here many years. One of the younger servants may have a lover. It is easy to take an impression of a key and have one cut. There are many possibilities. Then there is another person who, I should judge, is exceedingly likely to have such a thing.'

'Who is that?'

'Madame Daubreuil,' said the detective.

'Eh, eh!' said the magistrate. 'So you have heard about that, have you?'

'I hear everything,' said Giraud imperturbably.

'There is one thing I could swear you have not heard,' said M. Hautet, delighted to be able to show superior knowledge, and without more ado he retailed the story of the mysterious visitor the night before. He also touched on the cheque made out to 'Duveen', and finally handed Giraud the letter signed 'Bella'.

'All very interesting. But my theory remains unaffected.'

'And your theory is?'

'For the moment I prefer not to say. Remember, I am only just beginning my investigations.'

'Tell me one thing, Monsieur Giraud,' said Poirot suddenly. 'Your theory allows for the door being opened. It does not explain why it was *left* open. When they departed, would it not have been natural for them to close it behind them? If a *sergent de ville* had chanced to come up to the house, as is sometimes done to see that all is well, they might have been discovered and overtaken almost at once.'

'Bah! They forgot it. A mistake, I grant you.'

Then, to my surprise, Poirot uttered almost the same words as he had uttered to Bex the previous evening:

'*I do not agree with you.* The door being left open was the result of either design or necessity, and any theory that does not admit that fact is bound to prove vain.'

We all regarded the little man with a good deal of astonishment. The confession of ignorance drawn from him over the match end had, I thought, been bound to humiliate him, but here he was self-satisfied as ever, laying down the law to Giraud without a tremor.

The detective twisted his moustache, eyeing my friend in a somewhat bantering fashion.

'You don't agree with me, eh? Well, what strikes you particularly about the case? Let's hear your views.'

'One thing presents itself to me as being significant. Tell me, Monsieur Giraud, does nothing strike you as familiar about this case? Is there nothing it reminds you of?'

'Familiar? Reminds me of? I can't say off-hand. I don't think so, though.'

'You are wrong,' said Poirot quietly. 'A crime almost precisely similar has been committed before.'

'When? And where?'

'Ah, that, unfortunately, I cannot for the moment remember, but I shall do so. I had hoped *you* might be able to assist me.'

Giraud snorted incredulously.

'There have been many affairs of masked men. I cannot remember the details of them all. The crimes all resemble each other more or less.'

'There is such a thing as the individual touch.' Poirot suddenly assumed his lecturing manner, and addressed us collectively. 'I am speaking to you now of the psychology of crime. Monsieur Giraud knows quite well that each criminal has his particular method, and that the police, when called in to investigate, say, a case of burglary, can often make a shrewd guess at the offender, simply by the peculiar methods he has employed. (Japp would tell you the same, Hastings.) Man is an unoriginal animal. Unoriginal within the law in his daily respectable life, equally unoriginal outside the law. If a man commits a crime, any other crime he commits will resemble it closely. The English murderer who disposed of his wives in succession by drowning them in their baths was a case in point. Had he varied his methods, he might have escaped detection to this day. But he obeyed the common dictates of human nature, arguing that what had once succeeded would succeed again, and he paid the penalty of his lack of originality.'

'And the point of all this?' sneered Giraud.

'That, when you have two crimes precisely similar in design and execution, you find the same brain behind them both. I am looking for that brain, Monsieur Giraud, and I shall find it. Here we have a true clue – a psychological clue. You may know all about cigarettes and match ends, Monsieur Giraud, but I, Hercule Poirot, know the mind of man.'

Giraud remained singularly unimpressed.

'For your guidance,' continued Poirot, 'I will also advise you of one fact which might fail to be brought to your notice. The wristwatch of Madame Renauld, on the day following the tragedy, had gained two hours.'

Giraud stared.

'Perhaps it was in the habit of gaining?'

'As a matter of fact, I am told it did.'

'Very well, then.'

'All the same, two hours is a good deal,' said Poirot softly. 'Then there is the matter of the footprints in the flower-bed.'

He nodded his head towards the open window. Giraud took two eager strides, and looked out.

'But I see no footprints?'

'No,' said Poirot, straightening a little pile of books on a table. 'There are none.'

For a moment an almost murderous rage obscured Giraud's face. He took two strides towards his tormentor, but at that moment the salon door was opened, and Marchaud announced:

'Monsieur Stonor, the secretary, has just arrived from England. May he enter?'

CHAPTER 10

GABRIEL STONOR

The man who now entered the room was a striking figure. Very tall, with a well-knit, athletic frame, and a deeply bronzed face and neck, he dominated the assembly. Even Giraud seemed anaemic beside him. When I knew him better I realized that Gabriel Stonor was quite an unusual personality. English by birth, he had knocked about all over the world. He had shot big game in Africa, travelled in Korea, ranched in California, and traded in the South Sea islands.

His unerring eye picked out M. Hautet.

'The examining magistrate in charge of the case? Pleased to meet you, sir. This is a terrible business. How's Mrs Renauld?

Is she bearing up fairly well? It must have been an awful shock to her.'

'Terrible, terrible,' said M. Hautet. 'Permit me to introduce Monsieur Bex, our commissary of police, Monsieur Giraud of the Sûreté. This gentleman is Monsieur Hercule Poirot. Mr Renauld sent for him, but he arrived too late to do anything to avert the tragedy. A friend of Monsieur Poirot's, Captain Hastings.'

Stonor looked at Poirot with some interest.

'Sent for you, did he?'

'You did not know, then, that Monsieur Renauld contemplated calling a detective?' interposed M. Bex.

'No, I didn't. But it doesn't surprise me a bit.'

'Why?'

'Because the old man was rattled. I don't know what it was all about. He didn't confide in me. We weren't on those terms. But rattled he was – and badly.'

'H'm!' said M. Hautet. 'But you have no notion of the cause?'

'That's what I said, sir.'

'You will pardon me, Monsieur Stonor, but we must begin with a few formalities. Your name?'

'Gabriel Stonor.'

'How long ago was it that you became secretary to Monsieur Renauld?'

'About two years ago, when he first arrived from South America. I met him through a mutual friend, and he offered me the post. A thundering good boss he was too.'

'Did he talk to you much about his life in South America?'

'Yes, a good bit.'

'Do you know if he was ever in Santiago?'

'Several times, I believe.'

'He never mentioned any special incident that occurred there – anything that might have provoked some vendetta against him?'

'Never.'

'Did he speak of any secret that he had acquired while sojourning there?'

'Not that I can remember. But, for all that, there *was* a mystery about him. I've never heard him speak of his boyhood, for instance, or of any incident prior to his arrival in South America. He was a French-Canadian by birth, I believe, but I've never heard him speak of his life in Canada. He could shut up like a clam if he liked.'

'So, as far as you know, he had no enemies, and you can give us no clue as to any secret to obtain possession of which he might have been murdered?'

'That's so.'

'Monsieur Stonor, have you ever heard the name of Duveen in connexion with Monsieur Renauld?'

'Duveen. Duveen.' He tried the name over thoughtfully. 'I don't think I have. And yet it seems familiar.'

'Do you know a lady, a friend of Monsieur Renauld's, whose Christian name is Bella?'

Again Mr Stonor shook his head.

'Bella Duveen? Is that the full name? It's curious. I'm sure I know it. But for the moment I can't remember in what connexion.'

The magistrate coughed.

'You understand, Monsieur Stonor – the case is like this. *There must be no reservations*. You might, perhaps, through a feeling of consideration for Madame Renauld – for whom, I gather, you have a great esteem and affection – you might – in fact!' said M. Hautet, getting rather tied up in his sentence, 'there must absolutely be no reservations.'

Stonor stared at him, a dawning light of comprehension in his eyes.

'I don't quite get you,' he said gently. 'Where does Mrs Renauld come in? I've an immense respect and affection for that lady; she's a very wonderful and unusual type, but I don't quite see how my reservations, or otherwise, could affect her.'

'Not if this Bella Duveen should prove to have been something more than a friend to her husband?'

'Ah!' said Stonor. 'I get you now. But I'll bet my bottom dollar that you're wrong. The old man never so much as looked at a petticoat. He just adored his own wife. They were the most devoted couple I know.'

M. Hautet shook his head gently.

'Monsieur Stonor, we hold absolute proof – a love-letter written by this Bella to Monsieur Renauld, accusing him of having tired of her. Moreover, we have further proof that, at the time of his death, he was carrying on an intrigue with a Frenchwoman, a Madame Daubreuil, who rents the adjoining villa.'

The secretary's eyes narrowed.

'Hold on, sir. You're barking up the wrong tree. I knew Paul Renauld. What you've just been saying is plumb impossible. There's some other explanation.'

The magistrate shrugged his shoulders.

'What other explanation could there be?'

'What leads you to think it was a love affair?'

'Madame Daubreuil was in the habit of visiting him here in the evenings. Also, since Monsieur Renauld came to the Villa Geneviève, Madame Daubreuil has paid large sums of money into the bank in notes. In all, the amount totals four thousand pounds of your English money.'

'I guess that's right,' said Stonor quietly. 'I transmitted him those sums in notes at his request. But it wasn't an intrigue.'

'What else could it be?'

'*Blackmail*,' said Stonor sharply, bringing down his hand with a slam on the table. 'That's what it was.'

'Ah!' cried the magistrate, shaken in spite of himself.

'Blackmail,' repeated Stonor. 'The old man was being bled – and at a good rate too. Four thousand in a couple of months. Whew! I told you just now there was a mystery about Renauld. Evidently this Madame Daubreuil knew enough of it to put the screw on.'

'It is possible,' the commissary cried excitedly. 'Decidedly it is possible.'

'Possible?' roared Stonor. 'It's certain. Tell me, have you asked Mrs Renauld about this love-affair stunt of yours?'

'No, monsieur. We did not wish to occasion her any distress if it could reasonably be avoided.'

'Distress? Why, she'd laugh in your face. I tell you, she and Renauld were a couple in a hundred.'

'Ah, that reminds me of another point,' said M. Hautet. 'Did Monsieur Renauld take you into his confidence at all as to the dispositions of his will?'

'I know all about it – took it to the lawyers for him after he'd drawn it out. I can give you the name of his solicitors if you want to see it. They've got it there. Quite simple. Half in trust to his wife for her lifetime, the other half to his son. A few legacies. I rather think he left me a thousand.'

'When was this will drawn up?'

'Oh, about a year and a half ago.'

'Would it surprise you very much, Monsieur Stonor, to hear that Monsieur Renauld had made another will, less than a fortnight ago?'

Stonor was obviously very much surprised.

'I'd no idea of it. What's it like?'

'The whole of his vast fortune is left unreservedly to his wife. There is no mention of his son.'

Mr Stonor gave vent to a prolonged whistle.

'I call that rather rough on the lad. His mother adores him of course, but to the world at large it looks rather like a want of confidence on his father's part. It will be rather galling to his pride. Still, it all goes to prove what I told you, that Renauld and his wife were on first-rate terms.'

'Quite so, quite so,' said M. Hautet. 'It is possible we shall have to revise our ideas on several points. We have, of course, cabled to Santiago, and are expecting a reply from there any minute. In all probability, everything will then be perfectly clear and straightforward. On the other hand, if your suggestion of blackmail is true, Madame Daubreuil ought to be able to give us valuable information.'

Poirot interjected a remark:

'Monsieur Stonor, the English chauffeur, Masters, had he been long with Monsieur Renauld?'

'Over a year.'

'Have you any idea whether he has ever been in South America?'

'I'm quite sure he hasn't. Before coming to M. Renauld he had been for many years with some people in Gloucestershire whom I know well.'

'In fact, you can answer for him as being above suspicion?'

'Absolutely.'

Poirot seemed somewhat crestfallen.

Meanwhile the magistrate had summoned Marchaud.

'My compliments to Madame Renauld, and I should be glad to speak to her for a few minutes. Beg her not to disturb herself. I will wait upon her upstairs.'

Marchaud saluted and disappeared.

We waited some minutes, and then, to our surprise, the door opened, and Mrs Renauld, deathly pale in her heavy mourning, entered the room.

M. Hautet brought forward a chair, uttering vigorous protestations, and she thanked him with a smile. Stonor was holding one hand of hers in his with an eloquent sympathy. Words evidently failed him. Mrs Renauld turned to M. Hautet.

'You wish to ask me something?'

'With your permission, madame. I understand your husband was a French-Canadian by birth. Can you tell me anything of his youth or upbringing?'

She shook her head.

'My husband was always very reticent about himself, monsieur. He came from the North-West, I know, but I fancy that he had an unhappy childhood, for he never cared to speak of that time. Our life was lived entirely in the present and the future.'

'Was there any mystery in his past life?'

Mrs Renauld smiled a little and shook her head.

'Nothing so romantic, I am sure, monsieur.'

M. Hautet also smiled.

'True, we must not permit ourselves to get melodramatic. There is one thing more –' He hesitated.

Stonor broke in impetuously:

'They've got an extraordinary idea into their heads, Mrs Renauld. They actually fancy that Mr Renauld was carrying on an intrigue with a Madame Daubreuil who, it seems, lives next door.'

The scarlet colour flamed into Mrs Renauld's cheeks. She flung her head up, then bit her lip, her face quivering. Stonor stood looking at her in astonishment, but M. Bex leaned forward and said gently:

'We regret to cause you pain, madame, but have you any reason to believe that Madame Daubreuil was your husband's mistress?'

With a sob of anguish, Mrs Renauld buried her face in her hands. Her shoulders heaved convulsively. At last she lifted her head and said brokenly:

'She may have been.'

Never, in all my life, have I seen anything to equal the blank amazement on Stonor's face. He was thoroughly taken aback.

CHAPTER 11

JACK RENAULD

What the next development of the conversation would have been I cannot say, for at that moment the door was thrown open violently and a tall young man strode into the room.

Just for a moment I had the uncanny sensation that the dead man had come to life again. Then I realized that this dark head was untouched with grey, and that, in point of fact, it was a mere boy who now burst in among us with so little ceremony. He went straight to Mrs Renauld with an impetuosity that took no heed of the presence of others.

'Mother!'

'Jack!' With a cry she folded him in her arms. 'My dearest! But what brings you here? You were to sail on the *Anzora* from Cherbourg two days ago?' Then, suddenly recalling to herself the presence of others, she turned with a certain dignity: 'My son, messieurs.'

'Aha!' said M. Hautet, acknowledging the young man's bow. 'So you did not sail on the *Anzora*?'

'No, monsieur. As I was about to explain, the *Anzora* was detained twenty-four hours through engine trouble. I should have sailed last night instead of the night before, but, happening to buy an evening paper, I saw in it an account of the – the awful tragedy that had befallen us –' His voice broke and the tears came into his eyes. 'My poor father – my poor, poor father.'

Staring at him like one in a dream, Mrs Renauld repeated:

'So you did not sail?' And then, with a gesture of infinite weariness, she murmured as though to herself: 'After all, it does not matter – now.'

'Sit down, Monsieur Renauld, I beg of you,' said M. Hautet, indicating a chair. 'My sympathy for you is profound. It must have been a terrible shock to you to learn the news as you did. However, it is most fortunate that you were prevented from sailing. I am in hopes that you may be able to give us just the information we need to clear up this mystery.'

'I am at your disposal, monsieur. Ask me any questions you please.'

'To begin with, I understand that this journey was being undertaken at your father's request?'

'Quite so, monsieur. I received a telegram bidding me to proceed without delay to Buenos Aires, and from thence *via* the Andes to Valparaiso, and on to Santiago.'

'Ah! And the object of this journey?'

'I have no idea.'

'What?'

'No. See, here in the telegram.'

The magistrate took it and read it aloud:

'"Proceed immediately Cherbourg embark *Anzora* sailing tonight Buenos Aires. Ultimate destination Santiago. Further instructions will await you Buenos Aires. Do not fail. Matter is of utmost importance. RENAULD." And there had been no previous correspondence on the matter?'

Jack Renauld shook his head.

'That is the only intimation of any kind. I knew, of course, that my father, having lived so long out there, had necessarily many interests in South America. But he had never mooted any suggestion of sending me out.'

'You have, of course, been a good deal in South America, M. Renauld?'

'I was there as a child. But I was educated in England, and spent most of my holidays in that country, so I really know far less of South America than might be supposed. You see, the War broke out when I was seventeen.'

'You served in the English Flying Corps, did you not?'

'Yes, monsieur.'

M. Hautet nodded his head and proceeded with his inquiries along the, by now, well-known lines. In response, Jack Renauld declared definitely that he knew nothing of any enmity his father might have incurred in the city of Santiago or elsewhere in the South American continent, that he had noticed no change in his father's manner of late, and that he had never heard him refer to a secret. He had regarded the mission to South America as connected with business interests.

As M. Hautet paused for a minute, the quiet voice of Giraud broke in:

'I should like to put a few questions of my own, Monsieur le juge.'

'By all means, Monsieur Giraud, if you wish,' said the magistrate coldly.

Giraud edged his chair a little nearer to the table.

'Were you on good terms with your father, Monsieur Renauld?'

'Certainly I was,' returned the lad haughtily.

'You assert that positively?'

'Yes.'

'No little disputes, eh?'

Jack shrugged his shoulders. 'Everyone may have a difference of opinion now and then.'

'Quite so, quite so. But, if anyone were to assert that you had a violent quarrel with your father on the eve of your departure for Paris, that person, without doubt, would be lying?'

I could not but admire the ingenuity of Giraud. His boast, 'I know everything,' had been no idle one. Jack Renauld was clearly disconcerted by the question.

'We – we did have an argument,' he admitted.

'Ah, an argument! In the course of that argument, did you use this phrase: "When you are dead I can do as I please"?'

'I may have done,' muttered the other. 'I don't know.'

'In response to that, did your father say: "But I am not dead yet!"? To which you responded: "I wish you were!"'

The boy made no answer. His hands fiddled nervously with the things on the table in front of him.

'I must request an answer, please, Monsieur Renauld,' said Giraud sharply.

With an angry exclamation, the boy swept a heavy paper-knife to the floor.

'What does it matter? You might as well know. Yes, I did quarrel with my father. I dare say I said all those things – I was so angry I cannot even remember what I said! I was furious – I could almost have killed him at that moment – there, make the most of that!' He leant back in his chair, flushed and defiant.

Giraud smiled, then, moving his chair back a little, said:

'That is all. You would, without doubt, prefer to continue the interrogatory, Monsieur Hautet.'

'Ah, yes, exactly,' said M. Hautet. 'And what was the subject of your quarrel?'

'That I decline to state.'

M. Hautet sat up in his chair.

'Monsieur Renauld, it is not permitted to trifle with the law!' he thundered. 'What was the subject of the quarrel?'

Young Renauld remained silent, his boyish face sullen and overcast. But another voice spoke, imperturbable and calm, the voice of Hercule Poirot:

'I will inform you, if you like, monsieur.'

'You know?'

'Certainly I know. The subject of the quarrel was Mademoiselle Marthe Daubreuil.'

Renauld sprang round, startled. The magistrate leaned forward.

'Is that so, monsieur?'

Jack Renauld bowed his head.

'Yes,' he admitted. 'I love Mademoiselle Daubreuil, and I wish to marry her. When I informed my father of the fact he flew at once into a violent rage. Naturally, I could not stand hearing the girl I loved insulted, and I, too, lost my temper.'

M. Hautet looked across at Mrs Renauld.

'You were aware of this – attachment, madame?'

'I feared it,' she replied simply.

'Mother,' cried the boy. 'You too! Marthe is as good as she is beautiful. What can you have against her?'

'I have nothing against Mademoiselle Daubreuil in any way. But I should prefer you to marry an Englishwoman, or if a Frenchwoman, not one who has a mother of doubtful antecedents!'

Her rancour against the older woman showed plainly in her voice, and I could well understand that it must have been a bitter blow to her when her only son showed signs of falling in love with the daughter of her rival.

Mrs Renauld continued, addressing the magistrate:

'I ought, perhaps, to have spoken to my husband on the subject, but I hoped that it was only a boy and girl flirtation which would blow over all the quicker if no notice was taken of it. I blame myself now for my silence, but my husband, as I told you, had seemed so anxious and careworn, different altogether from his normal self, that I was chiefly concerned not to give him any additional worry.'

M. Hautet nodded.

'When you informed your father of your intentions towards

Mademoiselle Daubreuil,' he resumed, 'he was surprised?'

'He seemed completely taken aback. Then he ordered me peremptorily to dismiss any such idea from my mind. He would never give his consent to such a marriage. Nettled, I demanded what he had against Mademoiselle Daubreuil. To that he could give no satisfactory reply, but spoke in slighting terms of the mystery surrounding the lives of the mother and daughter. I answered that I was marrying Marthe and not her antecedents, but he shouted me down with a peremptory refusal to discuss the matter in any way. The whole thing must be given up. The injustice and high-handedness of it all maddened me – especially since he himself always seemed to go out of his way to be attentive to the Daubreuils and was always suggesting that they should be asked to the house. I lost my head, and we quarrelled in earnest. My father reminded me that I was entirely dependent on him, and it must have been in answer to that that I made the remark about doing as I pleased after his death –'

Poirot interrupted with a quick question:

'You were aware, then, of the terms of your father's will?'

'I knew that he had left half his fortune to me, the other half in trust for my mother, to come to me at her death,' replied the lad.

'Proceed with your story,' said the magistrate.

'After that we shouted at each other in sheer rage, until I suddenly realized that I was in danger of missing my train to Paris. I had to run for the station, still in a white heat of fury. However, once well away, I calmed down. I wrote to Marthe, telling her what had happened, and her reply soothed me still further. She pointed out to me that we had only to be steadfast, and any opposition was bound to give way at last. Our affection for each other must be tried and proved, and when my parents realized that it was no light infatuation on my part they would doubtless relent towards us. Of course, to her, I had not dwelt on my father's principal objection to the match. I soon saw that I should do my cause no good by violence.'

'To pass to another matter, are you acquainted with the name of Duveen, Monsieur Renauld?'

'Duveen?' said Jack. 'Duveen?' He leant forward and slowly picked up the paper-knife he had swept from the table. As he lifted his head his eyes met the watching ones of Giraud. 'Duveen? No, I can't say I do.'

'Will you read this letter, Monsieur Renauld? And tell me if you have any idea as to who the person was who addressed it to your father.'

Jack Renauld took the letter and read it through, the colour mounting in his face as he did so.

'Addressed to my father?' The emotion and indignation in his tones were evident.

'Yes. We found it in the pocket of his coat.'

'Does –' He hesitated, throwing the merest fraction of a glance towards his mother.

The magistrate understood.

'As yet – no. Can you give us any clue as to the writer?'

'I have no idea whatsoever.'

M. Hautet sighed.

'A most mysterious case. Ah, well, I suppose we can now rule out the letter altogether. Let me see, where were we? Oh, the weapon. I fear this may give you pain, Monsieur Renauld. I understand it was a present from you to your mother. Very sad – very distressing –'

Jack Renauld leaned forward. His face, which had flushed during the perusal of the letter, was now deadly white.

'Do you mean – that it was with an aeroplane wire paper-cutter that my father was – was killed? But it's impossible! A little thing like that!'

'Alas, Monsieur Renauld, it is only too true! An ideal little tool, I fear. Sharp and easy to handle.'

'Where is it? Can I see it? Is it still in the – the body?'

'Oh no, it has been removed. You would like to see it? To make sure? It would be as well, perhaps, though madame has already identified it. Still – Monsieur Bex, might I trouble you?'

'Certainly. I will fetch it immediately.'

'Would it not be better to take Monsieur Renauld to the shed?' suggested Giraud smoothly. 'Without doubt he would wish to see his father's body.'

The boy made a shivering gesture of negation, and the magistrate, always disposed to cross Giraud whenever possible, replied:

'But no – not at present. Monsieur Bex will be so kind as to bring it to us here.'

The commissary left the room. Stonor crossed to Jack and

wrung him by the hand. Poirot had risen, and was adjusting a pair of candlesticks that struck his trained eye as being a shade askew. The magistrate was reading the mysterious love-letter through a last time, clinging desperately to his first theory of jealousy and a stab in the back.

Suddenly the door burst open and the commissary rushed in.

'Monsieur le juge! Monsieur le juge!'

'But yes. What is it?'

'The dagger! It is gone!'

'What – gone?'

'Vanished. Disappeared. The glass jar that contained it is empty!'

'What?' I cried. 'Impossible. Why, only this morning I saw –' The words died on my tongue.

But the attention of the entire room was diverted to me.

'What is that you say?' cried the commissary. 'This morning?'

'I saw it there this morning,' I said slowly. 'About an hour and a half ago, to be accurate.'

'You went to the shed, then? How did you get the key?'

'I asked the *sergent de ville* for it.'

'And you went there? Why?'

I hesitated, but in the end I decided that the only thing to do was to make a clean breast of it.

'Monsieur Hautet,' I said, 'I have committed a grave fault, for which I must crave your indulgence.'

'Proceed, monsieur.'

'The fact of the matter is,' I said, wishing myself anywhere else but where I was, 'that I met a young lady, an acquaintance of mine. She displayed a great desire to see everything that was to be seen, and I – well, in short, I took the key to show her the body.'

'Ah!' cried the magistrate indignantly. 'But it is a grave fault you have committed there, Captain Hastings. It is altogether most irregular. You should not have permitted yourself this folly.'

'I know,' I said meekly. 'Nothing that you can say could be too severe, monsieur.'

'You did not invite this lady to come here?'

'Certainly not. I met her quite by accident. She is an English lady who happens to be staying in Merlinville, though I was not aware of that until my unexpected meeting with her.'

'Well, well,' said the magistrate, softening. 'It was most irregular, but the lady is without doubt young and beautiful. What it is to be young!' And he sighed sentimentally.

But the commissary, less romantic and more practical, took up the tale:

'But did you not reclose and lock the door when you departed?'

'That's just it,' I said slowly. 'That's what I blame myself for so terribly. My friend was upset at the sight. She nearly fainted. I got her some brandy and water, and afterwards insisted on accompanying her back to the town. In the excitement I forgot to relock the door. I only did so when I got back to the villa.'

'Then for twenty minutes at least –' said the commissary slowly. He stopped.

'Exactly,' I said.

'Twenty minutes,' mused the commissary.

'It is deplorable,' said M. Hautet, his sternness of manner returning. 'Without precedent.'

Suddenly another voice spoke.

'You find it deplorable?' asked Giraud.

'Certainly I do.'

'I find it admirable!' said the other imperturbably.

This unexpected ally quite bewildered me.

'Admirable, Monsieur Giraud?' asked the magistrate, studying him cautiously out of the corner of his eye.

'Precisely.'

'And why?'

'Because we know now that the assassin, or an accomplice of the assassin, has been near the villa only an hour ago. It will be strange if, with that knowledge, we do not shortly lay hands upon him.' There was a note of menace in his voice. He continued: 'He risked a good deal to gain possession of that dagger. Perhaps he feared that fingerprints might be discovered on it.'

Poirot turned to Bex.

'You said there were none?'

Giraud shrugged his shoulders.

'Perhaps he could not be sure.'

Poirot looked at him.

'You are wrong, Monsieur Giraud. The assassin wore gloves. So he must have been sure.'

'I do not say it was the assassin himself. It may have been an accomplice who was not aware of that fact.'

The magistrate's clerk was gathering up the papers on the table. M. Hautet addressed us:

'Our work here is finished. Perhaps, Monsieur Renauld, you will listen while your evidence is read over to you. I have purposely kept all the proceedings as informal as possible. I have been called original in my methods, but I maintain that there is much to be said for originality. The case is now in the clever hands of the renowned Monsieur Giraud. He will without doubt distinguish himself. Indeed, I wonder that he has not already laid his hands upon the murderers! Madame, again let me assure you of my heartfelt sympathy. Messieurs, I wish you all good day.' And, accompanied by his clerk and the commissary, he took his departure.

Poirot tugged out that large turnip of a watch of his and observed the time.

'Let us return to the hotel for lunch, my friend,' he said. 'And you shall recount to me in full the indiscretions of this morning. No one is observing us. We need make no adieux.'

We went quietly out of the room. The examining magistrate had just driven off in his car. I was going down the steps when Poirot's voice arrested me:

'One little moment, my friend.' Dexterously he whipped out his yard measure and proceeded, quite solemnly, to measure an overcoat hanging in the hall, from the collar to the hem. I had not seen it hanging there before, and guessed that it belonged to either Mr Stonor or Jack Renauld.

Then, with a little satisfied grunt, Poirot returned the measure to his pocket and followed me out into the open air.

CHAPTER 12

POIROT ELUCIDATES CERTAIN POINTS

'Why did you measure that overcoat?' I asked, with some curiosity, as we walked down the hot white road at a leisurely pace.

'*Parbleu!* to see how long it was,' replied my friend imperturbably.

I was vexed. Poirot's incurable habit of making a mystery out of nothing never failed to irritate me. I relapsed into silence, and followed a train of thought of my own. Although I had not noticed them specially at the time, certain words Mrs Renauld had addressed to her son now recurred to me, fraught with a new significance. 'So you did not sail?' she had said, and then had added: '*After all, it does not matter – now.*'

What had she meant by that? The words were enigmatical – significant. Was it possible that she knew more than we supposed? She had denied all knowledge of the mysterious mission with which her husband was to have entrusted his son. But was she really less ignorant than she pretended? Could she enlighten us if she chose, and was her silence part of a carefully thought out and preconceived plan?

The more I thought about it, the more I was convinced that I was right. Mrs Renauld knew more than she chose to tell. In her surprise at seeing her son, she had momentarily betrayed herself. I felt convinced that she knew, if not the assassins, at least the motive for the assassination. But some very powerful considerations must keep her silent.

'You think profoundly, my friend,' remarked Poirot, breaking in upon my reflections. 'What is it that intrigues you so?'

I told him, sure of my ground, though feeling expectant that he would ridicule my suspicions. But to my surprise he nodded thoughtfully.

'You are quite right, Hastings. From the beginning I have been sure that she was keeping something back. At first I suspected her, if not of inspiring, at least of conniving at the crime.'

'You suspected *her*?' I cried.

'But certainly. She benefits enormously – in fact, by this new will, she is the only person to benefit. So, from the start, she was singled out for attention. You may have noticed that I took an early opportunity of examining her wrists. I wished to see whether there was any possibility that she had gagged and bound herself. *Eh bien*, I saw at once that there was no fake, the cords had actually been drawn so tight as to cut into the flesh. That ruled out the possibility of her having committed the crime single-handed. But it was still possible for her to have connived at it, or to have been the instigator with an accomplice. Moreover, the story, as she told it, was singularly familiar to me – the masked men that she could not recognize, the mention of "the secret" – I had heard, or read, all these things before. Another little detail confirmed my belief that she was not speaking the truth. *The wristwatch, Hastings, the wristwatch!*'

Again that wristwatch! Poirot was eyeing me curiously.

'You see, *mon ami*? You comprehend?'

'No,' I replied with some ill humour. 'I neither see nor comprehend. You make all these confounded mysteries, and it's useless asking you to explain. You always like keeping something up your sleeve to the last minute.'

'Do not enrage yourself, my friend,' said Poirot, with a smile. 'I will explain if you wish. But not a word to Giraud, *c'est entendu*? He treats me as an old one of no importance! *We shall see!* In common fairness I gave him a hint. If he does not choose to act upon it, that is his own lookout.'

I assured Poirot that he could rely upon my discretion.

'*C'est bien!* Let us then employ our little grey cells. Tell me, my friend, at what time, according to you, did the tragedy take place?'

'Why, at two o'clock or thereabouts,' I said, astonished. 'You remember, Mrs Renauld told us that she heard the clock strike while the men were in the room.'

'Exactly, and on the strength of that, you, the examining magistrate, Bex, and everyone else, accept the time without further question. But I, Hercule Poirot, say that Madame Renauld lied. *The crime took place at least two hours earlier.*'

'But the doctors –'

'They declared, after examination of the body, that death had taken place between ten and seven hours previously. *Mon ami*, for some reason it was imperative that the crime should seem to have taken place later than it actually did. You have read of a smashed watch or clock recording the exact hour of a crime? So that the time should not rest on Madame Renauld's testimony alone, someone moved on the hands of that wristwatch to two o'clock, and then dashed it violently to the ground. But, as is often the case, they defeated their own object. The glass was smashed, but the mechanism of the watch was uninjured. It was a most disastrous manœuvre on their part, for it at once drew my attention to two points – first, that Madame Renauld was lying; secondly, that there must be some vital reason for the postponement of the time.'

'But what reason could there be?'

'Ah, that is the question! There we have the whole mystery. As yet, I cannot explain it. There is only one idea that presents itself to me as having a possible connexion.'

'And that is?'

'The last train left Merlinville at seventeen minutes past twelve.'

I followed it out slowly.

'So that, the crime apparently taking place some two hours later, anyone leaving by that train would have an unimpeachable alibi!'

'Perfect, Hastings! You have it!'

I sprang up.

'But we must inquire at the station! Surely they cannot have failed to notice two foreigners who left by that train! We must go there at once!'

'You think so, Hastings?'

'Of course. Let us go there now.'

Poirot restrained my ardour with a light touch upon the arm.

'Go by all means if you wish, *mon ami* – but if you go, I should not ask for particulars of two foreigners.'

I stared and he said rather impatiently:

'*Là, là*, you do not believe all that rigmarole, do you? The masked men and all the rest of *cette histoire-là!*'

His words took me so much aback, that I hardly knew how to respond. He went on serenely:

'You heard me say to Giraud, did you not, that all the details of this crime were familiar to me? *Eh bien*, that presupposes one of two things, either the brain that planned the first crime also planned this one, or else an account read of a *cause célèbre* unconsciously remained in our assassin's memory and prompted the details. I shall be able to pronounce definitely on that after –' He broke off.

I was revolving sundry matters in my mind.

'But Mr Renauld's letter? It distinctly mentions a secret and Santiago!'

'Undoubtedly there was a secret in Monsieur Renauld's life – there can be no doubt of that. On the other hand, the word Santiago, to my mind, is a red herring, dragged continually across the track to put us off the scent. It is possible that it was used in the same way on Monsieur Renauld, to keep him from directing his suspicions to a quarter nearer at hand. Oh, be assured, Hastings, the danger that threatened him was not in Santiago, it was near at hand, in France.'

He spoke so gravely, and with such assurance, that I could not fail to be convinced. But I essayed one final objection:

'And the match and cigarette end found near the body? What of them?'

A light of pure enjoyment lit up Poirot's face.

'Planted! Deliberately planted there for Giraud or one of his tribe to find! Ah, he is smart, Giraud, he can do his tricks! So can a good retriever dog. He comes in so pleased with himself. For hours he has crawled on his stomach. "See what I have found," he says. And then again to me: "What do you see here?" Me, I answer, with profound and deep truth, "Nothing." And Giraud, the great Giraud, he laughs, he thinks to himself, "Oh, he is imbecile, this old one!" *But we shall see . . .*'

But my mind had reverted to the main facts.

'Then all this story of the masked men –?'

'Is false.'

'What really happened?'

Poirot shrugged his shoulders.

'One person could tell us – Madame Renauld. But she will not speak. Threats and entreaties would not move her. A remarkable woman that, Hastings. I recognized as soon as I saw her that I had to deal with a woman of unusual character. At first, as I told you, I was inclined to suspect her of being concerned in the crime. Afterwards I altered my opinion.'

'What made you do that?'

'Her spontaneous and genuine grief at the sight of her husband's body. I could swear that the agony in that cry of hers was genuine.'

'Yes,' I said thoughtfully, 'one cannot mistake these things.'

'I beg your pardon, my friend – one can always be mistaken. Regard a great actress, does not her acting of grief carry you away and impress you with its reality? No, however strong my own impression and belief, I needed other evidence before I allowed myself to be satisfied. The great criminal can be a great actor. I base my certainty in this case not upon my own impression, but upon the undeniable fact that Madame Renauld actually fainted. I turned up her eyelids and felt her pulse. There was no deception – the swoon was genuine. Therefore I was satisfied that her anguish was real and not assumed. Besides, a small additional point without interest, it was unnecessary for Madame Renauld to exhibit unrestrained grief. She had had one paroxysm on learning of her husband's death, and there would be no need for her to simulate another such a violent one on beholding his body. No, Madame Renauld was not her husband's murderess. But why has she lied? She lied about the wristwatch, she lied about the masked men – she lied about a third thing. Tell me, Hastings, what is your explanation of the open door?'

'Well,' I said, rather embarrassed, 'I suppose it was an oversight. They forgot to shut it.'

Poirot shook his head, and sighed.

'That is the explanation of Giraud. It does not satisfy me. There is a meaning behind that open door which for the moment I cannot fathom. One thing I am fairly sure of – they did not leave through the door. They left by the window.'

'What?'

'Precisely.'

'But there were no footmarks in the flower-bed underneath.'

'No – and there ought to have been. Listen, Hastings. The gardener, Auguste, as you heard him say, planted both those beds the preceding afternoon. In the one there are plentiful impressions of his big hobnailed boots – in the other, *none!* You see? Someone had passed that way, someone who, to obliterate their footprints, smoothed over the surface of the bed with a rake.'

'Where did they get a rake?'

'Where they got the spade and the gardening gloves,' said Poirot impatiently. 'There is no difficulty about that.'

'What makes you think that they left that way, though? Surely it is more probable that they entered by the window, and left by the door?'

'That is possible, of course. Yet I have a strong idea that they left by the window.'

'I think you are wrong.'

'Perhaps, *mon ami*.'

I mused, thinking over the new field of conjecture that Poirot's deductions had opened up to me. I recalled my wonder at his cryptic allusion to the flower-bed and the wristwatch. His remarks had seemed so meaningless at the moment, and now, for the first time, I realized how remarkably, from a few slight incidents, he had unravelled much of the mystery that surrounded the case. I paid a belated homage to my friend.

'In the meantime,' I said, considering, 'although we know a great deal more than we did, we are no nearer to solving the mystery of who killed Mr Renauld.'

'No,' said Poirot cheerfully. 'In fact we are a great deal farther off.'

The fact seemed to afford him such peculiar satisfaction that I gazed at him in wonder. He met my eye and smiled.

Suddenly a light burst upon me.

'Poirot! Mrs Renauld! I see it now. She must be shielding somebody.'

From the quietness with which Poirot received my remark, I could see that the idea had already occurred to him.

'Yes,' he said thoughtfully. 'Shielding someone – or screening someone. One of the two.'

Then, as we entered our hotel, he enjoined silence on me with a gesture.

CHAPTER 13

THE GIRL WITH THE ANXIOUS EYES

We lunched with an excellent appetite. For a while we ate in silence, and then Poirot observed maliciously: '*Eh bien!* And your indiscretions! You recount them not?'

I felt myself blushing.

'Oh, you mean this morning?' I endeavoured to adopt a tone of absolute nonchalance.

But I was no match for Poirot. In a very few minutes he had extracted the whole story from me, his eyes twinkling as he did so.

'*Tiens!* A story of the most romantic. What is her name, this charming young lady?'

I had to confess that I did not know.

'Still more romantic! The first *rencontre* in the train from Paris, the second here. Journeys end in lovers' meetings, is not that the saying?'

'Don't be an ass, Poirot.'

'Yesterday it was Mademoiselle Daubreuil, today it is Mademoiselle – Cinderella! Decidedly you have the heart of a Turk, Hastings! You should establish a harem!'

'It's all very well to rag me. Mademoiselle Daubreuil is a very beautiful girl, and I do admire her immensely – I don't mind admitting it. The other's nothing – I don't suppose I shall ever see her again.'

'You do not propose to see the lady again?'

His last words were almost a question, and I was aware of the sharpness with which he darted a glance at me. And before my eyes, writ large in letters of fire, I saw the words 'Hôtel du Phare', and I heard again her voice saying, 'Come and look me up', and my own answering with *empressement* 'I will.'

I answered Poirot lightly enough:

'She asked me to look her up, but, of course, I shan't.'

'Why "of course"?'

'Well, I don't want to.'

'Mademoiselle Cinderella is staying at the Hôtel d'Angleterre you told me, did you not?'

'No. Hôtel du Phare.'

'True, I forgot.'

A moment's misgiving shot across my mind. Surely I had never mentioned any hotel to Poirot. I looked across at him and felt reassured. He was cutting his bread into neat little squares, completely absorbed in his task. He must have fancied I had told him where the girl was staying.

We had coffee outside facing the sea. Poirot smoked one of his tiny cigarettes, and then drew his watch from his pocket.

'The train to Paris leaves at 2.25,' he observed. 'I should be starting.'

'Paris?' I cried.

'That is what I said, *mon ami*.'

'You are going to Paris? But why?'

He replied very seriously:

'To look for the murderer of Monsieur Renauld.'

'You think he is in Paris?'

'I am quite certain that he is not. Nevertheless, it is there that I must look for him. You do not understand, but I will explain it all to you in good time. Believe me, this journey to Paris is necessary. I shall not be away long. In all probability I shall return tomorrow.

I do not propose that you should accompany me. Remain here and keep an eye on Giraud. Also cultivate the society of Monsieur Renauld *fils*.'

'That reminds me,' I said. 'I meant to ask you how you knew about those two?'

'*Mon ami* – I know human nature. Throw together a boy like young Renauld and a beautiful girl like Mademoiselle Marthe and the result is almost inevitable. Then, the quarrel! It was money, or a woman, and, remembering Léonie's description of the lad's anger, I decided on the latter. So I made my guess – and I was right.'

'You already suspected that she loved young Renauld?' Poirot smiled.

'At any rate, *I saw that she had anxious eyes*. That is how I always think of Mademoiselle Daubreuil – *as the girl with the anxious eyes*.'

His voice was so grave that it impressed me uncomfortably.

'What do you mean by that, Poirot?'

'I fancy, my friend, that we shall see before very long. But I must start.'

'I will come and see you off,' I said, rising.

'You will do nothing of the sort. I forbid it.'

He was so peremptory that I stared at him in surprise. He nodded emphatically.

'I mean it, *mon ami*. Au revoir.'

I felt rather at a loose end after Poirot had left me. I strolled down to the beach and watched the bathers, without feeling energetic enough to join them. I rather fancied that Cinderella might be disporting herself among them in some wonderful costume, but I saw no signs of her. I strolled aimlessly along the sands towards the farther end of the town. It occurred to me that, after all, it would only be decent feeling on my part to inquire after the girl. And it would save trouble in the end. The matter would then be finished with. There would be no need for me to trouble about her any further. But if I did not go at all, she might quite possibly come and look me up at the villa.

Accordingly, I left the beach, and walked inland. I soon found the Hôtel du Phare, a very unpretentious building. It was annoying in the extreme not to know the lady's name and, to save my dignity, I decided to stroll inside and look around. Probably I should find her in the lounge. I went in, but there was no sign of her. I waited for some time, till my impatience got the better of me. I took the concierge aside and slipped five francs into his hand.

'I wish to see a lady who is staying here. A young English lady, small and dark. I am not sure of her name.'

The man shook his head and seemed to be suppressing a grin.

'There is no such lady as you describe staying here.'

'But the lady told me she was staying here.'

'Monsieur must have made a mistake – or it is more likely the lady did, since there has been another gentleman here inquiring for her.'

'What is that you say?' I cried, surprised.

'But yes, monsieur. A gentleman who described her just as you have done.'

'What was he like?'

'He was a small gentleman, well dressed, very neat, very spotless, the moustache very stiff, the head of a peculiar shape, and the eyes green.'

Poirot! So that was why he refused to let me accompany him to the station. The impertinence of it! I would thank him not to meddle in my concerns. Did he fancy I needed a nurse to look after me?

Thanking the man, I departed, somewhat at a loss, and still much incensed with my meddlesome friend.

But where was the lady? I set aside my wrath and tried to puzzle it out. Evidently, through inadvertence, she had named the wrong hotel. Then another thought struck me. Was it inadvertence? Or had she deliberately withheld her name and given me the wrong address?

The more I thought about it, the more I felt convinced that this last surmise of mine was right. For some reason or other she did not wish to let the acquaintance ripen into friendship. And, though half an hour earlier this had been precisely my own view, I did not enjoy having the tables turned upon me. The whole affair was profoundly unsatisfactory, and I went up to the Villa Geneviève in a condition of distinct ill humour. I did not go to the house, but went up the path to the little bench by the shed, and sat there moodily enough.

I was distracted from my thoughts by the sound of voices close at hand. In a second or two I realized that they came, not from the garden I was in, but from the adjoining garden of the Villa Marguerite, and that they were approaching rapidly. A girl's voice was speaking, a voice that I recognized as that of the beautiful Marthe.

'*Chéri*,' she was saying, 'is it really true? Are all our troubles over?'

'You know it, Marthe,' Jack Renauld replied. 'Nothing can part us now, beloved. The last obstacle to our union is removed. Nothing can take you from me.'

'Nothing?' the girl murmured. 'Oh Jack, Jack – I am afraid.'

I had moved to depart, realizing that I was quite unintentionally eavesdropping. As I rose to my feet, I caught sight of them through a gap in the hedge. They stood together facing me, the man's arm round the girl, his eyes looking into hers. They were a splendid-looking couple, the dark, well-knit boy, and the fair young goddess. They seemed made for each other as they stood there, happy in spite of the terrible tragedy that overshadowed their young lives.

But the girl's face was troubled, and Jack Renauld seemed to recognize it, as he held her closer to him and asked:

'But what are you afraid of, darling? What is there to fear – now?'

And then I saw the look in her eyes, the look Poirot had spoken of, as she murmured, so that I almost guessed at the words:

'I am afraid – for *you*.'

I did not hear young Renauld's answer, for my attention was distracted by an unusual appearance a little farther down the hedge. There appeared to be a brown bush there, which seemed odd, to say the least of it, so early in the summer. I stepped along to investigate, but, at my advance, the brown bush withdrew itself precipitately, and faced me with a finger to its lips. It was Giraud.

Enjoining caution, he led the way round the shed until we were out of ear-shot.

'What were you doing there?' I asked.

'Exactly what you were doing – listening.'

'But I was not there on purpose!'

'Ah!' said Giraud. 'I was.'

As always, I admired the man while disliking him. He looked me up and down with a sort of contemptuous disfavour.

'You didn't help matters by butting in. I might have heard something useful in a minute. What have you done with your old fossil?'

'Monsieur Poirot has gone to Paris,' I replied coldly.

Giraud snapped his fingers disdainfully. 'So he has gone to Paris, has he? Well, a good thing. The longer he stays there the better. But what does he think he will find there?'

I thought I read in the question a tinge of uneasiness. I drew myself up.

'That I am not at liberty to say,' I said quietly.

Giraud subjected me to a piercing stare.

'He has probably enough sense not to tell *you*,' he remarked rudely. 'Good afternoon. I'm busy.' And with that he turned on his heel, and left me without ceremony.

Matters seemed at a standstill at the Villa Geneviève. Giraud evidently did not desire my company and, from what I had seen, it seemed fairly certain that Jack Renauld did not either.

I went back to the town, had an enjoyable bathe, and returned to the hotel. I turned in early, wondering whether the following day would bring forth anything of interest.

I was wholly unprepared for what it did bring forth. I was eating my *petit déjeuner* in the dining-room, when the waiter, who had been talking to someone outside, came back in obvious excitement. He hesitated for a minute, fidgeting with his napkin, and then burst out:

'Monsieur will pardon me, but he is connected, is he not, with the affair at the Villa Geneviève?'

'Yes,' I said eagerly. 'Why?'

'Monsieur has not heard the news, though?'

'What news?'

'That there has been another murder there last night!'

'*What?*'

Leaving my breakfast, I caught up my hat and ran as fast as I could. Another murder – and Poirot away! What fatality. But who had been murdered?

I dashed in at the gate. A group of servants were in the drive, talking and gesticulating. I caught hold of Françoise.

'What has happened?'

'Oh, monsieur! monsieur! Another death! It is terrible. There is a curse upon the house. But yes, I say it, a curse! They should send for Monsieur le Curé to bring some holy water. Never will I sleep another night under that roof. It might be my turn, who knows?'

She crossed herself.

'Yes,' I cried, 'but who has been killed?'

'Do I know – me? A man – a stranger. They found him up there – in the shed – not a hundred yards from where they found poor Monsieur. And that is not all. He is stabbed – stabbed to the heart *with the same dagger!*'

CHAPTER 14

THE SECOND BODY

Waiting for no more, I turned and ran up the path to the shed. The two men on guard there stood aside to let me pass and, filled with excitement, I entered.

The light was dim, the place was a mere rough wooden erection to keep old pots and tools in. I had entered impetuously, but on the threshold I checked myself, fascinated by the spectacle before me.

Giraud was on his hands and knees, a pocket torch in his hand with which he was examining every inch of the ground. He looked up with a frown at my entrance, then his face relaxed a little in a sort of good-humoured contempt.

'There he is,' said Giraud, flashing his torch to the far corner.

I stepped across.

The dead man lay straight upon his back. He was of medium height, swarthy of complexion, and possibly about fifty years of age. He was neatly dressed in a dark blue suit, well cut, and probably made by an expensive tailor, but not new. His face was terribly convulsed, and on his left side, just over the heart, the hilt of a dagger stood up, black and shining. I recognized it. It was the same dagger I had seen reposing in the glass jar the preceding morning!

'I'm expecting the doctor any minute,' explained Giraud. 'Although we hardly need him. There's no doubt what the man died of. He was stabbed to the heart, and death must have been pretty well instantaneous.'

'When was it done? Last night?'

Giraud shook his head.

'Hardly. I don't lay down the law on medical evidence, but the man's been dead well over twelve hours. When do you say you last saw that dagger?'

'About ten o'clock yesterday morning.'

'Then I should be inclined to fix the crime as being done not long after that.'

'But people were passing and repassing this shed continually.'

Giraud laughed disagreeably.

'You progress to a marvel! Who told you he was killed in this shed?'

'Well –' I felt flustered. 'I – I assumed it.'

'Oh, what a fine detective! Look at him. Does a man stabbed to the heart fall like that – neatly with his feet together, and his arms to his sides? No. Again, does a man lie down on his back and permit himself to be stabbed without raising a hand to defend himself? It is absurd, is it not? But see here – and here –' He flashed the torch along the ground. I saw curious irregular marks in the soft dirt. 'He was dragged here after he was dead. Half dragged, half carried by two people. Their tracks do not show on the hard ground outside, and here they have been careful to obliterate them; but one of the two was a woman, my young friend.'

'A woman?'

'Yes.'

'But if the tracks are obliterated, how do you know?'

'Because, blurred as they are, the prints of the woman's shoe are unmistakable. Also, by *this*.' And, leaning forward, he drew something from the handle of the dagger and held it up for me to see. It was a woman's long black hair, similar to the one Poirot had taken from the armchair in the library.

With a slightly ironic smile he wound it round the dagger again.

'We will leave things as they are as much as possible,' he explained. 'It pleases the examining magistrate. Well, do you notice anything else?'

I was forced to shake my head.

'Look at his hands.'

I did. The nails were broken and discoloured and the skin was hard. It hardly enlightened me as much as I should have liked it to have done. I looked up at Giraud.

'They are not the hands of a gentleman,' he said, answering my look. 'On the contrary, his clothes are those of a well-to-do man. That is curious, is it not?'

'Very curious,' I agreed.

'And none of his clothing is marked. What do we learn from that? This man was trying to pass himself off as other than he was. He was masquerading. Why? Did he fear something? Was he trying to escape by disguising himself? As yet we do not know, but one thing we do know – he was as anxious to conceal his identity as we are to discover it.'

He looked down at the body again.

'As before, there are no fingerprints on the handle of the dagger. The murderer again wore gloves.'

'You think, then, that the murderer was the same in both cases?' I asked eagerly.

Giraud became inscrutable.

'Never mind what I think. We shall see. Marchaud!'

The *sergent de ville* appeared at the door.

'Monsieur?'

'Why is Madame Renauld not here? I sent for her a quarter of an hour ago.'

'She is coming up the path now, monsieur, and her son with her.'

'Good. I only want one at a time, though.'

Marchaud saluted and disappeared again. A moment later he reappeared with Mrs Renauld.

'Here is Madame.'

Giraud came forward with a curt bow.

'This way, madame.' He led her across, and then, standing suddenly aside, 'Here is the man. Do you know him?'

And as he spoke, his eyes, gimlet-like, bored into her face, seeking to read her mind, noting every indication of her manner.

But Mrs Renauld remained perfectly calm – too calm, I felt. She looked down at the corpse almost without interest, certainly without any sign of agitation or recognition.

'No,' she said. 'I have never seen him in my life. He is quite a stranger to me.'

'You are sure?'

'Quite sure.'

'You do not recognize in him one of your assailants, for instance?'

'No.' She seemed to hesitate, as though struck by the idea. 'No, I do not think so. Of course they wore beards – false ones the examining magistrate thought – but still, no.' Now she seemed to make her mind up definitely. 'I am sure neither of the two was this man.'

'Very well, madame. That is all, then.'

She stepped out with head erect, the sun flashing on the silver threads in her hair. Jack Renauld succeeded her. He, too, failed to identify the man in a completely natural manner.

Giraud merely grunted. Whether he was pleased or chagrined I could not tell. He called to Marchaud.

'You have got the other there?'

'Yes, monsieur.'

'Bring her in, then.'

'The other' was Madame Daubreuil. She came indignantly, protesting with vehemence.

'I object, monsieur! This is an outrage! What have I to do with all this?'

'Madame,' said Giraud brutally, 'I am investigating not one murder, but two murders! For all I know you may have committed them both.'

'How dare you?' she cried. 'How dare you insult me by such a wild accusation! It is infamous!'

'Infamous, is it? What about this?' Stooping, he again detached the hair, and held it up. 'Do you see this, madame?' He advanced towards her. 'You permit that I see whether it matches?'

With a cry she started backwards, white to the lips.

'It is false, I swear it. I know nothing of the crime – of either crime. Anyone who says I do lies! Ah, *mon Dieu*, what shall I do?'

'Calm yourself, madame,' said Giraud coldly. 'No one has accused you as yet. But you will do well to answer my questions without more ado.'

'Anything you wish, monsieur.'

'Look at the dead man. Have you ever seen him before?'

Drawing nearer, a little of the colour creeping back to her face, Madame Daubreuil looked down at the victim with a certain amount of interest and curiosity. Then she shook her head.

'I do not know him.'

It seemed impossible to doubt her, the words came so naturally. Giraud dismissed her with a nod of the head.

'You are letting her go?' I asked in a low voice. 'Is that wise? Surely that black hair is from her head.'

'I do not need teaching my business,' said Giraud dryly. 'She is under surveillance. I have no wish to arrest her as yet.'

Then, frowning, he gazed down at the body.

'Should you say that was a Spanish type at all?' he asked suddenly.

I considered the face carefully.

'No,' I said at last. 'I should put him down as a Frenchman most decidedly.'

Giraud gave a grunt of dissatisfaction.

'Same here.'

He stood there for a moment, then with an imperative gesture he waved me aside, and once more, on hands and knees, he continued his search of the floor of the shed. He was marvellous. Nothing escaped him. Inch by inch he went over the floor, turning over pots, examining old sacks. He pounced on a bundle by the door, but it proved to be only a ragged coat and trousers, and he flung it down again with a snarl. Two pairs of old gloves interested him, but in the end he shook his head and laid them aside. Then he went back to the pots, methodically turning them over one by one. In the end he rose to his feet, and shook his head thoughtfully. He seemed baffled and perplexed. I think he had forgotten my presence.

But at that moment a stir and bustle was heard outside, and our old friend, the examining magistrate, accompanied by his clerk and M. Bex, with the doctor behind them, came bustling in.

'But this is extraordinary, Monsieur Giraud,' cried M. Hautet. 'Another crime! Ah, we have not got to the bottom of this case. There is some deep mystery here. But who is the victim this time?'

'That is just what nobody can tell us, monsieur. He has not been identified.'

'Where is the body?' asked the doctor.

Giraud moved aside a little.

'There in the corner. He has been stabbed to the heart, as you see. And with the dagger that was stolen yesterday morning. I fancy that the murder followed hard upon the theft – but that is for you to say. You can handle the dagger freely – there are no fingerprints on it.'

The doctor knelt down by the dead man, and Giraud turned to the examining magistrate.

'A pretty little problem, is it not? But I shall solve it.'

'And so no one can identify him,' mused the magistrate. 'Could it possibly be one of the assassins? They may have fallen out among themselves.'

Giraud shook his head.

'The man is a Frenchman – I would take my oath on that –'

But at that moment they were interrupted by the doctor, who was sitting back on his heels with a perplexed expression.

'You say he was killed yesterday morning?'

'I fix it by the theft of the dagger,' explained Giraud. 'He may, of course, have been killed later in the day.'

'Later in the day? Fiddlesticks! This man has been dead at least forty-eight hours, and probably longer.'

We stared at each other in blank amazement.

CHAPTER 15

A PHOTOGRAPH

The doctor's words were so surprising that we were all momentarily taken aback. Here was a man stabbed with a dagger which we knew to have been stolen only twenty-four hours previously, and yet Dr Durand asserted positively that he had been dead at least forty-eight hours! The whole thing was fantastic to the last extreme.

We were still recovering from the surprise of the doctor's announcement, when a telegram was brought to me. It had been sent up from the hotel to the villa. I tore it open. It was from Poirot, and announced his return by the train arriving at Merlinville at 12.28.

I looked at my watch and saw that I had just time to get comfortably to the station and meet him there. I felt that it was of the utmost importance that he should know at once of the new and startling developments in the case.

Evidently, I reflected, Poirot had had no difficulty in finding what he wanted in Paris. The quickness of his return proved that. Very few hours had sufficed. I wondered how he would take the exciting news I had to impart.

The train was some minutes late, and I strolled aimlessly up and down the platform, until it occurred to me that I might pass the time by asking a few questions as to who had left Merlinville by the last train on the evening of the tragedy.

I approached the chief porter, an intelligent-looking man, and had little difficulty in persuading him to enter upon the subject. It was a disgrace to the police, he hotly affirmed, that such brigands or assassins should be allowed to go about unpunished. I hinted that there was some possibility they might have left by the midnight train, but he negatived the idea decidedly. He would have noticed two foreigners – he was sure of it. Only about twenty people had left by the train, and he could not have failed to observe them.

I do not know what put the idea into my head – possibly it was the deep anxiety underlying Marthe Daubreuil's tones – but I asked suddenly:

'Young Monsieur Renauld – he did not leave by that train, did he?'

'Ah, no, monsieur. To arrive and start off again within half an hour, it would not be amusing, that!'

I stared at the man, the significance of his words almost escaping me. Then I saw.

'You mean,' I said, my heart beating a little, 'that Monsieur Jack Renauld arrived at Merlinville that evening?'

'But yes, monsieur. By the last train arriving the other way, the 11.40.'

My brain whirled. That, then, was the reason of Marthe's poignant anxiety. Jack Renauld had been in Merlinville on the night of the crime. But why had he not said so? Why, on the contrary, had he led us to believe that he had remained in Cherbourg? Remembering his frank boyish countenance, I could hardly bring myself to believe that he had any connexion with the crime. Yet why this silence on his part about so vital a matter? One thing was certain, Marthe had known all along. Hence her anxiety, and her eager questioning of Poirot as to whether anyone was suspected.

My cogitations were interrupted by the arrival of the train, and in another moment I was greeting Poirot. The little man was radiant. He beamed and vociferated and, forgetting my English reluctance, embraced me warmly on the platform.

'*Mon cher ami*, I have succeeded – but succeeded to a marvel!'

'Indeed? I'm delighted to hear it. Have you heard the latest here?'

'How would you that I should hear anything? There have been some developments, eh? The brave Giraud, he has made an arrest? Or even arrests, perhaps? Ah, but I will make him look foolish, that one! But where are you taking me, my friend? Do we not go to the hotel? It is necessary that I attend to my moustaches – they are deplorably limp from the heat of travelling. Also, without doubt, there is dust on my coat. And my tie, that I must rearrange.'

I cut short his remonstrances.

'My dear Poirot – never mind all that. We must go to the villa at once. *There has been another murder!*'

Never have I seen a man so flabbergasted. His jaw dropped. All the jauntiness went out of his bearing. He stared at me open-mouthed.

'What is that you say? Another murder? Ah, then, but I am all wrong. I have failed. Giraud may mock himself at me – he will have reason!'

'You did not expect it, then?'

'I? Not the least in the world. It demolishes my theory – it ruins everything – it – Ah, no!' He stopped dead, thumping himself on the chest. 'It is impossible. I *cannot* be wrong! The facts, taken methodically, and in their proper order, admit of only one explanation. I must be right! I *am* right!'

'But then –'

He interrupted me.

'Wait, my friend. I must be right, therefore this new murder is impossible unless – unless – Oh, wait, I implore you. Say no word.'

He was silent for a moment or two, then resuming his normal manner, he said in a quiet assured voice:

'The victim is a man of middle age. His body was found in the locked shed near the scene of the crime and had been dead at least forty-eight hours. And it is most probable that he was stabbed in a similar manner to Mr Renauld, though not necessarily in the back.'

It was my turn to gape – and gape I did. In all my knowledge of Poirot he had never done anything so amazing as this. And, almost inevitably, a doubt crossed my mind.

'Poirot,' I cried, 'you're pulling my leg. You've heard all about it already.'

He turned his earnest gaze upon me reproachfully.

'Would I do such a thing? I assure you that I have heard nothing whatsoever. Did you not observe the shock your news was to me?'

'But how on earth could you know all that?'

'I was right, then? But I knew it. The little grey cells, my friend, the little grey cells! They told me. Thus, and in no other way, could there have been a second death. Now tell me all. If we go round to the left here, we can take a short cut across the golf links which will bring us to the back of the Villa Geneviève much more quickly.'

As we walked, taking the way he had indicated, I recounted all I knew. Poirot listened attentively.

'The dagger was in the wound, you say? That is curious. You are sure it was the same one?'

'Absolutely certain. That's what makes it so impossible.'

'Nothing is impossible. There may have been two daggers.'

I raised my eyebrows.

'Surely that is in the highest degree unlikely? It would be a most extraordinary coincidence.'

'You speak as usual, without reflection, Hastings. In some cases two identical weapons *would* be highly improbable. But not here. This particular weapon was a war souvenir which was made to Jack Renauld's orders. It is really highly unlikely, when you come to think of it, that he should have had only one made. Very probably he would have another for his own use.'

'But nobody has mentioned such a thing,' I objected.

A hint of the lecturer crept into Poirot's tone.

'My friend, in working upon a case, one does not take into account only the things that are "mentioned". There is no reason to mention many things which may be important. Equally, there is often an excellent reason for *not* mentioning them. You can take your choice of the two motives.'

I was silent, impressed in spite of myself. Another few minutes brought us to the famous shed. We found all our friends there, and after an interchange of polite amenities, Poirot began his task.

Having watched Giraud at work, I was keenly interested. Poirot bestowed but a cursory glance on the surroundings. The only thing he examined was the ragged coat and trousers by the door. A disdainful smile rose to Giraud's lips, and, as though noting it, Poirot flung the bundle down again.

'Old clothes of the gardener's?' he queried.

'Exactly,' said Giraud.

Poirot knelt down by the body. His fingers were rapid but methodical. He examined the texture of the clothes, and satisfied himself that there were no marks on them. The boots he subjected to special care, also the dirty and broken fingernails. While examining the latter he threw a quick question at Giraud.

'You saw them?'

'Yes, I saw them,' replied the other. His face remained inscrutable.

Suddenly Poirot stiffened.

'Dr Durand!'

'Yes?' The doctor came forward.

'There is foam on the lips. You observed it?'

'I didn't notice it, I must admit.'

'But you observe it now?'

'Oh, certainly.'

Poirot again shot a question at Giraud.

'You noticed it without doubt?'

The other did not reply. Poirot proceeded. The dagger had been withdrawn from the wound. It reposed in a glass jar by the side of the body. Poirot examined it, then he studied the wound closely. When he looked up, his eyes were excited and shone with the green light I knew so well.

'It is a strange wound, this! It has not bled. There is no stain on the clothes. The blade of the dagger is slightly discoloured, that is all. What do you think, *monsieur le docteur*?'

'I can only say that it is most abnormal.'

'It is not abnormal at all. It is most simple. The man was stabbed *after he was dead.*' And, stilling the clamour of voices that arose with a wave of his hand, Poirot turned to Giraud and added: 'M. Giraud agrees with me, do you not, monsieur?'

Whatever Giraud's real belief, he accepted the position without moving a muscle. Calmly and almost scornfully he replied:

'Certainly I agree.'

The murmur of surprise and interest broke out again.

'But what an idea!' cried M. Hautet. 'To stab a man after he is dead! Barbaric! Unheard of! Some unappeasable hate perhaps.'

'No,' said Poirot. 'I should fancy it was done quite cold-bloodedly – to create an impression.'

'What impression?'

'The impression it nearly did create,' returned Poirot oracularly.

M. Bex had been thinking.

'How, then, was the man killed?'

'He was not killed. He died. He died, if I am not much mistaken, of an epileptic fit!'

This statement of Poirot's again aroused considerable excitement. Dr Durand knelt down again, and made a searching examination. At last he rose to his feet.

'Monsieur Poirot, I am inclined to believe that you are correct in your assertion. I was misled to begin with. The incontrovertible fact that the man had been stabbed distracted my attention from any other indications.'

Poirot was the hero of the hour. The examining magistrate was profuse in compliments. Poirot responded gracefully, and then excused himself on the pretext that neither he nor I had yet lunched, and that he wished to repair the ravages of the journey. As we were about to leave the shed, Giraud approached us.

'One other thing, Monsieur Poirot,' he said, in his suave mocking voice. 'We found this coiled round the handle of the dagger – a woman's hair.'

'Ah!' said Poirot. 'A woman's hair? What woman's, I wonder?'

'I wonder also,' said Giraud. Then, with a bow, he left us.

'He was insistent, the good Giraud,' said Poirot thoughtfully, as we walked towards the hotel. 'I wonder in what direction he hopes to mislead me? A woman's hair – h'm!'

We lunched heartily, but I found Poirot somewhat distrait and inattentive. Afterwards we went up to our sitting-room, and there I begged him to tell me something of his mysterious journey to Paris.

'Willingly, my friend. I went to Paris to find *this*.'

He took from his pocket a small faded newspaper cutting. It was the reproduction of a woman's photograph. He handed it to me. I uttered an exclamation.

'You recognize it, my friend?'

I nodded. Although the photo obviously dated from very many years back, and the hair was dressed in a different style, the likeness was unmistakable.

'Madame Daubreuil!' I exclaimed.

Poirot shook his head with a smile.

'Not quite correct, my friend. She did not call herself by that name in those days. That is a picture of the notorious Madame Beroldy!'

Madame Beroldy! In a flash the whole thing came back to me. The murder trial that had evoked such world-wide interest.

The Beroldy Case.

CHAPTER 16

THE BEROLDY CASE

Some twenty years or so before the opening of the present story, Monsieur Arnold Beroldy, a native of Lyons, arrived in Paris accompanied by his pretty wife and their little daughter, a mere babe. Monsieur Beroldy was a junior partner in a firm of wine merchants, a stout middle-aged man, fond of the good things of life, devoted to his charming wife, and altogether unremarkable in every way. The firm in which Monsieur Beroldy was a partner was a small one and, although doing well, it did not yield a large income to the junior partner. The Beroldys had a small apartment and lived in a very modest fashion to begin with.

But, unremarkable though Monsieur Beroldy might be, his wife was plentifully gilded with the brush of Romance. Young and good-looking, and gifted withal with a singular charm of manner, Madame Beroldy at once created a stir in the quarter, especially when it began to be whispered that some interesting mystery surrounded her birth. It was rumoured that she was the illegitimate daughter of a Russian Grand Duke. Others asserted that it was an Austrian Arch-duke, and that the union was legal, though morganatic. But all stories agreed upon one point, that Jeanne Beroldy was the centre of an interesting mystery.

Among the friends and acquaintances of the Beroldys was a young lawyer, Georges Conneau. It was soon evident that the fascinating Jeanne had completely enslaved his heart. Madame Beroldy encouraged the young man in a discreet fashion, but always being careful to affirm her complete devotion to her middle-aged husband. Nevertheless, many spiteful persons did not hesitate to declare that young Conneau was her lover – and not the only one!

When the Beroldys had been in Paris about three months, another personage came upon the scene. This was Mr Hiram P. Trapp, a native of the United States, and extremely wealthy. Introduced to the charming and mysterious Madame Beroldy, he fell a prompt victim to her fascinations. His admiration was obvious, though strictly respectful.

About this time, Madame Beroldy became more outspoken in her confidences. To several friends, she declared herself greatly worried on her husband's behalf. She explained that he had been drawn into several schemes of a political nature, and also referred to some important papers that had been entrusted to him for safe-keeping and which concerned a 'secret' of far-reaching European importance. They had been entrusted to his custody to throw pursuers off the track, but Madame Beroldy was nervous, having recognized several important members of the Revolutionary Circle in Paris.

On the 28th day of November the blow fell. The woman who came daily to clean and cook for the Beroldys was surprised to find the door of the apartment standing wide open. Hearing faint moans issuing from the bedroom, she went in. A terrible sight met her eyes. Madame Beroldy lay on the floor bound hand and foot, uttering feeble moans, having managed to free her mouth from a gag. On the bed was Monsieur Beroldy, lying in a pool of blood, with a knife driven through his heart.

Madame Beroldy's story was clear enough. Suddenly awakened from sleep, she had discerned two masked men bending over her. Stifling her cries, they had bound and gagged her. They had then demanded of Monsieur Beroldy the famous 'secret'.

But the intrepid wine merchant refused point-blank to accede to their request. Angered by his refusal, one of the men incontinently stabbed him through the heart. With the dead man's keys, they had opened the safe in the corner, and had carried away with them a mass of papers. Both men were heavily bearded, and had worn masks, but Madame Beroldy declared positively that they were Russians.

The affair created an immense sensation. Time went on, and the mysterious bearded men were never traced. And then, just as public interest was beginning to die down, a startling development occurred: Madame Beroldy was arrested and charged with the murder of her husband.

The trial, when it came on, aroused widespread interest. The youth and beauty of the accused, and her mysterious history, were sufficient to make of it a *cause célèbre*.

It was proved beyond doubt that Jeanne Beroldy's parents were a highly respectable and prosaic couple, fruit merchants, who lived on the outskirts of Lyons. The Russian Grand Duke, the court intrigues, and the political schemes – all the stories current were traced back to the lady herself! Remorselessly, the whole story of her life was laid bare. The motive for the murder was found in Mr Hiram P. Trapp. Mr Trapp did his best, but, relentlessly and agilely cross-questioned, he was forced to admit that he loved the lady, and that, had she been free, he would have asked her to be his wife. The fact that the relations between them were admittedly platonic strengthened the case against the accused. Debarred from becoming his mistress by the simple honourable nature of the man, Jeanne Beroldy had conceived the monstrous project of ridding herself of her elderly, undistinguished husband and becoming the wife of the rich American.

Throughout, Madame Beroldy confronted her accusers with complete sang-froid and self-possession. Her story never varied. She continued to declare strenuously that she was of royal birth and that she had been substituted for the daughter of the fruit-seller at an early age. Absurd and completely unsubstantiated as these statements were, a great number of people believed implicitly in their truth.

But the prosecution was implacable. It denounced the masked 'Russians' as a myth, and asserted that the crime had been committed by Madame Beroldy and her lover, Georges Conneau. A warrant was issued for the arrest of the latter, but he had wisely disappeared. Evidence showed that the bonds which secured Madame Beroldy were so loose that she could easily have freed herself.

And then, towards the close of the trial, a letter, posted in Paris, was sent to the Public Prosecutor. It was from Georges Conneau and, without revealing his whereabouts, it contained a full confession of the crime. He declared that he had indeed struck the fatal blow at Madame Beroldy's instigation. The crime had been planned between them. Believing that her husband ill-treated her, and maddened by his own passion for her, a passion which he believed her to return, he had planned the crime and struck the fatal blow that should free the woman he loved from a hateful bondage. Now, for the first time, he learnt of Mr Hiram P. Trapp, and realized that the woman he loved had betrayed him! Not for his sake did she wish to be free, but in order to marry the wealthy American. She had used him as a cat's paw, and now, in his jealous rage, he turned and denounced her, declaring that throughout he had acted at her instigation.

And then Madame Beroldy proved herself the remarkable woman she undoubtedly was. Without hesitation, she dropped her previous defence, and admitted that the 'Russians' were a pure invention on her part. The real murderer was Georges Conneau. Maddened by passion, he had committed the crime, vowing that if she did not keep silence he would exact a terrible vengeance from her. Terrified by his threats, she had consented – also fearing it likely that if she told the truth she might be accused of conniving at the crime. But she had steadfastly refused to have anything more to do with her husband's murderer, and it was in revenge for this attitude on her part that he had written this letter accusing her. She swore solemnly that she had had nothing to do with the planning of the crime, that she had awoke on that memorable night to find Georges Conneau standing over her, the blood-stained knife in his hand.

It was a touch-and-go affair. Madame Beroldy's story was hardly credible. But her address to the jury was a masterpiece. The tears streaming down her face, she spoke of her child, of her woman's honour – of her desire to keep her reputation untarnished for the child's sake. She admitted that, Georges Conneau having been her lover, she might perhaps be held morally responsible for the crime – but, before God, nothing more! She knew that she had committed a grave fault in not denouncing Conneau to the law, but she declared in a broken voice that that was a thing no woman could have done. She had loved him! Could she let her hand be the one to send him to the guillotine? She had been guilty of much, but she was innocent of the terrible crime imputed to her.

However that may have been, her eloquence and personality won the day. Madame Beroldy, amidst a scene of unparalleled excitement, was acquitted.

Despite the utmost endeavours of the police, Georges Conneau was never traced. As for Madame Beroldy, nothing more was heard of her. Taking the child with her, she left Paris to begin a new life.

CHAPTER 17

WE MAKE FURTHER INVESTIGATIONS

I have set down the Beroldy case in full. Of course all the details did not present themselves to my memory as I have recounted them here. Nevertheless, I recalled the case fairly accurately. It had attracted a great deal of interest at the time, and had been fully reported by the English papers, so that it did not need much effort of memory on my part to recollect the salient details.

Just for the moment, in my excitement, it seemed to clear up the whole matter. I admit that I am impulsive, and Poirot deplores my custom of jumping to conclusions, but I think I had some excuse in this instance. The remarkable way in which this discovery justified Poirot's point of view struck me at once.

'Poirot,' I said, 'I congratulate you. I see everything now.'

Poirot lit one of his little cigarettes with his usual precision. Then he looked up.

'And since you see everything now, *mon ami*, what exactly is it that you see?'

'Why, that it was Madame Daubreuil – Beroldy – who murdered Mr Renauld. The similarity of the two cases proves that beyond a doubt.'

'Then you consider that Madame Beroldy was wrongly acquitted? That in actual fact she was guilty of connivance in her husband's murder?'

I opened my eyes wide.

'Of course! Don't you?'

Poirot walked to the end of the room, absent-mindedly straightened a chair, and then said thoughtfully:

'Yes, that is my opinion. But there is no "of course" about it, my friend. Technically speaking, Madame Beroldy is innocent.'

'Of that crime, perhaps. But not of this.'

Poirot sat down again, and regarded me, his thoughtful air more marked than ever.

'So it is definitely your opinion, Hastings, that Madame Daubreuil murdered Monsieur Renauld?'

'Yes.'

'Why?'

He shot the question at me with such suddenness that I was taken aback.

'Why?' I stammered. 'Why? Oh, because –' I came to a stop.

Poirot nodded his head at me.

'You see, you come to a stumbling-block at once. Why should Madame Daubreuil (I shall call her that for clearness' sake) murder Monsieur Renauld? We can find no shadow of a motive. She does not benefit by his death; considered as either mistress or blackmailer she stands to lose. You cannot have a murder without motive. The first crime was different – there we had a rich lover waiting to step into her husband's shoes.'

'Money is not the only motive for murder,' I objected.

'True,' agreed Poirot placidly. 'There are two others, the *crime passionnel* is one. And there is the third rare motive, murder for an idea, which implies some form of mental derangement on the part of the murderer. Homicidal mania and religious fanaticism belong to that class. We can rule it out here.'

'But what about the *crime passionnel*? Can you rule that out? If Madame Daubreuil was Renauld's mistress, if she found that his affection was cooling, or if her jealousy was aroused in any way, might she not have struck him down in a moment of anger?'

Poirot shook his head.

'If – I say *if*, you note – Madame Daubreuil was Renauld's

mistress, he had not had time to tire of her. And in any case you mistake her character. She is a woman who can simulate great emotional stress. She is a magnificent actress. But, looked at dispassionately, her life disproves her appearance. Throughout, if we examine it, she has been cold-blooded and calculating in her motives and actions. It was not to link her life with that of her young lover that she connived at her husband's murder. The rich American, for whom she probably did not care a button, was her objective. If she committed a crime, she would always do so for gain. Here there was no gain. Besides, how do you account for the digging of the grave? That was a man's work.'

'She might have had an accomplice,' I suggested, unwilling to relinquish my belief.

'I pass to another objection. You have spoken of the similarity between the two crimes. Wherein does that lie, my friend?'

I stared at him in astonishment.

'Why, Poirot, it was you who remarked on that! The story of the masked men, the "secret", the papers!'

Poirot smiled a little.

'Do not be so indignant, I beg of you. I repudiate nothing. The similarity of the two stories links the two cases together inevitably. But reflect now on something very curious. It is not Madame Daubreuil who tells us this tale – if it were, all would indeed be plain sailing – it is Madame Renauld. Is she then in league with the other?'

'I can't believe that,' I said slowly. 'If she is, she must be the most consummate actress the world has ever known.'

'Ta-ta-ta!' said Poirot impatiently. 'Again you have the sentiment and not the logic! If it is necessary for a criminal to be a consummate actress, then by all means assume her to be one. But is it necessary? I do not believe Mrs Renauld to be in league with Madame Daubreuil for several reasons, some of which I have already enumerated to you. The others are self-evident. Therefore, that possibility eliminated, we draw very near to the truth, which is, as always, very curious and interesting.'

'Poirot,' I cried, 'what more do you know?'

'*Mon ami*, you must make your own deductions. You have "access to the facts". Concentrate your grey cells. Reason – not like Giraud – but like Hercule Poirot!'

'But are you *sure*?'

'My friend, in many ways I have been an imbecile. But at last I see clearly.'

'You know everything?'

'I have discovered what Monsieur Renauld sent for me to discover.'

'And you know the murderer?'

'I know one murderer.'

'What do you mean?'

'We talk a little at cross-purposes. There are here not one crime, but two. The first I have solved, the second – *eh bien*, I will confess, I am not sure!'

'But, Poirot, I thought you said the man in the shed had died a natural death?'

'Ta-ta-ta!' Poirot made his favourite ejaculation of impatience. 'Still you do not understand. One may have a crime without a murderer, but for two crimes it is essential to have two bodies.'

His remark struck me as so peculiarly lacking in lucidity that I looked at him in some anxiety. But he appeared perfectly normal. Suddenly he rose and strolled to the window.

'Here he is,' he observed.

'Who?'

'Monsieur Jack Renauld. I sent a note up to the Villa to ask him to come here.'

That changed the course of my ideas, and I asked Poirot if he knew that Jack Renauld had been in Merlinville on the night of the crime. I had hoped to catch my astute little friend napping, but as usual he was omniscient. He, too, had inquired at the station.

'And without doubt we are not original in the idea, Hastings. The excellent Giraud, he also has probably made his inquiries.'

'You don't think –' I said, and then stopped. 'Ah, no, it would be too horrible!'

Poirot looked inquiringly at me, but I said no more. It had just occurred to me that though there were seven women, directly and indirectly connected with the case – Mrs Renauld, Madame Daubreuil and her daughter, the mysterious visitor, and the three servants – there was, with the exception of old Auguste, who could hardly count, only one man – Jack Renauld. *And a man must have dug the grave.*

I had no time to develop farther the appalling idea that had occurred to me, for Jack Renauld was ushered into the room.

Poirot greeted him in business-like manner.

'Take a seat, monsieur. I regret infinitely to derange you, but you will perhaps understand that the atmosphere of the villa is not too congenial to me. Monsieur Giraud and I do not see eye to eye about everything. His politeness to me has not been striking, and you will comprehend that I do not intend any little discoveries I may make to benefit him in any way.'

'Exactly, Monsieur Poirot,' said the lad. 'That fellow Giraud is an ill-conditioned brute, and I'd be delighted to see someone score at his expense.'

'Then I may ask a little favour of you?'

'Certainly.'

'I will ask you to go to the railway station and take a train to the next station along the line, Abbalac. Ask at the cloakroom whether two foreigners deposited a valise there on the night of the murder. It is a small station, and they are almost certain to remember. Will you do this?'

'Of course I will,' said the boy, mystified, though ready for the task.

'I and my friend, you comprehend, have business elsewhere,' explained Poirot. 'There is a train in a quarter of an hour, and I will ask you not to return to the villa, as I have no wish for Giraud to get an inkling of your errand.'

'Very well, I will go straight to the station.'

He rose to his feet. Poirot's voice stopped him:

'One moment, Monsieur Renauld, there is one little matter that puzzles me. Why did you not mention to Monsieur Hautet this morning that you were in Merlinville on the night of the crime?'

Jack Renauld's face went crimson. With an effort he controlled himself.

'You have made a mistake. I was in Cherbourg as I told the examining magistrate this morning.'

Poirot looked at him, his eyes narrowed, cat-like, until they only showed a gleam of green.

'Then it is a singular mistake that I have made there – for it is shared by the station staff. They say you arrived by the 11.40 train.'

For a moment Jack Renauld hesitated, then he made up his mind.

'And if I did? I suppose you do not mean to accuse me of

participating in my father's murder?' He asked the question haughtily, his head thrown back.

'I should like an explanation of the reason that brought you here.'

'That is simple enough. I came to see my fiancée, Mademoiselle Daubreuil. I was on the eve of a long voyage, uncertain as to when I should return. I wished to see her before I went, to assure her of my unchanging devotion.'

'And did you see her?' Poirot's eyes never left the other's face.

There was an appreciable pause before Renauld replied. Then he said:

'Yes.'

'And afterwards?'

'I found I had missed the last train. I walked to St Beauvais, where I knocked up a garage and got a car to take me back to Cherbourg.'

'St Beauvais? That is fifteen kilometres. A long walk, M. Renauld.'

'I – I felt like walking.'

Poirot bowed his head as a sign that he accepted the explanation. Jack Renauld took up his hat and cane and departed. In a trice Poirot jumped to his feet.

'Quick, Hastings. We will go after him.'

Keeping a discreet distance behind our quarry, we followed him through the streets of Merlinville. But when Poirot saw that he took the turning to the station he checked himself.

'All is well. He has taken the bait. He will go to Abbalac, and will inquire for the mythical valise left by the mythical foreigners. Yes, *mon ami*, all that was a little invention of my own.'

'You wanted him out of the way!' I exclaimed.

'Your penetration is amazing, Hastings! Now, if you please, we will go up to the Villa Geneviève.'

CHAPTER 18

GIRAUD ACTS

Arrived at the villa, Poirot led the way up to the shed where the second body had been discovered. He did not, however, go in, but paused by the bench which I have mentioned before as being set some few yards away from it. After contemplating it for a moment or two, he paced carefully from it to the hedge which marked the boundary between the Villa Geneviève and the Villa Marguerite. Then he paced back again, nodding his head as he did so. Returning again to the hedge, he parted the bushes with his hands.

'With good fortune,' he remarked to me over his shoulder, 'Mademoiselle Marthe may find herself in the garden. I desire to speak to her and would prefer not to call formally at the Villa Marguerite. Ah, all is well, there she is. Pst, Mademoiselle! Pst! *Un moment, s'il vous plaît.*'

I joined him at the moment that Marthe Daubreuil, looking slightly startled, came running up to the hedge at his call.

'A little word with you, mademoiselle, if it is permitted?'

'Certainly, Monsieur Poirot.'

Despite her acquiescence, her eyes looked troubled and afraid.

'Mademoiselle, do you remember running after me on the road the day that I came to your house with the examining magistrate? You asked me if anyone were suspected of the crime.'

'And you told me two Chileans.' Her voice sounded rather breathless, and her left hand stole to her breast.

'Will you ask me the same question again, mademoiselle?'

'What do you mean?'

'This. If you were to ask me that question again, I should give you a different answer. Someone is suspected – but not a Chilean.'

'Who?' The word came faintly between her parted lips.

'Monsieur Jack Renauld.'

'What?' It was a cry. 'Jack? Impossible. Who dares to suspect him?'

'Giraud.'

'Giraud!' The girl's face was ashy. 'I am afraid of that man. He is cruel. He will – he will –' She broke off. There was courage gathering in her face, and determination. I realized in that moment that she was a fighter. Poirot, too, watched her intently.

'You know, of course, that he was here on the night of the murder?' he asked.

'Yes,' she replied mechanically. 'He told me.'

'It was unwise to have tried to conceal the fact,' ventured Poirot.

'Yes, yes,' she replied impatiently. 'But we cannot waste time on regrets. We must find something to save him. He is innocent, of course; but that will not help him with a man like Giraud, who has his reputation to think of. He must arrest someone, and that someone will be Jack.'

'The facts will tell against him,' said Poirot. 'You realize that?'

She faced him squarely.

'I am not a child, monsieur. I can be brave and look facts in the face. He is innocent, and we must save him.'

She spoke with a kind of desperate energy, then was silent, frowning as she thought.

'Mademoiselle,' said Poirot, observing her keenly, 'is there not something that you are keeping back that you could tell us?'

She nodded perplexedly.

'Yes, there is something, but I hardly know whether you will believe it – it seems so absurd.'

'At any rate, tell us, mademoiselle.'

'It is this. M. Giraud sent for me, as an afterthought, to see if I could identify the man in there.' She signed with her head towards the shed. 'I could not. At least I could not at the moment. But since I have been thinking –'

'Well?'

'It seems so queer, and yet I am almost sure. I will tell you. On the morning of the day Monsieur Renauld was murdered, I was walking in the garden here, when I heard a sound of men's voices quarrelling. I pushed aside the bushes and looked through. One of the men was Monsieur Renauld and the other was a tramp, a dreadful-looking creature in filthy rags. He was alternately whining and threatening. I gathered he was asking for money, but at that moment *maman* called me from the house, and I had to go. That is all, only – I am almost sure that the tramp and the dead man in the shed are one and the same.'

Poirot uttered an exclamation.

'But why did you not say at the time, mademoiselle?'

'Because at first it only struck me that the face was vaguely familiar in some way. The man was differently dressed, and apparently belonged to a superior station in life.'

A voice called from the house.

'*Maman*,' whispered Marthe: 'I must go.' And she slipped away through the trees.

'Come,' said Poirot and, taking my arm, turned in the direction of the villa.

'What do you really think?' I asked in some curiosity. 'Was that story true, or did the girl make it up in order to divert suspicion from her lover?'

'It is a curious tale,' said Poirot, 'but I believe it to be the absolute truth. Unwittingly, Mademoiselle Marthe told us the truth on another point – and incidentally gave Jack Renauld the lie. Did you notice his hesitation when I asked him if he saw Marthe Daubreuil on the night of the crime? He paused and then said "Yes". I suspected that he was lying. It was necessary for me to see Mademoiselle Marthe before he could put her on her guard. Three little words gave me the information I wanted. When I asked her if she knew that Jack Renauld was here that night, she answered, "He *told* me". Now, Hastings, what was Jack Renauld doing here on that eventful evening, and if he did not see Mademoiselle Marthe whom did he see?'

'Surely, Poirot,' I cried, aghast, 'you cannot believe that a boy like that would murder his own father!'

'*Mon ami*,' said Poirot. 'You continue to be of a sentimentality unbelievable! I have seen mothers who murdered their little children for the sake of the insurance money! After that, one can believe anything.'

'And the motive?'

'Money of course. Remember that Jack Renauld thought that he would come into half his father's fortune at the latter's death.'

'But the tramp. Where does he come in?'

Poirot shrugged his shoulders.

'Giraud would say that he was an accomplice – an apache who helped young Renauld to commit the crime, and who was conveniently put out of the way afterwards.'

'But the hair round the dagger? The woman's hair?'

'Ah!' said Poirot, smiling broadly. 'That is the cream of Giraud's little jest. According to him, it is not a woman's hair at all. Remember that the youths of today wear their hair brushed straight back from the forehead with pomade or hair wash to make it lie flat. Consequently some of the hairs are of considerable length.'

'And you believe that too?'

'No,' said Poirot, with a curious smile. 'For I know it to be the hair of a woman – and more, which woman!'

'Madame Daubreuil,' I announced positively.

'Perhaps,' said Poirot, regarding me quizzically. But I refused to allow myself to get annoyed.

'What are we going to do now?' I asked, as we entered the hall of the Villa Geneviève.

'I wish to make a search among the effects of M. Jack Renauld. That is why I had to get him out of the way for a few hours.'

Neatly and methodically, Poirot opened each drawer in turn, examined the contents, and returned them exactly to their places. It was a singularly dull and uninteresting proceeding. Poirot waded on through collars, pyjamas, and socks. A purring noise outside drew me to the window. Instantly I became galvanized into life.

'Poirot!' I cried. 'A car has just driven up. Giraud is in it, and Jack Renauld, and two gendarmes.'

'*Sacré tonnerre!*' growled Poirot. 'That animal of a Giraud, could he not wait? I shall not be able to replace the things in this last drawer with the proper method. Let us be quick.'

Unceremoniously he tumbled out the things on the floor, mostly ties and handkerchiefs. Suddenly with a cry of triumph Poirot pounced on something, a small square of cardboard, evidently a photograph. Thrusting it into his pocket, he returned the things pell-mell to the drawer, and seizing me by the arm dragged me out of the room and down the stairs. In the hall stood Giraud, contemplating his prisoner.

'Good afternoon, Monsieur Giraud,' said Poirot. 'What have we here?'

Giraud nodded his head towards Jack.

'He was trying to make a getaway, but I was too sharp for him. He's under arrest for the murder of his father, Monsieur Paul Renauld.'

Poirot wheeled round to confront the boy, who was leaning limply against the door, his face ashy pale.

'What do you say to that, *jeune homme*?'

Jack Renauld stared at him stonily.

'Nothing,' he said.

CHAPTER 19

I USE MY GREY CELLS

I was dumbfounded. Up to the last, I had not been able to bring myself to believe Jack Renauld guilty. I had expected a ringing proclamation of his innocence when Poirot challenged him. But now, watching him as he stood, white and limp against the wall, and hearing the damning admission fall from his lips, I doubted no longer.

But Poirot had turned to Giraud.

'What are your grounds for arresting him?'

'Do you expect me to give them to you?'

'As a matter of courtesy, yes.'

Giraud looked at him doubtfully. He was torn between a desire to refuse rudely and the pleasure of triumphing over his adversary.

'You think I have made a mistake, I suppose?' he sneered.

'It would not surprise me,' replied Poirot, with a soupçon of malice.

Giraud's face took on a deeper tinge of red.

'*Eh bien*, come in here. You shall judge for yourself.'

He flung open the door of the salon, and we passed in, leaving Jack Renauld in the care of the two other men.

'Now, Monsieur Poirot,' said Giraud, laying his hat on the table, and speaking with the utmost sarcasm, 'I will treat you to a little lecture on detective work. I will show how we moderns work.'

'*Bien!*' said Poirot, composing himself to listen. 'I will show you how admirably the Old Guard can listen.' And he leaned back and closed his eyes, opening them for a moment to remark: 'Do not fear that I shall sleep. I will attend most carefully.'

'Of course,' began Giraud, 'I soon saw through all that Chilean tomfoolery. Two men were in it – but they were not mysterious foreigners! All that was a blind.'

'Very creditable so far, my dear Giraud,' murmured Poirot. 'Especially after that clever trick of theirs with the match and cigarette end.'

Giraud glared, but continued.

'A man must have been connected with the case, in order to dig the grave. There is no man who actually benefits by the crime, but there was a man who *thought* he would benefit. I heard of Jack Renauld's quarrel with his father, and of the threats that he had used. The motive was established. Now as to means. Jack Renauld was in Merlinville that night. He concealed the fact – which turned suspicion into certainty. Then we found a second victim – *stabbed with the same dagger*. We know when that dagger was stolen. Captain Hastings here can fix the time. Jack Renauld, arriving from Cherbourg, was the only person who could have taken it. I have accounted for all the other members of the household.'

Poirot interrupted.

'You are wrong. There is one other person who could have taken the dagger.'

'You refer to Monsieur Stonor? He arrived at the front door, in an automobile which had brought him straight from Calais. Ah! believe me, I have looked into everything. Monsieur Jack Renauld arrived by train. An hour elapsed between his arrival and the moment when he presented himself at the house. Without doubt, he saw Captain Hastings and his companion leave the shed, slipped in himself and took the dagger, stabbed his accomplice in the shed –'

'Who was already dead!'

Giraud shrugged his shoulders.

'Possibly he did not observe that. He may have judged him to be sleeping. Without doubt they had a rendezvous. In any case he knew this apparent second murder would greatly complicate the case. It did.'

'But it could not deceive Monsieur Giraud,' murmured Poirot.

'You mock at me! But I will give you one last irrefutable proof. Madame Renauld's story was false – a fabrication from beginning to end. We believe Madame Renauld to have loved her husband – *yet she lied to shield his murderer*. For whom will a woman lie? Sometimes for herself, usually for the man she loves, *always* for her children. That is the last – the irrefutable proof. You cannot get round it.'

Giraud paused, flushed and triumphant. Poirot regarded him steadily.

'That is my case,' said Giraud. 'What have you to say to it?'

'Only that there is one thing you have failed to take into account.'

'What is that?'

'Jack Renauld was presumably acquainted with the planning out of the golf course. He knew that the body would be discovered almost at once, when they started to dig the bunker.'

Giraud laughed out loud.

'But it is idiotic what you say there! He wanted the body to be found! Until it was found, he could not presume death, and would have been unable to enter into his inheritance.'

I saw a quick flash of green in Poirot's eyes as he rose to his feet.

'Then why bury it?' he asked very softly. 'Reflect, Giraud. Since it was to Jack Renauld's advantage that the body should be found without delay, *why dig a grave at all?*'

Giraud did not reply. The question found him unprepared. He shrugged his shoulders as though to intimate that it was of no importance.

Poirot moved towards the door. I followed him.

'There is one more thing that you have failed to take into account,' he said over his shoulder.

'What is that?'

'The piece of lead piping,' said Poirot, and left the room.

Jack Renauld still stood in the hall, with a white dumb face, but as we came out of the salon he looked up sharply. At the same moment there was the sound of a footfall on the staircase. Mrs Renauld was descending it. At the sight of her son, standing between the two myrmidons of the law, she stopped as though petrified.

'Jack,' she faltered. 'Jack, what is this?'

He looked up at her, his face set.

'They have arrested me, mother.'

'What?'

She uttered a piercing cry, and before anyone could get to her, swayed, and fell heavily. We both ran to her and lifted her up. In a minute Poirot stood up again.

'She has cut her head badly, on the corner of the stairs. I fancy there is slight concussion also. If Giraud wants a statement from her, he will have to wait. She will probably be unconscious for at least a week.'

Denise and Françoise had run to their mistress, and leaving her in their charge Poirot left the house. He walked with his head down, frowning thoughtfully. For some time I did not speak, but at last I ventured to put a question to him:

'Do you believe then, in spite of all appearances to the contrary, that Jack Renauld may not be guilty?'

Poirot did not answer at once, but after a long wait he said gravely:

'I do not know, Hastings. There is just a chance of it. Of course Giraud is all wrong – wrong from beginning to end. If Jack Renauld is guilty, it is in spite of Giraud's arguments, not *because* of them. And the gravest indictment against him is known only to me.'

'What is that?' I asked, impressed.

'If you would use your grey cells, and see the whole case clearly as I do, you too would perceive it, my friend.'

This was what I called one of Poirot's irritating answers. He went on, without waiting for me to speak:

'Let us walk this way to the sea. We will sit on that little mound there, overlooking the beach, and review the case. You shall know all that I know, but I would prefer that you should come at the truth by your own efforts – not by my leading you by thc hand.'

We established ourselves on the grassy knoll as Poirot had suggested, looking out to sea.

'Think, my friend,' said Poirot's voice encouragingly. 'Arrange your ideas. Be methodical. Be orderly. There is the secret of success.'

I endeavoured to obey him, casting my mind back over all the details of the case. And suddenly I started as an idea of bewildering luminosity shot into my brain. Tremblingly I built up my hypothesis.

'You have a little idea, I see, *mon ami!* Capital. We progress.'

I sat up, and lit a pipe.

'Poirot,' I said, 'it seems to me we have been strangely remiss. I say *we* – although I dare say *I* would be nearer the mark. But you must pay the penalty of your determined secrecy. So I say again we have been strangely remiss. There is someone we have forgotten.'

'And who is that?' inquired Poirot, with twinkling eyes.

'Georges Conneau!'

CHAPTER 20

AN AMAZING STATEMENT

The next moment Poirot embraced me warmly on the cheek.

'*Enfin!* You have arrived! And all by yourself. It is superb! Continue your reasoning. You are right. Decidedly we have done wrong to forget Georges Conneau.'

I was so flattered by the little man's approval that I could hardly continue. But at last I collected my thoughts and went on.

'Georges Conneau disappeared twenty years ago, but we have no reason to believe that he is dead.'

'*Aucunement*,' agreed Poirot. 'Proceed.'

'Therefore we will assume that he is alive.'

'Exactly.'

'Or that he was alive until recently.'

'*De mieux en mieux!*'

'We will presume,' I continued, my enthusiasm rising, 'that he has fallen on evil days. He has become a criminal, an apache, a tramp – a what you will. He chances to come to Merlinville. There he finds the woman he has never ceased to love.'

'Eh eh! The sentimentality,' warned Poirot.

'Where one hates one also loves,' I quoted or misquoted. 'At any rate he finds her there, living under an assumed name. But she has a new lover, the Englishman, Renauld. Georges Conneau, the memory of old wrongs rising in him, quarrels with this Renauld. He lies in wait for him as he comes to visit his mistress, and stabs him in the back. Then, terrified at what he has done, he starts to dig a grave. I imagine it likely that Madame Daubreuil comes out to look for her lover. She and Conneau have a terrible scene. He drags her into the shed, and there suddenly falls down in an epileptic fit. Now supposing Jack Renauld to appear. Madame Daubreuil tells him all, points out to him the dreadful consequences to her daughter if this scandal of the past is revived. His father's murderer is dead – let them do their best to hush it up. Jack Renauld consents – goes to the house and has an interview with his mother, winning her over to his point of view.

Primed with the story that Madame Daubreuil has suggested to him, she permits herself to be gagged and bound. There, Poirot, what do you think of that?' I leaned back, flushed with the pride of successful reconstruction.

Poirot looked at me thoughtfully.

'I think that you should write for the Kinema, *mon ami*,' he remarked at last.

'You mean –'

'It would mean a good film, the story that you have recounted to me there – but it bears no sort of resemblance to everyday life.'

'I admit that I haven't gone into all the details, but –'

'You have gone farther – you have ignored them magnificently. What about the way the two men were dressed? Do you suggest that after stabbing his victim, Conneau removed his suit of clothes, donned it himself, and replaced the dagger?'

'I don't see that that matters,' I objected rather huffily. 'He may have obtained clothes and money from Madame Daubreuil by threats earlier in the day.'

'By threats – eh? You seriously advance that supposition?'

'Certainly. He could have threatened to reveal her identity to the Renaulds, which would probably have put an end to all hopes of her daughter's marriage.'

'You are wrong, Hastings. He could not blackmail her, for she had the whip-hand. Georges Conneau, remember, is still wanted for murder. A word from her and he is in danger of the guillotine.'

I was forced, rather reluctantly, to admit the truth of this.

'*Your* theory,' I remarked acidly, 'is doubtless correct as to all the details?'

'My theory is the truth,' said Poirot quietly. 'And the truth is necessarily correct. In your theory you made a fundamental error. You permitted your imagination to lead you astray with midnight assignations and passionate love scenes. But in investigating crime we must take our stand upon the commonplace. Shall I demonstrate my methods to you?'

'Oh, by all means let us have a demonstration!'

Poirot sat very upright and began, wagging his forefinger emphatically to emphasize his points:

'I will start as you started from the basic fact of Georges Conneau. Now the story told by Madame Beroldy in court as to the "Russians" was admittedly a fabrication. If she was innocent of connivance in the crime, it was concocted by her, and by her only as she stated. If, on the other hand, she was *not* innocent, it might have been invented by either her or Georges Conneau.

'Now, in this case we are investigating, we meet the same tale. As I pointed out to you, the facts render it very unlikely that Madame Daubreuil inspired it. So we turn to the hypothesis that the story had its origin in the brain of Georges Conneau. Very good. Georges Conneau, therefore, planned the crime, with Mrs Renauld as his accomplice. She is in the limelight, and behind her is a shadowy figure whose present *alias* is unknown to us.

'Now let us go carefully over the Renauld Case from the beginning, setting down each significant point in its chronological order. You have a notebook and pencil? Good. Now what is the earliest point to note down?'

'The letter to you?'

'That was the first we knew of it, but it is not the proper beginning of the case. The first point of any significance, I should say, is the change that came over Monsieur Renauld shortly after arriving in Merlinville, and which is attested to by several witnesses. We have also to consider his friendship with Madame Daubreuil, and the large sums of money paid over to her. From thence we can come directly to the 23rd May.'

Poirot paused, cleared his throat, and signed to me to write:

'*23rd May.* M. Renauld quarrels with his son over latter's wish to marry Marthe Daubreuil. Son leaves for Paris.

'*24th May.* M. Renauld alters his will, leaving entire control of his fortune in his wife's hands.

'*7th June.* Quarrel with tramp in garden, witnessed by Marthe Daubreuil.

'Letter written to M. Hercule Poirot, imploring assistance.

'Telegram sent to M. Jack Renauld, bidding him proceed by the *Anzora* to Buenos Aires.

'Chauffeur, Masters, sent off on a holiday.

'Visit of a lady that evening. As he is seeing her out, his words are "Yes, yes – but for God's sake go now . . ."'

Poirot paused.

'There, Hastings, take each of those facts one by one, consider them carefully by themselves and in relation to the whole, and see if you do not get new light on the matter.'

I endeavoured conscientiously to do as he had said. After a moment or two, I said rather doubtfully:

'As to the first points, the question seems to be whether we adopt the theory of blackmail, or of an infatuation for this woman.'

'Blackmail, decidedly. You heard what Stonor said as to his character and habits.'

'Mrs Renauld did not confirm his view,' I argued.

'We have already seen that Madame Renauld's testimony cannot be relied upon in any way. We must trust to Stonor on that point.'

'Still, if Renauld had an affair with a woman called Bella, there seems no inherent improbability in his having another with Madame Daubreuil.'

'None whatever, I grant you, Hastings. But did he?'

'The letter, Poirot. You forget the letter.'

'No, I do not forget. But what makes you think that letter was written to Monsieur Renauld?'

'Why, it was found in his pocket, and – and –'

'And that is all!' cut in Poirot. 'There was no mention of any name to show to whom the letter was addressed. We assumed it was to the dead man because it was in the pocket of his overcoat. Now, *mon ami*, something about that overcoat struck me as unusual. I measured it, and made the remark that he wore his overcoat very long. That remark should have given you to think.'

'I thought you were just saying it for the sake of saying something,' I confessed.

'Ah, *quelle idée!* Later you observed me measuring the overcoat of Monsieur Jack Renauld. *Eh bien*, Monsieur Jack Renauld wears his overcoat very short. Put those two facts together with a third, namely, that Monsieur Jack Renauld flung out of the house in a hurry on his departure for Paris, and tell me what you make of it!'

'I see,' I said slowly, as the meaning of Poirot's remarks bore in upon me. 'That letter was written to Jack Renauld – not to his father. He caught up the wrong overcoat in his haste and agitation.'

Poirot nodded.

'*Précisément!* We can return to this point later. For the moment let us content ourselves with accepting the letter as having nothing to do with Monsieur Renauld *père*, and pass to the next chronological event.'

'"*23rd May.*"' I read: '"M. Renauld quarrels with his son over latter's wish to marry Marthe Daubreuil. Son leaves for Paris." I don't see anything much to remark upon there, and the altering of the will the following day seems straightforward enough. It was the direct result of the quarrel.'

'We agree, *mon ami* – at least as to the cause. But what exact motive underlay this procedure of Monsieur Renauld's?'

I opened my eyes in surprise.

'Anger against his son of course.'

'Yet he wrote him affectionate letters to Paris?'

'So Jack Renauld says, but he cannot produce them.'

'Well, let us pass from that.'

'Now we come to the day of the tragedy. You have placed the events of the morning in a certain order. Have you any justification for that?'

'I have ascertained that the letter to me was posted at the same time as the telegram was dispatched. Masters was informed he could take a holiday shortly afterwards. In my opinion the quarrel with the tramp took place anterior to these happenings.'

'I do not see that you can fix that definitely unless you question Madame Daubreuil again.'

'There is no need. I am sure of it. And if you do not see that, you see nothing, Hastings!'

I looked at him for a moment.

'Of course! I am an idiot. If the tramp was Georges Conneau, it was after the stormy interview with him that Mr Renauld apprehended danger. He sent away the chauffeur, Masters, whom he suspected of being in the other's pay, he wired to his son, and sent for you.'

A faint smile crossed Poirot's lips.

'You do not think it strange that he should use exactly the same expressions in his letter as Madame Renauld used, later in her story? If the mention of Santiago was a blind, why should Renauld speak of it, and – what is more – send his son there?'

'It is puzzling, I admit, but perhaps we shall find some explanation later. We come now to the evening, and the visit of the mysterious lady. I confess that that fairly baffles me, unless it was indeed Madame Daubreuil, as Françoise all along maintained.'

Poirot shook his head.

'My friend, my friend, where are your wits wandering? Remember the fragment of cheque, and the fact that the name Bella Duveen was faintly familiar to Stonor, and I think we may take it for granted that Bella Duveen is the full name of Jack's unknown correspondent, and that it was she who came to the Villa Geneviève that night. Whether she intended to see Jack, or whether she meant all along to appeal to his father, we cannot be certain, but I think we may assume that this is what occurred. She produced her claim upon Jack, probably showed letters that he had written her, and the older man tried to buy her off by writing a cheque. This she indignantly tore up. The terms of her letter are those of a woman genuinely in love, and she would probably deeply resent being offered money. In the end he got rid of her, and here the words that he used are significant.'

'"Yes, yes, but for God's sake go now",' I repeated. 'They seem to me a little vehement, perhaps, that is all.'

'That is enough. He was desperately anxious for the girl to go. Why? Not because the interview was unpleasant. No, it was the time that was slipping by, and for some reason time was precious.'

'Why should it be?' I asked bewildered.

'That is what we ask ourselves. Why should it be? But later we have the incident of the wristwatch – which again shows us that time plays a very important part in the crime. We are now fast approaching the actual drama. It is half past ten when Bella Duveen leaves, and by the evidence of the wristwatch we know that the crime was committed, or at any rate that it was staged, before twelve o'clock. We have reviewed all the events anterior to the murder, there remains only one unplaced. By the doctor's evidence, the tramp, when found, had been dead at least forty-eight hours – with a possible margin of twenty-four hours more. Now, with no other facts to help me than those we have discussed, I place the death as having occurred on the morning of 7th June.'

I stared at him, stupefied.

'But how? Why? How can you possibly know?'

'Because only in that way can the sequence of events be logically explained. *Mon ami*, I have taken you step by step along the way. Do you not now see what is so glaringly plain?'

'My dear Poirot, I can't see anything glaring about it. I did think I was beginning to see my way before, but I'm now hopelessly fogged. For goodness' sake, get on, and tell me who killed Mr Renauld.'

'That is just what I am not sure of as yet.'

'But you said it was glaringly clear!'

'We talk at cross-purposes, my friend. Remember, it is *two* crimes we are investigating – for which, as I pointed out to you, we have the necessary two bodies. There, there, *ne vous impatientez pas!* I explain all. To begin with, we apply our psychology. We find three points at which Monsieur Renauld displays a distinct change of view and action – three psychological points therefore. The first occurs immediately after arriving in Merlinville, the second after quarrelling with his son on a certain subject, the third on the morning of 7th June. Now for the three causes. We can attribute No 1 to meeting Madame Daubreuil. No 2 is indirectly connected with her, since it concerns a marriage between Monsieur Renauld's son and her daughter. But the cause of No 3 is hidden from us. We had to deduce it. Now, *mon ami*, let me ask you a question: whom do we believe to have planned this crime?'

'Georges Conneau,' I said doubtfully, eyeing Poirot warily.

'Exactly. Now Giraud laid it down as an axiom that a woman lies to save herself, the man she loves, and her child. Since we are satisfied that it was Georges Conneau who dictated the lie to her, and as Georges Conneau is not Jack Renauld, it follows that the third case is put out of court. And, still attributing the crime to Georges Conneau, the first is equally so. So we are forced to the second – that Madame Renauld lied for the sake of the man she loved – or in other words, for the sake of Georges Conneau. You agree to that?'

'Yes,' I admitted. 'It seems logical enough.'

'*Bien!* Madame Renauld loves Georges Conneau. Who, then, is Georges Conneau?'

'The tramp.'

'Have we any evidence to show that Madame Renauld loved the tramp?'

'No, but –'

'Very well then. Do not cling to theories where facts no longer support them. Ask yourself instead whom Madame Renauld *did* love.'

I shook my head perplexed.

'*Mais oui*, you know perfectly. Whom did Madame Renauld love so dearly that when she saw his dead body she fell down in a swoon?'

I stared dumbfounded.

'Her husband?' I gasped.

Poirot nodded.

'Her husband – or Georges Conneau, whichever you like to call him.'

I rallied myself.

'But it's impossible.'

'How "impossible"? Did we not agree just now that Madame Daubreuil was in a position to blackmail Georges Conneau?'

'Yes, but –'

'And did she not very effectively blackmail Monsieur Renauld?'

'That may be true enough, but –'

'And is it not a fact that we know nothing of Monsieur Renauld's youth and upbringing? That he springs suddenly into existence as a French-Canadian exactly twenty-two years ago?'

'All that is so,' I said more firmly, 'but you seem to me to be overlooking one salient point.'

'What is that, my friend?'

'Why, we have admitted that Georges planned the crime. That brings us to the ridiculous statement *that he planned his own murder!*'

'*Eh bien, mon ami*,' said Poirot placidly, 'that is just what he did do!'

CHAPTER 21

HERCULE POIROT ON THE CASE

In a measured voice Poirot began his exposition.

'It seems strange to you, *mon ami*, that a man should plan his own death? So strange, that you prefer to reject the truth as fantastic, and to revert to a story that is in reality ten times more impossible. Yes, Monsieur Renauld planned his own death, but there is one detail that perhaps escapes you – he did not intend to die.'

I shook my head, bewildered.

'But no, it is all most simple really,' said Poirot kindly. 'For the crime that Monsieur Renauld proposed a murderer was not necessary, as I told you, but a body was. Let us reconstruct, seeing events this time from a different angle.

'Georges Conneau flies from justice – to Canada. There, under an assumed name, he marries, and finally acquires a vast fortune in South America. But there is a nostalgia upon him for his own country. Twenty years have elapsed, he is considerably changed in appearance, besides being a man of such eminence that no one is likely to connect him with a fugitive from justice many years ago. He deems it quite safe to return. He takes up his headquarters in England, but intends to spend the summers in France. And ill fortune, or that obscure justice which shapes men's ends and will not allow them to evade the consequences of their acts, takes him to Merlinville. There, in the whole of France, is the one person who is capable of recognizing him. It is, of course, a gold mine to Madame Daubreuil, and a gold mine of which she is not slow to take advantage. He is helpless, absolutely in her power. And she bleeds him heavily.

'And then the inevitable happens. Jack Renauld falls in love with the beautiful girl he sees almost daily, and wishes to marry her. That rouses his father. At all costs, he will prevent his son marrying the daughter of this evil woman. Jack Renauld knows nothing of his father's past, but Madame Renauld knows everything. She is a woman of great force of character and passionately devoted to her husband. They take counsel together. Renauld sees only one way of escape – death. He must appear to die, in reality escaping to another country where he will start again under an assumed name and where Madame Renauld, having played the widow's part for a while, can join him. It is essential that she should have control of the money, so he alters his will. How they meant to manage the body business originally, I do not know – possibly an art student's skeleton and a fire – or something of the kind, but long before their plans have matured an event occurs which plays into their hands. A rough tramp, violent and abusive, finds his way into the garden. There is a struggle, Renauld seeks to eject him, and suddenly the tramp, an epileptic, falls down in a fit. He is dead. Renauld calls his wife. Together they drag him into the shed – as we know the event had occurred just outside – and they realize the marvellous opportunity that has been vouchsafed them. The man bears no resemblance to Renauld but he is middle-aged, of a usual French type. That is sufficient.

'I rather fancy that they sat on the bench up there, out of earshot from the house, discussing matters. Their plan was quickly made. The identification must rest solely on Madame Renauld's evidence. Jack Renauld and the chauffeur (who had been with his master two years) must be got out of the way. It was unlikely that the French women servants would go near the body, and in any case Renauld intended to take measures to deceive anyone not likely to appreciate details. Masters was sent off, a telegram dispatched to Jack, Buenos Aires being selected to give credence to the story that Renauld had decided upon. Having heard of me as a rather obscure elderly detective, he wrote his appeal for help, knowing that when I arrived, the production of the letter would have a profound effect upon the examining magistrate – which, of course, it did.

'They dressed the body of the tramp in a suit of Renauld's and left his ragged coat and trousers by the door of the shed, not daring to take them into the house. And then, to give credence to the tale Madame Renauld was to tell, they drove the aeroplane dagger through his heart. That night Renauld will first bind and gag his wife, and then, taking a spade, will dig a grave in that particular plot of ground where he knows a – how do you call it? – bunkair? is to be made. It is essential that the body should be found – Madame Daubreuil must have no suspicions. On the other hand, if a little time elapses, any dangers as to identity will be greatly lessened. Then, Renauld will don the tramp's rags, and shuffle off to the station, where he will leave, unnoticed, by the 12.10 train. Since the crime will be supposed to have taken place two hours later, no suspicion can possibly attach to him.

'You see now his annoyance at the inopportune visit of the girl, Bella. Every moment of delay is fatal to his plans. He gets rid of her as soon as he can, however. Then, to work! He leaves the front door slightly ajar to create the impression that assassins left that way. He binds and gags Madame Renauld, correcting his mistake of twenty-two years ago, when the looseness of the bonds caused suspicion to fall upon his accomplice, but leaving her primed with essentially the same story as he had invented before, proving the unconscious recoil of the mind against originality. The night is chilly, and he slips on an overcoat over his under-clothing, intending to cast it into the grave with the dead man. He goes out by the window, smoothing over the flower-bed carefully, and thereby furnishing the most positive evidence against himself. He goes out on to the lonely golf links, and he digs – And then –'

'Yes?'

'And then,' said Poirot gravely, 'the justice that he has so long eluded overtakes him. An unknown hand stabs him in the back . . . Now, Hastings, you understand what I mean when I talk of *two* crimes. The first crime, the crime that Monsieur Renauld, in his arrogance, asked us to investigate, is solved. But behind it lies a deeper riddle. And to solve that will be difficult – since the criminal, in his wisdom, has been content to avail himself of the devices prepared by Renauld. It has been a particularly perplexing and baffling mystery to solve.'

'You're marvellous, Poirot,' I said, with admiration. 'Absolutely marvellous. No one on earth but you would have done it!'

I think my praise pleased him. For once in his life he looked almost embarrassed.

'That poor Giraud,' said Poirot, trying unsuccessfully to look modest. 'Without doubt it is not all stupidity. He has had *la mauvaise chance* once or twice. That dark hair coiled round the dagger, for instance. To say the least, it was misleading.'

'To tell you the truth, Poirot,' I said slowly, 'even now I don't quite see – whose hair was it?'

'Madame Renauld's, of course. That is where *la mauvaise chance* came in. Her hair, dark originally, is almost completely silvered. It might just as easily have been a grey hair – and then, by no conceivable effort could Giraud have persuaded himself it came from the head of Jack Renauld! But it is all of a piece. Always the facts must be twisted to fit the theory!

'Without doubt, when Madame Renauld recovers, she will speak. The possibility of her son being accused of the murder never occurred to her. How should it, when she believed him safely at sea on board the *Anzora? Ah! voilà une femme*, Hastings! What force, what self-command! She only made one slip. On his unexpected return: "It does not matter – *now*." And no one noticed – no one realized the significance of those words. What a terrible part she has had to play, poor woman. Imagine the shock when she goes to identify the body and, instead of what she expects, sees the actual lifeless form of the husband she has believed miles away by now. No wonder she fainted! But since then, despite her grief and her despair, how resolutely she has played her part and how the anguish of it must wring her. She cannot say a word to set us on the track of the real murderers. For her son's sake, no one must know that Paul Renauld was Georges Conneau, the criminal. Final and most bitter blow, she has admitted publicly that Madame Daubreuil was her husband's mistress – for a hint of blackmail might be fatal to her secret. How cleverly she dealt with the examining magistrate when he asked her if there was any mystery in her husband's past life. "Nothing so romantic, I am sure, monsieur." It was perfect, the indulgent tone, the soupçon of sad mockery. At once Monsieur Hautet felt himself foolish and melodramatic. Yes, she is a great woman! If she loved a criminal, she loved him royally!'

Poirot lost himself in contemplation.

'One thing more, Poirot, what about the piece of lead-piping?'

'You do not see? To disfigure the victim's face so that it would be unrecognizable. It was that which first set me on the right track. And that imbecile of a Giraud, swarming all over it to look for match ends! Did I not tell you that a clue of two foot long was quite as good as a clue of two inches? You see, Hastings, we must now start again. Who killed Monsieur Renauld? Someone who was near the villa just before twelve o'clock that night, someone who would benefit by his death – the description fits Jack Renauld only too well. The crime need not have been premeditated. And then the dagger!'

I started, I had not realized that point.

'Of course,' I said, 'Mrs Renauld's dagger was the second one we found in the tramp. There *were* two, then?'

'Certainly, and since they were duplicates, it stands to reason that Jack Renauld was the owner. But that would not trouble me so much. In fact, I had a little idea as to that. No, the worst indictment against him is again psychological – heredity, *mon ami*, heredity! Like father, like son – Jack Renauld, when all is said or done, is the son of Georges Conneau.'

His tone was grave and earnest, and I was impressed in spite of myself.

'What is your little idea that you mentioned just now?' I asked.

For answer, Poirot consulted his turnip-faced watch, and then asked:

'What time is the afternoon boat from Calais?'

'About five, I believe.'

'That will do very well. We shall just have time.'

'You are going to England?'

'Yes, my friend.'

'Why?'

'To find a possible – witness.'

'Who?'

With a rather peculiar smile upon his face, Poirot replied:

'Miss Bella Duveen.'

'But how will you find her – what do you know about her?'

'I know nothing about her – but I can guess a good deal. We may take it for granted that her name *is* Bella Duveen, and since that name was faintly familiar to Monsieur Stonor, though evidently not in connexion with the Renauld family, it is probable that she is on the stage. Jack Renauld was a young man with plenty of money, and twenty years of age. The stage is sure to have been the home of his first love. It tallies, too, with Monsieur Renauld's attempt to placate her with a cheque. I think I shall find her all right – especially with the help of *this*.'

And he brought out the photograph I had seen him take from Jack Renauld's drawer. 'With love from Bella' was scrawled across the corner, but it was not that which held my eyes fascinated. The likeness was not first rate – but for all that it was unmistakable to me. I felt a cold sinking, as though some unutterable calamity had befallen me.

It was the face of Cinderella.

CHAPTER 22

I FIND LOVE

For a moment or two I sat as though frozen, the photograph still in my hand. Then summoning all my courage to appear unmoved, I handed it back. At the same time I stole a quick glance at Poirot. Had he noticed anything? But to my relief he did not seem to be observing me. Anything unusual in my manner had certainly escaped him.

He rose briskly to his feet.

'We have no time to lose. We must make our departure with all dispatch. All is well – the sea it will be calm!'

In the bustle of departure, I had no time for thinking, but once on board the boat, secure from Poirot's observation, I pulled myself together, and attacked the facts dispassionately. How much did Poirot know, and why was he bent on finding this girl? Did he suspect her of having seen Jack Renauld commit the crime? Or did he suspect – But that was impossible! The girl had no grudge against the elder Renauld, no possible motive for wishing his death. What had brought her back to the scene of the murder? I went over the facts carefully. She must have left the train at Calais where I parted from her that day. No wonder I had been unable to find her on the boat. If she had dined in Calais, and then taken a train out to Merlinville, she would have arrived at the Villa Geneviève just about the time that Françoise said. What had she done when she left the house just after ten? Presumably either gone to an hotel, or returned to Calais. And then? The crime had been committed on Tuesday night. On Thursday morning she was once more in Merlinville. Had she ever left France at all? I doubted it very much. What kept her there – the hope of seeing Jack Renauld? I had told her (as at the time we believed) that he was on the high seas *en route* to Buenos Aires. Possibly she was aware that the *Anzora* had not sailed. But to know that she must have seen Jack. Was that what Poirot was after? Had Jack Renauld, returning to see Marthe Daubreuil, come face to face instead with Bella Duveen, the girl he had heartlessly thrown over?

I began to see daylight. If that were indeed the case, it might furnish Jack with the alibi he needed. Yet under those circumstances his silence seemed difficult to explain. Why could he not have spoken out boldly? Did he fear for this former entanglement of his to come to the ears of Marthe Daubreuil? I shook my head, dissatisfied. The thing had been harmless enough, a foolish boy-and-girl affair, and I reflected cynically that the son of a millionaire was not likely to be thrown over by a penniless French girl, who moreover loved him devotedly, without a much graver cause.

Poirot reappeared brisk and smiling at Dover, and our journey to London was uneventful. It was past nine o'clock when we arrived, and I supposed that we should return straight away to our rooms and do nothing till the morning.

But Poirot had other plans.

'We must lose no time, *mon ami.* The news of the arrest will not be in the English papers until the day after tomorrow, but still we must lose no time.'

I did not quite follow his reasoning, but I merely asked how he proposed to find the girl.

'You remember Joseph Aarons, the theatrical agent? No? I assisted him in a little matter of a Japanese wrestler. A pretty little problem, I must recount it to you one day. He, without doubt, will be able to put us in the way of finding out what we want to know.'

It took us some time to run Mr Aarons to earth, and it was after midnight when we finally managed it. He greeted Poirot with every evidence of warmth, and professed himself ready to be of service to us in any way.

'There's not much about the profession I don't know,' he said, beaming genially.

'*Eh bien*, Monsieur Aarons, I desire to find a young girl called Bella Duveen.'

'Bella Duveen. I know the name, but for a moment I can't place it. What's her line?'

'That I do not know – but here is her photograph.'

Mr Aarons studied it for a moment, then his face lighted.

'Got it!' He slapped his thigh. 'The Dulcibella Kids, by the Lord!'

'The Dulcibella Kids?'

'That's it. They're sisters. Acrobats, dancers, and singers. Give quite a good little turn. They're in the provinces, somewhere, I believe – if they're not resting. They've been on in Paris for the last two or three weeks.'

'Can you find out for me exactly where they are?'

'Easy as a bird. You go home, and I'll send you round the dope in the morning.'

With this promise we took leave of him. He was as good as his word. About eleven o'clock the following day, a scribbled note reached us.

'The Dulcibella Sisters are on at the Palace in Coventry. Good luck to you.'

Without more ado, we started for Coventry. Poirot made no inquiries at the theatre, but contented himself with booking stalls for the variety performance that evening.

The show was wearisome beyond words – or perhaps it was only my mood that made it seem so. Japanese families balanced themselves precariously, would-be fashionable men, in greenish evening dress and exquisitely slicked hair, reeled off society patter and danced marvellously. Stout prima donnas sang at the top of the human register, a comic comedian endeavoured to be Mr George Robey and failed signally.

At last the number went up which announced the Dulcibella Kids. My heart beat sickeningly. There she was – there they both were, the pair of them, one flaxen-haired, one dark, matching as to size, with short fluffy skirts and immense 'Buster Brown' bows. They looked a pair of extremely piquant children. They began to sing. Their voices were fresh and true, rather thin and music-hally, but attractive.

It was quite a pretty little turn. They danced neatly, and did some clever little acrobatic feats. The words of their songs were crisp and catchy. When the curtain fell, there was a full meed of applause. Evidently the Dulcibella Kids were a success.

Suddenly I felt that I could remain no longer. I must get out into the air. I suggested leaving to Poirot.

'Go by all means, *mon ami.* I amuse myself, and will stay to the end. I will rejoin you later.'

It was only a few steps from the theatre to the hotel. I went up to the sitting-room, ordered a whisky and soda, and sat drinking it, staring meditatively into the empty grate. I heard the door open, and turned my head, thinking it was Poirot. Then I jumped to my feet. It was Cinderella who stood in the doorway. She spoke haltingly, her breath coming in little gasps.

'I saw you in front. You and your friend. When you got up to go, I was waiting outside and followed you. Why are you here – in Coventry? What were you doing there tonight? Is the man who was with you the – the detective?'

She stood there, the cloak she had wrapped round her stage dress slipping from her shoulders. I saw the whiteness of her cheeks under the rouge, and heard the terror in her voice. And in that moment I understood everything – understood why Poirot was seeking her, and what she feared, and understood at last my own heart . . .

'Yes,' I said gently.

'Is he looking for – me?' she half whispered.

Then, as I did not answer for a moment, she slipped down by the big chair, and burst into violent bitter weeping.

I knelt down by her, holding her in my arms, and smoothing the hair back from her face.

'Don't cry, child, don't cry, for God's sake. You're safe here. I'll take care of you. Don't cry, darling. Don't cry. I know – I know everything.'

'Oh, but you don't!'

'I think I do.' And after a moment, as her sobs grew quieter, I asked: 'It was you who took the dagger, wasn't it?'

'Yes.'

'That was why you wanted me to show you round? And why you pretended to faint?'

Again she nodded.

'Why did you take the dagger?' I asked presently.

She replied as simply as a child:

'I was afraid there might be finger-marks on it.'

'But didn't you remember that you had worn gloves?'

She shook her head as though bewildered, and then said slowly:

'Are you going to give me up to – to the police?'

'Good God! no.'

Her eyes sought mine long and earnestly, and then she asked in a little quiet voice that sounded afraid of itself:

'Why not?'

It seemed a strange place and a strange time for a declaration of love – and God knows, in all my imagining, I had never pictured love coming to me in such a guise. But I answered simply and naturally enough:

'Because I love you, Cinderella.'

She bent her head down, as though ashamed, and muttered in a broken voice:

'You can't – you can't – not if you knew –' And then, as though rallying herself, she faced me squarely, and asked, 'What do you know, then?'

'I know that you came to see Mr Renauld that night. He offered you a cheque and you tore it up indignantly. Then you left the house –' I paused.

'Go on – what next?'

'I don't know whether you knew Jack Renauld would be coming

that night, or whether you just waited about on the chance of seeing him, but you did wait about. Perhaps you were just miserable and walked aimlessly – but at any rate just before twelve you were still near there, and you saw a man on the golf links –'

Again I paused. I had leapt to the truth in a flash as she entered the room, but now the picture rose before me even more convincingly. I saw vividly the peculiar pattern of the overcoat on the dead body of Mr Renauld, and I remembered the amazing likeness that had startled me into believing for one instant that the dead man had risen from the dead when his son burst into our conclave in the salon.

'Go on,' repeated the girl steadily.

'I fancy his back was to you – but you recognized him, or thought you recognized him. The gait and the carriage were familiar to you, and the pattern of his overcoat.' I paused. 'You used a threat in one of your letters to Jack Renauld. When you saw him there, your anger and jealousy drove you mad – and you struck! I don't believe for a minute that you meant to kill him. But you did kill him, Cinderella.'

She had flung up her hands to cover her face, and in a choked voice she said:

'You're right . . . you're right . . . I can see it all as you tell it.' Then she turned on me almost savagely. 'And you love me? Knowing what you do, how can you love me?'

'I don't know,' I said a little wearily. 'I think love is like that – a thing one cannot help. I have tried, I know – ever since the first day I met you. And love has been too strong for me.'

And then suddenly, when I least expected it, she broke down again, casting herself down on the floor and sobbing wildly.

'Oh, I can't!' she cried. 'I don't know what to do. I don't know which way to turn. Oh, pity me, pity me, someone, and tell me what to do!'

Again I knelt by her, soothing her as best I could.

'Don't be afraid of me, Bella. For God's sake don't be afraid of me. I love you, that's true – but I don't want anything in return. Only let me help you. Love him still if you have to, but let me help you, as he can't.'

It was as though she had been turned to stone by my words. She raised her head from her hands and stared at me.

'You think that?' she whispered. 'You think that I love Jack Renauld?'

Then, half laughing, half crying, she flung her arms passionately round my neck, and pressed her sweet wet face to mine.

'Not as I love you,' she whispered. 'Never as I love you!'

Her lips brushed my cheek, and then, seeking my mouth, kissed me again and again with a sweetness and fire beyond belief. The wildness of it – and the wonder, I shall not forget – no, not as long as I live!

It was a sound in the doorway that made us look up. Poirot was standing there looking at us.

I did not hesitate. With a bound I reached him and pinioned his arms to his sides.

'Quick,' I said to the girl. 'Get out of here. As fast as you can. I'll hold him.'

With one look at me, she fled out of the room past us. I held Poirot in a grip of iron.

'*Mon ami*,' observed the latter mildly, 'you do this sort of thing very well. The strong man holds me in his grasp and I am helpless as a child. But all this is uncomfortable and slightly ridiculous. Let us sit down and be calm.'

'You won't pursue her?'

'*Mon Dieu!* no. Am I Giraud? Release me, my friend.'

Keeping a suspicious eye upon him, for I paid Poirot the compliment of knowing that I was no match for him in astuteness, I relaxed my grip, and he sank into an armchair, feeling his arms tenderly.

'It is that you have the strength of a bull when you are roused, Hastings! *Eh bien*, and do you think you have behaved well to your old friend? I show you the girl's photograph and you recognize it, but you never say a word.'

'There was no need if you knew that I recognized it,' I said rather bitterly. So Poirot had known all along! I had not deceived him for an instant.

'Ta-ta! You did not know that I knew that. And tonight you help the girl to escape when we have found her with so much trouble. *Eh bien!* it comes to this – are you going to work with me or against me, Hastings?'

For a moment or two I did not answer. To break with my old

friend gave me great pain. Yet I must definitely range myself against him. Would he ever forgive me, I wondered? He had been strangely calm so far, but I knew him to possess marvellous self-command.

'Poirot,' I said, 'I'm sorry. I admit I've behaved badly to you over this. But sometimes one has no choice. And in future I must take my own line.'

Poirot nodded his head several times.

'I understand,' he said. The mocking light had quite died out of his eyes, and he spoke with a sincerity and kindness that surprised me. 'It is that, my friend, is it not? It is love that has come – not as you imagined it, all cock-a-hoop with fine feathers, but sadly, with bleeding feet. Well, well – I warned you. When I realized that this girl must have taken the dagger, I warned you. Perhaps you remember. But already it was too late. But, tell me, how much do you know?'

I met his eyes squarely.

'Nothing that you could tell me would be any surprise to me, Poirot. Understand that. But in case you think of resuming your search for Miss Duveen, I should like you to know one thing clearly. If you have any idea that she was concerned in the crime, or was the mysterious lady who called upon Mr Renauld that night, you are wrong. I travelled home from France with her that day, and parted from her at Victoria that evening, so that it is clearly impossible for her to have been in Merlinville.'

'Ah!' Poirot looked at me thoughtfully. 'And you would swear to that in a court of law?'

'Most certainly I would.'

Poirot rose and bowed.

'*Mon ami! Vive l'amour!* It can perform miracles. It is decidedly ingenious what you have thought of there. It defeats even Hercule Poirot!'

CHAPTER 23

DIFFICULTIES AHEAD

After a moment of stress, such as I have just described, reaction is bound to set in. I retired to rest that night on a note of triumph, but I awoke to realize that I was by no means out of the wood. True, I could see no flaw in the alibi I had so suddenly conceived. I had but to stick to my story, and I failed to see how Bella could be convicted in face of it.

But I felt the need of treading warily. Poirot would not take defeat lying down. Somehow or other, he would endeavour to turn the tables on me, and that in the way, and at the moment, when I least expected it.

We met at breakfast the following morning as though nothing had happened. Poirot's good temper was imperturbable, yet I thought I detected a film of reserve in his manner which was new. After breakfast, I announced my intention of going out for a stroll. A malicious gleam shot through Poirot's eyes.

'If it is information you seek, you need not be at the pains of deranging yourself. I can tell you all you wish to know. The Dulcibella Sisters have cancelled their contract, and have left Coventry for an unknown destination.'

'Is that really so, Poirot?'

'You can take it from me, Hastings. I made inquiries the first thing this morning. After all, what else did you expect?'

True enough, nothing else could be expected under the circumstances. Cinderella had profited by the slight start I had been able to secure her, and would certainly not lose a moment in removing herself from the reach of the pursuer. It was what I had intended and planned. Nevertheless, I was aware of being plunged into a network of fresh difficulties.

I had absolutely no means of communicating with the girl, and it was vital that she should know the line of defence that had occurred to me, and which I was prepared to carry out. Of course it was possible that she might try to send word to me in some way or another, but I hardly thought it likely. She would know the risk she ran of a message being intercepted by Poirot, thus setting him on her track once more. Clearly her only course was to disappear utterly for the time being.

But, in the meantime, what was Poirot doing? I studied him attentively. He was wearing his most innocent air, and staring meditatively into the far distance. He looked altogether too placid and supine to give me reassurance. I had learned, with Poirot, that the less dangerous he looked, the more dangerous he was. His quiescence alarmed me. Observing a troubled quality in my glance, he smiled benignantly.

'You are puzzled, Hastings? You ask yourself why I do not launch myself in pursuit?'

'Well – something of the kind.'

'It is what you would do, were you in my place. I understand that. But I am not of those who enjoy rushing up and down a country seeking a needle in a haystack, as you English say. No – let Mademoiselle Bella Duveen go. Without doubt, I shall be able to find her when the time comes. Until then, I am content to wait.'

I stared at him doubtfully. Was he seeking to mislead me? I had an irritating feeling that, even now, he was master of the situation. My sense of superiority was gradually waning. I had contrived the girl's escape, and evolved a brilliant scheme for saving her from the consequences of her rash act – but I could not rest easy in my mind. Poirot's perfect calm awakened a thousand apprehensions.

'I suppose, Poirot,' I said rather diffidently, 'I mustn't ask what your plans are? I've forfeited the right.'

'But not at all. There is no secret about them. We return to France without delay.'

'*We?*'

'Precisely – "*we*"! You know very well that you cannot afford to let Papa Poirot out of your sight. Eh? is it not so, my friend? But remain in England by all means if you wish –'

I shook my head. He had hit the nail on the head. I could not afford to let him out of my sight. Although I could not expect his confidence after what had happened, I could still check his actions. The only danger to Bella lay with him. Giraud and the French police were indifferent to her existence. At all costs I must keep near Poirot.

Poirot observed me attentively as these reflections passed through my mind, and gave me a nod of satisfaction.

'I am right, am I not? And as you are quite capable of trying to follow me, disguised with some absurdity such as a false beard –

which everyone would perceive, *bien entendu* – I much prefer that we should voyage together. It would annoy me greatly that anyone should mock themselves at you.'

'Very well, then. But it's only fair to warn you –'

'I know – I know all. You are my enemy! Be my enemy, then. It does not worry me at all.'

'So long as it's all fair and above-board, I don't mind.'

'You have to the full the English passion for "fair play"! Now your scruples are satisfied, let us depart immediately. There is no time to be lost. Our stay in England has been short but sufficient. I know – what I wanted to know.'

The tone was light, but I read a veiled menace into the words.

'Still –' I began, and stopped.

'Still – as you say! Without doubt you are satisfied with the part you are playing. Me, I preoccupy myself with Jack Renauld.'

Jack Renauld! The words gave me a start. I had completely forgotten that aspect of the case. Jack Renauld, in prison, with the shadow of the guillotine looming over him. I saw the part I was playing in a more sinister light. I could save Bella – yes, but in doing so I ran the risk of sending an innocent man to his death.

I pushed the thought from me with horror. It could not be. He would be acquitted. Certainly he would be acquitted. But the cold fear came back. Suppose he were not? What then? Could I have it on my conscience – horrible thought! Would it come to that in the end? A decision. Bella or Jack Renauld? The promptings of my heart were to save the girl I loved at any cost to myself. But, if the cost were to another, the problem was altered.

What would the girl herself say? I remembered that no word of Jack Renauld's arrest had passed my lips. As yet she was in total ignorance of the fact that her former lover was in prison charged with a hideous crime which he had not committed. When she knew, how would she act? Would she permit her life to be saved at the expense of his? Certainly she must do nothing rash. Jack Renauld might, and probably would, be acquitted without any intervention on her part. If so, good. But if he was not! That was the terrible, the unanswerable problem. I fancied that she ran no risk of the extreme penalty. The circumstances of the crime were quite different in her case. She could plead jealousy and extreme provocation, and her youth and beauty would go for much. The fact that by a tragic mistake it was Mr Renauld, and not his son, who paid the penalty would not alter the motive of the crime. But in any case, however lenient the sentence of the Court, it must mean a long term of imprisonment.

No, Bella must be protected. And, at the same time, Jack Renauld must be saved. How this was to be accomplished I did not see clearly. But I pinned my faith to Poirot. He *knew*. Come what might, he would manage to save an innocent man. He must find some pretext other than the real one. It might be difficult, but he would manage it somehow. And with Bella unsuspected, and Jack Renauld acquitted, all would end satisfactorily.

So I told myself repeatedly, but at the bottom of my heart there still remained a cold fear.

CHAPTER 24

'SAVE HIM!'

We crossed from England by the evening boat, and the following morning saw us in St Omer, whither Jack Renauld had been taken. Poirot lost no time in visiting M. Hautet. As he did not seem disposed to make any objections to my accompanying him, I bore him company.

After various formalities and preliminaries, we were conducted to the examining magistrate's room. He greeted us cordially.

'I was told that you had returned to England, Monsieur Poirot. I am glad to find that such is not the case.'

'It is true I went there, monsieur, but it was only for a flying visit. A side issue, but one that I fancied might repay investigation.'

'And it did – eh?'

Poirot shrugged his shoulders. M. Hautet nodded, sighing.

'We must resign ourselves, I fear. That animal Giraud, his manners are abominable, but he is undoubtedly clever! Not much chance of that one making a mistake.'

'You think not?'

It was the examining magistrate's turn to shrug his shoulders.

'Oh, well, speaking frankly – in confidence, of course – can you come to any other conclusion?'

'Frankly, there seem to me to be many points that are obscure.'

'Such as –?'

But Poirot was not to be drawn.

'I have not yet tabulated them,' he remarked. 'It was a general reflection that I was making. I liked the young man, and should be sorry to believe him guilty of such a hideous crime. By the way, what has he to say for himself on the matter?'

The magistrate frowned.

'I cannot understand him. He seems incapable of putting up any sort of defence. It has been most difficult to get him to answer questions. He contents himself with a general denial, and beyond that takes refuge in a most obstinate silence. I am interrogating him again tomorrow, perhaps you would like to be present?'

We accepted the invitation with *empressement.*

'A distressing case,' said the magistrate with a sigh. 'My sympathy for Madame Renauld is profound.'

'How is Madame Renauld?'

'She has not yet recovered consciousness. It is merciful in a way, poor woman, she is being spared much. The doctors say that there is no danger, but that when she comes to herself she must be kept as quiet as possible. It was, I understand, quite as much the shock as the fall which caused her present state. It would be terrible if her brain became unhinged; but I should not wonder at all – no, really, not at all.'

M. Hautet leaned back, shaking his head, with a sort of mournful enjoyment, as he envisaged the gloomy prospect.

He roused himself at length, and observed with a start:

'That reminds me. I have here a letter for you, Monsieur Poirot. Let me see, where did I put it?'

He proceeded to rummage among his papers. At last he found the missive, and handed it to Poirot.

'It was sent under cover to me in order that I might forward it to you,' he explained. 'But as you left no address I could not do so.'

Poirot studied the letter curiously. It was addressed in a long, sloping, foreign hand, and the writing was decidedly a woman's. Poirot did not open it. Instead he put it in his pocket and rose to his feet.

'Till tomorrow then. Many thanks for your courtesy and amiability.'

'But not at all. I am always at your service.'

We were just leaving the building when we came face to face with Giraud, looking more dandified than ever, and thoroughly pleased with himself.

'Aha! Monsieur Poirot,' he cried airily. 'You have returned from England then?'

'As you see,' said Poirot.

'The end of the case is not far off now, I fancy.'

'I agree with you, Monsieur Giraud.'

Poirot spoke in a subdued tone. His crestfallen manner seemed to delight the other.

'Of all the milk-and-water criminals! Not an idea of defending himself. It is extraordinary!'

'So extraordinary that it gives one to think, does it not?' suggested Poirot mildly.

But Giraud was not even listening. He twirled his cane amicably.

'Well, good day, Monsieur Poirot. I am glad you're satisfied of young Renauld's guilt at last.'

'*Pardon!* But I am not in the least satisfied. Jack Renauld is innocent.'

Giraud stared for a moment – then burst out laughing, tapping his head significantly with the brief remark: '*Toqué!*'

Poirot drew himself up. A dangerous light showed in his eyes.

'Monsieur Giraud, throughout the case your manner to me has been deliberately insulting. You need teaching a lesson. I am prepared to wager you five hundred francs that I find the murderer of Monsieur Renauld before you do. Is it agreed?'

Giraud stared helplessly at him, and murmured again: '*Toqué!*'

'Come now,' urged Poirot, 'is it agreed?'

'I have no wish to take your money from you.'

'Make your mind easy – you will not!'

'Oh, well then, I agree! You speak of my manner to you being insulting. Well, once or twice, *your* manner has annoyed *me*.'

'I am enchanted to hear it,' said Poirot. 'Good morning, Monsieur Giraud. Come, Hastings.'

I said no word as we walked along the street. My heart was heavy. Poirot had displayed his intentions only too plainly. I doubted more than ever my powers of saving Bella from the consequences of her act. This unlucky encounter with Giraud had roused Poirot and put him on his mettle.

Suddenly I felt a hand laid on my shoulder, and turned to face Gabriel Stonor. We stopped and greeted him, and he proposed strolling with us back to our hotel.

'And what are you doing here, Monsieur Stonor?' inquired Poirot.

'One must stand by one's friends,' replied the other dryly. 'Especially when they are unjustly accused.'

'Then you do not believe that Jack Renauld committed the crime?' I asked eagerly.

'Certainly I don't. I know the lad. I admit that there have been one or two things in this business that have staggered me completely, but none the less, in spite of his fool way of taking it, I'll never believe that Jack Renauld is a murderer.'

My heart warmed to the secretary. His words seemed to lift a secret weight from my heart.

'I have no doubt that many people feel as you do,' I exclaimed. 'There is really absurdly little evidence against him. I should say that there was no doubt of his acquittal – no doubt whatever.'

But Stonor hardly responded as I could have wished.

'I'd give a lot to think as you do,' he said gravely. He turned to Poirot. 'What's your opinion, monsieur?'

'I think that things look very black against him,' said Poirot quietly.

'You believe him guilty?' said Stonor sharply.

'No. But I think he will find it hard to prove his innocence.'

'He's behaving so damned queerly,' muttered Stonor. 'Of course, I realize that there's a lot more in this affair than meets the eye. Giraud's not wise to that because he's an outsider, but the whole thing has been damned odd. As to that, least said soonest mended. If Mrs Renauld wants to hush anything up, I'll take my cue from her. It's her show, and I've too much respect for her judgement to shove my oar in, but I can't get behind this attitude of Jack's. Anyone would think he *wanted* to be thought guilty.'

'But it's absurd,' I cried, bursting in. 'For one thing, the dagger –' I paused, uncertain as to how much Poirot would wish me to reveal. I continued, choosing my words carefully, 'We know that the dagger could not have been in Jack Renauld's possession that evening. Mrs Renauld knows that.'

'True,' said Stonor. 'When she recovers, she will doubtless say all this and more. Well, I must be leaving you.'

'One moment.' Poirot's hand arrested his departure. 'Can you arrange for word to be sent to me at once should Mrs Renauld recover consciousness?'

'Certainly. That's easily done.'

'That point about the dagger is good, Poirot,' I urged as we went upstairs. 'I couldn't speak very plainly before Stonor.'

'That was quite right of you. We might as well keep the knowledge to ourselves as long as we can. As to the dagger, your point hardly helps Jack Renauld. You remember that I was absent for an hour this morning, before we started from London?'

'Yes?'

'Well, I was employed in trying to find the firm Jack Renauld employed to convert his souvenirs. It was not very difficult. *Eh bien*, Hastings, they made to his order not *two* paper knives, but *three*.'

'So that –'

'So that, after giving one to his mother and one to Bella Duveen, there was a third which he doubtless retained for his own use. No, Hastings, I fear the dagger question will not help us to save him from the guillotine.'

'It won't come to that,' I cried, stung.

Poirot shook his head uncertainly.

'You will save him,' I cried positively.

Poirot glanced at me dryly.

'Have you not rendered it impossible, *mon ami*?'

'Some other way,' I muttered.

'Ah! *Sapristi!* But it is miracles you ask from me. No – say no more. Let us instead see what is in this letter.'

And he drew out the envelope from his breast pocket.

His face contracted as he read, then he handed the one flimsy sheet to me.

'There are other women in the world who suffer, Hastings.'

The writing was blurred and the note had evidently been written in great agitation.

> Dear M. Poirot – If you get this, I beg of you to come to my aid. I have no one to turn to, and at all costs Jack must be saved. I implore of you on my knees to help us.
>
> Marthe Daubreuil

I handed it back, moved.

'You will go?'

'At once. We will command an auto.'

Half an hour later saw us at the Villa Marguerite. Marthe was at the door to meet us, and let Poirot in, clinging with both hands to one of his.

'Ah, you have come – it is good of you. I have been in despair, not knowing what to do. They will not let me go to see him in prison even. I suffer horribly. I am nearly mad.

'Is it true what they say, that he does not deny the crime? But that is madness. It is impossible that he should have done it! Never for one minute will I believe it.'

'Neither do I believe it, mademoiselle,' said Poirot gently.

'But then why does he not speak? I do not understand.'

'Perhaps because he is screening someone,' suggested Poirot, watching her.

Marthe frowned.

'Screening someone? Do you mean his mother? Ah, from the beginning I have suspected her. Who inherits all that vast fortune? She does. It is easy to wear widow's weeds and play the hypocrite. And they say that when he was arrested she fell down like *that!*' She made a dramatic gesture. 'And without doubt, Monsieur Stonor, the secretary, he helped her. They are thick as thieves, those two. It is true she is older than he – but what do men care – if a woman is rich!'

There was a hint of bitterness in her tone.

'Stonor was in England,' I put in.

'He says so – but who knows?'

'Mademoiselle,' said Poirot quietly, 'if we are to work together, you and I, we must have things clear. First, I will ask you a question.'

'Yes, monsieur?'

'Are you aware of your mother's real name?'

Marthe looked at him for a minute, then, letting her head fall forward on her arms, she burst into tears.

'There, there,' said Poirot, patting her on the shoulder. 'Calm yourself, *petite*, I see that you know. Now a second question – did you know who Monsieur Renauld was?'

'Monsieur Renauld,' she raised her head from her hands and gazed at him wonderingly.

'Ah, I see you do not know that. Now listen to me carefully.'

Step by step, he went over the case, much as he had done to

me on the day of our departure for England. Marthe listened spellbound. When he had finished, she drew a long breath.

'But you are wonderful – magnificent! You are the greatest detective in the world.'

With a swift gesture she slipped off her chair and knelt before him with an abandonment that was wholly French.

'Save him, monsieur,' she cried. 'I love him so. Oh, save him, save him – save him!'

CHAPTER 25

AN UNEXPECTED DÉNOUEMENT

We were present the following morning at the examination of Jack Renauld. Short as the time had been, I was shocked at the change that had taken place in the young prisoner. His cheeks had fallen in, there were deep black circles round his eyes, and he looked haggard and distraught, as one who had wooed sleep in vain for several nights. He betrayed no emotion at seeing us.

'Renauld,' began the magistrate, 'do you deny that you were in Merlinville on the night of the crime?'

Jack did not reply at once, then he said with a hesitancy of manner which was piteous:

'I – I – told you that I was in Cherbourg.'

The magistrate turned sharply.

'Send in the station witnesses.'

In a moment or two the door opened to admit a man whom I recognized as being a porter at Merlinville station.

'You were on duty on the night of 7th June?'

'Yes, monsieur.'

'You witnessed the arrival of the 11.40 train?'

'Yes, monsieur.'

'Look at the prisoner. Do you recognize him as having been one of the passengers to alight?'

'Yes, monsieur.'

'There is no possibility of your being mistaken?'

'No, monsieur. I know Monsieur Jack Renauld well.'

'Nor of your being mistaken as to the date?'

'No, monsieur. Because it was the following morning, 8th June, that we heard of the murder.'

Another railway official was brought in, and confirmed the first one's evidence. The magistrate looked at Jack Renauld.

'These men have identified you positively. What have you to say?'

Jack shrugged his shoulders.

'Nothing.'

'Renauld,' continued the magistrate, 'do you recognize this?'

He took something from the table by his side and held it out to the prisoner. I shuddered as I recognized the aeroplane dagger.

'Pardon,' cried Jack's counsel, Maître Grosier. 'I demand to speak to my client before he answers that question.'

But Jack Renauld had no consideration for the feelings of the wretched Grosier. He waved him aside, and replied quietly:

'Certainly I recognize it. It was a present given by me to my mother, as a souvenir of the war.'

'Is there, as far as you know, any duplicate of that dagger in existence?'

Again Maître Grosier burst out, and again Jack overrode him.

'Not that I know of. The setting was my own design.'

Even the magistrate almost gasped at the boldness of the reply. It did, in very truth, seem as though Jack was rushing on his fate. I realized, of course, the vital necessity he was under of concealing, for Bella's sake, the fact that there was a duplicate dagger in the case. So long as there was supposed to be only one weapon, no suspicion was likely to attach to the girl who had had the second paper-knife in her possession. He was valiantly shielding the woman he had once loved – but at what cost to himself! I began to realize the magnitude of the task I had so lightly set Poirot. It would not be easy to secure the acquittal of Jack Renauld by anything short of the truth.

M. Hautet spoke again, with a peculiarly biting inflection:

'Madame Renauld told us that this dagger was on her dressing-table on the night of the crime. But Madame Renauld is a mother! It will doubtless astonish you, Renauld, but I consider it highly likely that Madame Renauld was mistaken, and that, by inadvertence perhaps, you had taken it with you to Paris. Doubtless you will contradict me –'

I saw the lad's handcuffed hands clench themselves. The perspiration stood out in beads upon his brow, as with a supreme effort he interrupted M. Hautet in a hoarse voice:

'I shall not contradict you. It is possible.'

It was a stupefying moment. Maître Grosier rose to his feet, protesting:

'My client has undergone a considerable nervous strain. I should wish it put on record that I do not consider him answerable for what he says.'

The magistrate quelled him angrily. For a moment a doubt seemed to arise in his own mind. Jack Renauld had almost overdone his part. He leaned forward, and gazed at the prisoner searchingly.

'Do you fully understand, Renauld, that on the answers you have given me I shall have no alternative but to commit you for trial?'

Jack's pale face flushed. He looked steadily back.

'Monsieur Hautet, I swear that I did not kill my father.'

But the magistrate's brief moment of doubt was over. He laughed a short unpleasant laugh.

'Without doubt, without doubt – they are always innocent, our prisoners! By your own mouth you are condemned. You can offer no defence, no alibi – only a mere assertion which would not deceive a babe! – that you are not guilty. You killed your father, Renauld – a cruel and cowardly murder – for the sake of the money which you believed would come to you at his death. Your mother was an accessory after the fact. Doubtless, in view of the fact that she acted as a mother, the courts will extend an indulgence to her that they will not accord to you. And rightly so! Your crime was a horrible one – to be held in abhorrence by gods and men!'

M. Hautet was interrupted – to his intense annoyance. The door was pushed open.

'Monsieur le juge, Monsieur le juge,' stammered the attendant, 'there is a lady who says – who says –'

'Who says what?' cried the justly incensed magistrate. 'This is highly irregular. I forbid it – I absolutely forbid it.'

But a slender figure pushed the stammering gendarme aside. Dressed all in black, with a long veil that hid her face, she advanced into the room.

My heart gave a sickening throb. She had come then! All my efforts were in vain. Yet I could not but admire the courage that had led her to take this step so unfalteringly.

She raised her veil – and I gasped. For, though as like her as two peas, this girl was not Cinderella! On the other hand, now that I saw her without the fair wig she had worn on the stage, I recognized her as the girl of the photograph in Jack Renauld's room.

'You are the Juge d'Instruction, Monsieur Hautet?' she queried.

'Yes, but I forbid –'

'My name is Bella Duveen. I wish to give myself up for the murder of Mr Renauld.'

CHAPTER 26

I RECEIVE A LETTER

'My friend, – You will know all when you get this. Nothing that I can say will move Bella. She has gone out to give herself up. I am tired out with struggling.

'You will know now that I deceived you, that where you gave me trust I repaid you with lies. It will seem, perhaps, indefensible to you, but I should like, before I go out of your life for ever, to show you just how it all came about. If I knew that you forgave me, it would make life easier for me. It wasn't for myself I did it – that's the only thing I can put forward to say for myself.

'I'll begin from the day I met you in the boat train from Paris. I was uneasy then about Bella. She was just desperate about Jack Renauld, she'd have lain down on the ground for him to walk on, and when he began to change, and to stop writing so often, she began getting in a state. She got it into her head that he was keen on another girl – and of course, as it turned out afterwards, she was quite right there. She'd made up her mind to go to their villa at Merlinville, and try and see Jack. She knew I was against it, and tried to give me the slip. I found she was not on the train at Calais, and determined I would not go on to England without her. I'd an uneasy feeling that something awful was going to happen if I couldn't prevent it.

'I met the next train from Paris. She was on it, and set upon going out then and there to Merlinville. I argued with her for all I was worth, but it wasn't any good. She was all strung up and set upon having her own way. Well, I washed my hands of it. I'd done all I could. It was getting late. I went to an hotel, and Bella started for Merlinville. I still couldn't shake off my feeling of what the books call "impending disaster".

'The next day came – but no Bella. She'd made a date with me to meet at the hotel, but she didn't keep it. No sign of her all day. I got more and more anxious. Then came an evening paper with the news.

'It was awful! I couldn't be sure, of course – but I was terribly afraid. I figured it out that Bella had met Papa Renauld and told him about her and Jack, and that he'd insulted her or something like that. We've both got terribly quick tempers.

'Then all the masked foreigner business came out, and I began to feel more at ease. But it still worried me that Bella hadn't kept her date with me.

'By the next morning I was so rattled that I'd just got to go and see what I could. First thing, I ran up against you. You know all that . . . When I saw the dead man, looking so like Jack, and wearing Jack's fancy overcoat, I knew! And there was the identical paper-knife – wicked little thing! – that Jack had given Bella! Ten to one it had her fingermarks on it. I can't hope to explain to you the sort of helpless horror of that moment. I only saw one thing clearly – I must get hold of that dagger, and get right away with it before they found out it was gone. I pretended to faint, and while you were away getting water I took the thing and hid it away in my dress.

'I told you that I was staying at the Hôtel du Phare, but of course really I made a bee-line back to Calais, and then on to England by the first boat. When we were in mid-Channel I dropped that little devil of a dagger into the sea. Then I felt I could breathe again.

'Bella was in our digs in London. She looked like nothing on God's earth. I told her what I'd done, and that she was pretty safe for the time being. She stared at me, and then began laughing . . . laughing . . . laughing . . . it was horrible to hear her! I felt that the best thing to do was to keep busy. She'd go mad if she had time to brood on what she'd done. Luckily we got an engagement at once.

'And then, I saw you and your friend watching us that night . . . I was frantic. You must suspect, or you wouldn't have tracked us down. I had to know the worst, so I followed you. I was desperate. And then, before I'd had time to say anything, I tumbled to it that it was me you suspected, not Bella! Or at least that you thought I *was* Bella, since I'd stolen the dagger.

'I wish, honey, that you could see back into my mind at that moment . . . you'd forgive me, perhaps . . . I was so frightened, and muddled, and desperate . . . All I could get clearly was that you would try and save me – I didn't know whether you'd be willing to save her . . . I thought very likely not – It wasn't the same thing! And I couldn't risk it! Bella's my twin – I'd got to do the best for her. So I went on lying. I felt mean – I feel mean still . . . That's all – enough too, you'll say, I expect. I ought to have trusted you . . . If I had –

'As soon as the news was in the paper that Jack Renauld had been arrested, it was all up. Bella wouldn't even wait to see how things went . . .

'I'm very tired. I can't write any more.'

She had begun to sign herself Cinderella, but had crossed that out and written instead 'Dulcie Duveen.'

It was an ill-written, blurred epistle – but I have kept it to this day.

Poirot was with me when I read it. The sheets fell from my hand, and I looked across at him.

'Did you know all the time that it was – the other?'

'Yes, my friend.'

'Why did you not tell me?'

'To begin with, I could hardly believe it conceivable that you could make such a mistake. You had seen the photograph. The sisters are very alike, but by no means incapable of distinguishment.'

'But the fair hair?'

'A wig, worn for the sake of a piquant contrast on the stage. Is it conceivable that with twins one should be fair and one dark?'

'Why didn't you tell me that night at the hotel in Coventry?'

'You were rather high-handed in your methods, *mon ami*,' said Poirot dryly. 'You did not give me a chance.'

'But afterwards?'

'Ah, afterwards! Well, to begin with, I was hurt at your want of faith in me. And then, I wanted to see whether your – feelings would stand the test of time. In fact, whether it was love, or a flash in the pan, with you. I should not have left you long in your error.'

I nodded. His tone was too affectionate for me to bear resentment. I looked down on the sheets of the letter. Suddenly I picked them up from the floor, and pushed them across to him.

'Read that,' I said. 'I'd like you to.'

He read it through in silence, then he looked up at me.

'What is it that worries you, Hastings?'

This was quite a new mood in Poirot. His mocking manner seemed laid quite aside. I was able to say what I wanted without too much difficulty.

'She doesn't say – she doesn't say – well, not whether she cares for me or not?'

Poirot turned back the pages.

'I think you are mistaken, Hastings.'

'Where?' I cried, leaning forward eagerly.

Poirot smiled.

'She tells you that in every line of the letter, *mon ami*.'

'But where am I to find her? There's no address on the letter. There's a French stamp, that's all.'

'Excite yourself not! Leave it to Papa Poirot. I can find her for you as soon as I have five little minutes!'

CHAPTER 27

JACK RENAULD'S STORY

'Congratulations, Monsieur Jack,' said Poirot, wringing the lad warmly by the hand.

Young Renauld had come to us as soon as he was liberated – before starting for Merlinville to rejoin Marthe and his mother. Stonor accompanied him. His heartiness was in strong contrast to the lad's wan looks. It was plain that the boy was on the verge of a nervous breakdown. He smiled mournfully at Poirot, and said in a low voice:

'I went through it to protect her, and now it's all no use.'

'You could hardly expect the girl to accept the price of your life,' remarked Stonor dryly. 'She was bound to come forward when she saw you heading straight for the guillotine.'

'*Eh ma foi!* and you were heading for it too!' added Poirot, with a slight twinkle. 'You would have had Maître Grosier's death from rage on your conscience if you had gone on.'

'He was a well meaning ass, I suppose,' said Jack. 'But he worried me horribly. You see, I couldn't very well take him into my confidence. But, my God! what's going to happen about Bella?'

'If I were you,' said Poirot frankly, 'I should not distress myself unduly. The French Courts are very lenient to youth and beauty, and the *crime passionnel!* A clever lawyer will make out a great case of extenuating circumstances. It will not be pleasant for you –'

'I don't care about that. You see, Monsieur Poirot, in a way I *do* feel guilty of my father's murder. But for me, and my entanglement with this girl, he would be alive and well today. And then my cursed carelessness in taking away the wrong overcoat. I can't help feeling responsible for his death. It will haunt me for ever!'

'No, no,' I said soothingly.

'Of course it's horrible to me to think that Bella killed my father,' resumed Jack. 'But I'd treated her shamefully. After I met Marthe, and realized I'd made a mistake, I ought to have written and told her so honestly. But I was so terrified of a row, and of its coming to Marthe's ears, and her thinking there was more in it than there ever had been, that – well, I was a coward, and went on hoping the thing would die down of itself. I just drifted, in fact – not realizing that I was driving the poor kid desperate. If she'd really knifed me, as she meant to, I should have got no more than my deserts. And the way she's come forward now is downright plucky. I'd have stood the racket, you know – up to the end.'

He was silent for a moment or two, and then burst out on another tack:

'What gets me is why the Governor should be wandering about in underclothes and my overcoat at that time of night. I suppose he'd just given the foreign johnnies the slip, and my mother must have made a mistake about its being two o'clock when they came. Or – or, it wasn't all a frame-up, was it? I mean, my mother didn't think – couldn't think – that – that it was *me*?'

Poirot reassured him quickly.

'No, no, Monsieur Jack. Have no fears on that score. As for the rest, I will explain it to you one of these days. It is rather curious. But will you recount to us exactly what did occur on that terrible evening?'

'There's very little to tell. I came from Cherbourg, as I told you, in order to see Marthe before going to the other end of the world. The train was late, and I decided to take the short cut across the golf links. I could easily get into the grounds of the Villa Marguerite from there. I had nearly reached the place when –'

He paused and swallowed.

'Yes?'

'I heard a terrible cry. It wasn't loud – a sort of choke and gasp – but it frightened me. For a moment I stood rooted to the spot. Then I came round the corner of a bush. There was moonlight. I saw the grave, and a figure lying face downwards with a dagger sticking in the back. And then – and then – I looked up and saw *her*. She was looking at me as though she saw a ghost – it's what she must have thought me at first – all expression seemed frozen out of her face by horror. And then she gave a cry, and turned and ran.'

He stopped, trying to master his emotion.

'And afterwards?' asked Poirot gently.

'I really don't know. I stayed there for a time, dazed. And then I realized I'd better get away as fast as I could. It didn't occur to me that they would suspect me, but I was afraid of being called upon to give evidence against her. I walked to St Beauvais as I told you, and got a car from there back to Cherbourg.'

A knock came at the door, and a page entered with a telegram which he delivered to Stonor. He tore it open. Then he got up from his seat.

'Mrs Renauld has regained consciousness,' he said.

'Ah!' Poirot sprang to his feet. 'Let us all go to Merlinville at once!'

A hurried departure was made forthwith. Stonor, at Jack's insistence, agreed to stay behind and do all that could be done for Bella Duveen. Poirot, Jack Renauld, and I set off in the Renauld car.

The run took just over forty minutes. As we approached the doorway of the Villa Marguerite Jack Renauld shot a questioning glance at Poirot.

'How would it be if you went on first – to break the news to my mother that I am free –'

'While you break it in person to Mademoiselle Marthe, eh?' finished Poirot, with a twinkle. 'But yes, by all means, I was about to propose such an arrangement myself.'

Jack Renauld did not wait for more. Stopping the car, he swung himself out, and ran up the path to the front door. We went on in the car to the Villa Geneviève.

'Poirot,' I said, 'do you remember how we arrived here that first day? And were met by the news of Mr Renauld's murder?'

'Ah, yes, truly. Not so long ago either. But what a lot of things have happened since then – especially for *you, mon ami!*'

'Yes, indeed,' I sighed.

'You are regarding it from the sentimental standpoint, Hastings. That was not my meaning. We will hope that Mademoiselle Bella will be dealt with leniently, and after all Jack Renauld cannot marry both the girls! I spoke from a professional standpoint. This is not a crime well ordered and regular, such as a detective delights in. The *mise en scène* designed by Georges Conneau, that indeed is perfect, but the *dénouement* – ah, no! A man killed by accident in a girl's fit of anger – ah, indeed, what order or method is there in that?'

And in the midst of a fit of laughter on my part at Poirot's peculiarities, the door was opened by Françoise.

Poirot explained that he must see Mrs Renauld at once, and the old woman conducted him upstairs. I remained in the salon. It was some time before Poirot reappeared. He was looking unusually grave.

'*Vous voilà,* Hastings! *Sacré tonnerre!* but there are squalls ahead!'

'What do you mean?' I cried.

'I would hardly have credited it,' said Poirot thoughtfully, 'but women are very unexpected.'

'Here are Jack and Marthe Daubreuil,' I exclaimed, looking out of the window.

Poirot bounded out of the room, and met the young couple on the steps outside.

'Do not enter. It is better not. Your mother is very upset.'

'I know, I know,' said Jack Renauld. 'I must go up to her at once.'

'But no, I tell you. It is better not.'

'But Marthe and I –'

'In any case, do not take Mademoiselle with you. Mount, if you must, but you would be wise to be guided by me.'

A voice on the stairs behind made us all start.

'I thank you for your good offices, Monsieur Poirot, but I will make my own wishes clear.'

We stared in astonishment. Descending the stairs, leaning on Léonie's arm, was Mrs Renauld, her head still bandaged. The French girl was weeping, and imploring her mistress to return to bed.

'Madame will kill herself. It is contrary to all the doctor's orders!'

But Mrs Renauld came on.

'Mother,' cried Jack, starting forward.

But with a gesture she drove him back.

'I am no mother of yours! You are no son of mine! From this day and hour I renounce you.'

'Mother!' cried the lad, stupefied.

For a moment she seemed to waver, to falter before the anguish in his voice. Poirot made a mediating gesture. But instantly she regained command of herself.

'Your father's blood is on your head. You are morally guilty of his death. You thwarted and defied him over this girl, and by your heartless treatment of another girl, you brought about his death. Go out from my house. Tomorrow I intend to take such steps as shall make it certain that you shall never touch a penny of his money. Make your way in the world as best you can with the help of the girl who is the daughter of your father's bitterest enemy!'

And slowly, painfully, she retraced her way upstairs.

We were all dumbfounded – totally unprepared for such a demonstration. Jack Renauld, worn out with all he had already gone through, swayed and nearly fell. Poirot and I went quickly to his assistance.

'He is overdone,' murmured Poirot to Marthe. 'Where can we take him?'

'But home! To the Villa Marguerite. We will nurse him, my mother and I. My poor Jack!'

We got the lad to the villa, where he dropped limply on to a chair in a semi-dazed condition. Poirot felt his head and hands.

'He has fever. The long strain begins to tell. And now this shock on top of it. Get him to bed, and Hastings and I will summon a doctor.'

A doctor was soon procured. After examining the patient, he gave it as his opinion that it was simply a case of nerve strain. With perfect rest and quiet, the lad might be almost restored by the next day, but, if excited, there was a chance of brain fever. It would be advisable for someone to sit up all night with him.

Finally, having done all we could, we left him in the charge of

Marthe and her mother, and set out for the town. It was past our usual hour of dining, and we were both famished. The first restaurant we came to assuaged the pangs of hunger with an excellent omelette, and an equally excellent entrecôte to follow.

'And now for quarters for the night,' said Poirot, when at length *café noir* had completed the meal. 'Shall we try our old friend, the Hôtel de Bains?'

We traced our steps there without more ado. Yes, Messieurs could be accommodated with two good rooms overlooking the sea. Then Poirot asked a question which surprised me:

'Has an English lady, Miss Robinson, arrived?'

'Yes, Monsieur. She is in the little salon.'

'Ah!'

'Poirot,' I cried, keeping pace with him, as he walked along the corridor, 'who on earth is Miss Robinson?'

Poirot beamed kindly on me.

'It is that I have arranged you a marriage, Hastings.'

'But I say –'

'Bah!' said Poirot, giving me a friendly push over the threshold of the door. 'Do you think I wish to trumpet aloud in Merlinville the name of Duveen?'

It was indeed Cinderella who rose to greet us. I took her hand in both of mine. My eyes said the rest.

Poirot cleared his throat.

'*Mes enfants*,' he said, 'for the moment we have no time for sentiment. There is work ahead of us. Mademoiselle, were you able to do what I asked you?'

In response, Cinderella took from her bag an object wrapped up in paper, and handed it silently to Poirot. The latter unwrapped it. I gave a start – for it was the aeroplane dagger which I understood she had cast into the sea. Strange, how reluctant women always are to destroy the most compromising of objects and documents!

'*Très bien, mon enfant*,' said Poirot. 'I am pleased with you. Go now and rest yourself. Hastings here and I have work to do. You shall see him tomorrow.'

'Where are you going?' asked the girl, her eyes widening.

'You shall hear all about it tomorrow.'

'Because wherever you're going, I'm coming too.'

'But, mademoiselle –'

'I'm coming too, I tell you.'

Poirot realized that it was futile to argue. He gave in.

'Come then, mademoiselle. But it will not be amusing. In all probability nothing will happen.'

The girl made no reply.

Twenty minutes later we set forth. It was quite dark now, a close oppressive evening. Poirot led the way out of the town in the direction of the Villa Geneviève. But when he reached the Villa Marguerite he paused.

'I should like to assure myself that all goes well with Jack Renauld. Come with me, Hastings. Mademoiselle will perhaps remain outside. Madame Daubreuil might say something which would wound her.'

We unlatched the gate, and walked up the path. As we went round to the side of the house, I drew Poirot's attention to a window on the first floor. Thrown sharply on the blind was the profile of Marthe Daubreuil.

'Ah!' said Poirot. 'I figure to myself that that is the room where we shall find Jack Renauld.'

Madame Daubreuil opened the door to us. She explained that Jack was much the same, but perhaps we would like to see for ourselves. She led us upstairs and into the bedroom. Marthe Daubreuil was sitting by a table with a lamp on it, working. She put her finger to her lips as we entered.

Jack Renauld was sleeping an uneasy, fitful sleep, his head turning from side to side, and his face still unduly flushed.

'Is the doctor coming again?' asked Poirot in a whisper.

'Not unless we send. He is sleeping – that is the great thing. *Maman* made him a tisane.'

She sat down again with her embroidery as we left the room. Madame Daubreuil accompanied us down the stairs. Since I had learned of her past history, I viewed this woman with increased interest. She stood there with her eyes cast down, the same very faint enigmatical smile that I remembered on her lips. And suddenly I felt afraid of her, as one might feel afraid of a beautiful poisonous snake.

'I hope we have not deranged you, madame,' said Poirot politely, as she opened the door for us to pass out.

'Not at all, monsieur.'

'By the way,' said Poirot, as though struck by an after-thought, 'Monsieur Stonor has not been in Merlinville today, has he?'

I could not at all fathom the point of this question, which I well knew to be meaningless as far as Poirot was concerned.

Madame Daubreuil replied quite composedly:

'Not that I know of.'

'He has not had an interview with Madame Renauld?'

'How should I know that, monsieur?'

'True,' said Poirot. 'I thought you might have seen him coming or going, that is all. Goodnight, madame.'

'Why –' I began.

'No whys, Hastings. There will be time for that later.'

We rejoined Cinderella and made our way rapidly in the direction of the Villa Geneviève. Poirot looked over his shoulder once at the lighted window and the profile of Marthe as she bent over her work.

'He is being guarded at all events,' he muttered.

Arrived at the Villa Geneviève, Poirot took up his stand behind some bushes to the left of the drive, where, while enjoying a good view ourselves, we were completely hidden from sight. The villa itself was in total darkness, everybody was without doubt in bed and asleep. We were almost immediately under the window of Mrs Renauld's bedroom, which window, I noticed, was open. It seemed to me that it was upon this spot that Poirot's eyes were fixed.

'What are we going to do?' I whispered.

'Watch.'

'But –'

'I do not expect anything to happen for at least an hour, probably two hours, but the –'

His words were interrupted by a long, thin drawn cry:

'Help!'

A light flashed up in the first-floor room on the right-hand side of the front door. The cry came from there. And even as we watched there came a shadow on the blind as of two people struggling.

'*Mille tonnerres!*' cried Poirot. 'She must have changed her room.'

Dashing forward, he battered wildly on the front door. Then rushing to the tree in the flower-bed, he swarmed up it with the agility of a cat. I followed him, as with a bound he sprang in through the open window. Looking over my shoulder, I saw Dulcie reaching the branch behind me.

'Take care,' I exclaimed.

'Take care of your grandmother!' retorted the girl. 'This is child's play to me.'

Poirot had rushed through the empty room and was pounding on the door.

'Locked and bolted on the outside,' he growled. 'And it will take time to burst it open.'

The cries for help were getting noticeably fainter. I saw despair in Poirot's eyes. He and I together put our shoulders to the door.

Cinderella's voice, calm and dispassionate, came from the window:

'You'll be too late. I guess I'm the only one who can do anything.'

Before I could move a hand to stop her, she appeared to leap from the window into space. I rushed and looked out. To my horror, I saw her hanging by her hands from the roof, propelling herself along by jerks in the direction of the lighted window.

'Good heavens! She'll be killed,' I cried.

'You forget. She's a professional acrobat, Hastings. It was the providence of the good God that made her insist on coming with us tonight. I only pray that she may be in time. Ah!'

A cry of absolute terror floated out on to the night, as the girl disappeared through the window, and then in Cinderella's clear tones came the words:

'No, you don't! I've got you – and my wrists are just like steel.'

At the same moment the door of our prison was opened cautiously by Françoise. Poirot brushed her aside unceremoniously and rushed down the passage to where the other maids were grouped round the farther door.

'It's locked on the inside, monsieur.'

There was the sound of a heavy fall within. After a moment or two the key turned and the door swung slowly open. Cinderella, very pale, beckoned us in.

'She is safe?' demanded Poirot.

'Yes, I was just in time. She was exhausted.'

Mrs Renauld was half sitting, half lying on the bed. She was gasping for breath.

'Nearly strangled me,' she murmured painfully.

The girl picked up something from the floor and handed it to Poirot. It was a rolled-up ladder of silk rope, very fine but quite strong.

'A getaway,' said Poirot. 'By the window, while we were battering at the door. Where is – the other?'

The girl stood aside a little and pointed. On the ground lay a figure wrapped in some dark material, a fold of which hid the face.

'Dead?'

She nodded.

'I think so. Head must have struck the marble fender.'

'But who is it?' I cried.

'The murderer of Renauld, Hastings. And the would-be murderer of Madame Renauld.'

Puzzled and uncomprehending, I knelt down, and lifting the fold of cloth, looked into the dead beautiful face of Marthe Daubreuil!

CHAPTER 28

JOURNEY'S END

I have confused memories of the further events of that night. Poirot seemed deaf to my repeated questions. He was engaged in overwhelming Françoise with reproaches for not having told him of Mrs Renauld's change of sleeping quarters.

I caught him by the shoulder, determined to attract his attention, and make myself heard.

'But you *must* have known,' I expostulated. 'You were taken up to see her this afternoon.'

Poirot deigned to attend to me for a brief moment.

'She had been wheeled on a sofa into the middle room – her boudoir,' he explained.

'But, monsieur,' cried Françoise, 'Madame changed her room almost immediately after the crimes. The associations – they were too distressing!'

'Then why was I not told?' vociferated Poirot, striking the table, and working himself into a first-class passion. 'I demand of you – why – was – I – not – told? You are an old woman completely imbecile! And Léonie and Denise are no better. All of you are triple idiots! Your stupidity has nearly caused the death of your mistress. But for this courageous child –'

He broke off, and, darting across the room to where the girl was bending over ministering to Mrs Renauld, he embraced her with Gallic fervour – slightly to my annoyance.

I was aroused from my condition of mental fog by a sharp command from Poirot to fetch the doctor immediately on Mrs Renauld's behalf. After that, I might summon the police. And he added, to complete my dudgeon:

'It will hardly be worth your while to return here. I shall be too busy to attend to you, and of Mademoiselle here I make a *garde-malade*.'

I retired with what dignity I could command. Having done my errands, I returned to the hotel. I understood next to nothing of what had occurred. The events of the night seemed fantastic and impossible. Nobody would answer my questions. Nobody had seemed to hear them. Angrily, I flung myself into bed, and slept the sleep of the bewildered and utterly exhausted.

I awoke to find the sun pouring in through the open windows and Poirot, neat and smiling, sitting beside the bed.

'*Enfin*, you wake! But it is that you are a famous sleeper, Hastings! Do you know that it is nearly eleven o'clock?'

I groaned and put a hand to my head.

'I must have been dreaming,' I said. 'Do you know, I actually dreamt that we found Marthe Daubreuil's body in Mrs Renauld's room, and that you declared her to have murdered Mr Renauld?'

'You were not dreaming. All that is quite true.'

'But Bella Duveen killed Mr Renauld?'

'Oh no, Hastings, she did not! She said she did – yes – but that was to save the man she loved from the guillotine.'

'What?'

'Remember Jack Renauld's story. They both arrived on the scene on the same instant, and each took the other to be the perpetrator of the crime. The girl stares at him in horror, and then with a cry rushes away. But, when she hears that the crime has been brought home to him, she cannot bear it, and comes forward to accuse herself and save him from certain death.'

Poirot leaned back in his chair, and brought the tips of his fingers together in familiar style.

'The case was not quite satisfactory to me,' he observed judicially. 'All along I was strongly under the impression that we were dealing with a cold-blooded and premeditated crime committed by someone who had contented themselves (very cleverly) with using Monsieur Renauld's own plans for throwing the police off the track. The great criminal (as you may remember my remarking to you once) is always supremely simple.'

I nodded.

'Now, to support this theory, the criminal must have been fully cognizant of Monsieur Renauld's plans. That leads us to Mrs Renauld. But facts fail to support any theory of her guilt. Is there anyone else who might have known of them? Yes. From Marthe Daubreuil's own lips we have the admission that she overheard Mr Renauld's quarrel with the tramp. If she could overhear that, there is no reason why she should not have heard everything else, especially if Mr and Madame Renauld were imprudent enough to discuss their plans sitting on the bench. Remember how easily you overheard Marthe's conversation with Jack Renauld from that spot.'

'But what possible motive could Marthe have for murdering Mr Renauld?' I argued.

'What motive! Money! Renauld was a millionaire several times over, and at his death (or so she and Jack believed) half that vast fortune would pass to his son. Let us reconstruct the scene from the standpoint of Marthe Daubreuil.

'Marthe Daubreuil overhears what passes between Renauld and his wife. So far he has been a nice little source of income to the Daubreuil mother and daughter, but now he proposes to escape from their toils. At first, possibly, her idea is to prevent that escape. But a bolder idea takes its place, and one that fails to horrify the daughter of Jeanne Beroldy! At present Renauld stands inexorably in the way of her marriage with Jack. If the latter defies his father, he will be a pauper – which is not at all to the mind of Mademoiselle Marthe. In fact, I doubt if she has ever cared a straw for Jack Renauld. She can simulate emotion but in reality she is of the same cold, calculating type as her mother. I doubt, too, whether she was really very sure of her hold over the boy's affections. She had dazzled and captivated him, but separated from her, as his father could so easily manage to separate him, she might lose him. But with Renauld dead, and Jack the heir to half his millions, the marriage can take place at once, and at a stroke she will attain wealth – not the beggarly thousands that have been extracted from him so far. And her clever brain takes in the simplicity of the thing. It is all so easy. Renauld is planning all the circumstances of his death – she has only to step in at the right moment and turn the farce into a grim reality. And here comes in the second point which led me infallibly to Marthe Daubreuil – the dagger! Jack Renauld had *three* souvenirs made. One he gave to his mother, one to Bella Duveen – was it not highly probable that he had given the third one to Marthe Daubreuil?

'So, then, to sum up, there were four points of note against Marthe Daubreuil:

'1. Marthe Daubreuil could have overheard Renauld's plans.
'2. Marthe Daubreuil had a direct interest in causing Renauld's death.
'3. Marthe Daubreuil was the daughter of the notorious Madame Beroldy who in my opinion was morally and virtually the murderess of her husband, although it may have been Georges Conneau's hand which struck the actual blow.
'4. Marthe Daubreuil was the only person, besides Jack Renauld, likely to have the third dagger in her possession.'

Poirot paused and cleared his throat.

'Of course, when I learned of the existence of the other girl, Bella Duveen, I realized that it was quite possible that *she* might have killed Renauld. The solution did not commend itself to me, because, as I pointed out to you, Hastings, an expert, such as I am, likes to meet a foeman worthy of his steel. Still, one must take crimes as one finds them, not as one would like them to be. It did not seem very likely that Bella Duveen would be wandering about carrying a souvenir paper-knife in her hand, but of course she might have had some idea all the time of revenging herself on Jack Renauld. When she actually came forward and confessed to the murder, it seemed that all was over. And yet – I was not satisfied, *mon ami. I was not satisfied . . .*

'I went over the case again minutely, and I came to the same conclusion as before. If it was *not* Bella Duveen, the only other person who could have committed the crime was Marthe Daubreuil. But I had not one single proof against her!

'And then you showed me that letter from Mademoiselle Dulcie, and I saw a chance of settling the matter once for all. The original dagger was stolen by Dulcie Duveen and thrown into the sea – since, as she thought, it belonged to her sister. But if, by any chance, it was *not* her sister's, but the one given by Jack to Marthe Daubreuil – why then, Bella Duveen's dagger would be still intact! I said no word to you, Hastings (it was no time for romance), but I sought out Mademoiselle Dulcie, told her as much as I deemed needful, and set her to search among the effects of her sister. Imagine my elation, when she sought me out (according to my instructions) as Miss Robinson, with the precious souvenir in her possession!

'In the meantime I had taken steps to force Mademoiselle Marthe into the open. By my orders, Madame Renauld repulsed her son, and declared her intention of making a will on the morrow which should cut him off from ever enjoying even a portion of his father's fortune. It was a desperate step, but a necessary one, and Madame Renauld was fully prepared to take the risk – though unfortunately she also never thought of mentioning her change of room. I suppose she took it for granted that I knew. All happened as I thought. Marthe Daubreuil made a last bold bid for the Renauld millions – and failed!'

'What absolutely bewilders me,' I said, 'is how she ever got into the house without our seeing her. It seems an absolute miracle. We left her behind at the Villa Marguerite, we go straight to the Villa Geneviève – and yet she is there before us!'

'Ah, but we did not leave her behind. She was out of the Villa Marguerite by the back way while we were talking to her mother in the hall. That is where, as the Americans say, she "put it over" on Hercule Poirot!'

'But the shadow on the blind? We saw it from the road.'

'*Eh bien*, when we looked up, Madame Daubreuil had just had time to run upstairs and take her place.'

'Madame Daubreuil?'

'Yes. One is old, and one is young, one dark, and one fair, but, for the purpose of a silhouette on a blind, their profiles are singularly alike. Even I did not suspect – triple imbecile that I was! I thought I had plenty of time before me – that she would not try to gain admission to the villa until much later. She had brains, that beautiful Mademoiselle Marthe.'

'And her object was to murder Mrs Renauld?'

'Yes. The whole fortune would then pass to her son. But it would have been suicide, *mon ami!* On the floor by Marthe Daubreuil's body, I found a pad and a little bottle of chloroform and a hypodermic syringe containing a fatal dose of morphine. You understand? The chloroform first – then when the victim is unconscious the prick of the needle. By the morning the smell of the chloroform has quite disappeared, and the syringe lies where it has fallen from Madame Renauld's hand. What would he say, the excellent Monsieur Hautet? "Poor woman! What did I tell you? The shock of joy, it was too much on top of the rest! Did I not say that I should not be surprised if her brain became unhinged. Altogether a most tragic case, the Renauld Case!"

'However, Hastings, things did not go quite as Mademoiselle Marthe had planned. To begin with, Madame Renauld was awake and waiting for her. There is a struggle. But Madame Renauld is terribly weak still. There is a last chance for Marthe Daubreuil. The idea of suicide is at an end, but if she can silence Madame Renauld with her strong hands, make a getaway with her little silk ladder while we are still battering on the inside of the farther door, and be back at the Villa Marguerite before we return there, it will be hard to prove anything against her. But she was checkmated, not by Hercule Poirot, but by *la petite acrobate* with her wrists of steel.'

I mused over the whole story.

'When did you first begin to suspect Marthe Daubreuil, Poirot? When she told us she had overheard the quarrel in the garden?'

Poirot smiled.

'My friend, do you remember when we drove into Merlinville that first day? And the beautiful girl we saw standing at the gate? You asked me if I had noticed a young goddess, and I replied to you that I had seen only a girl with anxious eyes. That is how I have thought of Marthe Daubreuil from the beginning. *The girl with the anxious eyes!* Why was she anxious? Not on Jack Renauld's behalf, for she did not know then that he had been in Merlinville the previous evening.'

'By the way,' I exclaimed, 'how is Jack Renauld?'

'Much better. He is still at the Villa Marguerite. But Madame Daubreuil has disappeared. The police are looking for her.'

'Was she in with her daughter, do you think?'

'We shall never know. Madame is a lady who can keep her secrets. And I doubt very much if the police will ever find her.'

'Has Jack Renauld been – told?'

'Not yet.'

'It will be a terrible shock to him.'

'Naturally. And yet, do you know, Hastings, I doubt if his heart was ever seriously engaged? So far we have looked upon Bella Duveen as a siren, and Marthe Daubreuil as the girl he really loved. But I think that if we reversed the terms we should come nearer to the truth. Marthe Daubreuil was very beautiful. She set herself to fascinate Jack, and she succeeded, but remember his curious reluctance to break with the other girl. And see how he was willing to go to the guillotine rather than implicate her. I have a little idea that when he learns the truth, he will be horrified – revolted, and his false love will wither away.'

'What about Giraud?'

'He has a *crise* of the nerves, that one! He has been obliged to return to Paris.'

We both smiled.

Poirot proved a fairly true prophet. When at length the doctor pronounced Jack Renauld strong enough to hear the truth, it was Poirot who broke it to him. The shock was indeed terrific. Yet Jack rallied better than I could have supposed possible. His mother's devotion helped him to live through those difficult days. The mother and son were inseparable now.

There was a further revelation to come. Poirot had acquainted Mrs Renauld with the fact that he knew her secret, and had represented to her that Jack should not be left in ignorance of his father's past.

'To hide the truth, never does it avail, madame! Be brave and tell him everything.'

With a heavy heart Mrs Renauld consented, and her son learned that the father he had loved had been in actual fact a fugitive from justice. A halting question was promptly answered by Poirot.

'Reassure yourself, Monsieur Jack. The world knows nothing. As far as I can see, there is no obligation for me to take the police into my confidence. Throughout the case I have acted, not for them, but for your father. Justice overtook him at last, but no one need ever know that he and Georges Conneau were one and the same.'

There were, of course, various points in the case that remained puzzling to the police, but Poirot explained things in so plausible a fashion that all query about them was gradually stilled.

Shortly after we got back to London, I noticed a magnificent model of a foxhound adorning Poirot's mantelpiece. In answer to my inquiring glance, Poirot nodded.

'*Mais oui!* I got my five hundred francs! Is he not a splendid fellow? I call him Giraud!'

A few days later Jack Renauld came to see us with a resolute expression on his face.

'Monsieur Poirot, I've come to say goodbye. I'm sailing for South America almost immediately. My father had large interests over the continent, and I mean to start a new life out there.'

'You go alone, Monsieur Jack?'

'My mother comes with me – and I shall keep Stonor on as my secretary. He likes out-of-the-way parts of the world.'

'No one else goes with you?'

Jack flushed.

'You mean –?'

'A girl who loves you very dearly – who has been willing to lay down her life for you.'

'How could I ask her?' muttered the boy. 'After all that has happened, could I go to her and – Oh, what sort of a lame story could I tell?'

'*Les femmes* – they have a wonderful genius for manufacturing crutches for stories like that.'

'Yes, but – I've been such a damned fool.'

'So have all of us, one time and another,' observed Poirot philosophically.

But Jack's face had hardened.

'There's something else. I'm my father's son. Would anyone marry me, knowing that?'

'You are your father's son, you say. Hastings here will tell you that I believe in heredity –'

'Well, then –'

'Wait. I know a woman, a woman of courage and endurance, capable of great love, of supreme self-sacrifice –'

The boy looked up. His eyes softened.

'My mother!'

'Yes. You are your mother's son as well as your father's. Then go to Mademoiselle Bella. Tell her everything. Keep nothing back – and see what she will say!'

Jack looked irresolute.

'Go to her as a boy no longer, but a man – a man bowed by the fate of the Past, and the fate of Today, but looking forward to a new and wonderful life. Ask her to share it with you. You may not realize it, but your love for each other has been tested in the fire and not found wanting. You have both been willing to lay down your lives for each other.'

And what of Captain Arthur Hastings, humble chronicler of these pages?

There is some talk of his joining the Renaulds on a ranch across the seas, but for the end of this story I prefer to go back to a morning in the garden of the Villa Geneviève.

'I can't call you Bella,' I said, 'since it isn't your name. And Dulcie seems so unfamiliar. So it's got to be Cinderella. Cinderella married the Prince, you remember. I'm not a Prince, but –'

She interrupted me.

'Cinderella warned him, I'm sure. You see, she couldn't promise to turn into a princess. She was only a little scullion after all –'

'It's the Prince's turn to interrupt,' I interpolated. 'Do you know what he said?'

'No?'

'"Hell!" said the Prince – and kissed her!'

And I suited the action to the word.

THE MYSTERY OF THE BLUE TRAIN

To the two
distinguished members
of the O.F.D.
Carlotta and Peter

CONTENTS

CHAPTER 1

THE MAN WITH THE WHITE HAIR

It was close on midnight when a man crossed the Place de la Concorde. In spite of the handsome fur coat which garbed his meagre form, there was something essentially weak and paltry about him.

A little man with a face like a rat. A man, one would say, who could never play a conspicuous part, or rise to prominence in any sphere. And yet, in leaping to such a conclusion, an onlooker would have been wrong. For this man, negligible and inconspicuous as he seemed, played a prominent part in the destiny of the world. In an Empire where rats ruled, he was the king of the rats.

Even now, an Embassy awaited his return. But he had business to do first – business of which the Embassy was not officially cognizant. His face gleamed white and sharp in the moonlight. There was the least hint of a curve in the thin nose. His father had been a Polish Jew, a journeyman tailor. It was business such as his father would have loved that took him abroad tonight.

He came to the Seine, crossed it, and entered one of the less reputable quarters of Paris. Here he stopped before a tall, dilapidated house and made his way up to an apartment on the fourth floor. He had barely time to knock before the door was opened by a woman who had evidently been awaiting his arrival. She gave him no greeting, but helped him off with his overcoat and then led the way into the tawdrily furnished sitting-room. The electric light was shaded with dirty pink festoons, and it softened, but could not disguise, the girl's face with its mask of crude paint. Could not disguise, either, the broad Mongolian cast of her countenance. There was no doubt of Olga Demiroff's profession, nor of her nationality.

'All is well, little one?'

'All is well, Boris Ivanovitch.'

He nodded, murmuring: 'I do not think I have been followed.'

But there was anxiety in his tone. He went to the window, drawing the curtains aside slightly, and peering carefully out. He started away violently.

'There are two men – on the opposite pavement. It looks to me –' He broke off and began gnawing at his nails – a habit he had when anxious.

The Russian girl was shaking her head with a slow, reassuring action.

'They were here before you came.'

'All the same, it looks to me as though they were watching this house.'

'Possibly,' she admitted indifferently.

'But then –'

'What of it? Even if they *know* – it will not be *you* they will follow from here.'

A thin, cruel smile came to his lips.

'No,' he admitted, 'that is true.'

He mused for a minute or two, and then observed,

'This damned American – he can look after himself as well as anybody.'

'I suppose so.'

He went again to the window.

'Tough customers,' he muttered, with a chuckle. 'Known to the police, I fear. Well, well, I wish Brother Apache good hunting.'

Olga Demiroff shook her head.

'If the American is the kind of man they say he is, it will take more than a couple of cowardly apaches to get the better of him.' She paused. 'I wonder –'

'Well?'

'Nothing. Only twice this evening a man has passed along this street – a man with white hair.'

'What of it?'

'This. As he passed those two men, he dropped his glove. One of them picked it up and returned it to him. A threadbare device.'

'You mean – that the white-haired man is – their employer?'

'Something of the kind.'

The Russian looked alarmed and uneasy.

'You are sure – the parcel is safe? It has not been tampered with? There has been too much talk . . . much too much talk.'

He gnawed his nails again.

'Judge for yourself.'

She bent to the fireplace, deftly removing the coals. Underneath, from amongst the crumpled balls of newspaper, she selected from the very middle an oblong package wrapped round with grimy newspaper, and handed it to the man.

'Ingenious,' he said, with a nod of approval.

'The apartment has been searched twice. The mattress on my bed was ripped open.'

'It is as I said,' he muttered. 'There has been too much talk. This haggling over the price – it was a mistake.'

He had unwrapped the newspaper. Inside was a small brown paper parcel. This in turn he unwrapped, verified the contents, and quickly wrapped it up once more. As he did so, an electric bell rang sharply.

'The American is punctual,' said Olga, with a glance at the clock.

She left the room. In a minute she returned ushering in a stranger, a big, broad-shouldered man whose transatlantic origin was evident. His keen glance went from one to the other.

'M. Krassnine?' he inquired politely.

'I am he,' said Boris. 'I must apologize for – for the unconventionality of this meeting-place. But secrecy is urgent. I – I cannot afford to be connected with this business in any way.'

'Is that so?' said the American politely.

'I have your word, have I not, that no details of this transaction will be made public? That is one of the conditions of – sale.'

The American nodded.

'That has already been agreed upon,' he said indifferently. 'Now, perhaps, you will produce the goods.'

'You have the money – in notes?'

'Yes,' replied the other.

He did not, however, make any attempt to produce it. After a moment's hesitation, Krassnine gestured towards the small parcel on the table.

The American took it up and unrolled the wrapping paper. The contents he took over to a small electric lamp and submitted them to a very thorough examination. Satisfied, he drew from his pocket a thick leather wallet and extracted from it a wad of notes. These he handed to the Russian, who counted them carefully.

'All right?'

'I thank you, Monsieur. Everything is correct.'

'Ah!' said the other. He slipped the brown paper parcel negligently into his pocket. He bowed to Olga. 'Good evening, Mademoiselle. Good evening, M. Krassnine.'

He went out, shutting the door behind him. The eyes of the two in the room met. The man passed his tongue over his dry lips.

'I wonder – will he ever get back to his hotel?' he muttered.

By common accord, they both turned to the window. They were just in time to see the American emerge into the street below. He turned to the left and marched along at a good pace without once turning his head. Two shadows stole from a doorway and followed noiselessly. Pursuers and pursued vanished into the night. Olga Demiroff spoke.

'He will get back safely,' she said. 'You need not fear – or hope – whichever it is.'

'Why do you think he will be safe?' asked Krassnine curiously.

'A man who has made as much money as he has could not possibly be a fool,' said Olga. 'And talking of money –'

She looked significantly at Krassnine.

'Eh?'

'My share, Boris Ivanovitch.'

With some reluctance, Krassnine handed over two of the notes. She nodded her thanks, with a complete lack of emotion, and tucked them away in her stocking.

'That is good,' she remarked, with satisfaction.

He looked at her curiously.

'You have no regrets, Olga Vassilovna?'

'Regrets? For what?'

'For what has been in your keeping. There are women – most women, I believe, who go mad over such things.'

She nodded reflectively.

'Yes, you speak truth there. Most women have that madness. I – have not. I wonder now –' She broke off.

'Well?' asked the other curiously.

'The American will be safe with them – yes, I am sure of that. But afterwards –'

'Eh? What are you thinking of?'

'He will give them, of course, to some woman,' said Olga thoughtfully. 'I wonder what will happen then . . .'

She shook herself impatiently and went over to the window.

Suddenly she uttered an exclamation and called to her companion.

'See, he is going down the street now – the man I mean.'

They both gazed down together. A slim, elegant figure was progressing along at a leisurely pace. He wore an opera hat and a cloak. As he passed a street lamp, the light illuminated a thatch of thick white hair.

CHAPTER 2

M. LE MARQUIS

The man with the white hair continued on his course, unhurried, and seemingly indifferent to his surroundings. He took a side turning to the right and another one to the left. Now and then he hummed a little air to himself.

Suddenly he stopped dead and listened intently. He had heard a certain sound. It might have been the bursting of a tyre or it might have been – a shot. A curious smile played round his lips for a minute. Then he resumed his leisurely walk.

On turning a corner he came upon a scene of some activity. A representative of the law was making notes in a pocket-book, and one or two late passers-by had collected on the spot. To one of these the man with the white hair made a polite request for information.

'Something has been happening, yes?'

'*Mais oui*, Monsieur. Two apaches set upon an elderly American gentleman.'

'They did him no injury?'

'No, indeed.' The man laughed. 'The American, he had a revolver in his pocket, and before they could attack him, he fired shots so closely round them that they took alarm and fled. The police, as usual, arrived too late.'

'Ah!' said the inquirer.

He displayed no emotion of any kind.

Placidly and unconcernedly he resumed his nocturnal strolling. Presently he crossed the Seine and came into the richer areas of the city. It was some twenty minutes later that he came to a stop before a certain house in a quiet but aristocratic thoroughfare.

The shop, for shop it was, was a restrained and unpretentious one. D. Papopolous, dealer in antiques, was so known to fame that he needed no advertisement, and indeed most of his business was not done over a counter. M. Papopolous had a very handsome apartment of his own overlooking the Champs Elysées, and it might reasonably be supposed that he would have been found there and not at his place of business at such an hour, but the man with the white hair seemed confident of success as he pressed the obscurely placed bell, having first given a quick glance up and down the deserted street.

His confidence was not misplaced. The door opened and a man stood in the aperture. He wore gold rings in his ears and was of a swarthy cast of countenance.

'Good evening,' said the stranger. 'Your master is within?'

'The master is here, but he does not see chance visitors at this time of night,' growled the other.

'I think he will see me. Tell him that his friend M. le Marquis is here.'

The man opened the door a little wider and allowed the visitor to enter.

The man who gave his name as M. le Marquis had shielded his face with his hand as he spoke. When the man-servant returned with the information that M. Papopolous would be pleased to receive the visitor a further change had taken place in the stranger's appearance. The man-servant must have been very unobservant or very well trained, for he betrayed no surprise at the small black satin mask which hid the other's features. Leading the way to a door at the end of the hall, he opened it and announced in a respectful murmur: '*M. le Marquis.*'

The figure which rose to receive this strange guest was an imposing one. There was something venerable and patriarchal about M. Papopolous. He had a high domed forehead and a beautiful white beard. His manner had in it something ecclesiastical and benign.

'My dear friend,' said M. Papopolous.

He spoke in French and his tones were rich and unctuous.

'I must apologise,' said the visitor, 'for the lateness of the hour.'

'Not at all. Not at all,' said M. Papopolous – 'an interesting time of night. You have had, perhaps, an interesting evening?'

'Not personally,' said M. le Marquis.

'Not personally,' repeated M. Papopolous, 'no, no, of course not. And there is news, eh?'

He cast a sharp glance sideways at the other, a glance that was not ecclesiastical or benign in the least.

'There is no news. The attempt failed. I hardly expected anything else.'

'Quite so,' said M. Papopolous: 'anything crude –'

He waved his hand to express his intense distaste for crudity in any form. There was indeed nothing crude about M. Papopolous nor about the goods he handled. He was well known in most European courts, and kings called him Demetrius in a friendly manner. He had the reputation for the most exquisite discretion. That, together with the nobility of his aspect, had carried him through several very questionable transactions.

'The direct attack –' said M. Papopolous. He shook his head. 'It answers sometimes – but very seldom.'

The other shrugged his shoulders.

'It saves time,' he remarked, 'and to fail costs nothing – or next to nothing. The other plan – will not fail.'

'Ah,' said M. Papopolous, looking at him keenly.

The other nodded slowly.

'I have great confidence in your – er – reputation,' said the antique dealer.

M. le Marquis smiled gently.

'I think I may say,' he murmured, 'that your confidence will not be misplaced.'

'You have unique opportunities,' said the other, with a note of envy in his voice.

'I make them,' said M. le Marquis.

He rose and took up the cloak which he had thrown carelessly on the back of a chair.

'I will keep you informed, M. Papopolous, through the usual channels, but there must be no hitch in your arrangements.'

M. Papopolous was pained.

'There is *never* a hitch in my arrangements,' he complained.

The other smiled, and without any further word of adieu he left the room, closing the door behind him.

M. Papopolous remained in thought for a moment, stroking his venerable white beard, and then moved across to a second door which opened inwards. As he turned the handle, a young woman, who only too clearly had been leaning against it with her ear to the keyhole, stumbled headlong into the room. M. Papopolous displayed neither surprise nor concern. It was evidently all quite natural to him.

'Well, Zia?' he asked.

'I did not hear him go,' explained Zia.

She was a handsome young woman, built on Junoesque lines, with dark flashing eyes and such a general air of resemblance to M. Papopolous that it was easy to see they were father and daughter.

'It is annoying,' she continued vexedly, 'that one cannot see through a keyhole and hear through it at the same time.'

'It has often annoyed me,' said M. Papopolous, with great simplicity.

'So that is M. le Marquis,' said Zia slowly. 'Does he always wear a mask, Father?'

'Always.'

There was a pause.

'It is the rubies, I suppose?' asked Zia.

Her father nodded.

'What do you think, my little one?' he inquired, with a hint of amusement in his beady black eyes.

'Of M. le Marquis?'

'Yes.'

'I think,' said Zia slowly, 'that it is a very rare thing to find a well-bred Englishman who speaks French as well as that.'

'Ah!' said M. Papopolous, 'so that is what you think.'

As usual, he did not commit himself, but he regarded Zia with benign approval.

'I thought, too,' said Zia, 'that his head was an odd shape.'

'Massive,' said her father – 'a trifle massive. But then that effect is always created by a wig.'

They both looked at each other and smiled.

CHAPTER 3

HEART OF FIRE

Rufus Van Aldin passed through the revolving doors of the Savoy, and walked to the reception desk. The desk clerk smiled a respectful greeting.

'Pleased to see you back again, Mr Van Aldin,' he said.

The American millionaire nodded his head in a casual greeting.

'Everything all right?' he asked.

'Yes, sir. Major Knighton is upstairs in the suite now.'

Van Aldin nodded again.

'Any mail?' he vouchsafed.

'They have all been sent up, Mr Van Aldin. Oh! wait a minute.'

He dived into a pigeon-hole, and produced a letter.

'Just come this minute,' he explained.

Rufus Van Aldin took the letter from him, and as he saw the handwriting, a woman's flowing hand, his face was suddenly transformed. The harsh contours of it softened, and the hard line of his mouth relaxed. He looked a different man. He walked across to the lift with the letter in his hand and the smile still on his lips.

In the drawing-room of his suite, a young man was sitting at a desk nimbly sorting correspondence with the ease born of long practice. He sprang up as Van Aldin entered.

'Hallo, Knighton!'

'Glad to see you back, sir. Had a good time?'

'So so!' said the millionaire unemotionally. 'Paris is rather a one-horse city nowadays. Still – I got what I went over for.'

He smiled to himself rather grimly.

'You usually do, I believe,' said the secretary, laughing.

'That's so,' agreed the other.

He spoke in a matter-of-fact manner, as one stating a well-known fact. Throwing off his heavy overcoat, he advanced to the desk.

'Anything urgent?'

'I don't think so, sir. Mostly the usual stuff. I have not quite finished sorting it out.'

Van Aldin nodded briefly. He was a man who seldom expressed

either blame or praise. His methods with those he employed were simple; he gave them a fair trial and dismissed promptly those who were inefficient. His selections of people were unconventional. Knighton, for instance, he had met casually at a Swiss resort two months previously. He had approved of the fellow, looked up his war record, and found in it the explanation of the limp with which he walked. Knighton had made no secret of the fact that he was looking for a job, and indeed diffidently asked the millionaire if he knew of any available post. Van Aldin remembered, with a grim smile of amusement, the young man's complete astonishment when he had been offered the post of secretary to the great man himself.

'But – but I have no experience of business,' he had stammered.

'That doesn't matter a cuss,' Van Aldin had replied. 'I have got three secretaries already to attend to that kind of thing. But I am likely to be in England for the next six months, and I want an Englishman who – well, knows the ropes – and can attend to the social side of things for me.'

So far, Van Aldin had found his judgement confirmed. Knighton had proved quick, intelligent, and resourceful, and he had a distinct charm of manner.

The secretary indicated three or four letters placed by themselves on the top of the desk.

'It might perhaps be as well, sir, if you glanced at these,' he suggested. 'The top one is about the Colton agreement –'

But Rufus Van Aldin held up a protesting hand.

'I am not going to look at a durned thing tonight,' he declared. 'They can all wait till the morning. Except this one,' he added, looking down at the letter he held in his hand. And again that strange transforming smile stole over his face.

Richard Knighton smiled sympathetically.

'Mrs Kettering?' he murmured. 'She rang up yesterday and today. She seems very anxious to see you at once, sir.'

'Does she, now!'

The smile faded from the millionaire's face. He ripped open the envelope which he held in his hand and took out the enclosed sheet. As he read it his face darkened, his mouth set grimly in the line which Wall Street knew so well, and his brows knit themselves ominously. Knighton turned tactfully away, and went on opening letters and sorting them. A muttered oath escaped the millionaire, and his clenched fist hit the table sharply.

'I'll not stand for this,' he muttered to himself. 'Poor little girl, it's a good thing she has her old father behind her.'

He walked up and down the room for some minutes, his brows drawn together in a scowl. Knighton still bent assiduously over the desk. Suddenly Van Aldin came to an abrupt halt. He took up his overcoat from the chair where he had thrown it.

'Are you going out again, sir?'

'Yes, I'm going round to see my daughter.'

'If Colton's people ring up –?'

'Tell them to go to the devil,' said Van Aldin.

'Very well,' said the secretary unemotionally.

Van Aldin had his overcoat on by now. Cramming his hat upon his head, he went towards the door. He paused with his hand upon the handle.

'You are a good fellow, Knighton,' he said. 'You don't worry me when I am rattled.'

Knighton smiled a little, but made no reply.

'Ruth is my only child,' said Van Aldin, 'and there is no one on this earth who knows quite what she means to me.'

A faint smile irradiated his face. He slipped his hand into his pocket.

'Care to see something, Knighton?'

He came back towards the secretary.

From his pocket he drew out a parcel carelessly wrapped in brown paper. He tossed off the wrapping and disclosed a big, shabby, red velvet case. In the centre of it were some twisted initials surmounted by a crown. He snapped the case open, and the secretary drew in his breath sharply. Against the slightly dingy white of the interior, the stones glowed like blood.

'My God! sir,' said Knighton. 'Are they – are they real?'

Van Aldin laughed a quiet little cackle of amusement.

'I don't wonder at your asking that. Amongst these rubies are the three largest in the world. Catherine of Russia wore them, Knighton. That centre one there is known as "Heart of Fire". It's perfect – not a flaw in it.'

'But,' the secretary murmured, 'they must be worth a fortune.'

'Four or five hundred thousand dollars,' said Van Aldin nonchalantly, 'and that is apart from the historical interest.'

'And you carry them about – like that, loose in your pocket?'

Van Aldin laughed amusedly.

'I guess so. You see, they are my little present for Ruthie.'

The secretary smiled discreetly.

'I can understand now Mrs Kettering's anxiety over the telephone,' he murmured.

But Van Aldin shook his head. The hard look returned to his face.

'You are wrong there,' he said. 'She doesn't know about these; they are my little surprise for her.'

He shut the case, and began slowly to wrap it up again.

'It's a hard thing, Knighton,' he said, 'how little one can do for those one loves. I can buy a good portion of the earth for Ruth, if it would be any use to her, but it isn't. I can hang these things round her neck and give her a moment or two's pleasure, maybe, but –'

He shook his head.

'When a woman is not happy in her home –'

He left the sentence unfinished. The secretary nodded discreetly. He knew, none better, the reputation of the Hon. Derek Kettering. Van Aldin sighed. Slipping the parcel back in his coat pocket, he nodded to Knighton and left the room.

CHAPTER 4

IN CURZON STREET

The Hon. Mrs Derek Kettering lived in Curzon Street. The butler who opened the door recognized Rufus Van Aldin at once and permitted himself a discreet smile of greeting. He led the way upstairs to the big double drawing-room on the first floor.

A woman who was sitting by the window started up with a cry.

'Why, Dad, if that isn't too good for anything! I've been telephoning Major Knighton all day to try and get hold of you, but he couldn't say for sure when you were expected back.'

Ruth Kettering was twenty-eight years of age. Without being beautiful, or in the real sense of the word even pretty, she was striking-looking because of her colouring. Van Aldin had been called Carrots and Ginger in his time, and Ruth's hair was almost pure auburn. With it went dark eyes and very black lashes – the effect somewhat enhanced by art. She was tall and slender, and moved well. At a careless glance it was the face of a Raphael Madonna. Only if one looked closely did one perceive the same line of jaw and chin as in Van Aldin's face, bespeaking the same hardness and determination. It suited the man, but suited the woman less well. From her childhood upward Ruth Van Aldin had been accustomed to having her own way, and anyone who had ever stood up against her soon realized that Rufus Van Aldin's daughter never gave in.

'Knighton told me you'd 'phoned him,' said Van Aldin. 'I only got back from Paris half an hour ago. What's all this about Derek?'

Ruth Kettering flushed angrily.

'It's unspeakable. It's beyond all limits,' she cried. 'He – he doesn't seem to listen to anything I say.'

There was bewilderment as well as anger in her voice.

'He'll listen to me,' said the millionaire grimly.

Ruth went on.

'I've hardly seen him for the last month. He goes about everywhere with that woman.'

'With what woman?'

'Mirelle. She dances at the Parthenon, you know.'

Van Aldin nodded.

'I was down at Leconbury last week. I – I spoke to Lord Leconbury. He was awfully sweet to me, sympathized entirely. He said he'd give Derek a good talking to.'

'Ah!' said Van Aldin.

'What do you mean by "Ah!" Dad?'

'Just what you think I mean, Ruthie. Poor old Leconbury is a washout. Of course he sympathized with you, of course he tried to soothe you down. Having got his son and heir married to the daughter of one of the richest men in the States, he naturally doesn't want to mess the thing up. But he's got one foot in the grave already, everyone knows that, and anything he may say will cut darned little ice with Derek.'

'Can't *you* do anything, Dad?' urged Ruth, after a minute or two.

'I might,' said the millionaire. He waited a second reflectively, and then went on. 'There are several things I might do, but there's only one that will be any real good. How much pluck have you got, Ruthie?'

She stared at him. He nodded back at her.

'I mean just what I say. Have you got the grit to admit to all the world that you've made a mistake? There's only one way out of this mess, Ruthie. Cut your losses and start afresh.'

'You mean –?'

'Divorce.'

'Divorce!'

Van Aldin smiled drily.

'You say that word, Ruth, as though you'd never heard it before. And yet your friends are doing it all round you every day.'

'Oh! I know that. But –'

She stopped, biting her lip. Her father nodded comprehendingly.

'I know, Ruth. You're like me, you can't bear to let go. But I've learnt, and you've got to learn, that there are times when it's the only way. I might find ways of whistling Derek back to you, but it would all come to the same in the end. *He's no good*, Ruth; he's rotten through and through. And mind you, I blame myself for ever letting you marry him. But you were kind of set on having him, and he seemed in earnest about turning over a new leaf – and well, I'd crossed you once, honey . . .'

He did not look at her as he said the last words. Had he done so, he might have seen the swift colour that came up in her face.

'You did,' she said in a hard voice.

'I was too durned soft-hearted to do it a second time. I can't tell you how I wish I had, though. You've led a poor kind of life for the last few years, Ruth.'

'It has not been very – agreeable,' agreed Mrs Kettering.

'That's why I say to you that this thing has got to *stop*!' He brought his hand down with a bang on the table. 'You may have a hankering after the fellow still. *Cut it out.* Face facts. Derek Kettering married you for your money. That's all there is to it. Get rid of him, Ruth.'

Ruth Kettering looked down at the ground for some moments, then she said, without raising her head:

'Supposing he doesn't consent?'

Van Aldin looked at her in astonishment.

'He won't have a say in the matter.'

She flushed and bit her lip.

'No – no – of course not. I only meant –'

She stopped. Her father eyed her keenly.

'What did you mean?'

'I meant –' She paused, choosing her words carefully. 'He mayn't take it lying down.'

The millionaire's chin shot out grimly.

'You mean he'll fight the case? Let him! But, as a matter of fact, you're wrong. He won't fight. Any solicitor he consults will tell him he hasn't a leg to stand upon.'

'You don't think' – she hesitated – 'I mean – out of sheer spite against me – he might, well, try to make it awkward?'

Her father looked at her in some astonishment.

'Fight the case, you mean?'

He shook his head.

'Very unlikely. You see, he would have to have something to go upon.'

Mrs Kettering did not answer. Van Aldin looked at her sharply.

'Come, Ruth, out with it. There's something troubling you – what is it?'

'Nothing, nothing at all.'

But her voice was unconvincing.

'You are dreading the publicity, eh? Is that it? You leave it to me. I'll put the whole thing through so smoothly that there will be no fuss at all.'

'Very well, Dad, if you really think it's the best thing to be done.'

'Got a fancy for the fellow still, Ruth? Is that it?'

'No.'

The word came with no uncertain emphasis. Van Aldin seemed satisfied. He patted his daughter on the shoulder.

'It will be all right, little girl. Don't you worry any. Now let's forget about all this. I have brought you a present from Paris.'

'For me? Something very nice?'

'I hope you'll think so,' said Van Aldin, smiling.

He took the parcel from his coat pocket and handed it to her. She unwrapped it eagerly, and snapped open the case. A long-drawn 'Oh!' came from her lips. Ruth Kettering loved jewels – always had done so.

'Dad, how – how wonderful!'

'Rather in a class by themselves, aren't they?' said the millionaire with satisfaction. 'You like them, eh.'

'Like them? Dad, they're unique. How did you get hold of them?'

Van Aldin smiled.

'Ah! that's my secret. They had to be bought privately, of course. They are rather well known. See that big stone in the middle? You have heard of it, maybe; that's the historic "Heart of Fire".'

'"Heart of Fire"!' repeated Mrs Kettering.

She had taken the stones from the case and was holding them against her breast. The millionaire watched her. He was thinking of the series of women who had worn the jewels. The heartaches, the despairs, the jealousies. 'Heart of Fire,' like all famous stones, had left behind it a trail of tragedy and violence. Held in Ruth Kettering's assured hand, it seemed to lose its potency of evil. With her cool, equable poise, this woman of the western world seemed a negation to tragedy or heart-burnings. Ruth returned the stones to their case; then, jumping up, she flung her arms round her father's neck.

'Thank you, thank you, thank you, Dad. They are wonderful! You do give me the most marvellous presents always.'

'That's all right,' said Van Aldin, patting her shoulder. 'You are all I have, you know, Ruthie.'

'You will stay to dinner, won't you, Father?'

'I don't think so. You were going out, weren't you?'

'Yes, but I can easily put that off. Nothing very exciting.'

'No,' said Van Aldin. 'Keep your engagement. I have got a good deal to attend to. See you tomorrow, my dear. Perhaps if I 'phone you, we can meet at Galbraiths'?'

Messrs. Galbraith, Galbraith, Cuthbertson & Galbraith were Van Aldin's London solicitors.

'Very well, Dad.' She hesitated. 'I suppose it – this – won't keep me from going to the Riviera?'

'When are you off?'

'On the fourteenth.'

'Oh, that will be all right. These things take a long time to mature. By the way, Ruth, I shouldn't take those rubies abroad if I were you. Leave them at the bank.'

Mrs Kettering nodded.

'We don't want to have you robbed and murdered for the sake of "Heart of Fire",' said the millionaire jocosely.

'And yet you carried it about in your pocket loose,' retorted his daughter, smiling.

'Yes –'

Something, some hesitation, caught her attention.

'What is it, Dad?'

'Nothing.' He smiled. 'Thinking of a little adventure of mine in Paris.'

'An adventure?'

'Yes, the night I bought these things.'

He made a gesture towards the jewel case.

'Oh, do tell me.'

'Nothing to tell, Ruthie. Some apache fellows got a bit fresh and I shot at them and they got off. That's all.'

She looked at him with some pride.

'You're a tough proposition, Dad.'

'You bet I am, Ruthie.'

He kissed her affectionately and departed. On arriving back at the Savoy, he gave a curt order to Knighton.

'Get hold of a man called Goby; you'll find his address in my private book. He's to be here tomorrow morning at half-past nine.'

'Yes, sir.'

'I also want to see Mr Kettering. Run him to earth for me if you can. Try his Club – at any rate, get hold of him somehow, and arrange for me to see him here tomorrow morning. Better make it latish, about twelve. His sort aren't early risers.'

The secretary nodded in comprehension of these instructions. Van Aldin gave himself into the hands of his valet. His bath was prepared, and as he lay luxuriating in the hot water, his mind went back over the conversation with his daughter. On the whole he was well satisfied. His keen mind had long since accepted the fact that divorce was the only possible way out. Ruth had agreed to the proposed solution with more readiness than he had hoped for. Yet, in spite of her acquiescence, he was left with a vague sense of uneasiness. Something about her manner, he felt, had not been quite natural. He frowned to himself.

'Maybe I'm fanciful,' he muttered, 'and yet – I bet there's something she has not told me.'

CHAPTER 5

A USEFUL GENTLEMAN

Rufus Van Aldin had just finished the sparse breakfast of coffee and dry toast, which was all he ever allowed himself, when Knighton entered the room.

'Mr Goby is below, sir, waiting to see you.'

The millionaire glanced at the clock. It was just half-past nine.

'All right,' he said curtly. 'He can come up.'

A minute or two later, Mr Goby entered the room. He was a small, elderly man, shabbily dressed, with eyes that looked carefully all round the room, and never at the person he was addressing.

'Good morning, Goby,' said the millionaire. 'Take a chair.'

'Thank you, Mr Van Aldin.'

Mr Goby sat down with his hands on his knees, and gazed earnestly at the radiator.

'I have got a job for you.'

'Yes, Mr Van Aldin?'

'My daughter is married to the Hon. Derek Kettering, as you may perhaps know.'

Mr Goby transferred his gaze from the radiator to the left-hand drawer of the desk, and permitted a deprecating smile to pass over his face. Mr Goby knew a great many things, but he always hated to admit the fact.

'By my advice, she is about to file a petition for divorce. That, of course, is a solicitor's business. But, for private reasons, I want the fullest and most complete information.'

Mr Goby looked at the cornice and murmured:

'About Mr Kettering?'

'About Mr Kettering.'

'Very good, sir.'

Mr Goby rose to his feet.

'When will you have it ready for me?'

'Are you in a hurry, sir?'

'I'm always in a hurry,' said the millionaire.

Mr Goby smiled understandingly at the fender.

'Shall we say two o'clock this afternoon, sir?' he asked.

'Excellent,' approved the other. 'Good morning, Goby.'

'Good morning, Mr Van Aldin.'

'That's a very useful man,' said the millionaire as Goby went out and his secretary came in. 'In his own line he's a specialist.'

'What is his line?'

'Information. Give him twenty-four hours and he would lay the private life of the Archbishop of Canterbury bare for you.'

'A useful sort of chap,' said Knighton, with a smile.

'He has been useful to me once or twice,' said Van Aldin. 'Now then, Knighton, I'm ready for work.'

The next few hours saw a vast quantity of business rapidly transacted. It was half-past twelve when the telephone bell rang, and Mr Van Aldin was informed that Mr Kettering had called. Knighton looked at Van Aldin, and interpreted his brief nod.

'Ask Mr Kettering to come up, please.'

The secretary gathered up his papers and departed. He and the visitor passed each other in the doorway, and Derek Kettering stood aside to let the other go out. Then he came in, shutting the door behind him.

'Good morning, sir. You are very anxious to see me, I hear.'

The lazy voice with its slightly ironic inflection roused memories in Van Aldin. There was charm in it – there had always been charm in it. He looked piercingly at his son-in-law. Derek Kettering was thirty-four, lean of build, with a dark, narrow face, which had even now something indescribably boyish in it.

'Come in,' said Van Aldin curtly. 'Sit down.'

Kettering flung himself lightly into an arm-chair. He looked at his father-in-law with a kind of tolerant amusement.

'Not seen you for a long time, sir,' he remarked pleasantly. 'About two years, I should say. Seen Ruth yet?'

'I saw her last night,' said Van Aldin.

'Looking very fit, isn't she?' said the other lightly.

'I didn't know you had had much opportunity of judging,' said Van Aldin drily.

Derek Kettering raised his eyebrows.

'Oh, we sometimes meet at the same night club, you know,' he said airily.

'I am not going to beat about the bush,' Van Aldin said curtly. 'I have advised Ruth to file a petition for divorce.'

Derek Kettering seemed unmoved.

'How drastic!' he murmured. 'Do you mind if I smoke, sir?'

He lit a cigarette, and puffed out a cloud of smoke as he added nonchalantly:

'And what did Ruth say?'

'Ruth proposes to take my advice,' said her father.

'Does she really?'

'Is that all you have got to say?' demanded Van Aldin sharply.

Kettering flicked his ash into the grate.

'I think, you know,' he said, with a detached air, 'that she's making a great mistake.'

'From your point of view she doubtless is,' said Van Aldin grimly.

'Oh, come now,' said the other; 'don't let's be personal. I really wasn't thinking of myself at the moment. I was thinking of Ruth. You know my poor old Governor really can't last much longer; all the doctors say so. Ruth had better give it a couple more years, then I shall be Lord Leconbury, and she can be châtelaine of Leconbury, which is what she married me for.'

'I won't have any of your darned impudence,' roared Van Aldin.

Derek Kettering smiled at him unmoved.

'I agree with you. It's an obsolete idea,' he said. 'There's nothing in a title nowadays. Still, Leconbury is a very fine old place, and, after all, we are one of the oldest families in England. It will be very annoying for Ruth if she divorces me to find me marrying again, and some other woman queening it at Leconbury instead of her.'

'I am serious, young man,' said Van Aldin.

'Oh, so am I,' said Kettering. 'I am in very low water financially; it will put me in a nasty hole if Ruth divorces me, and, after all, if she has stood it for ten years, why not stand it a little longer? I give you my word of honour that the old man can't possibly last out another eighteen months, and, as I said before, it's a pity Ruth shouldn't get what she married me for.'

'You suggest that my daughter married you for your title and position?'

Derek Kettering laughed a laugh that was not all amusement.

'You don't think it was a question of a love match?' he asked.

'I know,' said Van Aldin slowly, 'that you spoke very differently in Paris ten years ago.'

'Did I? Perhaps I did. Ruth was very beautiful, you know –

rather like an angel or a saint, or something that had stepped down from a niche in a church. I had fine ideas, I remember, of turning over a new leaf, of settling down and living up to the highest traditions of English home-life with a beautiful wife who loved me.'

He laughed again, rather more discordantly.

'But you don't believe that, I suppose?' he said.

'I have no doubt at all that you married Ruth for her money,' said Van Aldin unemotionally.

'And that she married me for love?' asked the other ironically.

'Certainly,' said Van Aldin.

Derek Kettering stared at him for a minute or two, then he nodded reflectively.

'I see you believe that,' he said. 'So did I at the time. I can assure you, my dear father-in-law, I was very soon undeceived.'

'I don't know what you are getting at,' said Van Aldin, 'and I don't care. You have treated Ruth darned badly.'

'Oh, I have,' agreed Kettering lightly, 'but she's tough, you know. She's your daughter. Underneath the pink-and-white softness of her she's as hard as granite. You have always been known as a hard man, so I have been told, but Ruth is harder than you are. You, at any rate, love one person better than yourself. Ruth never has and never will.'

'That is enough,' said Van Aldin. 'I asked you here so that I could tell you fair and square what I meant to do. My girl has got to have some happiness, and remember this, I am behind her.'

Derek Kettering got up and stood by the mantelpiece. He tossed away his cigarette. When he spoke, his voice was very quiet.

'What exactly do you mean by that, I wonder?' he said.

'I mean,' said Van Aldin, 'that you had better not try to defend the case.'

'Oh,' said Kettering, 'is that a threat?'

'You can take it any way you please,' said Van Aldin.

Kettering drew a chair up to the table. He sat down fronting the millionaire.

'And supposing,' he said softly, 'that, just for argument's sake, I did defend the case?'

Van Aldin shrugged his shoulders.

'You have not got a leg to stand upon, you young fool. Ask

your solicitors, they will soon tell you. Your conduct has been notorious, the talk of London.'

'Ruth has been kicking up a row about Mirelle, I suppose. Very foolish of her. I don't interfere with her friends.'

'What do you mean?' said Van Aldin sharply.

Derek Kettering laughed.

'I see you don't know everything, sir,' he said. 'You are, perhaps naturally, prejudiced.'

He took up his hat and stick and moved towards the door.

'Giving advice is not much in my line.' He delivered his final thrust. 'But, in this case, I should advise most strongly perfect frankness between father and daughter.'

He passed quickly out of the room and shut the door behind him just as the millionaire sprang up.

'Now, what the hell did he mean by that?' said Van Aldin as he sank back into his chair again.

All his uneasiness returned in full force. There was something here that he had not yet got to the bottom of. The telephone was by his elbow; he seized it, and asked for the number of his daughter's house.

'Hallo! Hallo! Is that Mayfair 81907? Mrs Kettering in? Oh, she's out, is she? Yes, out to lunch. What time will she be in? You don't know? Oh, very good; no, there's no message.'

He slammed the receiver down again angrily. At two o'clock he was pacing the floor of his room waiting expectantly for Goby. The latter was ushered in at ten minutes past two.

'Well?' barked the millionaire sharply.

But little Mr Goby was not to be hurried. He sat down at the table, produced a very shabby pocket-book, and proceeded to read from it in a monotonous voice. The millionaire listened attentively, with an increasing satisfaction. Goby came to a full stop, and looked attentively at the wastepaper-basket.

'Um!' said Van Aldin. 'That seems pretty definite. The case will go through like winking. The hotel evidence is all right, I suppose?'

'Cast iron,' said Mr Goby, and looked malevolently at a gilt arm-chair.

'And financially he's in very low water. He's trying to raise a loan now, you say? Has already raised practically all he can upon his expectations from his father. Once the news of the divorce gets about, he won't be able to raise another cent, and not only that, his obligations can be bought up and pressure can be put upon him from that quarter. We have got him, Goby; we have got him in a cleft stick.'

He hit the table a bang with his fist. His face was grim and triumphant.

'The information,' said Mr Goby in a thin voice, 'seems satisfactory.'

'I have got to go round to Curzon Street now,' said the millionaire. 'I am much obliged to you, Goby. You are the goods all right.'

A pale smile of gratification showed itself on the little man's face.

'Thank you, Mr Van Aldin,' he said; 'I try to do my best.'

Van Aldin did not go direct to Curzon Street. He went first to the City, where he had two interviews which added to his satisfaction. From there he took the tube to Down Street. As he was walking along Curzon Street, a figure came out of No. 160, and turned up the street towards him, so that they passed each other on the pavement. For a moment, the millionaire had fancied it might be Derek Kettering himself; the height and build were not unlike. But as they came face to face, he saw that the man was a stranger to him. At least – no, not a stranger; his face awoke some call of recognition in the millionaire's mind, and it was associated definitely with something unpleasant. He cudgelled his brains in vain, but the thing eluded him. He went on, shaking his head irritably. He hated to be baffled.

Ruth Kettering was clearly expecting him. She ran to him and kissed him when he entered.

'Well, Dad, how are things going?'

'Very well,' said Van Aldin; 'but I have got a word or two to say to you, Ruth.'

Almost insensibly he felt the change in her; something shrewd and watchful replaced the impulsiveness of her greeting. She sat down in a big arm-chair.

'Well, Dad?' she asked. 'What is it?'

'I saw your husband this morning,' said Van Aldin.

'You saw Derek?'

'I did. He said a lot of things, most of which were darned cheek. Just as he was leaving, he said something that I didn't understand.

He advised me to be sure that there was perfect frankness between father and daughter. What did he mean by that, Ruthie?'

Mrs Kettering moved a little in her chair.

'I – I don't know, Dad. How should I?'

'Of course you know,' said Van Aldin. 'He said something else, about his having his friends and not interfering with yours. What did he mean by that?'

'I don't know,' said Ruth Kettering again.

Van Aldin sat down. His mouth set itself in a grim line.

'See here, Ruth. I am not going into this with my eyes closed. I am not at all sure that that husband of yours doesn't mean to make trouble. Now, he can't do it, I am sure of that. I have got the means to silence him, to shut his mouth for good and all, but I have got to know if there's any need to use those means. What did he mean by your having your own friends?'

Mrs Kettering shrugged her shoulders.

'I have got lots of friends,' she said uncertainly. 'I don't know what he meant, I am sure.'

'You do,' said Van Aldin.

He was speaking now as he might have spoken to a business adversary.

'I will put it plainer. Who is the man?'

'What man?'

'*The man*. That's what Derek was driving at. Some special man who is a friend of yours. You needn't worry, honey, I know there is nothing in it, but we have got to look at everything as it might appear to the Court. They can twist these things about a good deal, you know. I want to know who the man is, and just how friendly you have been with him.'

Ruth didn't answer. Her hands were kneading themselves together in intense nervous absorption.

'Come, honey,' said Van Aldin in a softer voice. 'Don't be afraid of your old Dad. I was not too harsh, was I, even that time in Paris? – By gosh!'

He stopped, thunderstruck.

'That's who it was,' he murmured to himself. 'I thought I knew his face.'

'What are you talking about, Dad? I don't understand.'

The millionaire strode across to her and took her firmly by the wrist.

'See here, Ruth, have you been seeing that fellow again?'

'What fellow?'

'The one we had all that fuss about years ago. You know who I mean well enough.'

'You mean' – she hesitated – 'you mean the Comte de la Roche?'

'Comte de la Roche!' snorted Van Aldin. 'I told you at the time that the man was no better than a swindler. You had entangled yourself with him then very deeply, but I got you out of his clutches.'

'Yes, you did,' said Ruth bitterly. 'And I married Derek Kettering.'

'You wanted to,' said the millionaire sharply.

She shrugged her shoulders.

'And now,' said Van Aldin slowly, 'you have been seeing him again – after all I told you. He has been in the house today. I met him outside, and couldn't place him for the moment.'

Ruth Kettering had recovered her composure.

'I want to tell you one thing, Dad; you are wrong about Armand – the Comte de la Roche, I mean. Oh, I know there were several regrettable incidents in his youth – he has told me about them; but – well, he has cared for me always. It broke his heart when you parted us in Paris, and now –'

She was interrupted by the snort of indignation her father gave.

'So you fell for that stuff, did you? You, a daughter of mine! My God!'

He threw up his hands.

'That women can be such darned fools!'

CHAPTER 6

MIRELLE

Derek Kettering emerged from Van Aldin's suite so precipitantly that he collided with a lady passing across the corridor. He apologized, and she accepted his apologies with a smiling reassurance and passed on, leaving with him a pleasant impression of a soothing personality and rather fine grey eyes.

For all his nonchalance, his interview with his father-in-law had shaken him more than he cared to show. He had a solitary lunch, and after it, frowning to himself a little, he went round to the sumptuous flat that housed the lady known as Mirelle. A trim Frenchwoman received him with smiles.

'But enter then, Monsieur. Madame reposes herself.'

He was ushered into the long room with its Eastern setting which he knew so well. Mirelle was lying on the divan, supported by an incredible number of cushions, all in varying shades of amber, to harmonize with the yellow ochre of her complexion. The dancer was a beautifully made woman, and if her face, beneath its mask of yellow, was in truth somewhat haggard, it had a bizarre charm of its own, and her orange lips smiled invitingly at Derek Kettering.

He kissed her, and flung himself into a chair.

'What have you been doing with yourself? Just got up, I suppose?'

The orange mouth widened into a long smile.

'No,' said the dancer. 'I have been at work.'

She flung out a long, pale hand towards the piano, which was littered with untidy music scores.

'Ambrose has been here. He has been playing me the new Opera.'

Kettering nodded without paying much attention. He was profoundly uninterested in Claud Ambrose and the latter's operatic setting of Ibsen's *Peer Gynt*. So was Mirelle, for that matter, regarding it merely as a unique opportunity for her own presentation as Anitra.

'It is a marvellous dance,' she murmured. 'I shall put all the passion of the desert into it. I shall dance hung over with jewels – ah! and, by the way, *mon ami*, there is a pearl that I saw yesterday in Bond Street – a black pearl.'

She paused, looking at him invitingly.

'My dear girl,' said Kettering, 'it's no use talking of black pearls to me. At the present minute, as far as I am concerned, the fat is in the fire.'

She was quick to respond to his tone. She sat up, her big black eyes widening.

'What is that you say, Dereek? What has happened?'

'My esteemed father-in-law,' said Kettering, 'is preparing to go off the deep end.'

'Eh?'

'In other words, he wants Ruth to divorce me.'

'How stupid!' said Mirelle. 'Why should she want to divorce you?'

Derek Kettering grinned.

'Mainly because of you, *chérie*!' he said.

Mirelle shrugged her shoulders.

'That is foolish,' she observed in a matter-of-fact voice.

'Very foolish,' agreed Derek.

'What are you going to do about it?' demanded Mirelle.

'My dear girl, what can I do? On the one side, the man with unlimited money; on the other side, the man with unlimited debts. There is no question as to who will come out on top.'

'They are extraordinary, these Americans,' commented Mirelle. 'It is not as though your wife were fond of you.'

'Well,' said Derek, 'what are we going to do about it?'

She looked at him inquiringly. He came over and took both her hands in his.

'Are you going to stick to me?'

'What do you mean? After –?'

'Yes,' said Kettering. 'After, when the creditors come down like wolves on the fold. I am damned fond of you, Mirelle; are you going to let me down?'

She pulled her hands away from him.

'You know I adore you, Dereek.'

He caught the note of evasion in her voice.

'So that's that, is it? The rats will leave the sinking ship.'

'Ah, Dereek!'

'Out with it,' he said violently. 'You will fling me over; is that it?'

She shrugged her shoulders.

'I am very fond of you, *mon ami* – indeed I am fond of you. You are very charming – *un beau garçon*, but *ce n'est pas practique*.'

'You are a rich man's luxury, eh? Is that it?'

'If you like to put it that way.'

She leaned back on the cushions, her head flung back.

'All the same, I am fond of you, Dereek.'

He went over to the window and stood there some time looking out, with his back to her. Presently the dancer raised herself on her elbow and stared at him curiously.

'What are you thinking of, *mon ami*?'

He grinned at her over his shoulder, a curious grin, that made her vaguely uneasy.

'As it happened, I was thinking of a woman, my dear.'

'A woman, eh?'

Mirelle pounced on something that she could understand.

'You are thinking of some other woman, is that it?'

'Oh, you needn't worry; it is purely a fancy portrait. "Portrait of a lady with grey eyes".'

Mirelle said sharply, 'When did you meet her?'

Derek Kettering laughed, and his laughter had a mocking, ironical sound.

'I ran into the lady in the corridor of the Savoy Hotel.'

'Well! What did she say?'

'As far as I can remember, I said "I beg your pardon," and she said, "It doesn't matter," or words to that effect.'

'And then?' persisted the dancer.

Kettering shrugged his shoulders.

'And then – nothing. That was the end of the incident.'

'I don't understand a word of what you are talking about,' declared the dancer.

'Portrait of a lady with grey eyes,' murmured Derek reflectively. 'Just as well I am never likely to meet her again.'

'Why?'

'She might bring me bad luck. Women do.'

Mirelle slipped quietly from her couch, and came across to him, laying one long, snake-like arm round his neck.

'You are foolish, Dereek,' she murmured. 'You are very foolish. You are *beau garçon*, and I adore you, but I am not made to be poor – no, decidedly I am not made to be poor. Now listen to me; everything is very simple. You must make it up with your wife.'

'I am afraid that's not going to be actually in the sphere of practical politics,' said Derek drily.

'How do you say? I do not understand.'

'Van Aldin, my dear, is not taking any. He is the kind of man who makes up his mind and sticks to it.'

'I have heard of him,' nodded the dancer. 'He is very rich, is he not? Almost the richest man in America. A few days ago, in Paris, he bought the most wonderful ruby in the world – "Heart of Fire" it is called.'

Kettering did not answer. The dancer went on musingly:

'It is a wonderful stone – a stone that should belong to a woman like me. I love jewels, Dereek; they say something to me. Ah! to wear a ruby like "Heart of Fire".'

She gave a little sigh, and then became practical once more.

'You don't understand these things. Dereek; you are only a man. Van Aldin will give these rubies to his daughter, I suppose. Is she his only child?'

'Yes.'

'Then when he dies, she will inherit all his money. She will be a rich woman.'

'She is a rich woman already,' said Kettering drily. 'He settled a couple of millions on her at her marriage.'

'A couple of million! But that is immense. And if she died suddenly, eh? That would all come to you?'

'As things stand at present,' said Kettering slowly, 'it would. As far as I know she has not made a will.'

'*Mon Dieu!*' said the dancer. 'If she were to die, what a solution that would be.'

There was a moment's pause, and then Derek Kettering laughed outright.

'I like your simple, practical mind, Mirelle, but I am afraid what you desire won't come to pass. My wife is an extremely healthy person.'

'*Eh bien!*' said Mirelle; 'there are accidents.'

He looked at her sharply but did not answer.

She went on.

'But you are right, *mon ami*, we must not dwell on possibilities. See now, my little Dereek, there must be no more talk of this divorce. Your wife must give up the idea.'

'And if she won't?'

The dancer's eyes narrowed to slits.

'I think she will, my friend. She is one of those who would not like the publicity. There are one or two pretty stories that she would not like her friends to read in the newspapers.'

'What do you mean?' asked Kettering sharply.

Mirelle laughed, her head thrown back.

'*Parbleu!* I mean the gentleman who calls himself the Comte de la Roche. I know all about him. I am Parisienne, you remember. He was her lover before she married you, was he not?'

Kettering took her sharply by the shoulders.

'That is a damned lie,' he said, 'and please remember that, after all, you are speaking of my wife.'

Mirelle was a little sobered.

'You are extraordinary, you English,' she complained. 'All the same, I dare say that you may be right. The Americans are so cold, are they not? But you will permit me to say, *mon ami*, that she was *in love with him* before she married you, and her father stepped in and sent the Comte about his business. And the little Mademoiselle, she wept many tears! But she obeyed. Still, you must know as well as I do, Dereek, that it is a very different story now. She sees him nearly every day, and on the 14th she goes to Paris to meet him.'

'How do you know all this?' demanded Kettering.

'Me? I have friends in Paris, my dear Dereek, who know the Comte intimately. It is all arranged. She is going to the Riviera, so she says, but in reality the Comte meets her in Paris and – who knows! Yes, yes, you can take my word for it, it is all arranged.'

Derek Kettering stood motionless.

'You see,' purred the dancer, 'if you are clever, you have her in the hollow of your hand. You can make things very awkward for her.'

'Oh, for God's sake be quiet,' cried Kettering. 'Shut your cursed mouth!'

Mirelle flung herself down on the divan with a laugh. Kettering caught up his hat and coat and left the flat, banging the door violently. And still the dancer sat on the divan and laughed softly to herself. She was not displeased with her work.

CHAPTER 7

LETTERS

'Mrs Samuel Harfield presents her compliments to Miss Katherine Grey and wishes to point out that under the circumstances Miss Grey may not be aware –'

Mrs Harfield, having written so far fluently, came to a dead stop, held up by what has proved an insuperable difficulty to many other people – namely, the difficulty of expressing oneself fluently in the third person.

After a minute or two of hesitation, Mrs Harfield tore up the sheet of notepaper and started afresh.

> Dear Miss Grey, – Whilst fully appreciating the adequate way you discharged your duties to my Cousin Emma (whose recent death has indeed been a severe blow to us all), I cannot but feel –

Again Mrs Harfield came to a stop. Once more the letter was consigned to the wastepaper-basket. It was not until four false starts had been made that Mrs Harfield at last produced an epistle that satisfied her. It was duly sealed and stamped and addressed to Miss Katherine Grey, Little Crampton, St Mary Mead, Kent, and it lay beside the lady's plate on the following morning at breakfast-time in company with a more important-looking communication in a long blue envelope.

Katherine Grey opened Mrs Harfield's letter first. The finished production ran as follows:

> Dear Miss Grey, – My husband and I wish to express our thanks to you for your services to my poor cousin, Emma. Her death has been a great blow to us, though we were, of course, aware that her mind has been failing for some time past. I understand that her latter testamentary dispositions have been of a most peculiar character, and they would not hold good, of course, in any court of law. I have no doubt that, with your usual good sense, you have already realized this fact. If these matters can be arranged privately it is always so much better, my husband says. We shall be pleased to recommend you most highly for a similar post, and hope that you will also accept a small present. Believe me, dear Miss Grey, yours cordially.
>
> Mary Anne Harfield.

Katherine Grey read the letter through, smiled a little, and read it a second time. Her face as she laid the letter down after the second reading was distinctly amused. Then she took up the second letter. After one brief perusal she laid it down and stared very straight in front of her. This time she did not smile. Indeed, it would have been hard for anyone watching her to guess what emotions lay behind that quiet, reflective gaze.

Katherine Grey was thirty-three. She came of good family, but her father had lost all his money, and Katherine had had to work for her living from an early age. She had been just twenty-three when she had come to old Mrs Harfield as companion.

It was generally recognized that old Mrs Harfield was 'difficult.' Companions came and went with startling rapidity. They arrived full of hope and they usually left in tears. But from the moment Katherine Grey set foot in Little Crampton, ten years ago, perfect peace had reigned. No one knows how these things come about. Snake-charmers, they say, are born, not made. Katherine Grey was born with the power of managing old ladies, dogs, and small boys, and she did it without any apparent sense of strain.

At twenty-three she had been a quiet girl with beautiful eyes. At thirty-three she was a quiet woman, with those same grey eyes, shining steadily out on the world with a kind of happy serenity that nothing could shake. Moreover, she had been born with, and still possessed, a sense of humour.

As she sat at the breakfast-table, staring in front of her, there was a ring at the bell, accompanied by a very energetic rat-a-tat-tat at the knocker. In another minute the little maid-servant opened the door and announced rather breathlessly:

'Dr Harrison.'

The big, middle-aged doctor came bustling in with the energy and breeziness that had been foreshadowed by his onslaught on the knocker.

'Good morning, Miss Grey.'

'Good morning, Dr Harrison.'

'I dropped in early,' began the doctor, 'in case you should have heard from one of those Harfield cousins. Mrs Samuel, she calls herself – a perfectly poisonous person.'

Without a word, Katherine picked up Mrs Harfield's letter from the table and gave it to him. With a good deal of amusement she watched his perusal of it, the drawing together of the bushy eyebrows, the snorts and grunts of violent disapproval. He dashed it down again on the table.

'Perfectly monstrous,' he fumed. 'Don't you let it worry you, my dear. They're talking through their hat. Mrs Harfield's intellect was as good as yours or mine, and you won't get anyone to say the contrary. They wouldn't have a leg to stand upon, and they know it. All that talk of taking it into court is pure bluff. Hence this attempt to get round you in a hole-and-corner way. And look here, my dear, don't let them get round you with soft soap either. Don't get fancying it's your duty to hand over the cash, or any tomfoolery of conscientious scruples.'

'I'm afraid it hasn't occurred to me to have scruples,' said Katherine. 'All these people are distant relatives of Mrs Harfield's husband, and they never came near her or took any notice of her in her lifetime.'

'You're a sensible woman,' said the doctor. 'I know, none better, that you've had a hard life of it for the last ten years. You're fully entitled to enjoy the old lady's savings, such as they were.'

Katherine smiled thoughtfully.

'Such as they were,' she repeated. 'You've no idea of the amount, doctor?'

'Well – enough to bring in five hundred a year or so, I suppose.'

Katherine nodded.

'That's what I thought,' she said. 'Now read this.'

She handed him the letter she had taken from the long blue envelope. The doctor read and uttered an exclamation of utter astonishment.

'Impossible,' he muttered. 'Impossible.'

'She was one of the original shareholders in Mortaulds. Forty years ago she must have had an income of eight or ten thousand a year. She has never, I am sure, spent more than four hundred a year. She was always terribly careful about money. I always believed that she was obliged to be careful about every penny.'

'And all the time the income has accumulated at compound interest. My dear, you're going to be a very rich woman.'

Katherine Grey nodded.

'Yes,' she said, 'I am.'

She spoke in a detached, impersonal tone, as though she were looking at the situation from outside.

'Well,' said the doctor, preparing to depart, 'you have all my congratulations.' He flicked Mrs Samuel Harfield's letter with his thumb. 'Don't worry about that woman and her odious letter.'

'It really isn't an odious letter,' said Miss Grey tolerantly. 'Under the circumstances, I think it's really quite a natural thing to do.'

'I have the gravest suspicions of you sometimes,' said the doctor.

'Why?'

'The things that you find perfectly natural.'

Katherine Grey laughed.

Doctor Harrison retailed the great news to his wife at lunch-time. She was very excited about it.

'Fancy old Mrs Harfield – with all that money. I'm glad she left it to Katherine Grey. That girl's a saint.'

The doctor made a wry face.

'Saints I always imagined must have been difficult people. Katherine Grey is too human for a saint.'

'She's a saint with a sense of humour,' said the doctor's wife, twinkling. 'And, though I don't suppose you've ever noticed the fact, she's extremely good looking.'

'Katherine Grey?' The doctor was honestly surprised. 'She's got very nice eyes, I know.'

'Oh, you men!' cried his wife. 'Blind as bats. Katherine's got all the makings of a beauty in her. All she wants is clothes!'

'Clothes? What's wrong with her clothes? She always looks very nice.'

Mrs Harrison gave an exasperated sigh, and the doctor rose preparatory to starting on his rounds.

'You might look in on her, Polly,' he suggested.

'I'm going to,' said Mrs Harrison, promptly.

She made her call about three o'clock.

'My dear, I'm so glad,' she said warmly, as she squeezed Katherine's hand. 'And everyone in the village will be glad too.'

'It's very nice of you to come and tell me,' said Katherine. 'I hoped you would come in because I wanted to ask about Johnnie.'

'Oh! Johnnie. Well –'

Johnnie was Mrs Harrison's youngest son. In another minute she was off, retailing a long history in which Johnnie's adenoids and tonsils bulked largely. Katherine listened sympathetically. Habits die hard. Listening had been her portion for ten years now. 'My dear, I wonder if I ever told you about the naval ball at Portsmouth? When Lord Charles admired my gown?' And composedly, kindly, Katherine would reply: 'I rather think you have, Mrs Harfield, but I've forgotten about it. Won't you tell it me again?' And then the old lady would start off full swing, with numerous corrections, and stops, and remembered details. And half of Katherine's mind would be listening, saying the right things mechanically when the old lady paused . . .

Now, with the same curious feeling of duality to which she was accustomed, she listened to Mrs Harrison.

At the end of half an hour, the latter recalled herself suddenly.

'I've been talking about myself all this time,' she exclaimed. 'And I came here to talk about you and your plans.'

'I don't know that I've got any yet.'

'My dear – you're not going to stay on *here*.'

Katherine smiled at the horror in the other's tone.

'No; I think I want to travel. I've never seen much of the world, you know.'

'I should think not. It must have been an awful life for you cooped up here all these years.'

'I don't know,' said Katherine. 'It gave me a lot of freedom.'

She caught the other's gasp, and reddened a little.

'It must sound foolish – saying that. Of course, I hadn't much freedom in the downright physical sense –'

'I should think not,' breathed Mrs Harrison, remembering that Katherine had seldom had that useful thing, a 'day off'.

'But in a way, being tied physically gives you lots of scope mentally. You're always free to think. I've had a lovely feeling always of mental freedom.'

Mrs Harrison shook her head.

'I can't understand that.'

'Oh! you would if you'd been in my place. But, all the same, I feel I want a change. I want – well, I want things to happen. Oh! not to me – I don't mean that. But to be in the midst of things – exciting things – even if I'm only the looker-on. You know, things don't happen in St Mary Mead.'

'They don't indeed,' said Mrs Harrison, with fervour.

'I shall go to London first,' said Katherine. 'I have to see the solicitors, anyway. After that, I shall go abroad, I think.'

'Very nice.'

'But of course, first of all –'

'Yes?'

'I must get some clothes.'

'Exactly what I said to Arthur this morning,' cried the doctor's wife. 'You know, Katherine, you could look possibly positively beautiful if you tried.'

Miss Grey laughed unaffectedly.

'Oh! I don't think you could ever make a beauty out of me,' she said sincerely. 'But I shall enjoy having some really good clothes. I'm afraid I'm talking about myself an awful lot.'

Mrs Harrison looked at her shrewdly.

'It must be quite a novel experience for you,' she said drily.

Katherine went to say goodbye to old Miss Viner before leaving the village. Miss Viner was two years older than Mrs Harfield, and her mind was mainly taken up with her own success in out-living her dead friend.

'You wouldn't have thought I'd have outlasted Jane Harfield, would you?' she demanded triumphantly of Katherine. 'We were at school together, she and I. And here we are, she taken, and I left. Who would have thought it?'

'You've always eaten brown bread for supper, haven't you?' murmured Katherine mechanically.

'Fancy your remembering that, my dear. Yes; if Jane Harfield had had a slice of brown bread every evening and taken a little stimulant with her meals she might be here today.'

The old lady paused, nodding her head triumphantly; then added in sudden remembrance:

'And so you've come into a lot of money, I hear? Well, well. Take care of it. And you're going up to London to have a good time? Don't think you'll get married, though, my dear, because you won't. You're not the kind to attract the men. And, besides, you're getting on. How old are you now?'

'Thirty-three,' Katherine told her.

'Well,' remarked Miss Viner doubtfully, 'that's not so very bad. You've lost your first freshness, of course.'

'I'm afraid so,' said Katherine, much entertained.

'But you're a very nice girl,' said Miss Viner kindly. 'And I'm sure there's many a man might do worse than take you for a wife instead of one of these flibbertigibbets running about nowadays showing more of their legs than the Creator ever intended them to. Goodbye, my dear, and I hope you'll enjoy yourself, but things are seldom what they seem in this life.'

Heartened by these prophecies, Katherine took her departure. Half the village came to see her off at the station, including the little maid of all work, Alice, who brought a stiff wired nosegay and cried openly.

'There ain't a many like her,' sobbed Alice when the train had finally departed. 'I'm sure when Charlie went back on me with that girl from the dairy, nobody could have been kinder than Miss Grey was, and though particular about the brasses and the dust, she was always one to notice when you'd give a thing an extra rub. Cut myself in little pieces for her, I would, any day. A real lady, that's what I call her.'

Such was Katherine's departure from St Mary Mead.

CHAPTER 8

LADY TAMPLIN WRITES A LETTER

'Well,' said Lady Tamplin, 'well.'

She laid down the continental *Daily Mail* and stared out across the blue waters of the Mediterranean. A branch of golden mimosa, hanging just above her head, made an effective frame for a very charming picture. A golden-haired, blue-eyed lady in a very becoming *négligé*. That the golden hair owed something to art, as did the pink-and-white complexion, was undeniable, but the blue of the eyes was Nature's gift, and at forty-four Lady Tamplin could still rank as a beauty.

Charming as she looked, Lady Tamplin was, for once, not thinking of herself. That is to say, she was not thinking of her appearance. She was intent on graver matters.

Lady Tamplin was a well-known figure on the Riviera, and her parties at the Villa Marguerite were justly celebrated. She was a woman of considerable experience, and had had four husbands. The first had been merely an indiscretion, and so was seldom referred to by the lady. He had had the good sense to die with commendable promptitude, and his widow thereupon espoused a rich manufacturer of buttons. He too had departed for another sphere after three years of married life – it was said after a congenial evening with some boon companions. After him came Viscount Tamplin, who had placed Rosalie securely on those heights where she wished to tread. She retained her title when she married for a fourth time. This fourth venture had been undertaken for pure pleasure. Mr Charles Evans, an extremely good-looking young man of twenty-seven, with delightful manners, a keen love of sport, and an appreciation of this world's goods, had no money of his own whatsoever.

Lady Tamplin was very pleased and satisfied with life generally, but she had occasional faint preoccupations about money. The button manufacturer had left his widow a considerable fortune, but, as Lady Tamplin was wont to say, 'what with one thing and another –' (one thing being the depreciation of stocks owing to the War, and the other the extravagances of the late Lord Tamplin). She was still comfortably off. But to be merely comfortably off was hardly satisfactory to one of Rosalie Tamplin's temperament.

So, on this particular January morning, she opened her blue eyes extremely wide as she read a certain item of news and uttered that non-committal monosyllable 'Well.' The only other occupant of the balcony was her daughter, the Hon. Lenox Tamplin. A daughter such as Lenox was a sad thorn in Lady Tamplin's side, a girl with no kind of tact, who actually looked older than her age, and whose peculiar sardonic form of humour was, to say the least of it, uncomfortable.

'Darling,' said Lady Tamplin, 'just fancy.'

'What is it?'

Lady Tamplin picked up the *Daily Mail*, handed it to her daughter, and indicated with an agitated forefinger the paragraph of interest.

Lenox read it without any of the signs of agitation shown by her mother. She handed back the paper.

'What about it?' she asked. 'It is the sort of thing that is always happening. Cheese-paring old women are always dying in villages and leaving fortunes of millions to their humble companions.'

'Yes, dear, I know,' said her mother, 'and I dare say the fortune is not anything like as large as they say it is; newspapers are so inaccurate. But even if you cut it down by half –'

'Well,' said Lenox, 'it has not been left to us.'

'Not exactly, dear,' said Lady Tamplin; 'but this girl, this Katherine Grey, is actually a cousin of mine. One of the Worcestershire Greys, the Edgeworth lot. My very own cousin! Fancy!'

'Ah-ha,' said Lenox.

'And I was wondering –' said her mother.

'What there is in it for us,' finished Lenox, with that sideways smile that her mother always found difficult to understand.

'Oh, darling,' said Lady Tamplin, on a faint note of reproach.

It was very faint, because Rosalie Tamplin was used to her daughter's outspokenness and to what she called Lenox's uncomfortable way of putting things.

'I was wondering,' said Lady Tamplin, again drawing her artistically pencilled brows together, 'whether – oh, good morning, Chubby darling: are you going to play tennis? How nice!'

Chubby, thus addressed, smiled kindly at her, remarked perfunctorily, 'How topping you look in that peach-coloured thing,' and drifted past them and down the steps.

'The dear thing,' said Lady Tamplin, looking affectionately after her husband. 'Let me see, what was I saying? Ah!' She switched her mind back to business once more. 'I was wondering –'

'Oh, for God's sake get on with it. That is the third time you have said that.'

'Well, dear,' said Lady Tamplin, 'I was thinking that it would be very nice if I wrote to dear Katherine and suggested that she should pay us a little visit out here. Naturally, she is quite out of touch with Society. It would be nicer for her to be launched by one of her own people. An advantage for her and an advantage for us.'

'How much do you think you would get her to cough up?' asked Lenox.

Her mother looked at her reproachfully and murmured:

'We should have to come to some financial arrangement, of course. What with one thing and another – the War – your poor father –'

'And Chubby now,' said Lenox. 'He is an expensive luxury if you like.'

'She was a nice girl as I remember her,' murmured Lady Tamplin, pursuing her own line of thought – 'quiet, never wanted to shove herself forward, not a beauty, and never a man-hunter.'

'She will leave Chubby alone, then?' said Lenox.

Lady Tamplin looked at her in protest. 'Chubby would never –' she began.

'No,' said Lenox, 'I don't believe he would; he knows a jolly sight too well which way his bread is buttered.'

'Darling,' said Lady Tamplin, 'you have such a coarse way of putting things.'

'Sorry,' said Lenox.

Lady Tamplin gathered up the *Daily Mail* and her *négligé*, a vanity bag, and various odd letters.

'I shall write to dear Katherine at once,' she said, 'and remind her of the dear old days at Edgeworth.'

She went into the house, a light of purpose shining in her eyes.

Unlike Mrs Samuel Harfield, correspondence flowed easily from her pen. She covered four sheets without pause or effort, and on re-reading it found no occasion to alter a word.

Katherine received it on the morning of her arrival in London. Whether she read between the lines of it or not is another matter. She put it in her handbag and started out to keep the appointment she had made with Mrs Harfield's lawyers.

The firm was an old-established one in Lincoln's Inn Fields, and after a few minutes' delay Katherine was shown into the presence of the senior partner, a kindly, elderly man with shrewd blue eyes and a fatherly manner.

They discussed Mrs Harfield's will and various legal matters for some twenty minutes, then Katherine handed the lawyer Mrs Samuel's letter.

'I had better show you this, I suppose,' she said, 'though it is really rather ridiculous.'

He read it with a slight smile.

'Rather a crude attempt, Miss Grey. I need hardly tell you, I suppose, that these people have no claim of any kind upon the estate, and if they endeavour to contest the will no court will uphold them.'

'I thought as much.'

'Human nature is not always very wise. In Mrs Samuel Harfield's place, I should have been more inclined to make an appeal to your generosity.'

'That is one of the things I want to speak to you about. I should like a certain sum to go to these people.'

'There is no obligation.'

'I know that.'

'And they will not take it in the spirit it is meant. They will probably regard it as an attempt to pay them off, though they will not refuse it on that account.'

'I can see that, and it can't be helped.'

'I should advise you, Miss Grey, to put that idea out of your mind.'

Katherine shook her head. 'You are quite right, I know, but I should like it done all the same.'

'They will grab at the money and abuse you all the more afterwards.'

'Well,' said Katherine, 'let them if they like. We all have our own ways of enjoying ourselves. They were, after all, Mrs Harfield's only relatives, and though they despised her as a poor relation and paid no attention to her when she was alive, it seems to me unfair that they should be cut off with nothing.'

She carried her point, though the lawyer was still unwilling, and she presently went out into the streets of London with a comfortable assurance that she could spend money freely and make what plans she liked for the future. Her first action was to visit the establishment of a famous dressmaker.

A slim, elderly Frenchwoman, rather like a dreaming duchess, received her, and Katherine spoke with a certain *naïveté*.

'I want, if I may, to put myself in your hands. I have been very poor all my life and know nothing about clothes, but now I have come into some money and want to look really well dressed.'

The Frenchwoman was charmed. She had an artist's temperament, which had been soured earlier in the morning by a visit from an Argentine meat queen, who had insisted on having those models least suited to her flamboyant type of beauty. She scrutinized Katherine with keen, clever eyes. 'Yes – yes, it will be a pleasure. Mademoiselle has a very good figure; for her the simple lines will be best. She is also *très anglaise*. Some people it would offend them if I said that, but Mademoiselle no. *Une belle Anglaise*, there is no style more delightful.'

The demeanour of a dreaming duchess was suddenly put off. She screamed out directions to various mannequins. 'Clothilde, Virginie, quickly, my little ones, the little *tailleur gris clair* and the *robe de soirée "soupir d'automne"*. Marcelle, my child, the little mimosa suit of crêpe de chine.'

It was a charming morning. Marcelle, Clothilde, Virginie, bored and scornful, passed slowly round, squirming and wriggling in the time-honoured fashion of mannequins. The Duchess stood by Katherine and made entries in a small notebook.

'An excellent choice, Mademoiselle. Mademoiselle has great

goût. Yes, indeed. Mademoiselle cannot do better than those little suits if she is going to the Riviera, as I suppose, this winter.'

'Let me see that evening dress once more,' said Katherine – 'the pinky mauve one.'

Virginie appeared, circling slowly.

'That is the prettiest of all,' said Katherine, as she surveyed the exquisite draperies of mauve and grey and blue. 'What do you call it?'

'*Soupir d'automne*; yes, yes, that is truly the dress of Mademoiselle.'

What was there in these words that came back to Katherine with a faint feeling of sadness after she had left the dressmaking establishment?

'"*Soupir d'automne; that is truly the dress of Mademoiselle.*"' Autumn, yes, it was autumn for her. She who had never known spring or summer, and would never know them now. Something she had lost never could be given to her again. These years of servitude in St Mary Mead – and all the while life passing by.

'I am an idiot,' said Katherine. 'I am an idiot. What do I want? Why, I was more contented a month ago than I am now.'

She drew out from her handbag the letter she had received that morning from Lady Tamplin. Katherine was no fool. She understood the *nuances* of that letter as well as anybody and the reason of Lady Tamplin's sudden show of affection towards a long-forgotten cousin was not lost upon her. It was for profit and not for pleasure that Lady Tamplin was so anxious for the company of her dear cousin. Well, why not? There would be profit on both sides.

'I will go,' said Katherine.

She was walking down Piccadilly at the moment, and turned into Cook's to clinch the matter then and there. She had to wait for a few minutes. The man with whom the clerk was engaged was also going to the Riviera. Everyone, she felt, was going. Well, for the first time in her life, she, too, would be doing what 'everybody' did.

The man in front of her turned abruptly, and she stepped into his place. She made her demand to the clerk, but at the same time half of her mind was busy with something else. That man's face – in some vague way it was familiar to her. Where had she seen him before? Suddenly she remembered. It was in the Savoy outside her room that morning. She had collided with him in the passage. Rather an odd coincidence that she should run into him twice in a day. She glanced over her shoulder, rendered uneasy by something, she knew not what. The man was standing in the doorway looking back at her. A cold shiver passed over Katherine; she had a haunting sense of tragedy, of doom impending . . .

Then she shook the impression from her with her usual good sense and turned her whole attention to what the clerk was saying.

CHAPTER 9

AN OFFER REFUSED

It was rarely that Derek Kettering allowed his temper to get the better of him. An easy-going insouciance was his chief characteristic, and it had stood him in good stead in more than one tight corner. Even now, by the time he had left Mirelle's flat, he had cooled down. He had need of coolness. The corner he was in now was a tighter one than he had ever been in before, and unforeseen factors had arisen with which, for the moment, he did not know how to deal.

He strolled along deep in thought. His brow was furrowed, and there was none of the easy, jaunty manner which sat so well upon him. Various possibilities floated through his mind. It might have been said of Derek Kettering that he was less of a fool than he looked. He saw several roads that he might take – one in particular. If he shrank from it, it was for the moment only. Desperate ills need desperate remedies. He had gauged his father-in-law correctly. A war between Derek Kettering and Rufus Van Aldin could end only one way. Derek damned money and the power of money vehemently to himself. He walked up St James's Street, across Piccadilly, and strolled along it in the direction of Piccadilly Circus. As he passed the offices of Messrs. Thomas Cook & Sons his footsteps slackened. He walked on, however, still turning the matter over in his mind. Finally, he gave a brief nod of his head, turned sharply – so sharply as to collide with a couple of pedestrians who were following in his footsteps, and went back the way he had come. This time he did not pass Cook's, but went in. The office was comparatively empty, and he got attended to at once.

'I want to go to Nice next week. Will you give me particulars?'

'What date, sir?'

'The fourteenth. What is the best train?'

'Well, of course, *the* best train is what they call "The Blue Train". You avoid the tiresome Customs business at Calais.'

Derek nodded. He knew all this, none better.

'The fourteenth,' murmured the clerk; 'that is rather soon. The Blue Train is nearly always all booked up.'

'See if there is a berth left,' said Derek. 'If there is not –' He left the sentence unfinished, with a curious smile on his face.

The clerk disappeared for a few minutes, and presently returned. 'That is all right, sir; still three berths left. I will book you one of them. What name?'

'Pavett,' said Derek. He gave the address of his rooms in Jermyn Street.

The clerk nodded, finished writing it down, wished Derek good morning politely, and turned his attention to the next client.

'I want to go to Nice – on the fourteenth. Isn't there a train called the Blue Train?'

Derek looked round sharply.

Coincidence – a strange coincidence. He remembered his own half-whimsical words to Mirelle. '*Portrait of a lady with grey eyes. I don't suppose I shall ever see her again.*' But he *had* seen her again, and, what was more, she proposed to travel to the Riviera on the same day as he did.

Just for a moment a shiver passed over him; in some ways he was superstitious. He had said, half-laughingly, that this woman might bring him bad luck. Suppose – suppose that should prove to be true. From the doorway he looked back at her as she stood talking to the clerk. For once his memory had not played him false. A lady – a lady in every sense of the word. Not very young, not singularly beautiful. But with something – grey eyes that might perhaps see too much. He knew as he went out of the door that in some way he was afraid of this woman. He had a sense of fatality.

He went back to his rooms in Jermyn Street and summoned his man.

'Take this cheque, Pavett, and go round to Cook's in Piccadilly. They will have some tickets there booked in your name, pay for them, and bring them back.'

'Very good, sir.'

Pavett withdrew.

Derek strolled over to a side-table and picked up a handful of letters. They were of a type only too familiar. Bills, small bills and large bills, one and all pressing for payment. The tone of the demands was still polite. Derek knew how soon that polite tone would change if – if certain news became public property.

He flung himself moodily into a large, leather-covered chair. A damned hole – that was what he was in. Yes, a damned hole! And ways of getting out of that damned hole were not too promising.

Pavett appeared with a discreet cough.

'A gentleman to see you – sir – Major Knighton.'

'Knighton, eh?'

Derek sat up, frowned, became suddenly alert. He said in a softer tone, almost to himself: 'Knighton – I wonder what is in the wind now?'

'Shall I – er – show him in, sir?'

His master nodded. When Knighton entered the room he found a charming and genial host awaiting him.

'Very good of you to look me up,' said Derek.

Knighton was nervous.

The other's keen eyes noticed that at once. The errand on which the secretary had come was clearly distasteful to him. He replied almost mechanically to Derek's easy flow of conversation. He declined a drink, and, if anything, his manner became stiffer than before. Derek appeared at last to notice it.

'Well,' he said cheerfully, 'what does my esteemed father-in-law want with me? You have come on his business, I take it?'

Knighton did not smile in reply.

'I have, yes,' he said carefully. 'I – I wish Mr Van Aldin had chosen someone else.'

Derek raised his eyebrows in mock dismay.

'Is it as bad as all that? I am not very thin skinned, I can assure you, Knighton.'

'No,' said Knighton; 'but this –'

He paused.

Derek eyed him keenly.

'Go on, out with it,' he said kindly. 'I can imagine my dear father-in-law's errands might not always be pleasant ones.'

Knighton cleared his throat. He spoke formally in tones that he strove to render free of embarrassment.

'I am directed by Mr Van Aldin to make you a definite offer.'

'An offer?' For a moment Derek showed his surprise. Knighton's opening words were clearly not what he had expected. He offered a cigarette to Knighton, lit one himself, and sank back in his chair, murmuring in a slightly sardonic voice:

'An offer? That sounds rather interesting.'

'Shall I go on?'

'Please. You must forgive my surprise, but it seems to me that my dear father-in-law has rather climbed down since our chat this morning. And climbing down is not what one associates with strong men, Napoleons of finance, etc. It shows – I think it shows that he finds his position weaker than he thought it.'

Knighton listened politely to the easy, mocking voice, but no sign of any kind showed itself on his rather stolid countenance. He waited until Derek had finished, and then he said quietly:

'I will state the proposition in the fewest possible words.'

'Go on.'

Knighton did not look at the other. His voice was curt and matter-of-fact.

'The matter is simply this. Mrs Kettering, as you know, is about to file a petition for divorce. If the case goes undefended you will receive one hundred thousand on the day that the decree is made absolute.'

Derek, in the act of lighting his cigarette, suddenly stopped dead. 'A hundred thousand!' he said sharply. 'Dollars?'

'Pounds.'

There was dead silence for at least two minutes. Kettering had his brows together thinking. A hundred thousand pounds. It meant Mirelle and a continuance of his pleasant, careless life. It meant that Van Aldin knew something. Van Aldin did not pay for nothing. He got up and stood by the chimney-piece.

'And in the event of my refusing his handsome offer?' he asked, with a cold, ironical politeness.

Knighton made a deprecating gesture.

'I can assure you, Mr Kettering,' he said earnestly, 'that it is with the utmost unwillingness that I came here with this message.'

'That's all right,' said Kettering. 'Don't distress yourself; it's not your fault. Now then – I asked you a question, will you answer it?'

Knighton also rose. He spoke more reluctantly than before.

'In the event of your refusing this proposition,' he said, 'Mr Van Aldin wished me to tell you in plain words that he proposes to break you. Just that.'

Kettering raised his eyebrows, but he retained his light, amused manner.

'Well, well!' he said, 'I suppose he can do it. I certainly should not be able to put up much of a fight against America's man of many millions. A hundred thousand! If you are going to bribe a man there is nothing like doing it thoroughly. Supposing I were to tell you that for two hundred thousand I'd do what he wanted, what then?'

'I would take your message back to Mr Van Aldin,' said Knighton unemotionally. 'Is that your answer?'

'No,' said Derek; 'funnily enough it is not. You can go back to my father-in-law and tell him to take himself and his bribes to hell. Is that clear?'

'Perfectly,' said Knighton. He got up, hesitated, and then flushed. 'I – you will allow me to say, Mr Kettering, that I am glad you have answered as you have.'

Derek did not reply. When the other had left the room he remained for a minute or two lost in thought. A curious smile came to his lips.

'And that is that,' he said softly.

CHAPTER 10

ON THE BLUE TRAIN

'Dad!'

Mrs Kettering started violently. Her nerves were not completely under control this morning. Very perfectly dressed in a long mink coat and a little hat of Chinese lacquer red, she had been walking along the crowded platform of Victoria deep in thought, and her father's sudden appearance and hearty greeting had an unlooked-for effect upon her.

'Why, Ruth, how you jumped!'

'I didn't expect to see you, I suppose, Dad. You said goodbye to me last night and said you had a conference this morning.'

'So I have,' said Van Aldin, 'but you are more to me than any number of darned conferences. I came to take a last look at you, since I am not going to see you for some time.'

'That is very sweet of you, Dad. I wish you were coming too.'

'What would you say if I did?'

The remark was merely a joking one. He was surprised to see the quick colour of flame in Ruth's cheeks. For a moment he almost thought he saw dismay flash out of her eyes. She laughed uncertainly and nervously.

'Just for a moment I really thought you meant it,' she said.

'Would you have been pleased?'

'Of course.' She spoke with exaggerated emphasis.

'Well,' said Van Aldin, 'that's good.'

'It isn't really for very long, Dad,' continued Ruth; 'you know, you are coming out next month.'

'Ah!' said Van Aldin unemotionally, 'sometimes I guess I will go to one of these big guys in Harley Street and have him tell me that I need sunshine and change of air right away.'

'Don't be so lazy,' cried Ruth; 'next month is ever so much nicer than this month out there. You have got all sorts of things you can't possibly leave just now.'

'Well, that's so, I suppose,' said Van Aldin, with a sigh. 'You had better be getting on board this train of yours, Ruth. Where is your seat?'

Ruth Kettering looked vaguely up at the train. At the door of one of the Pullman cars a thin, tall woman dressed in black was standing – Ruth Kettering's maid. She drew aside as her mistress came up to her.

'I have put your dressing-case under your seat, Madam, in case you should need it. Shall I take the rugs, or will you require one?'

'No, no, I shan't want one. Better go and find your own seat now, Mason.'

'Yes, Madam.'

The maid departed.

Van Aldin entered the Pullman car with Ruth. She found her seat, and Van Aldin deposited various papers and magazines on the table in front of her. The seat opposite to her was already taken, and the American gave a cursory glance at its occupant. He had a fleeting impression of attractive grey eyes and a neat travelling costume. He indulged in a little more desultory conversation with

Ruth, the kind of talk peculiar to those seeing other people off by train.

Presently, as whistles blew, he glanced at his watch.

'I had best be clearing out of here. Goodbye, my dear. Don't worry. I will attend to things.'

'Oh, Father!'

He turned back sharply. There had been something in Ruth's voice, something so entirely foreign to her usual manner, that he was startled. It was almost a cry of despair. She had made an impulsive movement towards him, but in another minute she was mistress of herself once more.

'Till next month,' she said carefully.

Two minutes later the train started.

Ruth sat very still, biting her under lip and trying hard to keep the unaccustomed tears from her eyes. She felt a sudden sense of horrible desolation. There was a wild longing upon her to jump out of the train and to go back before it was too late. She, so calm, so self-assured, for the first time in her life felt like a leaf swept by the wind. If her father knew – what would he say?

Madness! Yes, just that, madness! For the first time in her life she was swept away by emotion, swept away to the point of doing a thing which even she knew to be incredibly foolish and reckless. She was enough Van Aldin's daughter to realize her own folly, and level-headed enough to condemn her own action. But she was his daughter in another sense also. She had that same iron determination that would have what it wanted, and once it had made up its mind would not be balked. From her cradle she had been self-willed; the very circumstances of her life had developed that self-will in her. It drove her now remorselessly. Well, the die was cast. She must go through with it now.

She looked up, and her eyes met those of the woman sitting opposite. She had a sudden fancy that in some way this other woman had read her mind. She saw in those grey eyes understanding and – yes – compassion.

It was only a fleeting impression. The faces of both women hardened to well-bred impassiveness. Mrs Kettering took up a magazine, and Katherine Grey looked out of the window and watched a seemingly endless vista of depressing streets and suburban homes.

Ruth found an increasing difficulty in fixing her mind on the printed page in front of her. In spite of herself, a thousand apprehensions preyed on her mind. What a fool she had been! What a fool she was! Like all cool and self-sufficient people, when she did lose her self-control she lost it thoroughly. It was too late . . . Was it too late? Oh, for someone to speak to, for someone to advise her. She had never before had such a wish; she would have scorned the idea of relying on any judgment other than her own, but now – what was the matter with her? Panic. Yes, that would describe it best – panic. She, Ruth Kettering, was completely and utterly panic stricken.

She stole a covert glance at the figure opposite. If only she knew someone like that, some nice, cool, calm sympathetic creature. That was the sort of person one could talk to. But you can't, of course, confide in a stranger. And Ruth smiled to herself a little at the idea. She picked up the magazine again. Really she must control herself. After all she had thought all this out. She had decided of her own free will. What happiness had she ever had in her life up to now? She said to herself restlessly: 'Why shouldn't I be happy? No one will ever know.'

It seemed no time before Dover was reached. Ruth was a good sailor. She disliked the cold, and was glad to reach the shelter of the private cabin she had telegraphed for. Although she would not have admitted the fact, Ruth was in some ways superstitious. She was of the order of people to whom coincidence appeals. After disembarking at Calais and settling herself down with her maid in her double compartment in the Blue Train, she went along to the luncheon car. It was with a little shock of surprise that she found herself set down to a small table with, opposite her, the same woman who had been her *vis-à-vis* in the Pullman. A faint smile came to the lips of both women.

'This is quite a coincidence,' said Mrs Kettering.

'I know,' said Katherine; 'it is odd the way things happen.'

A flying attendant shot up to them with the wonderful velocity always displayed by the Compagnie Internationale des Wagons-Lits and deposited two cups of soup. By the time the omelette succeeded the soup they were chatting together in friendly fashion.

'It will be heavenly to get into the sunshine,' sighed Ruth.

'I am sure it will be a wonderful feeling.'

'You know the Riviera well?'

'No; this is my first visit.'

'Fancy that.'

'You go every year, I expect?'

'Practically. January and February in London are horrible.'

'I have always lived in the country. They are not very inspiring months there either. Mostly mud.'

'What made you suddenly decide to travel?'

'Money,' said Katherine. 'For ten years I have been a paid companion with just enough money of my own to buy myself strong country shoes; now I have been left what seems to me a fortune, though I dare say it would not seem so much to you.'

'Now I wonder why you said that – that it would not seem so to me.'

Katherine laughed. 'I don't really know. I suppose one forms impressions without thinking of it. I put you down in my own mind as one of the very rich of the earth. It was just an impression. I dare say I am wrong.'

'No,' said Ruth, 'you are not wrong.' She had suddenly become very grave. 'I wish you would tell me what other impressions you formed about me.'

'I –'

Ruth swept on, disregarding the other's embarrassment. 'Oh, please, don't be conventional. I want to know. As we left Victoria I looked across at you, and I had the sort of feeling that you – well, understood what was going on in my mind.'

'I can assure you I am not a mind reader,' said Katherine smiling.

'No, but will you tell me, please, just what you thought.' Ruth's eagerness was so intense and so sincere that she carried her point.

'I will tell you if you like, but you must not think me impertinent. I thought that for some reason you were in great distress of mind, and I was sorry for you.'

'You are right. You are quite right. I am in terrible trouble. I – I should like to tell you something about it, if I may.'

'Oh, dear,' Katherine thought to herself, 'how extraordinarily alike the world seems to be everywhere! People were always telling me things in St Mary Mead, and it is just the same thing here, and I don't really want to hear anybody's troubles!'

She replied politely:

'Do tell me.'

They were just finishing their lunch. Ruth gulped down her coffee, rose from her seat, and quite oblivious of the fact that Katherine had not begun to sip her coffee, said: 'Come to my compartment with me.'

They were two single compartments with a communicating door between them. In the second of them a thin maid, whom Katherine had noticed at Victoria, was sitting very upright on the seat, clutching a big scarlet morocco case with the initials R. V. K. on it. Mrs Kettering pulled the communicating door to and sank down on the seat. Katherine sat down beside her.

'I am in trouble and I don't know what to do. There is a man whom I am fond of – very fond of indeed. We cared for each other when we were young, and we were thrust apart most brutally and unjustly. Now we have come together again.'

'Yes?'

'I – I am going to meet him now. Oh! I dare say you think it is all wrong, but you don't know the circumstances. My husband is impossible. He has treated me disgracefully.'

'Yes,' said Katherine again.

'What I feel so badly about is this. I have deceived my father – it was he who came to see me off at Victoria today. He wishes me to divorce my husband, and, of course, he has no idea – that I am going to meet this other man. He would think it extraordinarily foolish.'

'Well, don't you think it is?'

'I – I suppose it is.'

Ruth Kettering looked down at her hands; they were shaking violently.

'But I can't draw back now.'

'Why not?'

'I – it is all arranged, and it would break his heart.'

'Don't you believe it,' said Katherine robustly; 'hearts are pretty tough.'

'He will think I have no courage, no strength of purpose.'

'It seems to me an awfully silly thing that you are going to do,' said Katherine. 'I think you realize that yourself.'

Ruth Kettering buried her face in her hands. 'I don't know – I don't know. Ever since I left Victoria I have had a horrible feeling of something – something that is coming to me very soon – that I can't escape.'

She clutched convulsively at Katherine's hand.

'You must think I am mad talking to you like this, but I tell you I know something horrible is going to happen.'

'Don't think it,' said Katherine; 'try to pull yourself together. You could send your father a wire from Paris, if you like, and he would come to you at once.'

The other brightened.

'Yes, I could do that. Dear old Dad. It is queer – but I never knew until today how terribly fond of him I am.' She sat up and dried her eyes with a handkerchief. 'I have been very foolish. Thank you so much for letting me talk to you. I don't know why I got into such a queer, hysterical state.'

She got up. 'I am quite all right now. I suppose, really, I just needed someone to talk to. I can't think now why I have been making such an absolute fool of myself.'

Katherine got up too.

'I am glad you feel better,' she said, trying to make her voice sound as conventional as possible. She was only too well aware that the aftermath of confidences is embarrassment. She added tactfully:

'I must be going back to my own compartment.'

She emerged into the corridor at the same time as the maid was also coming out from the next door. The latter looked towards Katherine, over her shoulder, and an expression of intense surprise showed itself on her face. Katherine turned also, but by that time whoever it was who had aroused the maid's interest had retreated into his or her compartment, and the corridor was empty. Katherine walked down it to regain her own place, which was in the next coach. As she passed the end compartment the door opened and a woman's face looked out for a moment and then pulled the door to sharply. It was a face not easily forgotten, as Katherine was to know when she saw it again. A beautiful face, oval and dark, very heavily made up in a bizarre fashion. Katherine had a feeling that she had seen it before somewhere.

She regained her own compartment without other adventure and sat for some time thinking of the confidence which had just been made to her. She wondered idly who the woman in the mink coat might be, wondered also how the end of her story would turn out.

'If I had stopped anyone from making an idiot of themselves,

I suppose I have done good work,' she thought to herself. 'But who knows? That is the kind of woman who is hard-headed and egotistical all her life, and it might be good for her to do the other sort of thing for a change. Oh, well – I don't suppose I shall ever see her again. She certainly won't want to see *me again.* That is the worst of letting people tell you things. They never do.'

She hoped that she would not be given the same place at dinner. She reflected, not without humour, that it might be awkward for both of them. Leaning back with her head against a cushion she felt tired and vaguely depressed. They had reached Paris, and the slow journey round the *ceinture*, with its interminable stops and waits, was very wearisome. When they arrived at the Gare de Lyon she was glad to get out and walk up and down the platform. The keen cold air was refreshing after the steam-heated train. She observed with a smile that her friend of the mink coat was solving the possible awkwardness of the dinner problem in her own way. A dinner basket was being handed up and received through the window by the maid.

When the train started once more, and dinner was announced by a violent ringing of bells, Katherine went along to it much relieved in mind. Her *vis-à-vis* tonight was of an entirely different kind – a small man, distinctly foreign in appearance, with a rigidly waxed moustache and an egg-shaped head which he carried rather on one side. Katherine had taken in a book to dinner with her. She found the little man's eyes fixed upon it with a kind of twinkling amusement.

'I see, Madame, that you have a *roman policier*. You are fond of such things?'

'They amuse me,' Katherine admitted.

The little man nodded with the air of complete understanding.

'They have a good sale always, so I am told. Now why is that, eh, Mademoiselle? I ask you as a student of human nature – why should that be?'

Katherine felt more and more amused.

'Perhaps they give one the illusion of living an exciting life,' she suggested.

He nodded gravely.

'Yes; there is something in that.'

'Of course, one knows that such things don't really happen,' Katherine was continuing, but he interrupted her sharply.

'Sometimes, Mademoiselle! Sometimes! I who speak to you – they have happened to *me*.'

She threw him a quick, interested glance.

'Some day, who knows, *you* might be in the thick of things,' he went on. 'It is all chance.'

'I don't think it is likely,' said Katherine. 'Nothing of that kind ever happens to me.'

He leaned forward.

'Would you like it to?'

The question startled her, and she drew in her breath sharply.

'It is my fancy, perhaps,' said the little man, as he dexterously polished one of the forks, 'but I think that you have a yearning in you for interesting happenings. *Eh bien*, Mademoiselle, all through my life I have observed one thing – "All one wants one gets!" Who knows?' His face screwed itself up comically. 'You may get more than you bargain for.'

'Is that a prophecy?' asked Katherine, smiling as she rose from the table.

The little man shook his head.

'I never prophesy,' he declared pompously. 'It is true that I have the habit of being always right – but I do not boast of it. Good-night, Mademoiselle, and may you sleep well.'

Katherine went back along the train amused and entertained by her little neighbour. She passed the open door of her friend's compartment and saw the conductor making up the bed. The lady in the mink coat was standing looking out of the window. The second compartment, as Katherine saw through the communicating door, was empty, with rugs and bags heaped up on the seat. The maid was not there.

Katherine found her own bed prepared, and since she was tired, she went to bed and switched off her light about half-past nine.

She woke with a sudden start; how much time had passed she did not know. Glancing at her watch, she found that it had stopped. A feeling of intense uneasiness pervaded her and grew stronger moment by moment. At last she got up, threw her dressing-gown round her shoulders, and stepped out into the corridor. The whole train seemed wrapped in slumber. Katherine let the window down and sat by it for some minutes, drinking in the cool night air and trying vainly to calm her uneasy fears. She presently decided that she would go along to the end and ask the conductor for the right time so that she could set her watch. She found, however, that his little chair was vacant. She hesitated for a moment and then walked through into the next coach. She looked down the long, dim line of the corridor and saw, to her surprise, that a man was standing with his hand on the door of the compartment occupied by the lady in the mink coat. That is to say, she thought it was the compartment. Probably, however, she was mistaken. He stood there for a moment or two with his back to her, seeming uncertain and hesitating in his attitude. Then he slowly turned, and with an odd feeling of fatality, Katherine recognized him as the same man whom she had noticed twice before – once in the corridor of the Savoy Hotel and once in Cook's offices. Then he opened the door of the compartment and passed in, drawing it to behind him.

An idea flashed across Katherine's mind. Could this be the man of whom the other woman had spoken – the man she was journeying to meet?

Then Katherine told herself that she was romancing. In all probability she had mistaken the compartment.

She went back to her own carriage. Five minutes later the train slackened speed. There was the long plaintive hiss of the Westinghouse brake, and a few minutes later the train came to a stop at Lyons.

CHAPTER 11

MURDER

Katherine wakened the next morning to brilliant sunshine. She went along to breakfast early, but met none of her acquaintances of the day before. When she returned to her compartment it had just been restored to its daytime appearance by the conductor, a dark man with a drooping moustache and melancholy face.

'Madame is fortunate,' he said; 'the sun shines. It is always a great disappointment to passengers when they arrive on a grey morning.'

'I should have been disappointed, certainly,' said Katherine.

The man prepared to depart.

'We are rather late, Madame,' he said. 'I will let you know just before we get to Nice.'

Katherine nodded. She sat by the window, entranced by the sunlit panorama. The palm trees, the deep blue of the sea, the bright yellow mimosa came with all the charm of novelty to the woman who for fourteen years had known only the drab winters of England.

When they arrived at Cannes, Katherine got out and walked up and down the platform. She was curious about the lady in the mink coat, and looked up at the windows of her compartment. The blinds were still drawn down – the only ones to be so on the whole train. Katherine wondered a little, and when she re-entered the train she passed along the corridor and noticed that these two compartments were still shuttered and closed. The lady of the mink coat was clearly no early riser.

Presently the conductor came to her and told her that in a few minutes the train would arrive at Nice. Katherine handed him a tip; the man thanked her, but still lingered. There was something odd about him. Katherine, who had at first wondered whether the tip had not been big enough, was now convinced that something far more serious was amiss. His face was of a sickly pallor, he was shaking all over, and looked as if he had been frightened out of his life. He was eyeing her in a curious manner. Presently he said abruptly: 'Madame will excuse me, but is she expecting friends to meet her at Nice?'

'Probably,' said Katherine. 'Why?'

But the man merely shook his head and murmured something that Katherine could not catch and moved away, not reappearing until the train came to rest at the station, when he started handing her belongings down from the window.

Katherine stood for a moment or two on the platform rather at a loss, but a fair young man with an ingenuous face came up to her and said rather hesitatingly:

'Miss Grey, is it not?'

Katherine said that it was, and the young man beamed upon her seraphically and murmured: 'I am Chubby, you know – Lady Tamplin's husband. I expect she mentioned me, but perhaps she forgot. Have you got your *billet de bagages*? I lost mine when I came out this year, and you would not believe the fuss they made about it. Regular French red tape!'

Katherine produced it, and was just about to move off beside him when a very gentle and insidious voice murmured in her ear:

'A little moment, Madame, if you please.'

Katherine turned to behold an individual who made up for insignificance of stature by a large quantity of gold lace and uniform. The individual explained. 'There were certain formalities. Madame would perhaps be so kind as to accompany him. The regulations of the police –' he threw up his arms. 'Absurd, doubtless, but there it was.'

Mr Chubby Evans listened with a very imperfect comprehension, his French being of a limited order.

'So like the French,' murmured Mr Evans. He was one of those staunch patriotic Britons who, having made a portion of a foreign country their own, strongly resent the original inhabitants of it. 'Always up to some silly dodge or other. They've never tackled people on the station before, though. This is something quite new. I suppose you'll have to go.'

Katherine departed with her guide. Somewhat to her surprise, he led her towards a siding where a coach of the departed train had been shunted. He invited her to mount into this, and, preceding her down the corridor, held aside the door of one of the compartments. In it was a pompous-looking official personage, and with him a nondescript being who appeared to be a clerk. The pompous-looking personage rose politely, bowed to Katherine, and said:

'You will excuse me, Madame, but there are certain formalities to be complied with. Madame speaks French, I trust?'

'Sufficiently, I think, Monsieur,' replied Katherine in that language.

'That is good. Pray be seated, Madame. I am M. Caux, the Commissary of Police.' He blew out his chest importantly, and Katherine tried to look sufficiently impressed.

'You wish to see my passport?' she inquired. 'Here it is.'

The Commissary eyed her keenly and gave a little grunt.

'Thank you, Madame,' he said, taking the passport from her. He cleared his throat. 'But what I really desire is a little information.'

'Information?'

The Commissary nodded his head slowly.

'About a lady who has been a fellow-passenger of yours. You lunched with her yesterday.'

'I am afraid I can't tell you anything about her. We fell into conversation over our meal, but she is a complete stranger to me. I have never seen her before.'

'And yet,' said the Commissary sharply, 'you returned to her compartment with her after lunch and sat talking for some time?'

'Yes,' said Katherine; 'that is true.'

The Commissary seemed to expect her to say something more. He looked at her encouragingly.

'Yes, Madame?'

'Well, Monsieur?' said Katherine.

'You can, perhaps, give me some kind of idea of that conversation?'

'I could,' said Katherine, 'but at the moment I see no reason to do so.'

In a somewhat British fashion she felt annoyed. This foreign official seemed to her impertinent.

'No reason?' cried the Commissary. 'Oh yes, Madame, I can assure you that there *is* a reason.'

'Then perhaps you will give it to me.'

The Commissary rubbed his chin thoughtfully for a minute or two without speaking.

'Madame,' he said at last, 'the reason is very simple. The lady in question was found dead in her compartment this morning.'

'Dead!' gasped Katherine. 'What was it – heart failure?'

'No,' said the Commissary in a reflective, dreamy voice. 'No – she was murdered.'

'Murdered!' cried Katherine.

'So you see, Madame, why we are anxious for any information we can possibly get.'

'But surely her maid –'

'The maid has disappeared.'

'Oh!' Katherine paused to assemble her thoughts.

'Since the conductor had seen you talking with her in her compartment, he quite naturally reported the fact to the police, and that is why, Madame, we have detained you, in the hope of gaining some information.'

'I am very sorry,' said Katherine; 'I don't even know her name.'

'Her name is Kettering. That we know from her passport and from the labels on her luggage. If we –'

There was a knock on the compartment door. M. Caux frowned. He opened it about six inches.

'What is the matter?' he said peremptorily. 'I cannot be disturbed.'

The egg-shaped head of Katherine's dinner acquaintance showed itself in the aperture. On his face was a beaming smile.

'My name,' he said, 'is Hercule Poirot.'

'Not,' the Commissary stammered, 'not *the* Hercule Poirot?'

'The same,' said M. Poirot. 'I remember meeting you once, M. Caux, at the *Sûreté* in Paris, though doubtless you have forgotten me?'

'Not at all, Monsieur, not at all,' declared the Commissary heartily. 'But enter, I pray you. You know of this –?'

'Yes, I know,' said Hercule Poirot. 'I came to see if I might be of any assistance?'

'We should be flattered,' replied the Commissary promptly. 'Let me present you, M. Poirot, to' – he consulted the passport he still held in his hand – 'to Madame – er – Mademoiselle Grey.'

Poirot smiled across at Katherine.

'It is strange, is it not,' he murmured, 'that my words should have come true so quickly?'

'Mademoiselle, alas! can tell us very little,' said the Commissary.

'I have been explaining,' said Katherine, 'that this poor lady was a complete stranger to me.'

Poirot nodded.

'But she talked to you, did she not?' he said gently. 'You formed an impression – is it not so?'

'Yes,' said Katherine thoughtfully. 'I suppose I did.'

'And that impression was –?'

'Yes, Mademoiselle' – the Commissary jerked himself forward – 'let us by all means have your impressions.'

Katherine sat turning the whole thing over in her mind. She felt in a way as if she were betraying a confidence, but with that ugly word 'Murder' ringing in her ears she dared not keep anything back. Too much might hang upon it. So, as nearly as she could, she repeated word for word the conversation she had had with the dead woman.

'That is interesting,' said the Commissary, glancing at the other. 'Eh, M. Poirot, that is interesting? Whether it has anything to do with the crime –' He left the sentence unfinished.

'I suppose it could not be suicide,' said Katherine, rather doubtfully.

'No,' said the Commissary, 'it could not be suicide. She was strangled with a length of black cord.'

'Oh!' Katherine shivered. M. Caux spread out his hands apologetically. 'It is not nice – no. I think that our train robbers are more brutal than they are in your country.'

'It is horrible.'

'Yes, yes' – he was soothing and apologetic – 'but you have great courage, Mademoiselle. At once, as soon as I saw you, I said to myself, "Mademoiselle has great courage." That is why I am going to ask you to do something more – something distressing, but I assure you very necessary.'

Katherine looked at him apprehensively.

He spread out his hands apologetically.

'I am going to ask you, Mademoiselle, to be so good as to accompany me to the next compartment.'

'Must I?' asked Katherine in a low voice.

'Someone must identify her,' said the Commissary, 'and since the maid has disappeared' – he coughed significantly – 'you appear to be the person who has seen most of her since she joined the train.'

'Very well,' said Katherine quietly; 'if it is necessary –'

She rose. Poirot gave her a little nod of approval.

'Mademoiselle is sensible,' he said. 'May I accompany you, M. Caux?'

'Enchanted, my dear M. Poirot.'

They went out into the corridor, and M. Caux unlocked the door of the dead woman's compartment. The blinds on the far side had been drawn half-way up to admit light. The dead woman lay on the berth to their left, in so natural a posture that one could have thought her asleep. The bedclothes were drawn up over her, and her head was turned to the wall, so that only the red auburn curls showed. Very gently M. Caux laid a hand on her shoulder and turned the body back so that the face came into view. Katherine flinched a little and dug her nails into her palms. A heavy blow had disfigured the features almost beyond recognition. Poirot gave a sharp exclamation.

'When was that done, I wonder?' he demanded. 'Before death or after?'

'The doctor says after,' said M. Caux.

'Strange,' said Poirot, drawing his brows together. He turned to Katherine. 'Be brave, Mademoiselle; look at her well. Are you sure that this is the woman you talked to in the train yesterday?'

Katherine had good nerves. She steeled herself to look long and earnestly at the recumbent figure. Then she leaned forward and took up the dead woman's hand.

'I am quite sure,' she replied at length. 'The face is too disfigured to recognize, but the build and carriage and hair are exact, and besides I noticed *this*' – she pointed to a tiny mole on the dead woman's wrist – 'while I was talking to her.'

'*Bon*,' approved Poirot. 'You are an excellent witness, Mademoiselle. There is, then, no question as to the identity, but it is strange, all the same.' He frowned down on the dead woman in perplexity.

M. Caux shrugged his shoulders.

'The murderer was carried away by rage, doubtless,' he suggested.

'If she had been struck down, it would have been comprehensible,' mused Poirot, 'but the man who strangled her slipped up behind and caught her unawares. A little choke – a little gurgle – that is all that would be heard, and then afterwards – that smashing blow on her face. Now why? Did he hope that if the face were unrecognizable she might not be identified? Or did he hate her so much that he could not resist striking that blow even after she was dead?'

Katherine shuddered, and he turned at once to her kindly.

'You must not let me distress you, Mademoiselle,' he said. 'To you this is all very new and terrible. To me, alas! it is an old story. One moment, I pray of you both.'

They stood against the door watching him as he went quickly round the compartment. He noted the dead woman's clothes neatly folded on the end of the berth, the big fur coat that hung from a hook, and the little red lacquer hat tossed on the rack. Then he passed through into the adjoining compartment, that in which Katherine had seen the maid sitting. Here the berth had not been made up. Three or four rugs were piled loosely on the seat; there was a hat-box and a couple of suit-cases. He turned suddenly to Katherine.

'You were in here yesterday,' he said. 'Do you see anything changed, anything missing?'

Katherine looked carefully round both compartments.

'Yes,' she said, 'there is something missing – a scarlet morocco case. It had the initials "R. V. K." on it. It might have been a small dressing-case or a big jewel-case. When I saw it, the maid was holding it.'

'Ah!' said Poirot.

'But, surely,' said Katherine, 'I – of course, I don't know anything about such things, but surely it is plain enough, if the maid and the jewel-case are missing?'

'You mean that it was the maid who was the thief? No, Mademoiselle, there is a very good reason against that.'

'What?'

'The maid was left behind in Paris.'

He turned to Poirot. 'I should like you to hear the conductor's story yourself,' he murmured confidentially. 'It is very suggestive.'

'Mademoiselle would doubtless like to hear it also,' said Poirot. 'You do not object, Monsieur le Commissaire?'

'No,' said the Commissary, who clearly did object very much. 'No, certainly, M. Poirot, if you say so. You have finished here?'

'I think so. One little minute.'

He had been turning over the rugs, and now he took one to the window and looked at it, picking something off it with his fingers.

'What is it?' demanded M. Caux sharply.

'Four auburn hairs.' He bent over the dead woman. 'Yes, they are from the head of Madame.'

'And what of it? Do you attach importance to them?'

Poirot let the rug drop back on the seat.

'What is important? What is not? One cannot say at this stage. But we must note each little fact carefully.'

They went back again into the first compartment, and in a minute or two the conductor of the carriage arrived to be questioned.

'Your name is Pierre Michel?' said the Commissary.

'Yes, Monsieur le Commissaire.'

'I should like you to repeat to this gentleman' – he indicated Poirot – 'the story that you told me as to what happened in Paris.'

'Very good, Monsieur le Commissaire. It was after we had left the Gare de Lyon I came along to make the beds, thinking that Madame would be at dinner, but she had a dinner-basket in her compartment. She said to me that she had been obliged to leave her maid behind in Paris, so that I only need make up one berth. She took her dinner basket into the adjoining compartment, and sat there while I made up the bed; then she told me that she did not wish to be wakened early in the morning, that she liked to sleep on. I told her I quite understood, and she wished me "good-night".'

'You yourself did not go into the adjoining compartment?'

'No, Monsieur.'

'Then you did not happen to notice if a scarlet morocco case was amongst the luggage there?'

'No, Monsieur, I did not.'

'Would it have been possible for a man to have been concealed in the adjoining compartment?'

The conductor reflected.

'The door was half open,' he said. 'If a man had stood behind the door I should not have been able to see him, but he would, of course, have been perfectly visible to Madame when she went in there.'

'Quite so,' said Poirot. 'Is there anything more you have to tell us?'

'I think that is all, Monsieur. I can remember nothing else.'

'And now this morning?' prompted Poirot.

'As Madame had ordered, I did not disturb her. It was not until just before Cannes that I ventured to knock at the door. Getting no reply, I opened it. The lady appeared to be in her bed asleep. I took her by the shoulder to rouse her, and then –'

'And then you saw what had happened,' volunteered Poirot. '*Très bien.* I think I know all I want to know.'

'I hope, Monsieur le Commissaire, it is not that I have been guilty of any negligence,' said the man piteously. 'Such an affair to happen on the Blue Train! It is horrible.'

'Console yourself,' said the Commissary. 'Everything will be done to keep the affair as quiet as possible, if only in the interests of justice. I cannot think you have been guilty of any negligence.'

'And Monsieur le Commissaire will report as much to the company?'

'But certainly, but certainly,' said M. Caux, impatiently. 'That will do now.'

The conductor withdrew.

'According to the medical evidence,' said the Commissary, 'the lady was probably dead before the train reached Lyons. Who then was the murderer? From Mademoiselle's story, it seems clear that somewhere on her journey she was to meet this man of whom she spoke. Her action in getting rid of the maid seems significant. Did the man join the train at Paris, and did she conceal him in the adjoining compartment? If so, they may have quarrelled, and he may have killed her in a fit of rage. That is one possibility. The other, and the more likely to my mind, is that her assailant was a train robber travelling on the train; that he stole along the corridor unseen by the conductor, killed her, and went off with the red morocco case, which doubtless contained jewels of some value. In all probability he left the train at Lyons, and we have already telegraphed to the station there for full particulars of anyone seen leaving the train.'

'Or he might have come on to Nice,' suggested Poirot.

'He might,' agreed the Commissary, 'but that would be a very bold course.'

Poirot let a minute or two go by before speaking, and then he said:

'In the latter case you think the man was an ordinary train robber?'

The Commissary shrugged his shoulders.

'It depends. We must get hold of the maid. It is possible that she has the red morocco case with her. If so, then the man of whom she spoke to Mademoiselle may be concerned in the case, and the affair is a crime of passion. I myself think the solution of a train robber is the more plausible. These bandits have become very bold of late.'

Poirot looked suddenly across at Katherine.

'And you, Mademoiselle,' he said, 'you heard and saw nothing during the night?'

'Nothing,' said Katherine.

Poirot turned to the Commissary.

'We need detain Mademoiselle no longer, I think,' he suggested.

The latter nodded.

'She will leave us her address?' he said.

Katherine gave him the name of Lady Tamplin's villa. Poirot made her a little bow.

'You permit that I see you again, Mademoiselle?' he said. 'Or have you so many friends that your time will be all taken up?'

'On the contrary,' said Katherine, 'I shall have plenty of leisure, and I shall be very pleased to see you again.'

'Excellent,' said Poirot, and gave her a little friendly nod. 'This shall be a *"roman policier" à nous*. We will investigate this affair together.'

CHAPTER 12

AT THE VILLA MARGUERITE

'Then you were really in the thick of it all!' said Lady Tamplin enviously. 'My dear, how thrilling!' She opened her china-blue eyes very wide and gave a little sigh.

'A real murder,' said Mr Evans gloatingly.

'Of course Chubby had no idea of anything of the kind,' went on Lady Tamplin; 'he simply could *not* imagine why the police wanted you. My dear, what an opportunity! I think, you know – yes, I certainly think something might be made out of this.'

A calculating look rather marred the ingenuousness of the blue eyes.

Katherine felt slightly uncomfortable. They were just finishing lunch, and she looked in turn at the three people sitting round the table. Lady Tamplin, full of practical schemes; Mr Evans, beaming with naïve appreciation, and Lenox with a queer crooked smile on her dark face.

'Marvellous luck,' murmured Chubby; 'I wish I could have gone along with you – and seen – all the exhibits.' His tone was wistful and childlike.

Katherine said nothing. The police had laid no injunctions of secrecy upon her, and it was clearly impossible to suppress the bare facts or try to keep them from her hostess. But she did rather wish it had been possible to do so.

'Yes,' said Lady Tamplin, coming suddenly out of her reverie, 'I do think something might be done. A little account, you know, cleverly written up. An eye-witness, a feminine touch: "*How I chatted with the dead woman, little thinking* –" that sort of thing, you know.'

'Rot!' said Lenox.

'You have no idea,' said Lady Tamplin in a soft, wistful voice, 'what newspapers will pay for a little titbit! Written, of course, by someone of really unimpeachable social position. You would not like to do it yourself, I dare say, Katherine dear, but just give me the bare bones of it, and *I* will manage the whole thing for you. Mr de Haviland is a special friend of mine. We have a little understanding together. A most delightful man – not at all reporterish. How does the idea strike you, Katherine?'

'I would much prefer to do nothing of the kind,' said Katherine bluntly.

Lady Tamplin was rather disconcerted at this uncompromising refusal. She sighed and turned to the elucidation of further details.

'A very striking-looking woman, you said? I wonder now who she could have been. You didn't hear her name?'

'It was mentioned,' Katherine admitted, 'but I can't remember it. You see, I was rather upset.'

'I should think so,' said Mr Evans; 'it must have been a beastly shock.'

It is to be doubted whether, even if Katherine had remembered the name, she would have admitted the fact. Lady Tamplin's remorseless cross-examination was making her restive. Lenox, who was observant in her own way, noticed this, and offered to take Katherine upstairs to see her room. She left her there, remarking kindly before she went: 'You mustn't mind Mother; she would make a few pennies' profit out of her dying grandmother if she could.'

Lenox went down again to find her mother and step-father discussing the newcomer.

'Presentable,' said Lady Tamplin, 'quite presentable. Her clothes are all right. That grey thing is the same model that Gladys Cooper wore in *Palm Trees in Egypt*.'

'Have you noticed her eyes – what?' interposed Mr Evans.

'Never mind her eyes, Chubby,' said Lady Tamplin tartly; 'we are discussing things that really matter.'

'Oh, quite,' said Mr Evans, and retired into his shell.

'She doesn't seem to me very – malleable,' said Lady Tamplin, rather hesitating to choose the right word.

'She has all the instincts of a lady, as they say in books,' said Lenox, with a grin.

'Narrow-minded,' murmured Lady Tamplin. 'Inevitable under the circumstances, I suppose.'

'I expect you will do your best to broaden her,' said Lenox, with a grin, 'but you will have your work cut out. Just now, you noticed, she stuck down her fore feet and laid back her ears and refused to budge.'

'Anyway,' said Lady Tamplin hopefully, 'she doesn't look to me at all mean. Some people, when they come into money, seem to attach undue importance to it.'

'Oh, you'll easily touch her for what you want,' said Lenox; 'and, after all, that is all that matters, isn't it? That is what she is here for.'

'She is my own cousin,' said Lady Tamplin, with dignity.

'Cousin, eh?' said Mr Evans, waking up again. 'I suppose I call her Katherine, don't I?'

'It is of no importance at all what you call her, Chubby,' said Lady Tamplin.

'Good,' said Mr Evans; 'then I will. Do you suppose she plays tennis?' he added hopefully.

'Of course not,' said Lady Tamplin. 'She has been a companion, I tell you. Companions don't play tennis – or golf. They might possibly play golf-croquet, but I have always understood that they wind wool and wash dogs most of the day.'

'O God!' said Mr Evans; 'do they really?'

Lenox drifted upstairs again to Katherine's room. 'Can I help you?' she asked rather perfunctorily.

On Katherine's disclaimer, Lenox sat on the edge of the bed and stared thoughtfully at her guest.

'Why did you come?' she said at last. 'To us, I mean. We're not your sort.'

'Oh, I am anxious to get into Society.'

'Don't be an ass,' said Lenox promptly, detecting the flicker of a smile. 'You know what I mean well enough. You are not a bit what I thought you would be. I say, you *have* got some decent clothes.' She sighed. 'Clothes are no good to me. I was born awkward. It's a pity, because I love them.'

'I love them too,' said Katherine, 'but it has not been much use my loving them up to now. Do you think this is nice?'

She and Lenox discussed several models with artistic fervour.

'I like you,' said Lenox suddenly. 'I came up to warn you not to be taken in by Mother, but I think now that there is no need to do that. You are frightfully sincere and upright and all those queer things, but you are not a fool. Oh hell! what is it now?'

Lady Tamplin's voice was calling plaintively from the hall:

'Lenox, Derek has just rung up. He wants to come to dinner tonight. Will it be all right? I mean, we haven't got anything awkward, like quails, have we?'

Lenox reassured her and came back into Katherine's room. Her face looked brighter and less sullen.

'I'm glad old Derek is coming,' she said; 'you'll like him.'

'Who is Derek?'

'He is Lord Leconbury's son, married a rich American woman. Women are simply potty about him.'

'Why?'

'Oh, the usual reason – very good-looking and a regular bad lot. Everyone goes off their head about him.'

'Do you?'

'Sometimes I do,' said Lenox, 'and sometimes I think I would like to marry a nice curate and live in the country and grow things in frames.' She paused a minute, and then added, 'An Irish curate would be best, and then I should hunt.'

After a minute or two she reverted to her former theme. 'There is something queer about Derek. All that family are a bit potty – mad gamblers, you know. In the old days they used to gamble away their wives and their estates, and did most reckless things just for the love of it. Derek would have made a perfect highwayman – debonair and gay, just the right manner.' She moved to the door. 'Well, come down when you feel like it.'

Left alone, Katherine gave herself up to thought. Just at present she felt thoroughly ill at ease and jarred by her surroundings. The shock of the discovery in the train and the reception of the news by her new friends jarred upon her susceptibilities. She thought long and earnestly about the murdered woman. She had been sorry for Ruth, but she could not honestly say that she had liked her. She had divined only too well the ruthless egoism that was the keynote of her personality, and it repelled her.

She had been amused and a trifle hurt by the other's cool dismissal of her when she had served her turn. That she had come to some decision, Katherine was quite certain, but she wondered now what that decision had been. Whatever it was, death had stepped in and made all decisions meaningless. Strange that it should have been so, and that a brutal crime should have been the ending of that fateful journey. But suddenly Katherine remembered a small fact that she ought, perhaps, to have told the police – a fact that had for the moment escaped her memory. Was it of any real importance? She had certainly thought that she had seen a man going into that particular compartment, but she realized that she might easily have been mistaken. It might have been the compartment next door, and certainly the man in question could be no train robber. She recalled him very clearly as she had seen him on those two previous occasions – once at the Savoy and once at Cook's office. No, doubtless she had been mistaken. He had not gone into the dead woman's compartment, and it was perhaps as well that she had said nothing to the police. She might have done incalculable harm by doing so.

She went down to join the others on the terrace outside. Through the branches of mimosa, she looked out over the blue of the Mediterranean, and, whilst listening with half an ear to Lady Tamplin's chatter, she was glad that she had come. This was better than St Mary Mead.

That evening she put on the mauvy pink dress that went by the name of *soupir d'automne*, and after smiling at her reflection in the mirror, went downstairs with, for the first time in her life, a faint feeling of shyness.

Most of Lady Tamplin's guests had arrived, and since noise was the essential of Lady Tamplin's parties, the din was already terrific. Chubby rushed up to Katherine, pressed a cocktail upon her, and took her under his wing.

'Oh, here you are, Derek,' cried Lady Tamplin, as the door opened to admit the last corner. 'Now at last we can have something to eat. I am starving.'

Katherine looked across the room. She was startled. So this – was Derek, and she realized that she was not surprised. She had always known that she would some day meet the man whom she had seen three times by such a curious chain of coincidences. She thought, too, that he recognized her. He paused abruptly in what he was saying to Lady Tamplin, and went on again as though with an effort. They all went in to dinner, and Katherine found that he was placed beside her. He turned to her at once with a vivid smile.

'I knew I was going to meet you soon,' he remarked, 'but I never dreamt that it would be here. It had to be, you know. Once at the

Savoy and once at Cook's – never twice without three times. Don't say you can't remember me or never noticed me. I insist upon your pretending that you noticed me, anyway.'

'Oh, I did,' said Katherine; 'but this is not the third time. It is the fourth time. I saw you on the Blue Train.'

'On the Blue Train!' Something undefinable came over his manner; she could not have said just what it was. It was as though he had received a check, a set-back. Then he said carelessly:

'What was the rumpus this morning? Somebody had died, hadn't they?'

'Yes,' said Katherine slowly; 'somebody had died.'

'You shouldn't die on a train,' remarked Derek flippantly. 'I believe it causes all sorts of legal and international complications, and it gives the train an excuse for being even later than usual.'

'Mr Kettering?' A stout American lady, who was sitting opposite, leaned forward and spoke to him with the deliberate intonation of her race. 'Mr Kettering, I do believe you have forgotten me, and I thought you such a perfectly lovely man.'

Derek leaned forward, answering her, and Katherine sat almost dazed.

Kettering! That was the name, of course! She remembered it now – but what a strange, ironical situation! Here was this man whom she had seen go into his wife's compartment last night, who had left her alive and well, and now he was sitting at dinner, quite unconscious of the fate that had befallen her. Of that there was no doubt. He did not know.

A servant was leaning over Derek, handing him a note and murmuring in his ear. With a word of excuse to Lady Tamplin, he broke it open, and an expression of utter astonishment came over his face as he read; then he looked at his hostess.

'This is most extraordinary. I say, Rosalie, I am afraid I will have to leave you. The Prefect of Police wants to see me at once. I can't think what about.'

'Your sins have found you out,' remarked Lenox.

'They must have,' said Derek; 'probably some idiotic nonsense, but I suppose I shall have to push off to the Prefecture. How dare the old boy rout me out from dinner? It ought to be something deadly serious to justify that,' and he laughed as he pushed back his chair and rose to leave the room.

CHAPTER 13

VAN ALDIN GETS A TELEGRAM

On the afternoon of the 15th February a thick yellow fog had settled down on London. Rufus Van Aldin was in his suite at the Savoy and was making the most of the atmospheric conditions by working double time. Knighton was overjoyed. He had found it difficult of late to get his employer to concentrate on the matters in hand. When he had ventured to urge certain courses, Van Aldin had put him off with a curt word. But now Van Aldin seemed to be throwing himself into work with redoubled energy, and the secretary made the most of his opportunities. Always tactful, he plied the spur so unobtrusively that Van Aldin never suspected it.

Yet in the middle of this absorption in business matters, one little fact lay at the back of Van Aldin's mind. A chance remark of Knighton's, uttered by the secretary in all unconsciousness, had given rise to it. It now festered unseen, gradually reaching further and further forward into Van Aldin's consciousness, until at last, in spite of himself, he had to yield to its insistence.

He listened to what Knighton was saying with his usual air of keen attention, but in reality not one word of it penetrated his mind. He nodded automatically, however, and the secretary turned to some other paper. As he was sorting them out, his employer spoke:

'Do you mind telling me that over again, Knighton?'

For a moment Knighton was at a loss.

'You mean about this, sir?' He held up a closely written Company report.

'No, no,' said Van Aldin; 'what you told me about seeing Ruth's maid in Paris last night. I can't make it out. You must have been mistaken.'

'I can't have been mistaken, sir; I actually spoke to her.'

'Well, tell me the whole thing again.'

Knighton complied.

'I had fixed up the deal with Bartheimers,' he explained, 'and had gone back to the Ritz to pick up my traps preparatory to having dinner and catching the nine o'clock train from the Gare du Nord. At the reception desk I saw a woman whom I was quite sure was Mrs Kettering's maid. I went up to her and asked if Mrs Kettering was staying there.'

'Yes, yes,' said Van Aldin. 'Of course. Naturally. And she told you that Ruth had gone on to the Riviera and had sent her to the Ritz to await further orders there?'

'Exactly that, sir.'

'It is very odd,' said Van Aldin. 'Very odd, indeed, unless the woman had been impertinent or something of that kind.'

'In that case,' objected Knighton, 'surely Mrs Kettering would have paid her down a sum of money, and told her to go back to England? She would hardly have sent her to the Ritz.'

'No,' muttered the millionaire; 'that's true.'

He was about to say something further, but checked himself. He was fond of Knighton and liked and trusted him, but he could hardly discuss his daughter's private affairs with his secretary. He had already felt hurt by Ruth's lack of frankness, and this chance information which had come to him did nothing to allay his misgivings.

Why had Ruth got rid of her maid in Paris? What possible object or motive could she have had in so doing?

He reflected for a moment or two on the curious combination of chance. How should it have occurred to Ruth, except as the wildest coincidence, that the first person that the maid should run across in Paris should be her father's secretary? Ah, but that was the way things happened. That was the way things got found out.

He winced at the last phrase; it had arisen with complete naturalness to his mind. Was there then 'something to be found out'? He hated to put this question to himself; he had no doubt of the answer. The answer was – he was sure of it – Armand de la Roche.

It was bitter to Van Aldin that a daughter of his should be gulled by such a man, yet he was forced to admit that she was in good company – that other well-bred and intelligent women had succumbed just as easily to the Count's fascination. Men saw through him, women did not.

He sought now for a phrase that would allay any suspicion that his secretary might have felt.

'Ruth is always changing her mind about things at a moment's notice,' he remarked, and then he added in a would-be careless tone: 'The maid didn't give any – er – reason for this change of plan?'

Knighton was careful to make his voice as natural as possible as he replied:

'She said, sir, that Mrs Kettering had met a friend unexpectedly.'

'Is that so?'

The secretary's practised ears caught the note of strain underlying the seemingly casual tone.

'Oh, I see. Man or woman?'

'I think she said a man, sir.'

Van Aldin nodded. His worst fears were being realized. He rose from his chair, and began pacing up and down the room, a habit of his when agitated. Unable to contain his feelings any longer, he burst forth:

'There is one thing no man can do, and that is to get a woman to listen to reason. Somehow or other, they don't seem to have any kind of *sense*. Talk of woman's instinct – why, it is well known all the world over that a woman is the surest mark for any rascally swindler. Not one in ten of them knows a scoundrel when she meets one; they can be preyed on by any good-looking fellow with a soft side to his tongue. If I had my way –'

He was interrupted. A page-boy entered with a telegram. Van Aldin tore it open, and his face went a sudden chalky white. He caught hold of the back of a chair to steady himself, and waved the page-boy from the room.

'What's the matter, sir?'

Knighton had risen in concern.

'Ruth!' said Van Aldin hoarsely.

'Mrs Kettering?'

'Killed!'

'An accident to the train?'

Van Aldin shook his head.

'No. From this it seems she has been robbed as well. They don't use the word, Knighton, but my poor girl has been murdered.'

'Oh, my God, sir!'

Van Aldin tapped the telegram with his forefinger.

'This is from the police at Nice. I must go out there by the first train.'

Knighton was efficient as ever. He glanced at the clock.

'Five o'clock from Victoria, sir.'

'That's right. You will come with me, Knighton. Tell my man,

Archer, and pack your own things. See to everything here. I want to go round to Curzon Street.'

The telephone rang sharply, and the secretary lifted the receiver.

'Yes; who is it?'

Then to Van Aldin:

'Mr Goby, sir.'

'Goby? I can't see him now. No – wait, we have plenty of time. Tell them to send him up.'

Van Aldin was a strong man. Already he had recovered that iron calm of his. Few people would have noticed anything amiss in his greeting to Mr Goby.

'I am pressed for time, Goby. Got anything important to tell me?'

Mr Goby coughed.

'The movements of Mr Kettering, sir. You wished them reported to you.'

'Yes – well?'

'Mr Kettering, sir, left London for the Riviera yesterday morning.'

'What?'

Something in his voice must have startled Mr Goby. That worthy gentleman departed from his usual practice of never looking at the person to whom he was talking, and stole a fleeting glance at the millionaire.

'What train did he go on?' demanded Van Aldin.

'The Blue Train, sir.'

Mr Goby coughed again and spoke to the clock on the mantelpiece.

'Mademoiselle Mirelle, the dancer from the Parthenon, went by the same train.'

CHAPTER 14

ADA MASON'S STORY

'I cannot repeat to you often enough, Monsieur, our horror, our consternation, and the deep sympathy we feel for you.'

Thus M. Carrège, the Juge d'Instruction, addressed Van Aldin. M. Caux, the Commissary, made sympathetic noises in his throat.

Van Aldin brushed away horror, consternation, and sympathy with an abrupt gesture. The scene was the Examining Magistrate's room at Nice. Besides M. Carrège, the Commissary, and Van Aldin, there was a further person in the room. It was that person who now spoke.

'M. Van Aldin,' he said, 'desires action – swift action.'

'Ah!' cried the Commissary, 'I have not yet presented you. M. Van Aldin, this is M. Hercule Poirot; you have doubtless heard of him. Although he has retired from his profession for some years now, his name is still a household word as one of the greatest living detectives.'

'Pleased to meet you, M. Poirot,' said Van Aldin, falling back mechanically on a formula that he had discarded some years ago. 'You have retired from your profession?'

'That is so, Monsieur. Now I enjoy the world.'

The little man made a grandiloquent gesture.

'M. Poirot happened to be travelling on the Blue Train,' explained the Commissary, 'and he has been so kind as to assist us out of his vast experience.'

The millionaire looked at Poirot keenly. Then he said unexpectedly:

'I am a very rich man, M. Poirot. It is usually said that a rich man labours under the belief that he can buy everything and everyone. That is not true. I am a big man in my way, and one big man can ask a favour from another big man.'

Poirot nodded a quick appreciation.

'That is very well said, M. Van Aldin. I place myself entirely at your service.'

'Thank you,' said Van Aldin. 'I can only say call upon me at any time, and you will not find me ungrateful. And now, gentlemen, to business.'

'I propose,' said M. Carrège, 'to interrogate the maid, Ada Mason. You have her here, I understand?'

'Yes,' said Van Aldin. 'We picked her up in Paris in passing through. She was very upset to hear of her mistress's death, but she tells her story coherently enough.'

'We will have her in, then,' said M. Carrège.

He rang the bell on his desk, and in a few minutes Ada Mason entered the room.

She was very neatly dressed in black, and the tip of her nose was red. She had exchanged her grey travelling gloves for a pair of black suède ones. She cast a look round the Examining Magistrate's office in some trepidation, and seemed relieved at the presence of her mistress's father. The Examining Magistrate prided himself on his geniality of manner, and did his best to put her at her ease. He was helped in this by Poirot, who acted as interpreter, and whose friendly manner was reassuring to the Englishwoman.

'Your name is Ada Mason; is that right?'

'Ada Beatrice I was christened, sir,' said Mason primly.

'Just so. And we can understand, Mason, that this has all been very distressing.'

'Oh, indeed it has, sir. I have been with many ladies and always given satisfaction, I hope, and I never dreamt of anything of this kind happening in any situation where I was.'

'No, no,' said M. Carrège.

'Naturally, I have read of such things, of course, in the Sunday papers. And then I always have understood that those foreign trains –' She suddenly checked her flow, remembering that the gentlemen who were speaking to her were of the same nationality as the trains.

'Now let us talk this affair over,' said M. Carrège. 'There was, I understand, no question of your staying in Paris when you started from London?'

'Oh no, sir. We were to go straight through to Nice.'

'Have you ever been abroad with your mistress before?'

'No, sir. I had only been with her two months, you see.'

'Did she seem quite as usual when starting on this journey?'

'She was worried like and a bit upset, and she was rather irritable and difficult to please.'

M. Carrège nodded.

'Now then, Mason, what was the first you heard of your stopping in Paris?'

'It was at the place they call the Gare de Lyon, sir. My mistress was thinking of getting out and walking up and down the platform. She was just going out into the corridor when she gave a sudden exclamation, and came back into her compartment with a gentleman. She shut the door between her carriage and mine, so that I didn't see or hear anything, till she suddenly opened it again and told me that she had changed her plans. She gave me some money and told me to get out and go to the Ritz. They knew her well there, she said, and would give me a room. I was to wait there until I heard from her; she would wire me what she wanted me to do. I had just time to get my things together and jump out of the train before it started off. It was a rush.'

'While Mrs Kettering was telling you this, where was the gentleman?'

'He was standing in the other compartment, sir, looking out of the window.'

'Can you describe him to us?'

'Well, you see, sir, I hardly saw him. He had his back to me most of the time. He was a tall gentleman and dark; that's all I can say. He was dressed very like another gentleman in a dark blue overcoat and a grey hat.'

'Was he one of the passengers on the train?'

'I don't think so, sir; I took it that he had come to the station to see Mrs Kettering in passing through. Of course he might have been one of the passengers; I never thought of that.'

Mason seemed a little flurried by the suggestion.

'Ah!' M. Carrège passed lightly to another subject. 'Your mistress later requested the conductor not to rouse her early in the morning. Was that a likely thing for her to do, do you think?'

'Oh yes, sir. The mistress never ate any breakfast and she didn't sleep well at nights, so that she liked sleeping on in the morning.'

Again M. Carrège passed to another subject.

'Amongst the luggage there was a scarlet morocco case, was there not?' he asked. 'Your mistress's jewel-case?'

'Yes, sir.'

'Did you take that case to the Ritz?'

'*Me* take the mistress's jewel-case to the Ritz! Oh no, indeed, sir.' Mason's tones were horrified.

'You left it behind you in the carriage?'

'Yes, sir.'

'Had your mistress many jewels with her, do you know?'

'A fair amount, sir; made me a bit uneasy sometimes, I can tell you, with those nasty tales you hear of being robbed in foreign countries. They were insured, I know, but all the same it seemed a frightful risk. Why, the rubies alone, the mistress told me, were worth several hundred thousand pounds.'

'The rubies! What rubies?' barked Van Aldin suddenly.

Mason turned to him. 'I think it was you who gave them to her, sir, not very long ago.'

'My God!' cried Van Aldin. 'You don't say she had those rubies with her? I told her to leave them at the bank.'

Mason gave once more the discreet cough which was apparently part of her stock-in-trade as a lady's maid. This time it expressed a good deal. It expressed far more clearly than words could have done, that Mason's mistress had been a lady who took her own way.

'Ruth must have been mad,' muttered Van Aldin. 'What on earth could have possessed her?'

M. Carrège in turn gave vent to a cough, again a cough of significance. It riveted Van Aldin's attention on him.

'For the moment,' said M. Carrège, addressing Mason, 'I think that is all. If you will go into the next room, Mademoiselle, they will read over to you the questions and answers, and you will sign accordingly.'

Mason went out escorted by the clerk, and Van Aldin said immediately to the Magistrate:

'Well?'

M. Carrège opened a drawer in his desk, took out a letter, and handed it across to Van Aldin.

'This was found in Madame's handbag.'

> Chere Amie, *(the letter ran)* – I will obey you; I will be prudent, discreet – all those things that a lover most hates. Paris would perhaps have been unwise, but the Isles d'Or are far away from the world, and you may be assured that nothing will leak out. It is like you and your divine sympathy to be so interested in the work on famous jewels that I am writing. It will, indeed, be an extraordinary privilege to actually see and handle these historic rubies. I am devoting a special passage to 'Heart of Fire'. My wonderful one! Soon I will make up to you for all those sad years of separation and emptiness.
>
> Your ever-adoring,
>
> Armand.

CHAPTER 15

THE COMTE DE LA ROCHE

Van Aldin read the letter through in silence. His face turned a dull angry crimson. The men watching him saw the veins start out on his forehead, and his big hands clench themselves unconsciously. He handed back the letter without a word. M. Carrège was looking with close attention at his desk, M. Caux's eyes were fixed upon the ceiling, and M. Hercule Poirot was tenderly brushing a speck of dust from his coat sleeve. With the greatest tact they none of them looked at Van Aldin.

It was M. Carrège, mindful of his status and his duties, who tackled the unpleasant subject.

'Perhaps, Monsieur,' he murmured, 'you are aware by whom – er – this letter was written?'

'Yes, I know,' said Van Aldin heavily.

'Ah?' said the magistrate inquiringly.

'A scoundrel who calls himself the Comte de la Roche.'

There was a pause; then M. Poirot leaned forward, straightened a ruler on the judge's desk, and addressed the millionaire directly.

'M. Van Aldin, we are all sensible, deeply sensible, of the pain it must give you to speak of these matters, but believe me, Monsieur, it is not the time for concealments. If justice is to be done, we must know everything. If you will reflect a little minute you will realize the truth of that clearly for yourself.'

Van Aldin was silent for a moment or two, then almost reluctantly he nodded his head in agreement.

'You are quite right, M. Poirot,' he said. 'Painful as it is, I have no right to keep anything back.'

The Commissary gave a sigh of relief, and the Examining Magistrate leaned back in his chair and adjusted a pince-nez on his long thin nose.

'Perhaps you will tell us in your own words, M. Van Aldin,' he said, 'all that you know of this gentleman.'

'It began eleven or twelve years ago – in Paris. My daughter was a young girl then, full of foolish, romantic notions, like all young girls are. Unknown to me, she made the acquaintance of this Comte de la Roche. You have heard of him, perhaps?'

The Commissary and Poirot nodded in assent.

'He calls himself the Comte de la Roche,' continued Van Aldin, 'but I doubt if he has any right to the title.'

'You would not have found his name in the *Almanac de Gotha*,' agreed the Commissary.

'I discovered as much,' said Van Aldin. 'The man was a good-looking, plausible scoundrel, with a fatal fascination for women. Ruth was infatuated with him, but I soon put a stop to the whole affair. The man was no better than a common swindler.'

'You are quite right,' said the Commissary. 'The Comte de la Roche is well known to us. If it were possible, we should have laid him by the heels before now, but *ma foi*! it is not easy; the fellow is cunning, his affairs are always conducted with ladies of high social position. If he obtains money from them under false pretences or as the fruit of blackmail, *eh bien*! naturally they will not prosecute. To look foolish in the eyes of the world, oh no, that would never do, and he has an extraordinary power over women.'

'That is so,' said the millionaire heavily. 'Well, as I told you, I broke the affair up pretty sharply. I told Ruth exactly what he was, and she had, perforce, to believe me. About a year afterwards, she met her present husband and married him. As far as I knew, that was the end of the matter; but only a week ago, I discovered, to my amazement, that my daughter had resumed her acquaintance with the Comte de la Roche. She had been meeting him frequently in London and Paris. I remonstrated with her on her imprudence, for I may tell you gentlemen that, on my insistence, she was preparing to bring a suit for divorce against her husband.'

'That is interesting,' murmured Poirot softly, his eyes on the ceiling.

Van Aldin looked at him sharply, and then went on.

'I pointed out to her the folly of continuing to see the Comte under the circumstances. I thought she agreed with me.'

The Examining Magistrate coughed delicately.

'But according to this letter –' he began, and then stopped.

Van Aldin's jaw set itself squarely.

'I know. It's no good mincing matters. However unpleasant, we have got to face facts. It seems clear that Ruth had arranged to go to Paris and meet de la Roche there. After my warnings to her, however, she must have written to the Count suggesting a change of rendezvous.'

'The Isles d'Or,' said the Commissary thoughtfully, 'are situated just opposite Hyères, a remote and idyllic spot.'

Van Aldin nodded.

'My God! How could Ruth be such a fool?' he exclaimed bitterly. 'All this talk about writing a book on jewels! Why, he must have been after the rubies from the first.'

'There are some very famous rubies,' said Poirot, 'originally part of the Crown jewels of Russia; they are unique in character, and their value is almost fabulous. There has been a rumour that they have lately passed into the possession of an American. Are we right in concluding, Monsieur, that you were the purchaser?'

'Yes,' said Van Aldin. 'They came into my possession in Paris about ten days ago.'

'Pardon me, Monsieur, but you have been negotiating for their purchase for some time?'

'A little over two months. Why?'

'These things became known,' said Poirot. 'There is always a pretty formidable crowd on the track of jewels such as these.'

A spasm distorted the other's face.

'I remember,' he said brokenly, 'a joke I made to Ruth when I gave them to her. I told her not to take them to the Riviera with her, as I could not afford to have her robbed and murdered for the sake of the jewels. My God! the things one says – never dreaming or knowing they will come true.'

There was a sympathetic silence, and then Poirot spoke in a detached manner.

'Let us arrange our facts with order and precision. According to our present theory, this is how they run. The Comte de la Roche knows of your purchase of these jewels. By an easy stratagem he induces Madame Kettering to bring the stones with her. He, then, is the man Mason saw in the train at Paris.'

The other three nodded in agreement.

'Madame is surprised to see him, but he deals with the situation promptly. Mason is got out of the way; a dinner basket is ordered. We know from the conductor that he made up the berth for the first compartment, but he did not go into the second compartment, and that a man could quite well have been concealed from him. So far the Comte could have been hidden to a marvel. No one knows of his presence on the train except Madame; he has been careful that the maid did not see his face. All that she could say is that he was tall and dark. It is all most conveniently vague. They are alone – and the train rushes through the night. There would be no outcry, no struggle, for the man is, so she thinks, her lover.'

He turned gently to Van Aldin.

'Death, Monsieur, must have been almost instantaneous. We will pass over that quickly. The Comte takes the jewel-case which lies ready to his hand. Shortly afterwards the train draws into Lyons.'

M. Carrège nodded his approval.

'Precisely. The conductor without descends. It would be easy for our man to leave the train unseen; it would be easy to catch a train back to Paris or anywhere he pleases. And the crime would be put down as an ordinary train robbery. But for the letter found in Madame's bag, the Comte would not have been mentioned.'

'It was an oversight on his part not to search that bag,' declared the Commissary.

'Without doubt he thought she had destroyed that letter. It was – pardon me, Monsieur – it was an indiscretion of the first water to keep it.'

'And yet,' murmured Poirot, 'it was an indiscretion the Comte might have foreseen.'

'You mean?'

'I mean we are all agreed on one point, and that is that the Comte de la Roche knows one subject *à fond*: Women. How was it that, knowing women as he does, he did not foresee that Madame would have kept that letter?'

'Yes – yes,' said the Examining Magistrate doubtfully, 'there is something in what you say. But at such times, you understand, a man is not master of himself. He does not reason calmly. *Mon Dieu!*' he added, with feeling, 'if our criminals kept their heads and acted with intelligence, how should we capture them?'

Poirot smiled to himself.

'It seems to me a clear case,' said the other, 'but a difficult one to prove. The Comte is a slippery customer, and unless the maid can identify him –'

'Which is most unlikely,' said Poirot.

'True, true.' The Examining Magistrate rubbed his chin. 'It is going to be difficult.'

'If he did indeed commit the crime –' began Poirot. M. Caux interrupted.

'If – you say *if*?'

'Yes, Monsieur le Commissaire, I say *if*.'

The other looked at him sharply. 'You are right,' he said at last, 'we go too fast. It is possible that the Comte may have an alibi. Then we should look foolish.'

'*Ah, ça par exemple*,' replied Poirot, 'that is of no importance whatever. Naturally, if he committed the crime he will have an alibi. A man with the Comte's experience does not neglect to take precautions. No, I said *if* for a very definite reason.'

'And what was that?'

Poirot wagged an emphatic forefinger. 'The psychology.'

'Eh?' said the Commissary.

'The psychology is at fault. The Comte is a scoundrel – yes. The Comte is a swindler – yes. The Comte preys upon women – yes. He proposes to steal Madame's jewels – again yes. Is he the kind of man to commit murder? I say *no*! A man of the type of the Comte is always a coward; he takes no risks. He plays the safe, the mean, what the English call the lowdown game; but murder, a hundred times no!' He shook his head in a dissatisfied manner.

The Examining Magistrate, however, did not seem disposed to agree with him.

'The day always comes when such gentry lose their heads and go too far,' he observed sagely. 'Doubtless that is the case here. Without wishing to disagree with you, M. Poirot –'

'It was only an opinion,' Poirot hastened to explain. 'The case is, of course, in your hands, and you will do what seems fit to you.'

'I am satisfied in my own mind the Comte de la Roche is the man we need to get hold of,' said M. Carrège. 'You agree with me, Monsieur le Commissaire?'

'Perfectly.'

'And you, M. Van Aldin?'

'Yes,' said the millionaire. 'Yes; the man is a thorough-paced villain, no doubt about it.'

'It will be difficult to lay hands on him, I am afraid,' said the Magistrate, 'but we will do our best. Telegraphed instructions shall go out at once.'

'Permit me to assist you,' said Poirot. 'There need be no difficulty.'

'Eh?'

The others stared at him. The little man smiled beamingly back at them.

'It is my business to know things,' he explained. 'The Comte is a man of intelligence. He is at present at a villa he has leased, the Villa Marina at Antibes.'

CHAPTER 16

POIROT DISCUSSES THE CASE

Everybody looked respectfully at Poirot. Undoubtedly the little man had scored heavily. The Commissary laughed – on a rather hollow note.

'You teach us all our business,' he cried. 'M. Poirot knows more than the police.'

Poirot gazed complacently at the ceiling, adopting a mock-modest air.

'What will you; it is my little hobby,' he murmured, 'to know things. Naturally I have the time to indulge it. I am not overburdened with affairs.'

'Ah!' said the Commissary shaking his head portentously. 'As for me –'

He made an exaggerated gesture to represent the cares that lay on his shoulders.

Poirot turned suddenly to Van Aldin.

'You agree, Monsieur, with this view? You feel certain that the Comte de la Roche is the murderer?'

'Why, it would seem so – yes, certainly.'

Something guarded in the answer made the Examining Magistrate look at the American curiously. Van Aldin seemed aware of his scrutiny and made an effort as though to shake off some preoccupation.

'What about my son-in-law?' he asked. 'You have acquainted him with the news? He is in Nice, I understand.'

'Certainly, Monsieur.' The Commissary hesitated, and then murmured very discreetly: 'You are doubtless aware, M. Van Aldin, that M. Kettering was also one of the passengers on the Blue Train that night?'

The millionaire nodded.

'Heard it just before I left London,' he vouchsafed laconically.

'He tells us,' continued the Commissary, 'that he had no idea his wife was travelling on the train.'

'I bet he hadn't,' said Van Aldin grimly. 'It would have been rather a nasty shock to him if he'd come across her on it.'

The three men looked at him questioningly.

'I'm not going to mince matters,' said Van Aldin savagely. 'No one knows what my poor girl has had to put up with. Derek Kettering wasn't alone. He had a lady with him.'

'Ah?'

'Mirelle – the dancer.'

M. Carrège and the Commissary looked at each other and nodded as though confirming some previous conversation. M. Carrège leaned back in his chair, joined his hands, and fixed his eyes on the ceiling.

'Ah!' he murmured again. 'One wondered.' He coughed. 'One has heard rumours.'

'The lady,' said M. Caux, 'is very notorious.'

'And also,' murmured Poirot softly, 'very expensive.'

Van Aldin had gone very red in the face. He leant forward and hit the table a bang with his fist.

'See here,' he cried, 'my son-in-law is a damned scoundrel!'

He glared at them, looking from one face to another.

'Oh, I don't know,' he went on. 'Good looks and a charming, easy manner. It took me in once upon a time. I suppose he pretended to be broken-hearted when you broke the news to him – that is, if he didn't know it already.'

'Oh, it came as a surprise to him. He was overwhelmed.'

'Darned young hypocrite,' said Van Aldin. 'Simulated great grief, I suppose?'

'N – no,' said the Commissary cautiously. 'I would not quite say that – eh, M. Carrège?'

The Magistrate brought the tips of his fingers together, and half closed his eyes.

'Shock, bewilderment, horror – these things, yes,' he declared judicially. 'Great sorrow – no – I should not say that.'

Hercule Poirot spoke once more.

'Permit me to ask, M. Van Aldin, does M. Kettering benefit by the death of his wife?'

'He benefits to the tune of a couple of millions,' said Van Aldin.

'Dollars?'

'Pounds. I settled that sum on Ruth absolutely on her marriage. She made no will and leaves no children, so the money will go to her husband.'

'Whom she was on the point of divorcing,' murmured Poirot. 'Ah, yes – *précisément*.'

The Commissary turned and looked sharply at him.

'Do you mean –?' he began.

'I mean nothing,' said Poirot. 'I arrange the facts, that is all.'

Van Aldin stared at him with awakening interest.

The little man rose to his feet.

'I do not think I can be of any further service to you, M. le Juge,' he said politely, bowing to M. Carrège. 'You will keep me informed of the course of events? It will be a kindness.'

'But certainly – most certainly.'

Van Aldin rose also.

'You don't want me any more at present?'

'No, Monsieur; we have all the information we need for the moment.'

'Then I will walk a little way with M. Poirot. That is, if he does not object?'

'Enchanted, Monsieur,' said the little man, with a bow.

Van Aldin lighted a large cigar, having first offered one to Poirot, who declined it and lit one of his own tiny cigarettes. A man of great strength of character, Van Aldin already appeared to be his everyday, normal self once more. After strolling along for a minute or two in silence, the millionaire spoke:

'I take it, M. Poirot, that you no longer exercise your profession?'

'That is so, Monsieur. I enjoy the world.'

'Yet you are assisting the police in this affair?'

'Monsieur, if a doctor walks along the street and an accident happens, does he say, "I have retired from my profession, I will continue my walk," when there is someone bleeding to death at his feet? If I had been already in Nice, and the police had sent to me and asked me to assist them, I should have refused. But this affair, the good God thrust it upon me.'

'You were on the spot,' said Van Aldin thoughtfully. 'You examined the compartment, did you not?'

Poirot nodded.

'Doubtless you found things that were, shall we say, suggestive to you?'

'Perhaps,' said Poirot.

'I hope you see what I am leading up to?' said Van Aldin. 'It seems to me that the case against this Comte de la Roche is perfectly clear, but I am not a fool. I have been watching you for this last hour or so, and I realize that for some reason of your own you don't agree with that theory?'

Poirot shrugged his shoulders.

'I may be wrong.'

'So we come to the favour I want to ask you. Will you act in this matter for me?'

'For you, personally?'

'That was my meaning.'

Poirot was silent for a moment or two. Then he said:

'You realize what you are asking?'

'I guess so,' said Van Aldin.

'Very well,' said Poirot. 'I accept. But in that case, I must have frank answers to my questions.'

'Why, certainly. That is understood.'

Poirot's manner changed. He became suddenly brusque and business-like.

'This question of a divorce,' he said. 'It was you who advised your daughter to bring the suit?'

'Yes.'

'When?'

'About ten days ago. I had had a letter from her complaining of her husband's behaviour, and I put it to her very strongly that divorce was the only remedy.'

'In what way did she complain of his behaviour?'

'He was being seen about with a *very* notorious lady – the one we have been speaking of – Mirelle.'

'The dancer. Ah-ha! And Madame Kettering objected? Was she very devoted to her husband?'

'I would not say that,' said Van Aldin, hesitating a little.

'It was not her heart that suffered, it was her pride – is that what you would say?'

'Yes, I suppose you might put it like that.'

'I gather that the marriage has not been a happy one from the beginning?'

'Derek Kettering is rotten to the core,' said Van Aldin. 'He is incapable of making any woman happy.'

'He is, as you say in England, a bad lot. That is right, is it not?'

Van Aldin nodded.

'*Très bien!* You advise Madame to seek a divorce, she agrees; you consult your solicitors. When does M. Kettering get news of what is in the wind?'

'I sent for him myself, and explained the course of action I proposed to take.'

'And what did he say?' murmured Poirot softly.

Van Aldin's face darkened at the remembrance.

'He was infernally impudent.'

'Excuse the question, Monsieur, but did he refer to the Comte de la Roche?'

'Not by name,' growled the other unwillingly, 'but he showed himself cognizant of the affair.'

'What, if I may ask, was Mr Kettering's financial position at the time?'

'How do you suppose I should know that?' asked Van Aldin, after a very brief hesitation.

'It seemed likely to me that you would inform yourself on that point.'

'Well – you are quite right, I did. I discovered that Kettering was on the rocks.'

'And now he has inherited two million pounds! *La vie* – it is a strange thing, is it not?'

Van Aldin looked at him sharply.

'What do you mean?'

'I moralize,' said Poirot, 'I reflect, I speak the philosophy. But to return to where we were. Surely M. Kettering did not propose to allow himself to be divorced without making a fight for it?'

Van Aldin did not answer for a minute or two, then he said:

'I don't exactly know what his intentions were.'

'Did you hold any further communications with him?'

Again a slight pause, then Van Aldin said:

'No.'

Poirot stopped dead, took off his hat, and held out his hand.

'I must wish you good-day, Monsieur. I can do nothing for you.'

'What are you getting at?' demanded Van Aldin angrily.

'If you do not tell me the truth, I can do nothing.'

'I don't know what you mean.'

'I think you do. You may rest assured, M. Van Aldin, that I know how to be discreet.'

'Very well, then,' said the millionaire. 'I'll admit that I was not speaking the truth just now. I *did* have further communication with my son-in-law.'

'Yes?'

'To be exact, I sent my secretary, Major Knighton, to see him, with instructions to offer him the sum of one hundred thousand pounds in cash if the divorce went through undefended.'

'A pretty sum of money,' said Poirot appreciatively: 'and the answer of Monsieur your son-in-law?'

'He sent back word that I could go to hell,' replied the millionaire succinctly.

'Ah!' said Poirot.

He betrayed no emotion of any kind. At the moment he was engaged in methodically recording facts.

'Monsieur Kettering has told the police that he neither saw nor spoke to his wife on the journey from England. Are you inclined to believe that statement, Monsieur?'

'Yes, I am,' said Van Aldin. 'He would take particular pains to keep out of her way, I should say.'

'Why?'

'Because he had got that woman with him.'

'Mirelle?'

'Yes.'

'How did you come to know that fact?'

'A man of mine, whom I had put on to watch him, reported to me that they both left by that train.'

'I see,' said Poirot. 'In that case, as you said before, he would not be likely to attempt to hold any communication with Madame Kettering.'

The little man fell silent for some time. Van Aldin did not interrupt his meditation.

CHAPTER 17

AN ARISTOCRATIC GENTLEMAN

'You have been to the Riviera before, Georges?' said Poirot to his valet the following morning.

George was an intensely English, rather wooden-faced individual.

'Yes, sir. I was here two years ago when I was in the service of Lord Edward Frampton.'

'And today,' murmured his master, 'you are here with Hercule Poirot. How one mounts in the world!'

The valet made no reply to this observation. After a suitable pause he asked:

'The brown lounge suit, sir? The wind is somewhat chilly today.'

'There is a grease spot on the waistcoat,' objected Poirot. 'A *morceau* of *filet de sole à la Jeanette* alighted there when I was lunching at the Ritz last Tuesday.'

'There is no spot there now, sir,' said George reproachfully. 'I have removed it.'

'*Très bien!*' said Poirot. 'I am pleased with you, Georges.'

'Thank you, sir.'

There was a pause, and then Poirot murmured dreamily:

'Supposing, my good Georges, that you had been born in the same social sphere as your late master, Lord Edward Frampton – that, penniless yourself, you had married an extremely wealthy wife, but that wife proposed to divorce you, with excellent reasons, what would you do about it?'

'I should endeavour, sir,' replied George, 'to make her change her mind.'

'By peaceful or by forcible methods?'

George looked shocked.

'You will excuse me, sir,' he said, 'but a gentleman of the aristocracy would not behave like a Whitechapel coster. He would not do anything low.'

'Would he not, Georges? I wonder now. Well, perhaps you are right.'

There was a knock on the door. George went to it and opened it a discreet inch or two. A low murmured colloquy went on, and then the valet returned to Poirot.

'A note, sir.'

Poirot took it. It was from M. Caux, the Commissary of Police.

'We are about to interrogate the Comte de la Roche. The Juge d'Instruction begs that you will be present.'

'Quickly, my suit, Georges! I must hasten myself.'

A quarter of an hour later, spick and span in his brown suit, Poirot entered the Examining Magistrate's room. M. Caux was already there, and both he and M. Carrège greeted Poirot with polite *empressement.*

'The affair is somewhat discouraging,' murmured M. Caux. 'It appears that the Comte arrived in Nice the day before the murder.'

'If that is true, it will settle your affair nicely for you,' responded Poirot.

M. Carrège cleared his throat.

'We must not accept this alibi without very cautious inquiry,' he declared. He struck the bell upon the table with his hand.

In another minute a tall dark man, exquisitely dressed, with a somewhat haughty cast of countenance, entered the room. So very aristocratic-looking was the Count, that it would have seemed sheer heresy even to whisper that his father had been an obscure corn-chandler in Nantes – which, as a matter of fact, was the case. Looking at him, one would have been prepared to swear that innumerable ancestors of his must have perished by the guillotine in the French Revolution.

'I am here, gentlemen,' said the Count haughtily. 'May I ask why you wish to see me?'

'Pray be seated, Monsieur le Comte,' said the Examining Magistrate politely. 'It is the affair of the death of Madame Kettering that we are investigating.'

'The death of Madame Kettering? I do not understand.'

'You were – ahem! – acquainted with the lady, I believe, Monsieur le Comte?'

'Certainly I was acquainted with her. What has that to do with the matter?'

Sticking an eyeglass in his eye, he looked coldly round the room, his glance resting longest on Poirot, who was gazing at him with a kind of simple, innocent admiration which was most pleasing to the Count's vanity. M. Carrège leaned back in his chair and cleared his throat.

'You do not perhaps know, Monsieur le Comte' – he paused – 'that Madame Kettering was murdered?'

'Murdered? *Mon Dieu*, how terrible!'

The surprise and the sorrow were excellently done – so well done, indeed, as to seem wholly natural.

'Madame Kettering was strangled between Paris and Lyons,' continued M. Carrège, 'and her jewels were stolen.'

'It is iniquitous!' cried the Count warmly; 'the police should do something about these train bandits. Nowadays no one is safe.'

'In Madame's handbag,' continued the Judge, 'we found a letter to her from you. She had, it seemed, arranged to meet you?'

The Count shrugged his shoulders and spread out his hands.

'Of what use are concealments,' he said frankly. 'We are all men of the world. Privately and between ourselves, I admit the affair.'

'You met her in Paris and travelled down with her, I believe?' said M. Carrège.

'That was the original arrangement, but by Madame's wish it was changed. I was to meet her at Hyères.'

'You did not meet her on the train at Gare de Lyon on the evening of the 14th?'

'On the contrary, I arrived in Nice on the morning of that day, so what you suggest is impossible.'

'Quite so, quite so,' said M. Carrège. 'As a matter of form, you would perhaps give me an account of your movements during the evening and night of the 14th.'

The Count reflected for a minute.

'I dined in Monte Carlo at the Café de Paris. Afterwards I went to the Le Sporting. I won a few thousand francs,' he shrugged his shoulders. 'I returned home at perhaps one o'clock.'

'Pardon me, Monsieur, but how did you return home?'

'In my own two-seater car.'

'No one was with you?'

'No one.'

'You could produce witnesses in support of this statement?'

'Doubtless many of my friends saw me there that evening. I dined alone.'

'Your servant admitted you on your return to your villa?'

'I let myself in with my own latch-key.'

'Ah!' murmured the Magistrate.

Again he struck the bell on the table with his hand. The door opened, and a messenger appeared.

'Bring in the maid, Mason,' said M. Carrège.

'Very good, Monsieur le Juge.'

Ada Mason was brought in.

'Will you be so good, Mademoiselle, as to look at this gentleman. To the best of your ability was it he who entered your mistress's compartment in Paris?'

The woman looked long and searchingly at the Count, who was, Poirot fancied, rather uneasy under this scrutiny.

'I could not say, sir, I am sure,' said Mason at last. 'It might be and again it might not. Seeing as how I only saw his back, it's hard to say. I rather think it *was* the gentleman.'

'But you are not sure?'

'No-o,' said Mason unwillingly; 'n-no, I am not sure.'

'You have seen this gentleman before in Curzon Street?'

Mason shook her head.

'I should not be likely to see any visitors that come to Curzon Street,' she explained, 'unless they were staying in the house.'

'Very well, that will do,' said the Examining Magistrate sharply.

Evidently he was disappointed.

'One moment,' said Poirot. 'There is a question I would like to put to Mademoiselle, if I may?'

'Certainly, M. Poirot – certainly, by all means.'

Poirot addressed himself to the maid.

'What happened to the tickets?'

'The tickets, sir?'

'Yes; the tickets from London to Nice. Did you or your mistress have them?'

'The mistress had her own Pullman ticket, sir; the others were in my charge.'

'What happened to them?'

'I gave them to the conductor on the French train, sir; he said it was usual. I hope I did right, sir?'

'Oh, quite right, quite right. A mere matter of detail.'

Both M. Caux and the Examining Magistrate looked at him curiously. Mason stood uncertainly for a minute or two, and then the magistrate gave her a brief nod of dismissal, and she went out. Poirot scribbled something on a scrap of paper and handed it across to M. Carrège. The latter read it and his brow cleared.

'Well, gentlemen,' demanded the Count haughtily, 'am I to be detained further?'

'Assuredly not, assuredly not,' M. Carrège hastened to say, with a great deal of amiability. 'Everything is now cleared up as regards your own position in this affair. Naturally, in view of Madame's letter, we were bound to question you.'

The Count rose, picked up his handsome stick from the corner, and, with rather a curt bow, left the room.

'And that is that,' said M. Carrège. 'You were quite right, M. Poirot – much better to let him feel he is not suspected. Two of my men will shadow him night and day, and at the same time we will go into the question of the alibi. It seems to me rather – er – a fluid one.'

'Possibly,' agreed Poirot thoughtfully.

'I asked M. Kettering to come here this morning,' continued the Magistrate, 'though really I doubt if we have much to ask him, but there are one or two suspicious circumstances –' He paused, rubbing his nose.

'Such as?' asked Poirot.

'Well' – the Magistrate coughed – 'this lady with whom he is said to be travelling – Mademoiselle Mirelle. She is staying at one hotel and he at another. That strikes me – er – as rather odd.'

'It looks,' said M. Caux, 'as though they were being careful.'

'Exactly,' said M. Carrège triumphantly; 'and what should they have to be careful about?'

'An excess of caution is suspicious, eh?' said Poirot.

'*Précisément.*'

'We might, I think,' murmured Poirot, 'ask M. Kettering one or two questions.'

The Magistrate gave instructions. A moment or two later, Derek Kettering, debonair as ever, entered the room.

'Good morning, Monsieur,' said the Judge politely.

'Good morning,' said Derek Kettering curtly. 'You sent for me. Has anything fresh turned up?'

'Pray sit down, Monsieur.'

Derek took a seat and flung his hat and stick on the table.

'Well?' he asked impatiently.

'We have, so far, no fresh data,' said M. Carrège cautiously.

'That's very interesting,' said Derek drily. 'Did you send for me here in order to tell me that?'

'We naturally thought, Monsieur, that you would like to be informed of the progress of the case,' said the Magistrate severely.

'Even if the progress is non-existent.'

'We also wished to ask you a few questions.'

'Ask away.'

'You are quite sure that you neither saw nor spoke with your wife on the train.'

'I've answered that already. I did not.'

'You had, no doubt, your reasons.'

Derek stared at him suspiciously.

'I – did – not – know – she – was – on – the – train,' he explained, spacing his words elaborately, as though to someone dull of intellect.

'That is what you say, yes,' murmured M. Carrège.

A quick frown suffused Derek's face.

'I should like to know what you are driving at. Do you know what I think, M. Carrège?'

'What do you think, Monsieur?'

'I think the French police are vastly overrated. Surely you must have some data as to these gangs of train robbers. It's outrageous that such a thing could happen on a *train de luxe* like that, and that the French police should be helpless to deal with the matter.'

'We are dealing with it, Monsieur, never fear.'

'Madame Kettering, I understand, did not leave a will,' interposed Poirot suddenly. His finger-tips were joined together, and he was looking intently at the ceiling.

'I don't think she ever made one,' said Kettering. 'Why?'

'It is a very pretty little fortune that you inherit there,' said Poirot – 'a very pretty little fortune.'

Although his eyes were still on the ceiling, he managed to see the dark flush that rose to Derek Kettering's face.

'What do you mean, and who are you?'

Poirot gently uncrossed his knees, withdrew his gaze from the ceiling, and looked the young man full in the face.

'My name is Hercule Poirot,' he said quietly, 'and I am probably the greatest detective in the world. You are quite sure that you did not see or speak to your wife on that train?'

'What are you getting at? Do you – do you mean to insinuate that I – I killed her?'

He laughed suddenly.

'I mustn't lose my temper; it's too palpably absurd. Why, if I killed her I should have had no need to steal her jewels, would I?'

'That is true,' murmured Poirot, with a rather crestfallen air. 'I did not think of that.'

'If ever there were a clear case of murder and robbery this is it,' said Derek Kettering. 'Poor Ruth, it was those damned rubies did for her. It must have got about she had them with her. There has been murder done for those same stones before now, I believe.'

Poirot sat up suddenly in his chair. A very faint green light glowed in his eyes. He looked extraordinarily like a sleek, well-fed cat.

'One more question, M. Kettering,' he said. 'Will you give me the date when you last saw your wife?'

'Let me see,' Kettering reflected. 'It must have been – yes, over three weeks ago. I am afraid I can't give you the date exactly.'

'No matter,' said Poirot drily; 'that is all I wanted to know.'

'Well,' said Derek Kettering impatiently, 'anything further?'

He looked towards M. Carrège. The latter sought inspiration from Poirot, and received it in a very faint shake of the head.

'No, M. Kettering,' he said politely; 'no, I do not think we need trouble you any further. I wish you good morning.'

'Good morning,' said Kettering. He went out, banging the door behind him.

Poirot leaned forward and spoke sharply, as soon as the young man was out of the room.

'Tell me,' he said peremptorily, 'when did you speak of these rubies to M. Kettering?'

'I have not spoken of them,' said M. Carrège. 'It was only yesterday afternoon that we learnt about them from M. Van Aldin.'

'Yes; but there was a mention of them in the Comte's letter.'

M. Carrège looked pained.

'Naturally I did not speak of that letter to M. Kettering,' he said in a shocked voice. 'It would have been most indiscreet at the present juncture of affairs.'

Poirot leaned forward and tapped the table.

'*Then how did he know about them?*' he demanded softly. 'Madame could not have told him, for he has not seen her for three weeks. It seems unlikely that either M. Van Aldin or his secretary would have mentioned them; their interviews with him have been on entirely different lines, and there has not been any hint or reference to them in the newspapers.'

He got up and took his hat and stick.

'And yet,' he murmured to himself, 'our gentleman knows all about them. I wonder now, yes, I wonder!'

CHAPTER 18

DEREK LUNCHES

Derek Kettering went straight to the Negresco, where he ordered a couple of cocktails and disposed of them rapidly; then he stared moodily out over the dazzling blue sea. He noted the passers-by mechanically – a damned dull crowd, badly dressed, and painfully uninteresting; one hardly ever saw anything worthwhile nowadays. Then he corrected this last impression rapidly, as a woman placed herself at a table a little distance away from him. She was wearing a marvellous confection of orange and black, with a little hat that shaded her face. He ordered a third cocktail; again he stared out to sea, and then suddenly he started. A well-known perfume assailed his nostrils, and he looked up to see the orange-and-black lady standing beside him. He saw her face now, and recognized her. It was Mirelle. She was smiling that insolent, seductive smile he knew so well.

'Dereek!' she murmured. 'You are pleased to see me, no?'

She dropped into a seat the other side of the table.

'But welcome me, then, stupid one,' she mocked.

'This is an unexpected pleasure,' said Derek. 'When did you leave London?'

She shrugged her shoulders.

'A day or two ago?'

'And the Parthenon?'

'I have, how do you say it? – given them the chuck!'

'Really?'

'You are not very amiable, Dereek.'

'Do you expect me to be?'

Mirelle lit a cigarette and puffed at it for a few minutes before saying:

'You think, perhaps, that it is not prudent so soon?'

Derek stared at her, then he shrugged his shoulders, and remarked formally:

'You are lunching here?'

'*Mais oui.* I am lunching with you.'

'I am exceedingly sorry,' said Derek. 'I have a very important engagement.'

'*Mon Dieu!* But you men are like children,' exclaimed the dancer. 'But yes, it is the spoilt child that you act to me, ever since that day in London when you flung yourself out of my flat, you sulk. Ah! *mais c'est inouï!*'

'My dear girl,' said Derek, 'I really don't know what you are talking about. We agreed in London that rats desert a sinking ship, that is all that there is to be said.'

In spite of his careless words, his face looked haggard and strained. Mirelle leaned forward suddenly.

'You cannot deceive me,' she murmured. 'I know – I know what you have done for me.'

He looked up at her sharply. Some undercurrent in her voice arrested his attention. She nodded her head at him.

'Ah! have no fear; I am discreet. You are magnificent! You have a superb courage, but, all the same, it was I who gave you the idea that day, when I said to you in London that accidents sometimes happened. And you are not in danger? The police do not suspect you?'

'What the devil –?'

'Hush!'

She held up a slim olive hand with one big emerald on the little finger.

'You are right, I should not have spoken so in a public place. We will not speak of the matter again, but our troubles are ended; our life together will be wonderful – wonderful!'

Derek laughed suddenly – a harsh, disagreeable laugh.

'So the rats come back, do they? Two million makes a difference – of course it does. I ought to have known that.' He laughed again. 'You will help me to spend that two million, won't you, Mirelle? You know how, no woman better.' He laughed again.

'Hush!' cried the dancer. 'What is the matter with you, Dereek? See – people are turning to stare at you.'

'Me? I will tell you what is the matter. I have finished with you, Mirelle. Do you hear? Finished!'

Mirelle did not take it as he expected her to do. She looked at him for a minute or two, and then she smiled softly.

'But what a child! You are angry – you are sore, and all because I am practical. Did I not always tell you that I adored you?'

She leaned forward.

'But I know you, Dereek. Look at me – see, it is Mirelle who speaks to you. You cannot live without her, you know it. I loved you before, I will love you a hundred times more now. I will make life wonderful for you – but wonderful. There is no one like Mirelle.'

Her eyes burned into his. She saw him grow pale and draw in his breath, and she smiled to herself contentedly. She knew her own magic and power over men.

'That is settled,' she said softly, and gave a little laugh. 'And now, Dereek, will you give me lunch?'

'No.'

He drew in his breath sharply and rose to his feet.

'I am sorry, but I told you – I have got an engagement.'

'You are lunching with someone else? Bah! I don't believe it.'

'I am lunching with that lady over there.'

He crossed abruptly to where a lady in white had just come up the steps. He addressed her a little breathlessly.

'Miss Grey, will you – will you have lunch with me? You met me at Lady Tamplin's, if you remember.'

Katherine looked at him for a minute or two with those thoughtful grey eyes that said so much.

'Thank you,' she said, after a moment's pause; 'I should like to very much.'

CHAPTER 19

AN UNEXPECTED VISITOR

The Comte de la Roche had just finished *déjeuner*, consisting of an *omelette fines herbes*, an *entrecôte Bearnaise*, and a *savarin au rhum*. Wiping his fine black moustache delicately with his table napkin, the Comte rose from the table. He passed through the salon of the villa, noting with appreciation the few *objets d'art* which were carelessly scattered about. The Louis XV snuff-box, the satin shoe worn by Marie Antoinette, and the other historic trifles that were part of the Comte's *mise en scène*. They were, he would explain to his fair visitors, heirlooms in his family. Passing through on to the terrace the Comte looked out on to the Mediterranean with an unseeing eye. He was in no mood for appreciating the beauties of scenery. A fully matured scheme had been rudely brought to naught, and his plans had to be cast afresh. Stretching himself out in a basket chair, a cigarette held between his white fingers, the Comte pondered deeply.

Presently Hipolyte, his man-servant, brought out coffee and a choice of liqueurs. The Comte selected some very fine old brandy.

As the man-servant was preparing to depart, the Comte arrested him with a slight gesture. Hipolyte stood respectfully to attention. His countenance was hardly a prepossessing one, but the correctitude of his demeanour went far to obliterate the fact. He was now the picture of respectful attention.

'It is possible,' said the Comte, 'that in the course of the next few days various strangers may come to the house. They will endeavour to scrape acquaintance with you and with Marie. They will probably ask you various questions concerning me.'

'Yes, Monsieur le Comte.'

'Perhaps this has already happened?'

'No, Monsieur le Comte.'

'There have been no strangers about the place? You are certain?'

'There has been no one, Monsieur le Comte.'

'That is well,' said the Comte drily; 'nevertheless they will come – I am sure of it. They will ask questions.'

Hipolyte looked at his master in intelligent anticipation.

The Comte spoke slowly, without looking at Hipolyte.

'As you know, I arrived here last Tuesday morning. If the police or any other inquirer should question you, do not forget that fact. I arrived on Tuesday, the 14th – not Wednesday, the 15th. You understand?'

'Perfectly, Monsieur le Comte.'

'In an affair where a lady is concerned, it is always necessary to be discreet. I feel certain, Hipolyte, that you can be discreet.'

'I can be discreet, Monsieur.'

'And Marie?'

'Marie also. I will answer for her.'

'That is well then,' murmured the Comte.

When Hipolyte had withdrawn, the Comte sipped his black coffee with a reflective air. Occasionally he frowned, once he shook his head slightly, twice he nodded it. Into the midst of these cogitations came Hipolyte once more.

'A lady, Monsieur.'

'A lady?'

The Comte was surprised. Not that a visit from a lady was an unusual thing at the Villa Marina, but at this particular moment the Comte could not think who the lady was likely to be.

'She is, I think, a lady not known to Monsieur,' murmured the valet helpfully.

The Comte was more and more intrigued.

'Show her out here, Hipolyte,' he commanded.

A moment later a marvellous vision in orange and black stepped out in the terrace, accompanied by a strong perfume of exotic blossoms.

'Monsieur le Comte de la Roche?'

'At your service, Mademoiselle,' said the Comte, bowing.

'My name is Mirelle. You may have heard of me.'

'Ah, indeed, Mademoiselle, but who has not been enchanted by the dancing of Mademoiselle Mirelle? Exquisite!'

The dancer acknowledged this compliment with a brief mechanical smile.

'My descent upon you is unceremonious,' she began.

'But seat yourself, I beg of you, Mademoiselle,' cried the Comte, bringing forward a chair.

Behind the gallantry of his manner he was observing her narrowly. There were very few things that the Comte did not know about women. True, his experience had not lain much in ladies of Mirelle's class, who were themselves predatory. He and the dancer were, in a sense, birds of a feather. His arts, the Comte knew, would be thrown away on Mirelle. She was a Parisienne, and a shrewd one. Nevertheless, there was one thing that the Comte could recognize infallibly when he saw it. He knew at once that he was in the presence of a very angry woman, and an angry woman, as the Comte was well aware, always says more than is prudent, and is occasionally a source of profit to a level-headed gentleman who keeps cool.

'It is most amiable of you, Mademoiselle, to honour my poor abode thus.'

'We have mutual friends in Paris,' said Mirelle. 'I have heard of you from them, but I come to see you today for another reason. I have heard of you since I came to Nice – in a different way, you understand.'

'Ah?' said the Comte softly.

'I will be brutal,' continued the dancer; 'nevertheless, believe that I have your welfare at heart. They are saying in Nice, Monsieur le Comte, that you are the murderer of the English lady, Madame Kettering.'

'I! – the murderer of Madame Kettering? Bah! But how absurd!'

He spoke more languidly than indignantly, knowing that he would thus provoke her further.

'But yes,' she insisted, 'it is as I tell you.'

'It amuses people to talk,' murmured the Comte indifferently. 'It would be beneath me to take such wild accusations seriously.'

'You do not understand.' Mirelle bent forward, her dark eyes flashing. 'It is not the idle talk of those in the street. It is the police.'

'The police – ah?'

The Comte sat up, alert once more.

Mirelle nodded her head vigorously several times.

'Yes, yes. You comprehend me – I have friends everywhere. The Prefect himself –' She left the sentence unfinished, with an eloquent shrug of the shoulders.

'Who is not indiscreet where a beautiful woman is concerned?' murmured the Count politely.

'The police believe that you killed Madame Kettering. But they are wrong.'

'Certainly they are wrong,' agreed the Comte easily.

'You say that, but you do not know the truth. I do.'

The Comte looked at her curiously.

'You know who killed Madame Kettering? Is that what you would say, Mademoiselle?'

Mirelle nodded vehemently.

'Yes.'

'Who was it?' asked the Comte sharply.

'Her husband.' She leant across to the Comte, speaking in a low voice that vibrated with anger and excitement. 'It was her husband who killed her.'

The Comte leaned back in his chair. His face was a mask.

'Let me ask you, Mademoiselle – how do you know this?'

'How do I know it?' Mirelle sprang to her feet, with a laugh. 'He boasted of it beforehand. He was ruined, bankrupt, dishonoured. Only the death of his wife could save him. He told me so. He travelled on the same train – but she was not to know it. Why was that, I ask you? So that he might creep upon her in the night – Ah!' – she shut her eyes – 'I can see it happening . . .'

The Count coughed.

'Perhaps – perhaps,' he murmured. 'But surely, Mademoiselle, in that case he would not steal the jewels?'

'The jewels!' breathed Mirelle. 'The jewels. Ah! Those rubies . . .'

Her eyes grew misty, a far-away light in them. The Comte looked at her curiously, wondering for the hundredth time at the magical influence of precious stones on the female sex. He recalled her to practical matters.

'What do you want me to do, Mademoiselle?'

Mirelle became alert and business-like once more.

'Surely it is simple. You will go to the police. You will say to them that M. Kettering committed this crime.'

'And if they do not believe me? If they ask for proof?' He was eyeing her closely.

Mirelle laughed softly, and drew her orange-and-black wrap closer round her.

'Send them to me, Monsieur le Comte,' she said softly; 'I will give them the proof they want.'

Upon that she was gone, an impetuous whirlwind, her errand accomplished.

The Comte looked after her, his eyebrows delicately raised.

'She is in a fury,' he murmured. 'What has happened now to upset her? But she shows her hand too plainly. Does she really believe that Mr Kettering killed his wife? She would like me to believe it. She would even like the police to believe it.'

He smiled to himself. He had no intention whatsoever of going to the police. He saw various other possibilities; to judge by his smile, an agreeable vista of them.

Presently, however, his brow clouded. According to Mirelle, he was suspected by the police. That might be true or it might not. An angry woman of the type of the dancer was not likely to bother about the strict veracity of her statements. On the other hand, she might easily have obtained – inside information. In that case – his mouth set grimly – in that case he must take certain precautions.

He went into the house and questioned Hipolyte closely once more as to whether any strangers had been to the house. The valet was positive in his assurances that this was not the case. The Comte went up to his bedroom and crossed over to an old bureau that stood against the wall. He let down the lid of this, and his delicate fingers sought for a spring at the back of one of the pigeon-holes. A secret drawer flew out; in it was a small brown paper package. The Comte took this out and weighed it in his hand carefully for a minute or two. Raising his hand to his head, with a slight grimace he pulled out a single hair. This he placed on the lip of the drawer and shut it carefully. Still carrying the small parcel in his hand, he went downstairs and out of the house to the garage, where stood a scarlet two-seater car. Ten minutes later he had taken the road for Monte Carlo.

He spent a few hours at the Casino, then sauntered out into the town. Presently he re-entered the car and drove off in the direction of Mentone. Earlier in the afternoon he had noticed an inconspicuous grey car some little distance behind him. He noticed it again now. He smiled to himself. The road was climbing steadily upwards. The Comte's foot pressed hard on the accelerator. The little red car had been specially built to the Comte's design, and had a far more powerful engine than would have been suspected from its appearance. It shot ahead.

Presently he looked back and smiled; the grey car was following behind. Smothered in dust, the little red car leaped along the road. It was travelling now at a dangerous pace, but the Comte was a first-class driver. Now they were going down hill, twisting and curving unceasingly. Presently the car slackened speed, and finally came to a standstill before a Bureau de Poste. The Comte jumped out, lifted the lid of the tool chest, extracted the small brown paper parcel and hurried into the post office. Two minutes later he was driving once more in the direction of Mentone. When the grey car arrived there, the Comte was drinking English five o'clock tea on the terrace of one of the hotels.

Later, he drove back to Monte Carlo, dined there, and reached home once more at eleven o'clock. Hipolyte came out to meet him with a disturbed face.

'Ah! Monsieur le Comte has arrived. Monsieur le Comte did not telephone me, by any chance?'

The Comte shook his head.

'And yet at three o'clock I received a summons from Monsieur le Comte, to present myself to him at Nice, at the Negresco.'

'Really,' said the Comte; 'and you went?'

'Certainly, Monsieur, but at the Negresco they knew nothing of Monsieur le Comte. He had not been there.'

'Ah,' said the Comte, 'doubtless at that hour Marie was out doing her afternoon marketing?'

'That is so, Monsieur le Comte.'

'Ah, well,' said the Comte, 'it is of no importance. A mistake.'

He went upstairs, smiling to himself.

Once within his own room, he bolted his door and looked sharply round. Everything seemed as usual. He opened various drawers and cupboards. Then he nodded to himself. Things had been replaced almost exactly as he had left them, but not quite. It was evident that a very thorough search had been made.

He went over to the bureau and pressed the hidden spring. The drawer flew open, but the hair was no longer where he had placed it. He nodded his head several times.

'They are excellent, our French police,' he murmured to himself – 'excellent. Nothing escapes them.'

CHAPTER 20

KATHERINE MAKES A FRIEND

On the following morning Katherine and Lenox were sitting on the terrace of the Villa Marguerite. Something in the nature of a friendship was springing up between them, despite the difference in age. But for Lenox, Katherine would have found life at the Villa Marguerite quite intolerable. The Kettering case was the topic of the moment. Lady Tamplin frankly exploited her guest's connection with the affair for all it was worth. The most persistent rebuffs that Katherine could administer quite failed to pierce Lady Tamplin's self-esteem. Lenox adopted a detached attitude, seemingly amused at her mother's manoeuvres, and yet with a sympathetic understanding of Katherine's feelings. The situation was not helped by Chubby, whose naïve delight was unquenchable, and who introduced Katherine to all and sundry as:

'This is Miss Grey. You know that Blue Train business? She was in it up to the ears! Had a long talk with Ruth Kettering a few hours before the murder! Bit of luck for her, eh?'

A few remarks of this kind had provoked Katherine that morning to an unusually tart rejoinder, and when they were alone together Lenox observed in her slow drawl:

'Not used to exploitation, are you? You have a lot to learn, Katherine.'

'I am sorry I lost my temper. I don't, as a rule.'

'It is about time you learnt to blow off steam. Chubby is only an ass; there is no harm in him. Mother, of course, is trying, but you can lose your temper with her until Kingdom come, and it won't make any impression. She will open large, sad blue eyes at you and not care a bit.'

Katherine made no reply to this filial observation, and Lenox presently went on:

'I am rather like Chubby. I delight in a good murder, and besides – well, knowing Derek makes a difference.'

Katherine nodded.

'So you lunched with him yesterday,' pursued Lenox reflectively. 'Do you like him, Katherine?'

Katherine considered for a minute or two.

'I don't know,' she said very slowly.

'He is very attractive.'

'Yes, he is attractive.'

'What don't you like about him?'

Katherine did not reply to the question, or at any rate not directly. 'He spoke of his wife's death,' she said. 'He said he would not pretend that it had been anything but a bit of most marvellous luck for him.'

'And that shocked you, I suppose,' said Lenox. She paused, and then added in rather a queer tone of voice: 'He likes you, Katherine.'

'He gave me a very good lunch,' said Katherine, smiling.

Lenox refused to be side-tracked.

'I saw it the night he came here,' she said thoughtfully. 'The way he looked at you; and you are not his usual type – just the opposite. Well, I suppose it is like religion – you get it at a certain age.'

'Mademoiselle is wanted at the telephone,' said Marie, appearing at the window of the salon. 'M. Hercule Poirot desires to speak with her.'

'More blood and thunder. Go on, Katherine; go and dally with your detective.'

M. Hercule Poirot's voice came neat and precise in its intonation to Katherine's ear.

'That is Mademoiselle Grey who speaks? *Bon.* Mademoiselle, I have a word for you from M. Van Aldin, the father of Madame Kettering. He wishes very much to speak with you, either at the Villa Marguerite or at his hotel, whichever you prefer.'

Katherine reflected for a moment, but she decided that for Van Aldin to come to the Villa Marguerite would be both painful and unnecessary. Lady Tamplin would have hailed his advent with far too much delight. She never lost a chance to cultivate millionaires. She told Poirot that she would much rather come to Nice.

'Excellent, Mademoiselle. I will call for you myself in an auto. Shall we say in about three-quarters of an hour?'

Punctually to the moment Poirot appeared. Katherine was waiting for him, and they drove off at once.

'Well, Mademoiselle, how goes it?'

She looked at his twinkling eyes, and was confirmed in her first impression that there was something very attractive about M. Hercule Poirot.

'This is our own *roman policier*, is it not?' said Poirot. 'I made you the promise that we should study it together. And me, I always keep my promises.'

'You are too kind,' murmured Katherine.

'Ah, you mock yourself at me; but do you want to hear the developments of the case, or do you not?'

Katherine admitted that she did, and Poirot proceeded to sketch for her a thumbnail portrait of the Comte de la Roche.

'You think he killed her,' said Katherine thoughtfully.

'That is the theory,' said Poirot guardedly.

'Do you yourself believe that?'

'I did not say so. And you, Mademoiselle, what do you think?'

Katherine shook her head.

'How should I know? I don't know anything about those things, but I should say that –'

'Yes,' said Poirot encouragingly.

'Well – from what you say the Count does not sound the kind of man who would actually kill anybody.'

'Ah! Very good,' cried Poirot. 'You agree with me; that is just what I have said.' He looked at her sharply. 'But tell me, you have met Mr Derek Kettering?'

'I met him at Lady Tamplin's, and I lunched with him yesterday.'

'A *mauvais sujet*,' said Poirot, shaking his head; 'but *les femmes* – they like that, eh?'

He twinkled at Katherine and she laughed.

'He is the kind of man one would notice anywhere,' continued Poirot. 'Doubtless you observed him on the Blue Train?'

'Yes, I noticed him.'

'In the restaurant car?'

'No. I didn't notice him at meals at all. I only saw him once – going into his wife's compartment.'

Poirot nodded. 'A strange business,' he murmured. 'I believe you said you were awake, Mademoiselle, and looked out of your window at Lyons? You saw no tall dark man such as the Comte de la Roche leave the train?'

Katherine shook her head. 'I don't think I saw anyone at all,' she said. 'There was a youngish lad in a cap and overcoat who got out, but I don't think he was leaving the train, only walking up and down the platform. There was a fat Frenchman with a beard, in pyjamas and an overcoat, who wanted a cup of coffee. Otherwise, I think there were only the train attendants.'

Poirot nodded his head several times. 'It is like this, you see,' he confided, 'the Comte de la Roche has an alibi. An alibi, it is a very pestilential thing, and always open to the gravest suspicion. But here we are!'

They went straight up to Van Aldin's suite, where they found Knighton. Poirot introduced him to Katherine. After a few commonplaces had been exchanged, Knighton said: 'I will tell Mr Van Aldin that Miss Grey is here.'

He went through a second door into an adjoining room. There was a low murmur of voices, and then Van Aldin came into the room and advanced towards Katherine with outstretched hand, giving her at the same time a shrewd and penetrating glance.

'I am pleased to meet you, Miss Grey,' he said simply. 'I have been wanting very badly to hear what you can tell me about Ruth.'

The quiet simplicity of the millionaire's manner appealed to Katherine strongly. She felt herself in the presence of a very genuine grief, the more real for its absence of outward sign.

He drew forward a chair.

'Sit here, will you, and just tell me all about it.'

Poirot and Knighton retired discreetly into the other room, and Katherine and Van Aldin were left alone together. She found no difficulty in her task. Quite simply and naturally she related her conversation with Ruth Kettering, word for word as nearly as she could. He listened in silence, leaning back in his chair, with one hand shading his eyes. When she had finished he said quietly:

'Thank you, my dear.'

They both sat silent for a minute or two. Katherine felt that words of sympathy would be out of place. When the millionaire spoke, it was in a different tone:

'I am very grateful to you, Miss Grey. I think you did something to ease my poor Ruth's mind in the last hours of her life. Now I want to ask you something. You know – M. Poirot will have told you – about the scoundrel that my poor girl had got herself mixed up with. He was the man of whom she spoke to you – the man she was going to meet. In your judgment, do you think she might have changed her mind after her conversation with you? Do you think she meant to go back on her word?'

'I can't honestly tell you. She had certainly come to some decision, and seemed more cheerful in consequence of it.'

'She gave you no idea where she intended to meet the skunk – whether in Paris or at Hyères?'

Katherine shook her head.

'She said nothing as to that.'

'Ah!' said Van Aldin thoughtfully, 'and that is the important point. Well, time will show.'

He got up and opened the door of the adjoining room. Poirot and Knighton came back.

Katherine declined the millionaire's invitation to lunch, and Knighton went down with her and saw her into the waiting car. He returned to find Poirot and Van Aldin deep in conversation.

'If we only knew,' said the millionaire thoughtfully, 'what decision Ruth came to. It might have been any of half a dozen. She might have meant to leave the train at Paris and cable to me. She may have meant to have gone on to the south of France and have an explanation with the Count there. We are in the dark – absolutely in the dark. But we have the maid's word for it that she was both startled and dismayed at the Count's appearance at the station in Paris. That was clearly not part of the preconceived plan. You agree with me, Knighton?'

The secretary started. 'I beg your pardon, Mr Van Aldin. I was not listening.'

'Day-dreaming, eh?' said Van Aldin. 'That's not like you. I believe that girl has bowled you over.'

Knighton blushed.

'She is a remarkably nice girl,' said Van Aldin thoughtfully, 'very nice. Did you happen to notice her eyes?'

'Any man,' said Knighton, 'would be bound to notice her eyes.'

CHAPTER 21

AT THE TENNIS

Several days had elapsed. Katherine had been for a walk by herself one morning, and came back to find Lenox grinning at her expectantly.

'Your young man has been ringing you up, Katherine!'

'Who do you call my young man?'

'A new one – Rufus Van Aldin's secretary. You seem to have made rather an impression there. You are becoming a serious breaker of hearts, Katherine. First Derek Kettering, and now this young Knighton. The funny thing is that I remember him quite well. He was in Mother's War Hospital that she ran out here. I was only a kid of about eight at the time.'

'Was he badly wounded?'

'Shot in the leg, if I remember rightly – rather a nasty business. I think the doctors messed it up a bit. They said he wouldn't limp or anything, but when he left here he was still completely dot and go one.'

Lady Tamplin came out and joined them.

'Have you been telling Katherine about Major Knighton?' she asked. 'Such a dear fellow! Just at first I didn't remember him – one had so many – but now it all comes back.'

'He was a bit too unimportant to be remembered before,' said Lenox. 'Now that he is a secretary to an American millionaire, it is a very different matter.'

'Darling!' said Lady Tamplin in her vague reproachful voice.

'What did Major Knighton ring up about?' inquired Katherine.

'He asked if you would like to go to the tennis this afternoon. If so, he would call for you in a car. Mother and I accepted for you with *empressement*. Whilst you dally with a millionaire's secretary, you might give me a chance with the millionaire, Katherine. He is about sixty, I suppose, so that he will be looking about for a nice sweet young thing like me.'

'I should like to meet Mr Van Aldin,' said Lady Tamplin earnestly; 'one has heard so much of him. Those fine rugged figures of the Western world' – she broke off – 'so fascinating,' she murmured.

'Major Knighton was very particular to say it was Mr Van Aldin's invitation,' said Lenox. 'He said it so often that I began to smell a rat. You and Knighton would make a very nice pair, Katherine. Bless you, my children.'

Katherine laughed, and went upstairs to change her clothes.

Knighton arrived soon after lunch and endured manfully Lady Tamplin's transports of recognition.

When they were driving together towards Cannes he remarked to Katherine: 'Lady Tamplin has changed wonderfully little.'

'In manner or appearance?'

'Both. She must be, I suppose, well over forty, but she is a remarkably beautiful woman still.'

'She is,' agreed Katherine.

'I am very glad that you could come today,' went on Knighton. 'M. Poirot is going to be there also. What an extraordinary little man he is. Do you know him well, Miss Grey?'

Katherine shook her head. 'I met him on the train on the way here. I was reading a detective novel, and I happened to say something about such things not happening in real life. Of course, I had no idea of who he was.'

'He is a very remarkable person,' said Knighton slowly, 'and has done some very remarkable things. He has a kind of genius for going to the root of the matter, and right up to the end no one has any idea of what he is really thinking. I remember I was staying at a house in Yorkshire, and Lady Clanravon's jewels were stolen. It seemed at first to be a simple robbery, but it completely baffled the local police. I wanted them to call in Hercule Poirot, and said he was the only man who could help them, but they pinned their faith to Scotland Yard.'

'And what happened?' said Katherine curiously.

'The jewels were never recovered,' said Knighton drily.

'You really do believe in him?'

'I do indeed. The Comte de la Roche is a pretty wily customer. He has wriggled out of most things. But I think he has met his match in Hercule Poirot.'

'The Comte de la Roche,' said Katherine thoughtfully; 'so you really think he did it?'

'Of course.' Knighton looked at her in astonishment. 'Don't you?'

'Oh yes,' said Katherine hastily; 'that is, I mean, if it was not just an ordinary train robbery.'

'It might be, of course,' agreed the other, 'but it seems to me that the Comte de la Roche fits into this business particularly well.'

'And yet he has an alibi.'

'Oh, alibis!' Knighton laughed, his face broke into his attractive boyish smile.

'You confess that you read detective stories, Miss Grey. You must know that anyone who has a perfect alibi is always open to grave suspicion.'

'Do you think that real life is like that?' asked Katherine, smiling.

'Why not? Fiction is founded on fact.'

'But is rather superior to it,' suggested Katherine.

'Perhaps. Anyway, if I was a criminal I should not like to have Hercule Poirot on my track.'

'No more should I,' said Katherine, and laughed.

They were met on arrival by Poirot. As the day was warm he was attired in a white duck suit, with a white camellia in his buttonhole.

'*Bonjour*, Mademoiselle,' said Poirot. 'I look very English, do I not?'

'You look wonderful,' said Katherine tactfully.

'You mock yourself at me,' said Poirot genially. 'But no matter. Papa Poirot, he always laughs the last.'

'Where is Mr Van Aldin?' asked Knighton.

'He will meet us at our seats. To tell you the truth, my friend, he is not too well pleased with me. Oh, those Americans – the repose, the calm, they know it not! Mr Van Aldin, he would that I fly myself in the pursuit of criminals through all the byways of Nice.'

'I should have thought myself that it would not have been a bad plan,' observed Knighton.

'You are wrong,' said Poirot; 'in these matters one needs not energy but finesse. At the tennis one meets everyone. That is so important. Ah, there is Mr Kettering.'

Derek came abruptly up to them. He looked reckless and angry, as though something had arisen to upset him. He and Knighton greeted each other with some frigidity. Poirot alone seemed unconscious of any sense of strain, and chatted pleasantly in a laudable attempt to put everyone at their ease. He paid little compliments.

'It is amazing, M. Kettering, how well you speak the French,' he observed – 'so well that you could be taken for a Frenchman if you chose. That is a very rare accomplishment among Englishmen.'

'I wish I did,' said Katherine. 'I am only too well aware that my French is of a painfully British order.'

They reached their seats and sat down, and almost immediately Knighton perceived his employer signalling to him from the other end of the court, and went off to speak to him.

'Me, I approve of that young man,' said Poirot, sending a beaming smile after the departing secretary; 'and you, Mademoiselle?'

'I like him very much.'

'And you, M. Kettering?'

Some quick rejoinder was springing to Derek's lips, but he checked it as though something in the little Belgian's twinkling eyes had made him suddenly alert. He spoke carefully, choosing his words.

'Knighton is a very good fellow,' he said.

Just for a moment Katherine fancied that Poirot looked disappointed.

'He is a great admirer of yours, M. Poirot,' she said, and she related some of the things that Knighton had said. It amused her to see the little man plume himself like a bird, thrusting out his chest, and assuming an air of mock modesty that would have deceived no one.

'That reminds me, Mademoiselle,' he said suddenly, 'I have a little matter of business I have to speak to you about. When you were sitting talking to that poor lady in the train, I think you must have dropped a cigarette case.'

Katherine looked rather astonished. 'I don't think so,' she said. Poirot drew from his pocket a cigarette case of soft blue leather, with the initial 'K' on it in gold.

'No, that is not mine,' Katherine said.

'Ah, a thousand apologies. It was doubtless Madame's own. "K", of course, stands for Kettering. We were doubtful, because she had another cigarette case in her bag, and it seemed odd that she should have two.' He turned to Derek suddenly. 'You do not know, I suppose, whether this was your wife's case or not?'

Derek seemed momentarily taken aback. He stammered a little in his reply: 'I – I don't know. I suppose so.'

'It is not yours by any chance?'

'Certainly not. If it were mine it would hardly have been in my wife's possession.'

Poirot looked more ingenuous and childlike than ever.

'I thought perhaps you might have dropped it when you were in your wife's compartment,' he explained guilelessly.

'I never was there. I have already told the police that a dozen times.'

'A thousand pardons,' said Poirot, with his most apologetic

air. 'It was Mademoiselle here who mentioned having seen you going in.'

He stopped with an air of embarrassment.

Katherine looked at Derek. His face had gone rather white, but perhaps that was her fancy. His laugh, when it came, was natural enough.

'You made a mistake, Miss Grey,' he said easily. 'From what the police have told me, I gather that my own compartment was only a door or two away from that of my wife's – though I never suspected the fact at the time. You must have seen me going into my own compartment.' He got up quickly as he saw Van Aldin and Knighton approaching.

'I'm going to leave you now,' he announced. 'I can't stand my father-in-law at any price.'

Van Aldin greeted Katherine very courteously, but was clearly in a bad humour.

'You seem fond of watching tennis, M. Poirot,' he growled.

'It is a pleasure to me, yes,' replied Poirot placidly.

'It is as well you are in France,' said Van Aldin. 'We are made of sterner stuff in the States. Business comes before pleasure there.'

Poirot did not take offence; indeed, he smiled gently and confidingly at the irate millionaire.

'Do not enrage yourself, I beg of you. Everyone his own methods. Me, I have always found it a delightful and pleasing idea to combine business and pleasure together.'

He glanced at the other two. They were deep in conversation, absorbed in each other. Poirot nodded his head in satisfaction, and then leant towards the millionaire, lowering his voice as he did so.

'It is not only for pleasure that I am here, M. Van Aldin. Observe just opposite us that tall old man – the one with the yellow face and the venerable beard.'

'Well, what of him?'

'That,' Poirot said, 'is M. Papopolous.'

'A Greek, eh?'

'As you say – a Greek. He is a dealer in antiques of world-wide reputation. He has a small shop in Paris, and he is suspected by the police of being something more.'

'What?'

'A receiver of stolen goods, especially jewels. There is nothing as to the re-cutting and re-setting of gems that he does not know. He deals with the highest in Europe and with the lowest of the riff-raff of the underworld.'

Van Aldin was looking at Poirot with suddenly awakened attention.

'Well?' he demanded, a new note in his voice.

'I ask myself,' said Poirot, 'I, Hercule Poirot' – he thumped himself dramatically on the chest – 'ask myself *why is M. Papopolous suddenly come to Nice?*'

Van Aldin was impressed. For a moment he had doubted Poirot and suspected the little man of being past his job, a *poseur* only. Now, in a moment, he switched back to his original opinion. He looked straight at the little detective.

'I must apologize to you, M. Poirot.'

Poirot waved the apology aside with an extravagant gesture.

'Bah!' he cried, 'all that is of no importance. Now listen, M. Van Aldin; I have news for you.'

The millionaire looked sharply at him, all his interest aroused.

Poirot nodded.

'It is as I say. You will be interested. As you know, M. Van Aldin, the Comte de la Roche has been under surveillance ever since his interview with the Juge d'Instruction. The day after that, during his absence, the Villa Marina was searched by the police.'

'Well,' said Van Aldin, 'did they find anything? I bet they didn't.'

Poirot made him a little bow.

'Your acumen is not at fault, M. Van Aldin. They found nothing of an incriminating nature. It was not to be expected that they would. The Comte de la Roche, as your expressive idiom has it, was not born on the preceding day. He is an astute gentleman with great experience.'

'Well, go on,' growled Van Aldin.

'It may be, of course, that the Comte had nothing of a compromising nature to conceal. But we must not neglect the possibility. If, then, he has something to conceal, where is it? Not in his house – the police searched thoroughly. Not on his person, for he knows that he is liable to arrest at any minute. There remains – his car. As I say, he was under surveillance. He was followed on that day to Monte Carlo. From there he went by road to Mentone, driving himself. His car is a very powerful one, it outdistanced his pursuers, and for about a quarter of an hour they completely lost sight of him.'

'And during that time you think he concealed something by the roadside?' asked Van Aldin, keenly interested.

'By the roadside, no. *Ca n'est pas pratique.* But listen now – me, I have made a little suggestion to M. Carrège. He is graciously pleased to approve of it. In each Bureau de Poste in the neighbourhood it has been seen to that there is someone who knows the Comte de la Roche by sight. Because, you see, Monsieur, the best way of hiding a thing is by sending it away by the post.'

'Well?' demanded Van Aldin; his face was keenly alight with interest and expectation.

'Well – *voilà!*' With a dramatic flourish Poirot drew out from his pocket a loosely wrapped brown paper package from which the string had been removed.

'During that quarter of an hour's interval, our good gentleman mailed this.'

'The address?' asked the other sharply.

Poirot nodded his head.

'Might have told us something, but unfortunately it does not. The package was addressed to one of these little newspaper shops in Paris where letters and parcels are kept until called for on payment of a small commission.'

'Yes, but what is inside?' demanded Van Aldin impatiently.

Poirot unwrapped the brown paper and disclosed a square cardboard box. He looked round him.

'It is a good moment,' he said quietly. 'All eyes are on the tennis. Look, Monsieur!'

He lifted the lid of the box for a fraction of a second. An exclamation of utter astonishment came from the millionaire. His face turned as white as chalk.

'My God!' he breathed, 'the rubies.'

He sat for a minute as though dazed. Poirot restored the box to his pocket and beamed placidly. Then suddenly the millionaire seemed to come out of his trance; he leaned across to Poirot and wrung his hand so heartily that the little man winced with pain.

'This is great,' said Van Aldin. 'Great! You are the goods, M. Poirot. Once and for all, you are the goods.'

'It is nothing,' said Poirot modestly. 'Order, method, being prepared for eventualities beforehand – that is all there is to it.'

'And now, I suppose, the Comte de la Roche has been arrested?' continued Van Aldin eagerly.

'No,' said Poirot.

A look of utter astonishment came over Van Aldin's face.

'But why? What more do you want?'

'The Comte's alibi is still unshaken.'

'But that is nonsense.'

'Yes,' said Poirot; 'I rather think it is nonsense, but unfortunately we have to prove it so.'

'In the meantime he will slip through your fingers.'

Poirot shook his head very energetically.

'No,' he said, 'he will not do that. The one thing the Comte cannot afford to sacrifice is his social position. At all costs he must stop and brazen it out.'

Van Aldin was still dissatisfied.

'But I don't see –'

Poirot raised a hand. 'Grant me a little moment, Monsieur. Me, I have a little idea. Many people have mocked themselves at the little ideas of Hercule Poirot – and they have been wrong.'

'Well,' said Van Aldin, 'go ahead. What is this little idea?'

Poirot paused for a moment and then he said:

'I will call upon you at your hotel at eleven o'clock tomorrow morning. Until then, say nothing to anyone.'

CHAPTER 22

M. PAPOPOLOUS BREAKFASTS

M. Papopolous was at breakfast. Opposite him sat his daughter, Zia.

There was a knock at the sitting-room door, and a chasseur entered with a card which he brought to M. Papopolous. The latter scrutinized it, raised his eyebrows, and passed it over to his daughter.

'Ah!' said M. Papopolous, scratching his left ear thoughtfully, 'Hercule Poirot. I wonder now.'

Father and daughter looked at each other.

'I saw him yesterday at the tennis,' said M. Papopolous. 'Zia, I hardly like this.'

'He was very useful to you once,' his daughter reminded him.

'That is true,' acknowledged M. Papopolous; 'also he has retired from active work, so I hear.'

These interchanges between father and daughter had passed in their own language. Now M. Papopolous turned to the chasseur and said in French:

'*Faîtes monter ce monsieur*.'

A few minutes later Hercule Poirot, exquisitely attired, and swinging a cane with a jaunty air, entered the room.

'My dear M. Papopolous.'

'My dear M. Poirot.'

'And Mademoiselle Zia.' Poirot swept her a low bow.

'You will excuse us going on with our breakfast,' said M. Papopolous, pouring himself out another cup of coffee. 'Your call is – ahem! – a little early.'

'It is scandalous,' said Poirot, 'but you see, I am pressed.'

'Ah!' murmured M. Papopolous, 'you are on an affair then?'

'A very serious affair,' said Poirot; 'the death of Madame Kettering.'

'Let me see,' M. Papopolous looked innocently up at the ceiling, 'that was the lady who died on the Blue Train, was it not? I saw a mention of it in the papers, but there was no suggestion of foul play.'

'In the interests of justice,' said Poirot, 'it was thought best to suppress that fact.'

There was a pause.

'And in what way can I assist you, M. Poirot?' asked the dealer politely.

'*Voilà*,' said Poirot, 'I shall come to the point.' He took from his pocket the same box that he had displayed at Cannes, and, opening it, he took out the rubies and pushed them across the table to Papopolous.

Although Poirot was watching him narrowly, not a muscle of the old man's face moved. He took up the jewels and examined them with a kind of detached interest, then he looked across at the detective inquiringly:

'Superb, are they not?' asked Poirot.

'Quite excellent,' said M. Papopolous.

'How much should you say they are worth?'

The Greek's face quivered a little.

'Is it really necessary to tell you, M. Poirot?' he asked.

'You are shrewd, M. Papopolous. No, it is not. They are not, for instance, worth five hundred thousand dollars.'

Papopolous laughed, and Poirot joined with him.

'As an imitation,' said Papopolous, handing them back to Poirot, 'they are, as I said, quite excellent. Would it be indiscreet to ask, M. Poirot, where you came across them?'

'Not at all,' said Poirot; 'I have no objection to telling an old friend like yourself. They were in the possession of the Comte de la Roche.'

M. Papopolous' eyebrows lifted themselves eloquently.

'Indeed,' he murmured.

Poirot leaned forward and assumed his most innocent and beguiling air.

'M. Papopolous,' he said, 'I am going to lay my cards upon the table. The original of these jewels was stolen from Madame Kettering on the Blue Train. Now I will say to you first this: *I am not concerned with the recovery of these jewels. That is the affair of the police.* I am working not for the police but for M. Van Aldin. I want to lay hands on the man who killed Madame Kettering. I am interested in the jewels only in so far as they may lead me to the man. You understand?'

The last two words were uttered with great significance. M. Papopolous, his face quite unmoved, said quietly:

'Go on.'

'It seems to me probable, Monsieur, that the jewels will change hands in Nice – may already have done so.'

'Ah!' said M. Papopolous.

He sipped his coffee reflectively, and looked a shade more noble and patriarchal than usual.

'I say to myself,' continued Poirot, with animation, 'what good fortune! My old friend, M. Papopolous, is in Nice. He will aid me.'

'And how do you think I can aid you?' inquired M. Papopolous coldly.

'I said to myself, without doubt M. Papopolous is in Nice on business.

'Not at all,' said M. Papopolous, 'I am here for my health – by the doctor's orders.'

He coughed hollowly.

'I am desolated to hear it,' replied Poirot, with somewhat insincere sympathy. 'But to continue. When a Russian Grand Duke, an Austrian Archduchess, or an Italian Prince wish to dispose of their family jewels – to whom do they go? To M. Papopolous, is it not? He who is famous all over the world for the discretion with which he arranges these things.'

The other bowed.

'You flatter me.'

'It is a great thing, discretion,' mused Poirot, and was rewarded by the fleeting smile which passed across the Greek's face. 'I, too, can be discreet.'

The eyes of the two men met.

Then Poirot went on speaking very slowly, and obviously picking his words with care.

'I say to myself, this: if these jewels have changed hands in Nice, M. Papopolous would have heard of it. He has knowledge of all that passes in the jewel world.'

'Ah!' said M. Papopolous, and helped himself to a *croissant.*

'The police, you understand,' said M. Poirot, 'do not enter into the matter. It is a personal affair.'

'One hears rumours,' admitted M. Papopolous cautiously.

'Such as?' prompted Poirot.

'Is there any reason why I should pass them on?'

'Yes,' said Poirot, 'I think there is. You may remember, M. Papopolous, that seventeen years ago there was a certain article in your hands, left there as security by a very – er – Prominent Person. It was in your keeping and it unaccountably disappeared. You were, if I may use the English expression, in the soup.'

His eyes came gently round to the girl. She had pushed her cup and plate aside, and with both elbows on the table and her chin resting on her hands, was listening eagerly. Still keeping an eye on her he went on:

'I am in Paris at the time. You send for me. You place yourself in my hands. If I restore to you that – article, you say I shall earn your undying gratitude. *Eh bien!* I did restore it to you.'

A long sigh came from M. Papopolous.

'It was the most unpleasant moment of my career,' he murmured.

'Seventeen years is a long time,' said Poirot thoughtfully, 'but I believe that I am right in saying, Monsieur, that your race does not forget.'

'A Greek?' murmured Papopolous, with an ironical smile.

'It was not as a Greek I meant,' said Poirot.

There was a silence, and then the old man drew himself up proudly.

'You are right, M. Poirot,' he said quietly. 'I am a Jew. And, as you say, our race does not forget.'

'You will aid me then?'

'As regards the jewels, Monsieur, I can do nothing.'

The old man, as Poirot had done just now, picked his words carefully.

'I know nothing. I have heard nothing. But I can perhaps do you a good turn – that is, if you are interested in racing.'

'Under certain circumstances I might be,' said Poirot, eyeing him steadily.

'There is a horse running at Longchamps that would, I think, repay attention. I cannot say for certain, you understand; this news passed through so many hands.'

He stopped, fixing Poirot with his eyes, as though to make sure that the latter was comprehending him.

'Perfectly, perfectly,' said Poirot, nodding.

'The name of the horse,' said M. Papopolous, leaning back and joining the tips of his fingers together, 'is the Marquis. I think, but I am not sure, that it is an English horse, eh, Zia?'

'I think so too,' said the girl.

Poirot got up briskly.

'I thank you, Monsieur,' he said. 'It is a great thing to have what the English call a tip from the stable. Au revoir, Monsieur, and many thanks.'

He turned to the girl.

'Au revoir, Mademoiselle Zia. It seems to me but yesterday that I saw you in Paris. One would say that two years had passed at most.'

'There is a difference between sixteen and thirty-three,' said Zia ruefully.

'Not in your case,' declared Poirot gallantly. 'You and your father will perhaps dine with me one night.'

'We shall be delighted,' replied Zia.

'Then we will arrange it,' declared Poirot, 'and now – *je me sauve.*'

Poirot walked along the street humming a little tune to himself. He twirled his stick with a jaunty air, once or twice he smiled to himself quietly. He turned into the first Bureau de Poste he came to and sent off a telegram. He took some time in wording it, but it was in code and he had to call upon his memory. It purported to deal with a missing scarf-pin, and was addressed to Inspector Japp, Scotland Yard.

Decoded, it was short and to the point. '*Wire me everything known about man whose soubriquet is the Marquis.*'

CHAPTER 23

A NEW THEORY

It was exactly eleven o'clock when Poirot presented himself at Van Aldin's hotel. He found the millionaire alone.

'You are punctual, M. Poirot,' he said, with a smile, as he rose to greet the detective.

'I am always punctual,' said Poirot. 'The exactitude – always do I observe it. Without order and method –'

He broke off. 'Ah, but it is possible that I have said these things to you before. Let us come at once to the object of my visit.'

'Your little idea?'

'Yes, my little idea.' Poirot smiled.

'First of all, Monsieur, I should like to interview once more the maid, Ada Mason. She is here?'

'Yes, she's here.'

'Ah!'

Van Aldin looked at him curiously. He rang the bell, and a messenger was despatched to find Mason.

Poirot greeted her with his usual politeness, which was never without effect on that particular class.

'Good afternoon, Mademoiselle,' he said cheerfully. 'Be seated, will you not, if Monsieur permits.'

'Yes, yes, sit down, my girl,' said Van Aldin.

'Thank you, sir,' said Mason primly, and she sat down on the extreme edge of a chair. She looked bonier and more acid than ever.

'I have come to ask you yet more questions,' said Poirot. 'We must get to the bottom of this affair. Always I return to the question of the man in the train. You have been shown the Comte de la Roche. You say that it is possible he was the man, but you are not sure.'

'As I told you, sir, I never saw the gentleman's face. That is what makes it so difficult.'

Poirot beamed and nodded.

'Precisely, exactly. I comprehend well the difficulty. Now, Mademoiselle, you have been in the service of Madame Kettering two months, you say. During that time, how often did you see your master?'

Mason reflected a minute or two, and then said:

'Only twice, sir.'

'And was that near to, or far away?'

'Well once, sir, he came to Curzon Street. I was upstairs, and I looked over the banisters and saw him in the hall below. I was a bit curious like, you understand, knowing the way things – er – were.' Mason finished up with her discreet cough.

'And the other time?'

'I was in the Park, sir, with Annie – one of the housemaids, sir, and she pointed out the master to me walking with a foreign lady.'

Again Poirot nodded.

'Now listen, Mason, this man whom you saw in the carriage talking to your mistress at the Gare de Lyon, how do you know it was not your master?'

'The master, sir? Oh, I don't think it could have been.'

'But you are not sure,' Poirot persisted.

'Well – I never thought of it, sir.'

Mason was clearly upset at the idea.

'You have heard that your master was also on the train. What more natural than that it should be he who came along the corridor?'

'But the gentleman who was talking to the mistress must have come from outside, sir. He was dressed for the street. In an overcoat and soft hat.'

'Just so, Mademoiselle, but reflect a minute. The train has just arrived at the Gare de Lyon. Many of the passengers promenade themselves upon the quay. Your mistress was about to do so, and for that purpose had doubtless put on her fur coat, eh?'

'Yes, sir,' agreed Mason.

'Your master, then, does the same. The train is heated, but outside in the station it is cold. He puts on his overcoat and his hat and he walks along beside the train, and looking up at the lighted windows he suddenly sees Madame Kettering. Until then he has had no idea that she was on the train. Naturally, he mounts the carriage and goes to her compartment. She gives an exclamation of surprise at seeing him and quickly shuts the door between the two compartments since it is possible that their conversation may be of a private nature.'

He leaned back in his chair and watched the suggestion slowly take effect. No one knew better than Hercule Poirot that the class to which Mason belongs cannot be hurried. He must give her time to get rid of her own preconceived ideas. At the end of three minutes she spoke:

'Well, of course, sir, it might be so. I never thought of it that way. The master is tall and dark, and just about that build. It was seeing the hat and coat that made me say it was a gentleman from outside. Yes, it might have been the master. I would not like to say either way I'm sure.'

'Thank you very much, Mademoiselle. I shall not require you any further. Ah, just one thing more.' He took from his pocket the cigarette case he had already shown to Katherine. 'Is that your mistress's case?' he said to Mason.

'No, sir, it is not the mistress's – at least –'

She looked suddenly startled. An idea was clearly working its way to the forefront of her mind.

'Yes?' said Poirot encouragingly.

'I think, sir – I can't be sure, but I think – it is a case that the mistress bought to give to the master.'

'Ah,' said Poirot in a non-committal manner.

'But whether she ever did give it to him or not, I can't say, of course.'

'Precisely,' said Poirot, 'precisely. That is all, I think, Mademoiselle. I wish you good afternoon.'

Ada Mason retired discreetly, closing the door noiselessly behind her.

Poirot looked across at Van Aldin, a faint smile upon his face. The millionaire looked thunderstruck.

'You think – you think it was Derek?' he queried, 'but –

everything points the other way. Why, the Count has actually been caught red-handed with the jewels on him.'

'No.'

'But you told me –'

'What did I tell you?'

'That story about the jewels. You showed them to me.'

'No.'

Van Aldin stared at him.

'You mean to say you didn't show them to me?'

'No.'

'Yesterday – at the tennis?'

'No.'

'Are you crazy, M. Poirot, or am I?'

'Neither of us is crazy,' said the detective. 'You ask me a question; I answer it. You say have I not shown you the jewels yesterday? I reply – no. What I showed you, M. Van Aldin, was a first-class imitation, hardly to be distinguished except by an expert from the real ones.'

CHAPTER 24

POIROT GIVES ADVICE

It took the millionaire some few minutes to take the thing in. He stared at Poirot as though dumbfounded. The little Belgian nodded at him gently.

'Yes,' he said, 'it alters the position, does it not?'

'Imitation!'

He leaned forward.

'All along, M. Poirot, you have had this idea? All along this is what you have been driving at? You never believed that the Comte de la Roche was the murderer?'

'I have had doubts,' said Poirot quietly. 'I said as much to you. Robbery with violence and murder' – he shook his head energetically – 'no, it is difficult to picture. It does not harmonize with the personality of the Comte de la Roche.'

'But you believe that he meant to steal the rubies?'

'Certainly. There is no doubt as to that. See, I will recount to you the affair as I see it. The Comte knew of the rubies and he laid his plans accordingly. He made up a romantic story of a book he was writing, so as to induce your daughter to bring them with her. He provided himself with an exact duplicate. It is clear, is it not, that substitution is what he was after. Madame, your daughter, was not an expert on jewels. It would probably be a long time before she discovered what had occurred. When she did so – well – I do not think she would prosecute the Comte. Too much would come out. He would have in his possession various letters of hers. Oh yes, a very safe scheme from the Comte's point of view – one that he has probably carried out before.'

'It seems clear enough, yes,' said Van Aldin musingly.

'It accords with the personality of the Comte de la Roche,' said Poirot.

'Yes, but now –' Van Aldin looked searchingly at the other. 'What actually happened? Tell me that, M. Poirot.'

Poirot shrugged his shoulders.

'It is quite simple,' he said; 'someone stepped in ahead of the Comte.'

There was a long pause.

Van Aldin seemed to be turning things over in his mind. When he spoke it was without beating about the bush.

'How long have you suspected my son-in-law, M. Poirot?'

'From the very first. He had the motive and the opportunity. Everyone took for granted that the man in Madame's compartment in Paris was the Comte de la Roche. I thought so, too. Then you happened to mention that you had once mistaken the Comte for your son-in-law. That told me that they were of the same height and build, and alike in colouring. It put some curious ideas in my head. The maid had only been with your daughter a short time. It was unlikely that she would know Mr Kettering well by sight, since he had not been living in Curzon Street; also the man was careful to keep his face turned away.'

'You believe he – murdered her?' said Van Aldin hoarsely.

Poirot raised a hand quickly.

'No, no, I did not say that – but it is a possibility – a very strong possibility. He was in a tight corner, a very tight corner, threatened with ruin. This was the one way out.'

'But why take the jewels?'

'To make the crime appear an ordinary one committed by train robbers. Otherwise suspicion might have fallen on him straight away.'

'If that is so, what has he done with the rubies?'

'That remains to be seen. There are several possibilities. There is a man in Nice who may be able to help, the man I pointed out at the tennis.'

He rose to his feet and Van Aldin rose also and laid his hand on the little man's shoulder. His voice when he spoke was harsh with emotion.

'Find Ruth's murderer for me,' he said, 'that is all I ask.'

Poirot drew himself up.

'Leave it in the hands of Hercule Poirot,' he said superbly; 'have no fears. I will discover the truth.'

He brushed a speck of fluff from his hat, smiled reassuringly at the millionaire, and left the room. Nevertheless, as he went down the stairs some of the confidence faded from his face.

'It is all very well,' he murmured to himself, 'but there are difficulties. Yes, there are great difficulties.' As he was passing out of the hotel he came to a sudden halt. A car had drawn up in front of the door. In it was Katherine Grey, and Derek Kettering was standing beside it talking to her earnestly. A minute or two later the car drove off and Derek remained standing on the pavement looking after it. The expression on his face was an odd one. He gave a sudden impatient gesture of the shoulders, sighed deeply, and turned to find Hercule Poirot standing at his elbow. In spite of himself he started. The two men looked at each other. Poirot steadily and unwaveringly and Derek with a kind of light-hearted defiance. There was a sneer behind the easy mockery of his tone when he spoke, raising his eyebrows slightly as he did so.

'Rather a dear, isn't she?' he asked easily.

His manner was perfectly natural.

'Yes,' said Poirot thoughtfully, 'that describes Mademoiselle Katherine very well. It is very English, that phrase there, and Mademoiselle Katherine, she also is very English.'

Derek remained perfectly still without answering.

'And yet she is *sympathique*, is it not so?'

'Yes,' said Derek; 'there are not many like her.'

He spoke softly, almost as though to himself. Poirot nodded significantly. Then he leant towards the other and spoke in a different tone, a quiet, grave tone that was new to Derek Kettering.

'You will pardon an old man, Monsieur, if he says to you something that you may consider impertinent. There is one of your English proverbs that I would quote to you. It says that "It is well to be off with the old love, before being on with the new."'

Kettering turned on him angrily.

'What the devil do you mean?'

'You enrage yourself at me,' said Poirot placidly. 'I expected as much. As to what I mean – I mean, Monsieur, that there is a second car with a lady in it. If you turn your head you will see her.'

Derek spun round. His face darkened with anger.

'Mirelle, damn her!' he muttered. 'I will soon –'

Poirot arrested the movement he was about to make.

'Is it wise what you are about to do there?' he asked warningly. His eyes shone softly with a green light in them. But Derek was past noticing the warning signs. In his anger he was completely off his guard.

'I have broken with her utterly, and she knows it,' cried Derek angrily.

'You have broken with her, yes, but has *she* broken with you?'

Derek gave a sudden harsh laugh.

'She won't break with two million pounds if she can help it,' he murmured brutally; 'trust Mirelle for that.'

Poirot raised his eyebrows.

'You have the outlook cynical,' he murmured.

'Have I?' There was no mirth in his sudden wide smile. 'I have lived in the world long enough, M. Poirot, to know that all women are pretty much alike.' His face softened suddenly. 'All save one.'

He met Poirot's gaze defiantly. A look of alertness crept into his eyes, then faded again. 'That one,' he said, and jerked his head in the direction of Cap Martin.

'Ah!' said Poirot.

This quiescence was well calculated to provoke the impetuous temperament of the other.

'I know what you are going to say,' said Derek rapidly, 'the kind of life I have led, the fact that I am not worthy of her. You will say that I have no right to think even of such a thing. You will say that it is not a case of giving a dog a bad name – I know that it is not decent to be speaking like this with my wife dead only a few days, and murdered at that.'

He paused for breath, and Poirot took advantage of the pause to remark in his plaintive tone:

'But, indeed, I have not said anything at all.'

'But you will.'

'Eh?' said Poirot.

'You will say that I have no earthly chance of marrying Katherine.'

'No,' said Poirot, 'I would not say that. Your reputation is bad, yes, but with women – never does that deter them. If you were a man of excellent character, of strict morality who had done nothing that he should not do, and – possibly everything that he should do – *eh bien*! then I should have grave doubts of your success. Moral worth, you understand, it is not romantic. It is appreciated, however, by widows.'

Derek Kettering stared at him, then he swung round on his heel and went up to the waiting car.

Poirot looked after him with some interest. He saw the lovely vision lean out of the car and speak.

Derek Kettering did not stop. He lifted his hat and passed straight on.

'*Ca y est*,' said M. Hercule Poirot, 'it is time, I think, that I return *chez moi*.'

He found an imperturbable George pressing trousers.

'A pleasant day, Georges, somewhat fatiguing, but not without interest,' he said.

George received these remarks in his usual wooden fashion.

'Indeed, sir.'

'The personality of a criminal, Georges, is an interesting matter. Many murderers are men of great personal charm.'

'I always heard, sir, that Dr. Crippen was a pleasant-spoken gentleman. And yet he cut up his wife like so much mincemeat.'

'Your instances are always apt, Georges.'

The valet did not reply, and at that moment the telephone rang. Poirot took up the receiver.

''Allo – 'allo – yes, yes, it is Hercule Poirot who speaks.'

'This is Knighton. Will you hold the line a minute, M. Poirot. Mr Van Aldin would like to speak to you.'

There was a moment's pause, then the millionaire's voice came through.

'Is that you, M. Poirot? I just wanted to tell you that Mason came to me now of her own accord. She has been thinking it over, and she says that she is almost certain that the man at Paris was Derek Kettering. There was something familiar about him at the time, she says, but at the minute she could not place it. She seems pretty certain now.'

'Ah,' said Poirot, 'thank you, M. Van Aldin. That advances us.'

He replaced the receiver, and stood for a minute or two with a very curious smile on his face. George had to speak to him twice before obtaining an answer.

'Eh?' said Poirot. 'What is that that you say to me?'

'Are you lunching here, sir, or are you going out?'

'Neither,' said Poirot. 'I shall go to bed and take a *tisane*. The expected has happened, and when the expected happens, it always causes me emotion.'

CHAPTER 25

DEFIANCE

As Derek Kettering passed the car, Mirelle leant out.

'Dereek – I must speak to you for a moment –'

But, lifting his hat, Derek passed straight on without stopping.

When he got back to his hotel, the concierge detached himself from his wooden pen and accosted him.

'A gentleman is waiting to see you, Monsieur.'

'Who is it?' asked Derek.

'He did not give his name, Monsieur, but he said his business with you was important, and that he would wait.'

'Where is he?'

'In the little salon, Monsieur. He preferred it to the lounge, he said, as being more private.'

Derek nodded, and turned his steps in that direction.

The small salon was empty except for the visitor, who rose and bowed with easy foreign grace as Derek entered. As it chanced, Derek had only seen the Comte de la Roche once, but found no difficulty in recognizing that aristocratic nobleman, and he frowned angrily. Of all the consummate impertinence!

'The Comte de la Roche, is it not?' he said. 'I am afraid you have wasted your time in coming here.'

'I hope not,' said the Comte agreeably. His white teeth glittered.

The Comte's charm of manner was usually wasted on his own sex. All men, without exception, disliked him heartily. Derek Kettering was already conscious of a distinct longing to kick the Count bodily out of the room. It was only the realization that scandal would be unfortunate just at present that restrained him. He marvelled anew that Ruth could have cared, as she certainly had, for this fellow. A bounder, and worse than a bounder. He looked with distaste at the Count's exquisitely manicured hands.

'I called,' said the Comte, 'on a little matter of business. It would be advisable, I think, for you to listen to me.'

Again Derek felt strongly tempted to kick him out, but again he refrained. The hint of a threat was not lost upon him, but he interpreted it in his own way. There were various reasons why it would be better to hear what the Comte had to say.

He sat down and drummed impatiently with his fingers on the table.

'Well,' he said sharply, 'what is it?'

It was not the Comte's way to come out into the open at once.

'Allow me, Monsieur, to offer you my condolences on your recent bereavement.'

'If I have any impertinence from you,' said Derek quietly, 'you go out by that window.'

He nodded his head towards the window beside the Comte, and the latter moved uneasily.

'I will send my friends to you, Monsieur, if that is what you desire,' he said haughtily.

Derek laughed.

'A duel, eh? My dear Count, I don't take you seriously enough for that. But I should take a good deal of pleasure in kicking you down the Promenade des Anglais.'

The Comte was not at all anxious to take offence. He merely raised his eyebrows and murmured:

'The English are barbarians.'

'Well,' said Derek, 'what is it you have to say to me?'

'I will be frank,' said the Comte, 'I will come immediately to the point. That will suit us both, will it not?'

Again he smiled in his agreeable fashion.

'Go on,' said Derek curtly.

The Comte looked at the ceiling, joined the tips of his fingers together, and murmured softly:

'You have come into a lot of money, Monsieur.'

'What the devil has that got to do with you?'

The Comte drew himself up.

'Monsieur, my name is tarnished! I am suspected – accused – of foul crime.'

'The accusation does not come from me,' said Derek coldly; 'as an interested party I have not expressed any opinion.'

'I am innocent,' said the Comte. 'I swear before heaven' – he raised his hand to heaven – 'that I am innocent.'

'M. Carrège is, I believe, the Juge d'Instruction in charge of the case,' hinted Derek politely.

The Comte took no notice.

'Not only am I unjustly suspected of a crime that I did not commit, but I am also in serious need of money.'

He coughed softly and suggestively.

Derek rose to his feet.

'I was waiting for that,' he said softly; 'you blackmailing brute! I will not give you a penny. My wife is dead, and no scandal that you can make can touch her now. She wrote you foolish letters, I dare say. If I were to buy them from you for a round sum at this minute, I am pretty certain that you would manage to keep one or two back; and I will tell you this, M. de la Roche, blackmailing is an ugly word both in England and France. That is my answer to you. Good afternoon.'

'One moment' – the Comte stretched out a hand as Derek was turning to leave the room. 'You are mistaken, Monsieur. You are completely mistaken. I am, I hope, a "gentleman".' Derek laughed. 'Any letters that a lady might write to me I should hold sacred.' He flung back his head with a beautiful air of nobility. 'The proposition that I was putting before you was of quite a different nature. I am, as I said, extremely short of money, and my conscience might impel me to go to the police with certain information.'

Derek came slowly back into the room.

'What do you mean?'

The Comte's agreeable smile flashed forth once more.

'Surely it is not necessary to go into details,' he purred. 'Seek whom the crime benefits, they say, don't they? As I said just now, you have come into a lot of money lately.'

Derek laughed.

'If that is all –' he said contemptuously.

But the Comte was shaking his head.

'But it is not all, my dear sir. I should not come to you unless I had much more precise and detailed information than that. It is not agreeable, Monsieur, to be arrested and tried for murder.'

Derek came close up to him. His face expressed such furious anger that involuntarily the Comte drew back a pace or two.

'Are you threatening *me*?' the young man demanded angrily.

'You shall hear nothing more of the matter,' the Comte assured him.

'Of all the colossal bluffs that I have ever struck –'

The Comte raised a white hand.

'You are wrong. It is not a bluff. To convince you I will tell you this. My information was obtained from a certain lady. It is she who holds the irrefutable proof that you committed the murder.'

'She? Who?'

'Mademoiselle Mirelle.'

Derek drew back as though struck.

'Mirelle,' he muttered.

The Comte was quick to press what he took to be his advantage.

'A bagatelle of one hundred thousand francs,' he said. 'I ask no more.'

'Eh?' said Derek absently.

'I was saying, Monsieur, that a bagatelle of one hundred thousand francs would satisfy my – conscience.'

Derek seemed to recollect himself. He looked earnestly at the Comte.

'You would like my answer now?'

'If you please, Monsieur.'

'Then here it is. You can go to the devil. See?'

Leaving the Comte too astonished to speak, Derek turned on his heel and swung out of the room.

Once out of the hotel he hailed a taxi and drove to Mirelle's hotel. On inquiring, he learned that the dancer had just come in. Derek gave the concierge his card.

'Take this up to Mademoiselle and ask if she will see me.'

A very brief interval elapsed, and then Derek was bidden to follow a *chasseur*.

A wave of exotic perfume assailed Derek's nostrils as he stepped over the threshold of the dancer's apartments. The room was filled with carnations, orchids, and mimosa. Mirelle was standing by the window in a *peignoir* of foamy lace.

She came towards him, her hands outstretched.

'Dereek – you have come to me. I knew you would.'

He put aside the clinging arms and looked down on her sternly.

'Why did you send the Comte de la Roche to me?'

She looked at him in astonishment, which he took to be genuine.

'I? Send the Comte de la Roche to you? But for what?'

'Apparently – for blackmail,' said Derek grimly.

Again she stared. Then suddenly she smiled and nodded her head.

'Of course. It was to be expected. It is what he would do, *ce type là*. I might have known it. No, indeed, Dereek, I did not send him.'

He looked at her piercingly, as though seeking to read her mind.

'I will tell you,' said Mirelle. 'I am ashamed, but I will tell you. The other day, you comprehend, I was mad with rage, quite mad' – she made an eloquent gesture. 'My temperament, it is not a patient one. I want to be revenged on you, and so I go to the Comte de la Roche, and I tell him to go to the police and say so and so, and so and so. But have no fear, Dereek. Not completely did I lose my head; the proof rests with me alone. The police can do nothing without my word, you understand? And now – now?'

She nestled up close to him, looking at him with melting eyes.

He thrust her roughly away from him. She stood there, her breast heaving, her eyes narrowing to a cat-like slit.

'Be careful, Dereek, be very careful. You have come back to me, have you not?'

'I shall never come back to you,' said Derek steadily.

'Ah!'

More than ever the dancer looked like a cat. Her eyelids flickered.

'So there is another woman? The one with whom you lunched that day. Eh! am I right?'

'I intend to ask that lady to marry me. You might as well know.'

'That prim Englishwoman! Do you think that I will support that for one moment? Ah, no.' Her beautiful lithe body quivered. 'Listen, Dereek, do you remember that conversation we had in London? You said the only thing that could save you was the death of your wife. You regretted that she was so healthy. Then the idea of an accident came to your brain. And more than an accident.'

'I suppose,' said Derek contemptuously, 'that it was this conversation that you repeated to the Comte de la Roche.'

Mirelle laughed.

'Am I a fool? Could the police do anything with a vague story like that? See – I will give you a last chance. You shall give up this Englishwoman. You shall return to me. And then, *chéri*, never, never will I breathe –'

'Breathe what?'

She laughed softly. 'You thought no one saw you –'

'What do you mean?'

'As I say, you thought no one saw you – but *I* saw you, Dereek, *mon ami; I saw you coming out of the compartment of Madame your wife just before the train got into Lyons that night*. And I know more than that. I know that when you came out of her compartment she was dead.'

He stared at her. Then, like a man in a dream, he turned very slowly and went out of the room, swaying slightly as he walked.

CHAPTER 26

A WARNING

'And so it is,' said Poirot, 'that we are the good friends and have no secrets from each other.'

Katherine turned her head to look at him. There was something in his voice, some undercurrent of seriousness, which she had not heard before.

They were sitting in the gardens of Monte Carlo. Katherine had come over with her friends, and they had run into Knighton and Poirot almost immediately on arrival. Lady Tamplin had seized upon Knighton and had overwhelmed him with reminiscences, most of which Katherine had a faint suspicion were invented. They had moved away together, Lady Tamplin with her hand on the young man's arm. Knighton had thrown a couple of glances back over his shoulder, and Poirot's eyes twinkled a little as he saw them.

'Of course we are friends,' said Katherine.

'From the beginning we have been sympathetic to each other,' mused Poirot.

'When you told me that a "*roman policier*" occurs in real life.'

'And I was right, was I not?' he challenged her, with an emphatic forefinger. 'Here we are, plunged in the middle of one. That is natural for me – it is my *métier* – but for you it is different. Yes,' he added in a reflective tone, 'for you it is different.'

She looked sharply at him. It was as though he were warning her, pointing out to her some menace that she had not seen.

'Why do you say that I am in the middle of it? It is true that I had that conversation with Mrs Kettering just before she died, but now – now all that is over. I am not connected with the case any more.'

'Ah, Mademoiselle, Mademoiselle, can we ever say, "I have finished with this or that"?'

Katherine turned defiantly round to face him.

'What is it?' she asked. 'You are trying to tell me something – to convey it to me rather. But I am not clever at taking hints. I would much rather that you said anything you have to say straight out.'

Poirot looked at her sadly. '*Ah, mais c'est anglais ça*,' he murmured, 'everything in black and white, everything clear cut and well defined. But life, it is not like that, Mademoiselle. There are the things that are not yet, but which cast their shadow before.'

He dabbed his brow with a very large silk pocket-handkerchief and murmured:

'Ah, but it is that I become poetical. Let us, as you say, speak only of facts. And, speaking of facts, tell me what you think of Major Knighton.'

'I like him very much indeed,' said Katherine warmly; 'he is quite delightful.'

Poirot sighed.

'What is the matter?' asked Katherine.

'You reply so heartily,' said Poirot. 'If you had said in an indifferent voice, "Oh, quite nice," *eh bien*, do you know I should have been better pleased.'

Katherine did not answer. She felt slightly uncomfortable. Poirot went on dreamily:

'And yet, who knows? With *les femmes*, they have so many ways of concealing what they feel – and heartiness is perhaps as good a way as any other.'

He sighed.

'I don't see –' began Katherine.

He interrupted her.

'You do not see why I am being so impertinent, Mademoiselle? I am an old man, and now and then – not very often – I come across someone whose welfare is dear to me. We are friends, Mademoiselle. You have said so yourself. And it is just this – I should like to see you happy.'

Katherine stared very straight in front of her. She had a cretonne sunshade with her, and with its point she traced little designs in the gravel at her feet.

'I have asked you a question about Major Knighton, now I will ask you another. Do you like Mr Derek Kettering?'

'I hardly know him,' said Katherine.

'That is not an answer, that.'

'I think it is.'

He looked at her, struck by something in her tone. Then he nodded his head gravely and slowly.

'Perhaps you are right, Mademoiselle. See you, I who speak to you have seen much of the world, and I know that there are two things which are true. A good man may be ruined by his love for a bad woman – but the other way holds good also. A bad man may equally be ruined by his love for a good woman.'

Katherine looked up sharply.

'When you say ruined –'

'I mean from his point of view. One must be whole-hearted in crime as in everything else.'

'You are trying to warn me,' said Katherine in a low voice. 'Against whom?'

'I cannot look into your heart, Mademoiselle; I do not think you would let me if I could. I will just say this. There are men who have a strange fascination for women.'

'The Comte de la Roche,' said Katherine, with a smile.

'There are others – more dangerous than the Comte de la Roche. They have qualities that appeal – recklessness, daring, audacity. You are fascinated, Mademoiselle; I see that, but I think that it is no more than that. I hope so. This man of whom I speak, the emotion he feels is genuine enough, but all the same –'

'Yes?'

He got up and stood looking down at her. Then he spoke in a low, distinct voice:

'You could, perhaps, love a thief, Mademoiselle, *but not a murderer*.'

He wheeled sharply away on that and left her sitting there.

He heard the little gasp she gave and paid no attention. He had said what he meant to say. He left her there to digest that last unmistakable phrase.

Derek Kettering, coming out of the Casino into the sunshine, saw her sitting alone on the bench and joined her.

'I have been gambling,' he said, with a light laugh, 'gambling unsuccessfully. I have lost everything – everything, that is, that I have with me.'

Katherine looked at him with a troubled face. She was aware at once of something new in his manner, some hidden excitement that betrayed itself in a hundred different infinitesimal signs.

'I should think you were always a gambler. The spirit of gambling appeals to you.'

'Every day and in every way a gambler? You are about right. Don't *you* find something stimulating in it? To risk all on one throw – there is nothing like it.'

Calm and stolid as she believed herself to be, Katherine felt a faint answering thrill.

'I want to talk to you,' went on Derek, 'and who knows when I may have another opportunity? There is an idea going about that I murdered my wife – no, please don't interrupt. It is absurd, of course.' He paused for a minute or two, then went on, speaking more deliberately. 'In dealing with the police and Local Authorities here I have had to pretend to – well – a certain decency. I prefer not to pretend with you. I meant to marry money. I was on the lookout for money when I first met Ruth Van Aldin. She had the look of a slim Madonna about her, and – I – well – I made all sorts of good resolutions – and was bitterly disillusioned. My wife was in love with another man when she married me. She never cared for me in the least. Oh, I am not complaining; the thing was a perfectly respectable bargain. She wanted Leconbury and I wanted money. The trouble arose simply through Ruth's American blood. Without caring a pin for me, she would have liked me to be continually dancing attendance. Time and again she as good as told me that she had bought me and that I belonged to her. The result was that I behaved abominably to her. My father-in-law will tell you that, and he is quite right. At the time of Ruth's death, I was faced with absolute disaster.' He laughed suddenly. 'One *is* faced with absolute disaster when one is up against a man like Rufus Van Aldin.'

'And then?' asked Katherine in a low voice.

'And then,' Derek shrugged his shoulders, 'Ruth was murdered – very providentially.'

He laughed, and the sound of his laugh hurt Katherine. She winced.

'Yes,' said Derek, 'that wasn't in very good taste. But it is quite true. Now I am going to tell you something more. From the very first moment I saw you I knew you were the only woman in the world for me. I was – afraid of you. I thought you might bring me bad luck.'

'Bad luck?' said Katherine sharply.

He stared at her. 'Why do you repeat it like that? What have you got in your mind?'

'I was thinking of things that people have said to me.'

Derek grinned suddenly. 'They will say a lot to you about me, my dear, and most of it will be true. Yes, and worse things too – things that I shall never tell you. I have been a gambler always – and I have taken some long odds. I shan't confess to you now or at any other time. The past is done with. There is one thing I do wish you to believe. I swear to you solemnly that I did not kill my wife.'

He said the words earnestly enough, yet there was somehow a theatrical touch about them. He met her troubled gaze and went on:

'I know. I lied the other day. It *was* my wife's compartment I went into.'

'Ah,' said Katherine.

'It's difficult to explain just why I went in, but I'll try. I did it on an impulse. You see, I was more or less spying on my wife. I kept out of sight on the train. Mirelle had told me that my wife was meeting the Comte de la Roche in Paris. Well, as far as I had seen, that was not so. I felt ashamed, and I thought suddenly that it would be a good thing to have it out with her once and for all, so I pushed open the door and went in.'

He paused.

'Yes,' said Katherine gently.

'Ruth was lying on the bunk asleep – her face was turned away from me – I could only see the back of her head. I could have woken her up, of course. But suddenly I felt a reaction. What, after all, was there to say that we hadn't both of us said a hundred times before? She looked so peaceful lying there. I left the compartment as quietly as I could.'

'Why lie about it to the police?' asked Katherine.

'Because I'm not a complete fool. I've realized from the beginning that, from the point of view of motive, I'm the ideal murderer. If I once admitted that I had been in her compartment just before she was murdered, I'd do for myself once and for all.'

'I see.'

Did she see? She could not have told herself. She was feeling the magnetic attraction of Derek's personality, but there was something in her that resisted, that held back . . .

'Katherine –'

'I –'

'You know that I care for you. Do – do you care for me?'

'I – I don't know.'

Weakness there. Either she knew or she did not know. If – if only –

She cast a look round desperately as though seeking something that would help her. A soft colour rose in her cheeks as a tall fair man with a limp came hurrying along the path towards them – Major Knighton.

There was relief and an unexpected warmth in her voice as she greeted him.

Derek stood up, scowling, his face black as a thunder-cloud.

'Lady Tamplin having a flutter?' he said easily. 'I must join her and give her the benefit of my system.'

He swung round on his heel and left them together. Katherine sat down again. Her heart was beating rapidly and unevenly, but as she sat there, talking commonplaces to the quiet, rather shy man beside her, her self-command came back.

Then she realized with a shock that Knighton also was laying bare his heart, much as Derek had done, but in a very different manner.

He was shy and stammering. The words came haltingly with no eloquence to back them.

'From the first moment I saw you – I – I ought not to have spoken so soon – but Mr Van Aldin may leave here any day, and I might not have another chance. I know you can't care for me so soon – that is impossible. I dare say it is presumption anyway on my part. I have private means, but not very much – no, please don't answer now. I know what your answer would be. But in case I went away suddenly I just wanted you to know – that I care.'

She was shaken – touched. His manner was so gentle and appealing.

'There's one thing more. I just wanted to say that if – if you are ever in trouble, anything that I can do –'

He took her hand in his, held it tightly for a minute, then dropped it and walked rapidly away towards the Casino without looking back.

Katherine sat perfectly still, looking after him. Derek Kettering – Richard Knighton – two men so different – so very different. There was something kind about Knighton, kind and trustworthy. As to Derek –

Then suddenly Katherine had a very curious sensation. She felt that she was no longer sitting alone on the seat in the Casino gardens, but that someone was standing beside her, and that that someone was the dead woman, Ruth Kettering. She had a further impression that Ruth wanted – badly – to tell her something. The impression was so curious, so vivid, that it could not be driven away. She felt absolutely certain that the spirit of Ruth Kettering was trying to convey something of vital importance to her. The impression faded. Katherine got up, trembling a little. What was it that Ruth Kettering had wanted so badly to say?

CHAPTER 27

INTERVIEW WITH MIRELLE

When Knighton left Katherine he went in search of Hercule Poirot, whom he found in the Rooms, jauntily placing the minimum stake on the even numbers. As Knighton joined him, the number thirty-three turned up, and Poirot's stake was swept away.

'Bad luck!' said Knighton; 'are you going to stake again?'

Poirot shook his head.

'Not at present.'

'Do you feel the fascination of gambling?' asked Knighton curiously.

'Not at roulette.'

Knighton shot a swift glance at him. His own face became troubled. He spoke haltingly, with a touch of deference.

'I wonder, are you busy, M. Poirot? There is something I would like to ask you about.'

'I am at your disposal. Shall we go outside? It is pleasant in the sunshine.'

They strolled out together, and Knighton drew a deep breath.

'I love the Riviera,' he said. 'I came here first twelve years ago, during the War, when I was sent to Lady Tamplin's Hospital. It was like Paradise, coming from Flanders to this.'

'It must have been,' said Poirot.

'How long ago the War seems now!' mused Knighton.

They walked on in silence for some little way.

'You have something on your mind?' said Poirot.

Knighton looked at him in some surprise.

'You are quite right,' he confessed. 'I don't know how you knew it, though.'

'It showed itself only too plainly,' said Poirot drily.

'I did not know that I was so transparent.'

'It is my business to observe the physiognomy,' the little man explained, with dignity.

'I will tell you, M. Poirot. You have heard of this dancer woman – Mirelle?'

'She who is the *chère amie* of M. Derek Kettering?'

'Yes, that is the one; and, knowing this, you will understand that Mr Van Aldin is naturally prejudiced against her. She wrote to him, asking for an interview. He told me to dictate a curt refusal, which of course I did. This morning she came to the hotel and sent up her card, saying that it was urgent and vital that she should see Mr Van Aldin at once.'

'You interest me,' said Poirot.

'Mr Van Aldin was furious. He told me what message to send down to her. I ventured to disagree with him. It seemed to me both likely and probable that this woman Mirelle might give us valuable information. We know that she was on the Blue Train, and she may have seen or heard something that it might be vital for us to know. Don't you agree with me, M. Poirot?'

'I do,' said Poirot drily. 'M. Van Aldin, if I may say so, behaved exceedingly foolishly.'

'I am glad you take that view of the matter,' said the secretary. 'Now I am going to tell you something, M. Poirot. So strongly did I feel the unwisdom of Mr Van Aldin's attitude that I went down privately and had an interview with the lady.'

'*Eh bien?*'

'The difficulty was that she insisted on seeing Mr Van Aldin himself. I softened his message as much as I possibly could. In fact – to be candid – I gave it in a very different form. I said that Mr Van Aldin was too busy to see her at present, but that she might make any communication she wished to me. That, however, she could not bring herself to do, and she left without saying anything further. But I have a strong impression, M. Poirot, that that woman knows something.'

'This is serious,' said Poirot quietly. 'You know where she is staying?'

'Yes.' Knighton mentioned the name of the hotel.

'Good,' said Poirot; 'we will go there immediately.'

The secretary looked doubtful.

'And Mr Van Aldin?' he queried doubtfully.

'M. Van Aldin is an obstinate man,' said Poirot drily. 'I do not argue with obstinate men. I act in spite of them. We will go and see the lady immediately. I will tell her that you are empowered by M. Van Aldin to act for him, and you will guard yourself well from contradicting me.'

Knighton still looked doubtful, but Poirot took no notice of his hesitation.

At the hotel, they were told that Mademoiselle was in, and Poirot sent up both his and Knighton's cards, with 'From Mr Van Aldin' pencilled upon them.

Word came down that Mademoiselle Mirelle would receive them.

When they were ushered into the dancer's apartments, Poirot immediately took the lead.

'Mademoiselle,' he murmured, bowing very low, 'we are here on behalf of M. Van Aldin.'

'Ah! And why did he not come himself?'

'He is indisposed,' said Poirot mendaciously; 'the Riviera throat, it has him in its grip, but me I am empowered to act for him, as is Major Knighton, his secretary. Unless, of course, Mademoiselle would prefer to wait a fortnight or so.'

If there was one thing of which Poirot was tolerably certain, it was that to a temperament such as Mirelle's the mere word 'wait' was anathema.

'*Eh bien*, I will speak, Messieurs,' she cried. 'I have been patient. I have held my hand. And for what? That I should be insulted! Yes, insulted! Ah! Does he think to treat Mirelle like that? To throw her off like an old glove. I tell you never has a man tired of me. Always it is I who tire of them.'

She paced up and down the room, her slender body trembling with rage. A small table impeded her free passage, and she flung it from her into a corner, where it splintered against the wall.

'That is what I will do to him,' she cried, 'and that!'

Picking up a glass bowl filled with lilies she flung it into the grate, where it smashed into a hundred pieces.

Knighton was looking at her with cold British disapproval. He felt embarrassed and ill at ease. Poirot, on the other hand, with twinkling eyes was thoroughly enjoying the scene.

'Ah, it is magnificent!' he cried. 'It can be seen – Madame has a temperament.'

'I am an artist,' said Mirelle; 'every artist has a temperament. I told Dereek to beware, and he would not listen.' She whirled round on Poirot suddenly. 'It is true, is it not, that he wants to marry that English miss?'

Poirot coughed.

'*On m'a dit*,' he murmured, 'that he adores her passionately.'

Mirelle came towards them.

'He murdered his wife,' she screamed. 'There – now you have it! He told me beforehand that he meant to do it. He had got to an *impasse* – zut! he took the easiest way out.'

'You say that M. Kettering murdered his wife.'

'Yes, yes, yes. Have I not told you so?'

'The police,' murmured Poirot, 'will need proof of that – er – statement.'

'I tell you I saw him come out of her compartment that night on the train.'

'When?' asked Poirot sharply.

'Just before the train reached Lyons.'

'You will swear to that, Mademoiselle?'

It was a different Poirot who spoke now, sharp and decisive.

'Yes.'

There was a moment's silence. Mirelle was panting, and her eyes, half defiant, half frightened, went from the face of one man to the other.

'This is a serious matter, Mademoiselle,' said the detective. 'You realize how serious?'

'Certainly I do.'

'That is well,' said Poirot. 'Then you understand, Mademoiselle, that no time must be lost. You will, perhaps, accompany us immediately to the office of the Examining Magistrate.'

Mirelle was taken aback. She hesitated, but, as Poirot had foreseen, she had no loophole for escape.

'Ver well,' she muttered, 'I will fetch a coat.'

Left alone together, Poirot and Knighton exchanged glances.

'It is necessary to act while – how do you say it? – the iron is hot,' murmured Poirot. 'She is temperamental; in an hour's time, maybe, she will repent, and she will wish to draw back. We must prevent that at all costs.'

Mirelle reappeared, wrapped in a sand-coloured velvet wrap trimmed with leopard skin. She looked not altogether unlike a leopardess, tawny and dangerous. Her eyes still flashed with anger and determination.

They found M. Caux and the Examining Magistrate together. A few brief introductory words from Poirot, and Mademoiselle Mirelle was courteously entreated to tell her tale. This she did in much the same words as she had done to Knighton and Poirot, though with far more soberness of manner.

'This is an extraordinary story, Mademoiselle,' said M. Carrège slowly. He leant back in his chair, adjusted his pince-nez, and looked keenly and searchingly at the dancer through them.

'You wish us to believe M. Kettering actually boasted of the crime to you beforehand?'

'Yes, yes. She was too healthy, he said. If she were to die it must be an accident – he would arrange it all.'

'You are aware, Mademoiselle,' said M. Carrège sternly, 'that you are making yourself out to be an accessory before the fact?'

'Me? But not the least in the world, Monsieur. Not for a moment did I take that statement seriously. Ah no indeed! I know men, Monsieur; they say many wild things. It would be an odd state of affairs if one were to take all they said *au pied de la lettre.*'

The Examining Magistrate raised his eyebrows.

'We are to take it, then, that you regarded M. Kettering's threats as mere idle words? May I ask, Mademoiselle, what made you throw up your engagements in London and come out to the Riviera?'

Mirelle looked at him with melting black eyes.

'I wished to be with the man I loved,' she said simply. 'Was it so unnatural?'

Poirot interpolated a question gently.

'Was it, then, at M. Kettering's wish that you accompanied him to Nice?'

Mirelle seemed to find a little difficulty in answering this. She hesitated perceptibly before she spoke. When she did, it was with a haughty indifference of manner.

'In such matters I please myself, Monsieur,' she said.

That the answer was not an answer at all was noted by all three men. They said nothing.

'When were you first convinced that M. Kettering had murdered his wife?'

'As I tell you, Monsieur, I saw M. Kettering come out of his wife's compartment just before the train drew in to Lyons. There was a look on his face – ah! at the moment I could not understand it – a look haunted and terrible. I shall never forget it.'

Her voice rose shrilly, and she flung out her arms in an extravagant gesture.

'Quite so,' said M. Carrège.

'Afterwards, when I found that Madame Kettering was dead when the train left Lyons, then – then I knew!'

'And still – you did not go to the police, Mademoiselle,' said the Commissary mildly.

Mirelle glanced at him superbly; she was clearly enjoying herself in the rôle she was playing.

'Shall I betray my lover?' she asked. 'Ah no; do not ask a woman to do that.'

'Yet now –' hinted M. Caux.

'Now it is different. He has betrayed me! Shall I suffer that in silence? . . .'

The Examining Magistrate checked her.

'Quite so, quite so,' he murmured soothingly. 'And now, Mademoiselle, perhaps you will read over the statement of what you have told us, see that it is correct, and sign it.'

Mirelle wasted no time on the document.

'Yes, yes,' she said, 'it is correct.' She rose to her feet. 'You require me no longer, Messieurs?'

'At present, no, Mademoiselle.'

'And Dereek will be arrested?'

'At once, Mademoiselle.'

Mirelle laughed cruelly and drew her fur draperies closer about her.

'He should have thought of this before he insulted me,' she cried.

'There is one little matter' – Poirot coughed apologetically – 'just a matter of detail.'

'Yes?'

'What makes you think that Madame Kettering was dead when the train left Lyons?'

Mirelle stared.

'But she *was* dead.'

'Was she?'

'Yes, of course. I –'

She came to an abrupt stop. Poirot was regarding her intently, and he saw the wary look that came into her eyes.

'I have been told so. Everybody says so.'

'Oh,' said Poirot, 'I was not aware that the fact had been mentioned outside the Examining Magistrate's office.'

Mirelle appeared somewhat discomposed.

'One hears those things,' she said vaguely; 'they get about. Somebody told me. I can't remember who it was.'

She moved to the door. M. Caux sprang forward to open it for her, and as he did so, Poirot's voice rose gently once more.

'And the jewels? Pardon, Mademoiselle. Can you tell me anything about those?'

'The jewels? What jewels?'

'The rubies of Catherine the Great. Since you hear so much, you must have heard of them.'

'I know nothing about any jewels,' said Mirelle sharply.

She went out, closing the door behind her. M. Caux came back to his chair; the Examining Magistrate sighed.

'What a fury!' he said, 'but *diablement chic*. I wonder if she is telling the truth? I think so.'

'There is *some* truth in her story, certainly,' said Poirot. 'We have confirmation of it from Miss Grey. She was looking down the corridor a short time before the train reached Lyons, and she saw M. Kettering go into his wife's compartment.'

'The case against him seems quite clear,' said the Commissary, sighing: 'it is a thousand pities,' he murmured.

'How do you mean?' asked Poirot.

'It has been the ambition of my life to lay the Comte de la Roche by the heels. This time, *ma foi*, I thought we had got him. This other – it is not nearly so satisfactory.'

M. Carrège rubbed his nose.

'If anything goes wrong,' he observed cautiously, 'it will be most awkward. M. Kettering is of the aristocracy. It will get into the newspapers. If we have made a mistake –' He shrugged his shoulders forebodingly.

'The jewels now,' said the Commissary, 'what do you think he has done with them?'

'He took them for a plant, of course,' said M. Carrège; 'they must have been a great inconvenience to him and very awkward to dispose of.'

Poirot smiled.

'I have an idea of my own about the jewels. Tell me, Messieurs, what do you know of a man called the Marquis?'

The Commissary leant forward excitedly.

'The Marquis,' he said, 'the Marquis? Do you think he is mixed up in this affair, M. Poirot?'

'I ask you what you know of him.'

The Commissary made an expressive grimace.

'Not as much as we should like to,' he observed ruefully. 'He works behind the scenes, you understand. He has underlings who do his dirty work for him. But he is someone high up. That we are sure of. He does not come from the criminal classes.'

'A Frenchman?'

'Y-es. At least we believe so. But we are not sure. He has worked in France, in England, in America. There was a series of robberies in Switzerland last autumn which were laid at his door. By all accounts he is a *grand seigneur*, speaking French and English with equal perfection, and his origin is a mystery.'

Poirot nodded and rose to take his departure.

'Can you tell us nothing more, M. Poirot?' urged the Commissary.

'At present, no,' said Poirot, 'but I may have news awaiting me at my hotel.'

M. Carrège looked uncomfortable. 'If the Marquis is concerned in this –' he began, and then stopped.

'It upsets our ideas,' complained M. Caux.

'It does not upset mine,' said Poirot. 'On the contrary, I think it agrees with them very well. Au revoir, Messieurs; if news of any importance comes to me I will communicate it to you immediately.'

He walked back to his hotel with a grave face. In his absence, a telegram had come for him. Taking a paper-cutter from his pocket, he slit it open. It was a long telegram, and he read it over twice before slowly putting it in his pocket. Upstairs, George was awaiting his master.

'I am fatigued, Georges, much fatigued. Will you order for me a small pot of chocolate?'

The chocolate was duly ordered and brought, and George set it at the little table at his master's elbow. As he was preparing to retire, Poirot spoke:

'I believe, Georges, that you have a good knowledge of the English aristocracy?' murmured Poirot.

George smiled apologetically.

'I think that I might say that I have, sir,' he replied.

'I suppose that it is your opinion, Georges, that criminals are invariably drawn from the lower orders?'

'Not always, sir. There was great trouble with one of the Duke of Devize's younger sons. He left Eton under a cloud, and after that he caused great anxiety on several occasions. The police would not accept the view that it was kleptomania. A very clever young gentleman, sir, but vicious through and through, if you take my meaning. His Grace shipped him to Australia, and I hear he was convicted out there under another name. Very odd, sir, but there it is. The young gentleman, I need hardly say, was not in want financially.'

Poirot nodded his head slowly.

'Love of excitement,' he murmured, 'and a little kink in the brain somewhere. I wonder now –'

He drew out the telegram from his pocket and read it again.

'Then there was Lady Mary Fox's daughter,' continued the valet in a mood of reminiscence. 'Swindled tradespeople something shocking, she did. Very worrying to the best families, if I may say so, and there are many other queer cases I could mention.'

'You have a wide experience, Georges,' murmured Poirot. 'I often wonder having lived so exclusively with titled families that you demean yourself by coming as a valet to me. I put it down to love of excitement on your part.'

'Not exactly, sir,' said George. 'I happened to see in *Society Snippets* that you had been received at Buckingham Palace. That was just when I was looking for a new situation. His Majesty, so it said, had been most gracious and friendly and thought very highly of your abilities.'

'Ah,' said Poirot, 'one always likes to know the reason for things.'

He remained in thought for a few moments and then said:

'You rang up Mademoiselle Papopolous?'

'Yes, sir; she and her father will be pleased to dine with you tonight.'

'Ah,' said Poirot thoughtfully. He drank off his chocolate, set the cup and saucer neatly in the middle of the tray, and spoke gently, more to himself than to the valet.

'The squirrel, my good Georges, collects nuts. He stores them up in the autumn so that they may be of advantage to him later. To make a success of humanity, Georges, we must profit by the lessons of those below us in the animal kingdom. I have always done so. I have been the cat, watching the mouse hole. I have been the good dog following up the scent, and not taking my nose from the trail. And also, my good Georges, I have been the squirrel. I have stored away the little fact here, the little fact there. I go now to my store and I take out one particular nut, a nut that I stored away – let me see, seventeen years ago. You follow me, Georges?'

'I should hardly have thought, sir,' said George, 'that nuts would have kept so long as that, though I know one can do wonders with preserving bottles.'

Poirot looked at him and smiled.

CHAPTER 28

POIROT PLAYS THE SQUIRREL

Poirot started to keep his dinner appointment with a margin of three-quarters of an hour to spare. He had an object in this. The car took him, not straight to Monte Carlo, but to Lady Tamplin's house at Cap Martin, where he asked for Miss Grey. The ladies were dressing and Poirot was shown into a small salon to wait, and here, after a lapse of three or four minutes, Lenox Tamplin came to him.

'Katherine is not quite ready yet,' she said. 'Can I give her a message, or would you rather wait until she comes down?'

Poirot looked at her thoughtfully. He was a minute or two in replying, as though something of great weight hung upon his decision. Apparently the answer to such a simple question mattered.

'No,' he said at last, 'No, I do not think it is necessary that I should wait to see Mademoiselle Katherine. I think perhaps, that it is better that I should not. These things are sometimes difficult.'

Lenox waited politely, her eyebrows slightly raised.

'I have a piece of news,' continued Poirot. 'You will, perhaps, tell your friend. M. Kettering was arrested tonight for the murder of his wife.'

'You want me to tell Katherine that?' asked Lenox. She breathed rather hard, as though she had been running; her face, Poirot thought, looked white and strained – rather noticeably so.

'If you please, Mademoiselle.'

'Why?' said Lenox. 'Do you think Katherine will be upset? Do you think she cares?'

'I don't know, Mademoiselle,' said Poirot. 'See, I admit it frankly. As a rule I know everything, but in this case, I – well, I do not. You, perhaps, know better than I do.'

'Yes,' said Lenox, 'I know – but I am not going to tell you all the same.'

She paused for a minute or two, her dark brows drawn together in a frown.

'You believe he did it?' she said abruptly.

Poirot shrugged his shoulders.

'The police say so.'

'Ah,' said Lenox, 'hedging, are you? So there is something to hedge about.'

Again she was silent, frowning. Poirot said gently:

'You have known Derek Kettering a long time, have you not?'

'Off and on ever since I was a kid,' said Lenox gruffly. Poirot nodded his head several times without speaking.

With one of her brusque movements Lenox drew forward a chair and sat down on it, her elbows on the table and her face supported by her hands. Sitting thus, she looked directly across the table at Poirot.

'What have they got to go on?' she demanded. 'Motive, I suppose. Probably came into money at her death.'

'He came into two million.'

'And if she had not died he would have been ruined?'

'Yes.'

'But there must have been more than that,' persisted Lenox. 'He travelled by the same train, I know, but – that would not be enough to go on by itself.'

'A cigarette case with the letter "K" on it which did not belong to Mrs Kettering was found in her carriage, and he was seen by two people entering and leaving the compartment just before the train got into Lyons.'

'What two people?'

'Your friend Miss Grey was one of them. The other was Mademoiselle Mirelle, the dancer.'

'And he, Derek, what has he got to say about it?' demanded Lenox sharply.

'He denies having entered his wife's compartment at all,' said Poirot.

'Fool!' said Lenox crisply, frowning. 'Just before Lyons, you say? Does nobody know when – when she died?'

'The doctors' evidence necessarily cannot be very definite,' said Poirot; 'they are inclined to think that death was unlikely to have occurred after leaving Lyons. And we know this much, that a few moments after leaving Lyons Mrs Kettering was dead.'

'How do you know that?'

Poirot was smiling rather oddly to himself.

'Someone else went into her compartment and found her dead.'

'And they did not rouse the train?'

'No.'

'Why was that?'

'Doubtless they had their reasons.'

Lenox looked at him sharply.

'Do you know the reason?'

'I think so – yes.'

Lenox sat still turning things over in her mind. Poirot watched her in silence. At last she looked up. A soft colour had come into her cheeks and her eyes were shining.

'You think someone on the train must have killed her, but that need not be so at all. What is to stop anyone swinging themselves on to the train when it stopped at Lyons? They could go straight to her compartment, strangle her, and take the rubies and drop off the train again without anyone being the wiser. She may have been actually killed while the train was in Lyons station. Then she would have been alive when Derek went in, and dead when the other person found her.'

Poirot leant back in his chair. He drew a deep breath. He looked across at the girl and nodded his head three times, then he heaved a sigh.

'Mademoiselle,' he said, 'what you have said there is very just – very true. I was struggling in the darkness, and you have shown me a light. There was a point that puzzled me and you have made it plain.'

He got up.

'And Derek?' said Lenox.

'Who knows?' said Poirot, with a shrug of his shoulders. 'But I will tell you this, Mademoiselle. I am not satisfied; no, I, Hercule Poirot, am not yet satisfied. It may be that this very night I shall learn something more. At least, I go to try.'

'You are meeting someone?'

'Yes.'

'Someone who knows something?'

'Someone who might know something. In these matters one must leave no stone unturned. Au revoir, Mademoiselle.'

Lenox accompanied him to the door.

'Have I – helped?' she asked.

Poirot's face softened as he looked up at her standing on the doorstep above him.

'Yes, Mademoiselle, you have helped. If things are very dark, always remember that.'

When the car had driven off he relapsed into a frowning absorption, but in his eyes was that faint green light which was always the precursor of the triumph to be.

He was a few minutes late at the rendezvous, and found that M. Papopolous and his daughter had arrived before him. His apologies were abject, and he outdid himself in politeness and small attentions. The Greek was looking particularly benign and noble this evening, a sorrowful patriarch of blameless life. Zia was looking handsome and good humoured. The dinner was a pleasant one. Poirot was his best and most sparkling self. He told anecdotes, he made jokes, he paid graceful compliments to Zia Papopolous, and he told many interesting incidents of his career. The menu was a carefully selected one, and the wine was excellent.

At the close of dinner M. Papopolous inquired politely:

'And the tip I gave you? You have had your little flutter on the horse?'

'I am in communication with – er – my bookmaker,' replied Poirot.

The eyes of the two men met.

'A well-known horse, eh?'

'No,' said Poirot; 'it is what our friends, the English, call a dark horse.'

'Ah!' said M. Papopolous thoughtfully.

'Now we must step across to the Casino and have our little flutter at the roulette table,' cried Poirot gaily.

At the Casino the party separated, Poirot devoting himself solely to Zia, whilst Papopolous himself drifted away.

Poirot was not fortunate, but Zia had a run of good luck, and had soon won a few thousand francs.

'It would be as well,' she observed drily to Poirot, 'if I stopped now.'

Poirot's eyes twinkled.

'Superb!' he exclaimed. 'You are the daughter of your father, Mademoiselle Zia. To know when to stop. Ah! that is the art.'

He looked round the rooms.

'I cannot see your father anywhere about,' he remarked carelessly. 'I will fetch your cloak for you, Mademoiselle, and we will go out in the gardens.'

He did not, however, go straight to the cloakroom. His sharp eyes had seen but a little while before the departure of M. Papopolous. He was anxious to know what had become of the wily Greek. He ran him to earth unexpectedly in the big entrance hall. He was standing by one of the pillars, talking to a lady who had just arrived. The lady was Mirelle.

Poirot sidled unostentatiously round the room. He arrived at the other side of the pillar, and unnoticed by the two who were talking together in an animated fashion – or rather, that is to say, the dancer was talking, Papopolous contributing an occasional monosyllable and a good many expressive gestures.

'I tell you I must have time,' the dancer was saying. 'If you give me time I will get the money.'

'To wait' – the Greek shrugged his shoulders – 'it is awkward.'

'Only a very little while,' pleaded the other. 'Ah! but you must! A week – ten days – that is all I ask. You can be sure of your affair. The money will be forthcoming.'

Papopolous shifted a little and looked round him uneasily – to find Poirot almost at his elbow with a beaming innocent face.

'*Ah! vous voilà,* M. Papopolous. I have been looking for you. It is permitted that I take Mademoiselle Zia for a little turn in the gardens? Good evening, Mademoiselle.' He bowed very low to Mirelle. 'A thousand pardons that I did not see you immediately.'

The dancer accepted his greetings rather impatiently. She was clearly annoyed at the interruption of her *tête-à-tête*. Poirot was quick to take the hint. Papopolous had already murmured: 'Certainly – but certainly,' and Poirot withdrew forthwith.

He fetched Zia's cloak, and together they strolled out into the gardens.

'This is where the suicides take place,' said Zia.

Poirot shrugged his shoulders. 'So it is said. Men are foolish, are they not, Mademoiselle? To eat, to drink, to breathe the good air, it is a very pleasant thing, Mademoiselle. One is foolish to leave all that simply because one has no money – or because the heart aches. *L'amour*, it causes many fatalities, does it not?'

Zia laughed.

'You should not laugh at love, Mademoiselle,' said Poirot, shaking an energetic forefinger at her. 'You who are young and beautiful.'

'Hardly that,' said Zia; 'you forget that I am thirty-three, M. Poirot. I am frank with you, because it is no good being otherwise. As you told my father it is exactly seventeen years since you aided us in Paris that time.'

'When I look at you, it seems much less,' said Poirot gallantly. 'You were then very much as you are now, Mademoiselle, a little thinner, a little paler, a little more serious. Sixteen years old and fresh from your *pension*. Not quite the *petite pensionnaire*, not quite a woman. You were very delicious, very charming, Mademoiselle Zia; others thought so too, without doubt.'

'At sixteen,' said Zia, 'one is simple and a little fool.'

'That may be,' said Poirot; 'yes, that well may be. At sixteen one is credulous, is one not? One believes what one is told.'

If he saw the quick sideways glance that the girl shot at him, he pretended not to have done so. He continued dreamily: 'It was a curious affair that, altogether. Your father, Mademoiselle, has never understood the true inwardness of it.'

'No?'

'When he asked me for details, for explanations, I said to him thus: "Without scandal, I have got back for you that which was lost. You must ask no questions." Do you know, Mademoiselle, why I said these things?'

'I have no idea,' said the girl coldly.

'It was because I had a soft spot in my heart for a little *pensionnaire*, so pale, so thin, so serious.'

'I don't understand what you are talking about,' cried Zia angrily.

'Do you not, Mademoiselle? Have you forgotten Antonio Pirezzio?' He heard the quick intake of her breath – almost a gasp.

'He came to work as an assistant in the shop, but not thus could he have got hold of what he wanted. An assistant can lift his eyes to his master's daughter, can he not? If he is young and handsome with a glib tongue. And since they cannot make love all the time, they must occasionally talk of things that interest them both – such as that very interesting thing which was temporarily in M. Papopolous' possession. And since, as you say, Mademoiselle, the young are foolish and credulous, it was easy to believe him and to give him a sight of that particular thing, to show him where it was kept. And afterwards when it is gone – when the unbelievable catastrophe has happened. Alas! the poor little *pensionnaire*. What a terrible position she is in. She is frightened, the poor little one. To speak or not to speak? And then there comes along that excellent fellow, Hercule Poirot. Almost a miracle it must have been, the way things arranged themselves. The priceless heirlooms are restored and there are no awkward questions.'

Zia turned on him fiercely.

'You have known all the time? Who told you? Was it – was it Antonio?'

Poirot shook his head.

'No one told me,' he said quietly. 'I guessed. It was a good guess, was it not, Mademoiselle? You see, unless you are good at guessing, it is not much use being a detective.'

The girl walked along beside him for some minutes in silence. Then she said in a hard voice:

'Well, what are you going to do about it; are you going to tell my father?'

'No,' said Poirot sharply. 'Certainly not.'

She looked at him curiously.

'You want something from me?'

'I want your help, Mademoiselle.'

'What makes you think that I can help you?'

'I do not think so. I only hope so.'

'And if I do not help you, then – you will tell my father?'

'But no, but no! Debarrass yourself of that idea, Mademoiselle.

I am not a blackmailer. I do not hold your secret over your head and threaten you with it.'

'If I refuse to help you –?' began the girl slowly.

'Then you refuse, and that is that.'

'Then why –?' she stopped.

'Listen, and I will tell you why. Women, Mademoiselle, are generous. If they can render a service to one who has rendered a service to them, they will do it. I was generous once to you, Mademoiselle. When I might have spoken, I held my tongue.'

There was another silence; then the girl said, 'My father gave you a hint the other day.'

'It was very kind of him.'

'I do not think,' said Zia slowly, 'that there is anything that I can add to that.'

If Poirot was disappointed he did not show it. Not a muscle of his face changed.

'*Eh bien!*' he said cheerfully, 'then we must talk of other things.'

And he proceeded to chat gaily. The girl was *distraite*, however, and her answers were mechanical and not always to the point. It was when they were approaching the Casino once more that she seemed to come to a decision.

'M. Poirot?'

'Yes, Mademoiselle?'

'I – I should like to help you if I could.'

'You are very amiable, Mademoiselle – very amiable.'

Again there was a pause. Poirot did not press her. He was quite content to wait and let her take her own time.

'Ah bah,' said Zia, 'after all, why should I not tell you? My father is cautious – always cautious in everything he says. But I know that with you it is not necessary. You have told us it is only the murderer you seek, and that you are not concerned over the jewels. I believe you. You were quite right when you guessed that we were in Nice because of the rubies. They have been handed over here according to plan. My father has them now. He gave you a hint the other day as to who our mysterious client was.'

'The Marquis?' murmured Poirot softly.

'Yes, the Marquis.'

'Have you ever seen the Marquis, Mademoiselle Zia?'

'Once,' said the girl. 'But not very well,' she added. 'It was through a keyhole.'

'That always presents difficulties,' said Poirot sympathetically, 'but all the same you saw him. You would know him again?'

Zia shook her head.

'He wore a mask,' she explained.

'Young or old?'

'He had white hair. It may have been a wig, it may not. It fitted very well. But I do not think he was old. His walk was young, and so was his voice.'

'His voice?' said Poirot thoughtfully. 'Ah, his voice! Would you know it again, Mademoiselle Zia?'

'I might,' said the girl.

'You were interested in him, eh? It was that that took you to the keyhole?'

Zia nodded.

'Yes, yes. I was curious. One had heard so much – he is not the ordinary thief – he is more like a figure of history or romance.'

'Yes,' said Poirot thoughtfully; 'yes, perhaps so.'

'But it is not this that I meant to tell you,' said Zia. 'It was just one other little fact that I thought might be – well – useful to you.'

'Yes?' said Poirot encouragingly.

'The rubies, as I say, were handed over to my father here at Nice. I did not see the person who handed them over, but –'

'Yes?'

'I know one thing. *It was a woman.*'

CHAPTER 29

A LETTER FROM HOME

Dear Katherine, – Living among grand friends as you are doing now, I don't suppose you will care to hear any of our news; but as I always thought you were a sensible girl, perhaps you are a trifle less swollen-headed than I suppose. Everything goes on much the same here. There was great trouble about the new curate, who is scandalously high. In my view, he is neither more nor less than a Roman. Everybody has spoken to the Vicar about it, but you know what the Vicar is – all Christian charity and no proper spirit. I have had a lot of trouble with maids lately. That girl Annie was no good – skirts up to her knees and wouldn't wear sensible woollen stockings. Not one of them can bear being spoken to. I have had a lot of pain with my rheumatism one way and another, and Dr Harris persuaded me to go and see a London specialist – a waste of three guineas and a railway fare, as I told him; but by waiting until Wednesday I managed to get a cheap return. The London doctor pulled a long face and talked all round about and never straight out, until I said to him, 'I'm a plain woman, Doctor, and I like things to be plainly stated. Is it cancer, or is it not?' And then, of course, he had to say it was. They say a year with care, and not too much pain, though I'm sure I can bear pain as well as any other Christian woman. Life seems rather lonely at times, with most of my friends dead or gone before. I wish you were in St Mary Mead, my dear, and that is a fact. If you hadn't come into this money and gone off into grand society, I would have offered you double the salary poor Jane gave you to come and look after me; but there – there's no good wanting what we can't get. However, if things should go ill with you – and that is always possible. I have heard no end of tales of bogus noblemen marrying girls and getting hold of their money and then leaving them at the church door. I dare say you are too sensible for anything of the kind to happen to you, but one never knows; and never having had much attention of any kind it might easily go to your head now. So just in case, my dear, remember there is always a home for you here; and though a plain-spoken woman I am a warm-hearted one too.

Your affectionate old friend,
Amelia Viner.

PS. I saw a mention of you in the paper with your cousin, Viscountess Tamplin, and I cut it out and put it with my cuttings. I prayed for you on Sunday that you might be kept from pride and vainglory.

Katherine read this characteristic epistle through twice, then she laid it down and stared out of her bedroom window across the blue waters of the Mediterranean. She felt a curious lump in her throat.

A sudden wave of longing for St Mary Mead swept over her. So full of familiar, everyday, stupid little things – and yet – home. She felt very inclined to lay her head down on her arms and indulge in a real good cry.

Lenox, coming in at the moment, saved her.

'Hello, Katherine,' said Lenox. 'I say – what is the matter?'

'Nothing,' said Katherine, grabbing up Miss Viner's letter and thrusting it into her handbag.

'You looked rather queer,' said Lenox. 'I say – I hope you don't mind – I rang up your detective friend, M. Poirot, and asked him to lunch with us in Nice. I said you wanted to see him, as I thought he might not come for me.'

'Did you want to see him then?' asked Katherine.

'Yes,' said Lenox. 'I have rather lost my heart to him. I never met a man before whose eyes were really green like a cat's.'

'All right,' said Katherine. She spoke listlessly. The last few days had been trying. Derek Kettering's arrest had been the topic of the hour, and the Blue Train Mystery had been thrashed out from every conceivable standpoint.

'I have ordered the car,' said Lenox, 'and I have told Mother some lie or other – unfortunately I can't remember exactly what; but it won't matter, as she never remembers. If she knew where we were going, she would want to come too, to pump M. Poirot.'

The two girls arrived at the Negresco to find Poirot waiting.

He was full of Gallic politeness, and showered so many compliments upon the two girls that they were soon helpless with laughter; yet for all that the meal was not a gay one. Katherine was dreamy and distracted, and Lenox made bursts of conversation, interspersed by silences. As they were sitting on the terrace sipping their coffee she suddenly attacked Poirot bluntly.

'How are things going? You know what I mean?'

Poirot shrugged his shoulders. 'They take their course,' he said.

'And you are just letting them take their course?'

He looked at Lenox a little sadly.

'You are young, Mademoiselle, but there are three things that cannot be hurried – *le bon Dieu*, Nature, and old people.'

'Nonsense!' said Lenox. 'You are not old.'

'Ah, it is pretty, what you say there.'

'Here is Major Knighton,' said Lenox.

Katherine looked round quickly and then turned back again.

'He is with Mr Van Aldin,' continued Lenox. 'There is something I want to ask Major Knighton about. I won't be a minute.'

Left alone together, Poirot bent forward and murmured to Katherine:

'You are *distraite*, Mademoiselle; your thoughts, they are far away, are they not?'

'Just as far as England, no farther.'

Guided by a sudden impulse, she took the letter she had received that morning and handed it across to him to read.

'That is the first word that has come to me from my old life; somehow or other – it hurts.'

He read it through and then handed it back to her.

'So you are going back to St Mary Mead?' he said.

'No, I am not,' said Katherine; 'why should I?'

'Ah,' said Poirot, 'it is my mistake. You will excuse me one little minute.'

He strolled across to where Lenox Tamplin was talking to Van Aldin and Knighton. The American looked old and haggard. He greeted Poirot with a curt nod but without any other sign of animation.

As he turned to reply to some observation made by Lenox, Poirot drew Knighton aside.

'M. Van Aldin looks ill,' he said.

'Do you wonder?' asked Knighton. 'The scandal of Derek Kettering's arrest has about put the lid on things, as far as he is concerned. He is even regretting that he asked you to find out the truth.'

'He should go back to England,' said Poirot.

'We are going the day after tomorrow.'

'That is good news,' said Poirot.

He hesitated, and looked across the terrace to where Katherine was sitting.

'I wish,' he murmured, 'that you could tell Miss Grey that.'

'Tell her what?'

'That you – I mean that M. Van Aldin is returning to England.'

Knighton looked a little puzzled, but he readily crossed the terrace and joined Katherine.

Poirot saw him go with a satisfied nod of the head, and then joined Lenox and the American. After a minute or two they joined the others. Conversation was general for a few minutes, then the millionaire and his secretary departed. Poirot also prepared to take his departure.

'A thousand thanks for your hospitality, Mesdemoiselles,' he cried; 'it has been a most charming luncheon. *Ma foi*, I needed it!' He swelled out his chest and thumped it. 'I am now a lion – a giant. Ah, Mademoiselle Katherine, you have not seen me as I can be. You have seen the gentle, the calm Hercule Poirot; but there is another Hercule Poirot. I go now to bully, to threaten, to strike terror into the hearts of those who listen to me.'

He looked at them in a self-satisfied way, and they both appeared to be duly impressed, though Lenox was biting her underlip, and the corners of Katherine's mouth had a suspicious twitch.

'And I shall do it,' he said gravely. 'Oh yes, I shall succeed.'

He had gone but a few steps when Katherine's voice made him turn.

'M. Poirot, I – I want to tell you. I think you were quite right in what you said. I am going back to England almost immediately.'

Poirot stared at her very hard, and under the directness of his scrutiny she blushed.

'I see,' he said gravely.

'I don't believe you do,' said Katherine.

'I know more than you think, Mademoiselle,' he said quietly.

He left her, with an odd little smile upon his lips. Entering a waiting car, he drove to Antibes.

Hipolyte, the Comte de la Roche's wooden-faced man-servant, was busy at the Villa Marina polishing his master's beautiful cut table glass. The Comte de la Roche himself had gone to Monte Carlo for the day. Chancing to look out of the window, Hipolyte espied a visitor walking briskly up to the hall door, a visitor of so uncommon a type that Hipolyte, experienced as he was, had some difficulty in placing him. Calling to his wife, Marie, who was busy in the kitchen, he drew her attention to what he called *ce type là*.

'It is not the police again?' said Marie anxiously.

'Look for yourself,' said Hipolyte.

Marie looked.

'Certainly not the police,' she declared. 'I am glad.'

'They have not really worried us much,' said Hipolyte. 'In fact, but for Monsieur le Comte's warning, I should never have guessed that stranger at the wine-shop to be what he was.'

The hall bell pealed and Hipolyte, in a grave and decorous manner, went to open the door.

'M. le Comte, I regret to say, is not at home.'

The little man with the large moustaches beamed placidly.

'I know that,' he replied. 'You are Hipolyte Flavelle, are you not?'

'Yes, Monsieur, that is my name.'

'And you have a wife, Marie Flavelle?'

'Yes, Monsieur, but –'

'I desire to see you both,' said the stranger, and he stepped nimbly past Hipolyte into the hall.

'Your wife is doubtless in the kitchen,' he said. 'I will go there.'

Before Hipolyte could recover his breath, the other had selected the right door at the back of the hall and passed along the passage and into the kitchen, where Marie paused open-mouthed to stare at him.

'*Voilà*,' said the stranger, and sank into a wooden arm-chair; 'I am Hercule Poirot.'

'Yes, Monsieur?'

'You do not know the name?'

'I have never heard it,' said Hipolyte.

'Permit me to say that you have been badly educated. It is the name of one of the great ones of this world.'

He sighed and folded his hands across his chest.

Hipolyte and Marie were staring at him uneasily. They were at a loss what to make of this unexpected and extremely strange visitor. 'Monsieur desires –?' murmured Hipolyte mechanically.

'I desire to know why you have lied to the police.'

'Monsieur!' cried Hipolyte; 'I – lied to the police? Never have I done such a thing.'

M. Poirot shook his head.

'You are wrong,' he said; 'you have done it on several occasions. Let me see.' He took a small notebook from his pocket and consulted it. 'Ah, yes; on seven occasions at least. I will recite them to you.'

In a gentle unemotional voice he proceeded to outline the seven occasions.

Hipolyte was taken aback.

'But it is not of these past lapses that I wish to speak,' continued Poirot, 'only, my dear friend, do not get into the habit of thinking yourself too clever. I come now to the particular lie in which I am concerned – your statement that the Comte de la Roche arrived at this villa on the morning of 14th January.'

'But that was no lie, Monsieur; that was the truth. Monsieur le Comte arrived here on the morning of Tuesday, the 14th. That is so, Marie, is it not?'

Marie assented eagerly.

'Ah, yes, that is quite right. I remember it perfectly.'

'Oh,' said Poirot, 'and what did you give your good master for *déjeuner* that day?'

'I –' Marie paused, trying to collect herself.

'Odd,' said Poirot, 'how one remembers some things – and forgets others.'

He leant forward and struck the table a blow with his fist; his eyes flashed with anger.

'Yes, yes, it is as I say. You tell your lies and you think nobody knows. But there are two people who know. Yes – two people. One is *le bon Dieu* –'

He raised a hand to heaven, and then settling himself back in his chair and shutting his eyelids, he murmured comfortably:

'And the other is Hercule Poirot.'

'I assure you, Monsieur, you are completely mistaken. Monsieur le Comte left Paris on Monday night –'

'True,' said Poirot – 'by the Rapide. I do not know where he broke his journey. Perhaps you do not know that. What I do know is that he arrived here on Wednesday morning, and not on Tuesday morning.'

'Monsieur is mistaken,' said Marie stolidly.

Poirot rose to his feet.

'Then the law must take its course,' he murmured, 'A pity.'

'What do you mean, Monsieur?' asked Marie, with a shade of uneasiness.

'You will be arrested and held as accomplices concerned in the murder of Mrs Kettering, the English lady who was killed.'

'Murder!'

The man's face had gone chalk white, his knees knocked together. Marie dropped the rolling-pin and began to weep.

'But it is impossible – impossible. I thought –'

'Since you stick to your story, there is nothing to be said. I think you are both foolish.'

He was turning towards the door when an agitated voice arrested him.

'Monsieur, Monsieur, just a little moment. I – I had no idea that it was anything of this kind. I – I thought it was just a matter concerning a lady. There have been little awkwardnesses with the police over ladies before. But murder – that is very different.'

'I have no patience with you,' cried Poirot. He turned round on them and angrily shook his fist in Hipolyte's face. 'Am I to stop here all day, arguing with a couple of imbeciles thus? It is the truth I want. If you will not give it to me, that is your lookout. *For the last time, when did Monsieur le Comte arrive at the Villa Marina – Tuesday morning or Wednesday morning?*'

'Wednesday,' gasped the man, and behind him Marie nodded confirmation.

Poirot regarded them for a minute or two, then inclined his head gravely.

'You are wise, my children,' he said quietly. 'Very nearly you were in serious trouble.'

He left the Villa Marina, smiling to himself.

'One guess confirmed,' he murmured to himself. 'Shall I take a chance on the other?'

It was six o'clock when the card of Monsieur Hercule Poirot was brought up to Mirelle. She stared at it for a moment or two, and then nodded. When Poirot entered, he found her walking up and down the room feverishly. She turned on him furiously.

'Well?' she cried. 'Well? What is it now? Have you not tortured me enough, all of you? Have you not made me betray my poor Dereek? What more do you want?'

'Just one little question, Mademoiselle. After the train left Lyons, when you entered Mrs Kettering's compartment –'

'What is that?'

Poirot looked at her with an air of mild reproach and began again.

'I say when you entered Mrs Kettering's compartment –'

'I never did.'

'And found her –'

'I never did.'

'*Ah, sacré!*'

He turned on her in a rage and shouted at her, so that she cowered back before him.

'Will you lie to me? I tell you I know what happened as well as though I had been there. You went into her compartment and you found her dead. I tell you I know it. To lie to me is dangerous. Be careful, Mademoiselle Mirelle.'

Her eyes wavered beneath his gaze and fell.

'I – I didn't –' she began uncertainly, and stopped.

'There is only one thing about which I wonder,' said Poirot – 'I wonder, Mademoiselle, if you found what you were looking for or whether –'

'Whether what?'

'Or whether someone else had been before you.'

'I will answer no more questions,' screamed the dancer. She tore herself away from Poirot's restraining hand, and flinging herself down on the floor in a frenzy, she screamed and sobbed. A frightened maid came rushing in.

Hercule Poirot shrugged his shoulders, raised his eyebrows, and quietly left the room.

But he seemed satisfied.

CHAPTER 30

MISS VINER GIVES JUDGMENT

Katherine looked out of Miss Viner's bedroom window. It was raining, not violently, but with a quiet, well-bred persistence. The window looked out on a strip of front garden with a path down to the gate and neat little flower-beds on either side, where later roses and pinks and blue hyacinths would bloom.

Miss Viner was lying in a large Victorian bedstead. A tray with the remains of breakfast had been pushed to one side and she was busy opening her correspondence and making various caustic comments upon it.

Katherine had an open letter in her hand and was reading it through for the second time. It was dated from the Ritz Hotel, Paris.

Chère Mademoiselle Katherine, *(It began)* – I trust that you are in good health and that the return to the English winter has not proved too depressing. Me, I prosecute my inquiries with the utmost diligence. Do not think that it is the holiday that I take here. Very shortly I shall be in England, and I hope then to have the pleasure of meeting you once more. It shall be so, shall it not? On arrival in London I shall write to you. You remember that we are the colleagues in this affair? But indeed I think you know that very well. Be assured, Mademoiselle, of my most respectful and devoted sentiments.

Hercule Poirot.

Katherine frowned slightly. It was as though something in the letter puzzled and intrigued her.

'A choirboys' picnic indeed,' came from Miss Viner, 'Tommy Saunders and Albert Dykes ought to be left behind, and I shan't subscribe to it unless they are. What those two boys think they are doing in church on Sundays I don't know. Tommy sang, "O God, make speed to save us," and never opened his lips again, and if Albert Dykes wasn't sucking a mint humbug, my nose is not what it is and always has been.'

'I know, they are awful,' agreed Katherine.

She opened her second letter, and a sudden flush came to her cheeks. Miss Viner's voice in the room seemed to recede into the far distance.

When she came back to a sense of her surroundings Miss Viner was bringing a long speech to a triumphant termination.

'And I said to her, "Not at all. As it happens, Miss Grey is Lady Tamplin's own cousin." What do you think of that?'

'Were you fighting my battles for me? That was very sweet of you.'

'You can put it that way if you like. There is nothing to me in a title. Vicar's wife or no vicar's wife, that woman is a cat. Hinting you had bought your way into Society.'

'Perhaps she was not so very far wrong.'

'And look at you,' continued Miss Viner. 'Have you come back a stuck-up fine lady, as well you might have done? No, there you are, as sensible as ever you were, with a pair of good Balbriggan stockings on and your sensible shoes. I spoke to Ellen about it only yesterday. "Ellen," I said, "you look at Miss Grey. She has been hobnobbing with some of the greatest in the land, and does she go about as you do with skirts up to her knees and silk stockings that ladder when you look at them, and the most ridiculous shoes that ever I set eyes on?"'

Katherine smiled a little to herself. It had apparently been worthwhile to conform to Miss Viner's prejudices. The old lady went on with increasing gusto.

'It has been a great relief to me that you have not had your head turned. Only the other day I was looking for my cuttings. I have several about Lady Tamplin and her War Hospital and what not, but I cannot lay my hand upon them. I wish you would look, my dear; your eyesight is better than mine. They are all in a box in the bureau drawer.'

Katherine glanced down at the letter in her hand and was about to speak, but checked herself, and going over to the bureau found the box of cuttings and began to look over them. Since her return to St Mary Mead, her heart had gone out to Miss Viner in admiration of the old woman's stoicism and pluck. She felt that there was little she could do for her old friend, but she knew from experience how much those seemingly small trifles meant to old people.

'Here is one,' she said presently. '"Viscountess Tamplin, who is running her villa at Nice as an Officers' Hospital, has just been the victim of a sensational robbery, her jewels having been stolen. Amongst them were some very famous emeralds, heirlooms of the Tamplin family."'

'Probably paste,' said Miss Viner; 'a lot of these Society women's jewels are.'

'Here is another,' said Katherine. 'A picture of her. "A charming camera study of Viscountess Tamplin with her little daughter Lenox."'

'Let me look,' said Miss Viner. 'You can't see much of the child's face, can you? But I dare say that is just as well. Things go by contraries in this world and beautiful mothers have hideous children. I dare say the photographer realized that to take the back of the child's head was the best thing he could do for her.'

Katherine laughed.

'"One of the smartest hostesses on the Riviera this season is Viscountess Tamplin, who has a villa at Cap Martin. Her cousin, Miss Grey, who recently inherited a vast fortune in a most romantic manner, is staying with her there."'

'That is the one I wanted,' said Miss Viner. 'I expect there has been a picture of you in one of the papers that I have missed; you know the kind of thing. Mrs Somebody or other Jones-Williams, at the something or other Point-to-Point, usually carrying a shooting-stick and having one foot lifted up in the air. It must be a trial to some of them to see what they look like.'

Katherine did not answer. She was smoothing out the cutting with her finger, and her face had a puzzled, worried look. Then she drew the second letter out of its envelope and mastered its contents once more. She turned to her friend.

'Miss Viner? I wonder – there is a friend of mine, someone I met on the Riviera, who wants very much to come down and see me here.'

'A man?' said Miss Viner.

'Yes.'

'Who is he?'

'He is secretary to Mr Van Aldin, the American millionaire.'

'What is his name?'

'Knighton. Major Knighton.'

'H'm – secretary to a millionaire. And wants to come down here. Now, Katherine, I am going to say something to you for your own good. You are a nice girl and a sensible girl, and though you have your head screwed on the right way about most things, every woman makes a fool of herself once in her life. Ten to one that this man is after is your money.'

With a gesture she arrested Katherine's reply. 'I have been waiting for something of this kind. What is a secretary to a millionaire? Nine times out of ten it is a young man who likes living soft. A young man with nice manners and a taste for luxury and no brains and no enterprise, and if there is anything that is a softer job than being secretary to a millionaire it is marrying a rich woman for her money. I am not saying that you might not be some man's fancy. But you are not young, and though you have a very good complexion you are not a beauty, and what I say to you is, don't make a fool of yourself; but if you are determined to do so, do see that your money is properly tied up on yourself. There, now I have finished. What have you got to say?'

'Nothing,' said Katherine; 'but would you mind if he did come down to see me?'

'I wash my hands of it,' said Miss Viner. 'I have done my duty, and whatever happens now is on your own head. Would you like him to lunch or to dinner? I dare say Ellen could manage dinner – that is, if she didn't lose her head.'

'Lunch would be very nice,' said Katherine. 'It is awfully kind of you, Miss Viner. He asked me to ring him up, so I will do so and say that we shall be pleased if he will lunch with us. He will motor down from town.'

'Ellen does a steak with grilled tomatoes pretty fairly,' said Miss Viner. 'She doesn't do it well, but she does it better than anything else. It is no good having a tart because she is heavy-handed with pastry; but her little castle puddings are not bad, and I dare say you could find a nice piece of Stilton at Abbot's. I have always heard that gentlemen like a nice piece of Stilton, and there is a good deal of Father's wine left, a bottle of sparkling Moselle, perhaps.'

'Oh no, Miss Viner; that is really not necessary.'

'Nonsense, my child. No gentleman is happy unless he drinks something with his meal. There is some good pre-war whisky if you think he would prefer that. Now do as I say and don't argue. The key of the wine-cellar is in the third drawer down in the dressing-table, in the second pair of stockings on the left-hand side.'

Katherine went obediently to the spot indicated.

'The second pair, now mind,' said Miss Viner. 'The first pair has my diamond earrings and my filigree brooch in it.'

'Oh,' said Katherine, rather taken aback, 'wouldn't you like them put in your jewel-case?'

Miss Viner gave vent to a terrific and prolonged snort.

'No, indeed! I have much too much sense for that sort of thing, thank you. Dear, dear, I well remember how my poor father had a safe built in downstairs. Pleased as Punch he was with it, and he said to my mother, "Now, Mary, you bring me your jewels in their case every night and I will lock them away for you." My mother was a very tactful woman, and she knew that gentlemen like having their own way, and she brought him the jewel-case to be locked up just as he said.

'And one night burglars broke in, and of course – naturally – the first thing they went for was the safe! It would be, with my father talking up and down the village and bragging about it until you might have thought he kept all King Solomon's diamonds there. They made a clean sweep, got the tankards, the silver cups, and the presentation gold plate that my father had had presented to him, *and* the jewel-case.'

She sighed reminiscently. 'My father was in a great state over my mother's jewels. There was the Venetian set and some very fine cameos, and some pale pink corals, and two diamond rings with quite large stones in them. And then, of course, she had to tell him that, being a sensible woman, she had kept her jewellery rolled up in a pair of corsets, and there it was still as safe as anything.'

'And the jewel-case had been quite empty?'

'Oh no, dear,' said Miss Viner, 'it would have been too light a weight then. My mother was a very intelligent woman; she saw to that. She kept her buttons in the jewel-case, and a very handy place it was. Boot buttons in the top tray, trouser buttons in the second tray, and assorted buttons below. Curiously enough, my father was quite annoyed with her. He said he didn't like deceit. But I mustn't go chattering on; you want to go and ring up your friend, and mind you choose a nice piece of steak, and tell Ellen she is not to have holes in her stockings when she waits at lunch.'

'Is her name Ellen or Helen, Miss Viner? I thought –'

Miss Viner closed her eyes.

'I can sound my h's, dear, as well as anyone, but Helen is *not* a suitable name for a servant. I don't know what the mothers in the lower classes are coming to nowadays.'

The rain had cleared away when Knighton arrived at the cottage. The pale fitful sunshine shone down on it and burnished Katherine's head as she stood in the doorway to welcome him. He came up to her quickly, almost boyishly.

'I say, I hope you don't mind. I simply had to see you again soon. I hope the friend you are staying with does not mind.'

'Come in and make friends with her,' said Katherine. 'She can be most alarming, but you will soon find that she has the softest heart in the world.'

Miss Viner was enthroned majestically in the drawing-room, wearing a complete set of the cameos which had been so providentially preserved in the family. She greeted Knighton with dignity and an austere politeness which would have damped many men. Knighton, however, had a charm of manner which was not easily set aside, and after about ten minutes Miss Viner thawed perceptibly. Luncheon was a merry meal, and Ellen, or Helen, in a new pair of silk stockings devoid of ladders, performed prodigies of waiting. Afterwards, Katherine and Knighton went for a walk, and they came back to have tea *tête-à-tête*, since Miss Viner had gone to lie down.

When the car had finally driven off Katherine went slowly upstairs. A voice called her and she went in to Miss Viner's bedroom.

'Friend gone?'

'Yes. Thank you so much for letting me ask him down.'

'No need to thank me. Do you think I am the sort of old curmudgeon who never will do anything for anybody?'

'I think you are a dear,' said Katherine affectionately.

'Humph,' said Miss Viner, mollified.

As Katherine was leaving the room she called her back.

'Katherine?'

'Yes.'

'I was wrong about that young man of yours. A man when he is making up to anybody can be cordial and gallant and full of little attentions and altogether charming. But when a man is really in love he can't help looking like a sheep. Now, whenever that young man looked at you he looked like a sheep. I take back all I said this morning. It is genuine.'

CHAPTER 31

MR AARONS LUNCHES

'Ah!' said Mr Joseph Aarons appreciatively.

He took a long draught from his tankard, set it down with a sigh, wiped the froth from his lips, and beamed across the table at his host, Monsieur Hercule Poirot.

'Give me,' said Mr Aarons, 'a good Porterhouse steak and a tankard of something worth drinking, and anyone can have your French fallals and whatnots, your ordoovres and your omelettes and your little bits of quail. Give me,' he reiterated, 'a Porterhouse steak.'

Poirot, who had just complied with this request, smiled sympathetically.

'Not that there is much wrong with a steak and kidney pudding,' continued Mr Aarons. 'Apple tart? Yes, I will take apple tart, thank you, Miss, and a jug of cream.'

The meal proceeded. Finally, with a long sigh, Mr Aarons laid down his spoon and fork preparatory to toying with some cheese before turning his mind to other matters.

'There was a little matter of business I think you said, Monsieur Poirot,' he remarked. 'Anything I can do to help you I am sure I shall be most happy.'

'That is very kind of you,' said Poirot. 'I said to myself, "If you want to know anything about the dramatic profession there is one person who knows all that is to be known and that is my old friend, Mr Joseph Aarons."'

'And you don't say far wrong,' said Mr Aarons complacently; 'whether it is past, present, or future, Joe Aarons is the man to come to.'

'*Précisément*. Now I want to ask you, Monsieur Aarons, what you know about a young woman called Kidd.'

'Kidd? Kitty Kidd?'

'Kitty Kidd.'

'Pretty smart, she was. Male impersonator, song and a dance – That one?'

'That is the one.'

'*Very* smart, she was. Made a good income. Never out of an engagement. Male impersonation mostly, but, as a matter of fact, you could not touch her as a character actress.'

'So I have heard,' said Poirot; 'but she has not been appearing lately, has she?'

'No. Dropped right out of things. Went over to France and took up with some swell nobleman there. She quitted the stage then for good and all, I guess.'

'How long ago was that?'

'Let me see. Three years ago. And she has been a loss – let me tell you that.'

'She was clever?'

'Clever as a cartload of monkeys.'

'You don't know the name of the man she became friends with in Paris?'

'He was a swell, I know that. A Count – or was it a Marquis? Now I come to think of it, I believe it was a Marquis.'

'And you know nothing about her since?'

'Nothing. Never even run across her accidentally like. I bet she is tooling it round some of these foreign resorts. Being a Marquise to the life. You couldn't put one over on Kitty. She would give as good as she got any day.'

'I see,' said Poirot thoughtfully.

'I am sorry I can't tell you more, Monsieur Poirot,' said the other. 'I would like to be of use to you if I could. You did me a good turn once.'

'Ah, but we are quits on that; you, too, did me a good turn.'

'One good turn deserves another. Ha, ha!' said Mr Aarons.

'Your profession must be a very interesting one,' said Poirot.

'So-so,' said Mr Aarons non-committally. 'Taking the rough with the smooth, it is all right. I don't do so badly at it, all things considered, but you have to keep your eyes skinned. Never know what the public will jump for next.'

'Dancing has come very much to the fore in the last few years,' murmured Poirot reflectively.

'*I* never saw anything in this Russian ballet, but people like it. Too highbrow for me.'

'I met one dancer out on the Riviera – Mademoiselle Mirelle.'

'Mirelle? She is hot stuff, by all accounts. There is always money going to back her – though, so far as that goes, the girl can dance; I have seen her, and I know what I am talking about. I never had much to do with her myself, but I hear she is a terror to deal with. Tempers and tantrums all the time.'

'Yes,' said Poirot thoughtfully; 'yes, so I should imagine.'

'Temperament!' said Mr Aarons, 'temperament! That is what they call it themselves. My missus was a dancer before she married me, but I am thankful to say she never had any temperament. You don't want temperament in the home, Monsieur Poirot.'

'I agree with you, my friend; it is out of place there.'

'A woman should be calm and sympathetic, and a good cook,' said Mr Aarons.

'Mirelle has not been long before the public, has she?' asked Poirot.

'About two and a half years, that is all,' said Mr Aarons. 'Some French duke started her. I hear now that she has taken up with the ex-Prime Minister of Greece. These are the chaps who manage to put money away quietly.'

'That is news to me,' said Poirot.

'Oh, she's not one to let the grass grow under her feet. They say that young Kettering murdered his wife on her account. I don't know, I am sure. Anyway, he is in prison, and she had to look round for herself, and pretty smart she has been about it. They say she is wearing a ruby the size of a pigeon's egg – not that I have ever seen a pigeon's egg myself, but that is what they always call it in works of fiction.'

'A ruby the size of a pigeon's egg!' said Poirot. His eyes were green and cat-like. 'How interesting!'

'I had it from a friend of mine,' said Mr Aarons. 'But for all I know, it may be coloured glass. They are all the same, these women – they never stop telling tall stories about their jewels. Mirelle goes about bragging that it has got a curse on it. "Heart of Fire", I think she calls it.'

'But if I remember rightly,' said Poirot, 'the ruby that is named "Heart of Fire" is the centre stone in a necklace.'

'There you are! Didn't I tell you there is no end to the lies women will tell about their jewellery? This is a single stone, hung on a platinum chain round her neck; but, as I said before, ten to one it is a bit of coloured glass.'

'No,' said Poirot gently; 'no – somehow I do not think it is coloured glass.'

CHAPTER 32

KATHERINE AND POIROT COMPARE NOTES

'You have changed, Mademoiselle,' said Poirot suddenly. He and Katherine were seated opposite each other at a small table at the Savoy.

'Yes, you have changed,' he continued.

'In what way?'

'Mademoiselle, these *nuances* are difficult to express.'

'I am older.'

'Yes, you are older. And by that I do not mean that the wrinkles and the crows' feet are coming. When I first saw you, Mademoiselle, you were a looker-on at life. You had the quiet, amused look of one who sits back in the stalls and watches the play.'

'And now?'

'Now you no longer watch. It is an absurd thing, perhaps, that I say here, but you have the wary look of a fighter who is playing a difficult game.'

'My old lady is difficult sometimes,' said Katherine, with a smile; 'but I can assure you that I don't engage in deadly contests with her. You must go down and see her some day, Monsieur Poirot. I think you are one of the people who would appreciate her pluck and her spirit.'

There was a silence while the waiter deftly served them with chicken *en casserole*. When he had departed, Poirot said: 'You have heard me speak of my friend Hastings? – he who said that I was a human oyster. *Eh bien*, Mademoiselle, I have met my match in you. You, far more than I, play a lone hand.'

'Nonsense,' said Katherine lightly.

'Never does Hercule Poirot talk nonsense. It is as I say.'

Again there was a silence. Poirot broke it by inquiring:

'Have you seen any of our Riviera friends since you have been back, Mademoiselle?'

'I have seen something of Major Knighton.'

'A-ha. Is that so?'

Something in Poirot's twinkling eyes made Katherine lower hers.

'So Mr Van Aldin remains in London?'

'Yes.'

'I must try to see him tomorrow or the next day.'

'You have news for him?'

'What makes you think that?'

'I – wondered, that is all.'

Poirot looked across at her with twinkling eyes.

'And now, Mademoiselle, there is much that you wish to ask me, I can see that. And why not? Is not the affair of the Blue Train our own "*roman policier*"?'

'Yes, there are things I should like to ask you.'

'*Eh bien?*'

Katherine looked up with a sudden air of resolution.

'What were you doing in Paris, Monsieur Poirot?'

Poirot smiled slightly.

'I made a call at the Russian Embassy.'

'Oh.'

'I see that that tells you nothing. But I will not be a human oyster. No, I will lay my cards on the table, which is assuredly a thing that oysters never do. You suspect, do you not, that I am not satisfied with the case against Derek Kettering?'

'That is what I have been wondering. I thought, in Nice, that you had finished with the case.'

'You do not say all that you mean, Mademoiselle. But I admit everything. It was I – my researches – which placed Derek Kettering where he now is. But for me the Examining Magistrate would still be vainly trying to fasten the crime on the Comte de la Roche. *Eh bien*, Mademoiselle, what I have done I do not regret. I have only one duty – to discover the truth, and that way led straight to Mr Kettering. But did it end there? The police say yes, but I, Hercule Poirot, am not satisfied.'

He broke off suddenly. 'Tell me, Mademoiselle, have you heard from Mademoiselle Lenox lately?'

'One very short, scrappy letter. She is, I think, annoyed with me for coming back to England.'

Poirot nodded.

'I had an interview with her the night that Monsieur Kettering was arrested. It was an interesting interview in more ways than one.'

Again he fell silent, and Katherine did not interrupt his train of thought. 'Mademoiselle,' he said at last, 'I am now on delicate ground, yet I will say this to you. There is, I think, someone who loves Monsieur Kettering – correct me if I am wrong – and for her sake – well – for her sake I hope that I am right and the police are wrong. You know who that someone is?'

There was a pause, then Katherine said:

'Yes – I think I know.'

Poirot leant across the table towards her.

'I am not satisfied, Mademoiselle; no, I am not satisfied. The facts, the main facts, led straight to Monsieur Kettering. But there is one thing that has been left out of account.'

'And what is that?'

'The disfigured face of the victim. I have asked myself, Mademoiselle, a hundred times, "Was Derek Kettering the kind of man who would deal that smashing blow after having committed the murder?" What end would it serve? What purpose would it accomplish? Was it a likely action for one of Monsieur Kettering's temperament? And, Mademoiselle, the answer to these questions is profoundly unsatisfactory. Again and again I go back to that one point – "why?" And the only things I have to help me to a solution of the problem are these.'

He whipped out his pocket-book and extracted something from it which he held between his finger and thumb.

'Do you remember, Mademoiselle? You saw me take these hairs from the rug in the railway carriage.'

Katherine leant forward, scrutinizing the hairs keenly.

Poirot nodded his head slowly several times.

'They suggest nothing to you, I see that, Mademoiselle. And yet – I think somehow that you see a good deal.'

'I have had ideas,' said Katherine slowly, 'curious ideas. That is why I ask you what you were doing in Paris, Monsieur Poirot.'

'When I wrote to you –'

'From the Ritz?'

A curious smile came over Poirot's face.

'Yes, as you say, from the Ritz. I am a luxurious person sometimes – when a millionaire pays.'

'The Russian Embassy,' said Katherine, frowning. 'No, I don't see where that comes in.'

'It does not come in directly, Mademoiselle. I went there to get certain information. I saw a particular personage and I threatened him – yes, Mademoiselle, I, Hercule Poirot, threatened him.'

'With the police?'

'No,' said Poirot drily, 'with the Press – a much more deadly weapon.'

He looked at Katherine and she smiled at him, just shaking her head.

'Are you not just turning back into an oyster again, Monsieur Poirot?'

'No, no; I do not wish to make mysteries. See, I will tell you everything. I suspect this man of being the active party in the sale of the jewels of Monsieur Van Aldin. I tax him with it, and in the end I get the whole story out of him. I learn where the jewels were handed over, and I learn, too, of the man who paced up and down outside in the street – a man with a venerable head of white hair, but who walked with the light, springy step of a young man – and I give that man a name in my own mind – the name of "Monsieur le Marquis".'

'And now you have come to London to see Mr Van Aldin?'

'Not entirely for that reason. I had other work to do. Since I have been in London I have seen two more people – a theatrical agent and a Harley Street doctor. From each of them I have got certain information. Put these things together, Mademoiselle, and see if you can make of them the same as I do.'

'I?'

'Yes, you. I will tell you one thing, Mademoiselle. There has been a doubt all along in my mind as to whether the robbery and the murder were done by the same person. For a long time I was not sure –'

'And now?'

'And now I *know*.'

There was a silence. Then Katherine lifted her head. Her eyes were shining.

'I am not clever like you, Monsieur Poirot. Half the things that you have been telling me don't seem to me to point anywhere at all. The ideas that came to me came from such an entirely different angle –'

'Ah, but that is always so,' said Poirot quietly. 'A mirror shows the truth, but everyone stands in a different place for looking into the mirror.'

'My ideas may be absurd – they may be entirely different from yours, but –'

'Yes?'

'Tell me, does this help you at all?'

He took a newspaper cutting from her outstretched hand. He read it and, looking up, he nodded gravely.

'As I told you, Mademoiselle, one stands at a different angle for looking into the mirror, but it is the same mirror and the same things are reflected there.'

Katherine got up. 'I must rush,' she said. 'I have only just time to catch my train. Monsieur Poirot –'

'Yes, Mademoiselle.'

'It – it mustn't be much longer, you understand. I – I can't go on much longer.'

There was a break in her voice.

He patted her hand reassuringly.

'Courage, Mademoiselle, you must not fail now; the end is very near.'

CHAPTER 33

A NEW THEORY

'Monsieur Poirot wants to see you, sir.'

'Damn the fellow!' said Van Aldin.

Knighton remained sympathetically silent.

Van Aldin got up from his chair and paced up and down.

'I suppose you have seen the cursed newspapers this morning?'

'I have glanced at them, sir.'

'Still at it hammer and tongs?'

'I am afraid so, sir.'

The millionaire sat down again and pressed his hand to his forehead.

'If I had had an idea of this,' he groaned. 'I wish to God I had never got that little Belgian to ferret out the truth. Find Ruth's murderer – that was all I thought about.'

'You wouldn't have liked your son-in-law to go scot free?'

Van Aldin sighed.

'I would have preferred to take the law into my own hands.'

'I don't think that would have been a very wise proceeding, sir.'

'All the same – are you sure the fellow wants to see me?'

'Yes, Mr Van Aldin. He is very urgent about it.'

'Then I suppose he will have to. He can come along this morning if he likes.'

It was a very fresh and debonair Poirot who was ushered in. He did not seem to see any lack of cordiality in the millionaire's manner, and chatted pleasantly about various trifles. He was in London, he explained, to see his doctor. He mentioned the name of an eminent surgeon.

'No, no, *pas la guerre* – a memory of my days in the police force, a bullet of a rascally apache.'

He touched his left shoulder and winced realistically.

'I always consider you a lucky man, Monsieur Van Aldin; you are not like our popular idea of American millionaires, martyrs to dyspepsia.'

'I am pretty tough,' said Van Aldin. 'I lead a very simple life, you know; plain fare and not too much of it.'

'You have seen something of Miss Grey, have you not?' inquired Poirot, innocently turning to the secretary.

'I – yes; once or twice,' said Knighton.

He blushed slightly and Van Aldin exclaimed in surprise:

'Funny you never mentioned to me that you had seen her, Knighton.'

'I didn't think you would be interested, sir.'

'I like that girl very much,' said Van Aldin.

'It is a thousand pities that she should have buried herself once more in St Mary Mead,' said Poirot.

'It is very fine of her,' said Knighton hotly. 'There are very few people who would bury themselves down there to look after a cantankerous old woman who has no earthly claim on her.'

'I am silent,' said Poirot, his eyes twinkling a little; 'but all the same I say it is a pity. And now, Messieurs, let us come to business.'

Both the other men looked at him in some surprise.

'You must not be shocked or alarmed at what I am about to say. Supposing, Monsieur Van Aldin, that, after all, Monsieur Derek Kettering did not murder his wife?'

'What?'

Both men stared at him in blank surprise.

'Supposing, I say, that Monsieur Kettering did not murder his wife?'

'Are you mad, Monsieur Poirot?'

It was Van Aldin who spoke.

'No,' said Poirot, 'I am not mad. I am eccentric, perhaps – at least certain people say so; but as regards my profession, I am very much, as one says, "all there". I ask you, Monsieur Van Aldin, whether you would be glad or sorry if what I tell you should be the case?'

Van Aldin stared at him.

'Naturally I should be glad,' he said at last. 'Is this an exercise in suppositions, Monsieur Poirot, or are there any facts behind it?'

Poirot looked at the ceiling.

'There is an off-chance,' he said quietly, 'that it might be the Comte de la Roche after all. At least I have succeeded in upsetting his alibi.'

'How did you manage that?'

Poirot shrugged his shoulders modestly.

'I have my own methods. The exercise of a little tact, a little cleverness – and the thing is done.'

'But the rubies,' said Van Aldin, 'these rubies that the Count had in his possession were false.'

'And clearly he would not have committed the crime except for the rubies. But you are overlooking one point, Monsieur Van Aldin. Where the rubies were concerned, someone might have been before him.'

'But this is an entirely new theory,' cried Knighton.

'Do you really believe all this rigmarole, Monsieur Poirot?' demanded the millionaire.

'The thing is not proved,' said Poirot quietly. 'It is as yet only a theory, but I tell you this, Monsieur Van Aldin, the facts are worth investigating. You must come out with me to the south of France and go into the case on the spot.'

'You really think this is necessary – that I should go, I mean?'

'I thought it would be what you yourself would wish,' said Poirot.

There was a hint of reproach in his tone which was not lost upon the other.

'Yes, yes, of course,' he said. 'When do you wish to start, Monsieur Poirot?'

'You are very busy at present, sir,' murmured Knighton.

But the millionaire had now made up his mind, and he waved the other's objections aside.

'I guess this business comes first,' he said. 'All right, Monsieur Poirot, tomorrow. What train?'

'We will go, I think, by the Blue Train,' said Poirot, and he smiled.

CHAPTER 34

THE BLUE TRAIN AGAIN

'The Millionaires' Train', as it is sometimes called, swung round a curve of line at what seemed a dangerous speed. Van Aldin, Knighton, and Poirot sat together in silence. Knighton and Van Aldin had two compartments connecting with each other, as Ruth Kettering and her maid had had on the fateful journey. Poirot's own compartment was farther along the coach.

The journey was a painful one for Van Aldin, recalling as it did the most agonizing memories. Poirot and Knighton conversed occasionally in low tones without disturbing him.

When, however, the train had completed its slow journey round the *ceinture* and reached the Gare de Lyon, Poirot became suddenly galvanized into activity. Van Aldin realized that part of his object in travelling by the train had been to attempt to reconstruct the crime. Poirot himself acted every part. He was in turn the maid, hurriedly shut into her own compartment, Mrs Kettering, recognizing her husband with surprise and a trace of anxiety, and Derek Kettering discovering that his wife was travelling on the train. He tested various possibilities, such as the best way for a person to conceal himself in the second compartment.

Then suddenly an idea seemed to strike him. He clutched at Van Aldin's arm.

'*Mon Dieu*, but that is something I have not thought of! We must break our journey in Paris. Quick, quick, let us alight at once.'

Seizing suit-cases he hurried from the train. Van Aldin and Knighton, bewildered but obedient, followed him. Van Aldin having once more formed his opinion of Poirot's ability was slow to depart from it. At the barrier they were held up. Their tickets were in the charge of the conductor of the train, a fact which all three of them had forgotten.

Poirot's explanations were rapid, fluent, and impassioned, but they produced no effect upon the stolid-faced official.

'Let us get quit of this,' said Van Aldin abruptly. 'I gather you are in a hurry, Monsieur Poirot. For God's sake pay the fares from Calais and let us get right on with whatever you have got on your mind.'

But Poirot's flood of language had suddenly stopped dead, and he had the appearance of a man turned to stone. His arm, still outflung in an impassioned gesture, remained there as though stricken with paralysis.

'I have been an imbecile,' he said simply. '*Ma foi*, I lose my head nowadays. Let us return and continue our journey quietly. With reasonable luck the train will not have gone.'

They were only just in time, the train moving off as Knighton, the last of the three, swung himself and his suit-case on board.

The conductor remonstrated with them feelingly and assisted

them to carry their luggage back to their compartments. Van Aldin said nothing, but he was clearly disgusted at Poirot's extraordinary conduct. Alone with Knighton for a moment, or two, he remarked:

'This is a wild-goose chase. The man has lost his grip on things. He has got brains up to a point, but any man who loses his head and scuttles round like a frightened rabbit is no earthly darned good.'

Poirot came to them in a moment or two, full of abject apologies and clearly so crestfallen that harsh words would have been superfluous. Van Aldin received his apologies gravely, but managed to restrain himself from making acid comments.

They had dinner on the train, and afterwards, somewhat to the surprise of the other two, Poirot suggested that they should all three sit up in Van Aldin's compartment.

The millionaire looked at him curiously.

'Is there anything that you are keeping back from us, Monsieur Poirot?'

'I?' Poirot opened his eyes in innocent surprise. 'But what an idea.'

Van Aldin did not answer, but he was not satisfied. The conductor was told that he need not make up the beds. Any surprise he might have felt was obliterated by the largeness of the tip which Van Aldin handed to him. The three men sat in silence. Poirot fidgeted and seemed restless. Presently he turned to the secretary.

'Major Knighton, is the door of your compartment bolted? The door into the corridor, I mean.'

'Yes; I bolted it myself just now.'

'Are you sure?' said Poirot.

'I will go and make sure, if you like,' said Knighton, smiling.

'No, no, do not derange yourself. I will see for myself.'

He passed through the connecting door and returned in a second or two, nodding his head.

'Yes, yes, it is as you said. You pardon an old man's fussy ways.' He closed the connecting door and resumed his place in the right-hand corner.

The hours passed. The three men dozed fitfully, waking with uncomfortable starts. Probably never before had three people booked berths on the most luxurious train available, then declined to avail themselves of the accommodation they had paid for. Every now and then Poirot glanced at his watch, and then nodded his head and composed himself to slumber once more. On one occasion he rose from his seat and opened the connecting door, peered sharply into the adjoining compartment, and then returned to his seat, shaking his head.

'What is the matter?' whispered Knighton. 'You are expecting something to happen, aren't you?'

'I have the nerves,' confessed Poirot. 'I am like the cat upon the hot tiles. Every little noise it makes me jump.'

Knighton yawned.

'Of all the darned uncomfortable journeys,' he murmured. 'I suppose you know what you are playing at, Monsieur Poirot.'

He composed himself to sleep as best he could. Both he and Van Aldin had succumbed to slumber, when Poirot, glancing for the fourteenth time at his watch, leant across and tapped the millionaire on the shoulder.

'Eh? What is it?'

'In five or ten minutes, Monsieur, we shall arrive at Lyons.'

'My God!' Van Aldin's face looked white and haggard in the dim light. 'Then it must have been about this time that poor Ruth was killed.'

He sat staring straight in front of him. His lips twitched a little, his mind reverting back to the terrible tragedy that had saddened his life.

There was the usual long screaming sigh of the brake, and the train slackened speed and drew into Lyons. Van Aldin let down the window and leant out.

'If it wasn't Derek – if your new theory is correct, it is here that the man left the train?' he asked over his shoulder.

Rather to his surprise Poirot shook his head.

'No,' he said thoughtfully, 'no *man* left the train, but I think – yes, I think, a *woman* may have done so.'

Knighton gave a gasp.

'A woman?' demanded Van Aldin sharply.

'Yes, a woman,' said Poirot, nodding his head. 'You may not remember, Monsieur Van Aldin, but Miss Grey in her evidence mentioned that a youth in a cap and overcoat descended on to the platform ostensibly to stretch his legs. Me, I think that that youth was most probably a woman.'

'But who was she?'

Van Aldin's face expressed incredulity, but Poirot replied seriously and categorically:

'Her name – or the name under which she was known, for many years – is Kitty Kidd, but you, Monsieur Van Aldin, knew her by another name – *that of Ada Mason*.'

Knighton sprang to his feet.

'What?' he cried.

Poirot swung round to him.

'Ah! – before I forget it.' He whipped something from a pocket and held it out.

'Permit me to offer you a cigarette – out of your own cigarette-case. It was careless of you to drop it when you boarded the train on the *ceinture* at Paris.'

Knighton stood staring at him as though stupefied. Then he made a movement, but Poirot flung up his hand in a warning gesture.

'No, don't move,' he said in a silky voice; 'the door into the next compartment is open, and you are being covered from there this minute. I unbolted the door into the corridor when we left Paris, and our friends the police were told to take their places there. As I expect you know, the French police want you rather urgently, Major Knighton – or shall we say – Monsieur le Marquis?'

CHAPTER 35

EXPLANATIONS

'Explanations?'

Poirot smiled. He was sitting opposite the millionaire at a luncheon table in the latter's private suite at the Negresco. Facing him was a relieved but very puzzled man. Poirot leant back in his chair, lit one of his tiny cigarettes, and stared reflectively at the ceiling.

'Yes, I will give you explanations. It began with the one point that puzzled me. You know what that point was? *The disfigured face*. It is not an uncommon thing to find when investigating a crime and it rouses an immediate question, the question of identity. That naturally was the first thing that occurred to me. Was the dead woman really Mrs Kettering? But that line led me nowhere, for Miss Grey's evidence was positive and very reliable, so I put that idea aside. The dead woman *was* Ruth Kettering.'

'When did you first begin to suspect the maid?'

'Not for some time, but one peculiar little point drew my attention to her. The cigarette-case found in the railway carriage and which she told us was one which Mrs Kettering had given to her husband. Now that was, on the face of it, most improbable, seeing the terms they were on. It awakened a doubt in my mind as to the general veracity of Ada Mason's statements. There was the rather suspicious fact to be taken into consideration, that she had only been with her mistress for two months. Certainly it did not seem as if she could have had anything to do with the crime since she had been left behind in Paris and Mrs Kettering had been seen alive by several people afterwards, but –'

Poirot leant forward. He raised an emphatic forefinger and wagged it with intense emphasis at Van Aldin.

'But I am a good detective. I suspect. There is nobody and nothing that I do not suspect. I believe nothing that I am told. I say to myself: how do we know that Ada Mason was left behind in Paris? And at first the answer to that question seemed completely satisfactory. There was the evidence of your secretary, Major Knighton, a complete outsider, whose testimony might be supposed to be entirely impartial, and there were the dead woman's own words to the conductor of the train. But I put the latter point aside for the moment, because a very curious idea – an idea perhaps fantastic and impossible – was growing up in my mind. If by any outside chance it happened to be true, that particular piece of testimony was worthless.

'I concentrated on the chief stumbling-block to my theory, Major Knighton's statement that he saw Ada Mason at the Ritz after the Blue Train had left Paris. That seemed conclusive enough, but yet, on examining the facts carefully, I noted two things. First, that by a curious coincidence he, too, had been exactly two months in your service. Secondly, his initial letter was the same – K. Supposing – just supposing – that it was *his* cigarette-case which had been found in the carriage. Then, if Ada Mason and he were working together, and she recognized it when we showed it to her, would she not act precisely as she had done? At first, taken aback, she quickly evolved a plausible theory that would agree with Mr Kettering's guilt. *Bien entendu*, that was not the original idea. The Comte de la Roche was to be the scapegoat, though Ada Mason would not make her recognition of him too certain, in case he should be able to prove an alibi. Now, if you will cast your mind back to that time, you will remember a significant thing that happened. I suggested to Ada Mason that the man she had seen was not the Comte de la Roche, but Derek Kettering. She seemed uncertain at the time, but after I had got back to my hotel you rang me up and told me that she had come to you and said that, on thinking it over, she was now quite convinced that the man in question *was* Mr Kettering. I had been expecting something of the kind. There could be but one explanation of this sudden certainty on her part. After leaving your hotel, she had had time to consult with somebody, and had received instructions which she acted upon. Who had given her these instructions? Major Knighton. And there was another very small point, which might mean nothing or might mean a great deal. In casual conversation Knighton had talked of a jewel robbery in Yorkshire in a house where he was staying. Perhaps a mere coincidence – perhaps another small link in the chain.'

'But there is one thing I do not understand, Monsieur Poirot. I guess I must be dense or I would have seen it before now. Who was the man in the train at Paris? Derek Kettering or the Comte de la Roche?'

'That is the simplicity of the whole thing. *There was no man*. Ah – *mille tonnerres!* – do you not see the cleverness of it all? Whose word have we for it that there ever was a man there? Only Ada Mason's. And we believe in Ada Mason because of Knighton's evidence that she was left behind in Paris.'

'But Ruth herself told the conductor that she had left her maid behind there,' demurred Van Aldin.

'Ah! I am coming to that. We have Mrs Kettering's own evidence there, but, on the other hand, we have not really got her evidence, because, Monsieur Van Aldin, a dead woman cannot give evidence. It is not *her* evidence, but the evidence of the conductor of the train – a very different affair altogether.'

'So you think the man was lying?'

'No, no, not at all. He spoke what he thought to be the truth. But the woman who told him that she had left her maid in Paris was not Mrs Kettering.'

Van Aldin stared at him.

'Monsieur Van Aldin, Ruth Kettering was dead before the train arrived at the Gare de Lyon. It was Ada Mason, dressed in her mistress's very distinctive clothing, who purchased a dinner basket and who made that very necessary statement to the conductor.'

'Impossible!'

'No, no, Monsieur Van Aldin; not impossible. *Les femmes*, they look so much alike nowadays that one identifies them more by their clothing than by their faces. Ada Mason was the same height as your daughter. Dressed in that very sumptuous fur coat and the little red lacquer hat jammed down over her eyes, with just a bunch of auburn curls showing over each ear, it was no wonder that the conductor was deceived. He had not previously spoken to Mrs Kettering, you remember. True, he had seen the maid just for a moment when she handed him the tickets, but his impression had been merely that of a gaunt, black-clad female. If he had been an unusually intelligent man, he might have gone so far as to say that mistress and maid were not unlike, but it is extremely unlikely that he would even think that. And remember, Ada Mason, or Kitty Kidd, was an actress, able to change her appearance and tone of voice at a moment's notice. No, no; there was no danger of his recognizing the maid in the mistress's clothing, but there *was* the danger that when he came to discover the body he might realize it was not the woman he had talked to the night before. And now we see the reason for the disfigured face. The chief danger that Ada Mason ran was that Katherine Grey might visit her compartment after the train left Paris, and she provided against that difficulty by ordering a dinner basket and by locking herself in her compartment.'

'But who killed Ruth – and when?'

'First, bear it in mind that the crime was planned and undertaken by the two of them – Knighton and Ada Mason, working together. Knighton was in Paris that day on your business. He boarded the train somewhere on its way round the *ceinture*. Mrs Kettering would be surprised, but she would be quite unsuspicious. Perhaps he draws her attention to something out of the window, and as she turns to look he slips the cord round her neck – and the whole thing is over in a second or two. The door of the compartment is locked, and he and Ada Mason set to work. They strip off the dead woman's outer clothes. Mason and Knighton roll the body up in a rug and put it on the seat in the adjoining compartment amongst the bags and suit-cases. Knighton drops off the train, taking the jewel-case containing the rubies with him. Since the crime is not supposed to have been committed until nearly twelve hours later he is perfectly safe, and his evidence and the supposed Mrs Kettering's words to the conductor will provide a perfect alibi for his accomplice.

'At the Gare de Lyon Ada Mason gets a dinner basket and, shutting herself into the toilet compartment, she quickly changes into her mistress's clothes, adjusts two false bunches of auburn curls, and generally makes up to resemble her as closely as possible. When the conductor comes to make up the bed, she tells him the prepared story about having left her maid behind in Paris; and whilst he is making up the berth, she stands looking out of the window, so that her back is towards the corridor and people passing along there. That was a wise precaution, because, as we know, Miss Grey was one of those passing, and she, among others, was willing to swear that Mrs Kettering was still alive at that hour.'

'Go on,' said Van Aldin.

'Before getting to Lyons, Ada Mason arranged her mistress's body in the bunk, folded up the dead woman's clothes neatly on the end of it, and herself changed into a man's clothes and prepared to leave the train. When Derek Kettering entered his wife's compartment, and, as he thought, saw her asleep in her berth, the scene had been set, and Ada Mason was hidden in the next compartment waiting for the moment to leave the train unobserved. As soon as the conductor had swung himself down on to the platform at Lyons, she follows, slouching along as though just taking a breath of air. At a moment when she is unobserved, she hurriedly crosses to the other platform, and takes the first train back to Paris and the Ritz Hotel. Her name has been registered there as taking a room the night before by one of Knighton's female accomplices. She has nothing to do but wait there placidly for your arrival. The jewels are not, and never have been, in her possession. No suspicion attaches to him, and, as your secretary, he brings them to Nice without the least fear of discovery. Their delivery there to Monsieur Papopolous is already arranged for, and they are entrusted to Mason at the last moment to hand over to the Greek. Altogether a very neatly planned coup, as one would expect from a master of the game such as the Marquis.'

'And you honestly mean that Richard Knighton is a well-known criminal, who has been at this business for years?'

Poirot nodded.

'One of the chief assets of the gentleman called the Marquis was his plausible, ingratiating manner. You fell a victim of his charm, Monsieur Van Aldin, when you engaged him as a secretary on such a slight acquaintanceship.'

'I could have sworn that he never angled for the post,' cried the millionaire.

'It was very astutely done – so astutely done that it deceived a man whose knowledge of other men is as great as yours is.'

'I looked up his antecedents too. The fellow's record was excellent.'

'Yes, yes; that was part of the game. As Richard Knighton his life was quite free from reproach. He was well born, well connected, did honourable service in the War, and seemed altogether above suspicion; but when I came to glean information about the mysterious Marquis, I found many points of similarity. Knighton spoke French like a Frenchman, he had been in America, France, and England at much the same time as the Marquis was operating. The Marquis was last heard of as engineering various jewel robberies in Switzerland, and it was in Switzerland that you had come across Major Knighton; and it was at precisely that time that the first rumours were going round of your being in treaty for the famous rubies.'

'But why murder?' murmured Van Aldin brokenly. 'Surely a clever thief could have stolen the jewels without running his head into a noose.'

Poirot shook his head. 'This is not the first murder that lies to the Marquis's charge. He is a killer by instinct; he believes, too, in leaving no evidence behind him. Dead men and women tell no tales.

'The Marquis had an intense passion for famous and historical jewels. He laid his plans far beforehand by installing himself as your secretary and getting his accomplice to obtain the situation of maid with your daughter, for whom he guessed the jewels were destined. And, though this was his matured and carefully thought-out plan, he did not scruple to attempt a short-cut by hiring a couple of apaches to waylay you in Paris on the night you bought the jewels. The plan failed, which hardly surprised him, I think. This plan was, so he thought, completely safe. No possible suspicion could attach to Richard Knighton. But like all great men – and the Marquis was a great man – he had his weaknesses. He fell genuinely in love with Miss Grey, and, suspecting her liking for Derek Kettering, he could not resist the temptation to saddle him with the crime when the opportunity presented itself. And now, Monsieur Van Aldin, I am going to tell you something very curious. Miss Grey is not a fanciful woman by any means, yet she firmly believes that she felt your daughter's presence beside her one day in the Casino Gardens at Monte Carlo, just after she had been having a long talk with Knighton. She was convinced, she says, that the dead woman was urgently trying to tell her something, and it suddenly came to her that what the dead woman was trying to say was that Knighton was her murderer! The idea seemed so fantastic at the time that Miss Grey spoke of it to no one. But she was so convinced of its truth that she acted on it – wild as it seemed. She did not discourage Knighton's advances, and she pretended to him that she was convinced of Derek Kettering's guilt.'

'Extraordinary,' said Van Aldin.

'Yes, it is very strange. One cannot explain these things. Oh, by the way, there is one little point that baffled me considerably. Your secretary has a decided limp – the result of a wound that he received in the War. Now the Marquis most decidedly did not limp. That was a stumbling block. But Miss Lenox Tamplin happened to mention one day that Knighton's limp had been a surprise to the surgeon who had been in charge of the case in her mother's hospital. That suggested camouflage. When I was in London I went to the surgeon in question, and I got several technical details from him which confirmed me in that belief. I mentioned the name of that surgeon in Knighton's hearing the day before yesterday. The natural thing would have been for Knighton to mention that he had been attended by him during the War, but he said nothing – and that little point, if nothing else, gave me the last final assurance that my theory of the crime was correct. Miss Grey, too, provided me with a cutting, showing that there had been a robbery at Lady Tamplin's hospital during the time that Knighton had been there. She realized that I was on the same track as herself when I wrote to her from the Ritz in Paris.

'I had some trouble in my inquiries there, but I got what I wanted

– evidence that Ada Mason arrived on the morning after the crime and not on the evening of the day before.'

There was a long silence, then the millionaire stretched out a hand to Poirot across the table.

'I guess you know what this means to me, Monsieur Poirot,' he said huskily. 'I am sending you round a cheque in the morning, but no cheque in the world will express what I feel about what you have done for me. You are the goods, Monsieur Poirot. Every time, you are the goods.'

Poirot rose to his feet; his chest swelled.

'I am only Hercule Poirot,' he said modestly, 'yet, as you say, in my own way I am a big man, even as you also are a big man. I am glad and happy to have been of service to you. Now I go to repair the damages caused by travel. Alas! My excellent Georges is not with me.'

In the lounge of the hotel he encountered a friend – the venerable Monsieur Papopolous, his daughter Zia beside him.

'I thought you had left Nice, Monsieur Poirot,' murmured the Greek as he took the detective's affectionately proffered hand.

'Business compelled me to return, my dear Monsieur Papopolous.'

'Business?'

'Yes, business. And talking of business, I hope your health is better, my dear friend?'

'Much better. In fact, we are returning to Paris tomorrow.'

'I am enchanted to hear such good news. You have not completely ruined the Greek ex-Minister, I hope.'

'I?'

'I understand you sold him a very wonderful ruby which – strictly *entre nous* – is being worn by Mademoiselle Mirelle, the dancer?'

'Yes,' murmured Monsieur Papopolous; 'yes, that is so.'

'A ruby not unlike the famous "Heart of Fire".'

'It has points of resemblance, certainly,' said the Greek casually.

'You have a wonderful hand with jewels, Monsieur Papopolous. I congratulate you. Mademoiselle Zia, I am desolate that you are returning to Paris so speedily. I had hoped to see some more of you now that my business is accomplished.'

'Would one be indiscreet if one asked what that business was?' asked Monsieur Papopolous.

'Not at all, not at all. I have just succeeded in laying the Marquis by the heels.'

A far-away look came over Monsieur Papopolous' noble countenance.

'The Marquis?' he murmured; 'now why does that seem familiar to me? No – I cannot recall it.'

'You would not, I am sure,' said Poirot. 'I refer to a very notable criminal and jewel robber. He has just been arrested for the murder of the English lady, Madame Kettering.'

'Indeed? How interesting these things are!'

A polite exchange of farewells followed, and when Poirot was out of earshot, Monsieur Papopolous turned to his daughter.

'Zia,' he said, with feeling, 'that man is the devil!'

'I like him.'

'I like him myself,' admitted Monsieur Papopolous. 'But he is the devil, all the same.'

CHAPTER 36

BY THE SEA

The mimosa was nearly over. The scent of it in the air was faintly unpleasant. There were pink geraniums twining along the balustrade of Lady Tamplin's villa, and masses of carnations below sent up a sweet, heavy perfume. The Mediterranean was at its bluest. Poirot sat on the terrace with Lenox Tamplin. He had just finished telling her the same story that he had told to Van Aldin two days before. Lenox had listened to him with absorbed attention, her brows knitted and her eyes sombre.

When he had finished she said simply:

'And Derek?'

'He was released yesterday.'

'And he has gone – where?'

'He left Nice last night.'

'For St Mary Mead?'

'Yes, for St Mary Mead.'

There was a pause.

'I was wrong about Katherine,' said Lenox. 'I thought she did not care.'

'She is very reserved. She trusts no one.'

'She might have trusted me,' said Lenox, with a shade of bitterness.

'Yes,' said Poirot gravely, 'she might have trusted you. But Mademoiselle Katherine has spent a great deal of her life listening, and those who have listened do not find it easy to talk; they keep their sorrows and joys to themselves and tell no one.'

'I was a fool,' said Lenox; 'I thought she really cared for Knighton. I ought to have known better. I suppose I thought so because – well, I hoped so.'

Poirot took her hand and gave it a little friendly squeeze. 'Courage, Mademoiselle,' he said gently.

Lenox looked very straight out across the sea, and her face, in its ugly rigidity, had for the moment a tragic beauty.

'Oh, well,' she said at last, 'it would not have done. I am too young for Derek; he is like a kid that has never grown up. He wants the Madonna touch.'

There was a long silence, then Lenox turned to him quickly and impulsively. 'But I *did* help, Monsieur Poirot – at any rate I did help.'

'Yes, Mademoiselle. It was you who gave me the first inkling of the truth when you said that the person who committed the crime need not have been on the train at all. Before that, I could not see how the thing had been done.'

Lenox drew a deep breath.

'I am glad,' she said; 'at any rate – that is something.'

From far behind them there came a long-drawn-out scream of an engine's whistle.

'That is that damned Blue Train,' said Lenox. 'Trains are relentless things, aren't they, Monsieur Poirot? People are murdered and die, but they go on just the same. I am talking nonsense, but you know what I mean.'

'Yes, yes, I know. Life is like a train, Mademoiselle. It goes on. And it is a good thing that that is so.'

'Why?'

'Because the train gets to its journey's end at last, and there is a proverb about that in your language, Mademoiselle.'

'"Journeys end in lovers meeting."' Lenox laughed. 'That is not going to be true for me.'

'Yes – yes, it is true. You are young, younger than you yourself know. Trust the train, Mademoiselle, for it is *le bon Dieu* who drives it.'

The whistle of the engine came again.

'Trust the train, Mademoiselle,' murmured Poirot again. 'And trust Hercule Poirot – *He knows*.'

DEATH IN THE CLOUDS

To Ormond Beadle

CONTENTS

PLAN OF REAR CAR 'PROMETHEUS'

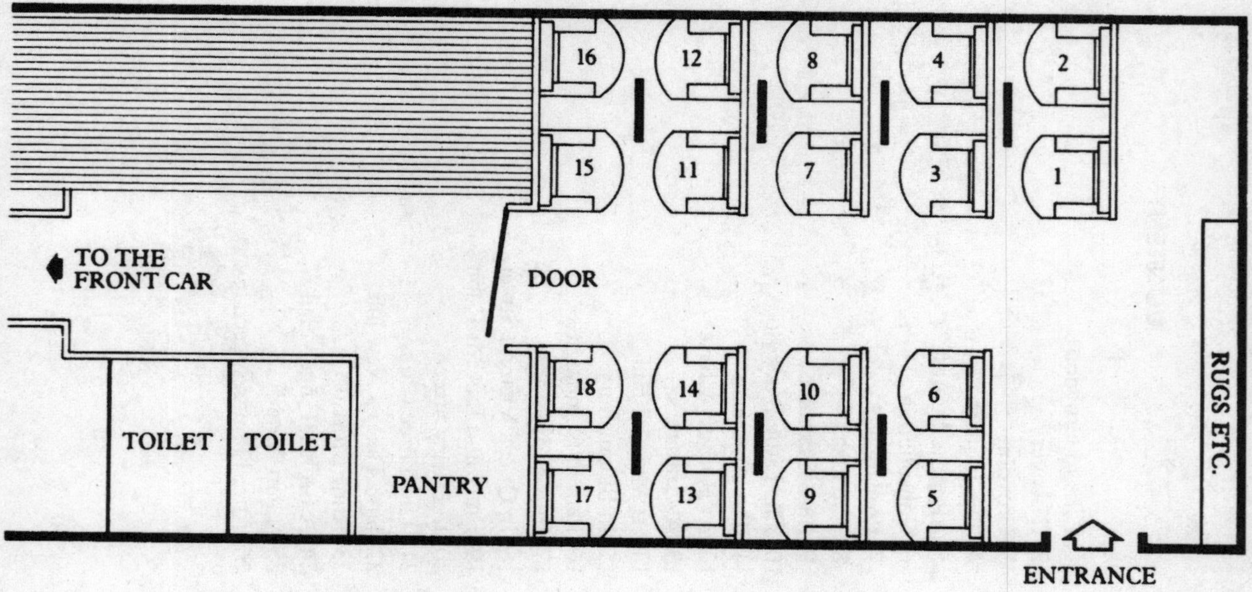

PASSENGERS

Seat	
No. 2	Madame Giselle
No. 4	James Ryder
No. 5	Monsieur Armand Dupont
No. 6	Monsieur Jean Dupont
No. 8	Daniel Clancy
No. 9	Hercule Poirot
No. 10	Doctor Bryant
No. 12	Norman Gale
No. 13	The Countess of Horbury
No. 16	Jane Grey
No. 17	The Hon. Venetia Kerr

CHAPTER 1

PARIS TO CROYDON

The September sun beat down hotly on Le Bourget aerodrome as the passengers crossed the ground and climbed into the air liner *Prometheus*, due to depart for Croydon in a few minutes' time.

Jane Grey was among the last to enter and take her seat, No. 16. Some of the passengers had already passed on through the centre door past the tiny pantry-kitchen and the two toilets to the front car. Most people were already seated. On the opposite side of the gangway there was a good deal of chatter – a rather shrill, high-pitched woman's voice dominating it. Jane's lips twisted slightly. She knew that particular type of voice so well.

'My dear – it's extraordinary – no idea – Where, do you say? Juan les Pins? Oh, yes. No – Le Pinet – Yes, just the same old crowd – But of *course* let's sit together. Oh, can't we? Who –? Oh, I see . . .'

And then a man's voice – foreign, polite:

'– With the greatest of pleasure, Madame.'

Jane stole a glance out of the corner of her eye.

A little elderly man with large moustaches and an egg-shaped head was politely moving himself and his belongings from the seat corresponding to Jane's on the opposite side of the gangway.

Jane turned her head slightly and got a view of the two women whose unexpected meeting had occasioned this polite action on the stranger's part. The mention of Le Pinet had stimulated her curiosity, for Jane also had been at Le Pinet.

She remembered one of the women perfectly – remembered how she had seen her last – at the baccarat table, her little hands clenching and unclenching themselves – her delicately made-up Dresden china face flushing and paling alternately. With a little effort, Jane thought, she could have remembered her name. A friend had mentioned it – had said: 'She's a peeress, she is, but not one of the proper ones – she was only some chorus girl or other.'

Deep scorn in the friend's voice. That had been Maisie, who had a first-class job as a masseuse 'taking off' flesh.

The other woman, Jane thought in passing, was the 'real thing'. The 'horsey, county type', thought Jane, and forthwith forgot the two women and interested herself in the view obtainable through the window of Le Bourget aerodrome. Various other machines were standing about. One of them looked like a big metallic centipede.

The one place she was obstinately determined not to look was straight in front of her, where, on the seat opposite, sat a young man.

He was wearing a rather bright periwinkle-blue pullover. Above the pullover Jane was determined not to look. If she did, she might catch his eye, and that would never do!

Mechanics shouted in French – the engine roared – relaxed – roared again – obstructions were pulled away – the plane started.

Jane caught her breath. It was only her second flight. She was still capable of being thrilled. It looked – it looked as though they must run into that fence thing – no, they were off the ground – rising – rising – sweeping round – there was Le Bourget beneath them.

The midday service to Croydon had started. It contained twenty-one passengers – ten in the forward carriage, eleven in the rear one. It had two pilots and two stewards. The noise of the engines was very skilfully deadened. There was no need to put cotton wool in the ears. Nevertheless there was enough noise to discourage conversation and encourage thought.

As the plane roared above France on its way to the Channel the passengers in the rear compartment thought their various thoughts.

Jane Grey thought: 'I won't look at him . . . I won't . . . It's much better not. I'll go on looking out of the window and thinking. I'll choose a definite thing to think about – that's always the best way. That will keep my mind steady. I'll begin at the beginning and go all over it.'

Resolutely she switched her mind back to what she called the beginning, that purchase of a ticket in the Irish Sweep. It had been an extravagance, but an exciting extravagance.

A lot of laughter and teasing chatter in the hairdressing establishment in which Jane and five other young ladies were employed.

'What'll you do if you win it, dear?'

'I know what I'd do.'

Plans – castles in the air – a lot of chaff.

Well, she hadn't won 'it' – 'it' being the big prize; but she *had* won a hundred pounds.

A hundred pounds.

'You spend half of it, dear, and keep the other half for a rainy day. You never know.'

'I'd buy a fur coat, if I was you – a real tip-top one.'

'What about a cruise?'

Jane had wavered at the thought of a 'cruise', but in the end she had remained faithful to her first idea. A week at Le Pinet. So many of her ladies had been going to Le Pinet or just come back from Le Pinet. Jane, her clever fingers patting and manipulating the waves, her tongue uttering mechanically the usual clichés, 'Let me see, how long is it since you had your perm, Madam?' 'Your hair's such an uncommon colour, Madam.' 'What a wonderful summer it has been, hasn't it, Madam?' had thought to herself, 'Why the devil can't *I* go to Le Pinet?' Well, now she could.

Clothes presented small difficulty. Jane, like most London girls employed in smart places, could produce a miraculous effect of fashion for a ridiculously small outlay. Nails, make-up and hair were beyond reproach.

Jane went to Le Pinet.

Was it possible that now, in her thoughts, ten days at Le Pinet had dwindled down to one incident?

An incident at the roulette table. Jane allowed herself a certain amount each evening for the pleasures of gambling. That sum she was determined not to exceed. Contrary to the prevalent superstition, Jane's beginner's luck had been bad. This was her fourth evening and the last stake of that evening. So far she had staked prudently on colour or on one of the dozens. She had won a little, but lost more. Now she waited, her stake in her hand.

There were two numbers on which nobody had staked, five and six. Should she put this, her last stake, on one of those numbers? If so, which of them? Five, or six? Which did she *feel*?

Five – five was going to turn up. The ball was spun. Jane stretched out her hand. Six, she'd put it on six.

Just in time. She and another player opposite staked simultaneously, she on six, he on five.

'*Rien ne va plus,*' said the croupier.

The ball clicked, settled.

'*Le numéro cinq, rouge, impair, manque.*'

Jane could have cried with vexation. The croupier swept away the stakes, paid out. The man opposite said: 'Aren't you going to take up your winnings?'

'Mine?'

'Yes.'

'But I put on six.'

'Indeed you didn't. I put on six and you put on five.'

He smiled – a very attractive smile. White teeth in a very brown face, blue eyes, crisp short hair.

Half unbelievingly Jane picked up her gains. Was it true? She felt a little muddled herself. Perhaps she *had* put her counters on five. She looked doubtingly at the stranger and he smiled easily back.

'That's right,' he said. 'Leave a thing lying there and somebody else will grab it who has got no right to it. That's an old trick.'

Then with a friendly little nod of the head he had moved away. That, too, had been nice of him. She might have suspected otherwise that he had let her take his winnings in order to scrape acquaintance with her. But he wasn't that kind of man. He was *nice* . . . (And here he was sitting opposite to her.)

And now it was all over – the money spent – a last two days (rather disappointing days) in Paris, and now home on her return air ticket.

'And what next?'

'Stop,' said Jane to her mind. 'Don't think of what's going to happen next. It'll only make you nervous.'

The two women had stopped talking.

She looked across the gangway. The Dresden china woman exclaimed petulantly, examining a broken fingernail. She rang the bell and when the white-coated steward appeared she said:

'Send my maid to me. She's in the other compartment.'

'Yes, my lady.'

The steward, very deferential, very quick and efficient, disappeared again. A dark-haired French girl dressed in black appeared. She carried a small jewel case.

Lady Horbury spoke to her in French:

'Madeleine, I want my red morocco case.'

The maid passed along the gangway. At the extreme end of the car were some piled-up rugs and cases.

The girl returned with a small red dressing-case.

Cicely Horbury took it and dismissed the maid.

'That's all right, Madeleine. I'll keep it here.'

The maid went out again. Lady Horbury opened the case and from the beautifully fitted interior she extracted a nail file. Then she looked long and earnestly at her face in a small mirror and touched it up here and there – a little powder, more lip salve.

Jane's lips curled scornfully; her glance travelled farther down the car.

Behind the two women was the little foreigner who had yielded his seat to the 'county' woman. Heavily muffled up in unnecessary mufflers, he appeared to be fast asleep. Perhaps made uneasy by Jane's scrutiny, his eyes opened, looked at her for a moment, then closed again.

Beside him sat a tall, grey-haired man with an authoritative face. He had a flute case open in front of him and was polishing the flute with loving care. Funny, Jane thought, he didn't look like a musician – more like a lawyer or a doctor.

Behind those two were a couple of Frenchmen, one with a beard and one much younger – perhaps his son. They were talking and gesticulating in an excited manner.

On her own side of the car Jane's view was blocked by the man in the blue pullover, the man at whom, for some absurd reason, she was determined not to look.

'Absurd to feel – so – so excited. I might be seventeen,' thought Jane disgustedly.

Opposite her, Norman Gale was thinking:

'She's pretty – really pretty – She remembers me all right. She looked so disappointed when her stakes were swept away. It was worth a lot more than that to see her pleasure when she won. I did that rather well . . . She's very attractive when she smiles – no pyorrhoea there – healthy gums and sound teeth . . . Damn it, I feel quite excited. Steady, my boy . . .'

He said to the steward who hovered at his side with the menu, 'I'll have cold tongue.'

The Countess of Horbury thought, 'My God, what shall I do? It's the hell of a mess – the hell of a mess. There's only one way out that I can see. If only I had the nerve. Can I do it? Can I bluff it out? My nerves are all to pieces. That's the coke. Why did I ever take to coke? My face looks awful, simply awful. That cat Venetia Kerr being here makes it worse. She always looks at me as though I were dirt. Wanted Stephen herself. Well, she didn't get him! That long face of hers gets on my nerves. It's exactly like a horse. I hate these county women. My God, what shall I do? I've got to make up my mind. The old bitch meant what she said . . .'

She fumbled in her vanity bag for her cigarette-case and fitted a cigarette into a long holder. Her hands shook slightly.

The Honourable Venetia Kerr thought: 'Bloody little tart. That's what she is. She may be technically virtuous, but she's a tart through and through. Poor old Stephen . . . if he could only get rid of her . . .'

She in turn felt for her cigarette-case. She accepted Cicely Horbury's match.

The steward said, 'Excuse me, ladies, no smoking.'

Cicely Horbury said, 'Hell!'

M. Hercule Poirot thought, 'She is pretty, that little one over there. There is determination in that chin. Why is she so worried over something? Why is she so determined not to look at the handsome young man opposite her? She is very much aware of him and he of her . . .' The plane dropped slightly. '*Mon estomac*,' thought Hercule Poirot, and closed his eyes determinedly.

Beside him Dr Bryant, caressing his flute with nervous hands, thought, 'I can't decide. I simply cannot decide. This is the turning point of my career . . .'

Nervously he drew out his flute from its case, caressingly, lovingly . . . Music . . . In music there was an escape from all your cares. Half smiling he raised the flute to his lips, then put it down again. The little man with the moustaches beside him was fast asleep. There had been a moment, when the plane had bumped a little, when he had looked distinctly green. Dr Bryant was glad that he himself was neither train-sick nor sea-sick nor air-sick . . .

M. Dupont *père* turned excitedly in his seat and shouted at M. Dupont *fils* sitting beside him.

'There is no doubt about it. They are *all* wrong – the Germans, the Americans, the English! They date the prehistoric pottery all wrong. Take the Samarra ware –'

Jean Dupont, tall, fair, with a false air of indolence, said:

'You must take the evidences from all sources. There is Tall Halaf, and Sakje Geuze –'

They prolonged the discussion.

Armand Dupont wrenched open a battered attaché case.

'Take these Kurdish pipes, such as they make today. The decoration on them is almost exactly similar to that on the pottery of 5000 BC.'

An eloquent gesture almost swept away the plate that a steward was placing in front of him.

Mr Clancy, writer of detective stories, rose from his seat behind Norman Gale and padded to the end of the car, extracted a continental Bradshaw from his raincoat pocket and returned with it to work out a complicated alibi for professional purposes.

Mr Ryder, in the seat behind him, thought, 'I'll have to keep my end up, but it's not going to be easy. I don't see how I'm going to raise the dibs for the next dividend . . . If we pass the dividend the fat's in the fire . . . Oh, hell!'

Norman Gale rose and went to the toilet. As soon as he had gone Jane drew out a mirror and surveyed her face anxiously. She also applied powder and lipstick.

A steward placed coffee in front of her.

Jane looked out of the window. The Channel showed blue and shining below.

A wasp buzzed round Mr Clancy's head just as he was dealing with 19.55 at Tzaribrod, and he struck at it absently. The wasp flew off to investigate the Duponts' coffee cups.

Jean Dupont slew it neatly.

Peace settled down on the car. Conversation ceased, but thoughts pursued their way.

Right at the end of the car, in seat No. 2, Madame Giselle's head lolled forward a little. One might have taken her to be asleep. But she was not asleep. She neither spoke nor thought.

Madame Giselle was dead . . .

CHAPTER 2

DISCOVERY

Henry Mitchell, the senior of the two stewards, passed swiftly from table to table depositing bills. In half an hour's time they would be at Croydon. He gathered up notes and silver, bowed, said, 'Thank you, sir. Thank you, Madam.' At the table where the two Frenchmen sat he had to wait a minute or two, they were so busy discussing and gesticulating. And there wouldn't be much of a tip anyway from them, he thought gloomily. Two of the passengers were asleep – the little man with the moustaches, and the old woman down at the end. She was a good tipper, though – he remembered her crossing several times. He refrained therefore from awaking her.

The little man with the moustaches woke up and paid for the bottle of soda water and the thin captain biscuits, which was all he had had.

Mitchell left the other passenger as long as possible. About five minutes before they reached Croydon he stood by her side and leant over her.

'Pardon, Madam, your bill.'

He laid a deferential hand on her shoulder. She did not wake. He increased the pressure, shaking her gently, but the only result was an unexpected slumping of the body down in the seat. Mitchell bent over her, then straightened up with a white face.

II

Albert Davis, second steward, said:

'Coo! You don't mean it!'

'I tell you it's true.'

Mitchell was white and shaking.

'You *sure*, Henry?'

'Dead sure. At least – well, I suppose it might be a fit.'

'We'll be at Croydon in a few minutes.'

'If she's just taken bad –'

They remained a minute or two undecided – then arranged their course of action. Mitchell returned to the rear car. He went from table to table, bending his head and murmuring confidentially:

'Excuse me, sir, you don't happen to be a doctor –?'

Norman Gale said, 'I'm a dentist. But if there's anything I can do –?' He half rose from his seat.

'I'm a doctor,' said Dr Bryant. 'What's the matter?'

'There's a lady at the end there – I don't like the look of her.'

Bryant rose to his feet and accompanied the steward. Unnoticed, the little man with the moustaches followed them.

Dr Bryant bent over the huddled figure in seat No. 2, the figure of a stoutish middle-aged woman dressed in heavy black.

The doctor's examination was brief.

He said: 'She's dead.'

Mitchell said, 'What do you think it was – kind of fit?'

'That I can't possibly say without a detailed examination. When did you last see her – alive, I mean?'

Mitchell reflected.

'She was all right when I brought her coffee along.'

'When was that?'

'Well, it might have been three-quarters of an hour ago – about that. Then, when I brought the bill along, I thought she was asleep . . .'

Bryant said, 'She's been dead at least half an hour.'

Their consultation was beginning to cause interest – heads were craned round looking at them. Necks were stretched to listen.

'I suppose it might have been a kind of fit, like?' suggested Mitchell hopefully.

He clung to the theory of a fit.

His wife's sister had fits. He felt that fits were homely things that any man might understand.

Dr Bryant had no intention of committing himself. He merely shook his head with a puzzled expression.

A voice spoke at his elbow, the voice of the muffled-up man with the moustaches.

'There is,' he said, 'a mark on her neck.'

He spoke apologetically, with a due sense of speaking to superior knowledge.

'True,' said Dr Bryant.

The woman's head lolled over sideways. There was a minute puncture mark on the side of her throat.

'Pardon –' the two Duponts joined in. They had been listening for the last few minutes. 'The lady is dead, you say, and there is a mark on the neck?'

It was Jean, the younger Dupont, who spoke.

'May I make a suggestion? There was a wasp flying about. I killed it.' He exhibited the corpse in his coffee saucer. 'Is it not possible that the poor lady has died of a wasp sting? I have heard such things happen.'

'It is possible,' agreed Bryant. 'I have known of such cases. Yes, that is certainly quite a possible explanation, especially if there were any cardiac weakness –'

'Anything I'd better do, sir?' asked the steward. 'We'll be at Croydon in a minute.'

'Quite, quite,' said Dr Bryant as he moved away a little. 'There's nothing to be done. The – er – body must not be moved, steward.'

'Yes, sir, I quite understand.'

Dr Bryant prepared to resume his seat and looked in some surprise at the small muffled-up foreigner who was standing his ground.

'My dear sir,' he said, 'the best thing to do is to go back to your seat. We shall be at Croydon almost immediately.'

'That's right, sir,' said the steward. He raised his voice. 'Please resume your seats, everybody.'

'*Pardon*,' said the little man. 'There is something –'

'Something?'

'*Mais oui*, something that has been overlooked.'

With the tip of a pointed patent-leather shoe he made his meaning clear. The steward and Dr Bryant followed the action with their eyes. They caught the glint of yellow and black on the floor half concealed by the edge of the black skirt.

'Another wasp?' said the doctor, surprised.

Hercule Poirot went down on his knees. He took a small pair of tweezers from his pocket and used them delicately. He stood up with his prize.

'Yes,' he said, 'it is very like a wasp; but it is not a wasp!'

He turned the object about this way and that so that both the doctor and the steward could see it clearly, a little knot of teased fluffy silk, orange and black, attached to a long, peculiar-looking thorn with a discoloured tip.

'Good gracious! Good gracious me!' The exclamation came from little Mr Clancy, who had left his seat and was poking his head desperately over the steward's shoulder. 'Remarkable, really very remarkable, absolutely the most remarkable thing I have ever come across in my life. Well, upon my soul, I should never have believed it.'

'Could you make yourself just a little clearer, sir?' asked the steward. 'Do you recognize this?'

'Recognize it? Certainly I recognize it.' Mr Clancy swelled with passionate pride and gratification. 'This object, gentlemen, is the native thorn shot from a blowpipe by certain tribes – er – I cannot be exactly certain now if it is South American tribes or whether it is the inhabitants of Borneo which I have in mind; but that is undoubtedly a native dart that has been aimed by a blowpipe, and I strongly suspect that on the tip –'

'Is the famous arrow poison of the South American Indians,' finished Hercule Poirot. And he added, '*Mais enfin! Est-ce que c'est possible?*'

'It is certainly very extraordinary,' said Mr Clancy, still full of blissful excitement. 'As I say, most extraordinary. I am myself a writer of detective fiction; but actually to meet, in real life –'

Words failed him.

The aeroplane heeled slowly over, and those people who were standing up staggered a little. The plane was circling round in its descent to Croydon aerodrome.

CHAPTER 3

CROYDON

The steward and the doctor were no longer in charge of the situation. Their place was usurped by the rather absurd-looking little man in the mufflers. He spoke with an authority and a certainty of being obeyed that no one thought of questioning.

He whispered to Mitchell, and the latter nodded, and, pushing his way through the passengers, he took up his stand in the doorway leading past the toilets to the front car.

The plane was running along the ground now. When it finally came to a stop Mitchell raised his voice:

'I must ask you, ladies and gentlemen, to keep your seats and remain here until somebody in authority takes charge. I hope you will not be detained long.'

The reasonableness of this order was appreciated by most of

the occupants of the car, but one person protested shrilly.

'Nonsense,' cried Lady Horbury angrily. 'Don't you know who I am? I insist on being allowed to leave at once.'

'Very sorry, my lady. Can't make exceptions.'

'But it's absurd, absolutely absurd,' Cicely tapped her foot angrily. 'I shall report you to the company. It's outrageous that we should be shut up here with a dead body.'

'Really, my dear,' Venetia Kerr spoke with her well-bred drawl, 'too devastating, but I fancy we'll have to put up with it.' She herself sat down and drew out a cigarette-case. 'Can I smoke now, steward?'

The harassed Mitchell said, 'I don't suppose it matters now, Miss.'

He glanced over his shoulder. Davis had disembarked the passengers from the front car by the emergency door and had now gone in search of orders.

The wait was not a long one, but it seemed to the passengers as though half an hour at least had passed before an erect soldierly figure in plain clothes, accompanied by a uniformed policeman, came hurriedly across the aerodrome and climbed into the plane by the door that Mitchell held open.

'Now, then, what's all this?' demanded the newcomer in brisk official tones.

He listened to Mitchell and then to Dr Bryant, and he flung a quick glance over the crumpled figure of the dead woman.

He gave an order to the constable and then addressed the passengers.

'Will you please follow me, ladies and gentlemen?'

He escorted them out of the plane and across the aerodrome, but he did not enter the usual customs department; instead, he brought them to a small private room.

'I hope not to keep you waiting any longer than is unavoidable, ladies and gentlemen.'

'Look here, Inspector,' said Mr James Ryder. 'I have an important business engagement in London.'

'Sorry, sir.'

'I am Lady Horbury. I consider it absolutely outrageous that I should be detained in this matter!'

'I'm sincerely sorry, Lady Horbury; but, you see, this is a very serious matter. It looks like a case of murder.'

'The arrow poison of the South American Indians,' murmured Mr Clancy deliriously, a happy smile on his face.

The inspector looked at him suspiciously.

The French archaeologist spoke excitedly in French, and the inspector replied to him slowly and carefully in the same language.

Venetia Kerr said, 'All this is a most crashing bore, but I suppose you have your duty to do, Inspector,' to which that worthy replied, 'Thank you, Madam,' in accents of some gratitude.

He went on:

'If you ladies and gentlemen will remain here, I want a few words with Doctor – er – Doctor –?'

'Bryant, my name is.'

'Thank you. Just come this way with me, Doctor.'

'May I assist at your interview?'

It was the little man with the moustaches who spoke.

The inspector turned on him, a sharp retort on his lips. Then his face changed suddenly.

'Sorry, M. Poirot,' he said. 'You're so muffled up, I didn't recognize you. Come along, by all means.'

He held the door open and Bryant and Poirot passed through, followed by the suspicious glance of the rest of the company.

'And why should he be allowed out and we made to stay here?' cried Cicely Horbury.

Venetia Kerr sat down resignedly on a bench.

'Probably one of the French police,' she said, 'or a customs spy.'

She lit a cigarette.

Norman Gale said rather diffidently to Jane:

'I think I saw you at – er – Le Pinet.'

'I was at Le Pinet.'

Norman Gale said, 'It's an awfully attractive place. I like the pine trees.'

Jane said, 'Yes, they smell so nice.'

And then they both paused for a minute or two, uncertain what to say next.

Finally Gale said, 'I – er – recognized you at once in the plane.'

Jane expressed great surprise. 'Did you?'

Gale said, 'Do you think that woman was really murdered?'

'I suppose so,' said Jane. 'It's rather thrilling in a way, but it's rather nasty too,' and she shuddered a little, and Norman Gale moved just a little nearer in a protective manner.

The Duponts were talking French to each other. Mr Ryder was making calculations in a little notebook and looking at his watch from time to time. Cicely Horbury sat with her foot tapping impatiently on the floor. She lit a cigarette with a shaking hand.

Against the door on the inside leaned a very large blue-clad impassive-looking policeman.

In a room nearby Inspector Japp was talking to Dr Bryant and Hercule Poirot.

'You've got a knack of turning up in the most unexpected places, M. Poirot.'

'Isn't Croydon aerodrome a little out of your beat, my friend?' asked Poirot.

'Ah, I'm after rather a big bug in the smuggling line. A bit of luck my being on the spot. This is the most amazing business I've come across for years. Now, then, let's get down to it. First of all, Doctor, perhaps you'll give me your full name and address.'

'Roger James Bryant. I am a specialist on diseases of the ear and throat. My address is 329 Harley Street.'

A stolid constable sitting at a table took down these particulars.

'Our own surgeon will, of course, examine the body,' said Japp, 'but we shall want you at the inquest, Doctor.'

'Quite so, quite so.'

'Can you give us any idea of the time of death?'

'The woman must have been dead at least half an hour when I examined her; that was a few minutes before we arrived at Croydon. I can't go nearer than that, but I understand from the steward that he had spoken to her about an hour before.'

'Well, that narrows it down for all practical purposes. I suppose it's no good asking you if you observed anything of a suspicious nature?'

The doctor shook his head.

'And me, I was asleep,' said Poirot with deep chagrin. 'I suffer almost as badly in the air as on the sea. Always I wrap myself up well and try to sleep.'

'Any idea as to the cause of death, Doctor?'

'I should not like to say anything definite at this stage. This is a case for post-mortem examination and analysis.'

Japp nodded comprehendingly.

'Well, Doctor,' he said, 'I don't think we need detain you now. I'm afraid you'll – er – have to go through certain formalities; all the passengers will. We can't make exceptions.'

Dr Bryant smiled.

'I should prefer you to make sure that I have no – er – blowpipes or other lethal weapons concealed upon my person,' he said gravely.

'Rogers here will see to that.' Japp nodded to his subordinate. 'By the way, Doctor, have you any idea what would be likely to be on this –?'

He indicated the discoloured thorn which was lying in a small box on the table in front of him.

Dr Bryant shook his head.

'Difficult to say without an analysis. Curare is the usual poison employed by the natives, I believe.'

'Would that do the trick?'

'It is a very swift and rapid poison.'

'But not very easy to obtain, eh?'

'Not at all easy for a layman.'

'Then we'll have to search you extra carefully,' said Japp, who was always fond of his joke. 'Rogers!'

The doctor and the constable left the room together.

Japp tilted back his chair and looked at Poirot.

'Rum business, this,' he said. 'Bit too sensational to be true. I mean, blowpipes and poisoned darts in an aeroplane – well, it insults one's intelligence.'

'That, my friend, is a very profound remark,' said Poirot.

'A couple of my men are searching the plane,' said Japp. 'We've got a fingerprint man and a photographer coming along. I think we'd better see the stewards next.'

He strode to the door and gave an order. The two stewards were ushered in. The younger steward had recovered his balance. He looked more excited than anything else. The other steward still looked white and frightened.

'That's all right, my lads,' said Japp. 'Sit down. Got the passports there? Good.'

He sorted through them quickly.

'Ah, here we are. Marie Morisot – French passport. Know anything about her?'

'I've seen her before. She crossed to and fro from England fairly often,' said Mitchell.

'Ah! in business of some kind. You don't know what her business was?'

Mitchell shook his head. The younger steward said, 'I remember her too. I saw her on the early service – the eight o'clock from Paris.'

'Which of you was the last to see her alive?'

'Him.' The younger steward indicated his companion.

'That's right,' said Mitchell. 'That's when I took her her coffee.'

'How was she looking then?'

'Can't say I noticed. I just handed her the sugar and offered her milk, which she refused.'

'What time was that?'

'Well, I couldn't say exactly. We were over the Channel at the time. Might have been somewhere about two o'clock.'

'Thereabouts,' said Albert Davis, the other steward.

'When did you see her next?'

'When I took the bills round.'

'What time was that?'

'About a quarter of an hour later. I thought she was asleep – Crikey, she must have been dead then!'

The steward's voice sounded awed.

'You didn't see any signs of this –' Japp indicated the little wasp-like dart.

'No, sir, I didn't.'

'What about you, Davis?'

'The last time I saw her was when I was handing the biscuits to go with the cheese. She was all right then.'

'What is your system of serving meals?' asked Poirot. 'Do each of you serve separate cars?'

'No, sir, we work it together. The soup, then the meat and vegetables and salad, then the sweet, and so on. We usually serve the rear car first, and then go out with a fresh lot of dishes to the front car.'

Poirot nodded.

'Did this Morisot woman speak to anyone on the plane, or show any signs of recognition?' asked Japp.

'Not that I saw, sir.'

'You, Davis?'

'No, sir.'

'Did she leave her seat at all during the journey?'

'I don't think so, sir.'

'There's nothing you can think of that throws any light on this business – either of you?'

Both the men thought, then shook their heads.

'Well, that will be all for now, then. I'll see you again later.'

Henry Mitchell said soberly:

'It's a nasty thing to happen, sir. I don't like it, me having been in charge, so to speak.'

'Well, I can't see that you're to blame in any way,' said Japp. 'Still, I agree, it's a nasty thing to happen.'

He made a gesture of dismissal. Poirot leaned forward.

'Permit me one little question.'

'Go ahead, M. Poirot.'

'Did either of you two notice a wasp flying about the plane?'

Both men shook their heads.

'There was no wasp that I know of,' said Mitchell.

'There *was* a wasp,' said Poirot. 'We have its dead body on the plate of one of the passengers.'

'Well, I didn't see it, sir,' said Mitchell.

'No more did I,' said Davis.

'No matter.'

The two stewards left the room. Japp was running his eye rapidly over the passports.

'Got a countess on board,' he said. 'She's the one who's throwing her weight about, I suppose. Better see her first before she goes right off the handle and gets a question asked in the House about the brutal methods of the police.'

'You will, I suppose, search very carefully all the baggage – the hand baggage – of the passengers in the rear car of the plane?'

Japp winked cheerfully.

'Why, what do you think, M. Poirot? We've got to find that blowpipe – if there *is* a blowpipe and we're not all dreaming! Seems like a kind of nightmare to me. I suppose that little writer chap hasn't gone off his onion and decided to do one of his crimes in the flesh instead of on paper? This poisoned dart business sounds like him.'

Poirot shook his head doubtfully.

'Yes,' continued Japp, 'everybody's got to be searched, whether they kick up rough or not; and every bit of truck they had with them has got to be searched too – and that's flat.'

'A very exact list might be made, perhaps,' suggested Poirot, 'a list of everything in these people's possession.'

Japp looked at him curiously.

'That can be done if you say so, M. Poirot. I don't quite see what you're driving at, though. We know what we're looking for.'

'*You* may, perhaps, *mon ami*, but *I* am not so sure. I look for something, but I know not what it is.'

'At it again, M. Poirot! You do like making things difficult, don't you? Now for her ladyship before she's quite ready to scratch my eyes out.'

Lady Horbury, however, was noticeably calmer in her manner. She accepted a chair and answered Japp's questions without the least hesitation. She described herself as the wife of the Earl of Horbury, gave her address as Horbury Chase, Sussex, and 315 Grosvenor Square, London. She was returning to London from Le Pinet and Paris. The deceased woman was quite unknown to her. She had noticed nothing suspicious during the flight over. In any case, she was facing the other way – towards the front of the plane – so had had no opportunity of seeing anything that was going on behind her. She had not left her seat during the journey. As far as she remembered no one had entered the rear car from the front one with the exception of the stewards. She could not remember exactly, but she thought that two of the men passengers had left the rear car to go to the toilets, but she was not sure of this. She had not observed anyone handling anything that could be likened to a blowpipe. No – in answer to Poirot – she had not noticed a wasp in the car.

Lady Horbury was dismissed. She was succeeded by the Honourable Venetia Kerr.

Miss Kerr's evidence was much the same as that of her friend. She gave her name as Venetia Anne Kerr, and her address as Little Paddocks, Horbury, Sussex. She herself was returning from the South of France. As far as she was aware she had never seen the deceased before. She had noticed nothing suspicious during the journey. Yes, she had seen some of the passengers farther down the car striking at a wasp. One of them, she thought, had killed it. That was after luncheon had been served.

Exit Miss Kerr.

'You seem very much interested in that wasp, M. Poirot.'

'The wasp is not so much interesting as suggestive, eh?'

'If you ask me,' said Japp, changing the subject, 'those two Frenchmen are the ones in this! They were just across the gangway from the Morisot woman. They're a seedy-looking couple, and that battered old suitcase of theirs is fairly plastered with outlandish foreign labels. Shouldn't be surprised if they'd been to Borneo or South America, or wherever it is. Of course, we can't get a line on the motive, but I dare say we can get that from Paris. We'll have to get the Sûreté to collaborate over this. It's their job more than ours. But, if you ask me, those two toughs are our meat.'

Poirot's eyes twinkled a little.

'What you say is possible, certainly, but as regards some of your points you are in error, my friend. Those two men are not toughs – or cut-throats, as you suggest. They are on the contrary two very distinguished and learned archaeologists.'

'Go on – you're pulling my leg!'

'Not at all. I know them by sight perfectly. They are M. Armand Dupont and his son, M. Jean Dupont. They have returned not long ago from conducting some very interesting excavations in Persia at a site not far from Susa.'

'Go on!'

Japp made a grab at a passport.

'You're right, M. Poirot,' he said, 'but you must admit they don't look up to much, do they?'

'The world's famous men seldom do! I myself – *moi, qui vous parle* – I have before now been taken for a hairdresser!'

'You don't say so,' said Japp with a grin. 'Well, let's have a look at our distinguished archaeologists.'

M. Dupont *père* declared that the deceased was quite unknown to him. He had noticed nothing of what had happened on the journey over as he had been discussing a very interesting point with his son. He had not left his seat at all. Yes, he had noticed a wasp towards the end of lunch. His son had killed it.

M. Jean Dupont confirmed this evidence. He had noticed nothing of what went on round about him. The wasp had annoyed him and he had killed it. What had been the subject of the discussion? The prehistoric pottery of the Near East.

Mr Clancy, who came next, came in for rather a bad time. Mr Clancy, so felt Inspector Japp, knew altogether too much about blowpipes and poisoned darts.

'Have you ever owned a blowpipe yourself?'

'Well – I – er – well, yes, as a matter of fact I have.'

'Indeed!' Inspector Japp pounced on the statement.

Little Mr Clancy fairly squeaked with agitation.

'You must not – er – misunderstand; my motives are quite innocent. I can explain . . .'

'Yes, sir, perhaps you *will* explain.'

'Well, you see, I was writing a book in which the murder was committed that way –'

'Indeed –'

Again that threatening intonation. Mr Clancy hurried on:

'It was all a question of fingerprints – if you understand me. It was necessary to have an illustration illustrating the point I meant – I mean – the fingerprints – the position of them – the position of them on the blowpipe, if you understand me, and having noticed such a thing – in the Charing Cross Road it was – at least two years ago now – and so I bought the blowpipe – and an artist friend of mine very kindly drew it for me – with the fingerprints – to illustrate my point. I can refer you to the book – *The Clue of the Scarlet Petal* – and my friend too.'

'Did you keep the blowpipe?'

'Why, yes – why, yes, I think so – I mean, yes, I did.'

'And where is it now?'

'Well, I suppose – well, it must be somewhere about.'

'What exactly do you mean by somewhere about, Mr Clancy?'

'I mean – well – somewhere – I can't say where. I – I am not a very tidy man.'

'It isn't with you now, for instance?'

'Certainly not. Why, I haven't seen the thing for nearly six months.'

Inspector Japp bent a glance of cold suspicion on him and continued his questions.

'Did you leave your seat at all in the plane?'

'No, certainly not – at least – well, yes, I did.'

'Oh, you *did*. Where did you go?'

'I went to get a continental Bradshaw out of my raincoat

pocket. The raincoat was piled with some rugs and suitcases by the entrance at the end.'

'So you passed close by the deceased's seat?'

'No – at least – well, yes, I must have done. But this was long before anything could have happened. I'd only just drunk my soup.'

Further questions drew negative answers. Mr Clancy had noticed nothing suspicious. He had been absorbed in the perfectioning of his cross-Europe alibi.

'Alibi, eh?' said the inspector darkly.

Poirot intervened with a question about wasps.

Yes, Mr Clancy had noticed a wasp. It had attacked him. He was afraid of wasps. When was this? Just after the steward had brought him his coffee. He struck at it and it went away.

Mr Clancy's name and address were taken and he was allowed to depart, which he did with relief on his face.

'Looks a bit fishy to me,' said Japp. 'He actually *had* a blowpipe; and look at his manner. All to pieces.'

'That is the severity of your official demeanour, my good Japp.'

'There's nothing for anyone to be afraid of if they're only telling the truth,' said the Scotland Yard man austerely.

Poirot looked at him pityingly.

'In verity, I believe that you yourself honestly believe that.'

'Of course I do. It's true. Now, then, let's have Norman Gale.'

Norman Gale gave his address as 14 Shepherd's Avenue, Muswell Hill. By profession he was a dentist. He was returning from a holiday spent at Le Pinet on the French coast. He had spent a day in Paris looking at various new types of dental instruments.

He had never seen the deceased, and had noticed nothing suspicious during the journey. In any case, he had been facing the other way – towards the front car. He had left his seat once during the journey to go to the toilet. He had returned straight to his seat and had never been near the rear end of the car. He had not noticed any wasp.

After him came James Ryder, somewhat on edge and brusque in manner. He was returning from a business visit to Paris. He did not know the deceased. Yes, he had occupied the seat immediately in front of hers, but he could not have seen her without rising and looking over the back of his seat. He had heard nothing –

no cry or exclamation. No one had come down the car except the stewards. Yes, the two Frenchmen had occupied the seats across the gangway from his. They had talked practically the whole journey. The younger of the two had killed a wasp at the conclusion of the meal. No, he hadn't noticed the wasp previously. He didn't know what a blowpipe was like, as he'd never seen one, so he couldn't say if he'd seen one on the journey or not –

Just at this point there was a tap on the door. A police constable entered, subdued triumph in his bearing.

'The sergeant's just found this, sir,' he said. 'Thought you'd like to have it at once.'

He laid his prize on the table, unwrapping it with care from the handkerchief in which it was folded.

'No fingerprints, sir, so as the sergeant can see, but he told me to be careful.'

The object thus displayed was an undoubted blowpipe of native manufacture.

Japp drew his breath in sharply.

'Good Lord! Then it *is* true? Upon my soul, I didn't believe it!'

Mr Ryder leant forward interestedly.

'So that's what the South Americans use, is it? Read about such things, but never seen one. Well, I can answer your question now. I didn't see anyone handling anything of this type.'

'Where was it found?' asked Japp sharply.

'Pushed down out of sight behind one of the seats, sir.'

'Which seat?'

'No. 9.'

'Very entertaining,' said Poirot.

Japp turned to him.

'What's entertaining about it?'

'Only that No. 9 was *my* seat.'

'Well, that looks a bit odd for you, I must say,' said Mr Ryder.

Japp frowned.

'Thank you, Mr Ryder, that will do.'

When Ryder had gone he turned to Poirot with a grin.

'This *your* work, old bird?'

'*Mon ami*,' said Poirot with dignity, 'when I commit a murder it will *not* be with the arrow poison of the South American Indians.'

'It *is* a bit low,' agreed Japp. 'But it seems to have worked.'

'That is what gives one so furiously to think.'

'Whoever it was must have taken the most stupendous chances. Yes, by Jove, they must. Lord, the fellow must have been an absolute lunatic. Who have we got left? Only one girl. Let's have her in and get it over. Jane Grey – sounds like a history book.'

'She is a pretty girl,' said Poirot.

'Is she, you old dog? So you weren't asleep all the time, eh?'

'She was pretty – and nervous,' said Poirot.

'Nervous, eh?' said Japp alertly.

'Oh, my dear friend, when a girl is nervous it usually means a young man – not crime.'

'Oh, well, I suppose you're right. Here she is.'

Jane answered the questions put to her clearly enough. Her name was Jane Grey and she was employed at Messrs. Antoine's hairdressing establishment in Bruton Street. Her home address was 10 Harrogate Street, NW5. She was returning to England from Le Pinet.

'Le Pinet – h'm!'

Further questions drew the story of the Sweep ticket.

'Ought to be made illegal, those Irish Sweeps,' growled Japp.

'I think they're marvellous,' said Jane. 'Haven't *you* ever put half a crown on a horse?'

Japp blushed and looked confused.

The questions were resumed. Shown the blowpipe, Jane denied having seen it at any time. She did not know the deceased, but had noticed her at Le Bourget.

'What made you notice her particularly?'

'Because she was so frightfully ugly,' said Jane truthfully.

Nothing else of any value was elicited from her, and she was allowed to go.

Japp fell back into contemplation of the blowpipe.

'It beats me,' he said. 'The crudest detective story dodge coming out trumps! What have we got to look for now? A man who's travelled in the part of the world this thing comes from? And where exactly does it come from? Have to get an expert on to that. It may be Malayan or South American or African.'

'Originally, yes,' said Poirot. 'But if you observe closely, my friend, you will notice a microscopic piece of paper adhering to the pipe. It looks to me very much like the remains of a torn-off price ticket. I fancy that this particular specimen has journeyed from the wilds *via* some curio dealer's shop. That will possibly make our search more easy. Just one little question.'

'Ask away.'

'You will still have that list made – the list of the passengers' belongings?'

'Well, it isn't quite so vital now, but it might as well be done. You're very set on that?'

'*Mais oui.* I am puzzled, very puzzled. If I could find something to help me –'

Japp was not listening. He was examining the torn price ticket.

'Clancy let out that he bought a blowpipe. These detective-story writers . . . always making the police out to be fools . . . and getting their procedure all wrong. Why, if I were to say the things to my super that their inspectors say to superintendents I should be thrown out of the Force tomorrow on my ear. Set of ignorant scribblers! This is just the sort of damn fool murder that a scribbler of rubbish would think he could get away with.'

CHAPTER 4

THE INQUEST

The inquest on Marie Morisot was held four days later. The sensational manner of her death had aroused great public interest, and the coroner's court was crowded.

The first witness called was a tall elderly Frenchman with a grey beard – Maître Alexandre Thibault. He spoke English slowly and precisely with a slight accent, but quite idiomatically.

After the preliminary questions the coroner asked, 'You have viewed the body of the deceased. Do you recognize it?'

'I do. It is that of my client, Marie Angélique Morisot.'

'That is the name on the deceased's passport. Was she known to the public by another name?'

'Yes, that of Madame Giselle.'

A stir of excitement went around. Reporters sat with pencils poised. The coroner said, 'Will you tell us exactly who this Madame Morisot – or Madame Giselle – was?'

'Madame Giselle – to give her her professional name, the name under which she did business – was one of the best-known moneylenders in Paris.'

'She carried on her business – where?'

'At the Rue Joliette, No. 3. That was also her private residence.'

'I understand that she journeyed to England fairly frequently. Did her business extend to this country?'

'Yes. Many of her clients were English people. She was very well known amongst a certain section of English society.'

'How would you describe that section of society?'

'Her clientèle was mostly among the upper and professional classes, in cases where it was important that the utmost discretion should be observed.'

'She had the reputation of being discreet?'

'Extremely discreet.'

'May I ask if you have an intimate knowledge of – er – her various business transactions?'

'No. I dealt with her legal business, but Madame Giselle was a first-class woman of business, thoroughly capable of attending to her own affairs in the most competent manner. She kept the control of her business entirely in her own hands. She was, if I may say so, a woman of very original character, and a well-known public figure.'

'To the best of your knowledge, was she a rich woman at the time of her death?'

'She was an extremely wealthy woman.'

'Had she, to your knowledge, any enemies?'

'Not to my knowledge.'

Maître Thibault then stepped down and Henry Mitchell was called.

The coroner said, 'Your name is Henry Charles Mitchell and you reside at 11 Shoeblack Lane, Wandsworth?'

'Yes, sir.'

'You are in the employment of Universal Airlines, Ltd?'

'Yes, sir.'

'You are the senior steward on the air liner *Prometheus*?'

'Yes, sir.'

'On Tuesday last, the eighteenth, you were on duty on the *Prometheus* on the twelve o'clock service from Paris to Croydon. The deceased travelled by that service. Had you ever seen the deceased before?'

'Yes, sir. I was on the 8.45 am service six months ago and I noticed her travelling by that once or twice.'

'Did you know her name?'

'Well, it must have been on my list, sir, but I didn't notice it special, so to speak.'

'Have you ever heard the name of Madame Giselle?'

'No, sir.'

'Please describe the occurrences of Tuesday last in your own way.'

'I'd served the luncheons, sir, and was coming round with the bills. The deceased was, as I thought, asleep. I decided not to wake her until about five minutes before we got in. When I tried to do so I discovered that she was dead or seriously ill. I discovered that there was a doctor on board. He said –'

'We shall have Dr Bryant's evidence presently. Will you take a look at this?'

The blowpipe was handed to Mitchell, who took it gingerly.

'Have you ever seen that before?'

'No, sir.'

'You are certain that you did not see it in the hands of any of the passengers?'

'Yes, sir.'

'Albert Davis.'

The younger steward took the stand.

'You are Albert Davis of 23 Barcome Street, Croydon. You are employed by Universal Airlines, Ltd?'

'Yes, sir.'

'You were on duty on the *Prometheus* as second steward on Tuesday last?'

'Yes, sir.'

'What was the first that you knew of the tragedy?'

'Mr Mitchell, sir, told me that he was afraid something had happened to one of the passengers.'

'Have you ever seen this before?'

The blowpipe was handed to Davis.

'No, sir.'

'You did not observe it in the hands of any of the passengers?'

'No, sir.'

'Did anything at all happen on the journey that you think might throw light on this affair?'

'No, sir.'

'Very good. You may stand down.'

'Dr Roger Bryant.'

Dr Bryant gave his name and address and described himself as a specialist in ear and throat diseases.

'Will you tell us in your own words, Dr Bryant, exactly what happened on Tuesday last, the eighteenth?'

'Just before getting into Croydon I was approached by the chief steward. He asked me if I was a doctor. On my replying in the affirmative, he told me that one of the passengers had been taken ill. I rose and went with him. The woman in question was lying slumped down in her seat. She had been dead some time.'

'What length of time in your opinion, Dr Bryant?'

'I should say at least half an hour. Between half an hour and an hour would be my estimate.'

'Did you form any theory as to the cause of death?'

'No. It would have been impossible to say without a detailed examination.'

'But you noticed a small puncture on the side of the neck?'

'Yes.'

'Thank you . . . Dr James Whistler.'

Dr Whistler was a thin, scraggy little man.

'You are the police surgeon for this district?'

'I am.'

'Will you give your evidence in your own words?'

'Shortly after three o'clock on Tuesday last, the eighteenth, I received a summons to Croydon aerodrome. There I was shown the body of a middle-aged woman in one of the seats of the air liner *Prometheus*. She was dead, and death had occurred, I should say, about an hour previously. I noticed a circular puncture on the side of the neck – directly on the jugular vein. This mark was quite consistent with having been caused by the sting of a wasp or by the insertion of a thorn which was shown to me. The body was removed to the mortuary, where I was able to make a detailed examination.'

'What conclusions did you come to?'

'I came to the conclusion that death was caused by the introduction of a powerful toxin into the blood stream. Death was due to acute paralysis of the heart, and must have been practically instantaneous.'

'Can you tell us what that toxin was?'

'It was a toxin I had never come across before.'

The reporters, listening attentively, wrote down 'Unknown poison.'

'Thank you . . . Mr Henry Winterspoon.'

Mr Winterspoon was a large, dreamy-looking man with a benignant expression. He looked kindly but stupid. It came as something of a shock to learn that he was chief Government analyst and an authority on rare poisons.

The coroner held up the fatal thorn and asked Mr Winterspoon if he recognized it.

'I do. It was sent to me for analysis.'

'Will you tell us the result of that analysis?'

'Certainly. I should say that originally the dart had been dipped in a preparation of native curare – an arrow poison used by certain tribes.'

The reporters wrote with gusto.

'You consider, then, that death may have been due to curare.'

'Oh, no,' said Mr Winterspoon. 'There was only the faintest trace of the original preparation. According to my analysis, the dart had recently been dipped in the venom of *Dispholidus typus*, better known as the boomslang or tree snake.'

'A boomslang? What is a boomslang?'

'It is a South African snake – one of the most deadly and poisonous in existence. Its effect on a human being is not known, but some idea of the intense virulence of the venom can be realized when I tell you that on injecting the venom into a hyena, the hyena died before the needle could be withdrawn. A jackal died as though shot by a gun. The poison causes acute haemorrhage under the skin and also acts on the heart, paralysing its action.'

The reporters wrote: '*Extraordinary Story. Snake Poison in Air Drama. Deadlier than the Cobra.*'

'Have you ever known the venom to be used in a case of deliberate poisoning?'

'Never. It is most interesting.'

Thank you, Mr Winterspoon.'

Detective-Sergeant Wilson deposed to the finding of the blow-pipe behind the cushion of one of the seats. There were no fingerprints on it. Experiments had been made with the dart and the blowpipe. What you might call the range of it was fairly accurate up to about ten yards.

'M. Hercule Poirot.'

There was a little stir of interest, but M. Poirot's evidence was very restrained. He had noticed nothing out of the way. Yes, it was he who had found the tiny dart on the floor of the car. It was in such a position as it would naturally have occupied if it had fallen from the neck of the dead woman.

'The Countess of Horbury.'

The reporters wrote: '*Peer's wife gives evidence in Air Death Mystery.*' Some of them put ' . . . *in Snake Poison Mystery.*'

Those who wrote for women's papers put, '*Lady Horbury wore one of the new collegian hats and fox furs,*' or '*Lady Horbury, who is one of the smartest women in town, wore black with one of the new collegian hats,*' or '*Lady Horbury, who before her marriage was Miss Cicely Bland, was smartly dressed in black with one of the new hats . . .*'

Everyone enjoyed looking at the smart and lovely young woman, though her evidence was of the briefest. She had noticed nothing; she had never seen the deceased before.

Venetia Kerr succeeded her, but was definitely less of a thrill.

The indefatigable purveyors of news for women wrote, '*Lord Cottesmore's daughter wore a well-cut coat and skirt with one of the new stocks,*' and noted down the phrase, '*Society Women at Inquest.*'

'James Ryder.'

'You are James Bell Ryder, and your address is 17 Blainberry Avenue, NW?'

'Yes.'

'What is your business or profession?'

'I am managing director of the Ellis Vale Cement Co.'

'Will you kindly examine this blowpipe.' (A pause.) 'Have you ever seen this before?'

'No.'

'You did not see any such thing in anybody's hand on board the *Prometheus*?'

'No.'

'You were sitting in seat No. 4, immediately in front of the deceased?'

'What if I was?'

'Please do not take that tone with me. You were sitting in seat

No. 4. From that seat you had a view of practically everyone in the compartment.'

'No, I hadn't. I couldn't see any of the people on my side of the thing. The seats have got high backs.'

'But if one of those people had stepped out into the gangway – into such a position as to be able to aim the blowpipe at the deceased – you would have seen them then?'

'Certainly.'

'And you saw no such thing?'

'No.'

'Did any of the people in front of you move from their seats?'

'Well, the man two seats ahead of me got up and went to the toilet compartment.'

'That was in a direction away from you and from the deceased?'

'Yes.'

'Did he come down the car towards you at all?'

'No, he went straight back to his seat.'

'Was he carrying anything in his hand?'

'Nothing at all.'

'You're sure of that?'

'Quite.'

'Did anyone else move from his seat?'

'The chap in front of me. He came the other way, past me to the back of the car.'

'I protest,' squeaked Mr Clancy, springing up from his seat in court. 'That was earlier – much earlier – about one o'clock.'

'Kindly sit down,' said the coroner. 'You will be heard presently. Proceed, Mr Ryder. Did you notice if this gentleman had anything in his hands?'

'I think he had a fountain-pen. When he came back he had an orange book in his hand.'

'Is he the only person who came down the car in your direction? Did you yourself leave your seat?'

'Yes, I went to the toilet compartment – and I didn't have any blowpipe in my hand either.'

'You are adopting a highly improper tone. Stand down.'

Mr Norman Gale, dentist, gave evidence of a negative character. Then the indignant Mr Clancy took the stand.

Mr Clancy was news of a minor kind, several degrees inferior to a Peeress.

'*Mystery Story Writer gives Evidence. Well-known author admits purchase of deadly weapon. Sensation in court.*'

But the sensation was perhaps a little premature.

'Yes, sir,' said Mr Clancy shrilly. 'I did purchase a blowpipe, and what is more, I have brought it with me today. I protest strongly against the inference that the blowpipe with which the crime was committed was my blowpipe. Here is my blowpipe.'

And he produced the blowpipe with a triumphant flourish.

The reporters wrote, '*Second blowpipe in court.*'

The coroner dealt severely with Mr Clancy. He was told that he was here to assist justice, not to rebut totally imaginary charges against himself. Then he was questioned about the occurrences on the *Prometheus*, but with very little result. Mr Clancy, as he explained at totally unnecessary length, had been too bemused with the eccentricities of foreign train services and the difficulties of the twenty-four hour times to have noticed anything at all going on round about him. The whole car might have been shooting snake-venomed darts out of blowpipes for all Mr Clancy would have noticed of the matter.

Miss Jane Grey, hairdresser's assistant, created no flutter among journalistic pens.

The two Frenchmen followed.

M. Armand Dupont deposed that he was on his way to London, where he was to deliver a lecture before the Royal Asiatic Society. He and his son had been very interested in a technical discussion and had noticed very little of what went on round them. He had not noticed the deceased until his attention was attracted by the stir of excitement caused by the discovery of her death.

'Did you know this Madame Morisot or Madame Giselle by sight?'

'No, Monsieur, I had never seen her before.'

'But she is a well-known figure in Paris, is she not?'

Old M. Dupont shrugged his shoulders.

'Not to me. In any case, I am not very much in Paris these days.'

'You have lately returned from the East, I understand?'

'That is so, Monsieur – from Persia.'

'You and your son have travelled a good deal in out-of-the-way parts of the world?'

'Pardon?'

'You have journeyed in wild places?'

'That, yes.'

'Have you ever come across a race of people that used snake venom as an arrow poison?'

This had to be translated, and when M. Dupont understood the question he shook his head vigorously.

'Never – never have I come across anything like that.'

His son followed him. His evidence was a repetition of his father's. He had noticed nothing. He had thought it possible that the deceased had been stung by a wasp, because he had himself been annoyed by one and had finally killed it.

The Duponts were the last witnesses.

The coroner cleared his throat and addressed the jury.

This, he said, was without doubt the most astonishing and incredible case with which he had ever dealt in this court. A woman had been murdered – they could rule out any question of suicide or accident – in mid-air, in a small enclosed space. There was no question of any outside person having committed the crime. The murderer or murderers must be of necessity one of the witnesses they had heard this morning. There was no getting away from that fact, and a very terrible and awful one it was. One of the persons present had been lying in a desperate and abandoned manner.

The manner of the crime was one of unparalleled audacity. In the full view of ten – or twelve, counting the stewards – witnesses, the murderer had placed a blowpipe to his lips and sent the fatal dart on its murderous course through the air and no one had observed the act. It seemed frankly incredible, but there was the evidence of the blowpipe, of the dart found on the floor, of the mark on the deceased's neck and of the medical evidence to show that, incredible or not, it had happened.

In the absence of further evidence incriminating some particular person, he could only direct the jury to return a verdict of murder against a person or persons unknown. Everyone present had denied any knowledge of the deceased woman. It would be the work of the police to find out how and where a connexion lay. In the absence of any motive for the crime he could only advise the verdict he had just mentioned. The jury would now consider the verdict.

A square-faced member of the jury with suspicious eyes leaned forward breathing heavily.

'Can I ask a question, sir?'

'Certainly.'

'You say as how the blowpipe was found down a seat? Whose seat was it?'

The coroner consulted his notes. Sergeant Wilson stepped to his side and murmured:

'Ah, yes. The seat in question was No. 9, a seat occupied by M. Hercule Poirot. M. Poirot, I may say, is a very well-known and respected private detective who has – er – collaborated several times with Scotland Yard.'

The square-faced man transferred his gaze to the face of M. Hercule Poirot. It rested with a far from satisfied expression on the little Belgian's long moustaches.

'Foreigners,' said the eyes of the square-faced man, 'you can't trust foreigners, not even if they *are* hand-and-glove with the police.'

Out loud he said:

'It was this Mr Poirot who picked up the dart, wasn't it?'

'Yes.'

The jury retired. They returned after five minutes, and the foreman handed a piece of paper to the coroner.

'What's all this?' The coroner frowned. 'Nonsense, I can't accept this verdict.'

A few minutes later the amended verdict was returned: 'We find that the deceased came to her death by poison, there being insufficient evidence to show by whom the poison was administered.'

CHAPTER 5

AFTER THE INQUEST

As Jane left the court after the verdict she found Norman Gale beside her.

He said, 'I wonder what was on that paper that the coroner wouldn't have at any price?'

'I can tell you, I think,' said a voice behind him.

The couple turned, to look into the twinkling eyes of M. Hercule Poirot.

'It was a verdict,' said the little man, 'of wilful murder against *me*.'

'Oh, surely –' cried Jane.

Poirot nodded happily.

'*Mais oui.* As I came out I heard one man say to the other, "That little foreigner – mark my words, *he done it!*" The jury thought the same.'

Jane was uncertain whether to condole or to laugh. She decided on the latter. Poirot laughed in sympathy.

'But, see you,' he said, 'definitely I must set to work and clear my character.'

With a smile and a bow he moved away.

Jane and Norman stared after his retreating figure.

'What an extraordinarily rum little beggar,' said Gale. 'Calls himself a detective. I don't see how *he* could do much detecting. Any criminal could spot him a mile off. I don't see how he *could* disguise himself.'

'Haven't you got a very old-fashioned idea of detectives?' asked Jane. 'All the false beard stuff is very out of date. Nowadays detectives just sit and think out a case psychologically.'

'Rather less strenuous.'

'Physically, perhaps; but of course you need a cool, clear brain.'

'I see. A hot muddled one won't do.'

They both laughed.

'Look here,' said Gale. A slight flush rose in his cheeks and he spoke rather fast. 'Would you mind – I mean, it would be frightfully nice of you – it's a bit late – but how about having some tea with me? I feel – comrades in misfortune – and –'

He stopped. To himself he said:

'What is the matter with you, you fool? Can't you ask a girl to have a cup of tea without stammering and blushing and making an utter ass of yourself? What will the girl think of you?'

Gale's confusion served to accentuate Jane's coolness and self-possession.

'Thank you very much,' she said. 'I *would* like some tea.'

They found a tea-shop and a disdainful waitress with a gloomy manner took their order with an air of doubt as of one who might say: 'Don't blame me if you're disappointed. They *say* we serve teas here, but *I* never heard of it.'

The tea-shop was nearly empty. Its emptiness served to emphasize the intimacy of tea drinking together. Jane peeled off her gloves and looked across the table at her companion. He *was* attractive – those blue eyes and that smile. And he was *nice* too.

'It's a queer show, this murder business,' said Gale, plunging hastily into talk. He was still not quite free from an absurd feeling of embarrassment.

'I know,' said Jane. 'I'm rather worried about it – from the point of view of my job, I mean. I don't know how they'll take it.'

'Ye-es. I hadn't thought of that.'

'Antoine's mayn't like to employ a girl who's been mixed up in a murder case and had to give evidence, and all that.'

'People are queer,' said Norman Gale thoughtfully. 'Life's so – so unfair. A thing like this that isn't your fault at all –' He frowned angrily. 'It's damnable!'

'Well, it hasn't happened yet,' Jane reminded him. 'No good getting hot and bothered about something that hasn't happened. After all, I suppose there is some point in it – I might be the person who murdered her! And when you've murdered one person they say you usually murder a lot more; and it wouldn't be very comfortable having your hair done by a person of that kind.'

'Anyone's only got to look at you to know you couldn't murder anybody,' said Norman, gazing at her earnestly.

'I'm not so sure about that,' said Jane. 'I'd like to murder some of my ladies sometimes – if I could be sure I'd get away with it! There's one in particular – she's got a voice like a corncrake and she grumbles at everything. I really think sometimes that murdering her would be a good deed and not a crime at all. So you see I'm quite criminally minded.'

'Well, you didn't do this particular murder, anyway,' said Gale. '*I* can swear to that.'

'And I can swear *you* didn't do it,' said Jane. 'But that won't help you if your patients think you have.'

'My patients, yes –' Gale looked rather thoughtful. 'I suppose you're right – I hadn't really thought of that. A dentist who might be a homicidal maniac – no, it's not a very alluring prospect.'

He added suddenly and impulsively:

'I say, you don't mind my being a dentist, do you?'

Jane raised her eyebrows.

'I? Mind?'

'What I mean is, there's always something rather – well, *comic* about a dentist. Somehow it's not a romantic profession. Now a doctor everyone takes seriously.'

'Cheer up,' said Jane. 'A dentist is decidedly a cut above a hairdresser's assistant.'

They laughed, and Gale said, 'I feel we're going to be friends. Do you?'

'Yes, I think I do.'

'Perhaps you'll dine with me one night and we might do a show?'

'Thank you.'

There was a pause, and then Gale said:

'How did you like Le Pinet?'

'It was great fun.'

'Had you ever been there before?'

'No, you see –'

Jane, suddenly confidential, came out with the story of the winning Sweep ticket. They agreed together on the general romance and desirability of Sweeps and deplored the attitude of an unsympathetic English Government.

Their conversation was interrupted by a young man in a brown suit who had been hovering uncertainly nearby for some minutes before they noticed him.

Now, however, he lifted his hat and addressed Jane with a certain glib assurance.

'Miss Jane Grey?' he said.

'Yes.'

'I represent the *Weekly Howl*, Miss Grey. I wondered if you would care to do us a short article on this Air Death Murder? Point of view of one of the passengers.'

'I think I'd rather not, thanks.'

'Oh, come now, Miss Grey. We'd pay well for it.'

'How much?' asked Jane.

'Fifty pounds – or, well – perhaps we'd make it a bit more. Say sixty.'

'No,' said Jane. 'I don't think I could. I shouldn't know what to say.'

'That's all right,' said the young man easily. 'You needn't actually *write* the article, you know. One of our fellows will just ask you for a few suggestions and work the whole thing up for you. It won't be the least trouble to you.'

'All the same,' said Jane, 'I'd rather not.'

'What about a hundred quid? Look here, I really will make it a hundred; and give us a photograph.'

'No,' said Jane. 'I don't like the idea.'

'So you may as well clear out,' said Norman Gale. 'Miss Grey doesn't want to be worried.'

The young man turned to him hopefully.

'Mr Gale, isn't it?' he said. 'Now look here, Mr Gale, if Miss Grey feels a bit squeamish about it, what about your having a shot? Five hundred words. And we'll pay you the same as I offered Miss Grey – and that's a good bargain, because a woman's account of another woman's murder is better news value. I'm offering you a good chance.'

'I don't want it. I shan't write a word for you.'

'It'll be good publicity apart from the pay. Rising professional man – brilliant career ahead of you – all your patients will read it.'

'That,' said Norman Gale, 'is mostly what I'm afraid of.'

'Well, you can't get anywhere without publicity in these days.'

'Possibly, but it depends on the kind of publicity. I'm hoping that just one or two of my patients may not read the papers and may continue in ignorance of the fact that I've been mixed up in a murder case. Now you've had your answer from both of us. Are you going quietly, or have I got to kick you out of here?'

'Nothing to get annoyed about,' said the young man, quite undisturbed by this threat of violence. 'Good evening, and ring me up at the office if you change your mind. Here's my card.'

He made his way cheerfully out of the tea-shop, thinking to himself as he did so: 'Not too bad. Made quite a decent interview.'

And in truth the next issue of the *Weekly Howl* had an important column on the views of two of the witnesses in the Air Murder Mystery. Miss Jane Grey had declared herself too distressed to talk about the matter. It had been a terrible shock to her and she hated to think about it. Mr Norman Gale had expressed himself at great length on the effect upon a professional man's career of being mixed up in a criminal case, however innocently. Mr Gale had humorously expressed the hope that some of his patients only read the fashion columns and so might not suspect the worst when they came for the ordeal of 'the chair'.

When the young man had departed Jane said:

'I wonder why he didn't go for the more important people?'

'Leaves that to his betters, probably,' said Gale grimly. 'He's probably tried there and failed.'

He sat frowning for a minute or two, then he said:

'Jane (I'm going to call you Jane. You don't mind, do you?) Jane – who do you think really murdered this Giselle woman?'

'I haven't the faintest idea.'

'Have you thought about it? *Really* thought about it?'

'Well, no, I don't suppose I have. I've been thinking about my own part in it, and worrying a little. I haven't really wondered seriously which – which of the others did it. I don't think I'd realized until today that one of them *must* have done it.'

'Yes, the coroner put it very plainly. I know *I* didn't do it, and I know *you* didn't do it, because – well, because I was watching you most of the time.'

'Yes,' said Jane. 'I know *you* didn't do it – for the same reason. And of course I know I didn't do it myself! So it *must* have been one of the others; but I don't know which. I haven't the slightest idea. Have you?'

'No.'

Norman Gale looked very thoughtful. He seemed to be puzzling out some train of thought. Jane went on:

'I don't see how we can have the least idea, either. I mean we didn't *see* anything – at least I didn't. Did you?'

Gale shook his head.

'Not a thing.'

'That's what seems so frightfully odd. I dare say *you* wouldn't have seen anything. You weren't facing that way. But I was. I was looking right along the middle. I mean – I could have been –'

Jane stopped and flushed. She was remembering that her eyes had been mostly fixed on a periwinkle-blue pullover, and that her mind, far from being receptive to what was going on around her, had been mainly concerned with the personality of the human being inside the periwinkle-blue pullover.

Norman Gale thought:

'I wonder what makes her blush like that . . . She's wonderful . . . I'm going to marry her . . . Yes, I am . . . But it's no good looking too far ahead. I've got to have some good excuse for seeing her often. This murder business will do as well as anything else . . .

Besides, I really think it would be as well to do something – that whipper-snapper of a reporter and his publicity . . .'

Aloud he said:

'Let's think about it now. Who killed her? Let's go over all the people. The stewards?'

'No,' said Jane.

'I agree. The women opposite us?'

'I don't suppose anyone like Lady Horbury would go killing people. And the other one, Miss Kerr, well, she's far too county. She wouldn't kill an old Frenchwoman, I'm sure.'

'Only an unpopular MFH? I expect you're not far wrong, Jane. Then there's moustachios, but he seems, according to the coroner's jury, to be the most likely person, so that washes him out. The doctor? That doesn't seem very likely, either.'

'If he'd wanted to kill her he could have used something quite untraceable and nobody would ever have known.'

'Ye-es,' said Norman doubtfully. 'These untraceable, tasteless, odourless poisons are very convenient, but I'm a bit doubtful if they really exist. What about the little man who owned up to having a blowpipe?'

'That's rather suspicious. But he seemed a very nice little man, and he needn't have said he had a blowpipe, so that looks as though he were all right.'

'Then there's Jameson – no – what's his name – Ryder?'

'Yes, it might be him.'

'And the two Frenchmen?'

'That's the most likely of all. They've been to queer places. And of course they may have had some reason we know nothing about. I thought the younger one looked very unhappy and worried.'

'You probably would be worried if you'd committed a murder,' said Norman Gale grimly.

'He looked nice, though,' said Jane; 'and the old father was rather a dear. I hope it isn't them.'

'We don't seem to be getting on very fast,' said Norman Gale.

'I don't see how we can get on without knowing a lot of things about the old woman who was murdered. Enemies, and who inherits her money, and all that.'

Norman Gale said thoughtfully:

'You think this is mere idle speculation?'

Jane said coolly, 'Isn't it?'

'Not quite.' Gale hesitated, then went on slowly, 'I have a feeling it may be useful –'

Jane looked at him inquiringly.

'Murder,' said Norman Gale, 'doesn't concern the victim and the guilty only. It affects the innocent too. You and I are innocent, but the shadow of murder has touched us. We don't know how that shadow is going to affect our lives.'

Jane was a person of cool common sense, but she shivered suddenly.

'Don't,' she said. 'You make me feel afraid.'

'I'm a little afraid myself,' said Gale.

CHAPTER 6

CONSULTATION

Hercule Poirot rejoined his friend Inspector Japp. The latter had a grin on his face.

'Hullo, old boy,' he said. 'You've had a pretty near squeak of being locked up in a police cell.'

'I fear,' said Poirot gravely, 'that such an occurrence might have damaged me professionally.'

'Well,' said Japp with a grin, 'detectives do turn out to be criminals sometimes – in story books.'

A tall thin man with an intelligent, melancholy face joined them, and Japp introduced him.

'This is Monsieur Fournier of the Sûreté. He has come over to collaborate with us about this business.'

'I think I have had the pleasure of meeting you once some years ago, M. Poirot,' said Fournier, bowing and shaking hands. 'I have also heard of you from M. Giraud.'

A very faint smile seemed to hover on his lips. And Poirot, who could well imagine the terms in which Giraud (whom he himself had been in the habit of referring to disparagingly as the 'human fox-hound') had spoken of him, permitted himself a small discreet smile in reply.

'I suggest,' said Poirot, 'that both you gentlemen should dine with me at my rooms. I have already invited Maître Thibault. That is, if you and my friend Japp do not object to my collaboration.'

'That's all right, old cock,' said Japp, slapping him heartily on the back. 'You're in on this on the ground floor.'

'We shall be indeed honoured,' murmured the Frenchman ceremoniously.

'You see,' said Poirot, 'as I said to a very charming young lady just now, I am anxious to clear my character.'

'That jury certainly didn't like the look of you,' agreed Japp with a renewal of his grin. 'Best joke I've heard for a long time.'

By common consent no mention of the case was made during the very excellent meal which the little Belgian provided for his friends.

'After all, it *is* possible to eat well in England,' murmured Fournier appreciatively as he made delicate use of a thoughtfully provided toothpick.

'A delicious meal, M. Poirot,' said Thibault.

'Bit Frenchified, but damn good,' pronounced Japp.

'A meal should always lie lightly on the *estomac*,' said Poirot. 'It should not be so heavy as to paralyse thought.'

'I can't say my stomach ever gives me much trouble,' said Japp. 'But I won't argue the point. Well, we'd better get down to business. I know that M. Thibault has got an appointment this evening, so I suggest that we should start by consulting him on any point that seems likely to be useful.'

'I am at your service, gentlemen. Naturally I can speak more freely here than in a coroner's court. I had a hurried conversation with Inspector Japp before the inquest, and he indicated a policy of reticence – the bare necessary facts.'

'Quite right,' said Japp. 'Don't ever spill the beans too soon. But now let's hear all you can tell us of this Giselle woman.'

'To speak the truth, I know very little. I know her as the world knew her – as a public character. Of her private life as an individual I know very little. Probably M. Fournier here can tell you more than I can. But I will say to you this: Madame Giselle was what you call in this country "a character". She was unique. Of her antecedents nothing is known. I have an idea that as a young woman she was good-looking. I believe that as a result of smallpox she lost her looks. She was – I am giving you my impressions – a woman who enjoyed power; she had power. She was a keen woman of business. She was the type of hard-headed Frenchwoman who would never allow sentiment to affect her business interests; but she had the reputation of carrying on her profession with scrupulous honesty.'

He looked for assent to Fournier. That gentleman nodded his dark melancholic head.

'Yes,' he said. 'She was honest – according to her lights. Yet the law could have called her to account if only evidence had been forthcoming; but that –' He shrugged his shoulders despondently. 'It is too much to ask, with human nature what it is.'

'You mean?'

'*Chantage.*'

'Blackmail?' echoed Japp.

'Yes, blackmail of a peculiar and specialized kind. It was Madame Giselle's custom to lend money on what I think you call in this country "note of hand alone". She used her discretion as to the sums she lent and the methods of repayment; but I may tell you that she had her own methods of getting paid.'

Poirot leaned forward interestedly.

'As Maître Thibault said today, Madame Giselle's clientèle lay amongst the upper and professional classes. Those classes are particularly vulnerable to the force of public opinion. Madame Giselle had her own intelligence service . . . It was her custom before lending money (that is, in the case of a large sum) to collect as many facts as possible about the client in question; and her intelligence system, I may say, was an extraordinarily good one. I will echo what our friend has said: according to her lights Madame Giselle was scrupulously honest. She kept faith with those who kept faith with her. I honestly believe that she has never made use of her secret knowledge to obtain money from anyone unless that money was already owed to her.'

'You mean,' said Poirot, 'that this secret knowledge was her form of security?'

'Exactly; and in using it she was perfectly ruthless and deaf to any finer shades of feeling; and I will tell you this, gentlemen: *her system paid!* Very, very rarely did she have to write off a bad debt. A man or woman in a prominent position would go to desperate lengths to obtain the money which would obviate a public scandal. As I say, we knew of her activities; but as for prosecution –' He shrugged his shoulders. 'That is a more difficult matter. Human nature is human nature.'

'And supposing,' said Poirot, 'that she did, as you say happened occasionally, have to write off a bad debt – what then?'

'In that case,' said Fournier slowly, 'the information she held was published, or was given to the person concerned in the matter.'

There was a moment's silence. Then Poirot said:

'Financially, that did not benefit her?'

'No,' said Fournier – 'not directly, that is.'

'But indirectly?'

'Indirectly,' said Japp, 'it made the others pay up, eh?'

'Exactly,' said Fournier. 'It was valuable for what you call the moral effect.'

'Immoral effect, I should call it,' said Japp. 'Well' – he rubbed his nose thoughtfully – 'it opens up a very pretty line in motives for murder – a very pretty line. Then there's the question of who is going to come into her money.' He appealed to Thibault. 'Can you help us there at all?'

'There was a daughter,' said the lawyer. 'She did not live with her mother – indeed I fancy that her mother has never seen her since she was a tiny child; but she made a will many years ago now leaving everything, with the exception of a small legacy to her maid, to her daughter Anne Morisot. As far as I know she has never made another.'

'And her fortune is large?' asked Poirot.

The lawyer shrugged his shoulders.

'At a guess eight or nine million francs.'

Poirot pursed his lips to a whistle. Japp said, 'Lord, she didn't look it. Let me see, what's the exchange – that's – why, that must be well over a hundred thousand pounds. Whew!'

'Mademoiselle Anne Morisot will be a very wealthy young woman,' said Poirot.

'Just as well she wasn't on that plane,' said Japp drily. 'She might have been suspected of bumping off her mother to get the dibs. How old would she be?'

'I really cannot say. I should imagine about twenty-four or five.'

'Well, there doesn't seem anything to connect her with the crime. We'll have to get down to this blackmailing business. Everyone on that plane denies knowing Madame Giselle. One of them is lying. We've got to find out which. An examination of her private papers might help, eh, Fournier?'

'My friend,' said the Frenchman, 'immediately the news came through, after I had conversed with Scotland Yard on the telephone, I went straight to her house. There was a safe there containing papers. All those papers had been burnt.'

'Burnt? Who by? Why?'

'Madame Giselle had a confidential maid, Elise. Elise had instructions in the event of anything happening to her mistress to open the safe (the combination of which she knew) and burn the contents.'

'What? But that's amazing!' Japp stared.

'You see,' said Fournier, 'Madame Giselle had her own code. She kept faith with those who kept faith with her. She gave her promise to her clients that she would deal honestly with them. She was ruthless, but she was also a woman of her word.'

Japp shook his head dumbly. The four men were silent, ruminating on the strange character of the dead woman . . .

Maître Thibault rose.

'I must leave you, Messieurs. I have to keep an appointment. If there is any further information I can give you at any time, you know my address.'

He shook hands with them ceremoniously and left the apartment.

CHAPTER 7

PROBABILITIES

With the departure of Maître Thibault, the three men drew their chairs a little closer to the table.

'Now, then,' said Japp, 'let's get down to it.' He unscrewed the cap of his fountain-pen. 'There were eleven passengers in that plane – in the rear car, I mean; the other doesn't come into it – eleven passengers and two stewards – that's thirteen people we've got. *One of the remaining twelve did the old woman in.* Some of the passengers were English, some were French. The latter I shall hand over to M. Fournier. The English ones I'll take on. Then there are inquiries to be made in Paris – that's your job too, Fournier.'

'And not only in Paris,' said Fournier. 'In the summer Giselle did a lot of business at the French watering-places – Deauville, Le

Pinet, Wimereux. She went down south too, to Antibes and Nice, and all those places.'

'A good point; one or two of the people in the *Prometheus* mentioned Le Pinet, I remember. Well, that's one line. Then we've got to get down to the actual murder itself – prove who could possibly be in a position to use that blowpipe.' He unrolled a large sketch plan of the car of the aeroplane and placed it in the centre of the table. 'Now, then, we're ready for the preliminary work. And, to begin with, let's go through the people one by one, and decide on the probabilities and – even more important – the possibilities.

'To begin with, we can eliminate M. Poirot here. That brings the number down to eleven.'

Poirot shook his head sadly.

'You are of too trustful a nature, my friend. You should trust nobody – nobody at all.'

'Well, we'll leave you in if you like,' said Japp good-temperedly. 'Then there are the stewards. Seems to me very unlikely it should be either of them from the probability point of view. They're not likely to have borrowed money on a grand scale and they've both got a good record – decent, sober men, both of them. It would surprise me very much if either of them had anything to do with this. On the other hand, from the possibility point of view we've got to include them. They were up and down the car. They could actually have taken up a position from which they could have used that blowpipe – from the right angle, I mean – though I don't believe that a steward could shoot a poisoned dart out of a blowpipe in a car full of people without someone noticing him do it. I know by experience that most people are blind as bats; but there are limits. Of course, in a way, the same thing applies to every blessed person. It was madness, absolute madness, to commit a crime that way. Only about a chance in a hundred that it would come off without being spotted. The fellow that did it must have had the luck of the devil. Of all the damn fool ways to commit a murder –'

Poirot, who had been sitting with his eyes down, smoking quietly, interposed a question.

'You think it was a foolish way of committing a murder, yes?'

'Of course it was. It was absolute madness.'

'And yet – it *succeeded*. We sit here, we three, we talk about it, but we have no knowledge of *who committed the crime*! That is success!'

'That's pure luck,' argued Japp. 'The murderer ought to have been spotted five or six times over.'

Poirot shook his head in a dissatisfied manner.

Fournier looked at him curiously.

'What is it that is in your mind, M. Poirot?'

'*Mon ami*,' said Poirot, 'my point is this: an affair must be judged by its results. This affair has succeeded. That is my point.'

'And yet,' said the Frenchman thoughtfully, 'it seems almost a miracle.'

'Miracle or no miracle, there it is,' said Japp. 'We've got the medical evidence, we've got the weapon; and if anyone had told me a week ago that I should be investigating a crime where a woman was killed with a poisoned dart with snake venom on it – well, I'd have laughed in his face! It's an insult – that's what this murder is – an insult.'

He breathed deeply. Poirot smiled.

'It is, perhaps, a murder committed by a person with a perverted sense of humour,' said Fournier thoughtfully. 'It is most important in a crime to get an idea of the psychology of the murderer.'

Japp snorted slightly at the word psychology, which he disliked and mistrusted.

'That's the sort of stuff M. Poirot likes to hear,' he said.

'I am very interested, yes, in what you both say.'

'You don't doubt that she was killed that way, I suppose?' Japp asked him suspiciously. 'I know your tortuous mind.'

'No, no, my friend. My mind is quite at ease on that point. The poisoned thorn that I picked up was the cause of death – that is quite certain. But nevertheless there are points about this case –'

He paused, shaking his head perplexedly.

Japp went on:

'Well, to get back to our Irish stew, we can't wash out the stewards absolutely, but I think myself it's very unlikely that either of them had anything to do with it. Do you agree, M. Poirot?'

'Oh, you remember what I said. Me – I would not wash out – what a term, *mon Dieu*! – anybody at this stage.'

'Have it your own way. Now, the passengers. Let's start up the end by the stewards' pantry and the toilets. Seat No. 16.' He jabbed a pencil on the plan. 'That's the hairdressing girl, Jane

Grey. Got a ticket in the Irish Sweep – blued it at Le Pinet. That means the girl's a gambler. She *might* have been hard up and borrowed from the old dame – doesn't seem likely, either, that she borrowed a large sum, or that Giselle could have a "hold" over her. Seems rather too small a fish for what we're looking for. And I don't think a hairdresser's assistant had the remotest chance of laying her hands on snake venom. They don't use it as a hair dye or for face massage.

'In a way it was rather a mistake to use snake venom; it narrows things down a lot. Only about two people in a hundred would be likely to have any knowledge of it and be able to lay hands on the stuff.'

'Which makes one thing, at least, perfectly clear,' said Poirot.

It was Fournier who shot a quick glance of inquiry at him.

Japp was busy with his own ideas.

'I look at it like this,' he said. 'The murderer has got to fall into one of two categories: either he's a man who's knocked about the world in queer places – a man who knows something of snakes and of the more deadly varieties and of the habits of the native tribes who use the venom to dispose of their enemies – that's category No. 1.'

'And the other?'

'The scientific line. Research. This boomslang stuff is the kind of thing they experiment with in high-class laboratories. I had a talk with Winterspoon. Apparently snake venom – cobra venom, to be exact – is sometimes used in medicine. It's used in the treatment of epilepsy with a fair amount of success. There's a lot being done in the way of scientific investigation into snake bite.'

'Interesting and suggestive,' said Fournier.

'Yes, but let's go on. Neither of those categories fit the Grey girl. As far as she's concerned, motive seems unlikely, chances of getting the poison – poor. Actual possibility of doing the blowpipe act very doubtful indeed – almost impossible. See here.'

The three men bent over the plan.

'Here's 16,' said Japp. 'And here's 2, where Giselle was sitting with a lot of people and seats intervening. If the girl didn't move from her seat – and everybody says she didn't – she couldn't possibly have aimed the thorn to catch Giselle on the side of the neck. I think we can take it she's pretty well out of it.

'Now then, 12, opposite. That's the dentist, Norman Gale. Very much the same applies to him. Small fry. I suppose he'd have a slightly better chance of getting hold of snake venom.'

'It is not an injection usually favoured by dentists,' murmured Poirot gently. 'It would be a case of kill rather than cure.'

'A dentist has enough fun with his patients as it is,' said Japp, grinning. 'Still, I suppose he might move in circles where you could get access to some funny business in drugs. He might have a scientific friend. But as regards *possibility* he's pretty well out of it. He *did* leave his seat, but only to go to the toilet – that's in the opposite direction. On his way back to his seat he couldn't be farther than the gangway here, and to shoot off a thorn from a blowpipe so as to catch the old lady in the neck he'd have to have a kind of pet thorn that would do tricks and make a right-angle turn. So *he's* pretty well out of it.'

'I agree,' said Fournier. 'Let us proceed.'

'We'll cross the gangway now. 17.'

'That was my seat originally,' said Poirot. 'I yielded it to one of the ladies since she desired to be near her friend.'

'That's the Honourable Venetia. Well, what about her? She's a big bug. She might have borrowed from Giselle. Doesn't look as though she had any guilty secrets in her life – but perhaps she pulled a horse in a point-to-point, or whatever they call it. We'll have to pay a little attention to her. The *position's* possible. If Giselle had got her head turned a little looking out of the window the Hon. Venetia could take a sporting shot (or do you call it a sporting puff?) diagonally across down the car. It would be a bit of a fluke, though. I rather think she'd have to stand up to do it. She's the sort of woman who goes out with the guns in the autumn. I don't know whether shooting with a gun is any help to you with a native blowpipe? I suppose it's a question of eye just the same – eye and practice; and she's probably got friends – men – who've been big-game hunting in odd parts of the globe. She might have got hold of some queer native stuff that way. What balderdash it all sounds, though! It doesn't make *sense*.'

'It does indeed seem unlikely,' said Fournier. 'Mademoiselle Kerr – I saw her at the inquest today –' He shook his head. 'One does not readily connect her with murder.'

'Seat 13,' said Japp. 'Lady Horbury. *She's* a bit of a dark horse. I know something about her I'll tell you presently. I shouldn't be surprised if she had a guilty secret or two.'

'I happen to know,' said Fournier, 'that the lady in question has been losing very heavily at the baccarat table at Le Pinet.'

'That's smart of you. Yes, she's the type of pigeon to be mixed up with Giselle.'

'I agree absolutely.'

'Very well, then – so far, so good. *But how did she do it?* She didn't leave her seat either, you remember. She'd have had to have knelt up in her seat and leaned over the top – with ten people looking at her. Oh, hell, let's get on.'

'9 and 10,' said Fournier, moving his finger on the plan.

'M. Hercule Poirot and Dr Bryant,' said Japp. 'What has M. Poirot to say for himself?'

Poirot shook his head sadly.

'*Mon estomac*,' he said pathetically. 'Alas, that the brain should be the servant of the stomach.'

'I, too,' said Fournier with sympathy. 'In the air I do not feel well.'

He closed his eyes and shook his head expressively.

'Now then, Dr Bryant. What about Dr Bryant? Big bug in Harley Street. Not very likely to go to a French woman money-lender; but you never know. And if any funny business crops up with a doctor he's done for life! Here's where my scientific theory comes in. A man like Bryant, at the top of the tree, is in with all the medical research people. He could pinch a test-tube of snake venom as easy as winking when he happens to be in some swell laboratory.'

'They check these things, my friend,' objected Poirot. 'It would not be just like plucking a buttercup in a meadow.'

'Even if they do check 'em, a clever man could substitute something harmless. It could be done, simply because a man like Bryant would be above suspicion.'

'There is much in what you say,' agreed Fournier.

'The only thing is, why did he draw attention to the thing? Why not say the woman died from heart failure – natural death?'

Poirot coughed. The other two looked at him inquiringly.

'I fancy,' he said, 'that that was the doctor's first – well, shall we say impression? After all, it looked very like natural death, possibly as the result of a wasp sting; there was a wasp, remember –'

'Not likely to forget that wasp,' put in Japp. 'You're always harping on it.'

'However,' continued Poirot, '*I* happened to notice the fatal thorn on the ground and picked it up. Once we had found that, everything pointed to murder.'

'The thorn would be bound to be found anyway.'

Poirot shook his head.

'There is just a chance that the murderer might have been able to pick it up unobserved.'

'Bryant?'

'Bryant or another.'

'H'm – rather risky.'

Fournier disagreed.

'You think so now,' he said, 'because you know that it is murder. But when a lady dies suddenly of heart failure, if a man is to drop his handkerchief and stoop to pick it up, who will notice the action or think twice about it?'

'That's true,' agreed Japp. 'Well, I fancy Bryant is definitely on the list of suspects. He could lean his head round the corner of his seat and do the blowpipe act – again diagonally across the car. But why nobody saw him –! However, I won't go into that again. Whoever did it *wasn't* seen!'

'And for that, I fancy, there must be a reason,' said Fournier. 'A reason that, by all I have heard,' he smiled, 'will appeal to M. Poirot. I mean a psychological reason.'

'Continue, my friend,' said Poirot. 'It is interesting what you say there.'

'Supposing,' said Fournier, 'that when travelling in a train you were to pass a house in flames. Everyone's eyes would at once be drawn to the window. Everyone would have their attention fixed on a certain point. A man in such a moment might whip out a dagger and stab a man, and nobody would see him do it.'

'That is true,' said Poirot. 'I remember a case in which I was concerned – a case of poison, where that very point arose. There was, as you call it, a psychological moment. If we discover that there was such a moment during the journey of the *Prometheus* –'

'We ought to find that out by questioning the stewards and the passengers,' said Japp.

'True. But if there *was* such a psychological moment, it must follow logically that the *cause* of that moment must have originated with the murderer. He must have been able to produce the particular effect that caused that moment.'

'Perfectly, perfectly,' said the Frenchman.

'Well, we'll note down that as a point for questions,' said Japp. 'I'm coming now to seat No. 8 – Daniel Michael Clancy.'

Japp spoke the name with a certain amount of relish.

'In my opinion he's the most likely suspect we've got. What's easier than for a mystery author to fake up an interest in snake venom and get some unsuspecting scientific chemist to let him handle the stuff? Don't forget he went down past Giselle's seat – the only one of the passengers who did.'

'I assure you, my friend,' said Poirot, 'that I have not forgotten that point.'

He spoke with emphasis.

Japp went on:

'He could have used that blowpipe from fairly close quarters without any need of a "psychological moment", as you call it. And he stood quite a respectable chance of getting away with it. Remember, he knows all about blowpipes – he said so.'

'Which makes one pause, perhaps.'

'Sheer artfulness,' said Japp. 'And as to this blowpipe he produced today, who is to say that it's the one he bought two years ago? The whole thing looks very fishy to me. I don't think it's healthy for a man to be always brooding over crime and detective stories, reading up all sorts of cases. It puts ideas into his head.'

'It is certainly necessary for a writer to have ideas in his head,' agreed Poirot.

Japp returned to his plan of the plane.

'No. 4 was Ryder – the seat slap in front of the dead woman. Don't think he did it. But we can't leave him out. He went to the toilet. He could have taken a pot shot on the way back from fairly close quarters; the only thing is he'd be right up against the archaeologist fellows when he did so. They'd notice it – couldn't help it.'

Poirot shook his head thoughtfully.

'You are not, perhaps, acquainted with many archaeologists? If these two were having a really absorbing discussion on some point at issue – *eh bien*, my friend, their concentration would be such that they would be quite blind and deaf to the outside world. They would be existing, you see, in five thousand or so BC. Nineteen hundred and thirty-five AD would have been non-existent for them.'

Japp looked a little sceptical.

'Well, we'll pass on to them. What can you tell us about the Duponts, Fournier?'

'M. Armand Dupont is one of the most distinguished archaeologists in France.'

'Then that doesn't get us anywhere much. Their position in the car is pretty good from my point of view – across the gangway but slightly farther forward than Giselle. And I suppose that they've knocked about the world and dug things up in a lot of queer places; they might easily have got hold of some native snake poison.'

'It is possible, yes,' said Fournier.

'But you don't believe it's likely?'

Fournier shook his head doubtfully.

'M. Dupont lives for his profession. He is an enthusiast. He was formerly an antique dealer. He gave up a flourishing business to devote himself to excavation. Both he and his son are devoted heart and soul to their profession. It seems to me unlikely – I will not say impossible, since the ramifications of the Stavisky business I will believe anything – *unlikely* that they are mixed up in this business.'

'All right,' said Japp.

He picked up the sheet of paper on which he had been making notes and cleared his throat.

'This is where we stand. *Jane Grey*. Probability – poor. Possibility – practically nil. *Gale*. Probability – poor. Possibility – again practically nil. *Miss Kerr*. Very improbable. Possibility – doubtful. *Lady Horbury*. Probability – good. Possibility – practically nil. *M. Poirot* – almost certainly the criminal; the only man on board who could create a psychological moment.'

Japp enjoyed a good laugh over his little joke, and Poirot smiled indulgently and Fournier a trifle diffidently. Then the detective resumed:

'*Bryant*. Probability and possibility – both good. *Clancy*. Motive doubtful – probability and possibility very good indeed. *Ryder*. Probability uncertain – possibility quite fair. *The two Duponts*. Probability poor as regards motive – good as to means of obtaining poison. Possibility – good.

'That's a pretty fair summary, I think, as far as we can go. We'll have to do a lot of routine inquiry. I shall take on Clancy and Bryant first – find out what they've been up to – if they've been hard up at any time in the past – if they've seemed worried or upset lately – their movements in the last year – all that sort of stuff. I'll do the same for Ryder. Then it won't do to neglect the others entirely. I'll get Wilson to nose round there. M. Fournier here will undertake the Duponts.'

The man from the Sûreté nodded.

'Be well assured – that will be attended to. I shall return to Paris tonight. There may be something to be got out of Elise, Giselle's maid, now that we know a little more about the case. Also, I will check up Giselle's movements very carefully. It will be well to know where she has been during the summer. She was, I know, at Le Pinet once or twice. We may get information as to her contacts with some of the English people involved. Ah, yes, there is much to do.'

They both looked at Poirot, who was absorbed in thought.

'You going to take a hand at all, M. Poirot?' asked Japp.

Poirot roused himself.

'Yes, I think I should like to accompany M. Fournier to Paris.'

'*Enchanté*,' said the Frenchman.

'What are you up to, I wonder?' said Japp. He looked at Poirot curiously. 'You've been very quiet over all this. Got some of your little ideas, eh?'

'One or two, one or two; but it is very difficult.'

'Let's hear about it.'

'One thing that worries me,' said Poirot slowly, 'is the place where the blowpipe was found.'

'Naturally! It nearly got you locked up.'

Poirot shook his head.

'I do not mean that. It is not because it was found pushed down beside my seat that it worries me – it was its being pushed down behind any seat.'

'I don't see anything in that,' said Japp. 'Whoever did it had got to hide the thing somewhere. He couldn't risk its being found on him.'

'*Evidemment*. But you may have noticed, my friend, when you examined the plane, that although the windows cannot be opened, there is in each of them a ventilator – a circle of small round holes in the glass which can be opened or closed by turning a fan of glass. Those holes are of a sufficient circumference to admit of the passage of our blowpipe. What could be simpler than to get rid of the blowpipe that way? It falls to the earth beneath, and it is extremely unlikely that it will ever be found.'

'I can think of an objection to that – the murderer was afraid of being seen. If he pushed the blowpipe through the ventilator someone might have noticed.'

'I see,' said Poirot. 'He was not afraid of being seen placing the blowpipe to his lips and dispatching the fatal dart, but he *was* afraid of being seen trying to push the blowpipe through the window!'

'Sounds absurd, I admit,' said Japp; 'but there it is. He *did* hide the blowpipe behind the cushion of a seat. We can't get away from that.'

Poirot did not answer, and Fournier asked curiously:

'It gives you an idea, that?'

Poirot bowed his head assentingly.

'It gives rise to, say, a speculation in my mind.'

With absent-minded fingers he straightened the unused ink-stand that Japp's impatient hand had set a little askew.

Then lifting his head sharply, he asked:

'*A propos*, have you that detailed list of the belongings of the passengers that I asked you to get me?'

CHAPTER 8

THE LIST

'I'm a man of my word, I am,' said Japp.

He grinned and dived his hand into his pocket, bringing out a mass of closely-typewritten paper.

'Here you are. It's all here – down to the minutest detail! And I'll admit that there is one rather curious thing in it. I'll talk to you about it when you've finished reading the stuff.'

Poirot spread out the sheets on the table and began to read. Fournier moved up and read them over his shoulder:

James Ryder.

Pockets. – Linen handkerchief marked J. Pigskin notecase – seven £1 notes, three business cards. Letter from partner George Ebermann hoping 'loan has been successfully negotiated . . . otherwise we're in Queer Street'. Letter signed Maudie making appointment Trocadero following evening (cheap paper, illiterate handwriting). Silver cigarette-case. Match-folder. Fountain-pen. Bunch of keys. Yale door key. Loose change in French and English money.

Attaché Case. – Mass of papers concerning dealings in cement. Copy of *Bootless Cup* (banned in this country). A box of 'Immediate Cold Cures'.

Dr Bryant.
Pockets. – Two linen handkerchiefs. Notecase containing £20 and 500 francs. Loose change in French and English money. Engagement book. Cigarette-case. Lighter. Fountain-pen. Yale door key. Bunch of keys. Flute in case. Carrying *Memoirs of Benvenuto Cellini* and *Les Maux de l'Oreille.*

Norman Gale.
Pockets. – Silk handkerchief. Wallet containing £1 in English and 600 francs. Loose change. Business cards of two French firms – makers of dental instruments. Bryant & May matchbox – empty. Silver lighter. Briar pipe. Rubber tobacco pouch. Yale door key.
Attaché Case. – White linen coat. Two small dental mirrors. Dental rolls of cottonwool. *La Vie Parisienne. The Strand Magazine. The Autocar.*

Armand Dupont.
Pockets. – Wallet containing 1000 francs and £10 in English. Spectacles in case. Loose change in French money. Cotton handkerchief. Packet of cigarettes, match-folder. Cards in case. Toothpick.
Attaché Case. – Manuscript of proposed address to Royal Asiatic Society. Two German archaeological publications. Two sheets of rough sketches of pottery. Ornamented hollow tubes (said to be Kurdish pipe stems). Small basketwork tray. Nine unmounted photographs – all of pottery.

Jean Dupont.
Pockets. – Notecase containing £5 in English and 300 francs. Cigarette-case. Cigarette-holder (ivory). Lighter. Fountain-pen.

Two pencils. Small notebook full of scribbled notes. Letter in English from L. Marriner giving invitation to lunch at restaurant near Tottenham Court Road. Loose change in French.

Daniel Clancy.
Pockets. – Handkerchief (ink-stained). Fountain-pen (leaking). Notecase containing £4 and 100 francs. Three newspaper cuttings dealing with recent crimes (one poisoning by arsenic and two embezzlement). Two letters from house agents with details of country properties. Engagement book. Four pencils. Pen-knife. Three receipted and four unpaid bills. Letter from 'Gordon' headed S.S. *Minotaur*. Half-done crossword puzzle cut from *Times*. Notebook containing suggestions for plots. Loose change in Italian, French, Swiss and English money. Receipted hotel bill, Naples. Large bunch of keys.
In overcoat pocket. – Manuscript notes of *Murder on Vesuvius*. Continental Bradshaw. Golf ball. Pair of socks. Toothbrush. Receipted hotel bill, Paris.

Miss Kerr.
Vanity bag. – Lipstick. Two cigarette-holders (one ivory and one jade). Flapjack. Cigarette-case. Match-folder. Handkerchief. £2 English. Loose change. One half letter of credit. Keys.
Dressing-case. – Shagreen fitted. Bottles, brushes, combs, etc. Manicure outfit. Washing bag containing toothbrush, sponge, toothpowder, soap. Two pairs of scissors. Five letters from family and friends in England. Two Tauchnitz novels. Photograph of two spaniels.

Carried *Vogue* and *Good Housekeeping*.

Miss Grey.
Handbag. – Lipstick, rouge, flapjack. Yale key and one trunk key. Pencil. Cigarette-case. Holder. Match-folder. Two handkerchiefs. Receipted hotel bill, Le Pinet. Small book, *French Phrases*. Notecase, 100 francs and 10s. Loose French and English change. One Casino counter value 5 francs.

In pocket of travelling coat. – Six postcards of Paris, two handkerchiefs and silk scarf. Letter signed 'Gladys'. Tube of aspirin.

Lady Horbury.

Vanity bag. – Two lipsticks, rouge, flapjack. Handkerchief. Three *mille* notes. £6 English. Loose change (French). A diamond ring. Five French stamps. Two cigarette-holders. Lighter with case.

Dressing-case. – Complete makeup outfit. Elaborate manicure set (gold). Small bottle labelled (in ink) Boracic Powder.

As Poirot came to the end of the list, Japp laid his finger on the last item.

'Rather smart of our man. He thought that didn't seem quite in keeping with the rest. Boracic powder my eye! The white powder in that bottle was cocaine.'

Poirot's eyes opened a little. He nodded his head slowly.

'Nothing much to do with our case, perhaps,' said Japp. 'But you don't need me to tell you that a woman who's got the cocaine habit hasn't got much moral restraint. I've an idea anyway that her ladyship wouldn't stick at much to get what she wanted, in spite of all that helpless feminine business. All the same, I doubt if she'd have the nerve to carry a thing like this through; and, frankly, I can't see that it was *possible* for her to do it. The whole thing is a bit of a teaser.'

Poirot gathered up the loose typewritten sheets and read them through once again. Then he laid them down with a sigh.

'On the face of it,' he said, 'it seems to point very plainly to one person as having committed the crime. And yet, I cannot see *why*, or even *how*.'

Japp stared at him.

'Are you pretending that by reading all this stuff you've got an idea who did it?'

'I think so.'

Japp seized the papers from him and read them through, handing each sheet over to Fournier as he had finished with it. Then he slapped them down on the table and stared at Poirot.

'Are you pulling my leg, Moosior Poirot?'

'No, no. *Quelle idée!*'

The Frenchman in his turn laid down the sheets.

'What about you, Fournier?'

The Frenchman shook his head. 'I may be stupid,' he said, 'but I cannot see that this list advances us much.'

'Not by itself,' said Poirot. 'But taken in conjunction with certain features of the case, no? Well, it may be that I am wrong – quite wrong.'

'Well, come out with your theory,' said Japp. 'I'll be interested to hear it at all events.'

Poirot shook his head.

'No, as you say it is a theory – a theory only. I hoped to find a certain object on that list. *Eh bien*, I have found it. It is there; but it seems to point in the wrong direction. The right clue on the wrong person. That means there is much work to be done, and truly there is much that is still obscure to me. I cannot see my way; only certain facts seem to stand out, to arrange themselves in a significant pattern. You do not find it so? No, I see you do not. Let us then each work to his own idea. I have no *certainty*, I tell you, only a certain suspicion . . .'

'I believe you're just talking through your hat,' said Japp. He rose. 'Well, let's call it a day. I work the London end, you return to Paris, Fournier – and what about our M. Poirot?'

'I still wish to accompany M. Fournier to Paris – more than ever now.'

'More than ever –? I'd like to know just what kind of maggot you've got in your brain.'

'Maggot? *Ce n'est pas joli, ça!*'

Fournier shook hands ceremoniously.

'I wish you good evening, with many thanks for your delightful hospitality. We will meet then at Croydon tomorrow morning?'

'Exactly. *A demain*.'

'Let us hope,' said Fournier, 'that nobody will murder us *en route*.'

The two detectives departed.

Poirot remained for a time as in a dream. Then he rose, cleared away any traces of disorder, emptied the ashtrays and straightened the chairs.

He went to a side table and picked up a copy of the *Sketch*. He turned the pages until he came to the one he sought.

'Two Sun Worshippers,' it was headed. 'The Countess of Horbury and Mr Raymond Barraclough at Le Pinet.' He looked at the two laughing figures in bathing-dresses, their arms entwined.

'I wonder,' said Hercule Poirot. 'One might do something along those lines . . . Yes, one might.'

CHAPTER 9

ELISE GRANDIER

The weather on the following day was of so perfect a nature that even Hercule Poirot had to admit that his *estomac* was perfectly peaceful.

On this occasion they were travelling by the 8.45 Air Service to Paris.

There were seven or eight travellers beside Poirot and Fournier in the compartment, and the Frenchman utilized the journey to make some experiments. He took from his pocket a small piece of bamboo and three times during the journey he raised this to his lips, pointing it in a certain direction. Once he did it bending himself round the corner of his seat, once with his head slightly turned sideways, once when he was returning from the toilet compartment; and on each occasion he caught the eye of some passenger or other eyeing him with mild astonishment. On the last occasion, indeed, every eye in the car seemed to be fixed upon him.

Fournier sank in his seat discouraged, and was but little cheered by observing Poirot's open amusement.

'You are amused, my friend? But you agree one must try experiments?'

'*Evidemment!* In truth I admire your thoroughness. There is nothing like ocular demonstration. You play the part of the murderer with blowpipe. The result is perfectly clear. Everybody sees you!'

'Not *everybody*.'

'In a sense, no. On each occasion there is *somebody* who does *not* see you; but for a successful murder that is not enough. You must be reasonably sure that *nobody* will see you.'

'And that is impossible given ordinary conditions,' said Fournier. 'I hold then to my theory that there must have been *extraordinary* conditions – the psychological moment! There *must* have been a psychological moment when everyone's attention was mathematically centred elsewhere.'

'Our friend Inspector Japp is going to make minute inquiries on that point.'

'Do you not agree with me, M. Poirot?'

Poirot hesitated a minute, then he said slowly:

'I agree that there was – that there must have been a psychological reason why nobody saw the murderer . . . But my ideas are running in a slightly different channel from yours. I feel that in this case mere ocular facts may be deceptive. Close your eyes, my friend, instead of opening them wide. Use the eyes of the *brain*, not of the *body*. Let the little grey cells of the mind function . . . Let it be their task to show you *what actually happened*.'

Fournier stared at him curiously.

'I do not follow you, M. Poirot.'

'Because you are deducing from things that you have *seen*. Nothing can be so misleading as observation.'

Fournier shook his head again and spread out his hands. 'I give up. I cannot catch your meaning.'

'Our friend Giraud would urge you to pay no attention to my vagaries. "Be up and doing," he would say. "To sit still in an armchair and think, that is the method of an old man past his prime." But I say that a young hound is often so eager upon the scent that he overruns it . . . For him is the trail of the red herring. There, it is a very good hint I have given you there . . .'

And, leaning back, Poirot closed his eyes, it may have been to think, but it is quite certain that five minutes later he was fast asleep.

On arrival in Paris they went straight to No. 3 Rue Joliette.

The Rue Joliette is on the south side of the Seine. There was nothing to distinguish No. 3 from the other houses. An aged concierge admitted them and greeted Fournier in a surly fashion.

'So we have the police here again! Nothing but trouble. This will give the house a bad name.'

He retreated grumbling into his apartment.

'We will go to Giselle's office,' said Fournier. 'It is on the first floor.'

He drew a key from his pocket as he spoke and explained that the French police had taken the precaution of locking and sealing the door whilst awaiting the result of the English inquest.

'Not, I fear,' said Fournier, 'that there is anything here to help us.'

He detached the seals, unlocked the door, and they entered.

Madame Giselle's office was a small, stuffy apartment. It had a somewhat old-fashioned type of safe in a corner, a writing desk of business-like appearance and several shabbily upholstered chairs. The one window was dirty and it seemed highly probable that it had never been opened.

Fournier shrugged his shoulders as he looked round.

'You see?' he said. 'Nothing. Nothing at all.'

Poirot passed round behind the desk. He sat down in the chair and looked across the desk at Fournier. He passed his hand gently across the surface of the wood, then down underneath it.

'There is a bell here,' he said.

'Yes, it rings down to the concierge.'

'Ah, a wise precaution. Madame's clients might sometimes become obstreperous.'

He opened one or two of the drawers. They contained stationery, a calendar, pens and pencils, but no papers and nothing of a personal nature.

Poirot merely glanced into them in a cursory manner.

'I will not insult you, my friend, by a close search. If there were anything to find you would have found it, I am sure.' He looked across at the safe. 'Not a very efficacious pattern, that?'

'Somewhat out of date,' agreed Fournier.

'It was empty?'

'Yes. That cursed maid had destroyed everything.'

'Ah, yes, the maid. The confidential maid. We must see her. This room, as you say, has nothing to tell us. It is significant that, do you not think so?'

'What do you mean by significant, M. Poirot?'

'I mean that there is in this room no personal touch . . . I find that interesting.'

'She was hardly a woman of sentiment,' said Fournier dryly.

Poirot rose.

'Come,' he said, 'let us see this maid – this highly confidential maid.'

Elise Grandier was a short stout woman of middle age with a florid face and small shrewd eyes that darted quickly from Fournier's face to that of his companion and then back again.

'Sit down, Mademoiselle Grandier,' said Fournier.

'Thank you, Monsieur.'

She sat down composedly.

'M. Poirot and I have returned today from London. The inquest – the inquiry, that is, into the death of Madame – took place yesterday. There is no doubt whatsoever. Madame was poisoned.'

The Frenchwoman shook her head gravely.

'It is terrible what you say there, Monsieur. Madame poisoned? Who would ever have dreamt of such a thing?'

'That is perhaps where you can help us, Mademoiselle.'

'Certainly, Monsieur, I will naturally do all I can to aid the police. But I know nothing – nothing at all.'

'You know that Madame had enemies?' said Fournier sharply.

'That is not true. Why should Madame have enemies?'

'Come, come, Mademoiselle Grandier,' said Fournier dryly. 'The profession of a moneylender – it entails certain unpleasantnesses.'

'It is true that sometimes the clients of Madame were not very reasonable,' agreed Elise.

'They made scenes, eh? They threatened her?'

The maid shook her head.

'No, no, you are wrong there. It was not *they* who threatened. They whined – they complained – they protested they could not pay – all that, yes.' Her voice held a very lively contempt.

'Sometimes, perhaps, Mademoiselle,' said Poirot, 'they could not pay.'

Elise Grandier shrugged her shoulders.

'Possibly. That is their affair! They usually paid in the end.'

Her tone held a certain amount of satisfaction.

'Madame Giselle was a hard woman,' said Fournier.

'Madame was justified.'

'You have no pity for the victims?'

'Victims – victims . . .' Elise spoke with impatience. 'You do not understand. Is it necessary to run into debt, to live beyond your means, to run and borrow, and then expect to keep the money as a gift? It is not reasonable, that! Madame was always fair and just. She lent – and she expected repayment. That is only fair. She herself had no debts. Always she paid honourably what she owed. Never, never were there any bills outstanding. And when you say that Madame was a hard woman it is not the truth! Madame was kind. She gave to the Little Sisters of the Poor when they came. She gave money to charitable institutions. When the wife of Georges, the concierge, was ill, Madame paid for her to go to a hospital in the country.'

She stopped, her face flushed and angry.

She repeated, 'You do not understand. No, you do not understand Madame at all.'

Fournier waited a moment for her indignation to subside and then said:

'You made the observation that Madame's clients usually managed to pay *in the end*. Were you aware of the means Madame used to compel them?'

She shrugged her shoulders.

'I know nothing, Monsieur – nothing at all.'

'You knew enough to burn Madame's papers.'

'I was following her instructions. If ever, she said, she were to meet with an accident, or if she were taken ill and died somewhere away from home, I was to destroy her business papers.'

'The papers in the safe downstairs?' asked Poirot.

'That is right. Her business papers.'

'And they were in the safe downstairs?'

His persistence brought the red up in Elise's cheeks.

'I obeyed Madame's instructions,' she said.

'I know that,' said Poirot, smiling. 'But the papers were not in the safe. That is so, is it not? That safe, it is far too old-fashioned – quite an amateur might have opened it. The papers were kept elsewhere – in Madame's bedroom, perhaps?'

Elise paused a moment and then answered:

'Yes, that is so. Madame always pretended to clients that papers were kept in the safe, but in reality the safe was a blind. Everything was in Madame's bedroom.'

'Will you show us where?'

Elise rose and the two men followed her. The bedroom was a fair-sized room, but was so full of ornate heavy furniture that it was hard to move about freely in it. In one corner was a large old-fashioned trunk. Elise lifted the lid and took out an old-fashioned alpaca dress with a silk underskirt. On the inside of the dress was a deep pocket.

'The papers were in this, Monsieur,' she said. 'They were kept in a large sealed envelope.'

'You told me nothing of this,' said Fournier sharply, 'when I questioned you three days ago.'

'I ask pardon, Monsieur. You asked me where were the papers that should be in the safe. I told you I had burned them. That was true. Exactly where the papers were kept seemed unimportant.'

'True,' said Fournier. 'You understand, Mademoiselle Grandier, that those papers should not have been burnt.'

'I obeyed Madame's orders,' said Elise sullenly.

'You acted, I know, for the best,' said Fournier soothingly. 'Now I want you to listen to me very closely, Mademoiselle: *Madame was murdered*. It is possible that she was murdered by a person or persons about whom she held certain damaging knowledge. That knowledge was in those papers you burnt. I am going to ask you a question, Mademoiselle, and do not reply too quickly without reflection. It is possible – *indeed in my view it is probable and quite understandable* – that you glanced through those papers before committing them to the flames. If that is the case, no blame will be attached to you for so doing. On the contrary, any information you have acquired may be of the greatest service to the police, and may be of material service in bringing the murderer to justice. Therefore, Mademoiselle, have no fear in answering truthfully. Did you, before burning the papers, glance over them?'

Elise breathed hard. She leant forward and spoke emphatically.

'No, Monsieur,' she said. 'I looked at nothing. I read nothing. I burnt the envelope without undoing the seal.'

CHAPTER 10

THE LITTLE BLACK BOOK

Fournier stared hard at her for a moment or two, then, satisfied that she was speaking the truth, he turned away with a gesture of discouragement.

'It is a pity,' he said. 'You acted honourably, Mademoiselle, but it is a pity.'

'I cannot help, Monsieur. I am sorry.'

Fournier sat down and drew a notebook from his pocket.

'When I questioned you before, you told me, Mademoiselle, that you did not know the names of Madame's clients. Yet just now you speak of them whining and asking for mercy. You did, therefore, know *something* about these clients of Madame Giselle's?'

'Let me explain, Monsieur. Madame never mentioned a name.

She never discussed her business. But all the same one is human, is one not? There are ejaculations – comments. Madame spoke to me sometimes as she would to herself.'

Poirot leaned forward.

'If you would give us an instance, Mademoiselle –' he said.

'Let me see – ah, yes – say a letter comes. Madame opens it. She laughs a short, dry laugh. She says, "*You whine and you snivel, my fine lady. All the same, you must pay.*" Or she would say to me, "*What fools! What fools! To think I would lend large sums without proper security. Knowledge is security, Elise. Knowledge is power.*" Something like that she would say.'

'Madame's clients who came to the house, did you ever see any of them?'

'No, Monsieur – at least hardly ever. They came to the first floor only, you understand, and very often they came after dark.'

'Had Madame Giselle been in Paris before her journey to England?'

'She returned to Paris only the afternoon before.'

'Where had she been?'

'She had been away for a fortnight to Deauville, Le Pinet, Paris-Plage and Wimereux – her usual September round.'

'Now think, Mademoiselle, did she say *anything* – anything at all that might be of use?'

Elise considered for some moments. Then she shook her head.

'No, Monsieur,' she said. 'I cannot remember anything. Madame was in good spirits. Business was going well, she said. Her tour had been profitable. Then she directed me to ring up Universal Airlines and book a passage to England for the following day. The early morning service was booked, but she obtained a seat on the 12 o'clock service.'

'Did she say what took her to England? Was there any urgency about it?'

'Oh, no, Monsieur. Madame journeyed to England fairly frequently. She usually told me the day before.'

'Did any clients come to see Madame that evening?'

'I believe there was one client, Monsieur, but I am not sure. Georges, perhaps, would know. Madame said nothing to me.'

Fournier took from his pockets various photographs – mostly snapshots taken by reporters, of various witnesses leaving the coroner's court.

'Can you recognize any of these, Mademoiselle?'

Elise took them and gazed at each in turn. Then she shook her head.

'No, Monsieur.'

'We must try Georges then.'

'Yes, Monsieur. Unfortunately, Georges has not very good eyesight. It is a pity.'

Fournier rose.

'Well, Mademoiselle, we will take our leave – that is, if you are quite sure that there is nothing – nothing at all – that you have omitted to mention.'

'I? What – what could there be?'

Elise looked distressed.

'It is understood, then. Come, M. Poirot. I beg your pardon. You are looking for something?'

Poirot was indeed wandering round the room in a vague searching way.

'It is true,' said Poirot. 'I am looking for something I do not see.'

'What is that?'

'Photographs. Photographs of Madame Giselle's relations – of her family.'

Elise shook her head.

'She had no family, Madame. She was alone in the world.'

'She had a daughter,' said Poirot sharply.

'Yes, that is so. Yes, she had a daughter.'

Elise sighed.

'But there is no picture of that daughter?' Poirot persisted.

'Oh, Monsieur does not understand. It is true that Madame had a daughter, but that was long ago, you comprehend. It is my belief that Madame had never seen that daughter since she was a tiny baby.'

'How was that?' demanded Fournier sharply.

Elise's hands flew out in an expressive gesture.

'I do not know. It was in the days when Madame was young. I have heard that she was pretty then – pretty and poor. She may have been married; she may not. Myself, I think not. Doubtless some arrangement was made about the child. As for Madame, she had the smallpox – she was very ill – she nearly died. When she got well her beauty was gone. There were no more follies, no more romance. Madame became a woman of business.'

'But she left her money to this daughter?'

'That is only right,' said Elise. 'Who should one leave one's money to except one's own flesh and blood? Blood is thicker than water; and Madame had no friends. She was always alone. Money was her passion – to make more and more money. She spent very little. She had no love for luxury.'

'She left you a legacy. You know that?'

'But yes, I have been informed. Madame was always generous. She gave me a good sum every year as well as my wages. I am very grateful to Madame.'

'Well,' said Fournier, 'we will take our leave. On the way out I will have another word with old Georges.'

'Permit me to follow you in a little minute, my friend,' said Poirot.

'As you wish.'

Fournier departed.

Poirot roamed once more round the room, then sat down and fixed his eyes on Elise.

Under his scrutiny the Frenchwoman got slightly restive.

'Is there anything more Monsieur requires to know?'

'Mademoiselle Grandier,' said Poirot, 'do you know who murdered your mistress?'

'No, Monsieur. Before the good God I swear it.'

She spoke very earnestly. Poirot looked at her searchingly, then bent his head.

'*Bien,*' he said. 'I accept that. But knowledge is one thing, suspicion is another. Have you any idea – an *idea* only – who might have done such a thing?'

'I have no idea, Monsieur. I have already said so to the agent of police.'

'You might say one thing to him and another thing to me.'

'Why do you say that, Monsieur? Why should I do such a thing?'

'Because it is one thing to give information to the police and another thing to give it to a private individual.'

'Yes,' admitted Elise. 'That is true.'

A look of indecision came over her face. She seemed to be thinking. Watching her very closely, Poirot leaned forward and spoke:

'Shall I tell you something, Mademoiselle Grandier? It is part of my business to believe nothing I am told – nothing that is, that is not *proved*. I do not suspect first this person and then that person. I suspect *everybody*. Anybody connected with a crime is regarded by me as a criminal until that person is proved innocent.'

Elise Grandier scowled at him angrily.

'Are you saying that you suspect me – *me* – of having murdered Madame? It is too strong, that! Such a thought is of a wickedness unbelievable!'

Her large bosom rose and fell tumultuously.

'No, Elise,' said Poirot. 'I do not suspect you of having murdered Madame. Whoever murdered Madame was a passenger in the aeroplane. Therefore it was not your hand that did the deed. But you might have been *an accomplice before the act*. You might have passed on to someone the details of Madame's journey.'

'I did not. I swear I did not.'

Poirot looked at her again for some minutes in silence. Then he nodded his head.

'I believe you,' he said. 'But, nevertheless, there is something that you conceal. Oh, yes there is! Listen, I will tell you something. In every case of a criminal nature one comes across the same phenomena when questioning witnesses. *Everyone keeps something back*. Sometimes – often indeed – it is something quite harmless, something, perhaps, quite unconnected with the crime; but – I say it again – there is always *something*. That is so with you. Oh, do not deny! I am Hercule Poirot and I *know*. When my friend M. Fournier asked you if you were sure there was nothing you had omitted to mention, you were troubled. You answered unconsciously, with an evasion. Again just now when I suggested that you might tell me something which you would not care to tell the police you very obviously turned the suggestion over in your mind. There is, then, *something*. I want to know what that something is.'

'It is nothing of importance.'

'Possibly not. But all the same, will you not tell me what it is? Remember,' he went on as she hesitated, 'I am not of the police.'

'That is true,' said Elise Grandier. She hesitated and went on, 'Monsieur, I am in a difficulty. I do not know what Madame herself would have wanted me to do.'

'There is a saying that two heads are better than one. Will you not consult me? Let us examine the question together.'

The woman still looked at him doubtfully. He said with a smile:

'You are a good watch-dog, Elise. It is a question, I see, of loyalty to your dead mistress?'

'That is quite right, Monsieur. Madame trusted me. Ever since I entered her service I have carried out her instructions faithfully.'

'You were grateful, were you not, for some great service she had rendered you?'

'Monsieur is very quick. Yes, that is true. I do not mind admitting it. I had been deceived, Monsieur, my savings stolen – and there was a child. Madame was good to me. She arranged for the baby to be brought up by some good people on a farm – a good farm, Monsieur, and honest people. It was then, at that time, that she mentioned to me that she, too, was a mother.'

'Did she tell you the age of her child, where it was, any details?'

'No, Monsieur, she spoke of a part of her life that was over and done with. It was best so, she said. The little girl was well provided for and would be brought up to a trade or profession. She would also inherit her money when she died.'

'She told you nothing further about this child or about its father?'

'No, Monsieur, but I have an idea –'

'Speak, Mademoiselle Elise.'

'It is an idea only, you understand.'

'Perfectly, perfectly.'

'I have an idea that the father of the child was an Englishman.'

'What exactly do you think gave you that impression?'

'Nothing definite. It is just that there was a bitterness in Madame's voice when she spoke of the English. I think, too, that in her business transactions she enjoyed having anyone English in her power. It is an impression only –'

'Yes, but it may be a very valuable one. It opens up possibilities . . . Your own child, Mademoiselle Elise? Was it a girl or a boy?'

'A girl, Monsieur. But she is dead – dead these five years now.'

'Ah – all my sympathy.'

There was a pause.

'And now, Mademoiselle Elise,' said Poirot, 'what is this something that you have hitherto refrained from mentioning?'

Elise rose and left the room. She returned a few minutes later with a small shabby black notebook in her hand.

'This little book was Madame's. It went with her everywhere. When she was about to depart for England she could not find it. It was mislaid. After she had gone I found it. It had dropped down behind the head of the bed. I put it in my room to keep until Madame should return. I burned the papers as soon as I heard of Madame's death, but I did not burn the book. There were no instructions as to that.'

'When did you hear of Madame's death?'

Elise hesitated a minute.

'You heard it from the police, did you not?' said Poirot. 'They came here and examined Madame's rooms. They found the safe empty and you told them that you had burnt the papers, but actually you did not burn the papers until afterwards.'

'It is true, Monsieur,' admitted Elise. 'Whilst they were looking in the safe I removed the papers from the trunk. I said they were burnt, yes. After all, it was very nearly the truth. I burnt them at the first opportunity. I had to carry out Madame's orders. You see my difficulty, Monsieur? You will not inform the police? It might be a very serious matter for me.'

'I believe, Mademoiselle Elise, that you acted with the best intentions. All the same, you understand, it is a pity . . . a great pity. But it does no good to regret what is done, and I see no necessity for communicating the exact hour of the destruction to the excellent M. Fournier. Now let me see if there is anything in this little book to aid us.'

'I do not think there will be, Monsieur,' said Elise, shaking her head. 'It is Madame's private memorandums, yes, but there are numbers only. Without the documents and files these entries are meaningless.'

Unwillingly she held out the book to Poirot. He took it and turned the pages. There were pencilled entries in a sloping foreign writing. They seemed to be all of the same kind. A number followed by a few descriptive details, such as:

CX 256. Colonel's wife. Stationed Syria. Regimental funds.
GF 342. French Deputy. Stavisky connexion.

The entries seemed to be all of the same kind. There were

perhaps twenty in all. At the end of the book were pencilled memoranda of dates or places, such as:

> Le Pinet, Monday. Casino, 10.30. Savoy Hotel, 5 o'clock. ABC. Fleet Street, 11 o'clock.

None of these were complete in themselves, and seemed to have been put down less as actual appointments than as aids to Giselle's memory.

Elise was watching Poirot anxiously.

'It means nothing, Monsieur, or so it seems to me. It was comprehensible to Madame, but not to a mere reader.'

Poirot closed the book and put it in his pocket.

'This may be very valuable, Mademoiselle. You did wisely to give it to me. And your conscience may be quite at rest. Madame never asked you to burn this book?'

'That is true,' said Elise, her face brightening a little.

'Therefore, having no instructions, it is your duty to hand this over to the police. I will arrange matters with M. Fournier so that you shall not be blamed for not having done so sooner.'

'Monsieur is very kind.'

Poirot rose.

'I will go now and join my colleague. Just one last question. When you reserved a seat in the aeroplane for Madame Giselle, did you ring up the aerodrome at Le Bourget or the office of the company?'

'I rang up the office of Universal Airlines, Monsieur.'

'And that, I think, is in the Boulevard des Capucines?'

'That is right, Monsieur, 254 Boulevard des Capucines.'

Poirot inscribed the number in his little book, then with a friendly nod he left the room.

CHAPTER 11

THE AMERICAN

Fournier was deep in conversation with old Georges. The detective was looking hot and annoyed.

'Just like the police,' the old man was grumbling in his deep hoarse voice. 'Ask one the same question over and over again. What do they hope for? That sooner or later one will give over speaking the truth and take to lies instead? Agreeable lies, naturally, lies that suit the book of *ces Messieurs*.'

'It is not lies I want, but the truth.'

'Very well, it is the truth that I have been telling you. Yes, a woman did come to see Madame the night before she left for England. You show me those photographs, you ask me if I recognize the woman among them. I tell you what I have told you all along – my present eyesight is not good – it was growing dark – I did not look closely. I did not recognize the lady. If I saw her face to face I should probably not recognize her. There! You have it plainly for the fourth or fifth time.'

'And you cannot even remember if she was tall or short, dark or fair, young or old? It is hardly to be believed, that.'

Fournier spoke with irritable sarcasm.

'Then do not believe it. What do I care? A nice thing – to be mixed up with the police! I am ashamed. If Madame had not been killed high up in the air you would probably pretend that I, Georges, had poisoned her. The police are like that.' Poirot forestalled an angry retort on Fournier's part by slipping a tactful arm through that of his friend.

'Come, *mon vieux*,' he said. 'The stomach calls. A simple but satisfying meal, that is what I prescribe. Let us say *omelette aux champignons, sole à la Normande* – a cheese of Port Salut, and with it red wine. What wine exactly?'

Fournier glanced at his watch.

'True,' he said. 'It is one o'clock. Talking to this animal here –' He glared at Georges.

Poirot smiled encouragingly at the old man.

'It is understood,' he said. 'The nameless lady was neither tall nor short, fair nor dark, thin nor fat, but this at least you can tell us: Was she chic?'

'Chic?' said Georges, rather taken aback.

'I am answered,' said Poirot. 'She was *chic*. And I have a little idea, my friend, that she would look well in a bathing-dress.'

Georges stared at him.

'A bathing-dress? What is this about a bathing-dress?'

'A little idea of mine. A charming woman looks still more

charming in a bathing-dress. Do you not agree? See here.'

He passed to the old man a page torn from the *Sketch*.

There was a moment's pause. The old man gave a very slight start.

'You agree, do you not?' asked Poirot.

'They look well enough, those two,' said the old man, handing the sheet back. 'To wear nothing at all would be very nearly the same thing.'

'Ah,' said Poirot. 'That is because nowadays we have discovered the beneficial action of sun on the skin. It is very convenient, that.'

Georges condescended to give a hoarse chuckle, and moved away as Poirot and Fournier stepped out into the sunlit street.

Over the meal as outlined by Poirot, the little Belgian produced the little black memorandum book.

Fournier was much excited, though distinctly irate with Elise. Poirot argued the point.

'It is natural – very natural. The police? It is always a word frightening to that class. It embroils them in they know not what. It is the same everywhere – in every country.'

'That is where *you* score,' said Fournier. 'The private investigator gets more out of witnesses than you ever get through official channels. However, there is the other side of the picture. We have official records – the whole system of a big organization at our command.'

'So let us work together amicably,' said Poirot, smiling. 'This omelette is delicious.'

In the interval between the omelette and the sole, Fournier turned the pages of the black book. Then he made a pencilled entry in his notebook.

He looked across at Poirot.

'You have read through this? Yes?'

'No. I have only glanced at it. You permit?'

He took the book from Fournier.

When the cheese was placed before them Poirot laid down the book on the table, and the eyes of the two men met.

'There are certain entries,' began Fournier.

'Five,' said Poirot.

'I agree – five.'

He read out from his pocket-book:

'CL 52. English Peeress. Husband.
RT 362. Doctor. Harley Street.
MR 24. Forged Antiquities.
XVB 724. English. Embezzlement.
GF 45. Attempted Murder. English.'

'Excellent, my friend,' said Poirot. 'Our minds march together to a marvel. Of all the entries in that little book, those five seem to me to be the only ones that can in any way bear a relation to the persons travelling in the aeroplane. Let us take them one by one.'

'*English Peeress. Husband*,' said Fournier. 'That may conceivably apply to Lady Horbury. She is, I understand, a confirmed gambler. Nothing could be more likely than that she should borrow money from Giselle. Giselle's clients are usually of that type. The word *husband* may have one of two meanings. Either Giselle expected the husband to pay up his wife's debts, or she had some hold over Lady Horbury, a secret which she threatened to reveal to the lady's husband.'

'Precisely,' said Poirot. 'Either of those two alternatives might apply. I favour the second one myself, especially as I would be prepared to bet that the woman who visited Giselle the night before the aeroplane journey was Lady Horbury.'

'Ah, you think that, do you?'

'Yes, and I fancy you think the same. There is a touch of chivalry, I think, in our *concierge's* disposition. His persistence in remembering nothing at all about the visitor seems rather significant. Lady Horbury is an extremely pretty woman. Moreover, I observed his start – oh, a very slight one – when I handed him a reproduction of her in bathing costume from the *Sketch*. Yes, it was Lady Horbury who went to Giselle's that night.'

'She followed her to Paris from Le Pinet,' said Fournier slowly. 'It looks as though she were pretty desperate.'

'Yes, yes, I fancy that may be true.'

Fournier looked at him curiously.

'But it does not square with your private ideas, eh?'

'My friend, as I tell you, I have what I am convinced is the right clue pointing to the wrong person . . . I am very much in the dark. My clue cannot be wrong; and yet –'

'You wouldn't like to tell me what it is?' suggested Fournier.

'No, because I may, you see, be wrong – totally and utterly wrong. And in that case I might lead you, too, astray. No, let us each work according to our own ideas. To continue with our selected items from the little book.'

'*RT 362. Doctor. Harley Street*,' read out Fournier.

'A possible clue to Dr Bryant. There is nothing much to go on, but we must not neglect that line of investigation.'

'That, of course, will be the task of Inspector Japp.'

'And mine,' said Poirot. 'I, too, have my finger in this pie.'

'*MR 24. Forged Antiquities*,' read Fournier. 'Far fetched, perhaps, but it is just possible that that might apply to the Duponts. I can hardly credit it. M. Dupont is an archaeologist of world-wide reputation. He bears the highest character.'

'Which would facilitate matters very much for him,' said Poirot. 'Consider, my dear Fournier, how high has been the character, how lofty the sentiments, and how worthy of admiration the life of most swindlers of note – *before they are found out*!'

'True, only too true,' agreed the Frenchman with a sigh.

'A high reputation,' said Poirot, 'is the first necessity of a swindler's stock in trade. An interesting thought. But let us return to our list.'

'*XVB 724* is very ambiguous. *English. Embezzlement*.'

'Not very helpful,' agreed Poirot. 'Who embezzles? A solicitor? A bank clerk? Anyone in a position of trust in a commercial firm. Hardly an author, a dentist or a doctor. Mr James Ryder is the only representative of commerce. He may have embezzled money, he may have borrowed from Giselle to enable his theft to remain undetected. As to the last entry – *GF 45. Attempted Murder. English* – that gives us a very wide field. Author, dentist, doctor, businessman, steward, hairdresser's assistant, lady of birth and breeding – any one of those might be *GF 45*. In fact only the Duponts are exempt by reason of their nationality.'

With a gesture he summoned the waiter and asked for the bill.

'And where next, my friend?' he inquired.

'To the Sûreté. They may have some news for me.'

'Good. I will accompany you. Afterwards I have a little investigation of my own to make in which, perhaps, you will assist me.'

At the Sûreté Poirot renewed acquaintance with the Chief of the Detective Force, whom he had met some years previously in the course of one of his cases. M. Gilles was very affable and polite.

'Enchanted to learn that you are interesting yourself in this case, M. Poirot.'

'My faith, my dear M. Gilles, it happened under my nose. It is an insult, that, you agree? Hercule Poirot to sleep while murder is committed!'

M. Gilles shook his head tactfully.

'These machines! On a day of bad weather they are far from steady, far from steady. I myself have felt seriously incommoded once or twice.'

'They say that an army marches on its stomach,' said Poirot. 'But how much are the delicate convolutions of the brain influenced by the digestive apparatus? When the *mal de mer* seizes me I, Hercule Poirot, am a creature with no grey cells, no order, no method – a mere member of the human race somewhat below average intelligence! It is deplorable, but there it is! And talking of these matters, how is my excellent friend Giraud?'

Prudently ignoring the significance of the words 'these matters', M. Gilles replied that Giraud continued to advance in his career.

'He is most zealous. His energy is untiring.'

'It always was,' said Poirot. 'He ran to and fro. He crawled on all fours. He was here, there and everywhere. Not for one moment did he ever pause and reflect.'

'Ah, M. Poirot, that is your little foible. A man like Fournier will be more to your mind. He is of the newest school – all for the psychology. That should please you.'

'It does. It does.'

'He has a very good knowledge of English. That is why we sent him to Croydon to assist in this case. A very interesting case, M. Poirot. Madame Giselle was one of the best-known characters in Paris. And the manner of her death – extraordinary! A poisoned dart from a blowpipe in an aeroplane. I ask you! Is it possible that such a thing could happen?'

'Exactly,' cried Poirot. 'Exactly. You hit the nail upon the head. You place a finger unerringly – Ah, here is our good Fournier. You have news, I see.'

The melancholy-faced Fournier was looking quite eager and excited.

'Yes, indeed. A Greek antique dealer, Zeropoulos, has reported the sale of a blowpipe and darts three days before the murder. I propose now, Monsieur' – he bowed respectfully to his chief – 'to interview this man.'

'By all means,' said Gilles. 'Does M. Poirot accompany you?'

'If you please,' said Poirot. 'This is interesting – very interesting.'

The shop of M. Zeropoulos was in the Rue St Honoré. It was by way of being a high-class antique dealer's. There was a good deal of Rhages ware and other Persian pottery. There were one or two bronzes from Louristan, a good deal of inferior Indian jewellery, shelves of silks and embroideries from many countries, and a large proportion of perfectly worthless beads and cheap Egyptian goods. It was the kind of establishment in which you could spend a million francs on an object worth half a million, or ten francs on an object worth fifty centimes. It was patronized chiefly by American tourists and knowledgeable connoisseurs.

M. Zeropoulos himself was a short, stout little man with beady black eyes. He talked volubly and at great length.

The gentlemen were from the police? He was delighted to see them. Perhaps they would step into his private office. Yes, he had sold a blowpipe and darts – a South American curio – 'you comprehend, gentlemen, me, I sell a little of everything! I have my specialities. Persia is my speciality. M. Dupont, the esteemed M. Dupont he will answer for me. He himself comes always to see my collection – to see what new purchases I have made – to give his judgement on the genuineness of certain doubtful pieces. What a man! So learned! Such an eye! Such a *feel*. But I wander from the point. I have my collection – my valuable collection that all connoisseurs know – and also I have – well, frankly, Messieurs, let us call it junk! Foreign junk, that is understood, a little bit of everything – from the South Seas, from India, from Japan, from Borneo. No matter! Usually I have no fixed price for these things. If anyone takes an interest I make my estimate and I ask a price, and naturally I am beaten down, and in the end I take only half. And even then, I will admit it, the profit is good! These articles, I buy them from sailors usually at a very low price.'

M. Zeropoulos took a breath and went on happily, delighted with himself, his importance and the easy flow of his narration.

'This blowpipe and darts I have had it for a long time –

two years, perhaps. It was in that tray there, with a cowrie necklace and a Red Indian headdress, and one or two crude wooden idols and some inferior jade beads. Nobody remarks it, nobody notices it till there comes this American and asks me what it is.'

'An American?' said Fournier sharply.

'Yes, yes, an American – unmistakably an American. Not the best type of American, either – the kind that knows nothing about anything and just wants a curio to take home. He is of the type that makes the fortune of bead sellers in Egypt – that buys the most preposterous scarabs ever made in Czecho-Slovakia. Well, very quickly I size him up, I tell him about the habits of certain tribes, the deadly poisons they use. I explain how very rare and unusual it is that anything of this kind comes into the market. He asks the price and I tell him. It is my American price, not quite as high as formerly (alas! they have had the depression over there). I wait for him to bargain, but straightaway he pays my price. I am stupefied. It is a pity; I might have asked more! I give him the blowpipe and the darts wrapped up in a parcel and he takes them away. It is finished. But afterwards when I read in the paper of this astounding murder I wonder – yes, I wonder very much. And I communicate with the police.'

'We are much obliged to you, M. Zeropoulos,' said Fournier politely. 'This blowpipe and dart – you think you would be able to identify them? At the moment they are in London, you understand, but an opportunity will be given you of identifying them.'

'The blowpipe was about so long,' M. Zeropoulos measured a space on his desk, 'and so thick – you see, like this pen of mine. It was of a light colour. There were four darts. They were long pointed thorns, slightly discoloured at the tips, with a little fluff of red silk on them.'

'*Red silk*?' asked Poirot keenly.

'Yes, Monsieur. A cerise red – somewhat faded.'

'That is curious,' said Fournier. 'You are sure that there was not one of them with a black and yellow fluff of silk?'

'Black and yellow? No, Monsieur.'

The dealer shook his head.

Fournier glanced at Poirot. There was a curious satisfied smile on the little man's face.

Fournier wondered why. Was it because Zeropoulos was lying, or was it for some other reason?

Fournier said doubtfully, 'It is very possible that this blowpipe and dart has nothing whatever to do with the case. It is just one chance in fifty, perhaps. Nevertheless, I should like as full a description as possible of this American.'

Zeropoulos spread out a pair of Oriental hands.

'He was just an American. His voice was in his nose. He could not speak French. He was chewing the gum. He had tortoise-shell glasses. He was tall and, I think, not very old.'

'Fair or dark?'

'I could hardly say. He had his hat on.'

'Would you know him again if you saw him?'

Zeropoulos seemed doubtful.

'I could not say. So many Americans come and go. He was not remarkable in any way.'

Fournier showed him the collection of snapshots, but without avail. None of them, Zeropoulos thought, was the man.

'Probably a wild-goose chase,' said Fournier as they left the shop.

'It is possible, yes,' agreed Poirot. 'But I do not think so. The price tickets were of the same shape and there are one or two points of interest about the story and about M. Zeropoulos's remarks. And now, my friend, having been upon one wild-goose chase, indulge me and come upon another.'

'Where to?'

'To the Boulevard des Capucines.'

'Let me see, that is –?'

'The office of Universal Airlines.'

'Of course. But we have already made perfunctory inquiries there. They could tell us nothing of interest.'

Poirot tapped him kindly on the shoulder.

'Ah, but, you see, an answer depends on the questions. You did not know what questions to ask.'

'And you do?'

'Well, I have a certain little idea.'

He would say no more, and in due course they arrived at the Boulevard des Capucines.

The office of Universal Airlines was quite small. A smart-looking dark man was behind a highly-polished wooden counter and a boy of about fifteen was sitting at a typewriter.

Fournier produced his credentials and the man, whose name was Jules Perrot, declared himself to be entirely at their service.

At Poirot's suggestion, the typewriting boy was dispatched to the farthest corner.

'It is very confidential what we have to say,' he explained.

Jules Perrot looked pleasantly excited.

'Yes, Messieurs?'

'It is this matter of the murder of Madame Giselle.'

'Ah, yes, I recollect. I think I have already answered some questions on the subject.'

'Precisely, precisely. But it is necessary to have the facts very exactly. Now Madame Giselle received her place – when?'

'I think that point has already been settled. She booked her seat by telephone on the 17th.'

'That was for the 12 o'clock service on the following day?'

'Yes, Monsieur.'

'But I understand from her maid that it was on the 8.45 am service that Madame reserved a seat.'

'No, no – at least this is what happened. Madame's maid asked for the 8.45 service, but that service was already booked up, so we gave her a seat on the 12 o'clock instead.'

'Ah, I see. I see.'

'Yes, Monsieur.'

'I see – I see – but all the same it is curious – decidedly it is curious.'

The clerk looked at him inquiringly.

'It is only that a friend of mine decided to go to England at a moment's notice, went to England on the 8.45 service that morning, and the plane was half empty.'

M. Perrot turned over some papers. He blew his nose.

'Possibly your friend has mistaken the day. The day before or the day after –'

'Not at all. It was the day of the murder, because my friend said that if he had missed the plane, as he nearly did, he would have actually been one of the passengers in the *Prometheus*.'

'Ah, indeed. Yes, very curious. Of course, sometimes people do not arrive at the last minute, and then, naturally, there are vacant places . . . and then sometimes there are mistakes. I have to get in touch with Le Bourget; they are not always accurate –'

The mild inquiring gaze of Hercule Poirot seemed to be upsetting to Jules Perrot. He came to a stop. His eyes shifted. A little bead of perspiration came out on his forehead.

'Two quite possible explanations,' said Poirot, 'but somehow, I fancy, not the true explanation. Don't you think it might perhaps be better to make a clean breast of the matter?'

'A clean breast of what? I don't understand you.'

'Come, come. You understand me very well. This is a case of murder – *murder*, M. Perrot. Remember that, if you please. If you withhold information it may well be very serious for you – very serious indeed. The police will take a very grave view. You are obstructing the ends of justice.'

Jules Perrot stared at him. His mouth fell open. His hands shook.

'Come,' said Poirot. His voice was authoritative, autocratic. 'We want precise information, if you please. How much were you paid, and who paid you?'

'I meant no harm – I had no idea – I never guessed . . .'

'How much, and who by?'

'F-five thousand francs. I never saw the man before. I – this will ruin me . . .'

'What will ruin you is not to speak out. Come, now, we know the worst. Tell us exactly how it happened.'

The perspiration rolling down his forehead, Jules Perrot spoke rapidly in little jerks.

'I meant no harm . . . Upon my honour, I meant no harm. A man came in. He said he was going to England on the following day. He wanted to negotiate a loan from – from Madame Giselle, but he wanted their meeting to be unpremeditated. He said it would give him a better chance. He said that he knew she was going to England on the following day. All I had to do was to tell her the early service was full up and to give her seat No. 2 in the *Prometheus*. I swear, Messieurs, that I saw nothing very wrong in that. What difference could it make? – that is what I thought. Americans are like that – they do business in unconventional ways –'

'Americans?' said Fournier sharply.

'Yes, this Monsieur was an American.'

'Describe him.'

'He was tall, stooped, had grey hair, horn-rimmed glasses and a little goatee beard.'

'Did he book a seat himself?'

'Yes, Monsieur, seat No. 1 – next to – to the one I was to keep for Madame Giselle.'

'In what name?'

'Silas – Silas Harper.'

'There was no one of that name travelling, and no one occupied seat No. 1.'

Poirot shook his head gently.

'I saw by the paper that there was no one of that name. That is why I thought there was no need to mention the matter. Since this man did not go by the plane –'

Fournier shot him a cold glance.

'You have withheld valuable information from the police,' he said. 'This is a very serious matter.'

Together he and Poirot left the office, leaving Jules Perrot staring after them with a frightened face.

On the pavement outside, Fournier removed his hat and bowed.

'I salute you, M. Poirot. What gave you this idea?'

'Two separate sentences. One this morning when I heard a man in our plane say that he had crossed on the morning of the murder in a nearly empty plane. The second sentence was that uttered by Elise when she said that she rung up the office of Universal Airlines and that there was no room on the early morning service. Now those two statements did not agree. I remembered the steward on the *Prometheus* saying that he had seen Madame Giselle before on the early service – so it was clearly her custom to go by the 8.45 am plane.

'*But somebody wanted her to go on the 12 o'clock* – somebody who was already travelling by the *Prometheus*. Why did the clerk say that the early service was booked up? A mistake, or a deliberate lie? I fancied the latter . . . I was right.'

'Every minute this case gets more puzzling,' cried Fournier. 'First we seem to be on the track of a woman. Now it is a man. This American –'

He stopped and looked at Poirot.

The latter nodded gently.

'Yes, my friend,' he said. 'It is so easy to be an American – here in Paris! A nasal voice – the chewing gum – the little goatee – the horn-rimmed spectacles – all the appurtenances of the stage American . . .'

He took from his pocket the page he had torn from the *Sketch.*

'What are you looking at?'

'At a countess in her bathing suit.'

'You think –? But no, she is petite, charming, fragile – she could not impersonate a tall stooping American. She has been an actress, yes, but to act such a part is out of the question. No, my friend, that idea will not do.'

'I never said it would,' said Hercule Poirot.

And still he looked earnestly at the printed page.

CHAPTER 12

AT HORBURY CHASE

Lord Horbury stood by the sideboard and helped himself absent-mindedly to kidneys.

Stephen Horbury was twenty-seven years of age. He had a narrow head and a long chin. He looked very much what he was – a sporting out-of-door kind of man without anything very spectacular in the way of brains. He was kind-hearted, slightly priggish, intensely loyal and invincibly obstinate.

He took his heaped plate back to the table and began to eat. Presently he opened a newspaper, but immediately, with a frown, he cast it aside. He thrust aside his unfinished plate, drank some coffee and rose to his feet. He paused uncertainly for a minute, then with a slight nod of the head he left the dining-room, crossed the wide hall and went upstairs. He tapped at a door and waited for a minute. From inside the room a clear high voice cried out, 'Come in.'

Lord Horbury went in.

It was a wide beautiful bedroom facing south. Cicely Horbury was in bed, a great carved oak Elizabethan bed. Very lovely she looked, too, in her rose chiffon draperies, with the curling gold of her hair. A breakfast tray with the remains of orange juice and coffee on it was on a table beside her. She was opening her letters. Her maid was moving about the room.

Any man might be excused if his breath came a little faster confronted by so much loveliness; but the charming picture his wife presented affected Lord Horbury not at all.

There had been a time, three years ago, when the breathtaking loveliness of his Cicely had set the young man's senses reeling. He had been madly, wildly, passionately in love. All that was over. He had been mad. He was now sane.

Lady Horbury said in some surprise:

'Why, Stephen?'

He said abruptly, 'I'd like to talk to you alone.'

'Madeleine.' Lady Horbury spoke to her maid. 'Leave all that. Get out.'

The French girl murmured, '*Très bien*, m'lady', shot a quick interested look out of the corner of her eye at Lord Horbury and left the room.

Lord Horbury waited till she had shut the door, then he said:

'I'd like to know, Cicely, just exactly what is behind this idea of coming down here.'

Lady Horbury shrugged her slender, beautiful shoulders.

'After all, why not?'

'Why not? It seems to me there are a good many reasons.'

His wife murmured, 'Oh, reasons . . .'

'Yes, reasons. You'll remember that we agreed that as things were between us, it would be as well to give up this farce of living together. You were to have the town house and a generous – an extremely generous – allowance. Within certain limits you were to go your own way. Why this sudden return?'

Again Cicely shrugged her shoulders.

'I thought it – better.'

'You mean, I suppose, that it's money?'

Lady Horbury said, 'My God, how I hate you. You're the meanest man alive.'

'Mean? Mean, you say, when it's because of you and your senseless extravagance that there's a mortgage on Horbury.'

'Horbury – Horbury – that's all you care for! Horses and hunting and shooting and crops and tiresome old farmers. God, what a life for a woman.'

'Some women enjoy it.'

'Yes, women like Venetia Kerr, who's half a horse herself. You ought to have married a woman like that.'

Lord Horbury walked over to the window.

'It's a little late to say that. I married you.'

'And you can't get out of it,' said Cicely. Her laugh was malicious, triumphant. 'You'd like to get rid of me, but you can't.'

He said, 'Need we go into all this?'

'Very much God and the Old School, aren't you? Most of my friends fairly laugh their heads off when I tell them the kind of things you say.'

'They are welcome to do so. Shall we get back to our original subject of discussion – your reason for coming here?'

But his wife would not follow his lead. She said:

'You advertised in the papers that you wouldn't be responsible for my debts. Do you call that a gentlemanly thing to do?'

'I regret having had to take that step. I warned you, you will remember. Twice I paid up. But there are limits. Your insensate passion for gambling – well, why discuss it? But I do want to know what prompted you to come down to Horbury. You've always hated the place, been bored to death here.'

Cicely Horbury, her small face sullen, said, 'I thought it better – just now.'

'Better – just now?' He repeated the words thoughtfully. Then he asked a question sharply: 'Cicely, had you been borrowing from that old French moneylender?'

'Which one? I don't know what you mean.'

'You know perfectly what I mean. I mean the woman who was murdered on the plane from Paris – the plane on which you travelled home. Had you borrowed money from her?'

'No, of course not. What an idea!'

'Now, don't be a little fool over this, Cicely. If that woman did lend you money, you'd better tell me about it. Remember the business isn't over and finished with. The verdict at the inquest was wilful murder by a person or persons unknown. The police of both countries are at work. It's only a matter of time before they come on the truth. The woman's sure to have left records of her dealings. If anything crops up to connect you with her we should be prepared beforehand. We must have ffoulkes's advice on the matter.' (ffoulkes, ffoulkes, Wilbraham and ffoulkes were the family solicitors who for generations had dealt with the Horbury estate.)

'Didn't I give evidence in that damned court and say I had never heard of the woman?'

'I don't think that proves very much,' said her husband dryly. 'If you did have dealings with this Giselle, you can be sure the police will find it out.'

Cicely sat up angrily in bed.

'Perhaps you think I killed her – stood up there in that plane and puffed darts at her from a blowpipe. Of all the crazy businesses!'

'The whole thing sounds mad,' Stephen agreed thoughtfully. 'But I do want you to realize your position.'

'What position? There isn't any position. You don't believe a word I say. It's damnable. And why be so anxious about me all of a sudden? A lot you care about what happens to me. You dislike me. You hate me. You'd be glad if I died tomorrow. Why pretend?'

'Aren't you exaggerating a little? In any case, old-fashioned though you think me, I do happen to care about my family name – an out-of-date sentiment which you will probably despise. But there it is.'

Turning abruptly on his heel, he left the room.

A pulse was beating in his temple. Thoughts followed each other rapidly through his head.

'Dislike? Hate? Yes, that's true enough. Should I be glad if she died tomorrow? My God, yes! I'd feel like a man who's been let out of prison. What a queer beastly business life is! When I first saw her in *Do It Now*, what a child, what an adorable child she looked! So fair and so lovely . . . Damned young fool! I was mad about her – crazy . . . She seemed everything that was adorable and sweet, and all the time she was what she is now – vulgar, vicious, spiteful, empty-headed . . . I can't even see her loveliness now.'

He whistled and a spaniel came running to him, looking up at him with adoring sentimental eyes.

He said, 'Good old Betsy,' and fondled the long, fringed ears.

He thought, 'Funny term of disparagement, to call a woman a bitch. A bitch like you, Betsy, is worth nearly all the women I've met put together.'

Cramming an old fishing hat on his head, he left the house accompanied by the dog.

This aimless saunter of his round the estate began gradually to soothe his jangled nerves. He stroked the neck of his favourite hunter, had a word with the groom, then he went to the Home Farm and had a chat with the farmer's wife. He was walking along a narrow lane, Betsy at his heels, when he met Venetia Kerr on her bay mare.

Venetia looked her best upon a horse. Lord Horbury looked up at her with admiration, fondness and a queer sense of homecoming.

He said, 'Hullo, Venetia.'

'Hullo, Stephen.'

'Where've you been? Out in the five-acre?'

'Yes, she's coming along nicely, isn't she?'

'First-rate. Have you seen that two-year-old of mine I bought at Chattisley's sale?'

They talked horses for some minutes, then he said:

'By the way, Cicely's here.'

'Here, at Horbury?'

Against Venetia's code to show surprise, but she could not quite keep the undertone of it out of her voice.

'Yes. Turned up last night.'

There was a silence between them. Then Stephen said, 'You were at that inquest, Venetia. How – how – er – did it go?'

She considered a moment.

'Well, nobody was saying very much, if you know what I mean.'

'Police weren't giving anything away?'

'No.'

Stephen said, 'Must have been rather an unpleasant business for you.'

'Well, I didn't exactly enjoy it. But it wasn't too devastating. The coroner was quite decent.'

Stephen slashed absent-mindedly at the hedge.

'I say, Venetia, any idea – have *you*, I mean – as to who did it?'

Venetia Kerr shook her head slowly.

'No.' She paused a minute, seeking how best and most tactfully to put into words what she wanted to say. She achieved it at last with a little laugh. 'Anyway, it wasn't Cicely or me. That I do know. She'd have spotted me and I'd have spotted her.'

Stephen laughed too.

'That's all right, then,' he said cheerfully.

He passed it off as a joke, but she heard the relief in his voice. So he *had* been thinking –

She switched her thoughts away.

'Venetia,' said Stephen, 'I've known you a long time, haven't I?'

'H'm, yes. Do you remember those awful dancing classes we used to go to as children?'

'Do I not? I feel I can say things to you –'

'Of course you can.' She hesitated, then went on in a calm, matter-of-fact tone: 'It's Cicely, I suppose?'

'Yes. Look here, Venetia. Was Cicely mixed up with this woman Giselle in any way?'

Venetia answered slowly.

'I don't know. I've been in the South of France, remember. I haven't heard the Le Pinet gossip yet.'

'What do you think?'

'Well, candidly, I shouldn't be surprised.'

Stephen nodded thoughtfully. Venetia said gently:

'Need it worry you? I mean you live pretty semi-detached lives, don't you? This business is her affair, not yours.'

'As long as she's my wife, it's bound to be my business too.'

'Can't you – er – agree to a divorce?'

'A trumped-up business, you mean? I doubt if she'd accept it.'

'Would you divorce her if you had the chance?'

'If I had a cause I certainly would.'

He spoke grimly.

'I suppose,' said Venetia thoughtfully, 'she knows that.'

'Yes.'

They were both silent. Venetia thought, 'She has the morals of a cat! I know that well enough. But she's careful. She's shrewd as they make 'em.' Aloud she said, 'So there's nothing doing?'

He shook his head. Then he said, 'If I were free, Venetia, would you marry me?'

Looking very straight between her horse's ears, Venetia said in a voice carefully devoid of emotion:

'I suppose I would.'

Stephen! She'd always loved Stephen, always since the old days of dancing classes and cubbing and birds' nesting. And Stephen had been fond of her, but not fond enough to prevent him from falling desperately, wildly, madly in love with a clever calculating cat of a chorus girl . . .

Stephen said, 'We could have a marvellous life together . . .'

Pictures floated before his eyes: hunting – tea and muffins –

the smell of wet earth and leaves – children . . . All the things that Cicely could never share with him, that Cicely would never give him. A kind of mist came over his eyes. Then he heard Venetia speaking, still in that flat, emotionless voice:

'Stephen, if you care – what about it? If we went off together Cicely would have to divorce you.'

He interrupted her fiercely. 'My God, do you think I'd let you do a thing like that?'

'I shouldn't care.'

'I should.'

He spoke with finality.

Venetia thought, 'That's that. It's a pity, really. He's hopelessly prejudiced, but rather a dear. I wouldn't like him to be different.'

Aloud she said, 'Well, Stephen, I'll be getting along.'

She touched her horse gently with her heel. As she turned to wave goodbye to Stephen their eyes met, and in that glance was all the feeling that their careful words had avoided.

As she rounded the corner of the lane Venetia dropped her whip. A man walking picked it up and returned it to her with an exaggerated bow.

'A foreigner,' she thought as she thanked him. 'I seem to remember his face.' Half of her mind searched through the summer days at Juan les Pins while the other half thought of Stephen.

Only just as she reached home did memory suddenly pull her half-dreaming brain up with a jerk.

'*The little man who gave me his seat in the aeroplane. They said at the inquest he was a detective.*' And hard on that came another thought: '*What is he doing down here?*'

CHAPTER 13

AT ANTOINE'S

Jane presented herself at Antoine's on the morning after the inquest with some trepidation of spirit.

The person who was usually regarded as M. Antoine himself, and whose real name was Andrew Leech and whose claims to foreign nationality consisted of having had a Jewish mother, greeted her with an ominous frown.

It was by now second nature to him to speak in broken English once within the portals of Bruton Street.

He upbraided Jane as a complete *imbécile.* Why did she wish to travel by air, anyway? What an idea! Her escapade would do his establishment infinite harm. Having vented his spleen to the full, Jane was permitted to escape, receiving as she did so a large-sized wink from her friend Gladys.

Gladys was an ethereal blonde with a haughty demeanour and a faint, faraway professional voice. In private her voice was hoarse and jocular.

'Don't you worry, dear,' she said to Jane. 'The old brute's sitting on the fence watching which way the cat will jump. And it's my belief it isn't going to jump the way he thinks it is. Ta ta, dearie, here's my old devil coming in, damn her eyes. I suppose she'll be in seventeen tantrums as usual. I hope she hasn't brought that damned lap-dog with her.'

A moment later Gladys's voice could be heard with its faint, faraway notes . . .

'Good morning, Madam, not brought your sweet little Pekingese with you? Shall we get on with the shampoo, and then we'll be all ready for M. Henri.'

Jane had just entered the adjoining cubicle where a henna-haired woman was sitting waiting, examining her face in the glass and saying to a friend:

'Darling, my face is really *too* frightful this morning, it really is . . .'

The friend, who in a bored manner was turning over the pages of a three-weeks-old *Sketch*, replied uninterestedly:

'Do you think so, my sweet? It seems to me much the same as usual.'

On the entrance of Jane the bored friend stopped her languid survey of the *Sketch* and subjected Jane to a piercing stare instead.

Then she said, 'It is, darling. I'm sure of it.'

'Good morning, Madam,' said Jane with that airy brightness expected of her and which she could now produce quite mechanically and without any effort whatsoever. 'It's quite a long time since we've seen you here. I expect you've been abroad.'

'Antibes,' said the henna-haired woman, who in her turn was staring at Jane with the frankest interest.

'How lovely,' said Jane with false enthusiasm. 'Let me see, is it a shampoo and set, or are you having a tint today?'

Momentarily diverted from her scrutiny, the henna-haired woman leaned forward and examined her hair attentively.

'I think I could go another week. Heavens, what a fright I look!'

The friend said, 'Well, darling, what can you expect at this time of the morning?'

Jane said, 'Ah! wait until M. Georges has finished with you.'

'Tell me,' the woman resumed her stare, 'are you the girl who gave evidence at the inquest yesterday – the girl who was in the aeroplane?'

'Yes, Madam.'

'How too terribly thrilling! Tell me about it.'

Jane did her best to please.

'Well, Madam, it was all rather dreadful, really –' She plunged into narration, answering questions as they came. What had the old woman looked like? Was it true that there were two French detectives aboard and that the whole thing was mixed up with the French Government scandals? Was Lady Horbury on board? Was she really as good-looking as everyone said? Who did she, Jane, think had actually done the murder? They said the whole thing was being hushed up for Government reasons, and so on and so on . . .

This first ordeal was only a forerunner of many others all on the same lines. Everyone wanted to be done by 'the girl who was on the plane'. Everyone was able to say to their friends, 'My dear, positively too marvellous. The girl at my hairdresser's is *the* girl . . . Yes, I should go there if I were you – they do your hair very well . . . Jeanne, her name is . . . rather a little thing, big eyes. She'll tell you all about it if you ask her nicely . . .'

By the end of the week Jane felt her nerves giving way under the strain. Sometimes she felt that if she had to go through the recital once again she would scream or attack her questioner with the dryer.

However, in the end she hit upon a better way of relieving her feelings. She approached M. Antoine and boldly demanded a rise of salary.

'You ask that? You have the impudence, when it is only out of kindness of heart that I keep you here, after you have been mixed up in a murder case? Many men, less kindhearted than I, would have dismissed you immediately.'

'That's nonsense,' said Jane coolly. 'I'm a draw in this place and you know it. If you want me to go, I'll go. I'll easily get what I want from Henri's or the Maison Richet.'

'And who is to know you have gone there? Of what importance are you anyway?'

'I met one or two reporters at that inquest,' said Jane. 'One of them would give my change of establishment any publicity needed.'

Because he feared that this was indeed so, grumblingly M. Antoine agreed to Jane's demands. Gladys applauded her friend heartily.

'Good for you, dear,' she said. 'Ikey Andrew was no match for you that time. If a girl couldn't fend for herself a bit I don't know where we'd all be. Grit, dear, that's what you've got, and I admire you for it.'

'I can fight for my own hand all right,' said Jane, her small chin lifting itself pugnaciously. 'I've had to all my life.'

'Hard lines, dear,' said Gladys. 'But keep your end up with Ikey Andrew. He likes you all the better for it, really. Meekness doesn't pay in this life – but I don't think we're either of us troubled by too much of that.'

Thereafter Jane's narrative, repeated daily with little variation, sank into the equivalent of a part played on the stage.

The promised dinner and theatre with Norman Gale had duly come off. It was one of those enchanting evenings when every word and confidence exchanged seemed to reveal a bond of sympathy and shared tastes.

They liked dogs and disliked cats. They both hated oysters and loved smoked salmon. They liked Greta Garbo and disliked Katharine Hepburn. They didn't like fat women and admired really jet-black hair. They disliked very red nails. They disliked loud voices, noisy restaurants and negroes. They preferred buses to tubes.

It seemed almost miraculous that two people should have so many points of agreement.

One day at Antoine's, opening her bag, Jane let a letter from Norman fall out. As she picked it up with a slightly heightened colour, Gladys pounced upon her.

'Who's your boy friend, dear?'

'I don't know what you mean,' retorted Jane, her colour rising.

'Don't tell me! I know that letter isn't from your mother's great-uncle. I wasn't born yesterday. Who is he, Jane?'

'It's someone – a man – that I met at Le Pinet. He's a dentist.'

'A dentist,' said Gladys with lively distaste. 'I suppose he's got very white teeth and a smile.'

Jane was forced to admit that this was indeed the case.

'He's got a very brown face and very blue eyes.'

'Anyone can have a brown face,' said Gladys. 'It may be the seaside or it may come out of a bottle, 2s. 11d. at the chemist's. *Handsome Men are Slightly Bronzed.* The eyes sound all right. But a dentist! Why, if he was going to kiss you you'd feel he was going to say, "Open a little wider, please".'

'Don't be an idiot, Gladys.'

'You needn't be so touchy, my dear. I see you've got it badly. Yes, Mr Henry, I'm just coming . . . Drat Henry! Thinks he's God Almighty, the way he orders us girls about!'

The letter had been to suggest dinner on Saturday evening. At lunch-time on Saturday when Jane received her augmented pay she felt full of high spirits.

'And to think,' said Jane to herself, 'that I was worrying so, that day coming over in the aeroplane. Everything's turned out beautifully . . . Life is really too marvellous.'

So full of exuberance did she feel that she decided to be extravagant and lunch at the Corner House and enjoy the accompaniment of music to her food.

She seated herself at a table for four, where there were already a middle-aged woman and a young man sitting. The middle-aged woman was just finishing her lunch. Presently she called for her bill, picked up a large collection of parcels and departed.

Jane, as was her custom, read a book as she ate. Looking up as she turned a page, she noticed the young man opposite her staring at her very intently, and at the same moment realized that his face was vaguely familiar to her.

Just as she made these discoveries the young man caught her eye and bowed.

'Excuse me, Mademoiselle, you do not recognize me?'

Jane looked at him more attentively. He had a fair boyish-looking face, attractive more by reason of its extreme mobility than because of any actual claim to good looks.

'We have not been introduced, it is true,' went on the young man, 'unless you call murder an introduction and the fact that we both gave evidence in the coroner's court.'

'Of course,' said Jane. 'How stupid of me! I thought I knew your face. You are –?'

'Jean Dupont,' said the man and gave a funny, rather engaging little bow.

A remembrance flashed into Jane's mind of a dictum of Gladys's, expressed perhaps without undue delicacy.

'If there's one fellow after you, there's sure to be another. Seems to be a law of Nature. Sometimes it's three or four.'

Now Jane had always led an austere, hard-working life (rather like the description after the act of girls who were missing – 'She was a bright, cheerful girl with no men friends, etc.'). Jane had been 'a bright, cheerful girl with no men friends'. Now it seemed that men friends were rolling up all round. There was no doubt about it, Jean Dupont's face as he leaned across the table held more than mere interested politeness. He was pleased to be sitting opposite Jane. He was more than pleased – he was delighted.

Jane thought to herself with a touch of misgiving:

'He's French, though. You've got to look out with the French, they always say so.'

'You're still in England, then,' said Jane, and silently cursed herself for the extreme inanity of her remark.

'Yes. My father has been to Edinburgh to give a lecture there, and we have stayed with friends also. But now – tomorrow – we return to France.'

'I see.'

'The police, they have not made an arrest yet?' said Jean Dupont.

'No, there's not even been anything about it in the papers lately. Perhaps they've given it up.'

Jean Dupont shook his head. 'No, no, they will not have given it up. They work silently' – he made an expressive gesture – 'in the dark.'

'Don't,' said Jane uneasily. 'You give me the creeps.'

'Yes, it is not a very nice feeling, to have been so close when a murder was committed . . .' He added, 'And I was closer than you were. I was very close indeed. Sometimes I do not like to think of that . . .'

'Who do you think did it?' asked Jane. 'I've wondered and wondered.'

Jean Dupont shrugged his shoulders.

'It was not I. She was far too ugly!'

'Well,' said Jane, 'I suppose you would rather kill an ugly woman than a good-looking one?'

'Not at all. If a woman is good-looking you are fond of her – she treats you badly – she makes you jealous, mad with jealousy. "Good," you say, "I will kill her. It will be a satisfaction".'

'And is it a satisfaction?'

'That, Mademoiselle, I do not know, because I have not yet tried.' He laughed, then shook his head. 'But an ugly old woman like Giselle – who would want to bother to kill her?'

'Well, that's one way of looking at it,' said Jane. She frowned. 'It seems rather terrible, somehow, to think that perhaps she was young and pretty once.'

'I know, I know.' He became suddenly grave. 'It is the great tragedy of life, that women grow old.'

'You seem to think a lot about women and their looks,' said Jane.

'Naturally. It is the most interesting subject possible. That seems strange to you because you are English. An Englishman thinks first of his work – his job, he calls it – and then of his sport, and last – a good way last – of his wife. Yes, yes, it is really so. Why, imagine, in a little hotel in Syria was an Englishman whose wife had been taken ill. He himself had to be somewhere in Iraq by a certain date. *Eh bien*, would you believe it, he left his wife and went on so as to be "on duty" in time. And both he and his wife thought that quite natural; they thought him noble, unselfish. But the doctor, who was not English, thought him a barbarian. A wife, a human being – that should come first; to do one's job – that is something much less important.'

'I don't know,' said Jane. 'One's work has to come first, I suppose.'

'But why? You see, you too have the same point of view. By doing one's work one obtains money – by indulging and looking after a woman one spends it – so the last is much more noble an ideal than the first.'

Jane laughed.

'Oh, well,' she said. 'I think I'd rather be regarded as a mere luxury and self-indulgence, than regarded sternly as a First Duty. I'd rather a man felt that he was enjoying himself looking after me than that he should feel I was a duty to be attended to.'

'No one, Mademoiselle, would be likely to feel that with you.'

Jane blushed slightly at the earnestness of the young man's tone. He went on talking quickly:

'I have only been in England once before. It was very interesting to me the other day at the – inquest, you call it? – to study three young and charming women, all so different from one another.'

'What did you think of us all?' asked Jane, amused.

'That Lady Horbury – bah, I know her type well. It is very exotic – very, very expensive. You see it sitting round the baccarat table – the soft face – the hard expression – and you know – you know so well what it will be like in, say fifteen years. She lives for sensation, that one. For high play, perhaps for drugs . . . *Au fond*, she is uninteresting!'

'And Miss Kerr?'

'Ah, she is very, very English. She is the kind that any shop-keeper on the Riviera will give credit to; they are very discerning, our shopkeepers. Her clothes are very well cut, but rather like a man's. She walks about as though she owns the earth. She is not conceited about it – she is just an Englishwoman. She knows which department of England different people come from. It is true. I have heard ones like her in Egypt. "What? The Etceteras are here? The Yorkshire Etceteras? Oh, the Shropshire Etceteras".'

His mimicry was good. Jane laughed at the drawling, well-bred tones.

'And then – me,' she said.

'And then you. And I say to myself, "How nice, how very nice it would be if I were to see her again one day." And here I am sitting opposite you. The gods arrange things very well sometimes.'

Jane said, 'You're an archaeologist, aren't you? You dig up things?'

And she listened with keen attention while Jean Dupont talked of his work.

Jane gave a little sigh at last.

'You've been in so many countries. You've seen so much. It all sounds so fascinating. And I shall never go anywhere or see anything.'

'You would like that – to go abroad – to see wild parts of the earth? You would not be able to get your hair waved, remember.'

'It waves by itself,' said Jane, laughing.

She looked up at the clock and hastily summoned the waitress for her bill.

Jean Dupont said with a little embarrassment, 'Mademoiselle, I wonder if you would permit – as I have told you, I return to France tomorrow – if you would dine with me tonight.'

'I'm so sorry, I can't. I'm dining with someone.'

'Ah! I'm sorry, very sorry. You will come again to Paris, soon?'

'I don't expect so.'

'And me, I do not know when I shall be in London again! It is sad!'

He stood a moment, holding Jane's hand in his.

'I shall hope to see you again, very much,' he said, and sounded as though he meant it.

CHAPTER 14

AT MUSWELL HILL

At about the time that Jane was leaving Antoine's, Norman Gale was saying in a hearty professional tone, 'Just a little tender, I'm afraid . . . Guide me if I hurt you –'

His expert hand guided the electric drill.

'There, that's all over. Miss Ross?'

Miss Ross was immediately at his elbow stirring a minute white concoction on a slab.

Norman Gale completed his filling and said, 'Let me see, it's next Tuesday you're coming for those others?'

His patient, rinsing her mouth ardently, burst into a fluent explanation. She was going away – so sorry – would have to cancel the next appointment. Yes, she would let him know when she got back.

And she escaped hurriedly from the room.

'Well,' said Gale, 'that's all for today.'

Miss Ross said, 'Lady Higginson rang up to say she must give up her appointment next week. She wouldn't make another. Oh, and Colonel Blunt can't come on Thursday.'

Norman Gale nodded. His face hardened.

Every day was the same. People ringing up. Cancelled appointments. All varieties of excuses – going away – going abroad – got a cold – may not be here –

It didn't matter what reason they gave, the real reason Norman had just seen quite unmistakably in his last patient's eye as he reached for the drill . . . a look of sudden panic . . .

He could have written down the woman's thoughts on paper.

'Oh, dear, of course he was in that aeroplane when that woman was murdered . . . I wonder . . . You do hear of people going off their heads and doing the most senseless crimes. It really isn't safe. The man might be a homicidal lunatic. They look the same as other people, I've always heard . . . I believe I always felt there was rather a peculiar look in his eye . . .'

'Well,' said Gale, 'it looks like being a quiet week next week, Miss Ross.'

'Yes, a lot of people have dropped out. Oh, well, you can do with a rest. You worked so hard earlier in the summer.'

'It doesn't look as though I were going to have a chance of working very hard in the autumn, does it?'

Miss Ross did not reply. She was saved from having to do so by the telephone ringing. She went out of the room to answer it.

Norman dropped some instruments into the sterilizer, thinking hard.

'Let's see how we stand. No beating about the bush. This business has about done for me professionally. Funny, it's done well for Jane. People come on purpose to gape at her. Come to think of it, that's what's wrong here – they *have* to gape at me, and they don't like it! Nasty helpless feeling you have in a dentist's chair. If the dentist were to run amuck . . .

'What a strange business murder is! You'd think it was a perfectly straightforward issue – and it isn't. It affects all sorts of queer things you'd never think of . . . Come back to facts. As a dentist I seem to be about done for . . . What would happen, I wonder, if they arrested the Horbury woman? Would my patients come trooping back? Hard to say. Once the rot's set in . . . Oh, well, what does it matter? I don't care. Yes, I do – because of

Jane . . . Jane's adorable. I want her. And I can't have her – yet . . . A damnable nuisance.'

He smiled. 'I feel it's going to be all right . . . She cares . . . She'll wait . . . Damn it, I shall go to Canada – yes, that's it – and make money there.'

He laughed to himself.

Miss Ross came back into the room.

'That was Mrs Lorrie. She's sorry –'

'– but she may be going to Timbuctoo,' finished Norman. '*Vive les rats*! You'd better look out for another post, Miss Ross. This seems to be a sinking ship.'

'Oh, Mr Gale, I shouldn't think of deserting you . . .'

'Good girl. You're not a rat, anyway. But seriously I mean it. If something doesn't happen to clear up this mess I'm done for.'

'Something *ought* to be done about it!' said Miss Ross with energy. 'I think the police are *disgraceful*. They're not *trying*.'

Norman laughed. 'I expect they're trying all right.'

'Somebody ought to do something.'

'Quite right. I've rather thought of trying to do something myself – though I don't quite know what.'

'Oh, Mr Gale, I should. You're so clever.'

'I'm a hero to that girl all right,' thought Norman Gale. 'She'd like to help me in my sleuth stuff; but I've got another partner in view.'

It was that same evening that he dined with Jane. Half-unconsciously he pretended to be in very high spirits, but Jane was too astute to be deceived. She noted his sudden moments of absent-mindedness, the little frown that showed between his brows, the sudden strained line of his mouth.

She said at last, 'Norman, are things going badly?'

He shot a quick glance at her, then looked away.

'Well, not too frightfully well. It's a bad time of year.'

'Don't be idiotic,' said Jane sharply.

'Jane!'

'I mean it. Don't you think I can see that you're worried to death?'

'I'm not worried to death. I'm just annoyed.'

'You mean people are fighting shy –'

'Of having their teeth attended to by a possible murderer? Yes.'

'How cruelly unfair!'

'It is, rather. Because frankly, Jane, I'm a jolly good dentist. And I'm not a murderer.'

'It's wicked. Somebody ought to do something.'

'That's what my secretary, Miss Ross, said this morning.'

'What's she like?'

'Miss Ross?'

'Yes.'

'Oh, I don't know. Big – lots of bones – nose rather like a rocking horse – frightfully competent.'

'She sounds quite nice,' said Jane graciously.

Norman rightly took this as a tribute to his diplomacy. Miss Ross's bones were not really quite as formidable as stated, and she had an extremely attractive head of red hair, but he felt, and rightly, that it was just as well not to dwell on the latter point to Jane.

'I'd like to do *something*,' he said. 'If I was a young man in a book I'd find a clue or I'd shadow somebody.'

Jane tugged suddenly at his sleeve.

'Look, there's Mr Clancy – you know, the author – sitting over there by the wall by himself. We might shadow him.'

'But we were going to the flicks?'

'Never mind the flicks. I feel somehow this might be *meant*. You said you wanted to shadow somebody, and here's somebody to shadow. You never know. We might find out something.'

Jane's enthusiasm was infectious. Norman fell in with the plan readily enough.

'As you say, one never knows,' he said. 'Whereabouts has he got to in his dinner? I can't see properly without turning my head, and I don't want to stare.'

'He's about level with us,' said Jane. 'We'd better hurry a bit and get ahead and then we can pay the bill and be ready to leave when he does.'

They adopted this plan. When at last little Mr Clancy rose and passed out into Dean Street, Norman and Jane were fairly close on his heels.

'In case he takes a taxi,' Jane explained.

But Mr Clancy did not take a taxi. Carrying an overcoat over one arm (and, occasionally allowing it to trail on the ground), he ambled gently through the London streets. His progress was somewhat erratic. Sometimes he moved forward at a brisk trot, sometimes he slowed down till he almost came to a stop. Once, on the very brink of crossing a road, he did come to a standstill, standing there with one foot hanging over the kerb and looking exactly like a slow-motion picture.

His direction, too, was erratic. Once he actually took so many right-angle turns that he traversed the same streets twice over.

Jane felt her spirits rise.

'You see?' she said excitedly. 'He's afraid of being followed. He's trying to put us off the scent.'

'Do you think so?'

'Of course. Nobody would go round in circles otherwise.'

'Oh!'

They had turned a corner rather quickly and had almost cannoned into their quarry. He was standing staring up at a butcher's shop. The shop itself was naturally closed, but it seemed to be something about the level of the first floor that was riveting Mr Clancy's attention.

He said aloud, 'Perfect. The very thing. What a piece of luck!'

He took out a little book and wrote something down very carefully. Then he started off again at a brisk pace, humming a little tune.

He was now heading definitely for Bloomsbury. Sometimes, when he turned his head, the two behind could see his lips moving.

'There is something up,' said Jane. 'He's in great distress of mind. He's talking to himself and he doesn't know it.'

As he waited to cross by some traffic lights, Norman and Jane drew abreast.

It was quite true; Mr Clancy was talking to himself. His face looked white and strained. Norman and Jane caught a few muttered words:

'Why doesn't she speak? Why? There must be a *reason* . . .'

The lights went green. As they reached the opposite pavement Mr Clancy said, 'I see now. Of course. That's why she's got to be silenced!'

Jane pinched Norman ferociously.

Mr Clancy set off at a great pace now. The overcoat dragged hopelessly. With great strides the little author covered the ground, apparently oblivious of the two people on his tracks.

Finally, with disconcerting abruptness, he stopped at a house, opened the door with a key and went in.

Norman and Jane looked at each other.

'It's his own house,' said Norman. '47 Cardington Square. That's the address he gave at the inquest.'

'Oh, well,' said Jane, 'perhaps he'll come out again by and by. And, anyway, we have heard *something*. Somebody – a woman – is going to be silenced, and some other woman won't speak. Oh, dear, it sounds dreadfully like a detective story.'

A voice came out of the darkness. 'Good evening,' it said.

The owner of the voice stepped forward. A pair of magnificent moustaches showed in the lamplight.

'*Eh bien*,' said Hercule Poirot. 'A fine evening for the chase, is it not?'

CHAPTER 15

IN BLOOMSBURY

Of the two startled young people, it was Norman Gale who recovered himself first.

'Of course,' he said, 'it's Monsieur – Monsieur Poirot. Are you still trying to clear your character, M. Poirot?'

'Ah, you remember our little conversation? And it is the poor Mr Clancy you suspect?'

'So do you,' said Jane acutely, 'or you wouldn't be here.'

He looked at her thoughtfully for a moment.

'Have you ever thought about murder, Mademoiselle? Thought about it, I mean, in the abstract – cold-bloodedly and dispassionately?'

'I don't think I've ever thought about it at all until just lately,' said Jane.

Hercule Poirot nodded.

'Yes, you think about it now because a murder has touched you personally. But me, I have dealt with crime for many years now. I have my own way of regarding things. What should you say the most important thing was to bear in mind when you are trying to solve a murder?'

'Finding the murderer,' said Jane.

Norman Gale said, 'Justice.'

Poirot shook his head. 'There are more important things than finding the murderer. And justice is a fine word, but it is sometimes difficult to say exactly what one means by it. In my opinion the important thing is to clear the innocent.'

'Oh, naturally,' said Jane. 'That goes without saying. If anyone is falsely accused –'

'Not even that. *There may be no accusation.* But until one person is proved guilty beyond any possible doubt, everyone else who is associated with the crime is liable to suffer in varying degrees.'

Norman Gale said with emphasis, 'How true that is.'

Jane said, 'Don't we know it!'

Poirot looked from one to the other.

'I see. Already you have been finding that out for yourselves.'

He became suddenly brisk.

'Come now, I have affairs to see to. Since our aims are the same, we three, let us combine together. I am about to call upon our ingenious friend, Mr Clancy. I would suggest that Mademoiselle accompanies me – in the guise of my secretary. Here, Mademoiselle, is a notebook and a pencil for the shorthand.'

'I can't write shorthand,' gasped Jane.

'But naturally not. But you have the quick wits – the intelligence – you can make plausible signs in pencil in the book, can you not? Good. As for Mr Gale, I suggest that he meets us in, say, an hour's time. Shall we say upstairs at Monseigneur's? *Bon!* We will compare notes then.'

And forthwith he advanced to the bell and pressed it.

Slightly dazed, Jane followed him, clutching the notebook.

Gale opened his mouth as though to protest, then seemed to think better of it.

'Right,' he said. 'In an hour, at Monseigneur's.'

The door was opened by a rather forbidding-looking elderly woman attired in severe black.

Poirot said, 'Mr Clancy?'

She drew back and Poirot and Jane entered.

'What name, sir?'

'Mr Hercule Poirot.'

The severe woman led them upstairs and into a room on the first floor.

'Mr Air Kule Prott,' she announced.

Poirot realized at once the force of Mr Clancy's announcement at Croydon to the effect that he was not a tidy man. The room, a long one, with three windows along its length and shelves and bookcases on the other walls, was in a state of chaos. There were papers strewn about, cardboard files, bananas, bottles of beer, open books, sofa cushions, a trombone, miscellaneous china, etchings, and a bewildering assortment of fountain-pens.

In the middle of this confusion Mr Clancy was struggling with a camera and a roll of film.

'Dear me,' said Mr Clancy, looking up as the visitors were announced. He put the camera down and the roll of film promptly fell on the floor and unwound itself. He came forward with outstretched hand. 'Very glad to see you, I'm sure.'

'You remember me, I hope?' said Poirot. 'This is my secretary, Miss Grey.'

'How d'you do, Miss Grey.' He shook her by the hand and then turned back to Poirot. 'Yes, of course I remember you – at least – now, where was it exactly? Was it at the Skull and Crossbones Club?'

'We were fellow passengers on an aeroplane from Paris on a certain fatal occasion.'

'Why, of course,' said Mr Clancy. 'And Miss Grey too! Only I hadn't realized she was your secretary. In fact, I had some idea that she was in a beauty parlour – something of that kind.'

Jane looked anxiously at Poirot.

The latter was quite equal to the situation.

'Perfectly correct,' he said. 'As an efficient secretary, Miss Grey has at times to undertake certain work of a temporary nature – you understand?'

'Of course,' said Mr Clancy. 'I was forgetting. You're a detective – the real thing. Not Scotland Yard. Private investigation. Do sit down, Miss Grey. No, not there; I think there's orange juice on that chair. If I shift this file – Oh, dear, now everything's tumbled out. Never mind. You sit here, M. Poirot – that's right, isn't it? – Poirot? The back's not *really* broken. It only creaks a little as you lean against it. Well, perhaps it's best not to lean *too* hard. Yes, a private investigator like my Wilbraham Rice. The public have taken very strongly to Wilbraham Rice. He bites his nails and eats a lot of bananas. I don't know why I made him bite his nails to start with – it's really rather disgusting – but there it is. He started by biting his nails, and now he has to do it in every single book.

So monotonous. The bananas aren't so bad; you get a bit of fun out of them – criminals slipping on the skin. I eat bananas myself – that's what put it into my head. But I don't bite my nails. Have some beer?'

'I thank you, no.'

Mr Clancy sighed, sat down himself, and gazed earnestly at Poirot.

'I can guess what you've come about – the murder of Giselle. I've thought and thought about that case. You can say what you like, it's amazing – poisoned darts and a blowpipe in an aeroplane. An idea I have used myself, as I told you, both in book and short story form. Of course it was a very shocking occurrence, but I must confess, M. Poirot, that I was thrilled, positively thrilled.'

'I can quite see,' said Poirot, 'that the crime must have appealed to you professionally, Mr Clancy.'

Mr Clancy beamed.

'Exactly. You would think that anyone – even the official police – could have understood that! But not at all. Suspicion – that is all I got, both from the inspector and at the inquest. I go out of my way to assist the course of justice, and all I get for my pains is palpable thick-headed suspicion!'

'All the same,' said Poirot, smiling, 'it does not seem to affect you very much.'

'Ah,' said Mr Clancy. 'But, you see, I have my methods, Watson. If you'll excuse my calling you Watson. No offence intended. Interesting, by the way, how the technique of the idiot friend has hung on. Personally I myself think the Sherlock Holmes stories grossly overrated. The fallacies – the really amazing fallacies that there are in those stories – But what was I saying?'

'You said that you had your methods.'

'Ah, yes.' Mr Clancy leaned forward. 'I'm putting that inspector – what is his name, Japp? – yes, I'm putting him in my next book. You should see the way Wilbraham Rice deals with him.'

'In between bananas, as one might say.'

'In between bananas – that's very good, that.' Mr Clancy chuckled.

'You have a great advantage as a writer, Monsieur,' said Poirot. 'You can relieve your feelings by the expedient of the printed word. You have the power of the pen over your enemies.'

Mr Clancy rocked gently back in his chair.

'You know,' he said, 'I begin to think this murder is going to be a really fortunate thing for me. I'm writing the whole thing exactly as it happened – only as fiction, of course, and I shall call it *The Air Mail Mystery*. Perfect pen portraits of all the passengers. It ought to sell like wildfire – if only I can get it out in time.'

'Won't you be had up for libel, or something?' asked Jane.

Mr Clancy turned a beaming face upon her.

'No, no, my dear lady. Of course, if I were to make one of the passengers the murderer – well, then, I might be liable for damages. But that is the strong part of it all – an entirely unexpected solution is revealed in the last chapter.'

Poirot leaned forward eagerly.

'And that solution is?'

Again Mr Clancy chuckled.

'Ingenious,' he said. 'Ingenious and sensational. Disguised as the pilot, a girl gets into the plane at Le Bourget and successfully stows herself away under Madame Giselle's seat. She has with her an ampoule of the newest gas. She releases this – everybody becomes unconscious for three minutes – she squirms out – fires the poisoned dart, and makes a parachute descent from the rear door of the car.'

Both Jane and Poirot blinked.

Jane said, 'Why doesn't she become unconscious from the gas too?'

'Respirator,' said Mr Clancy.

'And she descends into the Channel?'

'It needn't be the Channel – I shall make it the French coast.'

'And, anyway, nobody could hide under a seat; there wouldn't be room.'

'There will be room in my aeroplane,' said Mr Clancy firmly.

'*Epatant*,' said Poirot. 'And the motive of the lady?'

'I haven't quite decided,' said Mr Clancy meditatively. 'Probably Giselle ruined the girl's lover, who killed himself.'

'And how did she get hold of the poison?'

'That's the really clever part,' said Mr Clancy. 'The girl's a snake charmer. She extracts the stuff from her favourite python.'

'*Mon Dieu!*' said Hercule Poirot.

He said, 'You don't think, perhaps, it is just a *little* sensational?'

'You can't write anything too sensational,' said Mr Clancy firmly. 'Especially when you're dealing with the arrow poison of the South American Indians. I know it was snake juice, really; but the principle is the same. After all, you don't want a detective story to be like real life? Look at the things in the papers – dull as ditchwater.'

'Come, now, Monsieur, would you say this little affair of ours is dull as ditchwater?'

'No,' admitted Mr Clancy. 'Sometimes, you know, I can't believe it really happened.'

Poirot drew the creaking chair a little nearer to his host. His voice lowered itself confidentially.

'M. Clancy, you are a man of brains and imagination. The police, as you say, have regarded you with suspicion. They have not sought your advice. But I, Hercule Poirot, desire to consult you.'

Mr Clancy flushed with pleasure.

'I'm sure that's very nice of you.'

He looked flustered and pleased.

'You have studied the criminology. Your ideas will be of value. It would be of great interest to me to know who, in your opinion, committed the crime.'

'Well –' Mr Clancy hesitated, reached automatically for a banana and began to eat it. Then, the animation dying out of his face, he shook his head. 'You see, M. Poirot, it's an entirely different thing. When you're writing you can make it anyone you like; but, of course, in real life there is a real person. You haven't any command over the facts. I'm afraid, you know, that I'd be absolutely no good as a real detective.'

He shook his head sadly and threw the banana skin into the grate.

'It might be amusing, however, to consider the case together?' suggested Poirot.

'Oh, that, yes.'

'To begin with, supposing you had to make a sporting guess, who would you choose?'

'Oh, well, I suppose one of the two Frenchmen.'

'Now, why?'

'Well, she was French. It seems more likely, somehow. And they were sitting on the opposite side not too far away from her. But really I don't know.'

'It depends,' said Poirot thoughtfully, 'so much on motive.'

'Of course – of course. I suppose you tabulate all the motives very scientifically?'

'I am old-fashioned in my methods. I follow the old adage: seek whom the crime benefits.'

'That's all very well,' said Mr Clancy. 'But I take it that's a little difficult in a case like this. There's a daughter who comes into money, so I've heard. But a lot of the people on board might benefit, for all we know – that is if they owed her money and haven't got to pay it back.'

'True,' said Poirot. 'And I can think of other solutions. Let us suppose that Madame Giselle knew of something – attempted murder, shall we say? – on the part of one of those people.'

'Attempted murder?' said Mr Clancy. 'Now, why attempted murder? What a very curious suggestion.'

'In cases such as these,' said Poirot, 'one must think of everything.'

'Ah!' said Mr Clancy. 'But it's no good thinking. You've got to *know*.'

'You have reason – you have reason. A very just observation.'

Then he said, 'I ask your pardon, but this blowpipe that you bought –'

'Damn that blowpipe,' said Mr Clancy. 'I wish I'd never mentioned it.'

'You bought it, you say, at a shop in the Charing Cross Road? Do you, by any chance, remember the name of that shop?'

'Well,' said Mr Clancy, 'it might have been Absolom's – or there's Mitchell & Smith. I don't know. But I've already told all this to that pestilential inspector. He must have checked up on it by this time.'

'Ah,' said Poirot, 'but I ask for quite another reason. I desire to purchase such a thing and make a little experiment.'

'Oh, I see. But I don't know that you'll find one all the same. They don't keep sets of them, you know.'

'All the same I can try. Perhaps, Miss Grey, you would be so obliging as to take down those two names?'

Jane opened her notebook and rapidly performed a series of (she hoped) professional-looking squiggles. Then she surreptitiously wrote the names in longhand on the reverse side of the sheet in case these instructions of Poirot's should be genuine.

'And now,' said Poirot, 'I have trespassed on your time too long. I will take my departure with a thousand thanks for your amiability.'

'Not at all. Not at all,' said Mr Clancy. 'I wish you would have had a banana.'

'You are most amiable.'

'Not at all. As a matter of fact, I'm feeling rather happy tonight. I'd been held up in a short story I was writing – the thing wouldn't pan out properly, and I couldn't get a good name for the criminal. I wanted something with a flavour. Well, just a bit of luck, I saw just the name I wanted over a butcher's shop. Pargiter. Just the name I was looking for. There's a sort of genuine sound to it; and about five minutes later I got the other thing. There's always the same snag in stories – why won't the girl speak? The young man tries to make her and she says her lips are sealed. There's never any real reason, of course, why she shouldn't blurt out the whole thing at once, but you have to try to think of something that's not too definitely idiotic. Unfortunately it has to be a different thing every time!'

He smiled gently at Jane.

'The trials of an author!'

He darted past her to a bookcase.

'One thing you must allow me to give you.'

He came back with a book in his hand.

'*The Clue of the Scarlet Petal.* I think I mentioned at Croydon that that book of mine dealt with arrow poison and native darts.'

'A thousand thanks. You are too amiable.'

'Not at all. I see,' said Mr Clancy suddenly to Jane, 'that you don't use the Pitman system of shorthand.'

Jane flushed scarlet. Poirot came to her rescue.

'Miss Grey is very up to date. She uses the most recent system invented by a Czecho-Slovakian.'

'You don't say so? What an amazing place Czecho-Slovakia must be. Everything seems to come from there – shoes, glass, gloves, and now a shorthand system. Quite amazing.'

He shook hands with them both.

'I wish I could have been more helpful.'

They left him in the littered room smiling wistfully after them.

CHAPTER 16

PLAN OF CAMPAIGN

From Mr Clancy's house they took a taxi to the Monseigneur, where they found Norman Gale awaiting them.

Poirot ordered some *consommé* and a *chaud-froid* of chicken.

'Well?' said Norman. 'How did you get on?'

'Miss Grey,' said Poirot, 'has proved herself the super-secretary.'

'I don't think I did so very well,' said Jane. 'He spotted my stuff when he passed behind me. You know, he must be very observant.'

'Ah, you noticed that? This good Mr Clancy is not quite so absent-minded as one might imagine.'

'Did you really want those addresses?' asked Jane.

'I think they might be useful – yes.'

'But if the police –'

'Ah, the police! I should not ask the same questions as the police have asked. Though, as a matter of fact, I doubt whether the police have asked any questions at all. You see, they know that the blowpipe found in the plane was purchased in Paris by an American.'

'In Paris? An American? But there wasn't any American in the aeroplane.'

Poirot smiled kindly on her.

'Precisely. We have here an American just to make it more difficult. *Voilà tout.*'

'But it was bought by a man?' said Norman.

Poirot looked at him with rather an odd expression.

'Yes,' he said, 'it was *bought* by a man.'

Norman looked puzzled.

'Anyway,' said Jane, 'it wasn't Mr Clancy. He'd got one blow-pipe already, so he wouldn't want to go about buying another.'

Poirot nodded his head.

'That is how one must proceed. Suspect everyone in turn and then wipe him or her off the list.'

'How many have you wiped off so far?' asked Jane.

'Not so many as you might think, Mademoiselle,' said Poirot with a twinkle. 'It depends, you see, on the motive.'

'Has there been –?' Norman Gale stopped and then added apologetically: 'I don't want to butt in on official secrets, but is there no record of this woman's dealings?'

Poirot shook his head.

'All the records are burnt.'

'That's unfortunate.'

'*Evidemment!* But it seems that Madame Giselle combined a little blackmailing with her profession of moneylending, and that opens up a wider field. Supposing, for instance, that Madame Giselle had knowledge of a certain criminal offence – say, attempted murder on the part of someone.'

'Is there any reason to suppose such a thing?'

'Why, yes,' said Poirot slowly. 'There is – one of the few pieces of documentary evidence that we have in this case.'

He looked from one to the other of their interested faces and gave a little sigh.

'Ah, well,' he said, 'that is that. Let us talk of other matters – for instance, of how this tragedy has affected the lives of you two young people.'

'It sounds horrible to say so, but I've done well out of it,' said Jane.

She related her rise of salary.

'As you say, Mademoiselle, you have done well, but probably only for the time being. Even a nine-days' wonder does not last longer than nine days, remember.'

Jane laughed. 'That's very true.'

'I'm afraid it's going to last more than nine days in my case,' said Norman.

He explained the position. Poirot listened sympathetically.

'As you say,' he observed thoughtfully, 'it will take more than nine days – or nine weeks – or nine months. Sensationalism dies quickly – fear is long-lived.'

'Do you think I ought to stick it out?'

'Have you any other plan?'

'Yes – chuck up the whole thing. Go out to Canada or somewhere and start again.'

'I'm sure that would be a pity,' said Jane firmly.

Norman looked at her.

Poirot tactfully became engrossed with his chicken.

'I don't want to go,' said Norman.

'If I discover who killed Madame Giselle, you will not have to go,' said Poirot cheerfully.

'Do you really think you will?' asked Jane.

Poirot looked at her reproachfully.

'If one approaches a problem with order and method there should be no difficulty in solving it – none whatever,' said Poirot severely.

'Oh, I see,' said Jane, who didn't.

'But I should solve this problem quicker if I had help,' said Poirot.

'What kind of help?'

Poirot did not speak for a moment or two. Then he said:

'Help from Mr Gale. And perhaps, later, help from you also.'

'What can I do?' asked Norman.

Poirot shot a sideways glance at him.

'You will not like it,' he said warningly.

'What is it?' repeated the young man impatiently.

Very delicately, so as not to offend English susceptibilities, Poirot used a toothpick. Then he said: 'Frankly, what I need is a blackmailer.'

'A blackmailer?' exclaimed Norman. He stared at Poirot as a man does who cannot believe his ears.

Poirot nodded.

'Precisely,' he said. 'A blackmailer.'

'But what for?'

'*Parbleu!* To blackmail.'

'Yes, but I mean who? Why?'

'Why,' said Poirot, 'is my business. As to *whom* –' He paused for a moment, then went on in a calm business-like tone:

'Here is the plan I will outline for you. You will write a note – that is to say, *I* will write a note and *you* will copy it – to the Countess of Horbury. You will mark it "Personal". In the note you will ask for an interview. You will recall yourself to her memory as having travelled to England by air on a certain occasion. You will also refer to certain business dealings of Madame Giselle's having passed into your hands.'

'And then?'

'And then you will be accorded an interview. You will go and you will say certain things (in which I will instruct you). You will ask for – let me see – ten thousand pounds.'

'You're mad!'

'Not at all,' said Poirot. 'I am eccentric, possibly, but mad, no.'

'And suppose Lady Horbury sends for the police? I shall go to prison.'

'She will not send for the police.'

'You can't *know* that.'

'*Mon cher*, practically speaking, I know everything.'

'And, anyway, I don't like it.'

'You will not get the ten thousand pounds – if that makes your conscience any clearer,' said Poirot with a twinkle.

'Yes, but look here, M. Poirot – this is the sort of wildcat scheme that might ruin me for life.'

'Ta – ta – ta – the lady will not go to the police – that I assure you.'

'She may tell her husband.'

'She will not tell her husband.'

'I don't like it.'

'Do you like losing your patients and ruining your career?'

'No, but –'

Poirot smiled at him kindly.

'You have the natural repugnance, yes? That is very natural. You have, too, the chivalrous spirit. But I can assure you that Lady Horbury is not worth all this fine feeling – to use your idiom she is a very nasty piece of goods.'

'All the same, she can't be a murderess.'

'Why?'

'Why? Because we should have seen her. Jane and I were sitting just opposite.'

'You have too many preconceived ideas. Me, I desire to straighten things out; and to do that I must *know*.'

'I don't like the idea of blackmailing a woman.'

'Ah, *mon Dieu* – what there is in a word! There will be no blackmail. You have only to produce a certain effect. After that, when the ground is prepared, I will step in.'

Norman said, 'If you land me in prison –'

'No, no, no, I am very well known at Scotland Yard. If anything should occur I will take the blame. But nothing will occur other than what I have prophesied.'

Norman surrendered with a sigh.

'All right. I'll do it. But I don't half like it.'

'Good. This is what you will write. Take a pencil.'

He dictated slowly.

'*Voilà*,' he said. 'Later I will instruct you as to what you are to say. Tell me, Mademoiselle, do you ever go to the theatre?'

'Yes, fairly often,' said Jane.

'Good. Have you seen, for instance, a play called *Down Under*?'

'Yes. I saw it about a month ago. It's rather good.'

'An American play, is it not?'

'Yes.'

'Do you remember the part of Harry, played by Mr Raymond Barraclough?'

'Yes. He was very good.'

'You thought him attractive? Yes?'

'Frightfully attractive.'

'Ah, *il a le sex appeal*?'

'Decidedly,' said Jane, laughing.

'Just that – or is he a good actor as well?'

'Oh, I think he acts well too.'

'I must go and see him,' said Poirot.

Jane stared at him, puzzled.

What an odd little man he was – hopping from subject to subject like a bird from one branch to another!

Perhaps he read her thoughts. He smiled:

'You do not approve of me, Mademoiselle? Of my methods?'

'You jump about a good deal.'

'Not really. I pursue my course logically with order and method. One must not jump wildly to a conclusion. One must *eliminate*.'

'Eliminate?' said Jane. 'Is that what you're doing?' She thought a moment. 'I see. You've eliminated Mr Clancy –'

'Perhaps,' said Poirot.

'And you've eliminated us; and now you're going, perhaps, to eliminate Lady Horbury. Oh!'

She stopped as a sudden thought struck her.

'What is it, Mademoiselle?'

'That talk of attempted murder? Was that a *test*?'

'You are very quick, Mademoiselle. Yes, that was part of the course I pursue. I mention attempted murder and I watch Mr Clancy, I watch you, I watch Mr Gale – and in neither of you three is there any sign – not so much as the flicker of an eyelash. And let me tell you that I could not be deceived on that point. A murderer can be ready to meet any attack that he *foresees*. But that entry in a little notebook could not have been known to any of you. So, you see, I am satisfied.'

'What a horrible, tricky sort of person you are, M. Poirot,' said Jane, rising. 'I shall never know why you are saying things.'

'That is quite simple. I want to find out things.'

'I suppose you've got very clever ways of finding out things?'

'There is only one really simple way.'

'What is that?'

'To let people tell you.'

Jane laughed.

'Suppose they don't want to?'

'Everyone likes talking about themselves.'

'I suppose they do,' admitted Jane.

'That is how many a quack makes a fortune. He encourages patients to come and sit and tell him things. How they fell out of the perambulator when they were two, and how their mother ate a pear and the juice fell on her orange dress, and how when they were one and a half they pulled their father's beard; and then he tells them that now they will not suffer from the insomnia any longer, and he takes two guineas; and they go away, having enjoyed themselves – oh, so much – and perhaps they do sleep.'

'How ridiculous,' said Jane.

'No, it is not so ridiculous as you think. It is based on a fundamental need of human nature – the need to talk – to reveal oneself. You yourself, Mademoiselle, do you not like to dwell on your childhood memories – on your mother and your father?'

'That doesn't apply in my case. I was brought up in an orphanage.'

'Ah, that is different. It is not gay, that.'

'I don't mean that we were the kind of charity orphans who go out in scarlet bonnets and cloaks. It was quite fun really.'

'It was in England?'

'No, in Ireland – near Dublin.'

'So you are Irish. That is why you have the dark hair and the blue-grey eyes, with the look –'

'As though they had been put in with a smutty finger –' Norman finished with amusement.

'*Comment?* What is that you say?'

'That is a saying about Irish eyes – that they have been put in with a smutty finger.'

'Really? It is not elegant, that. And yet – it expresses it well.' He bowed to Jane. 'The effect is very good, Mademoiselle.'

Jane laughed as she got up.

'You'll turn my head, M. Poirot. Good night, and thank you for supper. You'll have to stand me another if Norman is sent to prison for blackmail.'

A frown came over Norman's face at the reminder.

Poirot bade the two young people good night.

When he got home he unlocked a drawer and took out a list of eleven names.

Against four of these names he put a light tick. Then he nodded his head thoughtfully.

'I think I know,' he murmured to himself. 'But I have got to be sure. *Il faut continuer.*'

CHAPTER 17

IN WANDSWORTH

Mr Henry Mitchell was just sitting down to a supper of sausage and mash when a visitor called to see him.

Somewhat to the steward's astonishment the visitor in question was the full-moustached gentleman who had been one of the passengers on the fatal plane.

M. Poirot was very affable, very agreeable in his manner. He insisted on Mr Mitchell's getting on with his supper, paid a graceful compliment to Mrs Mitchell, who was standing staring at him open-mouthed.

He accepted a chair, remarked that it was very warm for the time of year and then gently came round to the purpose of his call.

'Scotland Yard, I fear, is not making much progress with the case,' he said.

Mitchell shook his head.

'It was an amazing business, sir – amazing. I don't see what they've got to go on. Why, if none of the people on the plane saw anything, it's going to be difficult for anyone afterwards.'

'Truly, as you say.'

'Terribly worried, Henry's been, over it,' put in his wife. 'Not able to sleep of nights.'

The steward explained:

'It's lain on my mind, sir, something terrible. The company have been very fair about it. I must say I was afraid at first I might lose my job –'

'Henry, they couldn't. It would have been cruelly unfair.'

His wife sounded highly indignant. She was a buxom, highly-complexioned woman with snapping dark eyes.

'Things don't always happen fairly, Ruth. Still it turned out better than I thought. They absolve me from blame. But I felt it, if you understand me. I was in charge, as it were.'

'I understand your feelings,' said Poirot sympathetically. 'But I assure you that you are over-conscientious. Nothing that happened was your fault.'

'That's what *I* say, sir,' put in Mrs Mitchell.

Mitchell shook his head.

'I ought to have noticed that the lady was dead sooner. If I'd tried to wake her up when I first took round the bills –'

'It would have made little difference. Death, they think, was very nearly instantaneous.'

'He worries so,' said Mrs Mitchell. 'I tell him not to bother his head so. Who's to know what reason foreigners have for murdering each other; and if you ask me, I think it's a dirty trick to have done it in a British aeroplane.'

She finished her sentence with an indignant and patriotic snort.

Mitchell shook his head in a puzzled way.

'It weighs on me, so to speak. Every time I go on duty I'm in a state. And then the gentleman from Scotland Yard asking me again and again if nothing unusual or sudden occurred on the way over. Makes me feel as though I *must* have forgotten something – and yet I know I haven't. It was a most uneventful voyage in every way until – until *it* happened.'

'Blowpipes and darts – heathen, I call it,' said Mrs Mitchell.

'You are right,' said Poirot, addressing her with a flattering air of being struck by her remarks. 'Not so is an English murder committed.'

'You're right, sir.'

'You know, Mrs Mitchell, I can almost guess what part of England you come from.'

'Dorset, sir. Not far from Bridport. That's my home.'

'Exactly,' said Poirot. 'A lovely part of the world.'

'It is that. London isn't a patch on Dorset. My folk have been settled in Dorset for over two hundred years – and I've got Dorset in the blood, as you might say.'

'Yes, indeed.' He turned to the steward again. 'There's one thing I'd like to ask you, Mitchell.'

The man's brow contracted.

'I've told you all that I know – indeed I have, sir.'

'Yes, yes – this is a very trifling matter. I only wondered if anything on the table – Madame Giselle's table, I mean – was disarranged?'

'You mean when – when I found her?'

'Yes. The spoons and forks – the salt cellar – anything like that.'

The man shook his head.

'There wasn't anything of that kind on the tables. Everything was cleared away bar the coffee cups. I didn't notice anything myself. I shouldn't, though. I was much too flustered. But the police would know that, sir, they searched the plane through and through.'

'Ah, well,' said Poirot. 'It is no matter. Sometime I must have a word with your colleague – Davis.'

'He's on the early 8.45 am service now, sir.'

'Has this business upset him much?'

'Oh, well, sir, you see he's only a young fellow. If you ask me, he's almost enjoyed it all. The excitement, and everyone standing him drinks and wanting to hear about it.'

'Has he perhaps a young lady?' asked Poirot. 'Doubtless his connexion with the crime would be very thrilling to her.'

'He's courting old Johnson's daughter at the Crown and Feathers,' said Mrs Mitchell. 'But she's a sensible girl – got her head screwed on the right way. She doesn't approve of being mixed up with a murder.'

'A very sound point of view,' said Poirot, rising. 'Well, thank you, Mr Mitchell – and you, Mrs Mitchell – and I beg of you, my friend, do not let this weigh upon your mind.'

When he had departed Mitchell said, 'The thick heads in the jury at the inquest thought he'd done it. But if you ask me, he's secret service.'

'If you ask me,' said Mrs Mitchell, 'there's Bolshies at the back of it.'

Poirot had said that he must have a word with the other steward, Davis, sometime. As a matter of fact he had it not many hours later, in the bar of the Crown and Feathers.

He asked Davis the same question he had asked Mitchell.

'Nothing disarranged – no, sir. You mean upset? That kind of thing?'

'I mean – well, shall we say something missing from the table – or something that would not usually be there –'

Davis said slowly:

'There was *something* – I noticed it when I was clearing up, after the police had done with the place – but I don't suppose that it's the sort of thing you mean. It's only that the dead lady had two coffee spoons in her saucer. It does sometimes happen when we're serving in a hurry. I noticed it because there's a superstition about that; they say two spoons in a saucer means a wedding.'

'Was there a spoon missing from anyone else's saucer?'

'No, sir, not that I noticed. Mitchell or I must have taken the cup and saucer along that way – as I say one does sometimes what with the hurry and all. I laid two sets of fish knives and forks only a week ago. On the whole it's better than laying the table short, for then you have to interrupt yourself and go and fetch the extra knife, or whatever it is you've forgotten.'

Poirot asked one more question – a somewhat jocular one:

'What do you think of French girls, Davis?'

'English are good enough for me, sir.'

And he grinned at a plump, fair-haired girl behind the bar.

CHAPTER 18

IN QUEEN VICTORIA STREET

Mr James Ryder was rather surprised when a card bearing the name of M. Hercule Poirot was brought to him.

He knew that the name was familiar, but for the moment he could not remember why. Then he said to himself:

'Oh, *that* fellow!' and told the clerk to show the visitor in.

M. Hercule Poirot was looking very jaunty. In one hand he carried a cane, he had a flower in his buttonhole.

'You will forgive my troubling you, I trust,' said Poirot. 'It is this affair of the death of Madame Giselle.'

'Yes?' said Mr Ryder. 'Well, what about it? Sit down, won't you? Have a cigar?'

'I thank you, no. I smoke my own cigarettes. Perhaps you will accept one?'

Ryder regarded Poirot's tiny cigarettes with a somewhat dubious eye.

'Think I'll have one of my own, if it's all the same to you. Might swallow one of those by mistake.' He laughed heartily.

'The inspector was round here a few days ago,' said Mr Ryder when he had induced his lighter to work. 'Nosey, that's what those fellows are. Can't mind their own business.'

'They have, I suppose, to get information,' said Poirot mildly.

'They needn't be so damned offensive about it,' said Mr Ryder bitterly. 'A man's got his feelings – and his business reputation to think about.'

'You are, perhaps, a little over-sensitive.'

'I'm in a delicate position, I am,' said Mr Ryder. 'Sitting where I did, just in front of her – well, it looks fishy, I suppose. I can't help where I sat. If I'd known that woman was going to be murdered I wouldn't have come by that plane at all. I don't know, though, perhaps I would.'

He looked thoughtful for a moment.

'Has good come out of evil?' asked Poirot, smiling.

'It's funny your saying that. It has, and it hasn't, in a manner of speaking. I mean I've had a lot of worry. I've been badgered. Things have been insinuated. And why *me*? That's what I say. Why don't they go and worry that Dr Hubbard – Bryant, I mean. Doctors are the people who can get hold of high-falutin' undetectable poisons. How'd I get hold of snake juice? I ask you!'

'You were saying,' said Poirot, 'that although you had been put to a lot of inconvenience –?'

'Ah, yes, there was a bright side to the picture. I don't mind telling you I cleaned up a tidy little sum from the papers. Eyewitness stuff – though there was more of the reporter's imagination than of my eyesight; but that's neither here nor there.'

'It is interesting,' said Poirot, 'how a crime affects the lives of people who are quite outside it. Take yourself, for example –

you make suddenly a quite unexpected sum of money – a sum of money perhaps particularly welcome at the moment.'

'Money's always welcome,' said Mr Ryder.

He eyed Poirot sharply.

'Sometimes the need of it is imperative. For that reason men embezzle – they make fraudulent entries –' He waved his hands. 'All sorts of complications arise.'

'Well, don't let's get gloomy about it,' said Mr Ryder.

'True. Why dwell on the dark side of the picture? This money was grateful to you – since you failed to raise a loan in Paris –'

'How the devil did you know that?' asked Mr Ryder angrily.

Hercule Poirot smiled.

'At any rate it is true.'

'It's true enough, but I don't particularly want it to get about.'

'I will be discretion itself, I assure you.'

'It's odd,' mused Mr Ryder, 'how small a sum will sometimes put a man in Queer Street. Just a small sum of ready money to tide him over a crisis – and if he can't get hold of that infinitesimal sum, to hell with his credit. Yes, it's damned odd. Money's odd. Credit's odd. Come to that, life is odd!'

'Very true.'

'By the way, what was it you wanted to see me about?'

'It is a little delicate. It has come to my ears – in the course of my profession, you understand – that in spite of your denials you *did* have dealings with this woman Giselle.'

'Who says so? It's a lie! I never saw the woman.'

'Dear me, that is very curious!'

'Curious! It's damned libel.'

Poirot looked at him thoughtfully.

'Ah,' he said, 'I must look into the matter.'

'What do you mean? What are you getting at?'

Poirot shook his head.

'Do not enrage yourself; there must be – a mistake.'

'I should think there was. Catch me getting myself mixed up with these high-toned Society moneylenders. Society woman with gambling debts – that's their sort.'

Poirot rose.

'I must apologize for having been misinformed.' He paused at the door. 'By the way, just as a matter of curiosity, what made you call Dr Bryant Dr *Hubbard* just now?'

'Blessed if I know. Let me see – Oh, yes, I think it must have been the flute. The nursery rhyme, you know. Old Mother Hubbard's dog – *But when she came back he was playing the flute.* Odd thing how you mix up names.'

'Ah, yes, the flute . . . These things interest me, you understand, psychologically.'

Mr Ryder snorted at the word psychologically. It savoured to him of what he called that tom-fool business psychoanalysis.

He looked at Poirot with suspicion.

CHAPTER 19

ENTER AND EXIT MR ROBINSON

The Countess of Horbury sat in her bedroom at 315 Grosvenor Square in front of her toilet table. Gold brushes and boxes, jars of face cream, boxes of powder – dainty luxury all around her. But in the midst of the luxury Cicely Horbury sat with dry lips and a face on which the rouge showed up in unbecoming patches on her cheeks.

She read the letter for the fourth time.

> The Countess of Horbury.
>
> Dear Madam,
>
> *re*:Madame Giselle, deceased.
>
> I am the holder of certain documents formerly in the possession of the deceased lady. If you or Mr Raymond Barraclough are interested in the matter, I should be happy to call upon you with a view to discussing the affair.
>
> Or perhaps you would prefer me to deal with your husband in the matter?
>
> Yours truly,
>
> John Robinson.

Stupid, to read the same thing over and over again . . .

As though the words might alter their meaning.

She picked up the envelope – two envelopes, the first with 'Personal' on it, the second with 'Private and Very Confidential.'

'Private and Very Confidential . . .'

The beast . . . the beast . . .

And that lying old Frenchwoman, who had sworn that 'all arrangements were made to protect clients in case of her own sudden demise . . .'

Damn her . . . Life was hell – hell . . .

'Oh God, my nerves,' thought Cicely. 'It isn't fair. It isn't fair . . .'

Her shaking hand went out to a gold-topped bottle . . .

'It will steady me, pull me together . . .'

She snuffed the stuff up her nose.

There. Now she could think! What to do? See the man, of course. Though where she could raise any money – perhaps a lucky flutter at that place in Carlos Street . . .

But time enough to think of that later. See the man – find out what he knows.

She went over to the writing-table, dashed off in her big, unformed handwriting:

The Countess of Horbury presents her compliments to Mr John Robinson and will see him if he calls at eleven o'clock tomorrow morning . . .

II

'Will I do?' asked Norman.

He flushed a little under Poirot's startled gaze.

'Name of a name,' said Hercule Poirot. 'What kind of a comedy is it that you are playing?'

Norman Gale flushed even more deeply.

He mumbled, 'You said a slight disguise would be as well.'

Poirot sighed, then he took the young man by the arm and marched him to the looking-glass.

'Regard yourself,' he said. 'That is all I ask of you – regard yourself! What do you think you are – a Santa Claus dressed up to amuse the children? I agree that your beard is not white: no, it is black – the colour for villains. But what a beard – a beard that screams to Heaven! A cheap beard, my friend, and most imperfectly and amateurishly attached! Then there are your eyebrows. But it is that you have the mania for false hair? The spirit gum one smells it several yards away; and if you think that anyone will fail to perceive that you have a piece of sticking plaster attached to a tooth, you are mistaken. My friend, it is not your *métier* – decidedly not – to play the part.'

'I acted in amateur theatricals a good deal at one time,' said Norman Gale stiffly.

'I can hardly believe it. At any rate, I presume they did not let you indulge in your own ideas of makeup. Even behind the footlights your appearance would be singularly unconvincing. In Grosvenor Square in broad daylight –'

Poirot gave an eloquent shrug of the shoulders by way of finishing the sentence.

'No, *mon ami*,' he said. 'You are a blackmailer, not a comedian. I want her ladyship to fear you – not to die of laughing when she sees you. I observe that I wound you by what I am saying. I regret, but it is a moment when only the truth will serve. Take this and this –' He pressed various jars upon him. 'Go into the bathroom and let us have an end of what you call in this country the fooltommery.'

Crushed, Norman Gale obeyed. When he emerged a quarter of an hour later, his face a vivid shade of brick red, Poirot gave him a nod of approval.

'*Très bien.* The farce is over. The serious business begins. I will permit you to have a small moustache. But I will, if you please, attach it to you myself. There – and now we will part the hair differently – so. That is quite enough. Now let me see if you at least know your lines.'

He listened with attention, then nodded.

'That is good. *En avant* – and good luck to you.'

'I devoutly hope so. I shall probably find an enraged husband and a couple of policemen.'

Poirot reassured him.

'Have no anxiety. All will march to a marvel.'

'So you say,' muttered Norman rebelliously.

With his spirits at zero, he departed on his distasteful mission.

At Grosvenor Square he was shown into a small room on the first floor. There, after a minute or two, Lady Horbury came to him.

Norman braced himself. He must not – positively must not – show that he was new to this business.

'Mr Robinson?' said Cicely.

'At your service,' said Norman, and bowed.

'Damn it all – just like a shop-walker,' he thought disgustedly. 'That's fright.'

'I had your letter,' said Cicely.

Norman pulled himself together. 'The old fool said I couldn't act,' he said to himself with a mental grin.

Aloud he said rather insolently:

'Quite so – well, what about it, Lady Horbury?'

'I don't know what you mean.'

'Come, come. Must we really go into details? Everyone knows how pleasant a – well, call it a weekend at the seaside – can be; but husbands seldom agree. I think you know, Lady Horbury, just exactly what the evidence consists of. Wonderful woman, old Giselle. Always had the goods. Hotel evidence, etc., is quite first class. Now the question is who wants it most – you or Lord Horbury? That's the question.'

She stood there quivering.

'I'm a seller,' said Norman, his voice growing commoner as he threw himself more whole-heartedly into the part of Mr Robinson. 'Are you a buyer? That's the question.'

'How did you get hold of this – evidence?'

'Now really, Lady Horbury, that's rather beside the point. I've got it, that's the main thing.'

'I don't believe you. Show it to me.'

'Oh, no.' Norman shook his head with a cunning leer. 'I didn't bring anything with me. I'm not so green as that. If we agree to do business, that's another matter. I'll show you the stuff before you hand the money over. All fair and above board.'

'How – how much?'

'Ten thousand of the best – pounds, not dollars.'

'Impossible. I could never lay my hands on anything like that amount.'

'It's wonderful what you can do if you try. Jewels aren't fetching what they did, but pearls are still pearls. Look here, to oblige a lady I'll make it eight thousand. That's my last word. And I'll give you two days to think it over.'

'I can't get the money, I tell you.'

Norman sighed and shook his head.

'Well, perhaps it's only right Lord Horbury should know what's been going on. I believe I'm correct in saying that a divorced woman gets no alimony – and Mr Barraclough's a very promising young actor, but he's not touching big money. Now not another word. I'll leave you to think it over; and mind what I say – I mean it.'

He paused and then added:

'I mean it, just as Giselle meant it . . .'

Then quickly, before the wretched woman could reply, he had left the room.

'Ouch!' said Norman as he reached the street. He wiped his brow. 'Thank goodness *that's* over.'

III

It was a bare hour later when a card was brought to Lady Horbury.

'M. Hercule Poirot.'

She thrust it aside. 'Who is he? I can't see him!'

'He said, m'lady, that he was here at the request of Mr Raymond Barraclough.'

'Oh.' She paused. 'Very well, show him in.'

The butler departed, reappeared.

'M. Hercule Poirot.'

Exquisitely dressed in the most dandiacal style, M. Poirot entered, bowed.

The butler closed the door. Cicely took a step forward.

'Mr Barraclough sent you –?'

'Sit down, Madame.' His tone was kindly but authoritative.

Mechanically she sat. He took a chair near her. His manner was fatherly and reassuring.

'Madame, I entreat you, look upon me as a friend. I come to advise you. You are, I know, in grave trouble.'

She murmured faintly, 'I don't –'

'*Ecoutez*, Madame, I do not ask you to give away your secrets. It is unnecessary. I know them beforehand. That is the essence of being a good detective – to know.'

'A detective?' Her eyes widened. 'I remember – you were on the plane. It was you –'

'Precisely, it was me. Now, Madame, let us get to business. As I said just now, I do not press you to confide in me. You shall not start by telling *me* things. *I* will tell to *you*. This morning, not an hour ago, you had a visitor. That visitor – his name was Brown, perhaps?'

'Robinson,' said Cicely faintly.

'It is the same thing – Brown, Smith, Robinson – he uses them in turn. He came here to blackmail you, Madame. He has in his possession certain proofs of – shall we say – indiscretion? Those proofs were once in the keeping of Madame Giselle. Now this man has them. He offers them to you for, perhaps, seven thousand pounds.'

'Eight.'

'Eight, then. And you, Madame, will not find it easy to get that sum very quickly?'

'I can't do it – I simply can't do it . . . I'm in debt already. I don't know what to do . . .'

'Calm yourself, Madame. I come to assist you.'

She stared at him.

'How do you know all this?'

'Simply, Madame, because I am Hercule Poirot. *Eh bien*, have no fears – place yourself in my hands – I will deal with this Mr Robinson.'

'Yes,' said Cicely sharply. 'And how much will you want?'

Hercule Poirot bowed.

'I shall ask only a photograph, signed, of a very beautiful lady . . .'

She cried out, 'Oh, dear, I don't know what to do . . . My nerves . . . I'm going mad.'

'No, no, all is well. Trust Hercule Poirot. Only, Madame, I must have the truth – the whole truth – do not keep anything back or my hands will be tied.'

'And you'll get me out of this mess?'

'I swear to you solemnly that you will never hear of Mr Robinson again.'

She said, 'All right. I'll tell you everything.'

'Good. Now then, you borrowed money from this woman Giselle?'

Lady Horbury nodded.

'When was that? When did it begin, I mean?'

'Eighteen months ago. I was in a hole.'

'Gambling?'

'Yes. I had an appalling run of luck.'

'And she lent you as much as you wanted?'

'Not at first. Only a small sum to begin with.'

'Who sent you to her?'

'Raymond – Mr Barraclough told me that he had heard she lent money to Society women.'

'But later she lent you more?'

'Yes – as much as I wanted. It seemed like a miracle at the time.'

'It was Madame Giselle's special kind of miracle,' said Poirot drily. 'I gather that before then you and Mr Barraclough had become – er – friends?'

'Yes.'

'But you were very anxious that your husband should not know about it?'

Cicely cried angrily, 'Stephen's a prig. He's tired of me. He wants to marry someone else. He'd have jumped at the thought of divorcing me.'

'And you did not want – divorce?'

'No. I – I –'

'You liked your position – and also you enjoyed the use of a very ample income. Quite so. *Les femmes*, naturally, they must look after themselves. To proceed – there arose the question of repayment?'

'Yes, and I – I couldn't pay back the money. And then the old devil turned nasty. She knew about me and Raymond. She'd found out places and dates and everything – I can't think how.'

'She had her methods,' said Poirot drily. 'And she threatened, I suppose, to send all this evidence to Lord Horbury?'

'Yes, unless I paid up.'

'And you couldn't pay?'

'No.'

'So her death was quite providential?'

Cicely Horbury said earnestly, 'It seemed too, too wonderful.'

'Ah, precisely – too, too wonderful. But it made you a little nervous, perhaps?'

'Nervous?'

'Well, after all, Madame, you alone of anyone on the plane had a motive for desiring her death.'

She drew in her breath sharply.

'I know. It was awful. I was in an absolute state about it.'

'Especially since you had been to see her in Paris the night before, and had had something of a scene with her?'

'The old devil! She wouldn't budge an inch. I think she actually enjoyed it. Oh, she was a beast through and through! I came away like a rag.'

'And yet you said at the inquest that you had never seen the woman before?'

'Well, naturally, what else could I say?'

Poirot looked at her thoughtfully.

'*You*, Madame, could say nothing else.'

'It's been too ghastly – nothing but lies – lies – lies. That dreadful inspector man has been here again and again badgering me with questions. But I felt pretty safe. I could see he was only trying it on. He didn't know anything.'

'If one does guess, one should guess with assurance.'

'And then,' continued Cicely, pursuing her own line of thought, 'I couldn't help feeling that if anything *were* to leak out, it would have leaked out at once. I felt safe – till that awful letter yesterday.'

'You have not been afraid all this time?'

'Of course I've been afraid!'

'But of what? Of exposure, or of being arrested for murder?'

The colour ebbed away from her cheeks.

'Murder – but I didn't – Oh, you don't believe *that*! I didn't kill her. I didn't!'

'You wanted her dead . . .'

'Yes, but I didn't kill her . . . Oh, you must believe me – you must. I never moved from my seat. I –'

She broke off. Her beautiful blue eyes were fixed on him imploringly.

Hercule Poirot nodded soothingly.

'I believe you, Madame, for two reasons – first, because of your sex, and secondly because of – a wasp.'

She stared at him.

'A wasp?'

'Exactly. That does not make sense to you, I see. Now, then, let us attend to the matter in hand. I will deal with this Mr Robinson. I pledge you my word that you shall never see or hear of him again. I will settle his – his – I have forgotten the word – his bacon? No, his goat. Now in return for my services I will ask you two little questions. Was Mr Barraclough in Paris the day before the murder?'

'Yes, we dined together. But he thought it better I should go and see the woman alone.'

'Ah, he did, did he? Now, Madame, one further question: Your stage name before you were married was Cicely Bland. Was that your real name?'

'No, my real name is Martha Jebb. But the other –'

'Made a better professional name. And you were born – where?'

'Doncaster. But why –'

'Mere curiosity. Forgive me. And now, Lady Horbury, will you permit me to give you some advice? Why not arrange with your husband a discreet divorce?'

'And let him marry that woman?'

'And let him marry that woman. You have a generous heart, Madame; and besides, you will be safe – oh, so safe – and your husband he will pay you an income.'

'Not a very large one.'

'*Eh bien*, once you are free you will marry a millionaire.'

'There aren't any nowadays.'

'Ah, do not believe that, Madame. The man who had three millions perhaps now he has two millions – *eh bien*, it is still enough.'

Cicely laughed.

'You're very persuasive, M. Poirot. And are you really sure that dreadful man will never bother me again?'

'On the word of Hercule Poirot,' said that gentleman solemnly.

CHAPTER 20

IN HARLEY STREET

Detective-Inspector Japp walked briskly up Harley Street and stopped at a certain door.

He asked for Dr Bryant.

'Have you an appointment, sir?'

'No, I'll just write a few words.'

On an official card he wrote:

'Should be much obliged if you could spare me a few moments. I won't keep you long.'

He sealed up the card in an envelope and gave it to the butler.

He was shown into a waiting-room. There were two women there and a man. Japp settled down with an elderly copy of *Punch*.

The butler reappeared and, crossing the floor, said in a discreet voice:

'If you wouldn't mind waiting a short time, sir, the doctor will see you, but he's very busy this morning.'

Japp nodded. He did not in the least mind waiting – in fact he rather welcomed it. The two women had begun to talk. They had obviously a very high opinion of Dr Bryant's abilities. More patients came in. Evidently Dr Bryant was doing well in his profession.

'Fairly coining money,' thought Japp to himself. 'That doesn't look like needing to borrow; but of course the loan may have taken place a long time ago. Anyway, he's got a fine practice; a breath of scandal would burst it to bits. That's the worst of being a doctor.'

Quarter of an hour later the butler reappeared and said:

'The doctor will see you now, sir.'

Japp was shown into Dr Bryant's consulting-room – a room at the back of the house with a big window. The doctor was sitting at his desk. He rose and shook hands with the detective.

His fine-lined face showed fatigue, but he seemed in no way disturbed by the inspector's visit.

'What can I do for you, Inspector?' he said as he resumed his seat and motioned Japp to a chair opposite.

'I must apologize first for calling in your consulting hours, but I shan't keep you long, sir.'

'That is all right, I suppose it is about the aeroplane death?'

'Quite right, sir. We're still working on it.'

'With any result?'

'We're not as far on as we'd like to be. I really came to ask you some questions about the method employed. It's this snake venom business that I can't get the hang of.'

'I'm not a toxicologist, you know,' said Dr Bryant, smiling. 'Such things aren't in my line. Winterspoon's your man.'

'Ah, but you see, it's like this, Doctor. Winterspoon's an expert – and you know what experts are. They talk so that the ordinary man can't understand them. But as far as I can make out there's a medical side of this business. Is it true that snake venom is sometimes injected for epilepsy?'

'I'm not a specialist in epilepsy, either,' said Dr Bryant. 'But I believe that injections of cobra venom have been used in the treatment of epilepsy with excellent results. But, as I say, that's not really my line of country.'

'I know – I know. What it really amounts to is this: I felt that you'd take an interest, having been on the aeroplane yourself. I thought it possible that you'd have some ideas on the subject yourself that might be useful to me. It's not much good my going to an expert if I don't know what to ask him.'

Dr Bryant smiled.

'There is something in what you say, Inspector. There is probably no man living who can remain entirely unaffected by having come in close contact with murder . . . I am interested, I admit. I have speculated a good deal about the case in my quiet way.'

'And what do you think, sir?'

Bryant shook his head slowly.

'It amazes me – the whole thing seems almost – unreal – if I might put it that way. An astounding way of committing a crime. It seems a chance in a hundred that the murderer was not seen. He must be a person with a reckless disregard of risks.'

'Very true, sir.'

'The choice of poison is equally amazing. How could a would-be murderer possibly get hold of such a thing?'

'I know. It seems incredible. Why, I don't suppose one man in a thousand has ever heard of such a thing as a boomslang, much less actually handled the venom. You yourself, sir, now, you're a doctor – but I don't suppose you've ever handled the stuff.'

'There are certainly not many opportunities of doing so. I have a friend who works at tropical research. In his laboratory there are various specimens of dried snake venoms – that of the cobra, for instance – but I cannot remember any specimen of the boomslang.'

'Perhaps you can help me –' Japp took out a piece of paper and handed it to the doctor. 'Winterspoon wrote down these three names – said I might get information there. Do you know any of these men?'

'I know Professor Kennedy slightly. Heidler I know well; mention my name and I'm sure he'll do all he can for you. Carmichael's an Edinburgh man – I don't know him personally – but I believe they've done some good work up there.'

'Thank you, sir, I'm much obliged. Well, I won't keep you any longer.'

When Japp emerged into Harley Street he was smiling to himself in a pleased fashion.

'Nothing like tact,' he said to himself. 'Tact does it. I'll be bound he never saw what I was after. Well, that's that.'

CHAPTER 21

THE THREE CLUES

When Japp got back to Scotland Yard he was told that M. Hercule Poirot was waiting to see him.

Japp greeted his friend heartily.

'Well, M. Poirot, and what brings you along. Any news?'

'I came to ask you for news, my good Japp.'

'If that isn't just like you. Well, there isn't much and that's the truth. The dealer fellow in Paris has identified the blowpipe all right. Fournier's been worrying the life out of me from Paris about his *moment psychologique*. I've questioned those stewards till I'm blue in the face, and they stick to it that there wasn't a *moment psychologique*. Nothing startling or out of the way happened on the voyage.'

'It might have occurred when they were both in the front car.'

'I've questioned the passengers, too. Everyone can't be lying.'

'In one case I investigated everyone was!'

'You and your cases! To tell the truth, M. Poirot, I'm not very happy. The more I look into things the less I get. The Chief's inclined to look on me rather coldly. But what can I do? Luckily it's one of those semi-foreign cases. We can put it on the Frenchmen over here – and in Paris they say it was done by an Englishman and that it's our business.'

'Do you really believe the Frenchmen did it?'

'Well, frankly, I don't. As I look at it an archaeologist is a poor kind of fish. Always burrowing in the ground and talking through his hat about what happened thousands of years ago – and how do they know, I should like to know? Who's to contradict them? They say some rotten string of beads is five thousand three hundred and twenty-two years old, and who's to say it isn't? Well, there they are – liars, perhaps – though they seem to believe it themselves – but harmless. I had an old chap in here the other day who'd had a scarab pinched – terrible state he was in – nice old boy, but helpless as a baby in arms. No, between you and me, I don't think for a minute that pair of French archaeologists did it.'

'Who *do* you think did it?'

'Well – there's Clancy, of course. He's in a queer way. Goes about muttering to himself. He's got something on his mind.'

'The plot of a new book, perhaps.'

'It may be that – and it may be something else; but, try as I may, I can't get a line on motive. I still think CL 52 in the black book is Lady Horbury; but I can't get anything out of her. She's pretty hard-boiled, I can tell you.'

Poirot smiled to himself. Japp went on:

'The stewards – well, I can't find a thing to connect them with Giselle.'

'Dr Bryant?'

'I think I'm on to something there. Rumours about him and a patient. Pretty woman – nasty husband – takes drugs or something. If he's not careful he'll be struck off the medical council. That fits in with RT 362 well enough, and I don't mind telling you that I've got a pretty shrewd idea where he could have got the snake venom from. I went to see him and he gave himself away rather badly over that. Still, so far it is all surmise – no *facts*. Facts aren't any too easy to get at in this case. Ryder seems all square and above board – says he went to raise a loan in Paris and couldn't get it – gave names and addresses – all checked up. I've found out that the firm was nearly in Queer Street about a week or two ago, but they seem to be just pulling through. There you are again – unsatisfactory. The whole thing is a muddle.'

'There is no such thing as muddle – obscurity, yes – but muddle can exist only in a disorderly brain.'

'Use any word you choose. The result's the same. Fournier's stumped, too. I suppose you've got it all taped out, but you'd rather not tell!'

'You mock yourself at me. I have not got it all taped out. I proceed a step at a time, with order and method, but there is still far to go.'

'I can't help feeling glad to hear that. Let's hear about these orderly steps.'

Poirot smiled.

'I make a little table – so.' He took a paper from his pocket.

'My idea is this: A murder is an action performed to bring about a certain result.'

'Say that again slowly.'

'It is not difficult.'

'Probably not – but you make it sound so.'

'No, no, it is very simple. Say you want money – you get it when an aunt dies. *Bien* – you perform an action – this is to kill the aunt – and get the result – inherit the money.'

'I wish I had some aunts like that,' sighed Japp. 'Go ahead, I see your idea. You mean there's *got* to be a motive.'

'I prefer my own way of putting it. An action is performed – the action being murder – what now are the results of that action? By studying the different results we should get the answer to our conundrum. The results of a single action may be very varied – that particular action affects a lot of different people. *Eh bien*, I study today – three weeks after the crime – the result in eleven different cases.'

He spread out the paper.

Japp leaned forward with some interest and read over Poirot's shoulder:

> *Miss Grey*. Result – temporary improvement. Increased salary.
> *Mr Gale*. Result – bad. Loss of practice.
> *Lady Horbury*. Result good, if she's CL 52.
> *Miss Kerr*. Result – bad, since Giselle's death makes it more unlikely Lord Horbury will get the evidence to divorce his wife.

'H'm.' Japp interrupted his scrutiny. 'So you think she's keen on his lordship? You are a one for nosing out love affairs.'

Poirot smiled. Japp bent over the chart once more.

> *Mr Clancy*. Result – good – expects to make money by book dealing with the murder.
> *Dr Bryant*. Result – good if RT 362.
> *Mr Ryder*. Result – good, owing to small amount of cash obtained through articles on murder which tided firm over delicate time. Also good if Ryder is XVB 724.
> *M. Dupont*. Result – unaffected.

M. Jean Dupont. Result – the same.
Mitchell. Result – unaffected.
Davis. Result – unaffected.

'And you think that's going to help you?' asked Japp sceptically. 'I can't see that writing down "*I don't know. I don't know. I can't tell*," makes it any better.'

'It gives one a clear classification,' explained Poirot. 'In four cases – Mr Clancy, Miss Grey, Mr Ryder, and I think I may say Lady Horbury – there is a result on the credit side. In the cases of Mr Gale and Miss Kerr there is a result on the debit side – in four cases there is no result at all – so far as we know – and in one, Dr Bryant, there is either no result or a distinct gain.'

'And so?' asked Japp.

'And so,' said Poirot, 'we must go on seeking.'

'With precious little to go upon,' said Japp gloomily. 'The truth of it is that we're hung up until we can get what we want from Paris. It's the Giselle side that wants going into. I bet I could have got more out of that maid than Fournier did.'

'I doubt it, my friend. The most interesting thing about this case is the personality of the dead woman. A woman without friends – without relations – without, as one might *say* – any *personal* life. A woman who was once young, who once loved and suffered and then – with a firm hand pulled down the shutter – all that was over; not a photograph, not a souvenir, not a knick-knack. Marie Morisot became Madame Giselle – moneylender.'

'Do you think there is a clue in her past?'

'Perhaps.'

'Well, we could do with it! There aren't any clues in this case.'

'Oh, yes, my friend, there are.'

'The blowpipe, of course –'

'No, no, not the blowpipe.'

'Well, let's hear your ideas of the clues in the case.'

Poirot smiled.

'I will give them titles – like the names of Mr Clancy's stories: The Clue of the Wasp. The Clue in the Passenger's Baggage. The Clue of the Extra Coffee Spoon.'

'You're potty,' said Japp kindly, and added: 'What's this about a coffee spoon?'

'Madame Giselle had two spoons in her saucer.'

'That's supposed to mean a wedding.'

'In this case,' said Poirot, 'it meant a funeral.'

CHAPTER 22

JANE TAKES A NEW JOB

When Norman Gale, Jane and Poirot met for dinner on the night after the 'blackmailing incident' Norman was relieved to hear that his services as 'Mr Robinson' were no longer required.

'He is dead, the good Mr Robinson,' said Poirot. He raised his glass. 'Let us drink to his memory.'

'RIP,' said Norman with a laugh.

'What happened?' asked Jane of Poirot.

He smiled at her.

'I found out what I wanted to know.'

'Was she mixed up with Giselle?'

'Yes.'

'That was pretty clear from my interview with her,' said Norman.

'Quite so,' said Poirot. 'But I wanted a full and detailed story.'

'And you got it?'

'I got it.'

They both looked at him inquiringly, but Poirot, in a provoking manner, began to discuss the relationship between a career and life.

'There are not so many round pegs in square holes as one might think. Most people, in spite of what they tell you, choose the occupations that they secretly desire. You will hear a man say who works in an office, "I should like to explore – to rough it in far countries." But you will find that he likes reading the fiction that deals with that subject, but that he himself prefers the safety and moderate comfort of an office stool.'

'According to you,' said Jane, 'my desire for foreign travel isn't genuine – messing about with women's heads is my true vocation – well, that *isn't* true.'

Poirot smiled at her.

'You are young still. Naturally one tries this, that and the other, but what one eventually settles down into is the life one prefers.'

'And suppose I prefer being rich?'

'Ah, that, it is more difficult!'

'I don't agree with you,' said Gale. 'I'm a dentist by chance – not choice. My uncle was a dentist – he wanted me to come in with him, but I was all for adventure and seeing the world. I chucked dentistry and went off to farm in South Africa. However, that wasn't much good – I hadn't got enough experience. I had to accept the old man's offer and come and set up business with him.'

'And now you are thinking of chucking dentistry again and going off to Canada. You have a Dominion complex!'

'This time I shall be forced to do it.'

'Ah, but it is incredible how often things force one to do the thing one would like to do.'

'Nothing's forcing me to travel,' said Jane wistfully. 'I wish it would.'

'*Eh bien*, I make you an offer here and now. I go to Paris next week. If you like you can take the job of my secretary – I will give you a good salary.'

Jane shook her head.

'I mustn't give up Antoine's. It's a good job.'

'So is mine a good job.'

'Yes, but it's only temporary.'

'I will obtain you another post of the same kind.'

'Thanks, but I don't think I'll risk it.'

Poirot looked at her and smiled enigmatically.

Three days later he was rung up.

'M. Poirot,' said Jane, 'is that job still open?'

'But yes. I go to Paris on Monday.'

'You really mean it? I can come?'

'Yes, but what has happened to make you change your mind?'

'I've had a row with Antoine. As a matter of fact I lost my temper with a customer. She was an – an absolute – well, I can't say just what she was through the telephone. I was feeling nervy and instead of doing my soothing syrup stuff I just let rip and told her exactly what I thought of her.'

'Ah, the thought of the great wide open spaces.'

'What's that you say?'

'I say that your mind was dwelling on a certain subject.'

'It wasn't my mind, it was my tongue that slipped. I enjoyed it – her eyes looked just like her beastly Pekingese's – as though they were going to drop out – but here I am – thrown out on my ear, as you might say. I must get another job sometime, I suppose – but I'd like to come to Paris first.'

'Good, it is arranged. On the way over I will give you your instructions.'

Poirot and his new secretary did not travel by air, for which Jane was secretly thankful. The unpleasant experience of her last trip had shaken her nerve. She did not want to be reminded of that lolling figure in rusty black . . .

On their way from Calais to Paris they had the compartment to themselves, and Poirot gave Jane some idea of his plans.

'There are several people in Paris that I have to see. There is the lawyer – Maître Thibault. There is also M. Fournier of the Sûreté – a melancholy man, but intelligent. And there are M. Dupont *père* and M. Dupont *fils*. Now, Mademoiselle Jane, whilst I am taking on the father I shall leave the son to you. You are very charming, very attractive – I fancy that M. Dupont will remember you from the inquest.'

'I've seen him since then,' said Jane, her colour rising slightly.

'Indeed? And how was that?'

Jane, her colour rising a little more, described their meeting in the Corner House.

'Excellent – better and better. Ah, it was a famous idea of mine to bring you to Paris with me. Now listen carefully, Mademoiselle Jane. As far as possible do not discuss the Giselle affair, but do not avoid the subject if Jean Dupont introduces it. It might be well if, without actually saying so, you could convey the impression that Lady Horbury is suspected of the crime. My reason for coming to Paris, you can say, is to confer with M. Fournier and to inquire particularly into any dealings Lady Horbury may have had with the dead woman.'

'Poor Lady Horbury – you do make her a stalking horse!'

'She is not the type I admire – *eh bien*, let her be useful for once.'

Jane hesitated for a minute, then said:

'You don't suspect young M. Dupont of the crime, do you?'

'No, no, no – I desire information merely.' He looked at her sharply. 'He attracts you – eh – this young man? *Il a le sex appeal?*'

Jane laughed at the phrase.

'No, that's not how I would describe him. He's very simple, but rather a dear.'

'So that is how you describe him – very simple?'

'He *is* simple. I think it's because he's led a nice unworldly life.'

'True,' said Poirot. 'He has not, for instance, dealt with teeth. He has not been disillusioned by the sight of a public hero shivering with fright in the dentist's chair.'

Jane laughed.

'I don't think Norman's roped in any public heroes yet as patients.'

'It would have been a waste, since he is going to Canada.'

'He's talking of New Zealand now. He thinks I'd like the climate better.'

'At all events he is patriotic. He sticks to the British Dominions.'

'I'm hoping,' said Jane, 'that it won't be necessary.'

She fixed Poirot with an inquiring eye.

'Meaning that you put your trust in Papa Poirot? Ah, well – I will do the best I can – that I promise you. But I have the feeling very strongly, Mademoiselle, that there is a figure who has not yet come into the limelight – a part as yet unplayed –'

He shook his head, frowning.

'There is, Mademoiselle, an unknown factor in this case. Everything points to that . . .'

II

Two days after their arrival in Paris, M. Hercule Poirot and his secretary dined in a small restaurant, and the two Duponts, father and son, were Poirot's guests.

Old M. Dupont, Jane found as charming as his son, but she got little chance of talking to him. Poirot monopolized him severely from the start. Jane found Jean no less easy to get on with than she had done in London. His attractive, boyish personality pleased her now as it had then. He was such a simple friendly soul.

All the same, even while she laughed and talked with him, her ear was alert to catch snatches of the two older men's conversation. She wondered precisely what information it was that Poirot wanted. So far as she could hear, the conversation had never touched once on the murder. Poirot was skilfully drawing out his companion on the subject of the past. His interest in archaeological research in Persia seemed both deep and sincere. M. Dupont was enjoying his evening enormously. Seldom did he get such an intelligent and sympathetic listener.

Whose suggestion it was that the two young people should go to a cinema was not quite clear, but when they had gone Poirot drew his chair a little closer to the table and seemed prepared to take a still more practical interest in archaeological research.

'I comprehend,' he said. 'Naturally it is a great anxiety in these difficult financial days to raise sufficient funds. You accept private donations?'

M. Dupont laughed.

'My dear friend, we sue for them practically on bended knees! But our particular type of dig does not attract the great mass of humanity. They demand spectacular results! Above all, they like gold – large quantities of gold! It is amazing how little the average person cares for pottery. Pottery – the whole romance of humanity can be expressed in terms of pottery. Design – texture –'

M. Dupont was well away. He besought Poirot not to be led astray by the specious publications of B –, the really criminal misdating of L –, and the hopelessly unscientific stratification of G –. Poirot promised solemnly not to be led astray by any of the publications of these learned personages.

Then he said:

'Would a donation, for instance, of five hundred pounds –?'

M. Dupont nearly fell across the table in his excitement.

'You – you are offering that? To me? To aid our researches. But it is magnificent, stupendous! The biggest private donation we have had.'

Poirot coughed.

'I will admit – there is a favour –'

'Ah, yes, a *souvenir* – some specimens of pottery –'

'No, no, you misunderstand me,' said Poirot quickly before M. Dupont could get well away again. 'It is my secretary – that charming young girl you saw tonight – if she could accompany you on your expedition?'

M. Dupont seemed slightly taken aback for a moment.

'Well,' he said, pulling his moustache, 'it might possibly be arranged. I should have to consult my son. My nephew and his wife are to accompany us. It was to have been a family party. However, I will speak to Jean –'

'Mademoiselle Grey is passionately interested in pottery. The Past has for her an immense fascination. It is the dream of her life to dig. Also she mends socks and sews on buttons in a manner truly admirable.'

'A useful accomplishment.'

'Is it not? And now you were telling me – about the pottery of Susa –'

M. Dupont resumed a happy monologue on his own particular theories of Susa I and Susa II.

Poirot reached his hotel, to find Jane saying good night to Jean Dupont in the hall.

As they went up in the lift Poirot said:

'I have obtained for you a job of great interest. You are to accompany the Duponts to Persia in the spring.'

Jane stared at him.

'Are you quite mad?'

'When the offer is made to you, you will accept with every manifestation of delight.'

'I am certainly not going to Persia. I shall be in Muswell Hill or New Zealand with Norman.'

Poirot twinkled at her gently.

'My dear child,' he said, 'it is some months to next March. To express delight is not to buy a ticket. In the same way, I have talked about a donation – but I have not actually signed a cheque! By the way, I must obtain for you in the morning a handbook on Prehistoric Pottery of the Near East. I have said that you are passionately interested in the subject.'

Jane sighed.

'Being secretary to you is no sinecure, is it? Anything else?'

'Yes. I have said that you sew on buttons and darn socks to perfection.'

'Do I have to give a demonstration of that tomorrow, too?'

'It would be as well, perhaps,' said Poirot, 'if they took my word for it!'

CHAPTER 23

ANNE MORISOT

At half past ten on the following morning the melancholy M. Fournier walked into Poirot's sitting-room and shook the little Belgian warmly by the hand.

His own manner was far more animated than usual.

'Monsieur,' he said, 'there is something I want to tell you. I have, I think, at last seen the point of what you said in London about the finding of the blowpipe.'

'Ah!' Poirot's face lighted up.

'Yes,' said Fournier taking a chair. 'I pondered much over what you had said. Again and again I say to myself: *Impossible that the crime should have been committed as we believe*. And at last – at last – I see a connexion between that repetition of mine and what you said about the finding of the blowpipe.'

Poirot listened attentively, but said nothing.

'That day in London you said, *Why was the blowpipe found, when it might so easily have been passed out through the ventilator*? And I think now that I have the answer. *The blowpipe was found because the murderer wanted it to be found*.'

'Bravo!' said Poirot.

'That *was* your meaning, then? Good, I thought so. And I went on a step further. I ask myself: *Why did the murderer want the blowpipe to be found*? And to that I got the answer: *Because the blowpipe was not used*.'

'Bravo! Bravo! My reasoning exactly.'

'I say to myself: The poisoned dart, *yes*, but not the blowpipe. Then *something else* was used to send that dart through the air – something that a man or woman might put to their lips in a normal manner and which would cause no remark. And I remembered your insistence on a complete list of all that was found in the passengers' luggage and upon their persons. There were two things that especially attracted my attention – *Lady Horbury had two cigarette holders*, and on the table in front of the Duponts *were a number of Kurdish pipes*.'

M. Fournier paused. He looked at Poirot. Poirot did not speak.

'Both those things could have been put to the lips naturally without anyone remarking on it . . . I am right, am I not?'

Poirot hesitated, then he said:

'You are on the right track, yes, but go a little further; and do not forget the wasp.'

'The wasp?' Fournier stared. 'No, there I do not follow you. I cannot see where the wasp comes in.'

'You cannot see? But it is there that I –'

He broke off as the telephone rang.

He took up the receiver.

''Allo, 'allo. Ah, good morning. Yes, it is I myself, Hercule Poirot.' In an aside to Fournier he said, 'It is Thibault . . .'

'Yes – yes, indeed. Very well. And you? M. Fournier? Quite right. Yes, he has arrived. He is here at this moment.'

Lowering the receiver, he said to Fournier:

'He tried to get you at the Sûreté. They told him that you had come to see me here. You had better speak to him. He sounds excited.'

Fournier took the telephone.

''Allo – 'allo. Yes, it is Fournier speaking . . . What . . . *What* . . . In verity, is that so . . . ? Yes, indeed . . . Yes . . . Yes, I am sure he will. We will come round at once.'

He replaced the telephone on its hook and looked across at Poirot.

'It is the daughter. The daughter of Madame Giselle.'

'What?'

'Yes, she has arrived to claim her heritage.'

'Where has she come from?'

'America, I understand. Thibault has asked her to return at half past eleven. He suggests we should go round and see him.'

'Most certainly. We will go immediately . . . I will leave a note for Mademoiselle Grey.'

He wrote:

> Some developments have occurred which force me to go out. If M. Jean Dupont should ring up or call, be amiable to him. Talk of buttons and socks, but not as yet of prehistoric pottery. He admires you; but he is intelligent!
>
> Au revoir,
>
> Hercule Poirot.

'And now let us come, my friend,' he said, rising. 'This is what

I have been waiting for – the entry on the scene of the shadowy figure of whose presence I have been conscious all along. Now – soon – I ought to understand everything.'

II

Maître Thibault received Poirot and Fournier with great affability.

After an interchange of compliments and polite questions and answers, the lawyer settled down to the discussion of Madame Giselle's heiress.

'I received a letter yesterday,' he said, 'and this morning the young lady herself called upon me.'

'What age is Mademoiselle Morisot?'

'Mademoiselle Morisot – or rather Mrs Richards – for she is married, is exactly twenty-four years of age.'

'She brought documents to prove her identity?' asked Fournier.

'Certainly. Certainly.'

He opened a file at his elbow.

'To begin with, there is this.'

It was a copy of a marriage certificate between George Leman, bachelor, and Marie Morisot – both of Quebec. Its date was 1910. There was also the birth certificate of Anne Morisot Leman. There were various other documents and papers.

'This throws a certain light on the early life of Madame Giselle,' said Fournier.

Thibault nodded.

'As far as I can piece it out,' he said, 'Marie Morisot was nursery governess or sewing-maid when she met this man Leman.

'He was, I gather, a bad lot who deserted her soon after the marriage, and she resumed her maiden name.

'The child was received in the Institut de Marie at Quebec and was brought up there. Marie Morisot or Leman left Quebec shortly afterwards – I imagine with a man – and came to France. She remitted sums of money from time to time, and finally dispatched a lump sum of ready money to be given to the child on attaining the age of twenty-one. At that time Marie Morisot or Leman was, no doubt, living an irregular life, and considered it better to sunder any personal relations.'

'How did the girl realize that she was the heiress to a fortune?'

'We have inserted discreet advertisements in various journals.

It seems one of these came to the notice of the Principal of the Institut de Marie, and she wrote or telegraphed to Mrs Richards, who was then in Europe, but on the point of returning to the States.'

'Who is Richards?'

'I gather he is an American or Canadian from Detroit – by profession a maker of surgical instruments.'

'He did not accompany his wife?'

'No, he is still in America.'

'Is Mrs Richards able to throw any light upon a possible reason for her mother's murder?'

The lawyer shook his head.

'She knows nothing about her. In fact, although she had once heard the Principal mention it, she did not even remember what her mother's maiden name was.'

'It looks,' said Fournier, 'as though her appearance on the scene is not going to be of any help in solving the murder problem. Not, I must admit, that I ever thought it would. I am on quite another tack at present. My inquiries have narrowed down to a choice of three persons.'

'Four,' said Poirot.

'You think four?'

'It is not I who say four, but on the theory that you advanced to me you cannot confine yourself to three persons.' He made a sudden rapid motion with his hands. 'The two cigarette holders – the Kurdish pipes and a flute. Remember the flute, my friend.'

Fournier gave an exclamation, but at that moment the door opened and an aged clerk mumbled:

'The lady has returned.'

'Ah,' said Thibault. 'Now you will be able to see the heiress for yourself. Come in, Madame. Let me present to you M. Fournier of the Sûreté, who is in charge in this country of the inquiries into your mother's death. This is M. Hercule Poirot, whose name may be familiar to you and who is kindly giving us his assistance. Madame Richards.'

Giselle's daughter was a dark, chic-looking young woman. She was very smartly though plainly dressed.

She held out her hand to each of the men in turn, murmuring a few appreciative words.

'Though, I fear, Messieurs, that I have hardly the feeling of a daughter in the matter. I have been to all intents and purposes an orphan all my life.'

In answer to Fournier's questions she spoke warmly and gratefully of Mère Angélique, the head of the Institut de Marie.

'She has always been kindness itself to me.'

'You left the Institut – when, Madame?'

'When I was eighteen, Monsieur. I started to earn my living. I was, for a time, a manicurist. I have also been in a dressmaker's establishment. I met my husband in Nice. He was then just returning to the States. He came over again on business to Holland and we were married in Rotterdam a month ago. Unfortunately, he had to return to Canada. I was detained – but I am now about to rejoin him.'

Anne Richards's French was fluent and easy. She was clearly more French than English.

'You heard of the tragedy – how?'

'Naturally I read of it in the papers, but I did not know – that is, I did not *realize* – that the victim in the case was my mother. Then I received a telegram here in Paris from Mère Angélique giving me the address of Maître Thibault and reminding me of my mother's maiden name.'

Fournier nodded thoughtfully.

They talked a little further, but it seemed clear that Mrs Richards could be of little assistance to them in their search for the murderer. She knew nothing at all of her mother's life or business relations.

Having elicited the name of the hotel at which she was staying, Poirot and Fournier took leave of her.

'You are disappointed, *mon vieux*,' said Fournier. 'You had some idea in your brain about this girl? Did you suspect that she might be an impostor? Or do you, in fact, still suspect that she is an impostor?'

Poirot shook his head in a discouraged manner.

'No – I do not think she is an impostor. Her proofs of identity sound genuine enough . . . It is odd, though, I feel that I have either seen her before – or that she reminds me of someone . . .'

'A likeness to the dead woman?' suggested Fournier doubtfully. 'Surely not.'

'No – it is not that – I wish I could remember what it was. I am sure her face reminds me of someone . . .'

Fournier looked at him curiously.

'You have always, I think, been intrigued by the missing daughter.'

'Naturally,' said Poirot, his eyebrows rising a little. 'Of all the people who may or may not benefit by Giselle's death, this young woman does benefit – very definitely – in hard cash.'

'True – but does that get us anywhere?'

Poirot did not answer for a minute or two. He was following the train of his own thoughts. He said at last:

'My friend – a very large fortune passes to this girl. Do you wonder that from the beginning I speculated as to her being implicated. There were three women on that plane. One of them, Miss Venetia Kerr, was of well-known and authenticated family. But the other two? Ever since Elise Grandier advanced the theory that the father of Madame Giselle's child was an Englishman I have kept it in my mind that one of the two other women might conceivably be this daughter. They were both of approximately the right age. Lady Horbury was a chorus girl whose antecedents were somewhat obscure and who acted under a stage name. Miss Jane Grey, as she once told me, had been brought up in an orphanage.'

'Ah ha!' said the Frenchman. 'So that is the way your mind has been running? Our friend Japp would say that you were being over-ingenious.'

'It is true that he always accuses me of preferring to make things difficult.'

'You see?'

'But as a matter of fact it is not true – I proceed always in the simplest manner imaginable! And I never refuse to accept facts.'

'But you are disappointed? You expected more from this Anne Morisot?'

They were just entering Poirot's hotel. An object lying on the reception desk recalled Fournier's mind to something Poirot had said earlier in the morning.

'I have not thanked you,' he said, 'for drawing my attention to the error I had committed. I noted the two cigarette holders of Lady Horbury and the Kurdish pipes of the Duponts. It was unpardonable on my part to have forgotten the flute of Dr Bryant, though I do not seriously suspect him –'

'You do not?'

'No. He does not strike me as the kind of man to –'

He stopped. The man standing at the reception desk talking to the clerk turned, his hand on the flute case. His glance fell on Poirot and his face lit up in grave recognition.

Poirot went forward – Fournier discreetly withdrew into the background. As well that Bryant should not see him.

'Dr Bryant,' said Poirot, bowing.

'M. Poirot.'

They shook hands. A woman who had been standing near Bryant moved away towards the lift. Poirot sent just a fleeting glance after her.

He said:

'Well, *M. le docteur*, are your patients managing to do without you for a little?'

Dr Bryant smiled – that melancholy attractive smile that the other remembered so well. He looked tired, but strangely peaceful.

'I have no patients now,' he said.

Then, moving towards a little table, he said:

'A glass of sherry, M. Poirot, or some other *apéritif*?'

'I thank you.'

They sat down, and the doctor gave the order. Then he said slowly:

'No, I have no patients now. I have retired.'

'A sudden decision?'

'Not so very sudden.'

He was silent as the drinks were set before them. Then, raising the glass, he said:

'It is a necessary decision. I resign of my own free will before I am struck off the register.' He went on speaking in a gentle, faraway voice. 'There comes to everyone a turning-point in their lives, M. Poirot. They stand at the cross-roads and have to decide. My profession interests me enormously – it is a sorrow – a very great sorrow to abandon it. But there are other claims . . . There is, M. Poirot, the happiness of a human being.'

Poirot did not speak. He waited.

'There is a lady – a patient of mine – I love her very dearly. She has a husband who causes her infinite misery. He takes drugs. If you were a doctor you would know what that meant. She has no money of her own, so she cannot leave him . . .

'For some time I have been undecided – but now I have made

up my mind. She and I are now on our way to Kenya to begin a new life. I hope that at last she may know a little happiness. She has suffered so long . . .'

Again he was silent. Then he said in a brisker tone:

'I tell you this, M. Poirot, because it will soon be public property, and the sooner you know the better.'

'I understand,' said Poirot. After a minute he said, 'You take your flute, I see?'

Dr Bryant smiled.

'My flute, M. Poirot, is my oldest companion . . . When everything else fails – music remains.'

His hand ran lovingly over the flute case, then with a bow he rose.

Poirot rose also.

'My best wishes for your future, *M. le docteur* – and for that of Madame,' said Poirot.

When Fournier rejoined his friend, Poirot was at the desk making arrangements for a trunk call to Quebec.

CHAPTER 24

A BROKEN FINGER-NAIL

'What now?' cried Fournier. 'You are still preoccupied with this girl who inherits? Decidedly it is the *idée fixe* you have there.'

'Not at all, not at all,' said Poirot. 'But there must be in all things order and method. One must finish with one thing before proceeding to the next.'

He looked round.

'Here is Mademoiselle Jane. Suppose that you commence *déjeuner*. I will join you as soon as I can.'

Fournier acquiesced and he and Jane went into the dining-room.

'Well?' said Jane with curiosity. 'What is she like?'

'She is a little over medium height, dark, with a matte complexion, a pointed chin –'

'You're talking exactly like a passport,' said Jane. 'My passport description is simply insulting, I think. It's composed of mediums and ordinary. Nose, medium; mouth ordinary (how do they expect you to describe a mouth?); forehead, ordinary; chin, ordinary.'

'But not ordinary eyes,' said Fournier.

'Even they are grey, which is not a very exciting colour.'

'And who has told you, Mademoiselle, that it is not an exciting colour?' said the Frenchman, leaning across the table.

Jane laughed.

'Your command of the English language,' she said, 'is highly efficient. Tell me more about Anne Morisot – is she pretty?'

'*Assez bien*,' said Fournier cautiously. 'And she is not Anne Morisot. She is Anne Richards. She is married.'

'Was the husband there, too?'

'No.'

'Why not, I wonder?'

'Because he is in Canada or America.'

He explained some of the circumstances of Anne's life. Just as he was drawing his narrative to a close, Poirot joined them.

He looked a little dejected.

'Well, *mon cher*?' inquired Fournier.

'I spoke to the principal – to Mère Angélique herself. It is romantic, you know, the transatlantic telephone. To speak so easily to someone nearly halfway across the globe.'

'The telegraphed photograph – that too is romantic. Science is the greatest romance there is. But you were saying?'

'I talked with Mère Angélique. She confirmed exactly what Mrs Richards told us of the circumstances of her having been brought up at the Institut de Marie. She spoke quite frankly about the mother who left Quebec with a Frenchman interested in the wine trade. She was relieved at the time that the child would not come under her mother's influence. From her point of view Giselle was on the downward path. Money was sent regularly – but Giselle never suggested a meeting.'

'In fact your conversation was a repetition of what we heard this morning.'

'Practically – except that it was more detailed. Anne Morisot left the Institut de Marie six years ago to become a manicurist, afterwards she had a job as a lady's maid – and finally left Quebec for Europe in that capacity. Her letters were not frequent, but Mère Angélique usually heard from her about twice a year. When she saw an account of the inquest in the paper she realized that this Marie Morisot was in all probability the Marie Morisot who had lived in Quebec.'

'What about the husband?' asked Fournier. 'Now that we know definitely that Giselle was married, the husband might become a factor?'

'I thought of that. It was one of the reasons for my telephone call. George Leman, Giselle's blackguard of a husband, was killed in the early days of the war.'

He paused and then remarked abruptly:

'What was it that I just said – not my last remark – the one before? – I have an idea that – without knowing it – I said something of significance.'

Fournier repeated as well as he could the substance of Poirot's remarks, but the little man shook his head in a dissatisfied manner.

'No – no – it was not that. Well, no matter . . .'

He turned to Jane and engaged her in conversation.

At the close of the meal he suggested that they have coffee in the lounge.

Jane agreed and stretched out her hand for her bag and gloves, which were on the table. As she picked them up she winced slightly.

'What is it, Mademoiselle?'

'Oh, it's nothing,' laughed Jane. 'It's only a jagged nail. I must file it.'

Poirot sat down again very suddenly.

'*Nom d'un nom d'un nom*,' he said quietly.

The other two stared at him in surprise.

'M. Poirot?' cried Jane. 'What is it?'

'It is,' said Poirot, 'that I remember now why the face of Anne Morisot is familiar to me. I have seen her before . . . in the aeroplane on the day of the murder. Lady Horbury sent for her to get a nail file. *Anne Morisot was Lady Horbury's maid.*'

CHAPTER 25

'I AM AFRAID'

This sudden revelation had an almost stunning effect on the three people sitting round the luncheon table. It opened up an entirely new aspect of the case.

Instead of being a person wholly remote from the tragedy, Anne

Morisot was now shown to have been actually present on the scene of the crime. It took a minute or two for everyone to readjust their ideas.

Poirot made a frantic gesture with his hands – his eyes closed – his face contorted in agony.

'A little minute – a little minute,' he implored them. 'I have got to think, to see, to realize how this affects my ideas of the case. I must go back in my mind. I must remember . . . A thousand maledictions on my unfortunate stomach. I was preoccupied only with my internal sensations!'

'She was actually on the plane, then,' said Fournier. 'I see. I begin to see.'

'I remember,' said Jane. 'A tall, dark girl.' Her eyes half closed in an effort of memory. 'Madeleine, Lady Horbury called her.'

'That is it, Madeleine,' said Poirot.

'Lady Horbury sent her along to the end of the plane to fetch a case – a scarlet dressing-case.'

'You mean,' said Fournier, 'that this girl went right past the seat where her mother was sitting?'

'That is right.'

'The motive,' said Fournier. He gave a great sigh. 'And the opportunity . . . Yes, it is all there.'

Then with a sudden vehemence most unlike his usual melancholy manner, he brought down his hand with a bang on the table.

'But, *parbleu*!' he cried. 'Why did no one mention this before? Why was she not included amongst the suspected persons?'

'I have told you, my friend. I have told you,' said Poirot wearily. 'My unfortunate stomach.'

'Yes, yes, that is understandable. But there were other stomachs unaffected – the stewards', the other passengers'.'

'I think,' said Jane, 'that perhaps it was because it was so very early this happened. The plane had only just left Le Bourget; and Giselle was alive and well an hour or so after that. It seemed as though she must have been killed much later.'

'That is curious,' said Fournier thoughtfully. 'Can there have been a delayed action of the poison? Such things happen . . .'

Poirot groaned and dropped his head into his hands.

'I must think. I must think . . . Can it be possible that all along my ideas have been entirely wrong?'

'*Mon vieux*,' said Fournier, 'such things happen. They happen to me. It is possible that they have happened to you. One has occasionally to pocket one's pride and readjust one's ideas.'

'That is true,' agreed Poirot. 'It is possible that all along I have attached too much importance to one particular thing. I expected to find a certain clue. I found it, and I built up my case from it. But if I have been wrong from the beginning – if that particular article was where it was merely as the result of an *accident* . . . why, then – yes – I will admit that I have been wrong – completely wrong.'

'You cannot shut your eyes to the importance of this turn of events,' said Fournier. 'Motive and opportunity – what more can you want?'

'Nothing. It must be as you say. The delayed action of the poison is indeed extraordinary – practically speaking – one would say *impossible*. But where poisons are concerned the impossible does happen. One has to reckon with idiosyncrasy . . .'

His voice tailed off.

'We must discuss a plan of campaign,' said Fournier. 'For the moment it would, I think, be unwise to arouse Anne Morisot's suspicions. She is completely unaware that you have recognized her. Her *bona fide* have been accepted. We know the hotel at which she is staying and we can keep in touch with her through Thibault. Legal formalities can always be delayed. We have two points established – opportunity and motive. We have still to prove that Anne Morisot had snake venom in her possession. There is also the question of the American who bought the blowpipe and bribed Jules Perrot. It might certainly be the husband – Richards. We have only her word for it that he is in Canada.'

'As you say – the husband . . . Yes, the husband. Ah, wait – wait!'

Poirot pressed his hands upon his temples.

'It is all wrong,' he murmured. 'I do not employ the little grey cells of the brain in an orderly and methodical way. No, I leap to conclusions. I think, perhaps, what I am *meant* to think. No, that is wrong again. If my original idea were right, I could not be *meant* to think –'

He broke off.

'I beg your pardon,' said Jane.

Poirot did not answer for a moment or two; then he took his hands from his temples, sat very upright and straightened two forks and a salt-cellar which offended his sense of symmetry.

'Let us reason,' he said. 'Anne Morisot is either guilty or innocent of the crime. If she is innocent why has she lied? Why has she concealed the fact that she was lady's maid to Lady Horbury?'

'Why, indeed?' said Fournier.

'So we say Anne Morisot is guilty because she has lied. But wait. Suppose my first supposition was correct. Will that supposition fit in with Anne Morisot's guilt, or with Anne Morisot's lie? Yes – yes – it *might* – given one premise. But in that case – and if that premise is correct – *then Anne Morisot should not have been on the plane at all.*'

The others looked at him politely, if with, perhaps, a rather perfunctory interest.

Fournier thought:

'I see now what the Englishman, Japp, meant. He makes difficulties, this old one. He tries to make an affair which is now simple sound complicated. He cannot accept a straightforward solution without pretending that it squares with his preconceived ideas.'

Jane thought:

'I don't see in the least what he means . . . Why couldn't the girl be on the plane? She had to go wherever Lady Horbury wanted her to go . . . I think he's rather a mountebank, really . . .'

Suddenly Poirot drew in his breath with a hiss.

'Of course,' he said. 'It is a possibility; and it ought to be very simple to find out.'

He rose.

'What now, my friend?' asked Fournier.

'Again the telephone,' said Poirot.

'The transatlantic to Quebec?'

'This time it is merely a call to London.'

'To Scotland Yard?'

'No, to Lord Horbury's house in Grosvenor Square. If only I have the good fortune to find Lady Horbury at home.'

'Be careful, my friend. If any suspicion gets round to Anne Morisot that we have been making inquiries about her it would not suit our affairs. Above all, we must not put her upon her guard.'

'Have no fears. I will be discreet. I ask only one little question – a question of a most harmless nature.' He smiled. 'You shall come with me if you like.'

'No, no.'

'But yes. I insist.'

The two men went off, leaving Jane in the lounge.

It took some little time to put the call through; but Poirot's luck was in. Lady Horbury was lunching at home.

'Good. Will you tell Lady Horbury that it is M. Hercule Poirot speaking from Paris.' There was a pause. 'That is you, Lady Horbury? No, no, all is well. I assure you *all is well.* It is not that matter at all. I want you to answer me a question. Yes . . . When you go from Paris to England by air does your maid usually go with you, or does she go by train? By train . . . And so on that particular occasion . . . I see . . . You are sure? Ah, she has left you. I see. She left you very suddenly at a moment's notice. *Mais oui*, base ingratitude. It is too true. A most ungrateful class! Yes, yes, exactly. No, no, you need not worry. *Au revoir.* Thank you.'

He replaced the receiver and turned to Fournier, his eyes green and shining.

'Listen, my friend, *Lady Horbury's maid usually travelled by train and boat.* On the occasion of Giselle's murder Lady Horbury decided *at the last moment* that Madeleine had better go by air, too.'

He took the Frenchman by the arm.

'Quick, my friend,' he said. 'We must go to her hotel. If my little idea is correct – and I think it is – there is no time to be lost.'

Fournier stared at him. But before he could frame a question Poirot had turned away and was heading for the revolving doors leading out of the hotel.

Fournier hastened after him.

'But I do not understand. What is all this?'

The commissionaire was holding open the door of a taxi. Poirot jumped in and gave the address of Anne Morisot's hotel.

'And drive quickly, but quickly!'

Fournier jumped in after him.

'What fly is this that has bitten you? Why this mad rush – this haste?'

'Because, my friend, if, as I say, my little idea is correct – *Anne Morisot is in imminent danger.*'

'You think so?'

Fournier could not help a sceptical tone creeping into his voice.

'I am afraid,' said Poirot. 'Afraid. *Bon Dieu* – how this taxi crawls!'

The taxi at the moment was doing a good forty miles an hour and cutting in and out of traffic with a miraculous immunity due to the excellent eye of the driver.

'It crawls to such an extent that we shall have an accident in a minute,' said Fournier drily. 'And Mademoiselle Grey, we have left her planted there awaiting our return from the telephone, and instead we leave the hotel without a word. It is not very polite, that!'

'Politeness or impoliteness – what does it matter in an affair of life and death?'

'Life or death?' Fournier shrugged his shoulders.

He thought to himself:

'It is all very well, but this obstinate madman may endanger the whole business. Once the girl knows that we are on her track –'

He said in a persuasive voice:

'See now, M. Poirot, be reasonable. We must go carefully.'

'You do not understand,' said Poirot. 'I am afraid – afraid –'

The taxi drew up with a jerk at the quiet hotel where Anne Morisot was staying.

Poirot sprang out and nearly collided with a young man just leaving the hotel.

Poirot stopped dead for a moment, looking after him.

'Another face that I know – but where –? Ah, I remember – it is the actor Raymond Barraclough.'

As he stepped forward to enter the hotel, Fournier placed a restraining hand on his arm.

'M. Poirot, I have the utmost respect, the utmost admiration for your methods – but I feel very strongly that no precipitate action must be taken. I am responsible here in France for the conduct of this case . . .'

Poirot interrupted him:

'I comprehend your anxiety; but do not fear any "precipitate action" on my part. Let us make inquiries at the desk. If Madame Richards is here and all is well – then no harm is done – and we can discuss together our future action. You do not object to that?'

'No, no, of course not.'

'Good.'

Poirot passed through the revolving door and went up to the reception desk. Fournier followed him.

'You have a Mrs Richards staying here, I believe,' said Poirot.

'No, Monsieur. She was staying here, but she left today.'

'She has left?' demanded Fournier.

'Yes, Monsieur.'

'When did she leave?'

The clerk glanced up at the clock.

'A little over half an hour ago.'

'Was her departure unexpected? Where has she gone?'

The clerk stiffened at the questions and was disposed to refuse to answer; but when Fournier's credentials were produced the clerk changed his tone and was eager to give any assistance in his power.

No, the lady had not left an address. He thought her departure was the result of a sudden change of plans. She had formerly said she was making a stay of about a week.

More questions. The concierge was summoned, the luggage porters, the lift boys.

According to the concierge a gentleman had called to see the lady. He had come while she was out, but had awaited her return, and they had lunched together. What kind of gentleman? An American gentleman – very American. She had seemed surprised to see him. After lunch the lady gave orders for her luggage to be brought down and put in a taxi.

Where had she driven to? She had driven to the Gare du Nord – at least that is the order she had given to the taximan. Did the American gentleman go with her? No, she had gone alone.

'The Gare du Nord,' said Fournier. 'That means England on the face of it. The two o'clock service. But it may be a blind. We must telephone to Boulogne and also try and get hold of that taxi.'

It was as though Poirot's fears had communicated themselves to Fournier.

The Frenchman's face was anxious.

Rapidly and efficiently he set the machinery of the law in motion.

It was five o'clock when Jane, sitting in the lounge of the hotel with a book, looked up to see Poirot coming towards her.

She opened her mouth reproachfully, but the words remained unspoken. Something in his face stopped her.

'What was it?' she said. 'Has anything happened?'

Poirot took both her hands in his.

'Life is very terrible, Mademoiselle,' he said.

Something in his tone made Jane feel frightened.

'What is it?' she said again.

Poirot said slowly:

'When the boat train reached Boulogne they found a woman in a first-class carriage – dead.'

The colour ebbed from Jane's face.

'Anne Morisot?'

'Anne Morisot. In her hand was a little blue glass bottle which had contained hydrocyanic acid.'

'Oh!' said Jane. 'Suicide?'

Poirot did not answer for a moment or two. Then he said, with the air of one who chooses his words carefully:

'Yes, the police think it was suicide.'

'And you?'

Poirot slowly spread out his hands in an expressive gesture.

'What else – is there to think?'

'She killed herself – why? Because of remorse – or because she was afraid of being found out?'

Poirot shook his head.

'Life can be very terrible,' he said. 'One needs much courage.'

'To kill oneself? Yes, I suppose one does.'

'Also to live,' said Poirot, 'one needs courage.'

CHAPTER 26

AFTER DINNER SPEECH

The next day Poirot left Paris. Jane stayed behind with a list of duties to perform. Most of these seemed singularly meaningless to her, but she carried them out to the best of her powers. She saw Jean Dupont twice. He mentioned the expedition which she was to join, and Jane did not dare to undeceive him without orders from Poirot, so she hedged as best she could and turned the conversation to other matters.

Five days later she was recalled to England by a telegram.

Norman met her at Victoria and they discussed recent events.

Very little publicity had been given to the suicide. There had been a paragraph in the papers stating that a Canadian lady, a Mrs Richards, had committed suicide in the Paris–Boulogne express, but that was all. There had been no mention of any connexion with the aeroplane murder.

Both Norman and Jane were inclined to be jubilant. Their troubles, they hoped, were at an end. Norman was not so sanguine as Jane.

'They may suspect her of doing her mother in, but now that she's taken this way out they probably won't bother to go on with the case; and unless it is proved publicly I don't see what good it is going to be to all of us poor devils. From the point of view of the public we shall remain under suspicion just as much as ever!'

He said as much to Poirot, whom he met a few days later in Piccadilly.

Poirot smiled.

'You are like all the rest. You think I am an old man who accomplishes nothing! Listen, you shall come tonight to dine with me. Japp is coming, and also our friend Mr Clancy. I have some things to say that may be interesting.'

The dinner passed off pleasantly. Japp was patronizing and good humoured, Norman was interested, and little Mr Clancy was nearly as thrilled as when he had recognized the fatal thorn.

It seemed clear that Poirot was not above trying to impress the little author.

After dinner, when coffee had been drunk, Poirot cleared his throat in a slightly embarrassed manner, not free from self-importance.

'My friends,' he said, 'Mr Clancy here has expressed interest in what he would call "my methods, Watson". (*C'est ça, n'est-ce pas?*) I propose, if it will not bore you all' – he paused significantly, and Norman and Japp said quickly, 'No, no,' and 'Most interesting' – 'to give you a little résumé of my methods in dealing with this case.'

He paused and consulted some notes. Japp whispered to Norman:

'Fancies himself, doesn't he? Conceit's that little man's middle name.'

Poirot looked at him reproachfully and said, 'Ahem!'

Three politely interested faces were turned to him, and he began:

'I will start at the beginning, my friends. I will go back to the air liner *Prometheus* on its ill-fated journey from Paris to Croydon. I am going to tell you my precise ideas and impressions at the time – passing on to how I came to confirm or modify them in the light of future events.

'When, just before we reached Croydon, Dr Bryant was approached by the steward and went with him to examine the body, I accompanied him. I had a feeling that it might – who knows? – be something in my line. I have, perhaps, too professional a point of view where deaths are concerned. They are divided, in my mind, into two classes – deaths which are my affair and deaths which are not my affair – and though the latter class is infinitely more numerous – nevertheless whenever I come in contact with death I am like the dog who lifts his head and sniffs the scent.

'Dr Bryant confirmed the steward's fear that the woman was dead. As to the cause of death, naturally he could not pronounce on that without a detailed examination. It was at this point that a suggestion was made – by M. Jean Dupont – that death was due to shock following on a wasp sting. In furtherance of this hypothesis, he drew attention to a wasp that he himself had slaughtered shortly before.

'Now that was a perfectly plausible theory – and one quite likely to be accepted. There was the mark on the dead woman's neck – closely resembling the mark of a sting – and there was the fact that a wasp had been in the plane.

'But at that moment I was fortunate enough to look down and espy what might at first have been taken for the body of yet another wasp. In actuality it was a native thorn with a little teased yellow and black silk on it.

'At this point Mr Clancy came forward and made the statement that it was a thorn shot from a blowpipe after the manner of some native tribe. Later, as you all know, the blowpipe itself was discovered.

'By the time we reached Croydon several ideas were working in my mind. Once I was definitely on the firm ground, my brain began to work once more with its normal brilliance.'

'Go it, M. Poirot,' said Japp with a grin. 'Don't have any false modesty.'

Poirot threw him a look and went on.

'One idea presented itself very strongly to me (as it did to everyone else), and that was the audacity of a crime being committed in such a manner – and the astonishing fact that nobody noticed its being done!

'There were two other points that interested me. One was the convenient presence of the wasp. The other was the discovery of the blowpipe. As I remarked after the inquest to my friend Japp, why on earth did the murderer not get rid of it by passing it out through the ventilating hole in the window? The thorn itself might be difficult to trace or identify, but a blowpipe which still retained a portion of its price label was a very different matter.

'What was the solution? Obviously that the murderer *wanted* the blowpipe to be found.

'But why? Only one answer seemed logical. If a poisoned dart and a blowpipe were found, it would naturally be assumed that the murder had been committed by a thorn shot from a blowpipe. Therefore in reality the murder had *not* been committed that way.

'On the other hand, as medical evidence was to show, the cause of death *was* undoubtedly the poisoned thorn. I shut my eyes and asked myself – what is the surest and most reliable way of placing a poisoned thorn in the jugular vein? And the answer came immediately: *By hand.*

'And that immediately threw light on the necessity for the finding of the blowpipe. The blowpipe inevitably conveyed the suggestion of *distance.* If my theory was right, the person who killed Madame Giselle was a person who went right up to her table and bent over her.

'Was there such a person? Yes, there were two people. The two stewards. Either of them could go up to Madame Giselle, lean towards her, and nobody would notice anything unusual.

'Was there anyone else?

'Well, there was Mr Clancy. He was the only person in the car who had passed immediately by Madame Giselle's seat – and I remembered that it was he who had first drawn attention to the blowpipe and thorn theory.'

Mr Clancy sprang to his feet.

'I protest,' he cried. 'I protest. This is an outrage.'

'Sit down,' said Poirot. 'I have not finished yet. I have to show you all the steps by which I arrived at my conclusion.

'I had now three persons as possible suspects – Mitchell, Davis, and Mr Clancy. None of them at first sight appeared likely murderers, but there was much investigation to be done.

'I next turned my mind to the possibilities of the wasp. It was suggestive, that wasp. To begin with, no one had noticed it until about the time coffee was served. That in itself was rather curious. I constructed a certain theory of the crime. The murderer presented to the world two separate solutions of the tragedy. On the first or simplest, Madame Giselle was stung by a wasp and had succumbed to heart failure. The success of that solution depended on whether or no the murderer was in a position to retrieve the thorn. Japp and I agreed that that could be done easily enough – *so long as no suspicion of foul play had arisen.* There was the particular colouring of silk which I had no doubt was deliberately substituted for the original cerise so as to simulate the appearance of a wasp.

'Our murderer, then, approaches the victim's table, inserts the thorn and releases the wasp! The poison is so powerful that death would occur almost immediately. If Giselle cried out – it would probably not be heard owing to the noise of the plane. If it was just noticed, well, there was the wasp buzzing about to explain the cry. The poor woman had been stung.

'That, as I say, was plan No. 1. *But supposing that, as actually happened, the poisoned thorn was discovered* before the murderer could retrieve it. In that case the fat is in the fire. The theory of the natural death is impossible. Instead of getting rid of the blowpipe through the window, it is put in a place where it is bound to be discovered when the plane is searched; and at once it will be assumed that the blowpipe was the instrument of the crime. The proper atmosphere of distance will be created and when the blowpipe is traced it will focus suspicion in a definite and prearranged direction.

'I had now my theory of the crime, and I had three suspects with a barely possible fourth – M. Jean Dupont, who had outlined the "Death by a Wasp Sting theory", and who was sitting on the gangway so near Giselle that he might just possibly have moved from it without being noticed. On the other hand, I did not really think he would have dared to take such a risk.

'I concentrated on the problem of the wasp. If the murderer had brought the wasp on to the plane and released it at the psychological moment – he must have had something in the nature of a small box in which to keep it.

'Hence my interest in the contents of the passengers' pockets and hand luggage.

'And here I came up against a totally unexpected development. I found what I was looking for – but as it seemed to me on the wrong person. There was an empty small-sized Bryant & May's match-box in Mr Norman Gale's pocket. *But by everybody's evidence Mr Gale had never passed down the gangway of the car.* He had only visited the toilet compartment and returned to his own seat.

'Nevertheless, although it seems *impossible*, there *was* a method by which Mr Gale could have committed the crime – as the contents of his attaché case showed.'

'My attaché case?' said Norman Gale. He looked amused and puzzled. 'Why, I don't even remember now what was in it.'

Poirot smiled at him amiably.

'Wait a little minute. I will come to that. I am telling you my first ideas.

'To proceed – I had *four* persons who could have done the crime – from the point of view of *possibility*: the two stewards, Clancy and Gale.

'I now looked at the case from the *opposite* angle – that of motive – if a *motive* were to coincide with a *possibility* – well, I had my murderer! But alas, I could find nothing of the kind. My friend Japp has accused me of liking to make things difficult. On the contrary, I approached this question of motive with all the simplicity in the world. To whose benefit would it be if Madame Giselle were removed? Clearly to her unknown daughter's benefit – since that unknown daughter would inherit a fortune. There were also certain persons who were in Madame Giselle's power, or shall we say – who *might* be in Giselle's power, for aught we knew. That, then, was a task of elimination. Of the passengers in the plane I could only be certain of one who was undoubtedly mixed up with Giselle. That one was Lady Horbury.

'In Lady Horbury's case the motive was very clear. She had visited Giselle at her house in Paris the night before. She was desperate and she had a friend, a young actor, who might easily have impersonated the American who bought the blowpipe – and might also have bribed the clerk in Universal Airlines to ensure that Giselle travelled by the 12 o'clock service.

'I had, as it were, a problem in two halves. I did not see how it was *possible* for Lady Horbury to commit the crime; and I could not see for what *motive* the stewards, Mr Clancy, or Mr Gale should want to commit it.

'Always, in the back of my mind, I considered the problem of Giselle's unknown daughter and heiress. Were any of my four suspects married – and if so, could one of the wives be this Anne Morisot? If her father was English, the girl might have been brought up in England. Mitchell's wife I soon dismissed – she was of good old Dorset stock. Davis was courting a girl whose father and mother were alive. Mr Clancy was not married. Mr Gale was obviously head over ears in love with Miss Jane Grey.

'I may say that I investigated the antecedents of Miss Grey very carefully, having learned from her in casual conversation that she had been brought up in an orphanage near Dublin. But I soon satisfied myself that Miss Grey was *not* Madame Giselle's daughter.

'I made out a table of results – the stewards had neither gained nor lost by Madame Giselle's death – except that Mitchell was obviously suffering from shock. Mr Clancy was planning a book on the subject by which he hoped to make money. Mr Gale was fast losing his practice. Nothing very helpful there.

'And yet, at that time, *I was convinced that Mr Gale was the murderer* – there was the empty match-box – the contents of his attaché case. Apparently he *lost*, not gained, by the death of Giselle. But those appearances might be *false* appearances.

'I determined to cultivate his acquaintance. It is my experience that no one, in the course of conversation, can fail to give themselves away sooner or later . . . Everyone has an irresistible urge to talk about themselves.

'I tried to gain Mr Gale's confidence. I pretended to confide in him, and I even enlisted his help. I persuaded him to aid me in the fake blackmailing of Lady Horbury. And it was then that he made his first mistake.

'I had suggested a slight disguise. He arrived to play his part with a ridiculous and impossible outfit! The whole thing was a farce. No one, I felt sure, could play a part as *badly* as he was proposing to play one. What then was the reason for this? *Because his knowledge of his own guilt* made him chary of showing himself to be a good actor. When, however, I had adjusted his ridiculous makeup, his artistic skill showed itself. He played his part perfectly and Lady Horbury did not recognize him. I was convinced then that he could have disguised himself as an American in Paris and could also have played the necessary part in the *Prometheus*.

'By this time I was getting seriously worried about Mademoiselle Jane. Either she was in this business with him, or else she was entirely innocent – and in the latter case she was a victim. She might wake up one day to find herself married to a murderer.

'With the object of preventing a precipitate marriage, I took Mademoiselle Jane to Paris as my secretary.

'It was whilst we were there that the missing heiress appeared to claim her fortune. I was haunted by a resemblance that I could not place. I did place it in the end – but too late . . .

'At first the discovery that she had actually been in the plane *and had lied about it* seemed to overthrow all my theories. Here, overwhelmingly, was the guilty person.

'But if she were guilty she had an accomplice – the man who bought the blowpipe and bribed Jules Perrot.

'Who was that man? Was it conceivably her husband?

'And – then – suddenly I saw the true solution. True, that is, if one point could be verified.

'For my solution to be correct Anne Morisot ought not to have been on the plane.

'I rang up Lady Horbury and got my answer. The maid, Madeleine, travelled in the plane by a last-minute whim of her mistress.'

He stopped.

Mr Clancy said:

'Ahem – but – I'm afraid I'm not quite clear.'

'When did you stop pitching on me as the murderer?' asked Norman.

Poirot wheeled round on him.

'I never stopped. *You are the murderer* . . . Wait – I will tell you everything. For the last week Japp and I have been busy – It is true that you became a dentist to please your uncle – John Gale. You took his name when you came into partnership with him – but you were his *sister's* son – not his brother's. Your real name is *Richards*.

It was as Richards that you met the girl Anne Morisot at Nice last winter, when she was there with her mistress. The story she told us was true as to the facts of her childhood, but the latter part was edited carefully by you. She *did* know her mother's maiden name. Giselle was at Monte Carlo – she was pointed out and her real name was mentioned. You realized that there might be a large fortune to be got. It appealed to your gambler's nature. It was from Anne Morisot that you learnt of Lady Horbury's connexion with Giselle. The plan of the crime formed itself in your head. Giselle was to be murdered in such a way that suspicion would fall on Lady Horbury. Your plans matured and finally fructified. You bribed the clerk in Universal Airlines so that Giselle should travel on the same plane as Lady Horbury. Anne Morisot had told you that she herself was going to England by train – you never expected her to be on the plane – and it seriously jeopardized your plans. If it was once known that Giselle's daughter and heiress had been on the plane suspicion would naturally have fallen upon her. Your original idea was that she should claim the inheritance with a perfect alibi, since she would have been on a train or boat at the time of the crime; and then you would have married her.

'The girl was by this time infatuated with you. But it was money you were after – not the girl herself.

'There was another complication to your plans. At Le Pinet you saw Mademoiselle Jane Grey and fell madly in love with her. Your passion for her drove you on to play a much more dangerous game.

'You intended to have both the money and the girl you loved. You were committing a murder for the sake of money, and you were in no mind to relinquish the fruits of the crime. You frightened Anne Morisot by telling her that if she came forward at once to proclaim her identity she would certainly be suspected of the murder. Instead you induced her to ask for a few days' leave, and you went together to Rotterdam, where you were married.

'In due course you primed her how to claim the money. She was to say nothing of her employment as lady's maid, and it was very clearly to be made plain that she and her husband had been abroad at the time of the murder.

'Unfortunately, the date planned for Anne Morisot to go to Paris and claim her inheritance coincided with my arrival in Paris, where Miss Grey had accompanied me. That did not suit your book at all. Either Mademoiselle Jane or myself *might* recognize in Anne Morisot the Madeleine who had been Lady Horbury's maid.

'You tried to get in touch with her in time, but failed. You finally arrived in Paris yourself and found she had already gone to the lawyer. When she returned shc told you of her meeting with me. Things were becoming dangerous, and you made up your mind to act quickly.

'It had been your intention that your new-made wife should not survive her accession to wealth very long. Immediately after the marriage ceremony you had both made wills leaving all you had one to the other! A very touching business.

'You intended, I fancy, to follow a fairly leisurely course. You would have gone to Canada – ostensibly because of the failure of your practice. There you would have resumed the name of Richards and your wife would have rejoined you. All the same I do not fancy it would have been very long before Mrs Richards regrettably died, leaving a fortune to a seemingly inconsolable widower. You would then have returned to England as Norman Gale, having had the good fortune to make a lucky speculation in Canada! But now you decided that no time must be lost.'

Poirot paused and Norman Gale threw back his head and laughed.

'You are very clever at knowing what people intend to do! You ought to adopt Mr Clancy's profession!' His tone deepened to one of anger. 'I never heard such a farrago of nonsense. What you *imagined*, M. Poirot, is hardly evidence!'

Poirot did not seem put out. He said:

'Perhaps not. But, then, I *have* some evidence.'

'Really?' sneered Norman. 'Perhaps you have *evidence* as to how I killed old Giselle when everyone in the aeroplane knows perfectly well I never went near her?'

'I will tell you *exactly how you committed the crime*,' said Poirot. '*What about the contents of your dispatch-case?* You were on a holiday. *Why take a dentist's linen coat*? That is what I asked myself. And the answer is this – because it resembled so closely a *steward's coat* . . .

'That is what you did. When coffee was served and the stewards had gone to the other compartment you went to the toilet, put on your linen coat, padded your cheeks with cottonwool rolls, came out, seized a coffee spoon from the box in the pantry opposite, hurried down the gangway with the steward's quick run, spoon in hand, to Giselle's table. You thrust the thorn into her neck, opened the match-box and let the wasp escape, hurried back into the toilet, changed your coat and emerged leisurely to return to your table. The whole thing took only a couple of minutes.

'*Nobody notices a steward particularly*. The only person who might have recognized you was Mademoiselle Jane. But you know women! As soon as a woman is left alone (particularly when she is travelling with an attractive young man) she seizes the opportunity to have a good look in her hand mirror, powder her nose and adjust her makeup.'

'Really,' sneered Gale. 'A most interesting theory; but it didn't happen. Anything else?'

'Quite a lot,' said Poirot. 'As I have just said, in the course of conversation a man gives himself away . . . You were imprudent enough to mention that for a while you were *on a farm in South Africa*. What you did not say, but what I have since found out, is that it was a *snake farm* . . .'

For the first time Norman Gale showed fear. He tried to speak, but the words would not come.

Poirot continued:

'You were there under your own name of Richards; *a photograph of you transmitted by telephone has been recognized*. That same photograph has been identified in Rotterdam as the man Richards who married Anne Morisot.'

Again Norman Gale tried to speak and failed. His whole personality seemed to change. The handsome, vigorous young man turned into a rat-like creature with furtive eyes looking for a way of escape and finding none . . .

'It was haste ruined your plan,' said Poirot. 'The Superior of the Institut de Marie hurried things on by wiring to Anne Morisot. It would have looked suspicious to ignore that wire. You had impressed it upon your wife that unless she suppressed certain facts either she or you might be suspected of murder, since you had both unfortunately been in the plane when Giselle was killed. When you met her afterwards and you learnt that I had been present at the interview you hurried things on. You were afraid I might get the truth out of Anne – perhaps she herself was beginning to suspect you. You hustled her away out of the hotel and into the boat train. You administered prussic acid to her by force and you left the empty bottle in her hand.'

'A lot of damned lies . . .'

'Oh, no. There was a bruise on her neck.'

'Damned lies, I tell you.'

'You even left your fingerprints on the bottle.'

'You lie. I wore –'

'Ah, you wore gloves . . . ? I think, Monsieur, that little admission cooks your gander.'

'You damned interfering little mountebank!' Livid with passion, his face unrecognizable, Gale made a spring at Poirot. Japp, however, was too quick for him. Holding him in a capable unemotional grip, Japp said:

'James Richards, alias Norman Gale, I hold a warrant for your arrest on the charge of wilful murder. I must warn you that anything you say will be taken down and used in evidence.'

A terrible shudder shook the man. He seemed on the point of collapse.

A couple of plain-clothes men were waiting outside. Norman Gale was taken away.

Left alone with Poirot, little Mr Clancy drew a deep breath of ecstasy.

'M. Poirot,' he said. 'That has been absolutely the most thrilling experience of my life. You have been wonderful!'

Poirot smiled modestly.

'No, no. Japp deserves as much credit as I do. He has done wonders in identifying Gale as Richards. The Canadian police want Richards. A girl he was mixed up with there is supposed to have committed suicide, but facts have come to light which seem to point to murder.'

'Terrible,' Mr Clancy chirped.

'A killer,' said Poirot. 'And like many killers, attractive to women.'

Mr Clancy coughed.

'That poor girl, Jane Grey.'

Poirot shook his head sadly.

'Yes, as I said to her, life can be very terrible. But she has courage. She will come through.'

With an absent-minded hand he arranged a pile of picture papers that Norman Gale had disarranged in his wild spring.

Something arrested his attention – a snapshot of Venetia Kerr at a race meeting, 'talking to Lord Horbury and a friend.'

He handed it to Mr Clancy.

'You see that? In a year's time there will be an announcement: "*A marriage is arranged and will shortly take place between Lord Horbury and the Hon. Venetia Kerr.*" And do you know who will have arranged that marriage? Hercule Poirot! There is another marriage that I have arranged, too.'

'Lady Horbury and Mr Barraclough?'

'Ah, no, in that matter I take no interest.' He leaned forward. 'No – I refer to a marriage between M. Jean Dupont and Miss Jane Grey. You will see.'

II

It was a month later that Jane came to Poirot.

'I ought to hate you, M. Poirot.'

She looked pale and fine drawn with dark circles round her eyes.

Poirot said gently:

'Hate me a little if you will. But I think you are one of those who would rather look truth in the face than live in a fool's paradise; and you might not have lived in it so very long. Getting rid of women is a vice that grows.'

'He was so terribly attractive,' said Jane.

She added:

'I shall never fall in love again.'

'Naturally,' agreed Poirot. 'That side of life is finished for you.'

Jane nodded.

'But what I must do is to have work – something interesting that I could lose myself in.'

Poirot tilted back his chair and looked at the ceiling.

'I should advise you to go to Persia with the Duponts. That is interesting work, if you like.'

'But – but – I thought that was only camouflage on your part.'

Poirot shook his head.

'On the contrary – I have become so interested in archaeology and prehistoric pottery that I sent the cheque for the donation I had promised. I heard this morning that they were expecting you to join the expedition. Can you draw at all?'

'Yes, I was rather good at drawing at school.'

'Excellent. I think you will enjoy your season.'

'Do they really want me to come?'

'They are counting on it.'

'It would be wonderful,' said Jane, 'to get right away –'

A little colour rose in her face.

'M. Poirot –' She looked at him suspiciously. 'You're not – you're not – being kind?'

'Kind?' said Poirot with a lively horror at the idea. 'I can assure you, Mademoiselle – that where money is concerned I am strictly a man of business –'

He seemed so offended that Jane quickly begged his pardon.

'I think,' she said, 'that I'd better go to some museums and look at some prehistoric pottery.'

'A very good idea.'

At the doorway Jane paused and then came back.

'You mayn't have been kind in that particular way, but you *have* been kind – to me.'

She dropped a kiss on the top of his head and went out again.

'*Ça, c'est très gentil!*' said Hercule Poirot.

ALSO IN THIS SERIES

Agatha Christie

POIROT in the ORIENT

There is nothing exotic about murder, no matter where it takes place. Away from home, Hercule Poirot finds that he cannot escape death, even when travelling across the Mesopotamia, the Nile and Petra.

MURDER IN MESOPOTAMIA

At the Hassanieh dig deep in the Iraqi desert, the wife of a celebrated archaeologist is suffering from terrifying hallucinations. Apparent madness – until a murderer strikes.

DEATH ON THE NILE

The tranquillity of a Nile cruise is shattered by the discovery that a young girl has been shot through the head. Stylish and beautiful, she had everything – even enemies.

APPOINTMENT WITH DEATH

And among the towering red cliffs of Petra sits the corpse of Mrs Boynton. A tiny puncture mark on her wrist is the only sign of the fatal injection that killed her.

Based on Agatha Christie's own experiences in the 1930s travelling with her husband, archaeologist Sir Max Mallowan, this trilogy of bestselling novels represents crime fiction at its very best.

ALSO IN THIS SERIES

Agatha Christie

POIROT at WAR

It seems Hitler's Luftwaffe aren't the only ones responsible for the deaths of innocent people as World War II rages – it seems there are plenty of murderers willing to help them reduce Britain's war-torn population further. And it's up to Hercule Poirot to stop them . . .

ONE, TWO, BUCKLE MY SHOE

A dentist lies dead in his Harley Street surgery, a pistol lying on the floor near his out-flung right hand – but was it suicide or murder? Poirot finds his investigation isn't exactly child's play . . .

FIVE LITTLE PIGS

Hell hath no fury like a woman scorned, so they say – and beautiful Caroline Crale's husband found that out the hard way. He was poisoned after flaunting his mistress in front of his wife – but was Caroline truly '*deadlier than the male*'?

TAKEN AT THE FLOOD

When the wealthy Gordon Cloade is killed in the blitz, his new, young wife inherits everything, much to the anger of the Cloade family. Hercule Poirot receives a message from the 'spirits' – which confirms his suspicion that Mrs Cloade's position is a dangerous one.

This trilogy of bestselling novels represents a time in Agatha Christie's life during which her writing was at its most prolific and, many would argue, its most ingenious.